BIG BANG

Brainse Dhromchonnrach
Drumcondra Branch
Tel: 8377206

D0317195

Also by David Bowman

Let the Dog Drive

Bunny Modern

This Must Be the Place:
The Adventures of Talking Heads in the 20th Century

BIG BANG

A nonfiction novel

David Bowman

Introduction by Jonathan Lethem

corsair

CORSAIR

First published in the US in 2019 by Hachette Book Group
First published in Great Britain in 2019 by Corsair

1 3 5 7 9 10 8 6 4 2

This book is a work of fiction. Names, characters, places and incidents either are the product of the author's imagination or, if real, are used fictitiously.

A CIP catalogue record for this book is available from the British Library.

ISBN: 978-1-4721-5497-2

Printed and bound in Great Britain by Clays Ltd, Elcograf S.p.A.

Papers used by Corsair are from well-managed forests and other responsible sources.

Corsair
An imprint of
Little, Brown Book Group
Carmelite House
50 Victoria Embankment
London EC4Y 0DZ

An Hachette UK Company
www.hachette.co.uk
www.littlebrown.co.uk

Contents

The Furry Girl School of American Fiction: An Introduction by Jonathan Lethem vii

Foreword: Watching TV with Elvis in Hollywood, November 22, 1963 3

Book One: 1950–1959

1. The American Embassy, Mexico City, 1950 19
2. The Watergate, District of Columbia, 1951 31
3. Mayo Clinic, Minnesota, 1951 39
4. Hyannis Port, Massachusetts, 1951–1952 56
5. Whittier, California, 1952 72
6. Lewisburg Federal Penitentiary, Pennsylvania, 1952 86
7. The Cargo of Truth, an American Ship Floating in the Aegean Sea, 1952 93
8. Puget Sound, Washington, 1953 105
9. Opa-Locka Airport, Florida, 1953–1954 121
10. Suddenly, California, 1954 150
11. The American Embassy in Tokyo, Japan, 1954 173
12. Detroit, Michigan, 1955 182
13. Cody, Wyoming, 1955–1956 197
14. Bloomingdale's (Asylum), Westchester County, New York, 1956 210
15. Long Island, New York, 1956 237

16. Memphis, Tennessee, 1956 283
17. The American Embassy, Montevideo, Uruguay, 1956–1957 292
18. Black Mountain, North Carolina, 1957–1958 302
19. Aboard the *Chola Srivijaya* Bound for San Francisco, 1959 328
20. Alaska, 1959 347

Book Two: 1960–1963

1. Reno, Nevada, 1960 367
2. Hilldale, Somewhere in the U.S.A., 1960 385
3. Watergate Towne, District of Columbia, 1960 391
4. The Great Lakes, 1960–1961 408
5. The Island of Dr. Moreau, Somewhere off the Southern Coast of the United States, 1961–1962 434
6. Chinatown, Los Angeles, California, 1962 473
7. Teapot Dome, Wyoming, 1962–1963 482
8. The American Embassy, Saigon, South Viet-Nam, 1963 500
Revolution 9. Dallas, Texas, November 22, 1963 547

Epilogue: Reciting Poetry with Aristotle Onassis 591

The Furry Girl School of American Fiction

An Introduction by Jonathan Lethem

1. THEY ALSO WROTE

For years I thought I'd begin an essay with the title "They Also Wrote." This wasn't a plan, exactly, but a notion, barely more than a title. The idea was to write a kind of general manifesto on behalf of forgotten authors. I'd likely never have done it. By a certain point I'd made my eccentric preference for out-of-print and neglected fiction, for the noncanonical dark horses—Flann O'Brien over James Joyce, say—abundantly clear (probably irritatingly so, for any reader who was paying attention). With the help of the *New York Review of Books* imprint, and a few other heroic publishing programs, I'd been involved, a few times, in dragging a few of my pets back into view—Bernard Wolfe, Anna Kavan, Don Carpenter. Other times I'd simply been delighted to see it done, as if according to my whims, but without lifting a finger.

We may be living, in fact, in the great age of "rediscovered" authors. Younger readers want to talk to me, all the time, about Shirley Jackson and John Williams and, of course, Philip K. Dick, who's become so renowned that very few people remember that at the time of his death he was largely forgotten, and out of print. Perhaps at a time when canons have fragmented and been assaulted, and working authors seem compromised by social-media overfamiliarity and three-and-a-half-star verdicts, these honorably silent dark horses are the best repository for our old sacred feeling, the one cultivated in the semiprivacy between a reader and a favorite book. Living writers, now that we've gotten such a close look at them, are pretty embarrassing. Famous authors of the past? Mostly blowhards. Posthumously celebrated writers, on the other hand, all seem to walk under the grace of Kafka's umbrella, with Melville and Emily Dickinson.

Plenty of remarkable books still slip through the rediscovery net. I wouldn't have put money on David Bowman's chances. Certainly, I'd never have imagined that my largely forgotten old friend, author of two slim out-of-print novels and one out-of-print book of music journalism, would be reincarnated in the form of an epic novel about celebrity and power in the postwar twentieth century, one he didn't finish soon enough to submit to publishers before he died. Sure, I'd known *Big Bang*—which Bowman also sometimes liked to call *Tall Cool One*—existed. He'd shown me portions of it over the years. I'm probably not the only person who saw pages. But the notion that he'd reached a satisfying conclusion to what seemed his most quixotic writing journey, let alone that anyone would ever usher it into print—this never seemed remotely likely.

No, if Bowman were heard from again, I'd assumed it would be because some dedicated publisher had chosen to reprint his first novel, from 1992, *Let the Dog Drive.* It was his only success, really, among the three books published during his lifetime, despite being published by NYU Press, and therefore receiving barely anything in the way of a publicity campaign. (The early '90s were an unmatched era in the history of publicity campaigns for novels; it was Bowman who joked to me that when he witnessed Donna Tartt's rollout in *Vanity Fair* he thought, "Wow, I wish *I* had a novel out," and then, "Wait a minute, I do have a novel out!") *Let the Dog Drive,* an antic noir comedy about a dysfunctional family, interspersed literary and pop-cultural references with arresting sex and violence. It gained rave reviews in both the *Times Book Review* and *The New Yorker,* despite featuring nothing more in the way of jacket blurbs than an excerpt from a letter to Bowman from Joan Didion, thanking him for mentioning her in the novel. (That he'd written to Didion was, I'd learn, typical of Bowman's ingenuous approach to celebrities, literary and otherwise, who fascinated him; more on this soon.)

During Bowman's 1995 book tour for the Penguin paperback of *Let the Dog Drive* he visited Diesel Books, in Oakland, California. I was one of a handful who attended. I asked him to autograph my copy of the NYU hardcover and gave him a copy of my then-fresh first novel, *Gun, with Occasional Music.* Bowman inscribed my copy, "to Jonathan—six figures in your future!" Bowman candidly dreamed of glory for both of us, from the inception of our friendship. Yet it was our dual marginality that created the bond. From this point I'm implicated in every story I have to tell you about David Bowman. I'm incapable of introducing him without committing memoir.

2. THE BOWMAN TAPES

Bowman returned to New York, and I stayed, for the moment, in my garret in Berkeley. Almost immediately, we'd talk on the phone nearly every day. Bowman was my first conduit to the contemporary literary New York City of the late '90s, which I was now working my courage up to enter, and which was almost wholly mysterious to me; growing up in Brooklyn hadn't constituted any form of preliminary encounter. Bowman was marvelously charismatic on the phone. His tone amused and conspiratorial, he began every call in medias res, with the word "—so . . ." Then he'd leap in midstream, resuming some trailing thought from an earlier conversation, even if it was only one he'd been having with himself.

Yet the phone wasn't enough. Bowman besieged me with charmingly nutty handwritten letters, many of them containing scissor-and-glue pot collages, usually incorporating elements from the New York tabloids—Page Six squibs concerning the kinds of writers who generated Page Six squibs: Mailer, McInerney, his beloved Didion, or downtown figures who'd risen to stardom, like Patti Smith, Jim Jarmusch, David Byrne—combined with Bowman's own cartoonish Sharpie scribbles, or his personal erotic photography. He'd call these cut-ups "charms"—they were meant to convey writerly luck. One I still have tacked up over my desk was called the "Dancing DeLillos Charm": a row of Rockettes with Don DeLillo's head atop each dancer.

Yet there's more: the Bowman tapes. He and his wife regularly rented a cabin in Montauk, and while there he'd pace the beach, drinking beer, and monologuing to me into a tape recorder. The cassettes arrived in the mail, incoherently labeled. I'd pop them into my car or home tape player and listen. They were hypnotic, outlandish, and boring at once. Bowman's monologues were elaborately themed—usually some variation on his obsession with writerly ambition, and how it was cursed for him, for me, and nearly anybody, by the afflictions of personal fate. He'd inaugurate each rant with certain key phrases to which he'd return, as if in song. Bowman was a master at a kind of verbal plate-spinning routine, but he was also a helpless digressionist, and sometimes a plate on the far side of the stage would be forgotten for twenty minutes or more. Sometimes you'd have to flip the tape over to find out if he'd forgotten his theme.

This is improbable, but much about Bowman is improbable. He sent more tapes than I found time to listen to. I recall my girlfriend complaining about how they'd begun filling up the floor space in the passenger side of my Toyota Corolla. I did my best to keep up, but it was hopeless. On the tapes, Bowman's dreams and schemes were interspersed with the crunch of his feet on the wet Montauk beach at night, and though I haven't listened to one of the Bowman tapes in nearly two decades, I can still hear that gravel crunch and the heavy breathing of his pauses for thought, as if it recurs in my nightly dreams.

3. THE *LOT 49* METHOD

Bowman's loyalty and generosity were simply immense, in those first years, while I remained stranded in Berkeley, far from the action, and our friendship was conducted by phone, tape, and charm. After three books, I'd been orphaned at Harcourt Brace and needed a new publisher, but I was a pretty small fish. My agent had an offer from Doubleday, but Bowman, working behind the scenes, turned it into a small auction with his own publisher, Little, Brown. (I landed at Doubleday.) The book in question needed a new title, the first task I needed to perform for my shiny new publisher, and I was flailing. Bowman walked me through it: use the Lot 49 Method, he told me. I had to ask what he meant. "'The Crying of Lot 49' is the last line of *The Crying of Lot 49,*" he explained. "What's the last line of your book?" I looked: my last line included the phrase "as she climbed across the table." That same book was blurbless. Bowman, acting on his own, forced it on, of all people, Jim Harrison. Likely bewildered but charmed, as people tended to be on early encounter with Bowman's manic style, Jim Harrison improbably gave forth with a blurb. I doubt my new publisher had any idea how that happened—I barely understood it myself—but they probably assumed Harrison had been my teacher somewhere, or had been a friend of my dad's.

4. THE FURRY GIRL SCHOOL

At some point early on Bowman coined a name for us: the Furry Girl School of American Fiction. He'd named it after a character in my second novel, *Amnesia Moon*—a girl, specifically, who was furry. I don't mean "furry" in the modern polymorphously perverse sense of a fetish for dressing up in costumes and having sex—I mean that her body was covered in light fur. To Bowman, the character was an emblem of what he and I loved most in the books we loved: not "heart," exactly, but some eccentric character or motif, a tic or inside joke, almost, one that made the book *personal* to the author, and in turn to the reader who loved it. A book could be impressive without containing this quality, which was quickly shortened to "Furry." In Bowman's reasoning—always comprised of instantaneous certainties—almighty DeLillo, for instance, had written books both Furry (*End Zone, White Noise*) and not (*Players, Underworld*). Mailer had never been Furry in his life. Chandler was Furry, Ellroy not. And so on. Swept up, anointed, I consented even when it made no sense, and we indexed the whole world on the Furry Scale.

The Furry Girl School needed a female member—this was my suggestion, and I nominated a writer named Cathryn Alpert, who'd written a funny, Furry, and in some ways Bowmanesque novel called *Rocket City*. From the clues (small-press publication in hardcover, for one thing) Alpert was as much outsider, as much dark horse, as Bowman and I felt ourselves to be. We called or emailed, out of the blue; or possibly I turned up at a reading and announced us to her. Bowman's charms worked at a distance (perhaps they worked best at a distance), and Cathryn Alpert, who'd heard of neither of us before this, quickly consented. The Furry Girl School had three members now.

5. CHLOE AND SNOOT

David Bowman would turn out to be one of the most isolated people I've ever known—isolated on the profoundest levels by a certain traumatic displacement from ordinary human consolation. Yet on a day-to-day basis he wasn't strictly *alone*. Bowman had a wife. Chloe Wing was older than

Bowman, and seemed almost infinitely kind and patient with him, if sometimes also rather distant, impassive (later, I'd view this as a survival trait on Chloe's part). He also had a dog, the beloved Snoot, a tall black-and-white hound with sensitive paws. Snoot suffered: he endured treatments to his paws, and for digestive troubles, and other ailments. Bowman, helpless in his devotion, suffered with the dog.

When I moved back to New York City and first visited Bowman and Chloe and Snoot in their beautiful Manhattan apartment, his life seemed enviable. From the distance of California my new friend had appeared to know so many editors and writers. I was now ready to be swept up in his world, to begin our friendship in person, rather than long-distance. In fact, up close, my great friend was quickly exposed to me as a person whose stark limitations, whose damage, were the equal of his charisma and brilliance. Almost overnight, I began at some level to take care of Bowman, instead of the reverse.

6. DOGBOY AND SARGE

If David Bowman was such a dear friend, why do I keep calling him Bowman? Well, I never called him David. To others, I called him Bowman, as he'd called me Lethem, to others. It was Bowman's habit always and only to last-name writers (Didion, Lish, Moody, et al.). Then he'd adopt hard-and-fast nicknames for interpersonal address. At his suggestion, I called him Dogboy, and he called me, at first, Amnesia Boy, after my second novel, *Amnesia Moon*. Pretty soon he switched me to Sarge, which was how he addressed me for the rest of his life. Bowman called me Sarge because, he explained, he always followed my commands, as if in a war movie, as if we were going over a hill.

The "commands" in question? I'd tell Bowman *not* to do things. After I'd moved to New York I'd begun to realize how he was serially alienating the magazine editors upon whom he depended, as well as his book publicists and other editorial subordinates. He freaked people out with his bizarre pitches, his strange, insinuating late-night calls and emails, his impetuous rages over poorly specified minor betrayals. He knew many writers and editors, yes, but now I saw that nearly all of them had learned, or were learning, or would soon learn, to treat him with kid gloves. There came a point when I understood I'd never met anyone who devoted as large a share of his (vast) creative energy to impulses that were sheerly disastrous, that he had to be talked out of.

I failed, at the time, to concern myself with the recipients of Bowman's tirades. Some of the villains who incensed him might have earned it—like the businessman who'd once kicked at Snoot on Second Avenue—but this can't be true of all the publishing operatives at whom he uncorked. To my shame, my interventions weren't so much with his victims in mind as they were intended to save Bowman from himself.

7. LOVES

Bowman loved beer and traveled to a special warehouse in Brooklyn to purchase the exotic imported bottles he craved. This was nearly the only thing that could get him onto the subway—he otherwise preferred to walk Snoot on the Lower East Side, or to stay at home.

Bowman loved Bob Dylan, inordinately, and collected Dylan bootlegs, but to my astonishment had never been to see Dylan play live. Bowman loved Patti Smith, inordinately. He loved her earliest music, raging and foul-mouthed, and he seemed always to be searching for an equivalent in his curiosity about PJ Harvey, Thea Gilmore, and so forth. He loved Marianne Faithfull, too; fair to say he was electrified by foul-mouthed women in general. He loved Lou Reed, Gillian Welch, Thomas Carlyle, Elizabeth McCracken's *The Giant's House,* Cormac McCarthy's *Blood Meridian,* Dr. Seuss, and dogs.

Bowman loved New York City. He'd come from elsewhere—Wisconsin, then Vermont—but embraced the city without looking back. The city's greatest exponents seem to latch on to it as Balzac's Lucien Chardon latches on to Paris, in *Lost Illusions,* after arriving from the provinces: Dawn Powell, Andy Warhol, et al.

Bowman loved film noir, but I don't recall him caring particularly for film otherwise. I don't recall any affection for soul music, or science fiction, or food in general. He lived a few blocks from Veselka but declined ever to meet me there for the late-night plates of pierogies that reminded me so much of my teenage years—frequenting Veselka's again had been one of the several things I was sure I'd moved back to New York City to do.

8. THE TRUCK

On Montauk, in 1989, Bowman had been walking alone on a road when he was hit and nearly killed by a truck (his *Times* obituary reads "car," but he always called it a truck when we spoke). He suffered major head trauma and was in a coma for a month, during which he was ministered to by his wife, Chloe, to whom he said he owed his life. *Let the Dog Drive* was largely finished before the accident, but when he awoke from his coma he wasn't aware he'd written a book, and had to read the draft dozens of times before he understood that it was up to him to finish it. His friend Eric Schneider, to whom it is dedicated, told his obituarist, Paul Vitello, that the book "helped him remember who he was."

This may be true. It surely is, in part. But it is also the case that the last portions of *Let the Dog Drive* portray scenes of torture and revenge that plunge the book into a darkness for which the earlier two-thirds have scantly prepared a reader to endure. I didn't have Chloe's or Eric Schneider's luck, of knowing Bowman both before and after the accident. I do know that one of Bowman's alternative nicknames for himself was Vengeance Boy—and that as long as I knew him he saw himself as wronged by the universe. I know that he saw himself as a person who suffered, on a daily basis, and sought alleviation in beer, rock and roll, and fantasies of righteous justice being inflicted on his many persecutors. He could offer humorous perspective on his condition, but it wasn't something over which he appeared to have any control.

David Bowman died, in 2012, of a massive brain hemorrhage. I'd moved back to California just a year before, and I learned of his death from Chloe, who reached me by telephone. I was stunned. Bowman and I had been out of touch for a year or more, and the news I feared was the reverse: I knew Chloe was mortally sick with cancer, and that Bowman might at some point tell me that he had been left even more alone in the world. (Chloe did follow, a year later.)

"He walked into our bedroom and told me he had a terrible headache,"

Chloe told me, and explained that he then fell to the floor and was dead within minutes. "It was a good death," she added, whether to console me or herself or because she felt it was so, I don't know. It seemed to me a parenthesis had closed, as though the truck had come to claim him. How strange to consider that the years between the injury and his death, the twenty-three years in which he published three books and wrote at least two more, the years in which I'd known him, could be seen as merely a kind of dispensation.

The question I can't avoid: how much was Vengeance Boy a product of brain trauma?

9. JUST LIKE TOM THUMB'S BLUES

In the first flush of my return to New York, in the period when I projected Bowman as one of my great life's companions, without qualification, and before I'd understood how difficult it was for him to be out of his self-soothing routines, without his Snoot walks, and away from his desk and telephone, I dragged him to a Bob Dylan concert. I saw this as my duty. I was seeing Dylan live a lot in that period.

The concert was in New Jersey, at the Performing Arts Center in Newark. I was riding there with my friend Michael, and others, and I arranged to pick Bowman up at his doorstep. This was a great calamitous carload of fools wreathed in pot smoke, and in retrospect I'm amazed that I lured Bowman into the back seat. He had a wide-eyed daft look that said he was amazed himself to have been lured. He wore a long trench coat, buttoned to the neck. "I just hope he plays 'Tom Thumb's Blues,'" Bowman said, and I warned him not to expect it; Dylan rarely plays that song, and never plays what you most wish to hear. Of course, we arrived late to the concert, in a crazy fever to park and go inside. We'd calculated our trip to miss the opening act, a regular sport for me and Michael when Dylangoing, so Dylan was already playing.

At the routine frisk inside the turnstiles, a security guard made Bowman open his trench coat. Immediately visible were two beers, Bowman's beloved imported bottles, one in each of his flannel shirt's pockets. Bowman gave a sheepish shrugging smile, one I'll never forget. The guard, shaking his head, confiscated the bottles. We rushed up to the highest level of the auditorium to find our seats in the dark. As we sat, Bowman frisked himself this time, reproducing the sheepish smile. He revealed a bottle that had survived the guard's inspection. Then another, and another—he still possessed *three* bottles, which had been secreted who-knows-where, in his sleeves or in the trench coat's interior pockets. As we took our seats, gazing down on Dylan and his band's heads from the upper deck, Dylan finished one song and began another: "Just Like Tom Thumb's Blues."

10. BUNNY HAS A HAIRBALL

Let the Dog Drive gave Bowman his chance to move to a major publisher. He followed his eccentric book with an even more eccentric one, called *Bunny Modern,* set in a future where electricity has vanished, and armed nannies protect a diminishing pool of babies from kidnappers while cranked up on a drug called Vengeance. Around the time I moved back to New York Bowman was revising the pages obsessively; his expectations for the book were immense. When he finally showed it to me he delivered it in what he called the Bunny Box—a kind of three-dimensional collage object, much larger than it needed to be to contain what was a very brief manuscript. His impatience for me to read it, and sanctify it as "Furry," was formidable.

There came a strange misadventure. This was before cell phones. I'd read the book overnight, and Bowman had stood by for my assessment, but I had some kind of urgent appointment, and had to leave word with my friend Maureen, knowing he'd call. The phrase I asked Maureen to pass along was "The Bunny is Furry." Maureen, panicked by Bowman's urgency, blurted out, "The Bunny has a hairball." Bowman exploded. She apologized, but it was too late. An hour or two later, when I was able to reach him directly, his only words for me were "The Bunny has a hairball? The Bunny has a *hairball?*" He'd sat stewing, drinking beer, and trying to interpret Maureen's colorful slip. The only interpretations he could hit on were dire ones. I worked to calm him down.

Maureen might have been prescient. There were U.S. writers who'd lately preceded Bowman in offering dystopian fantasias under the cover of traditional literary publishing: Steve Erickson, Katherine Dunn, Paul

Auster. Kirstin Bakis's *Lives of the Monster Dogs* had found a nice success in New York the year before. Bowman was envious—dogs were his thing—but also believed it auspicious for his book. Yet he was at least ten years ahead of the great fashion for dystopias in highbrow circles, and anyhow, hadn't judged how his book's slightness, and its vein of real perversity, might play against it.

Bowman had been a dark-horse success with *Let the Dog Drive,* but now he'd lost a major publisher some money, and, worse, exhausted their good faith with his badgering calls and office visits. The book's failure wasn't another truck, perhaps, but it sliced off another layer of Bowman's droll, perversely jubilant outlook, and deepened his sense of being misused by fate, perhaps even being conspired against—by whom, exactly, he wouldn't have been able to say.

11. SHIT ON YOUR SHOES

Yet Bowman was never self-pitying. Were I tempted to wallow or complain at some disappointment inflicted on my own aspirations—the fact that *As She Climbed across the Table* had gone completely unreviewed in the *New York Times,* say, leaving me, despite my new publisher's exertions, still a cult quantity—Bowman would offer a kind of non-commiseration commiseration. He'd invoke a favorite term: "Sarge," he'd say, "you've got shit on your shoes." I wish I could reproduce for you the tone of affectionate philosophical mordancy with which he'd pronounce it. (In fact, it's surely on the tapes, a dozen times over.)

By "shit on your shoes" Bowman meant, in my case, that I'd had my early stories published in science-fiction magazines, and attended science-fiction conventions, and traded blurbs with science-fiction writers, and not concealed or apologized for those facts. In his own case, he meant his publication with NYU Press—and in both our cases, the fact that (unlike Kirstin Bakis) we'd come in the door with no MFA program or Ivy League pedigree. We'd simply walked in with shit on our shoes, such that those with a nose averse to the kinds of shit we bore would reliably shun us. In fact, this isn't too lousy a diagnosis of an awful lot of literary fate-casting: that the first impression, or size of the first advance, was predeterminative in any but the luckiest or most tenacious of cases. For Bowman this was something to sigh over, to open a bottle of beer over. And then he'd resume work.

12. BOWMAN ALSO WROTE

The brevity of his two published novels notwithstanding, Bowman was a workaholic, and as voluminous on the page as on the tapes. Because his brain injury had made his eyesight difficult, and made him prone to headaches, he edited his pages at a giant font size, sixteen- or eighteen-point, as I remember it. (He blew his font up to an even more enormous size for public readings, I learned, when we gave one together at KGB, the two of us along with Amanda Fillipacci playing to an absolutely packed room for what was only my second-ever reading in New York City—a thrilling event for me.) In the years following *Bunny Modern* he worked on three fiction projects concurrently: *Big Bang* (or *Tall Cool One*); another novel in the phantasmagorical vein of *Bunny Modern,* called *Women on the Moon*; and a novella based on a conflation of Theodore Kaczyinski's antitechnological manifesto and Kafka's *Letter to His Father,* called either *The Unabomber's Letter to His Father* or, confusingly, *A Letter to His Unabomber.* Also confusingly, Bowman sent me portions of all three manuscripts, but never an entirety (perhaps superstitious of another hairball assessment), or even a first chapter. Even more confusingly, his spelling in first-draft work was always and persistently terrible, either because of some kind of dyslexia or because of his brain injury, I wasn't sure.

So much about Bowman was increasingly confusing and dismaying to me. Had he really telephoned X or Y and said aloud what he'd *told* me he'd said aloud to them? Why would anyone do these things? I'd run into writers Bowman had introduced me to, initially, and when his name came up, they'd shake their heads, and describe some kind of breach or ultimatum or farcical misconstruction that had come between them. I'd like to say I defended him, or apologized for him—there were times when I did. But Sarge couldn't work miracles, couldn't preempt every crisis, couldn't work in retrospect, or erase words he'd spoken aloud.

Gradually, to my shame, this sense that Bowman was making himself personally indefensible crept in and poisoned my belief in his writing. He was still one of my favorite writers, just as he was still my friend. But the non-long-term viability of his persona, of his personal approach, began to seem to me analogous to the notion that very many people weren't likely to agree with me about his writing. Besides, his fiction wasn't going into print, where I could advocate for it. It was piling up in his house, and in the email excerpts, which he'd fling my way, increasingly, confusingly, at random intervals, without clarifying the purpose to which he'd shared the particular sequence he'd shared. The emails appeared to be like the tapes, meant for me alone, even if they contained many brilliant, singular passages—lines I'd quote, or be thrilled to have written myself. The whole problem of Bowman was becoming something like the oversupply of tapes on the passenger-side floor of my old Toyota Corolla.

Nevertheless, I encouraged each project in turn. The Unabomber letter seemed especially promising to me, not merely for its clever hook, and newsy relevance. I knew Bowman was enraged at his parents (he hadn't spoken to anyone from his immediate family for over fifteen years, he claimed). I felt this unprocessed rage impeded his art, and his life. So, the reference to Kafka's famous outpouring seemed to suggest Bowman might use the project as a vehicle to confront all that went unconfronted. But no. In the pages he sent, the emphasis, bizarrely, was on *literary* injustices, on outrages within the publishing world of contemporary New York—it read like a Bowman tape, transcribed. I demoted the project in my regard, and encouraged him to work on *Women on the Moon* instead. It had that wonderful title, and seemed to capture some of his daffy reverence for Chloe, for all women. The mammoth project, the one about the Kennedys, Lou Reed, Howard Hunt, J. D. Salinger, Elvis, the one about everything and anything that he'd ever known or read or intuited about the postwar American backdrop against which we'd both come of age, all of which haunted his work implicitly, haunted every line, but was here being treated *explicitly*—that couldn't possibly work. Could it?

To my shame, I didn't think Bowman could carry it off. It seemed like something Norman Mailer would try for, and something Norman Mailer would fail at. Possibly Bowman had miscast himself, as Mailer or DeLillo or Doctorow, a white elephant novelist, when he really ought to have stuck to his Richard Brautigan dreams, his termite operations. This was also a matter of publishing pragmatics—who, after *Bunny Modern,* was going to sign on the dotted line for a thousand Bowman pages? Most simply, I couldn't imagine he'd finish it.

I should have known better.

13. THE FALL OF THE FURRY GIRL SCHOOL

The fall of the Furry Girl School of American Fiction took the form, on one side, of abrupt tragic farce and, on the other side, of slow degradation, and my long shame. The tragic farce was this: Cathryn Alpert and her husband had never met Bowman, and were coming to New York on other business and had planned a rendezvous. As I recall it, they were staying in a Midtown hotel. Time was tight. Some plan was in place—surely it had been difficult, for Bowman, to make such a plan, since meeting people, new people, at an appointed time and place would have been difficult for him. I believe it had been getting increasingly difficult. And the day in question was the same day as the annual Blessing of the Animals at the Cathedral Church of Saint John the Divine, on Amsterdam Avenue and 112th Street. Bowman was taking Snoot there, to be blessed.

Some misunderstanding occurred. Cathryn wanted to change the time of the rendezvous, I think, and telephoned to suggest it. She'd come a long distance, a Californian who rarely visited New York, and she was traveling with family. Bowman lived in New York, and had no children—surely it wasn't much to ask for him to emend a plan? Yet her proposal conflicted with Snoot's voyage to Harlem for the blessing. When Bowman presented this conflict, Cathryn, heartbreakingly for them both, teased him a little. His dog required blessing? So urgently he couldn't see her?

Cathryn, as one would expect, took Bowman's brilliant ironies, his tone of self-amused eccentricity and provocation, to mean he was capable of seeing himself in an absurd light. This was understandable—it was precisely what I'd done, falling in love with him long-distance, as I had. Yet there was nothing humorous about the blessing, from Bowman's side. California was a long way from New York, but for Bowman and Snoot, the ride to Harlem from the Lower East Side might have been equivalent.

Bowman, on the telephone, flipped his lid. Bowman blew his stack. It was a perfect misunderstanding, between two strangers who'd been jollied into conjunction by a go-between—me, that is. I doubt they ever did meet. Likely that day was the last time they spoke or emailed. But they both telephoned me, in a spirit of injury—Bowman enraged, as though his dog had again been attacked, kicked at on the street by an officious passerby, and Cathryn, on her side, utterly confused and appalled.

The slow degradation, and long shame, were mine. There came what we now call a tipping point—well, it was a tipping point for a lot of things—9/11. Bowman adopted the view that black helicopters had surveyed the scene minutes before the first airplane's impact. Disarranged by the fear that gripped us all during those anthrax weeks that followed, but with fewer regular human contacts to provide solace, Bowman's self-skepticism betrayed him totally. On his favorite instrument, the telephone, he plagued a magazine editor with his paranoid theories concerning the attack. She was not only one of the last editors regularly commissioning pieces from him, one of the last bridges he'd failed to burn, but she was one of my oldest friends. She complained to me, rightly—I'd put them together.

This, and other less flamboyant confusions, estranged us. I guess I couldn't take it, and I put Bowman on a kind of management course of contact and encouragement, as if Sarge had turned into a kind of methadone nurse. It wasn't necessary to exile him; he'd done it himself supremely well, as though systematically. By the time Bowman died our contacts were sporadic, our phone calls brief, and it had been years since he'd mailed me a charm. I'd quit having to defend him, or having to decide not to, to other writers, because other writers weren't raising his name to me (along with raising an eyebrow, as they'd done for so long). Either Bowman was reaching outside of his keep less frequently, or he wasn't dropping my name when he did. Likely some of both was the case. There wasn't anything Furry about this situation in the least.

14. SHIT BEFORE TRUCK

There was a deeper trauma in David Bowman, something predating the Montauk truck. The real shit on David Bowman's shoes when he walked through the door of adult life was a thing barely revealed, a darkness in his childhood. This wasn't a story he retailed, a play he made for sympathy. When he told me the story it wasn't really a story at all, but a single image.

I'd been pressing him to explain how he could go so long without contact with his living mother. My mother had died when I was a teenager, and I'd have given my right arm for one conversation with her in adulthood. In another sense I also identified with Bowman—in the wake of my mother's death, in my high school years, I'd left my siblings and my father behind. After one year of college I'd run west, like the characters in *Let the Dog Drive.* For much of my twenties I'd barely seen my family, and rarely called my father. Only now I was back in touch, and glad to be, and I thought Bowman should consider the cost to his life, and perhaps to his art, of the wall he'd placed between himself and his personal past.

That day I'd pushed him just enough. He laid one single card on the table to justify his ban. I don't remember the words he used; I remember his body, and the pantomime he offered me as he described the scene, a kind of somatic reenactment. His father had beaten him while his mother stood by and watched and did nothing, but the unforgettable detail, the story Bowman wanted to show me with his body, was that his father had beat him, not once, but in a sustained way, *across the hood of the family car.* I never asked for more.

This is probably the place to say even more clearly that I have no authority to speak of these matters. I'm neither a member of David's surviving extended family nor his biographer. My only claim is the memoirist's: these things happened to *me,* and I'm telling them to you as I recall them. I'll draw a curtain now on any further speculations (some may think I should have drawn a curtain sooner). The fact is, I had my own Bowman, and for most of a decade, since the brief flare of remembrances that accompanied the appearance of his obituary in the *New York Times,* I felt pretty certain I'd be alone with him for as long as I lived, and then he'd be gone. I never once expected that I'd try to give him to *you.*

15. *BIG BANG*

When the editor Judith Clain approached me—it was at another literary gala, one of those things I'm routinely invited to and David Bowman never was—and told me Little, Brown was to publish *Big Bang,* I couldn't have been more astonished if you'd hit me with, well, a truck. It was only then that I understood not only that Bowman had finished his most improbable work, but that his talent wasn't my private possession, to be marveled at and pitied in my secret garden, but that it belonged, would now belong, to any reader who cared to pick it up. The kinky adoration he was able to lavish on the cultural materials he picked up and looked at in his books—the way he makes, for instance, Jackie Onassis into a very Furry character indeed—was never exclusively mine to know. Bowman is a language dervish—the pleasure in hearing him describe the adding machine, the source of William S. Burroughs's family, as "the rosary of capitalism" belongs not to me, but to literature.

Big Bang isn't a place to go for straight facts about the Kennedy assassination—as if there are "straight facts" about it!—nor is it a place to go for a philosophical fugue on the instability of conspiracy theories, in the manner of DeLillo's *Libra.* Indeed, though Bowman's book is full of facts, none of them is to be considered strictly reliable. When you learn, for instance, that Jimi Hendrix's "first electric guitar was a Supro Ozark. It was white plastic with a black headstock. The white was known in the music-store business as 'mother-of-toilet-seat finish,'" you will only have yourself or Google to trust, and who can trust Google? In this opus David Bowman has written a vast docu-fiction, one in which facts have been fused in the Ecko Hi-Speed Calrod Pressure Cooker of his imagination into something stranger and deeper—a psychic X-ray of the century previous to this one, an enlivening dream voyage into the mystery of the world that made ours and which still haunts it.

None of it is mine, really, to defend or explain. I'm just Bowman's reader now, like you. It only happened that I had a front-row seat to a show I never believed could open, and now has opened.

What belongs to me are the tapes.

Tell it slant

—*Emily Dickinson*

What a drag it is getting old...

—*'Mother's Little Helper,' the Rolling Stones*

BIG
BANG

Foreword

Watching TV with Elvis in Hollywood, November 22, 1963

Where were you when you first heard President Kennedy had been shot? We can all answer this question, even if the answer is 'I wasn't born yet.' A few weeks before Norman Mailer—that magnificent narcissist—died of old age, he was asked the Kennedy Question at what would be his last press conference. 'Where was I when I heard that JFK had been shot?' Mailer repeated. He smiled. He liked this question. It was the first time he had been asked that in decades. He was eighty-four years old.

His answer is coming.

After Mailer finished with the press, he was caught sitting alone in an office waiting for his wife. Mailer was a short man with two short canes. He had a big head and big hands. His hair was white. He had more hair than most men twenty, thirty years younger. He was handed a first edition of his third novel, *The Deer Park*, to sign. It was published in 1955 and it is his only Hollywood novel. The old man peered at the cover with another smile. Back in the twentieth century, back when John F. Kennedy was running for the presidency, Mailer interviewed the candidate in Hyannis, located on the under-muscle of Cape Cod. Kennedy had told Mailer, 'I've read your books.'

Everyone Mailer interviewed claimed that. Seldom was it true. Everyone who told Mailer, 'I've read your books,' next said that they had read *The Naked and the Dead,* Mailer's first novel, the one that put him on the map in 1948. Kennedy told Mailer, 'I've read *The Deer Park*'—a novel critics had maligned when it was published. *The Deer Park* was Mailer's orphan and thus his favorite child. Mailer did not believe Kennedy had actually read the novel, but was flattered that this politician's handlers had done their homework.

Here in the twenty-first century, Norman Mailer signed *The Deer Park* and asked, 'Ever read *The House of the Seven Gables*?'

'A long long long time ago.'

'Remember how the photographer character says something like, *The past lies upon the present like the body of a dead giant and we have to drag him around*?'

'Yeah. He says that we all are stuck crying at dead men's pathos and laughing at dead men's jokes.'

'And reading dead men's books,' Mailer said deadpan. 'Hawthorne also created that magnificent image of the young dragging a giant dead body of a grandfather.'

'Like Barthelme's novel *The Dead Father.*'

'Yeah. Barthelme stole it from Hawthorne,' Mailer said. 'Jack Kennedy has been our dead giant, don't you think? We've been dragging him across the deserts and plains for forty years.'

* * *

Jack Kennedy was America's first president of the century who had actually been born in the twentieth century. Marilyn Monroe was the last woman to sing the actual song 'Happy Birthday' to Jack Kennedy during his lifetime. The song was sung on May 19, 1962—ten days before the man's actual birthday—at Madison Square Garden in Manhattan. A Saturday night. Kennedy was publicly celebrating his forthcoming forty-fifth birthday. Kennedy would live for another year and a half. Marilyn Monroe was thirty-five. She would be dead in less than three months.

President Kennedy's last birthday party, on May 23, 1963, also occurred in Manhattan, but it was a private affair at the Waldorf Astoria. Sultry twenty-two-year-old Sweden-born actress and sophisticated Las Vegas singer Ann-Margret sang for President Kennedy. Ann-Margret was limber legs and tasteful full décolleté. She serenaded the president with 'Baby Won't You Please Come Home':

> I've got the blues, I feel so lonely; I'd give the world if I could only make you understand; it surely would be grand. I'm gonna telephone my baby, ask him *won't you please come home.*

Kennedy was aroused with deep animal magnetism for Ann-Margret, with her Swedish curves and milk skin. The President of the United States of America wanted her.

No member of the public knew in 1963 how powerful and thorough the Kennedy seduction machine was—brother Bobby and the Secret Service, as well as other minions, all playing a part in the capture of female game for the president's pleasure, a pleasure that often consisted of almost immediate fornication. Before the pull cord of this sex machine could be yanked, Ann-Margret bolted the Waldorf, riding a cab from Manhattan to Idlewild to catch a TWA overnight to Los Angeles where this young woman had a ten o'clock meeting with Elvis Presley.

Elvis was twenty-eight. If the chemistry between them was any good, Ann-Margret would be Elvis's costar in a picture to be called *Viva Las Vegas.*

Elvis and Ann-Margret spent their first three days together in a Hollywood recording studio singing songs for the soundtrack. Their chemistry was $C_3H_5(NO_3)_3$. Nitroglycerin. They danced simpatico around the mics. Ann-Margret saw that Elvis was herself in a man's body. To Elvis, Ann-Margret was his female counterpart. Even though Elvis was older, it was as if the pair had once been twins curled around each other in the womb, and then separated at birth like in some Greek soap opera.

Now, Elvis and Ann-Margret had reunited.

When the pair was not flirting for the movie cameras, they went home and watched TV. They ate hamburgers together. They crawled on the lawn together singing Jimmy Reed blues. When they rode separate motorcycles together through Beverly Hills, it was as if they were the same driver. These two shared the loveliest form of narcissism.

By September '63, *Viva Las Vegas* was in the can and Ann-Margret traveled to England to do publicity for the British opening of her hit American movie *Bye Bye Birdie,* a motion picture about a young rock star named Conrad Birdie who is about to be drafted into the Army (just as Elvis had once been). Ann-Margret got herself into London trouble. A British tabloid quoted her announcing that she was 'in love' with Elvis Presley. 'I cannot say when, or if, we will marry, but [Elvis] is a real man.'

★ ★ ★

Back in L.A., Elvis's official fiancée, Priscilla, breezes into town unannounced. She is only eighteen. Priscilla has heard and read what

Ann-Margret had said and throws a flower vase at Elvis. The singer dodges it and grabs Priscilla by the waist and throws her on a king-size bed and tells her that he wants a woman who will understand that things like Ann-Margret 'might just happen.'

I'm gonna telephone my baby... Ann-Margret phoned Elvis transatlantic and swore she had not said any of those things to the British press.

Elvis knew she had not.

She told him she would be home on November 21 or 22.

Baby, won't you please come home?

The year, as you recall, is 1963.

* * *

It is Friday morning in Dallas, Texas, on November 22, nine a.m. Richard Nixon is at Love Field Airport reading about himself in the *Dallas Morning News,* how on the previous night a group that included Nixon and actress Joan Crawford had gone nightclubbing at the Empire Room in downtown Dallas. The article gives sketchy background about the two. The ex-vice president was now a lawyer toiling in private practice; one of his firm's clients was Pepsi-Cola. Nixon was in town for the Pepsi-Cola board meeting. The movie star Joan Crawford was the widow of the chairman of Pepsi and now sat on the board along with a dozen male stuffed shirts. Dick Nixon read how when he had walked into the nightclub the band was playing 'April in Portugal.' Nixon said that it was his wife's favorite song.

This was true.

The MC introduced Nixon as 'either you like him or you don't.' This 'broke up Nixon.'

Not true—the 'broke up' part. Nixon had only creased his face into a polite smile. When the band returned, 'La Crawford, looking every inch the movie star with a white fur hat, was first on the dance floor and requested twists all evening.'

Yes and no. She and Richard Nixon were only twisting at first. Nixon was fifty and Crawford fifty-eight, but the actress was in perfect shape. She whispered that she wasn't wearing a girdle. Nixon wasn't comfortable moving his hips back and forth, but as he 'twisted,' he energetically punched his arms in and out by picturing the similar moves of Cassius Clay in his mind's eye. After their second twist, Nixon raised his finger to Crawford and hurried to the bandleader. Nixon could tell the man with the baton was from Southern California and had been moving toward the east and just got stuck in Texas. Nixon slipped him a fin and asked for a Balboa.

The bandleader obliged. Nixon returned to Crawford and they began to dance close. He held her tight so she would know that he wasn't a square. Truth be told, he was a little tight as well. Her fur hat made him want to sneeze. She was mashing her tits into him and he was getting hard.

They drank only Pepsi that night. Not because anyone was on the wagon—the restaurants and hash houses in Dallas were dry. About four hours later, Crawford had invited her Pepsi crew back to her hotel room. Everyone left before sunrise, leaving only Joan Crawford and Richard Nixon.

Now at Love Field—Nixon has had no sleep. He looks doggy. He shaved an hour ago, but already his chin is layered with the sandpaper grit of stubble. The loudspeaker calls Nixon's flight. He is flying TWA—a company that is 78 percent owned by Nixon's personal money goat, Howard Hughes. The plane is still scheduled to be leaving on time. Everything is running like Berlin in Dallas because President Kennedy is coming to town. This morning, Kennedy is over in Forth Worth having breakfast with LBJ and other Texas yahoos. During Nixon's morning ride to Love Field, the cab radio had reported that the mayor of Fort Worth had given Kennedy the gift of a genuine Texan cowboy hat, but the president hadn't put it on. 'Doesn't want to muss his Catholic hair,' the cab driver said.

* * *

Ann-Margret has returned to Los Angeles from England the day before. On Friday, November 22, the actress drives into Beverly Hills to shop. She parks and steps out of her car. People are stumbling on the sidewalk. Their faces stricken. Stunned. Groups crowd around parked cars listening to the news coming over the radio. Ann-Margret pushes her way to a station wagon. She can't tell what the radio is saying.

'What happened?' she asks a girl her age wearing a ponytail.

'President Kennedy has been shot in Texas,' the girl answers and then starts bawling.

Ann-Margret runs back to her car and floors it to Elvis's place. She lets herself in. She finds Elvis sitting with the guys around the TV set. No one in the room is older than Elvis. Everyone is smoking and no one smokes regularly. Lamar gets off the couch to make room for Ann-Margret.

'Elvis, how is the president?' she asks.

* * *

Norman Mailer had quoted Nathaniel Hawthorne's complaints against the dead, but the words did not originate from Hawthorne. They were originally Thomas Jefferson's beef. America's foremost American swore that the U.S.A. needed neither the culture of dead Europeans nor the laws of dead American politicians. Jefferson calculated the productive adult life of a generation was nineteen years. (It's probably forty years now.) Jefferson suggested that all legislation and laws be reviewed every nineteen years to ensure that dead Americans held no sway. 'The earth is for the living, not the dead. Rights and powers can only belong to persons, not to things.'

Jefferson added, 'The dead are not even things.'

Say it aloud: 'The dead are not even things.'

That's hard-boiled. That's modern.

* * *

President John F. Kennedy has no idea that he is a dead man waiting to happen as he sits beside his wife in the back seat of a two-year-old Lincoln Continental as it heads toward downtown Dallas on this the last Friday before Thanksgiving. In front of Kennedy, John Connally, the governor of Texas, sits in the right jump seat and his wife, Nellie, sits in the left. Beside Kennedy on the seat lies a bouquet of roses for his wife. Beside the flowers sits Jacqueline. Remember? The first lady was wearing a pink Chanel suit with a matching pillbox hat. This was modern. This was haute couture. This was *très chic.* It's easy to forget that America had not experienced such an influential first lady since Eleanor Roosevelt. Jacqueline was blue blood and European cultured. Months earlier, in the middle of summer, Jacqueline Kennedy turned thirty-four and then gave birth to her third child and second son, Patrick Bouvier Kennedy. The baby died of hyaline membrane disease three days later, his father by Patrick's bedside. To recuperate from her loss, Jacqueline had taken a twenty-day cruise in the Mediterranean aboard Aristotle Onassis's yacht, the *Christina*. Onassis was like a James Bond villain—the richest of the rich who was an untouchable criminal. Onassis had just stolen opera diva Maria Callas from her husband. She was now Aristotle's moll. When the American press learned of Jacqueline's plans, they turned her trip into a soap opera. In living rooms all over the country, Avon ladies and their customers talked over coffee about how wrong it was for Jacqueline to be in the Mediterranean without her husband or her two living children. Jackie partying! Jackie wearing a bathing suit!

—with *that* man!

Still, during Jacqueline's absence, Texas's Governor Connally traveled to Washington to personally plead with the president to bring the first lady with him when he and LBJ began their unofficial campaign for reelection in Dallas that November. The president shrugged. He wouldn't force his wife to do anything.

After the first lady returned from the Mediterranean, she surprised her husband by saying, 'Okay. I'll go with you to Texas.' They flew to San Antonio on Thursday, November 21. Before Jacqueline showed herself in the open door of Air Force One, she took a desperate breath. She then stood in the doorway and looked down the exit stairs. Below on the tarmac, more than a hundred Texans, mostly women, were waiting to observe her passage down the stairs from the plane. Below were the Johnsons and the Connallys and the Lubells and the Rinks. Wealthy politicians. Oil money. Most of these Texas wives wanted to hate Jacqueline and the East Coast class she represented. Three years earlier, even the vice president's wife, Lady Bird, had been attacked while campaigning in her own state by the so called Mink Coat Mob, the ugly wives of ugly Texas cattle barons, who first herded Lady Bird away and spat in her direction.

What would the Mink Coat Mob do to Jackie? Jacqueline was more European than American, more French than mere European. She now stood revealed to them all at the top of the airplane stairway. Jacqueline was wearing a tasteful tailored dress—attire that a prosperous Avon lady would wear to church. Jacqueline eyed the women down on the tarmac and then looked down at her own feet. She then raised her face and gave a shy smile, a smile that was about to relax away when Jackie stood straighter and gave the Texans a beaming grin as if she couldn't believe her good fortune to be in their presence. Writer Barbara Learning would report that Lady Bird Johnson felt that '[Jackie's] emphatic hesitation, as if she wasn't sure the crowd was here for her, was utterly disarming... it drew people's interest. It signaled humility. It conveyed that Jacqueline understood that her triumphs around the world didn't count here.'

Here in Texas.

The women in the crowd began screaming Jackie's name in excited joy.

Because Jacqueline Kennedy's first day in Texas was a triumph, she made her decision: 'I will wear Chanel tomorrow.' There was no need to hide her cultured taste. She would be pretty in pink.

The next day, Friday, in Dallas, Jacqueline is wearing a pink Chanel suit with a matching pillbox hat.

French pink.

Houston Street in downtown Dallas is delightful pandemonium. Hundreds, thousands jam both sides of the street to cheer Jackie. In places, the limousine must snail along at five miles an hour to nudge bodies out of the way.

Then the car turns on Elm Street. This is the end of the parade. The limos are heading for the highway. The crowd on the street is thin enough that they all can fit comfortably side by side on the curb. A few of these pedestrians hear the crack of a gun or else the echo of a shot. A bullet hurls into the back of the president's neck. Supposedly, this single bullet tears out of the president's throat below his vocal cords and plows into Governor Connally's right shoulder. The governor is forty-six years old, the same age as Kennedy. Connally cries out, 'My God, they are going to kill us all!'

Kennedy raises his arms to his neck. After this first shot, the limo driver, William Greer, looks back instead of flooring it to speed out of the line of fire. A moment later, another bullet hits Kennedy's head. There is blood vapor above the seat and brain matter splatters everywhere. Jacqueline in pink and raspberry and blood scrambles out of the car over the trunk. She is tackled by a running Secret Service agent and pushed back in the vehicle.

It's 12:28:54 CST. The limo now speeds to Parkland, the only major hospital in Dallas.

★ ★ ★

By 2:00 CST, every third American had heard the news of the gundown. By 3:00 CST, 92 percent of the population knew—about half learning it on television or radio. Lou Reed would write a song about where he was when he heard. He was then a twenty-one-year-old college student standing in the Orange, the only bar near Syracuse University. The TV was on, its glowing blue B&W screen competing with the bar's beer signs and the already strung Christmas lights. It was a little after 1:45 EST when a newsman interrupted to announce that there were unconfirmed reports that the president had been shot. Everyone, including Reed, left the bar and crowded on the street. Statistics say that at this moment, a little over half of all Americans wanted to be with others to discuss the news, while a slightly smaller proportion wanted to be by themselves.

In Lou Reed's Syracuse, a guy in a Porsche suddenly hit his horn and repeated what his radio had just reported, 'The president, he was shot twice in the head in Dallas and they don't know by *whom*.'

★ ★ ★

Margaret Salinger was seven years old in November 1963 and was a third grader in Meridan Elementary School in New Hampshire. The town of Meridan sat in the frosty gulag of the U.S.A.—

Desolate. Endless snow. Many citizens inbred.

After recess on the Friday before Thanksgiving, the school principal, Mrs. Spaulding, entered the classroom and asked Margaret's teacher, Mrs. Beaupre, to come out to the hallway. Before leaving, Mrs. Beaupre appointed Marilyn Percy, who sat in the front row, to be monitor and fink on any students who acted up during the teacher's absence. Miss Percy vigilantly turned her head quickly from side to side to keep her eye on her peers. Mrs. Beaupre returned to the classroom and said, 'Children, President Kennedy has just been shot.'

The classroom erupted with agitated kids. Several boys jumped on their chairs and began applauding and hooting, acting out the views of their New Hampshire parents. In fact, during recess an hour before, six big girls had circled Margaret. Each one took her turn kicking the younger child. As an adult, Margaret would describe these girls as 'some pack of feral Rockettes.' At least once a week, they kicked Margaret during recess. Margaret would one day ask an older boy, 'Why do the big girls hate me?'

'Because your dad is a Communist.'

Margaret Salinger's mother picked her daughter up after school at the usual time. The late November ground was already covered with four feet of snow. No wonder her mother had become irrefutably shell-shocked by their isolation in New Hampshire.

Margaret got into the car. Her mother started to tell her about the president. 'I already know about it,' the child said.

* * *

Watching television with Elvis—

Huntley and Brinkley together were reporting about the gunplay. Statistics state that eight out of ten Americans owned a television in 1963. One out of fifty owned a color set. Elvis had a color Zenith with the biggest screen they made, twenty-six inches by twenty-six inches.

Elvis and his entourage of five plus Ann-Margret were staring dumbly at the screen. Every minute or so, someone said, 'I can't believe this is happening.' Someone else said, 'Shhh!'

The Zapruder footage hadn't been discovered yet. It was still early afternoon. No one knew much of anything. The television showed dozens of Texans shocked and crying. All the women wore women's hats. The portions of their coiffures that stuck out from under their hats were evidence of perhaps the ugliest hairdos in recorded history. Elvis said, 'Let's see if Cronkite knows what's going on. Change the channel, Lamar, will you please.'

Ann-Margret started talking. 'I sang for President Kennedy.'

'What?' Elvis said. 'When?'

'The day before I first met you.'

'What? You didn't say anything about that.'

'I just put it out of my mind. I had been so bedazzled by President Kennedy, but then I met you.'

'Why were you singing to him?'

'For his birthday. He turned forty-six. There was a party at the Waldorf in New York City.'

'You sang for the president like Marilyn Monroe did last year?'

'Yes. I mean, no. I didn't sing "Happy Birthday." I sang "Baby Won't You Please Come Home."'

Elvis began softly snapping his fingers. Lamar Fike, who was now sitting on the floor, instinctively turned the TV sound off. Both Elvis and Ann-Margret sang softly, 'I've got the blues, I feel so lonely; I'd give the world if I could only make you understand; it surely would be grand. I'm gonna telephone my baby. Ask him, won't you please come home . . .'

Ann-Margret burst into tears mid-note. Elvis held her tight. He started crying himself. All the guys in the room began wiping their eyes. All morning they had wanted to start bawling about Kennedy, but couldn't. They were guys. Ann-Margret crying first made their tears okay.

Ann-Margret got up and went into the bathroom to wash her face. Elvis stayed on the couch and felt sudden shame. Kennedy had been such a young president. Just last week one of the boys had suggested to Elvis that he run for president in 1970 when Elvis would be thirty-five. This idea stayed at the back of his mind.

President Elvis.

Now, Elvis felt kicked in the stomach. *They shoot presidents.* His fantasy of running for office blew out of his mind like a tumbleweed.

* * *

Years from now, Margaret Salinger will still remember her father watching television coverage of Kennedy's assassination; her father slumped in his armchair hypnotized by TV grief—his face ashen, tears slipping down his cheeks. Margaret's father was only two years younger than Kennedy. This would be the only time Margaret would ever see her father cry. Those older girls were wrong to kick Margaret, because her father was not a Communist. In 1963 rural New Hampshire, the psychic calendar still read 1952. Oddballs or nonconformists were assumed Reds. The name of Margaret's father was Jerome David Salinger.

He was not a Communist.

He was the short story writer and novelist who wrote *Catcher in the Rye* twelve years previously under the name J. D. Salinger.

* * *

Ann-Margret returned from the bathroom. 'Do they know what happened yet?'

Four guys said 'No.'

Ann-Margret sat back down. 'After President Kennedy's birthday party at the Waldorf, I was invited to a party on the Upper East Side. Somebody's penthouse. The president asked me to sit beside him on the couch. He had a small pillow tucked behind him for his bad back. You know the first thing he said? He said, *You're a long ways from Valsjobyn*. He did his homework. He pronounced *Valsjobyn* perfectly. Like he spoke Swedish.'

'What's Valsjobyn?' someone asked.

'The town in Sweden where Rusty was born,' Elvis said—Rusty being Elvis's pet name for Ann-Margret.

'Then Robert, the president's brother, came over. He asked if I'd sing another song. I said I'd sing "Bye Bye Blackbird." But only if everyone would sing—including the president. And he did.' Rusty looked like she was going to break down again. 'I coaxed the president of the United States to sing "Bye Bye Blackbird."' Then she said, 'And now he's blackbird gone.'

* * *

The spring before the November shooting, the first lady had been planning a presidential gathering honoring American artists. President Kennedy himself had sent an invitation to J. D. Salinger and his wife, Claire. This was during a time when Salinger had been in deep hibernation for almost a decade.

He was more than just secluded.

He gave no interviews.

Salinger failed to RSVP.

Jacqueline Kennedy had telephoned the Salingers herself long-distance in New Hampshire. She talked with Claire Salinger, who could only say, 'You know my husband needs his privacy.'

'Can you put your husband on the line?' Jacqueline asked.

'I'll give it a go.' Claire set the receiver down.

Jacqueline sat listening to the Salingers' living room hundreds of miles away in New Hampshire. She heard a grandfather clock. It gave a quaint bonging for ten a.m.

Jacqueline waited.

Jacqueline never had to wait for anybody or anything.

Finally, Jacqueline heard footsteps. They sounded feminine. Claire came on. 'I am very sorry, Mrs. Kennedy,' she said.

'Say no more,' Jacqueline replied.

* * *

> 'We read in dead men's books!'
>
> —*The House of the Seven Gables*

'Where were you when you heard Kennedy had been shot?'

Norman Mailer answered: 'I was having lunch with Norman Podhoretz [then a *liberal* intellectual]. I don't think we were at Smith and Wollensky, but it was a steak joint somewhere in Manhattan. The news came in that Kennedy had been shot. I remember in my arrogance and stupidity saying, *I don't think he's seriously wounded. He wants us to believe he's seriously wounded so we realize how much we care about him and need him.* Of course, the news came in about half an hour later that Kennedy was dead.' Mailer paused. 'That was a great lesson in humility, let me tell you.... Instant humility.... What I will remember is my own contestation—that my acumen was so skewed, that I was so wrong.' Mailer threw up his hands. 'When you're a novelist you don't like to think that you're ever wrong.'

It is fascinating that Norman Mailer saw himself as a novelist when the seminal works that he is remembered for, such as *Armies of the Night* and *The Executioner's Song,* are nonfiction.

* * *

There was an old show, probably the genesis of all TV police dramas, called *Dragnet.* The show always began with a very serious male voice speaking these words, 'The story you are about to see is true. Some names were changed to protect the innocent.'

The novel you are about to read is true. All the people who are mentioned—just as Bob Dylan sang—I had to rearrange their faces and give them all another name. Still, this novel is true history.

Book One

1950–1959

Chapter 1

The American Embassy, Mexico City, 1950

Go back to 1950, thirteen years prior to Kennedy's gundown in Dallas. Three young male American expatriates are living in Mexico City.

The word *young* is used with its 1950s implication. This is and was a decade when even men in their late thirties were considered *young*.

One of the men is thirty-two. On his deathbed many years after November 22, 1963, he will claim that he was part of the conspiracy to murder President Kennedy. In 1950, this man brought his wife and their three-year-old daughter to this 5.2-square-mile capital built by the Aztecs in 1325. The Aztecs named it Tenochtitlán. The city had once been a Venice-like metropolis crisscrossed with canals as well as pyramids where the hearts of prisoners were ripped out from their chests. The Aztecs had faith this bloodletting kept the sun arcing across the sky.

This book's eldest expatriate is thirty-six. He brought his common law wife, his son, and his stepdaughter with him to Mexico City.

The youngest expatriate is twenty-seven. He brought only his wife, as they had no children. Each of these American men is unknown in 1950. The eldest will become a notorious modernist writer, his reputation greater than the number of actual readers who opened his books. The man whose age was in the middle will commit numerous political crimes, but will only be charged with a specific burglary that will force the resignation of an American president. The youngest of the three will become the enemy of this decade's relentless fecundity, this Baby Big Bang—year after year in the 1950s nearly four million newborns pop up in suburban hospitals situated discreetly on the peripheries of clusters of cookie-cutter fake-colonial snout houses where each parent keeps a well-thumbed copy of Dr. Spock's *The Common Sense Book of Baby and Child Care* beside the bed.

This trio's brief Mexican exile is a poignant lens to use to view the U.S.A. from.

—Norte America.

—Gringolandia.

★ ★ ★

The youngest expatriate is Carl Djerassi—pronounced *Ger-AH-see.* Djerassi looks a bit like a Semitic Desi Arnaz. Djerassi arrives in Mexico City around Día de los Muertos (Day of the Dead). Djerassi was born in Vienna when Sigmund Freud had still been alive. When he was sixteen, Carl's parents sent him to New York City to escape Hitler's imminent Blitzkrieg. Djerassi would attend college in Missouri and Ohio, finally earning a PhD from the University of Wisconsin. This man, who will exhibit a lifelong dedication to women and sex, and sex and women, was a carnal numbskull in college. He knew that possession of an automobile was the only way his generation could enjoy sex or a reasonably close facsimile, yet Djerassi never learned to drive. In fact, in Ohio, he took cello lessons instead of driving classes. At the start of the war, Djerassi was both a virgin and 4-F. He transcends that first affliction in 1943—his wedding night spent with his bride, Virginia, in a Pullman compartment clacking through the dark toward an Atlantic shore honeymoon.

Professionally, Djerassi would become a steroid man. 'Steroids are solid alcohols that occur widely in plants and animals,' he'd explain. 'The best-known steroid is cholesterol.' If you didn't stop him, Djerassi would tell how all steroids (and all sterols) are based on a chemical skeleton that consists of carbon and hydrogen atoms arranged in four fused rings, generically known as 'perhydrocyclopentanophenanthrene'—Djerassi always enunciating that boa constrictor word with smug fluidity.

Djerassi's first job was working in New Jersey for a Swiss chemical company called CIBA. They held a patent for cholesterol, a steroid that was considered a good thing back then as cholesterol was a thinking man or woman's steroid—10 percent of the brain is composed of cholesterol. Djerassi was part of the team that invented a powerful antihistamine for CIBA called pribenzamine. A chemical triumph. Djerassi was hot. He was recruited by a Mexico City pharmaceutical company called Syntex (from *Syn*thesis and M*ex*ico), led by Budapest-born chemist George Rosenkranz, who found himself exiled in Mexico after the war.

Djerassi's New Jersey colleagues think he is crazy moving down to Mexico. Djerassi defends his decision: 'Everyone assumes that serious chemistry stops at the Rio Grande. It doesn't. I'm gambling that being in the backwater I can establish a scientific reputation.' Then he speaks Latin, '*Quod licet Iovi non licet bovi*' and translates, 'What is allowed to God is not permitted to an ox.'

No one in New Jersey ever asks him what this means. Additionally, no one in New Jersey ever asks what his wife, Virginia, thinks about this Mexican relocation.

★ ★ ★

The gringo of the middle comparative age of thirty-two is an American spy named Howard Hunt. He is the head of the CIA office stationed in Mexico City. This town serves as the espionage portal to all of Central America. Spies are as numerous as drunks sleeping it off in city doorways and gutters.

Hunt works out of Uncle Sugar's embassy in Mexico City. (Uncle Sugar = Uncle Sam = U.S.A.) It is a nondescript *Latin moderne* eighteen-story office building on the Reforma.

Hunt is a spy who could look good posing for a photo wearing an ascot.

In the 3-D of real life, Hunt's face has more than a few Bob Hope angles. This is the difference between a handsome man and a comedian. In addition, Hunt's complexion is permanently pale as if he were some eternal Norwegian. Hunt even spent time in Hollywood and never tanned. In Mexico, he has remained relentlessly white. Hunt is a gringo's gringo. Often, his cover name is 'Mr. White.'

Hunt's spycraft is not assassination or molehood. He is an expert in Black Propaganda—forging reports or counterfeiting documents—stating something untrue, then planting fake spots in radio news or newspapers. Misinformation has always been as powerful as revealed secrets.

Hunt's thirty-year-old wife, Dorothy, is also a spy. She was born Dorothy Wetzel in Ohio on an April Fools' Day. After the Second World War, she worked for the OSS (progenitor of the CIA). She was adept at tracking down Nazi money and artwork for nineteenth-century-born William Averell Harriman. This man was the same Yale Bonesman Harriman who along with his cohort Prescott Bush had invested money for and with the Nazis in Berlin until FDR made such activities illegal. Dot's travels for Harriman took her to Calcutta and New Delhi. She suffered a brief marriage to an alcoholic French count. She ended up stationed in Shanghai. There, she met E. Howard Hunt, also of the OSS.

Dot Hunt is not conventionally pretty. She is more an askew beauty. Her face is severe and masculine. Her hair, short. She has an Indira Gandhi profile. There is some Oglala Sioux in her blood. Her smile and laugh are never generous, but regal—you pleased her so rather than kill you she would laugh at you.

In Mexico City, Dot primarily functions as Howard's confidante. She possesses security clearance so her husband can tell her his secrets. She also just found out that she is pregnant with their second child. Dorothy Hunt is perhaps the only expatriate mother in Mexico who never opened Dr. Spock. Why bother? A nanny dealt with the baby.

'Another nanny will deal with the new one when it comes.'

* * *

Virginia Djerassi. Curly black hair. Ice-cream-scoop chin. Glasses. In early 1950, Carl Djerassi divorces Virginia in Cuernavaca so he can marry his pregnant mistress, Norma—petite, pleasant face. It never fully penetrates Djerassi's consciousness that both his wives are gentiles. And even though divorce is anathema up in Gringolandia, Djerassi's soul remains more European than American. Divorce is not a life-or-death situation. Djerassi's own parents divorced when he was six and didn't inform him until he was thirteen. Soon after Virginia Djerassi's Mexican divorce, she marries a Mexican national and gets pregnant.

* * *

Our eldest gringo is William Seward Burroughs II—or 'Seward,' as the Mexican newspapers will call him one year from now after he shoots a woman in the head. He was born in safe-as-milk St. Louis, the grandson of the inventor of the rosary of capitalism, the adding machine. Young Burroughs never held a job, except once as an exterminator in Chicago. His mother sent him $200 a month allowance (about $1,500 in modern funds). During WWII, Burroughs had been drafted and classified 1-A in the infantry. His mother managed to get her son a civilian disability discharge.

His mother also wrote books on flower arranging.

During the war, Burroughs was in Manhattan and met a married woman nine years his junior named Joan Vollmer. She is now a divorcé living as Burroughs's common-law wife. She already had a daughter before giving birth to Burroughs's son. Before Mexico City, both Joan and Burroughs were arrested and jailed and even did time in American asylums. Their last stop in the U.S.A. was Texas, where Burroughs was a passenger in a car that was stopped by cops who found marijuana stashed in the glove compartment. Burroughs was arrested. Trial was set for late October. A week before Halloween, Burroughs and Joan packed Joan's daughter and the couple's son in their car and fled down the dove-gray Pan American Highway to Mexico City.

On good days in Mexico City, Burroughs does not look like a desperado. He is tall and lanky and dresses like he was born to the gentry. He's always been that way. He looked like a middle-aged lawyer even as a kid going to boarding school in pre–atom bomb Los Alamos. In Mexico City, Burroughs's good days become far and few. Mostly the man looks cadaverously beat. Joan's looks suffer as well. She was once a tall-drink-of-water five-foot-six Botticelli beauty. In Mexico City, she often appears more beat than even Burroughs does. Her slight childhood polio limp becomes pronounced. She has open sores on her arms. She lives on Benzedrine and hundreds of daily sips of tequila. Her husband has stopped sleeping with her and returned to sex with street boy-meat. Her husband also has a healthy appetite for bennies and horse. He is a local feature on Dolores Street where the Chinese junkies give him a nod as they slouch against the glass windows of the Exquisito Chop Suey joint. Junk is cheap on Dolores Street. A habit for horse only costs thirty dollars a month; up in the U.S.A. it's three hundred per month. On Dolores Street, Burroughs avoids pantopon cut with milk sugar. Burroughs loves eating yen pox—opium ash with coffee. He knows that Our Lady of Chalma is the patron saint of junkies. Finally, Burroughs possesses, as the Mexican police will one day say, a 'dedication' to alcohol.

* * *

Carl Djerassi has a mixed view of Mexico City. He likes that in a city spread over such a large area, most people leave you alone—everywhere except certain neighborhoods near Colonia Guerrero where strangers are always asking '¿Qué buscas, amigo?'

What are you looking for, friend?

'Nothing. Besides, I'm no friend.'

Djerassi likes the steam of the tamale stalls under the statues of the Angel of Independence and Diana the Huntress on Paseo de la Reforma. The traffic of Mexico City is Cairo mixed with Florence. The population—Calcutta mixed with Beverly Hills.

As for William Burroughs, he loves the calves' heads bobbing in the boiling cauldrons of soup at outdoor stalls. He loves the city's scent of wormseed—a smell like gasoline mixed with orange juice. The hoarse voices of Mexican women who smoke Faros amuse Burroughs. Faros are Mex cigarettes so poignant they are wrapped in rice paper sweetened with sugar. Burroughs believes Mexico is an 'Oriental country' amplifying centuries of 'disease and poverty and degradation and stupidity and slavery and brutality and psychic and physical terrorism.' Mexico is chaotic in that way dreams are chaotic. 'I like it myself,' Burroughs writes in a letter to his young friend Jack Kerouac, 'but it isn't everybody's taste.'

★ ★ ★

Howard Hunt was not just a spy.

He was a novelist.

He already had four hardcover novels published as well as two cheap paperback originals scheduled to come out that year. Hunt had once been a Promising Young Writer. One year after Pearl Harbor, his first novel, *East of Farewell,* a realistic war tale about a U.S. destroyer in the North Atlantic, was excerpted twice in the sophisticated magazine *The New Yorker* before publication by Alfred Knopf. The reviews were good, but the novel was topped by the daily war news in the *Sunday Mercury* or *Chicago Tribune*, making the book out-of-date on a daily basis. Still, Hunt won a Guggenheim Fellowship. He wrote three more novels that were best sellers, then forgotten. Like everyone else's, Hunt's postwar literary career was overshadowed by Norman Mailer's. Mailer was a Jew five years Hunt's junior. Mailer's first book, a Pacific theater war novel, *The Naked and the Dead,* was published in 1948. It got raves and glory and was a best seller. The *Providence Journal* in Rhode Island proclaimed it 'The most important American novel since *Moby-Dick*.' No newspaper in Rhode Island, or anywhere else, had or would ever compare anything Howard Hunt wrote to *Moby-Dick*.

* * *

Howard Hunt and Norman Mailer were both Magnificent Narcissists, as were many of the ex-G.I. alpha dogs who fathered the Baby Big Bang of the 1950s. Mailer married six years earlier when he was twenty. In the years immediately after the war, young men had been expected to marry at ages twenty to twenty-two, getting hitched one and a half years earlier than their fathers had. By 1950, Mailer had fathered only one child—social leprosy as an American marriage was expected to produce 2.2 kids per family. The social pressure against single-child households was even stronger than that against childless marriages.

Mailer would come through before his death. He would prove himself an unconventional patriarch who would burn through six wives and contribute his seed to the production of at least eight children.

Perhaps more important, Mailer would have written thirty-one books.

* * *

Carl Djerassi was a narcissist but not magnificent. You already know that he was 4-F during the war. He had always been a realist when it came to offspring. 'Americans mistakenly believe that we are creating an extension of ourselves,' he said often. 'But in the animal world sex is merely extending the species.' Mailer's nine children were not and would never be little Mailers according to Djerassian logic.

They were little Americans.

Little Semitic Americans.

* * *

William Burroughs was a junkie with newfound aspirations to be a writer. Until Mexico City, Burroughs abhorred writing. It disgusted him to put thoughts or feelings in words on paper. Now he was working on a novel, egged on by his comrade Allen Ginsberg, a twenty-four-year-old aspiring poet (and the son of a card-carrying Communist mother). Their friend Jack Kerouac was twenty-eight. Harcourt Brace was about to publish Kerouac's first novel, *The Town and the City,* that spring. Burroughs followed Kerouac's tenet that a novel was only a memoir with the names changed. The book Burroughs was writing concerned being a junkie in New York City and New Orleans and Mexico City. It was titled *Junky.* Burroughs wrote to Kerouac: 'There are some students at Mexico City University who are successful writers. I am trying to make a deal with one of them to rewrite *Junky* in a saleable form. It is doubtful whether I am capable of writing anything saleable.'

* * *

Joan and Bill Burroughs's kids, Julie and Bill Jr., are six and three, respectively. Joan was never exactly sure who Julie's real father was, but she convinced the soldier she was married to at the time that Julie was his. The girl is already six, yet she has not been toilet trained. Joan could not be bothered. Bill Jr. had been produced by Burroughs's seed in a New York hotel room. Bill Jr. did not use the potty either.

Dr. Spock had no advice for this situation.

If Dr. Spock had been dead, he would have rolled over in his grave to hear of a six-year-old American-born child who was not toilet trained.

'Children are innocent like animals,' Joan once said to Burroughs. He was cleaning his shoes after stepping in an arrangement of small child turds.

'You don't know the nonsense you speak,' Burroughs replied. 'Everything defaults to evil. America was old and dirty and evil before the settlers, even before the Indians. There is even worse evil down here in the heart of Mexico.'

'Oh, pasha, you old poop. You sound like some sour pilgrim. Bill, you're a Calvinist. You were born guilty. Everyone else was born innocent. The rest of us only get dirtied up after we become adults. Our mind gets Swiss cheesed by the disturbances of life. Listen to the kids talking while they're still kids. They are candid and immaculate and have all the finesse of'—she pointed to her chest—'their mother.' Then Joan unconsciously strutted in a circle around the room. 'Bill Jr. told me that he was going to run away from home. I asked him, *Where to?* He said, *I am running away to Vermont or maybe Asia.*' Joan started her second circle. 'I showed Julie a picture in a book of Adam and Eve. She asked me, *Which one is Adam and which one is Eve? I can't tell. They don't have any clothes on.*'

★ ★ ★

Howard Hunt needs a writer to translate a book written in Spanish by Peruvian ex-Communist Eudocio Ravines revealing his disdain for Marxism. Hunt summons a twenty-five-year-old kid down to Mexico City to do it.

The kid is named William Buckley Jr.

Buckley is good at brownnosing.

Nose. Nosing. Noses. This elitist pup of a papist talks through his nose with a pretentious drawl. Buckley is even more of a nasal conservative snob than his boss Hunt. The lad has a book coming in 1951. Not a novel. An intellectual memoir titled *God and Man at Yale*. Knopf is not his publisher. It will be the first title from a new conservative publisher named Regnery. In his book, Buckley claims Yale University undermined 'her' students' Christian beliefs while promoting Keynesian economics, which are only one step from collectivism, i.e., Communism.

Buckley is Roman Catholic, but that didn't stop him from becoming a Bonesman (as had George H. W. Bush, etc.). Catholicism was working-class, but Buckley was born with a silver spoon down his throat. Hunt was the one who had to work his way through Brown University playing trumpet for the Frank Rollin Orchestra.

Playing music was the only time Howard Hunt transcended his Jim Crow soul. The most ethereal experience he'd ever had with another man or even woman was with an African-American man—Charlie Christian, Benny Goodman's electric guitarist, who had died in 1942 at the age of twenty-five. Their encounter was at a Manhattan jam party after a Benny Goodman show. Hunt had only been in the audience, but he brought his horn. Now Hunt was in a cellar filled elbow-to-elbow with professional pipes and amateur blowers. Hunt was just a kid in college and he suddenly blew out of the ruckus and began a piercing solo. Hunt was not sure where his breath was coming from, but Hunt knew his breath was genius. Everyone stopped playing. They were listening. Everyone except Charlie Christian. He picked his electric guitar faster to keep up with Hunt. Charlie Christian anticipated Hunt's every note before Hunt blew it. Hunt was furious at first. Hunt didn't want to be shadowed by any black alley cat. Then Christian stopped anticipating what Hunt would blow, and he and that white trumpeter found themselves playing a heartfelt duet. The notes rounded around each other, sometimes in harmony, sometimes dissonance. Sometimes Hunt was the goat and Christian was the leopard. Other times Hunt sharked while Christian oystered up. Hunt closed his eyes, and then was afraid to open them because he was crying. When the jam was over, Christian passed him by, two swarthy women playfully gripping his arms. 'Cool as a jewel, cry-baby,' Charlie Christian said to Howard Hunt with a smile. Christian then escorted his women away.

★ ★ ★

The acid guitarist who went by the moniker Jimi Hendrix will become a character in this narration. Why not mention him now? Jimi Hendrix was born Johnny Allen Hendrix in 1942. He was a mutt before Obama—part black (Al, his father), part Cherokee (Lucille, his mother). Lucille was just seventeen when she had Jimi. Al was twenty-three and stationed in the South Pacific. Al returned to Seattle in '45 and discovered his first son had been dumped with his grandmother down in Berkeley. Al drove south from Washington, through Oregon, into California to retrieve his kid. Al Hendrix changed that shirttail's name to James Marshall.

Jimi Marshall Hendrix.

Life with father and son—strangers actually—was chaotic. Relatives would all tell different stories. Al would even write a biography, but much of what he would write would be pure fiction or at best an embellishment of what really happened.

In Seattle, Al gets back together with Lucille. They have more kids. Lucille gives birth to a boy she names Joseph. Al isn't the father. It will be said that the father is Filipino, but that could be wrong.

★ ★ ★

In the beginning of his career, William Buckley Jr. used snobbery as self-defense. It would transform into Buckley's unpleasant first-strike airs. One morning at Uncle's embassy, Hunt passed by Buckley's desk and said, 'Mistah Buckley, at the Colombian embassy cocktail party last night, a woman whom I shall not name said that Mexico was a country ruled by *innocent Fascism*. I didn't ask what she meant.'

Buckley furrowed his eyes.

'What did she mean, young Buckley?'

'She probably meant something akin to *innocent homosexuality*.'

'What's that?'

'Unconsummated man love.'

'Any form of homosexuality is guilty, Mistah Buckley!'

The young man smiled using his thin lips and showing his well-bred teeth: 'She probably meant *soft* Fascism.'

Hunt gave a theatrical frown. 'Which is?'

'Criminality without ideology. Mexican politics has always been criminal, yet Mexicans have burrito ambitions. The presidency is limited to a single term of six years. Since the president doesn't have to worry about reelection or impeachment, he can spend six years doing whatever he wants.'

'Hmm. The woman who used that term is an elitist [crude term for *vagina*].'

Buckley smiled. 'The elite in Mexico City are anti-American in public, while in private they fight tooth 'n' nail to protect their membership in the Chapultepec Country Club.'

Hunt gave a Disney-wicked smile. 'I have a membership in the Chapultepec Country Club.'

Buckley had no reaction.

'I'll take you there for cocktails someday if you continue to be a good lad.'

* * *

William Burroughs was as Ivy League as Hunt and Buckley—Burroughs being a Harvard man. Back in '41, Burroughs's father told his son that a Columbia alumni, Colonel Donovan, class of '38, was creating a 'spy outfit' in D.C. 'Bill' Burroughs took a train to the capital and met Colonel Donovan at his office. Donovan's nickname was 'Wild Bill.' The two Bills got along. It seemed certain that Burroughs would join the CIA, making him a peer with Howard Hunt.

But this was not to be.

Donovan's second-in-command came into the office to check out the new recruit. It turned out the guy, James Phinney Baxter, had been Burroughs's housemaster at Harvard. Baxter despised Burroughs. After the recruit left the interview, Baxter told Donovan what a misfit Burroughs was.

William Burroughs did not become a spy.

Chapter 2

The Watergate, District of Columbia, 1951

Saturday night in Mexico City.

The Djerassis and the Hunts went as separate couples to see *Uncle Vanya* performed at Mexico City College. (Howard Hunt only tolerated Chekhov because the Russian doctor was pre-Stalin.) Both couples ended up separately at a popular student hangout afterward, the Bounty Bar. This semi-dive was decorated with a nautical theme. The bar was comfortably empty—that is, there were just enough other customers drinking at tables so the two couples didn't feel they were alone on a stage. The bartender was black-skinned, but he was smiling and drinking a Pepsi. Safe. The two couples recognized each other from the Chekhov audience and then sat down at a table together. The wives ordered cocktails. The men, Carta Blanca. The beer was served in ceramic mugs like coffee. The gringos sipped their drinks. Made small talk. 'Mexican beer is supposed to be so good because of all the Nazi brewers that came here after the War.' While they chatted, the men checked out the cleavage of each other's wife. The women considered, without getting into details, what it would be like to sleep with the other's husband. By the time the first round was over, the women were laughing. Dot's laugh was deep. Norma's was shrill and annoying. Yet, as she laughed, she displayed an open yap filled with flawless dentality. Someone's wife pointed to the stuffed fish on the wall and said, 'I don't get it. The sailor theme—the name.'

'Yes,' said the other wife. 'What's with the Bounty Bar? Bounty for what?'

'*Mutiny on the Bounty,*' Djerassi said with a generous smile.

* * *

In the middle of the second round, one wife said to the other, 'Let's go powder our noses.' They rose and went as a pair to the 'Señoritas' Inodoro.' The men watched the legs of each other's wife. Djerassi then began a monologue about his work with steroids. Hunt felt like cutting in to brag about his au courant triumph, his men successfully sneaking into the Guatemalan embassy, but he couldn't talk about that to a civilian.

CIA work. For Your Eyes and Ears Only.

The Guatemalan embassy was located two blocks from Uncle's. Hunt could stand at his office window with binoculars and peer into all the Guatemalan offices facing his building. Guatemala had a legally elected president. The president was a liberal. Guatemala was on Hunt's anti-commie radar. Getting into the Guatemalan embassy pulled on Hunt's psyche the way a particular mountain tugs a mountaineer.

First, Hunt mounted twenty-four-hour surveillance of the building. His crew got blueprints. They recruited a maid, Juanita García, who planted a microphone in the Guatemalan ambassador's office. The CIA listening post was located in an apartment inside the embassy's very building, recording on tape recorders every sound the microphone picked up. Juanita even made a putty imprint of the ambassador's safe's keyhole. She also supplied Hunt with a key to the embassy service door.

Hunt had another agent make friends with the night watchman. In 1972 at the Watergate Hotel, it never dawned on Howard Hunt to cultivate the night watchman, Frank Wills. The Guatemalan embassy's night watchman was a janitor named José Corrida Detoros. Hunt's undercover man and Señor Detoros became card-playing/tequila-drinking buddies.

Hunt decided his burglars would go in Friday night, just as he would with his first attempt at breaking into Watergate.

* * *

Do you remember that when the Watergate burglars were arrested it had been their fourth failed attempt to bug the offices of the Democratic National Committee? First, Howard Hunt's men will try to break into the office on the Friday of Memorial Day weekend. Hunt will stage a fake business dinner for the 'Ameritas Corporation' at the Continental Room, a sublevel restaurant inside the Watergate complex. He'll round up around eight Cubans to pretend that they're businessmen. The plan will be: After watching bogus business movies while eating a tough steak dinner, everyone will leave the restaurant but Hunt and a Cuban. The two will hide inside a closet. After the Continental Room closes down for the night, they will sneak into the Watergate's stairwell and creep up to the Democrats' office on the sixth floor.

Here goes: Hunt and the Cuban slip out of the closet. The pair find the stairwell door locked. The entrance to the restaurant is also locked. The entire front wall of the Continental Room is glass. Hunt and his Cuban can be seen in the now empty hallway. The two hear custodians talking. Then a night watchman. Hunt and the Cuban spend the rest of the night hiding together again in the closet. On Saturday night things go better. Hunt's Cubans make it up to the DNC's door, but the lock man doesn't have the right pick. The mission is aborted. On Memorial Day itself, the lock man flies all the way down to Florida to get the right jimmies and flies back to D.C. as the sun is going down. They'll try to burglarize the Democrats for a third time.

This time they get in. They open safes. They photograph documents. They plant bugs. They leave.

Tuesday morning, Hunt finds that none of the bugs works. Two weeks later, Hunt and his Cubans return to the Watergate. They have new state-of-the-art bugs. One of the burglars, a non-Cuban, needlessly slips a strip of tape over the latch of the door in the stairwell. Here comes the night watchman, Mr. Frank Wills, the guy Howard Hunt ignored. Wills notices the tape and peels it off. Next, the non-Cuban comes by and sees that the tape is missing. He retapes the lock. Ten minutes after that, the night watchman sees that the tape has returned! He telephones the Washington, D.C., Police Department.

★ ★ ★

Yet, twenty-one years earlier in Mexico City—

Friday night, six p.m. The CIA agent is playing cards and drinking tequila down in the basement with Señor Detoros. Everyone else who works in the Guatemalan embassy has left early. Hunt has agents following each one back to their homes or to a bar. Juanita's bug inside the Guatemalan embassy reveals a silent office. Hunt telephones the embassy. The bug picks up the ringing telephone. That's all. No one answers. (No one in Mexico City had a 'phone answering' machine as such devices were as big as suitcases.) The phone in the Guatemalan embassy keeps ringing. Hunt hangs up.

The burglary is a *go.*

Hunt's team creeps into the Guatemalan embassy through the service door. They cover the embassy's windows with opaque black muslin so no one outside can see their flashlights. The team cracks the safe. They photograph everything inside with a new CIA Instamatic film so after the pictures develop everything can be returned exactly as it was found. The burglars set up a conventional camera and for three hours photograph every document in that safe. There is also $30,000 in American currency inside. Hunt's men let the money be and just copy the serial numbers.

After the burglars finish, they take down the black drapes.

Within an hour, every member of the team but Hunt is at the Mexico City airport, boarding a flight to Love Field in Dallas. They change their identities and fly to Washington, D.C., where the film is taken to the CIA and the NSA.

The photographs will reveal the names of all the prominent Mexico City citizens the Guatemalans have on their payroll as well as the names of contacts in the Soviet embassy.

Hunt's mission was perfect. Watergate will be a comedy of errors—yet as time will show Hunt intended for that burglary to fail, thus implicating the Committee to Re-Elect the President, aka CREEP.

The president will be, of course, Richard Milhous Nixon.

* * *

Inside the Bounty Bar in Mexico City, 1951.

Howard Hunt did not, because he could not, tell Carl Djerassi anything about the Guatemalan embassy job. Instead, Hunt had to nod his head as Djerassi jawed about cortisone. 'Arthritics get a shot of cortisone and jump up to dance.' Djerassi told about making cortisone on the cheap from raw plant material, an extraordinarily complex process involving thirty-six different chemical transformations beginning with animal bile acids. 'I was just in *Life* magazine,' Djerassi told Hunt. 'I got cortisone from a giant yam. They took a photo. The caption was *Scientists with average age of twenty-seven find big supply in Mexican root*. We were also in *Newsweek* as well. I discovered the yam plant Barbasco yields more diosgenin than *cabeza de negro.* I found the raw material grown in Veracruz and Oaxaca and Chiapas—areas difficult to reach, let me tell you.'

Djerassi then spoke the word *perhydrocyclopentanophenanthrene.*

—at that moment the arrow of coincidence struck—

William Burroughs walked into the Bounty Bar. He had signed up for cultural anthropology classes at Mexico City College on the G.I. Bill. 'Always feed at the public trough' was his adage. He was learning to speak Mayan—a tongue dead everywhere but in the Yucatán bush and among anthropologists. Burroughs knew a little about everything, but knew everything there was to know about drugs. When he heard 'perhydrocyclopentanophenanthrene' he made a gun with his hand and said 'Steroid man' to Djerassi. The latter looked surprised. He and Hunt invited the gaunt, but respectably dressed stranger to join them for a cerveza. Djerassi said, 'I was telling Hunt here about the opportunities for advancement in science down here in Mexico—*quod licet Iovi non licet bovi.*'

Burroughs said in his undertaker's drawl, 'You mean *ox* ironically?'

Before Djerassi could answer, Hunt bent low over the table and said to the 'steroid man': 'Please, friend, stop the priest talk.' Djerassi and Burroughs peered at Hunt. 'The pig Latin. Catholic tongue.' Neither Djerassi nor Burroughs was wearing a crucifix so Hunt assumed they wouldn't be offended.

Hunt didn't explain himself to these strangers. If you had to know, Hunt was a Presbyterian.

Dot was Catholic.

When they got married, Hunt refused to convert. So, his wife was excommunicated. The priests refused to baptize his daughter, Lisa. There in the Bounty Bar, a wave of hot rage sheened Hunt's face. He thought of Buckley. That prig-punk cake eater. Buckley agreed with a sneer with Saint Augustine's conjecture that unbaptized babies were sent to hell as demonstration of God's merciful love toward the baptized.

Dot was pregnant again, but not showing. Those papist mackerels would refuse to baptize his next child as well.

★ ★ ★

'So, what useful thing are you doing with your steroids, Señor Djerassi?' Burroughs asked.

It was a complicated question. Djerassi made something up. 'Sterilizing insects,' he said.

'I was an exterminator once,' Burroughs drawled. 'Steroids better than poison?'

Djerassi answered, 'A steroid won't harm the crops like poisons. It will just make the insects sterile, unable to lay eggs and reproduce. Once the prevalent generation dies, no more bugs.'

A beautiful Mexican woman in a green dress walked in and Burroughs felt particularly misogynistic—'If we could sterilize all the women in Mexico, the Mexican race would stop here.' He said that and then gave a sinister chuckle.

Hunt said, 'I'd like to sterilize every Communist. That would fix their wagon.'

The two wives returned and their husbands introduced Burroughs. 'What are you doing in these parts, Mr. Burroughs?' Dot asked.

Burroughs told them about the Aztecs. Burroughs told them he was a student. Burroughs told them he had a wife and two kids. He didn't mention the G.I. Bill. In the light from the bar, Burroughs actually appeared handsome at that moment. He was taller than the other two husbands. He was wearing a suit, but it didn't register as something for a special occasion or for work. It was as if he had been born in a suit like a good undertaker.

A group of men stumbled in and sat at a nearby table. One of them peered at Burroughs's table and said in Spanish, '*Valorar este libro gringos alerta cuando hay nuevos títulos de clásica*'—a sentiment that translated into 'Gringos are like the rooster who believes the sun has risen to hear him crow.'

Djerassi said to his table, '*Gringos.* Anyone know the origin of that word?'

Burroughs said, 'When Spain was Muslim, foreigners were called Greeks—*griegos.*'

'Yes,' Djerassi said. 'Strangers were *Greeks* regardless of the land of their origin. The noun *griegos* then took an etymological journey with Cortez across the Atlantic and the citizens of Norte America became the new Greeks—gringos.' Both Burroughs and Hunt then started to say something at the same time. They stopped. Burroughs nodded to Hunt to be the one to continue, but Djerassi kept right on talking. 'I for one am arrogant. I am an arrogant man. But I am not an arrogant gringo or Greek. My arrogance is deeper than nationality. My arrogance is the foundation of my identity. I don't try to hide it.' He then leaned forward and said conspiratorially without lowering his voice, 'I don't tell a waiter my order more than once. I don't talk to cabdrivers. I'm a very impatient person. I'm also an honest person. Why should I pretend that I'm not arrogant when I am? The arrogance that I'm referring to is an intellectual arrogance. It is not just social arrogance by any means. It's related to my impatience.'

Dot had placed his European accent. 'Does your arrogance have anything to do with being Viennese?'

Djerassi gave a dry half-hearted chuckle. 'It has more to do with being Jewish.' He gave a sly smile. 'My mother was Ashkenazi. Arrogantly Ashkenazi.'

Hunt knew that Dot was going to ask 'What's that?' and shot her a stern look that said *shut up*. Hunt hated Jews. Hunt hated Jews almost as much as he hated Negroes [African-Americans] and the Japanese and the Communists. Nevertheless, here in Mexico City all fellow gringos were comrades unless they were fruits or Communists. Hunt didn't figure Burroughs was fagged out—not with a wife and kids.

'Arrogance is a complicated word,' Burroughs was saying. 'There are snobs in leper colonies.'

This struck Norma Djerassi as funny. She laughed. 'The hubris of lepers.'

'Pride goeth before a fall,' Dot said.

Norma Djerassi asked, 'What Shakespeare play is that from?'

Djerassi was momentarily confused by his wife's question and was about to say *Macbeth,* when Burroughs said dryly, 'Proverbs sixteen: eighteen.'

Norma looked confused. 'Proverbs?' Her husband was aghast. At that moment, a drunken student—radiating American-hood and smelling of cheap something or other—staggered up to their table and reached into his sport coat and pulled out a .32 pistol and slammed it on their table. 'Burroughs,' he yelled, 'I bet you don't know what the Boy Scout motto is!'

Burroughs's lack of surprise meant that he knew the gunboy. Burroughs reached in his own coat and pulled out a Colt .45 that he set beside the .32.

Burroughs's .45 was much plumper than the .32.

'Yes I do,' Burroughs said. '*Be prepared.*'

* * *

This was a Chekhovian moment. You know how that goes: a gun introduced in the first act goes off in the third.

Yet everyone in Mexico carried a gun. Your barber was armed. Surgeons never removed their pistols when they performed a cut. In a different bar in a different part of town, the Spanish expatriate filmmaker Luis Buñuel (age fifty) was telling his table (in Spanish of course), 'I visit Esmeralda Studio in Xochimilco to see the orchestra run through the soundtrack to *Ensayo de un Crimen*. Thirty musicians show up. The studio is hot.' Buñuel fans his face. 'Each musician takes off his coat.' He makes that gesture in pantomime—you now noticed that this man with the squat head is remarkably ugly. 'All the violists, a few woodwinds and even'—Buñuel gives a shrug—'a cello player are wearing shoulder holsters, butt out, the guns ready to be gripped.'

Chapter 3

Mayo Clinic, Minnesota, 1951

It was July 1951. Early evening. A weekday. Hunt's phone rang at home. It was a Mexican phone so it didn't ring—instead it sounded like an old man clearing his throat. Hunt answered. Washington on the line.

'Listen to this, Hunt, Jersey Joe Walcott K.O.'d Ezzard Charles in the seventh.'

'Hello, Darwin,' Hunt said. 'Good for Jersey Joe.'

This call was being placed by another Joe—Joseph K. Darwin. Hunt had never met Joe K. Darwin face-to-face, yet Joe's voice was instantly recognizable just as Walter Winchell's voice was.

'Who is Jersey Joe?' Hunt asked.

'The oldest boxer to win the Heavyweight Championship.'

'How old is he?'

'Thirty-seven. How old are you?'

'Thirty-three.'

Darwin was no-nonsense brusque. 'Fug you, Hunt. I'm forty-two.'

Winchell spoke up to 197 words per minute. Darwin spoke 199—'Listen to this, Hunt. They put Dash Hammett in jail today.'

'The *Maltese Falcon* Sam Spade Hammett?'

'Right.'

'For what?'

—the damn Mexican phone line always crackling, static, silence; you had to shout into the phone—

'Not being a good American. He wouldn't spill the beans about some Reds he fox-trotted with.'—Darwin speaking those two sentences in under two seconds.

* * *

Hunt had become acquainted with Joe K. Darwin just after Hunt had arrived in Mexico City. The CIA hijacked the office that the FBI had occupied. The Mexicans had kicked the FBI back home and J. Edgar Buddha was enraged. Why? The FBI's presence in a foreign country was more thoroughly illegal than the CIA's.

J. Edgar's G-men had trashed the office before they left.

Uncle's embassy head in Mexico City, Ambassador O'Dwyer, hated the CIA on principle as much as he had hated the FBI. O'Dwyer refused to share office supplies. Hunt went above everyone's head and found a sympathetic ear north in Washington, D.C.—a quasi-Justice Department honcho named Joe K. Darwin. He was a fixer. Darwin provided Hunt with basic supplies such as typewriter ribbons and paper clips. Darwin took care of Hunt. He sent Hunt fresh bottles of Chivas Regal via diplomatic pouch.

'Hammett is a Red?' Hunt said. 'My God. He was once a strike-breaker for the Pinkertons. You'd think he'd know by now which side of the toast to butter.'

'What's your favorite Hammett?' Darwin asked.

'*The Maltese Falcon.*'

'*The Glass Key.*'

'I woulda figured a lush like yourself would pick *The Thin Man.*'

'I saw *Thin Man* movies, never read the book. Listen to me, I took my kid to the movies the other day—my youngest, Billy. We saw a horse opera, *The Cimarron Kid,* starring that war hero—what's his name?'

'Audie Murphy?'

'Yeah, Audie Murphy. He plays this kid cowboy who is falsely accused of being a thief, so he rides away into the desert and joins a family of bank robbers and becomes a thief for real.'

'Yeah? So?'

'Well my kid says to me, *Pop, listen to me. You have to be careful of who you call a Communist. Why is that?* I asked. *Cuz if you're wrong, they'll have no choice but to join the Communist Party like the Cimarron Kid.* This from a seven-year-old. Who puts these things in their heads?'

'Dr. Spock.'

* * *

Up in Minnesota, Dr. Benjamin Spock brings home a copy of *The Catcher in the Rye.*

Benjamin Spock is forty-eight years old. He works at the Mayo Clinic. His wife, Jane, is four years younger. She hates Minnesota as much as J. D. Salinger's wife will hate New Hampshire.

('Land of 10,000 Lakes' indeed.)

The Mayo Clinic sits near the bottom of the state. Residents say 'bottom' or 'downstate' because there is nothing 'southern' about Minnesota. The winters are Siberian.

Snow brute.

Land of 10,000 Blizzards. Land of 10,000 Snowmen.

From November till late February, the sun never rises higher than the tree line. Worse for Jane, Ben is never home and his wife has no Minnesotan companions to converse with. Other Mayo wives are just wives. Housewives. Dull as dishwater no matter where they were born. Jane was expected to be like them. She couldn't do it. She was the uncredited coauthor of *Baby and Child Care,* for Pete's sake! She was an intellectual who had once lived in Manhattan with her husband.

Jane Spock was an East Coast cosmopolitan.

'I've heard about this *Catcher in the Rye* thing,' Jane says. 'Why are you readin' it?'

'Someone told me I appear in the book.'

'What? It's a novel!'

'I know. The kid who narrates gives a tirade about me. He calls me a phony.'

'By name?'

'Yeah. *Dr. Spock is a phony.*'

'Want me to read the book for you?'

'Yeah. That would be great. I don't have the time to waste on a dumb novel.'

* * *

The waning Mexican summer of 1951.

William Seward Burroughs splits Mexico City to travel south into

Ecuador. He leaves Joan home with the kids. Burroughs is accompanied into the jungle by a young pseudo-bisexual male named Rolfe. Bounty trash. Burroughs plans to search for *yagé,* a mystical hallucinogenic vine.

In her husband's absence, Joan entertains their two old friends from the north, twenty-five-year-old Allen Ginsberg and twenty-six-year-old Lucien Carr. To Joan, Carr still looks like a mischievous little prick. He's not queer. Joan wants to rut with him as soon as it is prudent. Carr was born in St. Louis so that's how he knows Bill Burroughs. Last year, Kerouac typed an autobiographical novel about Neal Cassady in Carr's apartment on West 21st Street on a roll of teletype paper. Kerouac's novel will not be published for six years. It will be titled *On the Road.*

Ginsberg spends hours playing with Bill Jr.

Ginsberg and Burroughs had been lovers for a while during the mid-1940s in New York City. Ginsberg was the one who set Joan up with Burroughs. If Lucien Carr was the catalyst of the Beat Generation, Joan was the queen bee of those junkies and lowlifes and drugstore philosophers as well as one William Seward Burroughs who had just been honorably discharged out of the Army. Joan's original husband returned at the war's end to find his nineteen-year-old wife sitting cat-legged in bed with five disheveled men, everyone rambling about Kant and Rimbaud while Joan gave this soliloquy: 'The entire country is being driven by Pilgrim fear. Puritan fear. *Good Housekeeping* fear. We fear that we have B.O., halitosis, or cavities. We pray for redemption at the Church of Madison Avenue—*O tell us the products to buy—the deodorants, the toothpaste, the girdles, the toupee. . . .*'

Joan's husband left the apartment and procured an immediate divorce.

Joan was simpatico with Burroughs even though the man was gay. Allen Ginsberg egged on a 'relationship' between the two—one a 'skeptical genius of failure and self-annihilation' and the other 'a woman of blasé brittleness.' Joan had a diaphragm, terribly daring for a teenager in the 1940s. She told someone that Burroughs made love to her 'like a pimp.' (How did she know how a pimp did it?) When Joan gave birth to Bill Jr. in 1947, Ginsberg wrote a commemorative poem called 'Birthday Ode,' a 'lamentation against the possibility of homosexuality.' A poem that hoped Bill Jr. would grow up straight. Ginsberg felt differently once he saw the growing child in Mexico City. Ginsberg had a fantasy that when Bill Jr. was eighteen, Ginsberg would seduce the lad. As for Burroughs's heterosexual activities, Ginsberg had received a letter from Mexico City where Burroughs wrote, 'I have been laying women for the past 15 years and haven't heard any complaints.' Joan added the word *Correct!* The letter goes on to say, 'What does that prove except I was hard up at the time? Laying a woman, so far as I am concerned, is O.K. if I can't score a boy.'

No historian has ever suggested what I'm about to suggest: the procreative power of the postwar Dr. Spock/Baby Big Bang was so strong that Burroughs, against all sexual reasoning, had thrust his loins inside a female's to beget an American baby.

* * *

Jane Spock was always surprised that *The Common Sense Book of Baby and Child Care* was intellectually accessible across America, as the book was a product of the intellectual climate of Manhattan during the 1930s. Even in 1950s Iowa, newly married farm couples approved of Dr. Spock's plainspoken advice:

> Children want what they want when they want it.
>
> Everyone wets the bed until they learn how to stay dry.

The Spock newlyweds had moved from New England to Manhattan into an apartment on West 8th Street where Dr. Spock soon became the pediatrician of choice for intellectual Manhattanites during a time when psychology à la Freud was the rage. Dr. Spock developed his baby book in Manhattan and began actually writing the thing down in Washington, D.C., during World War II. Spock toiled as a Navy psychiatrist writing up forms for schizophrenic deserters so they could be discharged from the Navy in such a manner that absolved the Navy from ever paying disability. Spock wrote the baby book after work and on the weekends. He and Jane snuck sugarcoated Freud into his text. For example, they addressed the rivalry of boys with their fathers for their mothers-wives; how a boy of three will declare, 'I'm gonna marry Mommy.' Dr. Spock did not use the term *Oedipus complex*. If a little girl said the same about Dad, Spock wrote, 'Don't worry. This is natural.' If a brother and sister viewed each other naked—*be careful!* The shock of one sibling possessing a penis that the other sibling lacks can have more impact than just a curiosity soon forgotten. Spock didn't use the C word—*castration*. Ben and Jane had worked these major Freudian tenets into the book's pages, hiding them in plain sight.

★ ★ ★

Mexico City. It is the first Monday in August 1951. Hunt is the first in the empty office. A red light blinks on the teletype decoder. Hunt uses his key to turn it on. The thing starts marking a racket as it prints out a message, a secret message sent in code from Washington that the machine is now decoding.

Hunt read:

> Was closed on Sunday in Havana inflamed August 1951. In the study of the limpid Chibás CMQ Launches peroration incendiary. Shouts and gestures in the cabin, but was unable to provide evidence against Aureliano Sánchez Arango (that promised). Has planned a jump shot that he rubbed his leg, but the nervousness is unloaded gun in the groin. The denim dress is soaked with blood 100. Havana sees the whole agony.

What the hell! This machine never worked!

Cuba wasn't on Hunt's official beat, but Darwin had alerted Hunt that he should learn as much as he could about that island, telling his protégé, 'Listen to me, before the 1950s are done, Cuba will be the next Korea.' So, Hunt put his name in the queue of station directors who got top-secret information about Cuba, where the great mulatto dictator Batista ruled both overtly and behind the scenes.

Hunt was motivated to study Havana less because of Joe K. Darwin than because Havana possessed deep personal mythology for him.

It was about his father.

In New York City 1920-something, Father Hunt had been in business with a guy who one Sunday morning cleared out their company safe and hightailed it to Cuba. Hunt's dad followed down after packing a .45. Father Hunt found the thief in a cantina. Hunt's father cocked his .45 and stuck the barrel in the guy's ear. Real cowboy stuff. The guy gave his father's money back. Howard Hunt told this story about his father to everybody. Sometimes his father stuck the gun in the guy's ear. Other times his father stuck the gun discreetly into the guy's kidney.

In Hunt's story, his pop always got his money back.

★ ★ ★

Now in 1951, Howard Hunt was only writing paperback thrillers. Dr. Spock's book was a paperback original as well.

Pocket Books.

Just before Spock signed the contract to write the book, his editor said: 'The book doesn't have to be very good, because we are only going to charge a quarter and can sell ten thousand copies a year easily!'

No one at Pocket Books expected *The Common Sense Book of Baby and Child Care* to make any real money. No one expected it to outsell the Holy Bible (which it did year after year).

★ ★ ★

Howard Hunt goes to Hotel Inexistente on Revolución 333 to buy some foreign newspapers to find out what the 'uncoded' message is all about. Apparently, a Cuba politico named Eduardo René Chibás Rivas spoke on Radio Havana yesterday. Eduardo René was a great denouncer of Cuban gangsterdom. On the Sunday before, Eduardo René had promised that on his next broadcast he would present his listening audience with evidence that the Ministro en Educación, Aureliano Sánchez Arango, was an embezzler. Yesterday, when Chibás came on the air, he told his listeners that the politico who was going to provide him with the information of denunciation did not follow through. Eduardo René next said that Fulgencio Batista was preparing a military coup. Then Eduardo René was cut off.

What no Cuban heard or knew was that Eduardo René had then shot himself in front of the microphone. Eduardo René believed that performing such an act was the only way to uphold his honor after failing to expose Sánchez. Eduardo René assumed that he was still on the air when he pulled the trigger.

No, René. You were not.

Hunt ponders the secret message and what the newspaper said. According to reports, Eduardo René Chibás is expected to live. The secret message Hunt received appeared to be information that Eduardo René Chibás had shot himself in the groin. His gun was cheap and accidentally went off as he pulled it out from his pants intending to raise it to his forehead.

★ ★ ★

Meanwhile, Joan Vollmer and the kids and the other two gringos decide to take a drive to the Pacific Ocean in Lucien's Chevrolet. The trip takes a day now, but in those days, the way out of Mexico City was limited to a dirt road winding through the mountains.

Lucien drives.

Joan sits next to him shotgun—a bottle of tequila between them.

Allen is in the back with the kids.

Lucien tears up and down the mountains at fifty, sixty, then eighty miles an hour, egged on by Joan. Both kids look to Ginsberg for a clue as to how to act. Ginsberg is terrified, but Lucien has a recklessness about him that is blessed. Lucien is pure Rimbaud. Lucien had been the one who formed Ginsberg's aesthetic. Lucien told him the books to read. A few years from now, Ginsberg will write his great poem *Howl*.

There in the mountains outside Mexico City, Carr stopped his car at a fantastic river that reminded Ginsberg of Blake's drawing of the Rivers of Eden. Joan stripped and flipped into the water. The river abruptly became something primal from a landscape painted by Henri Rousseau—dozens of snakes began swimming downstream—long and fat and green—long and fat and green like garden hoses. Where was Joan? The men and the kids raced down the river shore. Joan was nowhere to be seen. For some reason, Ginsberg recalled how Carr had stabbed a man in '44 using a Boy Scout knife and then weighted the body with rocks and thrown it in the Hudson River. Green snakes did not swim downstream in the Hudson. Friend Burroughs helped Carr get rid of the guy's blood-drenched package of cigarettes by flushing it down the toilet. Friend Kerouac helped Carr ditch the knife, then he and Carr went to the movies. What did the two see? Some western about a cowboy with a bullwhip. In the aftermath of the stabbing, Kerouac and Burroughs were arrested as material witnesses.

Carr claimed the dead man was this old guy who stalked him from St. Louis and then tried to rape him in Riverside Park. Carr did two years in Elmira for manslaughter.

Ginsberg and Carr eventually find Joan downriver, lying on the shore naked and exhilarated and exhausted.

More tequila.

—Joan driving, clutching the wheel, using her good leg to work the brake and clutch. Carr lying on his belly on the floor pushing the gas pedal with his hand—

This is a woman with a death wish.

* * *

What about Djerassi? A Mexican-born chemist named Luis Miramontes, working at Syntex, had synthesized a pure progesterone compound called norethisterone. Djerassi was his boss so Miramontes had to share credit. The two started testing norethisterone. They had a hunch norethisterone would relieve menstrual disorder as well as recurrent miscarriage.

* * *

Up in Minnesota, Dr. Spock and Jane both occasionally and separately remembered sex twenty-five years ago before they married. Birth control was a momentous issue in the 1920s. Dr. Spock's mother was a literal Victorian. Premarital sex was unthinkable. Furthermore, Mother Spock was repulsed by the concept of married couples practicing birth control. Ben Spock was not born modern. He was raised a mama's boy until he escaped to Yale in the 1920s. There, he didn't even consider becoming a Bonesman. At the end of the college term, he found a girl—Jane. She was more plain than pretty. Both their parents were not enthusiastic about the marriage because of the couple's economic situation, i.e., *they had no money.* Like all parents, they did understand the magnetism of sex. They believed in the adage 'better to marry than to burn.' So, the families approved the marriage.

Unknown to everyone, certainly Mother Spock, her boy Ben and Jane lost their virginity together by engaging in modern enthusiastic sex several months before their actual wedding. The pair fornicated freely in friends' families' unoccupied vacation houses in Connecticut. The two used condoms. In those days, there was only one 'style.' Condoms were not sold above the checkout counter of convenience stores. They were under the counter at pharmacies only. Spock was twenty-four years old and lived at home and kept his condoms in a lockbox. Finally, Spock and Jane were married at five o'clock on June 25, 1927, in Hartford, Connecticut. (Two of Jane's bridesmaids had caused a stir when they landed in Hartford as passengers aboard a monoplane—this still being the age of Red Baron–style biplanes such as the ones that would shoot King Kong down from the Empire State Building.) During the first years of their marriage, Jane had several miscarriages. Doctors define *miscarriage* as the spontaneous loss of a fetus before the twentieth week of pregnancy. Sometimes all of the fetal debris exits the woman's body. Sometimes not. Near the end of the 1920s, Jane gave birth prematurely to a three-pound baby boy who quickly died. As modern as Benjamin Spock had become, the animal-guilt lobe of his brain believed the sin of premarital sex with Jane was responsible.

Dry facts: in 1951 there were likely 254,666 miscarriages in the U.S.A., a phenomenal number.

A phenomenal number that no one discussed.

★ ★ ★

It's now the morning in 1951 just after Djerassi met Burroughs at the Bounty Bar. Djerassi awakens and instantly remembers that skinny guy armed with *la pistola*. Burroughs. What a slim customer. Burroughs babbled something about sterilizing Mexican women. Then that other guy named Hunt talked about sterilizing Reds. There are many ways to sterilize a woman—all of them permanent. Then Djerassi's mind spins back to sterilizing insects. His progesterone did this by keeping each bug in a prepubescent state. Can you give a girl progesterone to keep her prepubescent forever? He visualizes the child prostitutes in Vienna. What was he thinking of?

Then a new idea hits him.

He is a genius.

Everyone is having babies because modern sex is so much fun. What if he can create a steroid that would simply keep a healthy, sexually functioning woman from ovulating?

That would be the world's most perfect form of contraception.

Norethisterone.

Norethisterone can do it.

That very day, Djerassi takes an airplane north carrying a satchel with samples of norethisterone. He plans to deliver them in person to a thoroughly gringo lab to be tested.

* * *

Early September. Burroughs returned to Mexico City *yagé*-less, his trip a failure. Worse, the straight kid who had agreed to let Burroughs fug him once a week had reneged. Burroughs walks by the Bounty Bar. Burroughs walks to 210 Orizaba Street and climbs the stairs to his apartment. Joan and the kids aren't there. Burroughs's young traveling companion has already met up with a straight buddy, so Burroughs assumes he'll be sleeping alone that night. Yet, Burroughs is back in Mexico City. He can get boy ass anytime he wants. He just needs money. He goes back over to the Bounty. Someone talks to someone else. A deal is made to sell one of Burroughs's pistols that very night. The transaction can be completed in an upstairs apartment above the Bounty. It's where the bartender lives. After sunset, Burroughs hears the whistle of the local knife grinder cart. Down in Ecuador, he'd bought a knife. He now strolls out and follows the whistle to get that knife sharpened. While he walks, he feels himself possessed.

It is an awareness.

There is something foreign inside him. He will subsequently name it the Ugly Spirit. A scientific mind like Carl Djerassi's would have deduced that Burroughs's brain was adjusting to Mexico City's high altitude of 7,300 feet—one and a half miles high. Up here, the boiling point of benzene and toluene were different from in Ohio. At any rate, Burroughs got his knife sharpened and returned to the apartment at 210 Orizaba Street, his head consumed with ugliness.

Psychic raw sewage.

Raw meat.

He was reminded that he had raw sores on his feet from jungle rot.

Burroughs opened the door to his apartment.

Joan was back.

* * *

Carl Djerassi was sitting in the perfect seat on the droning airplane. An aisle seat. Three different women were sitting in three successive seats kitty-corner from his row. They each had long lanky legs.

Then there was the stewardess.

Djerassi recited a rhyme to himself. 'Banish air from air. Divide light if you dare.' Djerassi was a man's man who possessed dedication to both an intellectual and carnal appreciation of women.

Djerassi's father appreciated women. He was a Viennese doctor whose specialty was, of all things, venereal disease. Infirmities such as *gonorrhö* and *syphilisartig* were the unspoken rampancy of Viennese society. Those were prepenicillin days and patients had to be treated with arsenicals for several years. Citizens of Vienna suffering from venereal disease didn't wish to be seen in a specialist's waiting room, so der Doktor made house calls. Djerassi's papa always brought the kid with him on visits to Fräulein Pfeiffer. She suffered from no disease. Fräulein Pfeiffer was his father's mistress. Carl would wait alone in a sitting room, listening to the mechanical sound of Fräulein Pfeiffer's mattress squeaking. The boy heard a variety of other noises. Young Djerassi tried to form a narration in his mind of what the two were doing.

* * *

On September 6, 1951, William Burroughs's life *stood with a loaded gun.* He was with Joan in the bartender's apartment above the Bounty Bar. Burroughs was holding the revolver he intended to sell, but shot his common-law wife in the forehead instead.

Neither Howard Hunt nor Carl Djerassi had stayed in touch with each other, let alone that weird fellow Burroughs, yet separately both Americans recognized Burroughs's gaunt face when it appeared on the front page of the Mexico City papers. The newspapers claimed the couple were reenacting some sort of William Tell escapade. Everyone was drunk. Burroughs tried to shoot a glass that Joan had balanced on top of her head.

He missed the glass. He had aimed too low.

The story changed the next day. Now the thirty-seven-year-old

Burroughs had been 'cleaning' his pistol and it went off 'accidentally.' The bullet divided the air, striking twenty-eight-year-old Joan Vollmer in the center of her forehead.

The Mexican headlines:

THE AMERICAN SEWARD TRIES TO MOCK JUSTICE

THE COVER-UP OF THE AMERICAN WITH BAD AIM

NOW THE NORTH-AMERICAN WHO KILLED HIS WIFE SAYS IT WAS AN ACCIDENT

IT APPEARS THAT SEWARD USED HIS WIFE AS A BULL'S-EYE

The newspapers confused Burroughs's middle name with the *apellido paterno* of the duo of Spanish surnames. His last name was misinterpreted to be his mother's *apellido materno.*

The newspapers are not consistent:

BURROUGHS CHANGES HIS VERSION ABOUT THE DEATH OF HIS YOUNG AND LOVELY WIFE

SEWARD CONSTANTLY CHANGES HIS STORY

ENORMOUS SUSPICIONS THAT BURROUGHS DID NOT KILL HIS WIFE ACCIDENTALLY

SEWARD TRIES TO MOCK THE AUTHORITIES

A SERIES OF CONTRADICTIONS IN WHAT THE NORTH-AMERICAN WHO KILLED HIS WIFE SAYS

Burroughs was caged in Lecumberri Prison, aka the Black Palace. Pancho Villa was the only prisoner who ever escaped from this place. Burroughs was only imprisoned there a day less than two weeks. His parents bailed their son out by paying $23,000, money spent on both legitimate legal fees and *mordidas* (bribes).

* * *

The landlady of the building where the shooting had taken place had been housemaid to Leon Trotsky fourteen years before when he began his exile in Mexico City.

Trotsky was one of the original Bolsheviks of the February Revolution in 1917 along with Stalin and Lenin. Then Lenin died. Stalin was a malignant narcissist and took power. Trotsky convinced or fooled many into believing he was the true socialist. Trotsky slipped into exile just before the American Depression in 1929. First, Trotsky hunkered on the island of Büyükada off the coast of Istanbul. Then he partook in a French exile, followed by exile in Norway. Finally, in 1937, Mexican president Lázaro Cárdenas welcomed Trotsky to Mexico.

* * *

During America's Depression, reputable intellectuals worth their salt (that left Burroughs out) flirted with and outright joined the Communist Party because the Republicans caused the Depression (if not the Dust Bowl as well), and Democrats were all liberal bluster with no actuality or action. Almost none of these Red intellectuals reinvented Marxist Communism in an American fashion the way Washington and Jefferson reinvented Greek democracy for the thirteen colonies. No. These intellectuals bought the party line that:

Communism
Was a
Universal Political Philosophy
& There Was Only
One
Communist Party
Centered in the Glorious
Union of Soviet Socialist Republics

It was as if Russia had the copyright on Communism the way Swiss chemical company CIBA held the patent on cholesterol.

In the Depression, American Reds were split between aligning themselves with Stalin or Trotsky. According to memoirs of the times, pretty girls were always Trotskyites, while macho fellows were Stalinists.

Stalinists called Trotskyites 'Trotskyists.'

★ ★ ★

Leslie Fiedler is an American character in this book. Back in 1943, Fiedler was a barrel-chested intellectual/heterosexual college student. First, Fiedler became a Stalinist. Six months later he changed and joined the Trotskyites.

★ ★ ★

When Leon Trotsky arrived in Mexico in 1937, he lived for a while at Diego Rivera's digs, cuckolding the muralist with Rivera's wife, Frida Kahlo, while plotting his own return to the U.S.S.R.

Rivera kicked Trotsky out.

Next, the Russian rented a hacienda in the suburb of Coyoacán owned by the woman who also owned the building that housed the Bounty Bar in Mexico City.

Trotsky spent most of his time tending to his rabbits and chickens in his walled-in garden. A small battalion of Stalinists tried to overrun Trotsky's place with machine guns and bombs, killing most of his rabbits and chickens, but not harming Trotsky himself, who hid in a corner with a child's intuition. Several months later, in August 1940, a twenty-seven-year-old Stalinesque mole in the Trotsky household named Jaime Ramón Mercader del Río Hernández sank an ice pick into Trotsky's skull. The sixty-year-old Red lived for a day before he joined Vladimir Ilyich Lenin in the Godless Void.

Leslie Fiedler was in an elevator in Madison, Wisconsin, when he heard about Ramón Mercader murdering Trotsky. Fiedler recalled having met Mercader once at a pro lefto cocktail party in Manhattan. Mercader had been messy and arrogant and had hit on everyone's girlfriend.

In Mexico in 1951 there had never been proof that the Bounty Bar's landlord had anything to do with Trotsky's assassination, but the stink of her karma alone should have been strong enough to have alerted a hare-brained American intellectual like Burroughs to neither rent nor even visit an apartment in any building she owned.

William Burroughs didn't believe in karma and so he shot Joan in September of 1951. As he lingered in the Black Palace, Jaime Ramón

Mercader del Río Hernández was still a resident there as well. One day, Burroughs and Mercader were placed in adjoining cells.

* * *

Joe K. Darwin was the one who introduced Howard Hunt to Leslie Fiedler's writing. Darwin sent Hunt by courier a copy of an egghead literary magazine, *Partisan Review.* In those days, people read things called essays, the text of which actually mattered and could sometimes become more influential than cocktail chatter. Darwin had earmarked a particular piece titled 'Come Back to the Raft Ag'in, Huck Honey!'—written by someone named Leslie Fiedler. Hunt checked before he read it—'Leslie' was a man. After Hunt read 'Huck Honey' he banged up Darwin on the horn, gripping the telephone receiver so hard the veins on his wrist resembled stalks of blue celery. 'What the hell is this *Partisan Review* bovine fecal matter? Huckleberry Finn as a nigger-loving queer—'

'As queer as Ishmael and Queequeg!'

'Sweet Jesus!'

'Listen to me, the Company is sponsoring this magazine,' Darwin told Hunt.

'Whaddya mean?

'The Company is funding the *Partisan Review*—not in the open, of course.'

'Angleton's too smart.'

'Sure. But he's not an egghead. He doesn't understand eggheads. *Partisan Review* does. It will help eggheads make the transition from Trotskyism to anti-Communism.'

'What does that have to do with Huck Finn? *Overt homosexuality has always been a threat to American sentimentality*?'

'Sure, Hunt. Think about it. We believe in chaste masculine faith. We believe in the camaraderie of the locker room. Listen to me, pederasty in a Boy Scout troop is unthinkable.'

'Fiedler compares Huckleberry Finn's scenes of *a fugitive slave and the no-account white boy lying side by side on a raft borne by the endless river toward an impossible escape* to a scene in *Moby-Dick* of Queequeg asleep with Ishmael forehead-against-forehead, Queequeg's arm wrapped around Ishmael's waist, hugging him as if Ishmael was *his wife.* What intellectual trash!'

'Hunt, listen to Fiedler. We white men have the nightmare that someday when the coloreds take over, we will be cast aside not in anger, but in irrelevance.'

> —what Fiedler actually wrote was: 'Behind the white American's nightmare that someday, no longer tourist, inheritor, or liberator, he will be rejected and refused, he dreams of his acceptance at the breast he has most utterly offended.'

Hunt replied, 'I don't have that nightmare because it's never gonna happen.' He paused and added, 'Anyway, Queequeg isn't colored. He's a tattooed Polynesian.'

'Hunt, would you tolerate Queequeg sitting next to you at a lunch counter in Alabama any more than you would let Nigger Jim?'

Chapter 4

Hyannis Port, Massachusetts, 1951–1952

Mexico City. The Black Palace. The guards moved William Burroughs to a different cell on a different floor in the middle of the night. They refused to tell why. At dawn, Burroughs saw his new accommodation sat kitty-corner from the pen that held Jaime Ramón Mercader del Río Hernández. This prisoner was nearing the midpoint of his twenty-five-year sentence for puncturing the rear of Leon Trotsky's skull with an ice pick.

Ten years earlier in New England, the Catholic girl Rosemary Kennedy was twenty-three and she had the cortex of her brain severed with a leucotome, medicine's ultra-sophisticated ice pick.

The leucotome was a tool for lobotomists. Their craft, lobotomy, was a modern, but crude, surgical method of mental hygiene that involved slicing into the back of the brain. The motive for Rosemary's lobotomy was opaque. It was said the girl was mildly retarded or mildly schizophrenic combined with a late attack of puberty. Perhaps Rosemary Kennedy was only a languid girl overwhelmed by being one of Joe Kennedy's children—four sons and five daughters—every sibling but herself competitive in maximum fashion because of Kennedy blood and the family motto, *Finish First*. The sorry brain robbers botched Rosemary's lobotomy and reduced the girl to a permanent infantile state. Initially the catastrophe broke her father's heart.

Joe Kennedy got over it.

By 1951, Rosemary had been institutionalized for ten years.

* * *

In 1951, every citizen well read in politics knew who Joe Kennedy was. The man was born in Boston in the nineteenth century. He was an Irish Catholic's Irish Catholic. Joe became a millionaire during the '20s by stock investment. It has been alleged that Joe Kennedy was a member of the unscrupulous bear raider investors who provoked Black Thursday in 1929. (If true, the Great Depression should be called the Kennedy Depression.) In the Roosevelt 1930s, Kennedy bought an ambassadorship to England. Three years after Rosemary was institutionalized in '41, his firstborn, Joe Jr., was killed when his experimental bomber aircraft exploded over England. In '48, Joe Sr.'s fourth child and second daughter, 'Kick,' died in a civilian plane crash over France. Only Joe Sr. came to Kick's requiem mass, just as he was the only family member who came to her wedding before the war. Joe Sr.'s wife, Rose, forbade her other children to attend both ceremonies because Kick had married an Anglican and died still married to the man. By 1951, there were six functioning adult Kennedy children left.

The eldest of the Kennedy siblings was Jack, a thirty-four-year-old congressman from Massachusetts. This book finds him in late spring of '51, around midnight, a passenger in a taxi driving him from the train station to the family compound in Hyannis Port, Massachusetts (located midway in the elbow of Cape Cod).

'Put it on my tab, willya,' Kennedy said, getting out of the cab.

'Yah, you bet,' the driver answered, sounding sour. Jack Kennedy never carried cash. The driver would only be reimbursed by the Kennedy accountant for the meter. No tip.

Jack Kennedy was oblivious to money.

Above Jack's head: a sideways Cheshire cat moon. Jack enjoyed walking from the front gate along the summer grass. He would have taken his shoes off but he was lugging two heavy suitcases and wanted to continue the initial momentum of his wandering. He heard crickets. A lazy airplane droning somewhere in the night. Then a girl's giggle. She giggled again. It was either sister Pat or sister Eunice. Pat was twenty-seven. Eunice, twenty-nine. Both women were long in the tooth to still be single in the Baby Big Bang. But then, Jack himself was a long-in-the-tooth bachelor. Baby brother Ted was nineteen and single. Younger brother Bobby was twenty-five and he had already been married for one year.

More giggling.

Jack set his suitcases down on the grass and crept toward the giggles that were coming from the outdoor swimming pool. He then saw the naked back of Eunice, below her waist a modest bikini bottom. He saw her raised elbows. She was apparently covering her bare chest. A man stood facing her, waving a bikini top just out of her grasp. He was whispering something at the girl.

It was Joe McCarthy.

Joseph McCarthy was jowly and dowdy and had a crude doughiness about him, but sister Eunice evidently found the man cute enough.

McCarthy was Irish Catholic and a forty-two-year-old bachelor. McCarthy was Irish Catholic and a Republican senator. Joe Kennedy had contributed a quarter of a million dollars to Irish Catholic Joe McCarthy's Senate campaign. Joe Kennedy liked Joe McCarthy because he acted younger than his years. This Irish Catholic had no airs. In the early 1950s, McCarthy was in his heyday gutting Washington Reds and pinkos.

Jack Kennedy, himself, felt ambivalent about Joe. This Kennedy first met McCarthy in the Solomon Islands in the Pacific during the war. McCarthy was a leatherneck. Jack took McCarthy on a ride one night on his PT boat and let McCarthy fire a machine gun into the dark. McCarthy was a fun enough guy.

That was then. He'd seen Joe in action stalking Communists in Washington. McCarthy was a bully. McCarthy was no Cicero. McCarthy was often tongue-tied, pontificating about nothing. Jack Kennedy couldn't believe that his father was pimping Eunice to McCarthy. Besides, Adlai Stevenson told Jack on the Q.T. that the 'Pepsi-Cola Kid' was as queer as ketchup on a banana.

Joseph McCarthy earned the Pepsi slur because the Pepsi-Cola Bottling Company allegedly bribed him to fight the federal sugar-rationing program. Remember that the CEO of Pepsi was a fifty-one-year-old white man named Alfred Steele. He will find himself married to Joan Crawford in four years.

★ ★ ★

Mexico City. Howard Hunt had not written a paperback thriller in almost seven months. Dot's second pregnancy had gone rough. She took a northbound train by herself to give birth among the Yankees. She took three days to deliver—by the second day, the doctors told Hunt on the telephone that Dot was shrieking and pounding the mattress because the medicinal pain dope had stopped working. Finally, the baby arrived. Hunt had wanted a son. He got a daughter. He and his wife named her Kevan. Sister Lisa, three years and a few months older, would grow up to be the Trouble. Kevan would be the Good Daughter. When Lisa becomes a teenager in the 1960s, she will be institutionalized for a year or two.

For now, neither Kevan nor Lisa had been baptized. Around Christmas, Hunt's wife and infant daughter returned to Mexico City. Hunt's writing urge returned as well. The man began pounding his typewriter in his home office one Thursday night after work.

I Came to Kill . . . by Howard Hunt.

No. Time to use a pseudonym.

I Came to Kill . . . by Gordon Davis.

Midnight came and went. Friday. Hunt/Davis typed until one in the morning. He placed his Royal typewriter on a rolled-up bath towel to soften the clacks so the baby and the rest of his household could sleep. He went to work Friday morning. Friday night, he came home from work and continued typing. Earlier in the day, he had phoned Dot to tell her to cancel their attendance at the cocktail party at the Italian embassy. This writer typed until two a.m., the baby sleeping in his lap. Hunt woke up around nine on Saturday morning. Touch-typed *clack clack clack*. He couldn't stop now. He typed all day. He took a nap around six p.m. He awoke and gulped a benny and was back at the typewriter sizzling. Hunt was almost done. He could feel it. He typed all of Saturday night and Sunday's dogwatch. He lay on the rug. When he opened his eyes, it was Sunday noon. He heard a multitude of Mexican church bells clanging. Hunt stacked his pages. He skimmed them for the rest of the afternoon. Then he gulped another benny and typed until nine o'clock.

'Gordon Davis' wrote a novel in three days

★ ★ ★

After Bill Jr.'s father shot his mother in the brain, the boy was sent north to live with his grandparents in St. Louis. Joan's own parents spirited granddaughter Julie away. William Burroughs and Julie never saw each other again. What happened to Julie remains a mystery in Burroughs literary scholarship.

Burroughs's slightly older brother, Mortimer, rushed down to Mexico

City to aid his errant sibling. Mortimer stayed in the swanky—*ostentoso*—Casa de la Condesa Reforma Hotel in the Distrito Federal. He doled out several considerable bribes around town. William Seward Burroughs was let out of the Black Palace pending trial.

'I don't want to go back to Mexican jail, Morty.'

'You're not gonna go to Mexican jail, Billy.'

'Can we buy our way out of a trial?'

'Already been done. Mother and Father put up the cash.'

'To bribe the judge?'

'To bribe the judge.'

'Good.'

'And Billy, I'm not going to tell Mother that every morning you wash down Benzedrine, sanicin, and hop with black coffee and a shot of tequila.'

'Thanks.'

'You're welcome, Billy.'

'Did I ever tell you I had hallucinations as a child?'

'No.'

'Did you hallucinate, Morty?'

'Uh-uh.'

'Junk can take you into that state of childhood innocence. I will shoot up and remember being a boy lying on the bed with Mother beside me, we watched headlights from the street move across the ceiling and down the walls.'

The brothers were silent. Then Bill asked, 'Remember that German maid?'

'No.'

'She told me that smoking opium brings sweet dreams. I told her I was going to smoke opium when I grew up.'

'You were always the one with ambition.'

The brothers went silent again. Small bells started jingling from the street.

'Ice cream truck?' Mortimer asked.

'Knife sharpener.' Silence. 'I never told you this, but when we were growing up on Pleasant Street, I looked down the hallway one night toward Mom and Dad's bedroom door and was struck by a feeling of animal despair. I was feeling such things that no animal should feel, let alone a boy.' Mortimer wiped his brother's forehead with a napkin. 'I felt those feelings again just before I shot Joan. About an hour before I pulled the trigger, I heard the bells and went to get a knife sharpened...'

* * *

Across town, Hunt told O'Dwyer's secretary, Donna—the one always covered with costume jewelry—to send his manuscript by diplomatic post to the M Building on M Street in Washington, D.C., so someone in Central Intelligence Censoring could glance it over to make sure the author didn't spill secret beans. Several days later, Hunt walked into the office to find Donna standing in the middle of the room weeping in hysterics.

'I lost your book, Mr. Hunt,' the girl whimpered. She hadn't tucked it into the diplomatic pouch because she'd started reading it and couldn't put it down. Back at her apartment, her roommate threw the manuscript away thinking it was 'just' papers. Donna had rushed to the Mexico City dump to search for it. No luck. Hunt wasn't aware that this same literary disaster had happened to Thomas Carlyle (1795–1881) after the influential Scottish writer gave the only handwritten copy of the manuscript of *The French Revolution* to his best friend to read. His friend's maid set the manuscript on fire by accident. Carlyle rewrote his four-hundred-page book from memory.

So did Howard Hunt/Gordon Davis.

It took another three days. Carlyle took much longer.

* * *

William Seward Burroughs's case came to trial. He was not charged with any form of homicide—deliberate or accidental. The Mexican judge charged Burroughs with *imprudencia criminal.*

Criminal imprudence.

Burroughs was not sent to Mexican prison. He merely had to report to the Black Palace every Monday so the police could determine that he hadn't fled Mexico City or been arrested for another imprudent crime. Burroughs was stunned at such lax punishment. God bless *imprudencia criminal.* 'Poor Jaime Ramón Mercader del Río Hernández,' Burroughs thought. 'Instead of an ice pick, he should have placed a glass on Trotsky's head and then tried to shoot it off.'

Burroughs had forgotten that Mortimer had bribed the judge, making Burroughs, in fact, innocent of nothing.

* * *

I Came to Kill by 'Gordon Davis' was published in the summer of 1953 as a paperback original. The cover illustration shows a woman wearing a dressing gown that reveals zero cleavage. She looks vaguely Mexican or Italian. She is about to use a lighter to fire up the cigarette dangling off her lip. A man lurks behind her—dressed in a brown suit the color of a grocery bag, wearing a brown Stetson as well as a loud yellow tie. Both his hands are balled into fists. You realize the woman about to light the cigarette must be sitting in front of a mirror and that she is eyeing him standing behind her. She doesn't look panicked. Her expression says that she assumed he was dead. *Damn. He's back.* Now she must manipulate him again. The caption over the title of the book says: *They wanted a tyrant liquidated and cash could hire him to do it.* What more did a potential reader need to know about this book?

* * *

Several months earlier in Lecumberri Prison/the Black Palace. William Burroughs in one cell. Jaime Ramón Mercader del Río Hernández, Trotsky's assassin, in an adjoining cell. 'My name is Jaime Ramón Mercader del Río Hernández,' the prisoner said. He looked Spanish. He was prison skinny. 'What is your name, señor?'

'Willy Lee,' William Burroughs lied in a sour voice. He'd been in jail now for nine days.

'Ah! You know what it is like to kill a man. I can see that. You have killed a man?'

'No. I have not.'

'Why be ashamed? Oh, wait. I see. You killed a woman. You killed your wife.'

'That is what the papers say. Our jailers want you to get me to confess so they can shake me down. The shooting was accidental.'

'Just as it was an accident when I plunged an ice pick into Leon Davidovich's [Trotsky's] brain!' Jaime Ramón Mercader del Río Hernández laughed.

'What kind of ice pick?'

'I don't understand.'

'A bartender's ice pick?'

'No no no. It was for mountain climbing.'

'Whyja do it?'

'To change the world. You kill an insignificant man, what have you done? You have blood on your hands, big deal. But to kill an important man is to change destiny.'

'Trotsky's time had come and gone. He was in exile . . . in Mexico. He had no destiny.'

'That is where you are wrong, Willy Lee. Stalin and Hitler had just signed the Molotov-Ribbentrop Pact. Leon Davidovich Trotsky was the only Bolshevik voice of note against it.'

'So, you killed Trotsky for Stalin?'

'I killed Trotsky for Jaime Ramón Mercader del Río Hernández. I will not be in jail forever. I now have a pedigree. I am like John Wilkes Booth.'

'John Wilkes Booth was shot dead.'

'But he became revered.'

'Who helped you kill Trotsky?'

'No one. I did it myself.'

'I heard that there were two different accomplices in motorcars prepared to drive you away after the killing.'

'Yes. Escape was the plan. That is why I used the ice pick—no noise. And I was even carrying a pistol. After I stabbed him, I was going to walk out of the office and tell Leon Davidovich's wife that he was busy working and asked not to be disturbed.'

'What went wrong?'

'Leon Davidovich gave out a howl and jumped out of his chair. Then he staggered to the door to his office and called for Natasha.'

'Who is Natasha?'

'His wife.'

'Oh.'

Jaime Ramón Mercader del Río Hernández said, 'Leon Davidovich died the next day.'

* * *

Leon Davidovich Trotsky's grandson, Vsievolod Platonovich 'Esteban' Volkov (born in 1926), remained in Mexico City after his granddad's killing. The grandson was a chemist and in the late 1940s began working for Syntex. Carl Djerassi never mentioned Vsievolod Platonovich. It was whispered that Carl Djerassi was jealous of the man's pedigree.

* * *

Even before Cuba went Red, amateur cartographers would say that Cuba was the 'size of Pennsylvania.' 'This is true by the square mile,' Howard Hunt would say and then snort. 'That comparison is useless from a tactical viewpoint. The regions are two different shapes.'

Even worse to say that Viet-Nam* was the size of New Mexico. It is, but New Mexico is boxy. Viet-Nam is shaped like an hourglass. At its narrowest, Viet-Nam is only fifty kilometers wide.

Viet-Nam had and still has two major cities, one in the north and one in the south. The distance between them is slightly longer than that between San Diego and San Francisco. There was Hanoi in the north. In the south was Saigon-Cholon. The latter was a single town separated by the Saigon River like San Francisco and Oakland. In four years, the burgh will just be called Saigon.

It's October. Congressman Jack Kennedy sits in a room in the Palace Hotel in Saigon-Cholon watching a slight green lizard zip along the wall-paper. This isn't Kennedy's room. Its occupant is journalist Bob Stone (not his real name). Most journalists stay at the Continental Hotel. Stone prefers solitude so he stays here. Stone writes for the *Saturday Evening Post.*

'The lizards eat the mosquitoes,' Stone tells Kennedy as he fills his guest's empty glass from a carafe of ice cubes and mineral water. Kennedy nods thanks, although he does not intend to drink it. He can't trust the ice cubes.

Stone's room has air-conditioning, but just barely. He has a rotating electric fan running on a sidebar.

---

* *Washington Post* spelling circa the 1950s.

'As I told you, I'm on a congressional fact-finding mission to be briefed by the French on the military situation between them and the Viet Minh, those goddamn Oriental Communists.'

'And the snails just told you happy time shit,' Stone said.

'Snails? Ah, the French. Yes. They told me they would have the Viet Minh wiped out within the year.'

'The snails will not have the Viet Minh wiped out within the year.'

'They told me that this is a Catholic country.'

'This is a Buddhist country.'

'Who are these Montagnards I read about?'

'They are like the Apaches and Iroquois of Viet-Nam. They're a tribal people who live in the central highlands that include the Koho and Mnong and Bahnars.'

'And they're Buddhist.'

'Most are Presbyterians.'

'Can you excuse me?' Kennedy said, standing gingerly. 'The bathroom?'

Stone pointed. Kennedy disappeared. When he returned he said, 'You know I've drunk nothing but mineral water. Why am I sick as a dog?'

'Your system isn't copasetic with malaria pills. You'll feel better in a few days.'

Kennedy returned to his indentation in the cushion of an exceedingly rococo French lounge. 'What can you tell me about the Oriental mind, Bob?'

Bob fished a cigarette out of a box with Asian writing on it. Kennedy was about to ask for one. Bob said, 'Thu Pzos. They say lepers roll these cigarettes.'

Kennedy didn't want a smoke that bad.

'Let me tell you about the snails first,' Bob Stone said. 'Most of the French behind the scene in Viet-Nam were part of the Vichy* government. After Pearl Harbor, those snails welcomed the Japs to Viet-Nam on a red carpet.' Then he added, 'I mean just a normal red carpet. Not a Moscow carpet.'

Kennedy suddenly winced. He made as if to rise.

'Your gut again?' Stone asked.

'My bad back,' Kennedy answered. 'You were explaining—'

---

* The Nazi puppet state in France, 1940–1944.

'Yeah. Well, Congressman, understand that in Viet-Nam, Communism and Catholicism have more similarities than differences.'

'How so?'

'Both Catholics and Marxists declare that time is a straight line moving toward the future. Time for Buddhists is cylindrical. In Viet-Nam, you must be as intimate with the past as you are with the present and future. What inspires the Viet Minh about Marx over Catholicism is that Marx is anticolonial. Viet-Nam broke away from China in the ninth century. The Vietnamese people held Viet-Nam until the French invaded Indochina one hundred years ago. No one owns Viet-Nam. Not the French. Certainly not the Red Chinese.'

'What about God?'

'What about God?'

'Don't the Vietnamese believe that God rules Viet-Nam?'

'The Catholic Vietnamese do because their particular God has been very good to them. The Vatican owns ninety percent of the land. The French only give government jobs to Catholics.'

'What about the Buddhists?'

'What about them?'

'Don't they own property?'

'They own very little. A dozen pagodas here and there. The Buddhists do not accumulate land the way the Catholics do.' Stone lit another leper's cigarette. 'Wait. Wait. There is another governing body in Viet-Nam. The Binh Xuyen. Organized crime. Saigon is like Chicago when Capone was in charge.'

'The syndicate owns Saigon?'

'Do you mean *American* gangsters?'

Kennedy nodded.

'No. The Binh Xuyen are Asians who work with the Corsicans.'

'Who are . . .'

'Snails. French organized crime. There are about forty thousand Binh Xuyen in Saigon. They run the only real economy Viet-Nam has. They run the brothels. They run the casinos. They run the opium factories. They supervise the protection rackets. The Binh Xuyen are like the mosquitoes—they will always be here.'

'What can you tell me about Ngô Diem?' Kennedy asked.

'Ngô Dinh Diem?'

'Yes. What's with Vietnamese names? Is his first name Ngô or Diem?'

'In Viet-Nam, the first name is the family name; the middle is often used to designate one's generation in the family. Diem is his personal name, his *Christian* name.'

'So, I should referred to him as Diem?'

'You got it, Congressman.'

'I understand that Diem is as Roman Catholic as the pope.'

'The Ngôs have been Catholic since the seventeenth century. They're also mandarins. Diem's father was the keeper of the Emperor of Viet-Nam's eunuchs.'

'This Diem is in America as we speak sucking up to Cardinal Spellman.'

'I hear he's drumming up the support of prominent American Catholics.'

'He's met with my father. I'm supposed to talk to Diem when I return to Washington.'

'Lucky you.'

'Why the cynicism, Bob?'

'Ngô Dinh Diem has always been just a pinch away from those in power. During the war, he cooperated with the Vichy colonial government, but showed desperation. The French wanted nothing to do with him. Diem might have aligned himself with Ho Chi Minh, except Ho's guerrillas buried one of Diem's brothers alive in the jungle.'

* * *

The rain stopped beating against the hotel windows. Bob Stone and Jack Kennedy left the room and walked down to Catinat Street. The air was not dry. There was a kind of dew that beaded up on everything.

'The French call this *saliver pluie*,' Stone said, wiping his face with a handkerchief.

'Spitting rain?' Kennedy said.

'Drooling rain.'

'My French is rusty.'

The street was filled with Triumphs and Lambretta motor scooters. They passed an Asian man standing by himself doing strange gestures.

'What's he doin'?' Kennedy asked. 'Ballet?'

'They call it t'ai chi. I recognize some of the gestures. That one is called Repelling the Monkey.'

Kennedy looked up at the trees. 'I don't see any monkeys.'

'It's metaphorical, Jack.'

Heat lightning flared in the patch of sky that was visible above the various clip joints.

'Saigon feels like Tijuana,' Kennedy said.

Stone thought a moment. 'Probably more accurate to say Tijuana feels like Saigon.'

'Why do you say that, Bob?'

'Saigon is four centuries old. Tijuana has only been around for fifty years.'

'Are you sure?'

'Yes.'

As they walked, huge indescribable spiders were hopping from leaf to leaf on the poinciana blossoms. The streets were filled with girls riding bicycles wearing white trousers and rice hats in the shape of flat mollusks. Something then happened that happened very quickly. An Asian man on a red motorbike raced down the curb and quickly raised his hand and jerked it forward in a pitching gesture. He had something in his hand. He was not pitching it. He was holding a pistol and used this throwing motion with each shot. His target was a man at a café with open French windows reading an early edition of *Miếng Ăn Hằng Ngày*. The fellow's head jerked back as his brains exploded out of the back of his head. His body and chair collapsed backward as well and hit a crowded table. Someone screamed and shoved the dead man and his chair sideways. He tumbled out of an open French window on the side of the café. His body landed on its back in a monsoon puddle. His newspaper floated out the window after him and landed covering his face.

Stone pulled Kennedy forward. 'Keep walking, Congressman. Don't look.'

People were now spilling out of the restaurant. Kennedy noted that the t'ai chi fellow had frozen in the act of Repelling the Monkey when the shooting started. Now, he continued his gestures.

'The guy with the gun was Viet Minh?' Kennedy asked Stone.

'Binh Xuyen.'

'Oh.'

Kennedy then noticed something new. A group of teenage girls were sitting at a restaurant table under an awning and were giggling at the shooting. They were not wearing skirts like teenagers in America. They were wearing white slacks. Kennedy saw that each had teeth that were jet black.

Stone eyed Kennedy and said under his breath, 'Lasses from the sticks. Saigon girls don't lacquer their teeth.' Stone pulled Kennedy fast down the sidewalk. 'Learn this quick, Congressman. Laughter in Viet-Nam seldom signifies amusement.'

Later that evening, Kennedy asked, 'So why were those girls laughing?'

'It's complicated,' Stone said. He looked like he wasn't going to say any more and then he did. 'They were laughing at you, Congressman.'

Kennedy sat upright in his chair. 'Why on earth—? Do I appear funny to them?'

'The Vietnamese are very superstitious people,' Stone answered. 'To those girls, you looked very lucky, Congressman.'

* * *

In early 1952, Carl Djerassi drives his second wife, Norma, and two-year-old daughter, Pamela, from Mexico City toward Detroit, where the man is accepting a tenured professorship at Wayne University, the Pontiac of American educational facilities. Professor Djerassi's wallet remains tied to Syntex—he still sits on the board of directors and he owns stock. As the twenty-eight-year-old drives his wife and daughter north across the border, they see billboards advertising products they had never heard of.

Ban Roll-On?

The Djerassis feel like wetbacks in their own country.

A day into the U.S.A., the family stays at an expensive motel that has 'the only rooms with television in Kansas.' American television was an amazing landscape for a virgin psyche. The Djerassis considered spending a day in Kansas just watching the TV, but decided to press northward like the pioneers they were.

Across the border in Nebraska, Djerassi saw the first snow he'd seen in three or four years. Plowed snow was piled up beside the highway and telephone poles. Dirty snow—snow and soot, a distinctive midwestern squalor.

He pulled to the side of the road. There was a flat surface of virgin white snow.

'Let's play in the snow, Pammy,' he said.

All daughter Pamela knew of life thus far was Mexican heat and Mexico City chaos. The American cold was wonderful. The cold was everywhere.

Americold.

Pamela began running over the snow. Her father laughed and chased her. She fell down face-first. The snow was hard like dirt. She started to howl. Her father tended to her. She told him she didn't like *'Merica.* Her father wiped off her face with the sleeve of his coat—a coat too thin for this weather.

'There, that's better,' he said.

'No, it isn't,' Pamela said. She reached up and grabbed the corner of his collar. He felt that she wanted him to pick her up, but she tugged on the collar. He lowered his head. His daughter didn't want to kiss him. She wanted to whisper in his ear. 'I don't like snow in 'Merica, Daddy. It hurts. I wanna go back to the motel and watch TV.'

* * *

The last thing that Jaime Ramón Mercader del Río Hernández said to 'Willy Lee' (aka William Burroughs) was a question. 'I read in the newspaper that after Leon Davidovich was dead, the Mexicans pried open the lid of his skull and took out his brains and weighed them. The scale said Trotsky's brain weighed almost fourteen hundred grams.' Jaime Ramón Mercader del Río Hernández waited for that to sink into his companion's head. 'That is very heavy, you think? Trotsky had a big brain?'

Burroughs answered dryly. 'What's that in American weight? Let's see.' He computed. 'Three pounds and eight ounces.' Burroughs paused. 'My friend, that's on the light side for a brain. That's what a woman's brain weighs.'

* * *

Texas doctors performing an autopsy...

They never weigh a dead man's brain if part of that brain is missing because of injury to his head. This will be especially true in 1963 in Parkland Hospital in Dallas where President Kennedy will be declared dead by Texan doctors and then again less than twelve hours later where an autopsy is performed on his body at the Naval Hospital in Bethesda, Maryland. This lack will create paranoia among fringe elements that another brain had been substituted for Kennedy's. Reminiscent of Igor the hunchback stealing the wrong encephalon in *Frankenstein,* don't you think? The Parkland doctors will make no effort to scrape the myelin of the president's brain off Jacqueline Kennedy's pink Chanel suit. If this lack was not sensible to history with a capital H, it was still very human.

Chapter 5

Whittier, California, 1952

New York City. Claire Douglas is a British-born eighteen-year-old sophomore at Radcliffe. She has spent the summer dating the thirty-three-year-old author of *The Catcher in the Rye*, J. D. Salinger.*

'How did you meet?' her friends would ask.

'At a shindig on the Upper East Side. We both came with dates, but we both were instantly smitten.'

'What were you wearing?'

'Philadelphia haute couture.'

'You were wearing a Nan Duskin?'

'Yup. Pewter blue.'

'Ooo! You must have been a knockout. What did he look like?'

Before her answer, consider Claire Douglas sitting beside a light talking on the telephone. The girl is blessed with the type of feminine face that will look perpetually young as an adult. She has high cheekbones. A peach chin. She even sits with regal posture.

No wonder Salinger was smitten.

'Jerry is lanky like Jimmy Stewart,' Claire said into the phone. 'He wore a black homburg and a charcoal suit.'

'His tie?'

'His tie was black with yellow polka dots.'

'Big polka dots or small?'

'Tiny.'

'What else about him?'

'There was something that I would call a *monastic gauze* spun around his face.'

'Like an El Greco saint?'

'Exactly! And he has gorgeous long eyelashes like a girl.'

---

* The novel had been published the year before, 1951.

'So you didn't talk to each other at all at the party?'

'At one point, Jerry mouthed some words to me. I couldn't tell what he was saying. His date noticed and frowned. Jerry disguised his fish mouthing into a yawn.'

'What did his date look like?'

'I forget.'

'So, what happened after the party?'

'Jerry called the hosts and got my number. He called me. We talked.'

'What did he say?'

'Hmm. Well, Jerry informed me that he had stopped meditating.'

* * *

September 23, 1952, 6:30 p.m. in Los Angeles.

Pat Nixon sits on a white cushioned chair with a floral design. The chair is sitting on a theater stage, stage left. Pat is forty years old, and is watching a very young and willowy woman puff makeup on the face of her husband, Dick Nixon.

My husband is about to talk his way out of death.

Pat would never tell Dick that was how she saw it. Two weeks ago Pat's whole family was on the campaign train chugging down California – *Ike & Dick, That's the Ticket!* War hero Dwight Eisenhower (age sixty-two) was running for president. Nixon was the candidate for the number two position. The Democratic candidates were über-liberal Adlai Stevenson (fifty-two), the governor of Illinois, and taciturn white supremacist Senator John Sparkman (fifty-three) of Alabama.

Richard Nixon was thirty-nine years old.

The *That's the Ticket!* train stopped in Modesto and a flunky stepped out to the station to get some newspapers. He returned bearing headlines that read, MILLIONAIRE'S CLUB ALLOWS CANDIDATE NIXON TO LIVE GOOD LIFE and SECRET RICH MEN'S TRUST FUND KEEPS NIXON IN STYLE FAR BEYOND HIS SALARY. Pat saw Dick read the headlines and actually crumple to his feet as if he'd been shot.

He had fainted.

Pat Nixon later insisted to her husband that he had to go on television to repair his reputation with the American public. 'One out of every ten Americans owns a television set, Dick!' NBC was willing to sell Nixon a half hour after Milton Berle's *Texaco Star Theatre*. Pat coached Dick to be forceful before the camera. 'Remember, you're not some pathetic contestant on *Queen for a Day*.' A week before the broadcast, all of Ike's people hammered on Pat's husband to just step down as a candidate. That bastard Dewey (of *Dewey Beats Truman*) phoned Dick early that morning to suggest that Dick should go ahead and give his speech, say his piece, and then announce he's stepping down. Dick Nixon stood with the phone to his ear, silent and sour. Dewey asked, 'So what you gonna do, Dick? What are you gonna say?' Pat's husband just said:

> 'I don't know. But if Eisenhower's *shitty sons of bitches* want to find out they'll just have to watch like everyone else.'

★ ★ ★

During the time of Nixon's speech, the text of *The Catcher in the Rye* had just been translated into Spanish. Down in Mexico City, *El Guardián entre el Centeno* by J. D. Salinger sat prominently in the windows of the half a dozen *real* bookstores off the *zócalo*.

The Spanish title translated back to English was: *The Guardian in the Rye*.

★ ★ ★

Los Angeles. Pat Nixon looked away from her husband into the glare of the TV lights. She was told the theater was empty but this glare was so strong there could be a full house out there for all Pat could see. The stage was set like the living room of some ghastly suburban home. It was by implication the Nixons' home. The props all looked cheap. There was a full bookcase. An abstract sculpture sitting on a table. Pat's chair was wobbly. 'This is supposed to be our house?' she had commented sternly to the director. 'The Ricardos live better on *I Love Lucy*.'

'Well, just think of this as *I Love Nixon*.'

She didn't laugh.

'The props aren't crummy, Mrs. Nixon,' the director said. He was doing this shoot free. He was some big shot. She'd heard he had just directed a movie based on a Mickey Spillane novel that ends with Malibu getting blown up by an 'atomic' bomb (it was actually a 'dirty bomb,' but that term hadn't been vocabulated yet). This director had blocked out all of Dick's movements in rehearsal. Dick was going to begin his monologue sitting at a desk and then stand up and talk and wave his hands around, make a fist, and sit on the edge of his desk. Pat was trying to think positive, but Dick reminded her of Shakespeare's lines about strutting and fretting one's half hour upon the stage and then is heard no more.

'Look, Mrs. Nixon,' the director said, peering down at her. 'The camera will mostly be on Dick.'

'I know that,' she answered in a soft voice. 'A tale full of sound and fury, signifying nothing.'

'What did you say?'

'Nothing.'

The director knelt to her eye level. He put his right elbow on a small table and raised that hand as if he was inviting her to Indian arm-wrestle him. 'Whenever Dick mentions your name, the camera will pan to you.'

'We've spent all afternoon rehearsing that over and over. And I shouldn't look at the camera. I know. I know.'

'Right, Mrs. Nixon. You just look at your husband. Look at him with admiration.'

Pat Nixon reflectively glanced over at Dick. She saw a very tall man with his face being powdered by a very tall woman who stood quite close to Dick. It even seemed like her breasts were pressed into him, but then her breasts were quite formidable—she must press her tits into everyone whose face she puffs. The woman was speaking softly to Dick, right into his ear. Maybe she was whispering. Pat turned back to the director. She had an impulse to grab his hand and bite his knuckles. She didn't. The director spoke again: 'Let me give you a television tip, Mrs. Nixon. This is going to be broadcast live and you may get scared. So just keep looking at your husband and say to yourself, *I admire you. I admire you.* Pretend this is just like a school play. A lot of time, greenhorns freeze up and look—'

'Excuse me. I am not a greenhorn. I am a novice.'

The director frowned. 'Just don't look scared, Mrs. Nixon. Be confident.'

'I am confident. And I do admire my husband. I admire him greatly.'

'Good. And don't wince if he flubs some lines.'

'But the camera won't be on me.'

'I mean if he flubs some lines when the camera is on you.'

The man stood up to leave.

'Look, Mr. Director, Dick won't listen to me. He refuses to take out the part about the *respectable Republican cloth coat*. Don't you dare point the camera at me when he says that. If you do, I'll— I'll stick out my tongue.'

'Okay, Mrs. Nixon. Control yourself. You're not going to stick your tongue out at anyone.'

Someone yelled, 'A minute to showtime, everyone.'

'I mean it about the *Republican cloth coat*!' Pat's voice was threatening.

⋆ ⋆ ⋆

Manhattan. During the time of this broadcast, Claire was now sleeping with J. D. Salinger in his sub-first-floor apartment on the Upper East Side. This neighborhood was still referred to as the Silk Stocking District. J. D. Salinger's double bed had black sheets.

'I've just become a Vedanta,' Jerry Salinger explained.

Claire understood.

The German translation of Salinger's novel *Der Fänger im Roggen* translated back to English perfectly, *The Catcher in the Rye.* The Bulgarian edition, however, Спасителят в ръжта, translated back as *The Savior in the Rye.*

—the Catalan version of *The Catcher in the Rye* translated back to *The Vigilant in the Rye Field*—

—in Serbian, the title was *The Hunter in the Rye.* Chinese, *The Watcher in the Rye.* Korean, *The Keeper in the Rye.* In Romanian, *Keeping Watch in the Field of Rye.*

⋆ ⋆ ⋆

Los Angeles. Richard Nixon on NBC: 'I come before you tonight as a candidate for the vice presidency and as a man whose honesty and integrity has been questioned.'

This was indeed showtime.

Pat Nixon sat at stage right eyeing her husband, who was wearing a camel coat, sitting at a desk. Behind her husband were a sheet of peculiar wallpaper and a fake window with peculiar curtains. To his right stood a bookcase full of prop books. Pat suddenly had to pee. This always happened when she was onstage with Dick. For some reason, Pat squinted and suddenly could make out the uniform titles on the spines of the books.

Nixon Is a Crook

There were three shelves of books. Each book had a different-colored spine, but all the spines read:

Nixon Is a Crook

Pat sat jiggling her legs. Was the camera on the bookcase? Could those titles be read on television?

Dick Tuck again!

This absolutely must have been the work of Dick Tuck—that awful and crazy man who sabotaged Dick's campaign with dirty trick after dirty trick. Tuck fooled Josephine Muller, Nixon's scheduling secretary, more than once into booking Nixon to speak at what turned out to be empty auditoriums. Five times that happened. Or in one case, Richard Nixon discovered that he was to give a speech at a slaughterhouse. A kosher poultry slaughterhouse. Once, Richard was in the back of the train, giving a speech from the caboose to a crowd gathered on the tracks. Tuck bribed the engineer to slowly pull the locomotive forward while Nixon was still speaking.

Why on earth did Tuck hate her husband so?

No one knew.

In pop nuance, one could say that Dick Tuck was to Dick Nixon what the Joker was to Batman.

Pat's husband was now explaining that the donations he received were for political expenses that it would be wrong to bill the state government for. Dick was talking toward the camera perpendicular to Dick Tuck's bookshelf.

Nixon: '—Well, then the question arises, you say, *Well, how do you pay for campaign expenses and how can you do it legally?* And there are several ways that it can be done. The first way is to be a rich man. I don't happen to be a rich man . . . like Governor Stevenson, who inherited a fortune from his father to run for president . . .' That was Pat's cue. The camera was moving on her. '—Another way that is used is to put your wife on the payroll . . .'

Pat was sitting there saying to herself, 'I admire you. I admire you. Oh, please, dear God, please keep the camera from showing those *Nixon Is a Crook* books. Oh please, God. I admire you. I admire you.'

* * *

Jane Spock was sipping her fifth martini and watching Nixon speak on television. She was not watching in Minnesota. Last year the Spocks had moved to Pittsburgh so Ben could teach at the university. 'Pittsburgh!' Jane would say out loud if goaded. 'Payroll. Polka! People speak pizzicato in Pittsburgh! People in Pittsburgh pick their words like pickles.' Jane sat in Pittsburgh watching Pat Nixon sitting on a chair staring up at her husband. Jane felt ever since Benjamin's goddamn *Common Sense Book of Baby and Child Care* hit the radar that she had been stuck on her own white chair, having to grimace up at her husband in adoration when in reality Ben was like a terrible toothache.

* * *

Los Angeles. The camera moved off Pat Nixon and back toward Dick. Pat was sure that she was off-camera and signaled the director. He saw her and shook his head. She signaled the director again. His face flashed panic. He hurried over. He lowered his ear to her lips. Pat whispered, 'Look at the books on the bookcase.' He glanced up. He squinted. He saw. He ran back off the set with his head down like modern people do when they exit or enter helicopters. He spoke softly into the ear of the makeup girl. Pat saw that the camera was panning back to her. She stared at her husband. *I admire you. I admire you. I admire you.* Nixon kept talking. Pat saw the makeup girl hurry over toward Dick and lift the books off the visible shelves. Pat's husband was so transfixed he just kept talking, peering outward as if the camera was on him. Pat was sure that it was not. She could not move her head away from her husband to find out. She could end up peering straight into the camera lens like an amateur. In Pat's all encompassing gaze at her husband, she saw the makeup girl filled the empty shelf with the books that were in a carton on the floor. Pat could not read any of their titles, but one.

Pat's husband stood up from behind the desk. The camera must be on him. Pat did not care. She continued to peer at him in admiration. Then it was like she was floating above her own body. She looked at her own expression. The admiration on her face looked real.

It was.

* * *

Jane Spock watching Nixon in Pittsburgh. The camera angle changed on Nixon. A sideways angle. A bookcase on a side wall was revealed. Not many books on it. The bookcase looked as cheap as the other furniture.

Nixon: '—this is unprecedented in the history of American politics—I am going at this time to give to this television and radio audience a complete financial history, everything I've earned, everything I've spent, everything I own. And I want you to know the facts.'

Then Jane squinted. She raised her hand to her mouth. The spine of one book clearly read: *Dr. Spock's The Common Sense Book of Baby and Child Care.*

She burst out laughing. Then she wondered why she was laughing. She did not feel ironic. Her laugh felt sour. She wanted to cry. She jumped up and made herself another martini.

* * *

The Catcher in the Rye in Turkish retranslated to *Kids in the Field of Rye.* In Polish, *Rummage around in the Corn.* In Danish, French, Hungarian, Italian, Norwegian, the novel was titled *The Savior; Cursed Youth; The Heartthrob; Oat Sharpener* (an expression that means 'Good for Nothing'); and lastly, *Young Holden.*

* * *

Nixon: '—Our family was one of modest circumstances, and most of my early life was spent in a store out in East Whittier. It was a grocery store. One of those family enterprises. My mother and dad had five boys, and we all worked in the store.'

Whittier. East Whittier actually. An hour's drive east from Hollywood. Whittier was flat. Whittier was one of those transplanted fake midwestern towns constructed in California.

Whittier was a Quaker town. The Nixons were Quakers. Whittier had even been named after abolitionist Quaker poet John Greenleaf Whittier (1807–1892). One of his poems goes:

The Quakers sank on their knees in praise
And thanks. A last low sunset blaze
Flashed out from under a cloud and shed
A golden glory on each bowed head
The tale is one of an evil time
When souls were fettered and thought was a crime

Prophetic poem. The year 1952 was an evil Communist time. Thinking Marxist thoughts in America was the basest of crimes.

* * *

Nixon on the TV: 'In 1940, probably the best thing that ever happened to me happened...'

Jane Spock in Pittsburgh—her brain neutered on Beefeater.

Nixon: '...I married Pat.'

Jane's mulled brain remembered her early married life on 8th Street in New York City.

Nixon: '...[Pat and I] had a rather difficult time after we were married, like so many of the young couples who may be listening to us—'

Jane Spock recalled that at least once a month she and Ben would go dancing with two other couples at ritzy nightclubs like El Morocco or Dave's Blue Room. Once at the Stork Club, Jane even danced with gossip columnist Ed Sullivan. The Spock entourage would also go to hole-in-the-wall joints that wanted to encourage Ivy League clientele—Spock and company always had their liquor comped. Jane's feet always hurt before her husband's did. Ben would continue dancing, fox-trotting with other married women. When they got home to 8th Street, Jane would nag him about his womanizing. He would retaliate by calling Jane a lush.

Were those days a difficult time?

Jane's first miscarriage had been a difficult time—what with Benjamin's obsession that premarital carnal joy cursed her to miscarry.

That was Ben's mother talking—the mother inside his brain.

* * *

Los Angeles, California. Pat Nixon on the stage sitting in her chair—relieved that the Tuck book business was over. She tuned in to what her husband was saying. She encouraged him to say what he was about to say. She had the abrupt realization how humiliating this must be. Every workingman in America would be humiliated having to reveal what Dick was going to reveal. Easier for a man to pull down his pants on live television—

'Now, what have I earned since I went into politics? Well, here it is. I've jotted it down. Let me read the notes. First of all, I have had my salary as a congressman and as a senator. Second, I have received a total in this past six years of sixteen hundred dollars from estates which were in my law firm...I have made an average of approximately fifteen hundred dollars a year from nonpolitical speaking engagements...And then, fortunately, we've inherited a little money. Pat sold her interest in her father's estate for three thousand dollars, and I inherited fifteen hundred dollars from my grandfather'

* * *

Jane Spock considered Nixon's finances and compared them to her husband's. She pondered how Pocket Books had just raised the price of the *Common Sense Book of Baby and Child Care* from thirty-five cents to forty cents. Ben received no profit from the price raise because back in '46, when Benjamin was trying to get the damn thing published, he agreed to take a lower-than-average royalty rate. Benjamin had made almost $37,000 in royalties from the *Common Sense Book of Baby and Child Care.* If he'd had a standard royalty agreement, he would have earned $200,0000.*

Ben and Jane wanted more money.

The president and founder of Pocket Books, Robert F. de Graff, brushed them off. Robert F. de Graff was a man who had been born in the late nineteenth century.

Jane Spock now watches as the camera moves again to Pat Nixon, the poor woman sitting as if she's balancing an apple on her head. William Tell's wife with a toothache.

Nixon: '—What did we do with this money . . . First of all, we've got a house in Washington, which cost forty-one thousand dollars and on which we owe twenty thousand dollars. We have a house in Whittier, California, which cost thirteen thousand dollars and on which we owe three thousand dollars. My folks are living there at the present time—'

★ ★ ★

'My folks . . .'

In the beginning, there had been five Nixon boys. By 1952, two were dead. The next-to-the-youngest son was named Francis Donald. He called himself Big Don. He was thirty-eight years old. Nixon's youngest brother, Edward, was only twenty-two—Ed obviously being Mother's 'mistake.'

Back to Big Don. He wasn't big because of weight, but because he had ambitions. This year, Big Don borrowed some money, and combined with savings, opened a drive-in called Nixon's in Whittier. Nixon's stood at a hot spot in town—Whittier Boulevard near Painter Avenue.

There was something that Big Don couldn't articulate intellectually, but nevertheless felt in his heart: Big Don was on the crest of the hamburger zeitgeist in the U.S.A. Get this example: In Washington, D.C., every day for lunch, Joe McCarthy would walk across the street to the Carroll Arms and order and eat the same thing—a medium hamburger with a slice of raw onion and tomato, and a milkshake. The hunger for burgers was as American as the Pledge of Allegiance. Yet, in 1952, there were only

---

★ Well over a million dollars in modern figures.

several In-N-Out burger joints in the suburbs of L.A. Down in Miami, Burger King's progenitor, David Edgerton, was two years away from opening the first Insta Burger King. The McDonald brothers (Richard and Maurice) only had their first McDonald's in San Bernardino, a town roughly sixty miles northeast of Whittier. The McDonald brothers' mascot was a cartoon character named Speedee, a chef with a hamburger for a head—Speedee's left eye in a perpetual wink. Hamburgers were fun and innocent and part of the American way in 1952. No one was vegetarian except maybe the gay British screenwriter Christopher Isherwood, out in Hollywood.

★ ★ ★

Nixon: '—I own a 1950 Oldsmobile car. We have our furniture ' He waves his hand as if the stage props were the furniture he spoke of. 'Now, that's what we have. What do we owe?'

Pat cringes. She can't help it. Nixon mentions a $20,000 mortgage on the Washington house and $3,000 on the house in Whittier. Dick and Pat owe $4,500 to the Riggs Bank in Washington, D.C. Dick owes $3,500 to his parents—'and the interest on that loan, which I pay regularly. . . . And that's what we owe '

Then Richard Nixon talks about The Dog.

A modern dog.

He doesn't dare mention that back in 1923, when Nixon was ten, he wrote a letter in the persona of a dog to a personage he addressed as 'Master.' The nineteenth-century poet Emily Dickinson also wrote letters to a mysterious correspondent she called 'Master.' In Emily's case, literary scholars have postulated more than half a dozen possibilities for Dickinson's Master. Young Nixon's Master was his mother, who was in Arizona nursing his older brother in a tuberculosis clinic.

Richard Nixon's letter to his mother began:

> My Dear Master:
>
> . . . While we were walking I saw a black round thing in a tree. I hit it with my paw. A swarm of black thing[s] came out of it. I started to

run and as both of my eyes swelled shut I fell into a pond. When I got home I was very sore. I wish you would come home right now.

Your good dog,
Richard

Nixon on television: '—We did get something, a gift, after the election. A man down in Texas heard Pat on the radio mention the fact that our two youngsters would like to have a dog. And believe it or not, the day before we left on this campaign trip we got a message from Union Station in Baltimore, saying they had a package for us. We went down to get it. You know what it was? It was a little cocker spaniel dog in a crate that he had sent all the way from Texas. The cocker spaniel was all the way from Texas, black and white, spotted. And our little girl Tricia, the six-year-old, named it *Checkers*...'

Dogs were not considered sentient in 1952. Pastors and ministers made a point of telling their congregations that animals had no souls. Even the few clergy who allowed animals to wait among the pews to be blessed on St. Francis Day always made it clear that those pets had no souls. In the 1950s, many were glad of this. It meant the family dog would not go to hell. Americans were innocent about dogs back then. Dogs themselves were innocent. Most dogs.

Dogs were for kids. Most kids.

* * *

Nixon on television: '...And you know, the kids, like all kids, love the dog.' Richard Nixon says: 'And I just want to say this, right now, that regardless of what they say about it, we're gonna keep it.'

Nixon folds his hands into knuckles and he's doing a tiddlywinks thing with his two thumbs. 'Pat and I have the satisfaction that every dime that we've got is honestly ours. I should say this...'

Now it comes. That line. Pat is drained of her blood. Her empty veins fill with humiliation.

'I should say this, that Pat doesn't have a mink coat...'

The humiliation.

'I should say this, that Pat doesn't have a mink coat...'

The humiliation. The humiliation. The horror of it.

'I should say this, that Pat doesn't have a mink coat. But she does have a respectable Republican cloth coat—'

Pat sitting there. '... she does have a respectable Republican cloth coat...'

Now Pat hears Dick's ad-lib. '...and I always tell her she'd look good in anything...'

Pat's face still burns. '...and I always tell her she'd look good in anything...' The ringing in her ears stops. '...and I always tell her she'd look good in anything...'

She guesses she loves him again.

Chapter 6

Lewisburg Federal Penitentiary, Pennsylvania, 1952

September 24, 4:30 a.m., Mexico City.

The Hunts had a TV, but just for looks. In Mexico, television was spooky new. The single station, XHTV, had been on the air for over one year only after a presidential panel convened to determine whether American commercial television was socially superior or inferior to Great Britain's public television system. PBS-style television won, only instead of any form of educational programming, XHTV broadcast raffles and bullfights and government propaganda. Flamboyant poet Salvador Novo López groused, 'Radio in Mexico is spiritual tequila and now television will become the monster daughter of incest between radio and cinema.'

It was ten hours or so after Richard Nixon's 'Respectable Republican Cloth Coat' speech. Hunt was snoring next to Dot. She was wearing a nightgown and he was wearing pajamas.* Hunt's pajamas were baby blue. He could never wear white PJs because of his ashen complexion. The Hunt telephone rang—Mexican ringing sounded like a choking macaw.

Hunt answered. 'Hello.'

'Hunt! Listen to me! Rocky Marciano just K.O.'d Jersey Joe Walcott in thirteen.'

'How old is Rocky Marciano?'

'Twenty-nine, Hunt.'

'Fug him.'

'Fug him is right. Hunt! I gotta ask—are you a papist?'

Nothing.

'Come on, Hunt, spill.'

---

* It was mandatory that American-born couples sleep in nightwear, never in the raw.

'Yeah. For the kids. I got two daughters now. We absolutely had to have them baptized.'

'I can't hear you.'

'I can't talk louder, Dot is asleep. Wait a minute.'

There was only one phone in Hunt's home as was the Mexican custom. It had a long cord that extended from the wall to the base of the white telephone. Hunt picked the phone up from the nightstand and stretched it as far as it could go out toward the bedroom door into the hallway. The base of the phone would only make it three feet from the door. He placed it on the bedroom floor and stretched the receiver out into the hallway and then shut the bedroom door. The receiver's curlicue wire was now so taut that Hunt could only talk by laying his head down on the hall carpet.

'Okay, is this better?' Hunt said.

'Yeah. Tell me about your papist nonsense.'

'I got two daughters now. We had to have them baptized.'

'No one *has* to have their kids baptized.'

'You don't want to debate ecclesiastic issues in the middle of the night with me.'

'You have them baptized in Mexico City?'

'Yeah. Sure. Better quality fire insurance down here.'

'Huh?'

'Priests. I'm talking about priests. The priests down here really really believe in hell.'

'Oh. Yeah.'

'My mother was just down here to see the new baby. I had to hide all our papist crap from her. Hide the crucifixes as if my mother was a goddamn vampire.'

'Hmmm.'

'So why did you call, Darwin?'

'To tell you how Nixon did.'

'On TV?'

'Yeah. Listen to me—fifty, sixty, seventy million Americans watched Richard the Lionhearted.'

'That's most of the country.'

'That's a third of the country. Right before Nixon gave the speech, Dewey phones Nixon to tell him that all Eisenhower's people want him to resign.

What you gonna do, Dick? Nixon says that he didn't know—*But if Eisenhower's shitty sons of bitches want to find out they'll just have to watch like everyone else.*'

Silence.

'It's real late, Darwin. Anything else?'

'*Eisenhower's shitty sons of bitches* is Nixon just getting started. Nixon's speech wasn't filmed inside his house. It was broadcast from inside an empty theater in Hollywood. All that crummy furniture was just stage props.'

Hunt tried to sit up. He couldn't. The cord wouldn't stretch that far. 'Why didn't Nixon film it in his château in Georgetown?' Hunt asked, head back on the floor.

'Maybe Pat is a terrible housekeeper, I dunno. But listen to me—immediately after the broadcast Nixon is talking to Eisenhower on the phone in Cleveland where Eisenhower's about to make a speech. Eisenhower still hadn't decided about Nixon's fate. Nixon blows up and says, *General, there comes a time in matters like this when you've either got to shit or get off the pot.* Can you believe it—sayin' that to old Dwight? *Shit or get off the pot.*'

'All I can say is *wow.*'

'Listen to me, all North America was moved by Nixon's talking. Richard Nixon was a thousand *Queen for a Day* contestants rolled into one. This was his majestic crucifixion. Crowds have been milling on the streets in all the major cities all night flapping their tongues about Nixon. It's a hundred to one pro-Dick.'

'Nixon's position on the ticket is safe?'

'Not yet. An hour after speaking to Nixon on the phone, Eisenhower sends his running mate a telegram that's just namby-pamby nothing-in-it I-don't-know-when-or-where-I'll-make-a-decision. And Nixon turns purple. He dictates a telegram to Rose Mary Woods to send to the Republican National Committee basically saying *Up yours; I'm resigning.*'

'And?'

'And what?'

'Did he send it?'

'What do you think?'

'No.'

'Well, he almost did. His campaign manager Chotiner cooled him down.'

* * *

During Nixon's thirty long minutes of jawing, he had evoked the full name of one Alger Hiss three times. Every viewer knew who Alger Hiss was. Everyone listening and watching that night assumed that Alger Hiss's name would evoke American infamy for a thousand years—a Charles Manson of political science.

This did not happen.

Who was Alger Hiss?

'I remember in the dark days of the Hiss case,' Nixon had said, moments before his speech was shut down, '—the same radio commentators who are attacking me now . . . were violently opposing me at the time I was after Alger Hiss. And I say that any man [like Adlai Stevenson] who called the Alger Hiss case a red herring isn't fit to be president of the United States.'

In the dead center of Pennsylvania sat Lewisburg Federal Penitentiary, where Alger Hiss was now serving two concurrent five-year sentences. This prisoner was fast approaching his forty-eighth birthday. Hiss had a masculine face that was handsome enough when he was a young man, but had not weathered well the slog through his forties. Even worse, he had perpetual prison stubble. Not because of Richard Nixonish testosterone, but because when a con got disgruntled with a guard in Lewisburg Federal Penitentiary, the con would stop shaving as a sign of disrespect. Most guards had no trouble with Hiss, yet there was always some screw with a patriotic grudge.

After Nixon's 'Respectable Republican Cloth Coat' speech, Hiss's fellow cons all kidded him that Nixon mentioned him on TV. His peers were all right with Hiss's Communist past. It had been the other cons on Hiss's cell block who talked the new ones with blood in their eye into not rubbing out Hiss. The entire cell block appreciated that Hiss didn't act like an egghead—the very identity that Nixon despised Hiss for. In jail, Alger Hiss did things like teach illiterate cons how to read. One con could now write a letter to his family without help. Another was reading *Robinson Crusoe.*

Hiss had an accuser named Whittaker Chambers. The latter was now fifty-one and had always had a physique like Fred Mertz on *I Love Lucy.* But where Fred was a jolly tub, Chambers was sloppy fat, going to seed. Whittaker Chambers was not a man you would let babysit your child.

When Chambers was subpoenaed to testify to the House Un-American Activities Committee (HUAC) (where Nixon was a member), Chambers claimed that all through the Depression, Alger Hiss (who worked at the State Department) would sneak home official documents that his wife, Posey, would retype (remember, there were no Kinkos in the 1930s) on an old Woodstock typewriter (serial number 230,099).

Posey had also used that Woodstock to 'work' on her novel.

When Mrs. Hiss was finished with her illicit typing, her husband would give the retyped documents to Chambers, who would pass them up the line, Posey's typing eventually reaching Stalin's desk in Moscow.

After Whittaker Chambers's testimony, Alger Hiss was subpoenaed to appear before the HUAC. He showed and not only claimed that he wasn't a spy, but that he didn't even know Whittaker Chambers. The whole matter would have stayed dead in the water as long as Hiss didn't sue Chambers for libel.

Hiss sued Chambers for libel.

Whittaker Chambers then revealed that he had saved some of Posey's typing as collateral if he ever got into a jam. Chambers had lived on a farm down in Maryland and hid the papers in a hollow pumpkin. What a Walt Disney gesture! These papers remained in the pumpkin for a decade. Chambers even showed the pumpkin to Nixon. The newspapers were filled with photos of Richard Nixon peering at a pumpkin with great concentration—as if all the mysteries of the universe were revealed inside. Back in December of '37, Posey had abandoned her novel and given her Woodstock typewriter away to her handyman's children. Now more than a decade later, the FBI tracked down the Woodstock typewriter, serial number 230,099. They did tests to try to prove it typed the so-called Pumpkin Papers.

* * *

Three days after the birth of David Rieff to Susan Sontag Rieff, Alger Hiss was standing on the prison grounds and heard a rose-breasted grosbeak singing from a tree. It was a complicated meandering song. A lot of nasal *weep* calls followed by a series of staccato whistles and some guttural tremolos that almost sounded like monkey talk in the background of a

Tarzan picture. Hiss adored birds. He stopped raking up leaves and just tilted his head and listened. Soon, the other dozen prisoners all stopped to listen to the bird's lovely little chirping too.

* * *

When the HUAC had questioned Chambers, the man had testified that he would go bird-watching with Hiss. When Hiss was testifying before the HUAC, answering a question put forth by someone or other, he saw Nixon lean toward a fellow representative named McDowell and whisper in his ear. When there was a pause in the questioning, McDowell casually asked Hiss, 'Did you ever seen a prothonotary warbler?'

Hiss smiled. 'I have. Right here on the Potomac.'

Richard Nixon turned to McDowell again and asked into the microphone if his colleague had ever seen such a bird. McDowell answered into his microphone, 'I saw one in Arlington.'

'They come back and nest in those swamps,' Hiss volunteered. 'Beautiful yellow head, a gorgeous bird.'

Both Nixon and McDowell were giving predatory grins. 'Like cats eating warblers,' someone said at the time. In Hiss's mind's ear, he heard the song of the prothonotary warbler. It is a shrill and manic patterned song that goes *sah-sah sah-sah sah-sot-sot-sot, sah-sah sah-sah sah-sot-sot-sot.* He didn't tell that to Nixon or McDowell. It wasn't until the interrogation was over that he overheard two reporters talking.

'Chambers said that Hiss was a bird-watcher. Chambers knew Hiss.'

'And vice versa.'

Hiss realized he'd put his bird in his mouth.

* * *

Last word on the Pumpkin Papers—how can a hollowed pumpkin last ten years without decaying? No one asked that question.

* * *

Incidentally, as every historian knows, Eisenhower kept Nixon on the ticket.

* * *

As everyone knows, during this time, babies were being born at an astonishing frequency—3.6 million babies in 1950, 3.8 million the next year.

And all this pregnancy was public!

Pregnant women didn't hide themselves away. They pushed their carts through the supermarket; they ferried their first and second children to Little League or Girl Scouts; pregnant women sat uncomfortably in wooden pews at church. In America you saw pregnant women everywhere you went, yet a pregnant woman had never appeared on television.

In 1952, Lucille Ball, the star of *I Love Lucy,* was pregnant. Her show premiered the year before. At that time, Lucy was only an RKO contract player married to another RKO actor, Desi Arnaz. He was Cuban. The pair had gone to CBS with an idea for a situation comedy—the adventures of a loony/daffy/zany redhead and her Cuban-born bandleader husband living in Manhattan. The studio thought it risky. So Ball and Arnaz formed their own production company, Desilu, and paid for the show themselves.

Comedies had existed on radio for years, yet it was Lucy and Desi who originated the television sitcom. Lucy expected to continue with her show during her growing pregnancy. Desi informed CBS of his wife's intentions. The network shouted, 'Absolutely not! You cannot show a pregnant woman on TV! That would be immoral!' Desi squired a minister, a priest, and a rabbi to CBS. The three clergymen assured CBS that televising a pregnant Lucille Ball was not an act of immorality. CBS relented, although no actor could utter the actual word *pregnant* on air.

Lucy was 'expecting.'

Or as Desi said in his Cuban brogue—'spectin'.

* * *

In Detroit, Mrs. Carl Djerassi was also 'spectin'.

Chapter 7

The Cargo of Truth, an American Ship Floating in the Aegean Sea, 1952

November 4, 1952. A Tuesday.

Eisenhower and Nixon won the election. The only states Stevenson and Sparkman took were Alabama, Mississippi, Louisiana, Kentucky, Arkansas, Georgia, West Virginia, and both Carolinas. Those states were for the southern conservative Sparkman, not for the ultra-liberal Stevenson. Four years from now, John Sparkman will be one of nineteen senators who will sign Strom Thurmond's 'Southern Manifesto' opposing any form of civil rights in Dixie.

★ ★ ★

Mexico City. The unpublished gringo writer Burroughs sneaks out of the country in December 1952. The published writer J. D. Salinger moves to Cornish, New Hampshire, for no particular reason on New Year's Day, 1953. This is also the day of the man's thirty-fourth birthday. J. D. Salinger never imagines that he will spend the remainder of his long life in this dinky town, located in the middle third of New Hampshire, close to the Vermont border.

Coed Claire Douglas visits Salinger in New Hampshire. He insists that she drop out and move in with him in Cornish. Claire shakes her head. She cries. She drives like hell back to Manhattan. She phones New Hampshire. Salinger never answers. Salinger doesn't answer her letters. Finally, Claire borrows someone's Dodge and drives back to New Hampshire.

Salinger's cabin was down a long road straight into the wooded nowhere. This house was as secluded as Adlai Stevenson was a liberal—very! Claire pulled up to the garage. She left the Dodge and rang the bell. Nothing. Peered in the windows. No one home. She opened a window and climbed in. She had the sense that Jerry had just left the house. The heat was still on, but barely. Did that mean something? Maybe the heat had to be on so the pipes wouldn't freeze. She rustled through his bedroom. She had the sense that some clothes were missing. No suitcase. No typewriter. She climbed out the window and returned to New York City. She drove all night.

Enter Richard Pavlick. Very little is now known about this lifelong resident of New Hampshire save that he was born in the nineteenth century, in 1887. He lived in Belmont, forty-five miles east as the crow flies from J. D. Salinger's Cornish or a two-hour car drive—the ungodly length of travel time because of the rough terrain.

Pavlick was a mailman in Belmont. This town was big enough to have a post office. A town hall. Half a dozen stores. Seventy houses. Yet there were no schools. The kids had to be bused up to Laconia on Lake Winnisquam. Apparently Pavlick never married. He appears to have been a crank loner. Seven years from now, in December of 1960, Pavlick will stalk President-elect John Kennedy to Florida with the intention of blowing the Catholic up with a suicide bomb. Pavlick will almost succeed. This would-be assassin will have no affiliation with 'organized crime' or Cubans or Russians or the CIA. Pavlick will be his own man. A lone wolf. An American lone wolf. A failed American assassin.

* * *

As a contrast to Richard Pavlick, consider Raymond Kaplan. He lives in Flushing. He is considered a 'good guy.'

Ray. A Jewish guy in his early forties, with a wife and kid.

During the war, Ray was an Army major. Now he works as a liaison between Massachusetts Institute of Technology and the Voice of America. The VOA is part of the State Department and broadcast White Propaganda to Russia—positive stories about the U.S.A. as well as world news such as riots behind the Iron Curtain, events that the Soviets censored. MIT oversaw the technical aspects of broadcasting over the immense boundaries of the U.S.S.R.

After Christmas, Kaplan was instructed to fly west to California and find a better location for a special VOA project, code name 'Baker West.'

In those days, the cross-country flight took all day—

Imagine you are sitting next to him on the flight to California. Ray Kaplan didn't look Hasidic. He looked more like Troy Donahue's older brother. Kaplan wasn't ashamed to talk to his seatmate(s) about VOA. Kaplan made VOA sound cloak-'n'-dagger: 'It's a game of chess. We make a move. The Reds make a move. We broadcast on shortwave because everyone in Russia has a shortwave radio. The Russian wilderness is so vast. Everyone needs a shortwave radio. Did you know that the U.S.S.R is as big as North America, that's the U.S.A. and Canada and Mexico combined? So, we broadcast on one wavelength and the Reds send a counter-broadcast on a wavelength just a tiny bit higher or lower than ours to scramble it up. It not only interferes with the broadcast but it makes a loud irritating whistle. Like a boiling teakettle. The Russians also broadcast squalls of a bagpipe. Ducks quacking. Annoying sounds that bleed into our broadcast. What we do at the VOA is use thirty-six stations. We tell our listeners to scan the dial for us. It takes the Kremlin at least twelve seconds to jam our particular frequency. You can broadcast a lot of news in twelve seconds.'

Kaplan landed in Los Angeles and rented a convertible—a long red Chevrolet shaped like a submarine. He put the ragtop down, but soon discovered Christmastime Los Angeles was too cold to drive in a convertible, even though there was no snow. It was eerie noticing Christmas decorations everywhere, but no snow. Kaplan enjoyed the lit menorahs in Beverly Hills. He had voted for Ike & Dick so he made a point to stop at Dick's brother's joint in Whittier to try a Nixon Burger.

* * *

There in Belmont, New Hampshire, Richard Pavlick would show up at public meetings to complain that the American flag was not being flown properly.

'Call to order. First order of business— Yes. What is it, Mr. Pavlick? We haven't seen you for a while.'

'The flag should be raised briskly and lowered ceremoniously. That fool at city hall does just the reverse.'

Pavlick also hated the water company. Pavlick hated Girl Scout cookies.

'Yes. What is it, Mr. Pavlick?'

'Are you aware that when the flag is hung over a street running east to west, the stars are always facing north?'

'No, I didn't know that, Mr. Pavlick.'

'Well, neither does the fool who hangs the flag at the First Presbyterian Church.'

No one visited Pavlick at his shack except girls selling Girl Scout cookies or Jehovah's Witnesses. Pavlick always came to the door carrying a shotgun.

'Yes, Mr. Pavlick.'

'Last Fourth of July parade—when the American flag was carried with the state flag and the Shriners flag, the American flag should have either been on the right of the line of flags or in the center. Those damn fool majorettes from the papists' school carried it on the left of the line.'

★ ★ ★

California.

Nixon's hamburger stand employed two six-hour shifts of six carhop girls. The youngest was seventeen; the oldest, twenty. Kaplan appreciated the girls' long Californian legs and their hind ends. The girls wore short-skirted uniforms that make them look like cheerleaders for hamburgers.

Cheerleaders for Nixon Burgers.

A peppery brunette bounced to his convertible and wedged a tray on the door.

'What can I getcha?'

'What's special?'

'Big Don's Double-Decker Nixon Burger with Cheese,' the brunette said.

'What's on it?'

'Well, a bun of course.'

'Yes, everyone has a bun.'

The brunette frowned. She didn't get it. 'Well, the Double-Decker Nixon Burger with Cheese has a bun and a dab of cheese and a burger and a bun and another burger and a dab of cheese and a pickle and the third bun.'

'Yum yum,' Kaplan said. 'I'll have two and a Dr. Pepper.'

'Who's Dr. Pepper?'

'I'll have a Pepsi.'

She frowned and shook her head. 'We don't serve Pepsi.' She spoke as if he'd asked for something obscene.

On the outskirts of Los Angeles, white people didn't drink Pepsi.

In the late 1940s and early 1950s, Pepsi marketed their cola to an overlooked demographic: Negroes. Pepsi's print ads showed African-Americans dressed in fine suburbanite clothes enjoying Pepsi with their hamburgers. Coca-Cola ads never had blacks sucking back a bottle of their soda.

Kaplan paid no attention to the ads. He liked the taste of Pepsi.

'Can I get a Coca-Cola?' Kaplan asked.

She smiled and nodded her head as if he was a stupid child who finally spit out the correct answer.

'Then that's it,' Kaplan said.

'No fries?'

'No fries.'

Kaplan's hamburger cheerleader bounced away. He began to beat on the dashboard like bongos. He was in California. He thought about the cheese on his double Double-Decker Nixon Burgers. The cheese would surely be processed cheese although Kaplan was never sure exactly what processed cheese was (it was unfermented dairy ingredients, emulsifiers, salt, whey, and food coloring).

* * *

For the record, Big Don doctored his Nixon Burgers with cracker meal. And just as Donald Nixon used filler in his Nixon Burgers, you might say his brother Dick's vision of democracy was filled with filler as well.

Between brother Dick's Checkers speech and Watergate, the man will weasel out of eight extensive accusations of money laundering. The impetus behind Dick Nixon's ordering Howard Hunt to have the Democratic National Committee headquarters burglarized at the Watergate complex in 1972 (a structure not even built yet) has its genesis here, at Donald's hamburger joint in 1952.

* * *

The hamburger cheerleader returned with Kaplan's twin Double-Decker Nixon Burgers. He thanked her. As Kaplan ate both his Double-Decker Nixon Burgers he considered the Voice of America broadcast team floating in the Aegean Sea at this very moment. Those Americans hadn't seen a hamburger let alone eaten one in two years. Their ship was named the *Courier*—a 338-foot, 5,500-ton cargo ship that had been retrofitted with twin diesel engines capable of generating 1.5 million watts of electrical power. These 1.5 million watts were used to power a radio that would broadcast nonstop American propaganda. Former president Harry S. Truman had called what the *Courier* carried 'The Cargo of Truth.'

The *Courier*'s crew was ninety Coast Guards and three Voice of America radio engineers. International law prohibited the *Courier* from broadcasting White Propaganda into the U.S.S.R. from the high seas. They could only broadcast from the territorial waters of agreeable countries. The *Courier* was now bobbing off the Turkish coast in the harbor of the Greek island of Rhodes.

The head *Courier* VOA deejay was John Roderigo Madison, thirty-two. He'd been educated with Leslie Fiedler in Wisconsin. John Roderigo Madison wanted to interject American poetry into VOA broadcasts, but no piece could be longer than thirty seconds because of Soviet jamming. Madison considered haiku. Short and sweet. But that was a Japanese form. Maybe limericks?

Ice, ice. Our wheels no longer move
Horseman your sword is in the groove

John Roderigo Madison's recitation of William Carlos Williams's poem 'The Red Wheelbarrow' caused an uproar in the Soviet Union. *What is this 'red wheelbarrow'?* 'Red' in the U.S.A. means Communist. *What is a 'wheelbarrow' code for? Obviously internal anti-Soviet agents within our Red borders.*

John Roderigo Madison's recitation of William Carlos Williams's 'The Red Wheelbarrow' caused an uproar at Voice of America as well. A top dog sent a cable to the ship: NO MORE RED WHEELBARROWS.

Madison shrugged. He figured the top minds in Washington, D.C., apparently knew what a Red Wheelbarrow was and didn't want the Communists to figure it out.

★ ★ ★

The poet himself, William Carlos Williams, was a pediatrician like Dr. Spock. Dr. Williams's beat was Rutherford, New Jersey, a place more rural than urban. Dr. Williams would estimate that he delivered more than two thousand babies in New Jersey. The man was now sixty-nine and looked good for his age. He had an 'old lawyer' intensity about him rather than 'old doctor.'

William Carlos Williams was also one of America's foremost poets. (After his death, he would even win a Pulitzer Prize.) During the time of the 'Red Wheelbarrow' broadcast, Williams had been invited to serve as a consultant in poetry for the Library of Congress.

The appointment enraged right-wing literates.

Forget 'The Red Wheelbarrow,' William Carlos Williams had once composed a poem titled 'Russia.' Williams's detractors said that poem 'lauded' the Communists.

None of his detractors had actually read 'Russia.' It contained the line: 'Russia [is the] idiot of the world, blind idiot.'

Williams had also written a poem titled 'The Pink Church.'

Pink. Pinko.

An abbreviated version of the poem without line breaks goes: 'Pink as a dawn in Galilee . . . the Pink Church trembles . . . to the light (of dawn) again . . . pink jade that is the light and is a stone and is a church if the image hold. . . . O Dewey! (John): O James! (William); O Whitehead!* teach well! . . . above and beyond your teaching stands the Pink Church: the nipples of a woman who never bore a child . . . suckled of its pink delight. . . . Joy! Joy! out of Elysium! chanted loud as a chorus from the Agonists; Milton, the unrhymer, singing among the rest like a Communist.'

Mrs. Virginia Kent Cummins, editor of a poetry magazine titled *The Lyric,* led the growing right-wing mob against Williams. 'To not write metered rhymed poetry is pure communism,' Mrs. Virginia Kent Cummins declared. Fulton Lewis Jr., a radio commentator, understood that Williams was a 'modernist.' 'Modernism is communism,' he told his listeners.

---

* References to three notable philosophers: John Dewey (1859–1952); William James (1842–1910), and Alfred North Whitehead (1861–1947).

* * *

Poems about Pink Churches and Red Wheelbarrows were one thing, but few English-language poets other than Carl Sandburg and W. H. Auden wrote poems about lawyers. As the weather got colder in December 1952 New York City, a young lawyer was invited to a party at the Biltmore in Manhattan. Somebody wanted to meet him. Somebody important.

A politician rather than a poet—Joseph McCarthy.

The young man will later say the scene at the Biltmore was like something from the Marx Brothers. Women all giving horse laughs. The men in tuxedos and mostly drunk out of their minds. The name of the young man was Roy Cohn. He was wearing a sport coat. Joe McCarthy, himself, was in tuxedo pants and suspenders over a sweaty T-shirt. 'Roy Cohn! My God, I'm glad to meet you,' McCarthy hollered.

'Likewise, sir,' Cohn said. Roy Cohn was a sleepy-eyed youth. Roy Cohn had bags under his eyes as prominent as golf balls.

'You can't possibly be one-tenth as good as everyone says you are.'

'Two-tenths, sir.' Cohn's father was a New York City judge. From the time he could talk, Roy knew how the deal was done. He now worked for the state. He had been part of the team that prosecuted the Rosenbergs for passing A-bomb secrets to Stalin. His greatest contribution to the case was (a) pulling strings and making sure Kaufman was the judge, and (b) pulling strings to seeing to it that the Rosenbergs would fry.

'Ha. A sense of humor,' McCarthy said. 'I like that. Have a drink.'

'You know, sir, that I'm a registered Democrat.'

'I couldn't care less about your politics. I just want you to help me ferret out Reds.' Then the older man put his hand on the younger man's shoulder. 'Give me a quick definition of a Communist.'

Cohn didn't hesitate a moment. 'A Communist, sir, is one who is under the discipline of an atheistic totalitarian movement that stands for the overthrow by force and by criminal means and by espionage and by sabotage of the government of the United States as well as every other free government throughout the world.'

* * *

The best way to get an idea of the Communist threat in 1952 is to compare the Reds' determination of leveling the U.S.A. with modern anti-West apocalyptic jihadists. I am well aware that for more than fifty years the 'Communist witch hunt of the 1950s' has been a dead horse that gets beaten over and over in books and movies because most of the citizens who had their careers justly and unjustly ruined were screenwriters and other writers.

Histories are, as you know, written by writers.

Surely, if the House Un-American Activities Committee (HUAC) had hauled ballet dancers to Washington, D.C., and accused them of performing Red choreography, the repertoire of the modern dance of today would be filled with anti-witch-trial pieces.

It's also easy in the fog of time to confuse the HUAC with Joseph McCarthy. Congressmen on the HUAC had been rooting out Communist spies all during the late 1940s. Joseph McCarthy was a senator, not a member of the House. He was a forty-four-year-old opportunistic Johnny-come-lately from Wisconsin who farted onto the national scene in the 1950s after giving a Lincoln Day speech to the Women's Republican Club of Wheeling, West Virginia, where he waved a sheet of paper in the air, howling that it contained the names of '205' Communists who worked in the State Department.

He didn't have 205 names. He was lying.

It is right-wing irony that the accomplishments of the HUAC are credited to 'McCarthyism.' He and they are now and forever pathetic Siamese twins.

* * *

Voice of America's Raymond Kaplan drove up the salty Pacific coast visiting local airports and meteorologists to talk about dipole and rhombic antennas. He even had access to some Navy weather balloons so he could take readings of the auroral absorption belt.

Ray liked driving in California. He liked talking to engineers. He liked talking to meteorologists. They both understood what he was talking about in a way that teenage girls who hopped hamburgers did not.

His second day in California, he spied a yellow Dodge following him. This same car had tailed him the day before in Santa Clara. He slowed. The yellow Dodge turned and disappeared. He listened to the NFL championship on the car radio. Detroit Lions vs. Cleveland Browns—

> 'Here's the pass . . . Banish air from air . . . Picked off by Lions' Rhys Traitor! He's gonna go! Talk about usurping the Browns' sovereignty . . . He's gonna go! Vin Kavel is a hair's breadth away on Rhys's tail—'

Ray was outside Santa Barbara when he again saw the yellow Dodge tailing him. Ray ignored the car and kept his appointment in Santa Clara with Dave Hope, meteorologist.

* * *

In Detroit, Carl Djerassi was out running errands. *Detroit* means 'strait' in French. Do you know that Detroit sits across from Canada on the western shore of Lake St. Clair? In those days, Detroit was the fourth-largest city in America. Djerassi's wife was home doing the dishes and listening to the Lions/Browns game on the Bakelite Crosley 'Musical Chef' radio they got as a premium for buying a refrigerator—

> 'Rhys Traitor is running. You can tell Rhys Traitor is running and thinking . . . Thinking hard . . . He's gonna go! He's gonna go! You think an ant can't run away with Achilles' head? He's gonna go!'

Carl Djerassi's wife begins slashing her fists into the soapy water while she bounces quickly foot-to-foot yelling, 'He's gonna go! He's gonna!'

> 'Touchdown! Hey-Hey! Rhys Traitor tosses his helmet off his head . . . He tilts his head back and starts laughing with joy . . . Hey-Hey-Hey!'

* * *

Santa Clara, California. Dave Hope had a small office cluttered with literally hundreds of weather maps folded and rolled, sitting on file cabinets and bookshelves and the floor. Hope himself was a messy child-sized man who looked cluttered. 'McKesson says Voice of America could save eighteen million dollars by moving the transmitters to Florida and California,' Hope was saying.

Ray shrugged.

'Senator McCarthy says the VOA is filled with commies,' Hope said. 'What do you think?'

Ray frowned big. 'The Army Corps of Engineers builds the antennas. You think they're in on it too?'

Hope raised his hand. 'Don't get me wrong, Ray. The only ones I want to pick a fight with are red-blooded Communists.'

Ray changed the subject. 'My kid David has a comic book that supposes the Russians start bombarding America with the Voice of the U.S.S.R. Only their radio show doesn't need a radio to be heard. You can't hear it in your ears. It's too high a frequency. The radio signal makes Americans start killing themselves. A deaf man saves the nation.' Kaplan then gave a shrug.

There now comes a moment when Kaplan opens his mouth to say something, but then doesn't.

Should he or shouldn't he?

He starts: 'I don't understand Jerome Wiesner. That's my boss. He supports building Baker West in Seattle. He's just thirty-six years old, the youngest *scientist* in the top-secret radio/radar department, and for less than one year, the director of that division at MIT. Before the war, Wiesner toured the rural South with some musicologist recording Negro sharecroppers singing songs. When the war started, Wiesner led Project Cadillac—'

'The airborne radar system?'

'Yeah.'

Dave emits a long whistle like a teakettle.

'At war's end,' Ray continues, 'Wiesner worked at Los Alamos. He designed electronic components used in the tests at Bikini Atoll. Then he came to MIT to run the Research Laboratory of Electronics. The guy now had a staff of three hundred fifty.' Kaplan went quiet. He started to speak. Then he didn't. What he wanted to say: *Everyone at MIT resents his youth and fears his terrible ambition.*

Dave Hope's phone rang. He frowned before answering. 'Yeah. I'm at my desk. We both are. We'll wait for his call.' He hung up.

'General Stoner is going to call.'

'I like him. He's no phony.'

'You ever hear him rasp poetic about the Army Signal Corps?'

'Not recently. You know Julius Rosenberg was in the Signal Corps.'

'No!' Hope began laughing out of his nose.

'But as I said, I like General Stoner. I've heard his speeches. He fought the Japs with radio signals.'

'The atmosphere being a more important battlefield than Iwo Jima.'

Kaplan began imitating Stoner's intoning speech. 'As the great man says: For every bullet an American soldier fired during World War Two, the Signal Corps fired eight words over radio and Morse code—'

Hope broke in: '. . . words that were parts of sentences that concerned maneuvers and supplies and reconnaissance information.'

'One bullet versus eight words,' said Kaplan.

'Words won the war.'

'Well at least General Stoner thinks in spherality, he thinks in hemispheres. Jerome Wiesner just thinks in terms of asses to kiss.'

'Well, last time I checked my ass was pretty spheral!'

The phone rang. Hope picked up. 'Hello, General Stoner.' He listened. He listened a long time. Kaplan could hear masculine murmuring coming from the phone's receiver. 'He's here. I'll put him on.' Hope handed Kaplan the receiver.

'Hello, General,' Kaplan says after he is handed the receiver. Kaplan listens. He grunts. He says, 'Okay, General. . . . Good-bye, sir.' Kaplan hands the phone to Hope to hang up. 'Stoner tells me to come home,' Kaplan says. 'The Baker West antenna is staying in Seattle. He can't stomach California.'

Chapter 8

Puget Sound, Washington, 1953

Seattle was more than a highly magnetic city or a flying saucer town. It had music. On the border between Darktown and the White.

Many who have never been to Seattle believe this city is located on the shores of the Pacific Ocean. It is not. It sprawls inside Puget Sound, a Pacific inlet. The summer that just passed in Seattle was already being called The Saucer Summer of '53. There had been more than five hundred sightings of UFOs. The flying saucers soared over downtown Seattle, over Tacoma, Bellingham, Enumclaw, Centralia, Hanford, Puget Sound and even Lake Sammamish. Terrestrial life in Seattle was a polyglot of Caucasians, Asians, Native American tribes native to the region, and Negroes. Yet, only white people reported seeing flying saucers. African-/Native American Jimi Hendrix was ten years old that summer. Everyone called him Buster. The boy had, in fact, seen a flying saucer once, only his dad told him to keep quiet.

There was a happenin' club named Birdland, although the sign out front had it spelled two words, *Bird Land*. It was named in honor of saxophonist supreme Charlie 'The Bird' Parker, just as the more famous club named in the man's honor, Birdland, was in Manhattan.

Birdland was one word.

In Seattle's Bird Land, bebop and R&B were in. There were also swinging clubs named the Mardi Gras Grill and the Pal Darwin Theater. A local star whose stage name was Bonnie Guitar (thirty) played fluid country jazz on her National Electric Spanish guitar at all these joints. She was on the verge of being discovered. Buster, himself, was said to strum the bristle end of a broom pretending it was a guitar. He wanted to play guitar when he grew up.

★ ★ ★

Detroit. Norma Djerassi gave birth to a son. Husband Carl had turned the pint-sized attic into a bedroom for daughter Pam because he believed in the American paraphrase of Virginia Woolf: A kid should have a room of their own.

Djerassi vowed that his next house would be twice as big. And it wouldn't have a pink bathroom and a pink kitchen full of pink appliances such as a pink refrigerator and a pink range. He never took to the craving of the new color called Mamie Pink, so named after the sequined pink gown the new first lady, Mamie Eisenhower, had worn to the inaugural ball in January.

No one criticized Mamie Eisenhower for her pinkness even though the slur *pinko* was coined for those liberals who were not totally committed to Communism (red); they were just leaning that way (pink). In fact, the American establishment embraced the first lady's color. 'Mamie Pink is a cross between pastel and baby pink,' stated Mrs. Margaret Hayden Rorke, the president of the Textile Color Card Association of the United States. She was the American woman in charge of regulating the colors in the American flag and the colors of military uniforms. Eight years from now, Mrs. Margaret Hayden Rorke will state that Jacqueline Kennedy's pink Chanel suit 'is a cross between baby pink and Venetian Ceruse.'

* * *

Mrs. Virginia Kent Cummins and Fulton Lewis Jr. and W. Cleon Skousen and George Dondero had blood in their eyes concerning Communists. Joe McCarthy didn't give a shit. Roy Cohn, McCarthy's aide-de-camp, will say, 'Joe McCarthy bought Communism in much the same way as other people purchase a new automobile. The salesman showed Joe the model; he studied it with interest, examined it more closely, kicked at the tires, sat at the wheel, squiggled in the seat, asked some questions and bought [it]. It was just as cold as that.'

If McCarthy soured his heart with bona fide human hatreds, the target of his wrath was not the Communists, but rather the United States Army. Just prior to his speech in Wheeling, Senator McCarthy had been in the middle of pursuing Army brass involved in the torture of Nazi storm troopers who in turn had been found guilty of atrocities against some Belgian and American prisoners of war. This resonates with us because of Abu Ghraib in 2004. It resonated with McCarthy in 1953 because there were six hundred thousand German-American voters in Wisconsin.

In the matter of the man's love life, he had not dated a Kennedy girl in one year. He had a different woman deep in his brain, so deep that she herself constructed all of Joseph McCarthy's anti-Communist thinking. She was a girl in her late twenties named Jean Kerr. She was his Girl Friday. Jean Kerr was as pretty as she needed to be and unmarried by choice just like the Kennedy sisters had been. Her personal hatred of Communism was so virulent she made writer Ayn Rand seem like a barrel of laughs. At night, Jean didn't pray, but silently recited a changing list of curses at Joseph Stalin calling him by his real name, Joseph Vissarionovich Dzhugashvili. She wrote the speeches Joe McCarthy gave that weren't off the cuff. She even ghostwrote his new book, *McCarthyism: The Fight for America*. It was 101 pages long. As slim as it was it contained 314 footnotes.

'Hello, Senator . . . It's Jean, silly. This is what we should do. We should bring down VOA . . . That's Voice of America, I said. VOA consumes forty percent of the State Department's budget. For cryin' out loud, VOA has a staff of ten thousand, most of them fags or pinkos . . . For now, the VOA broadcasts from radio boats, but they have a joint venture with MIT to— What? That's the Massachusetts Institute of Technology, I said. Up in Boston. They're planning to build two giant transmitters. One on the Atlantic coast and the other on the Pacific. The project is named *The Ring Plan* . . . Yes yes yes. The Ring Plan. Like some opera by Wagner . . . What? No, silly. Casanova didn't write operas. Wagner. *The Ring of the Nibelungen*. Yes, Hitler loved Wagner. Anyway, one transmitter will be in North Carolina. That's Baker East. The second will be outside Seattle. Baker West. And get this, Senator, a disgruntled Voice of America engineer named Louis McKesson— . . . What? No. For cryin' out loud, Senator, not a *train* engineer. A *radio* engineer, I said. Anyway, Seattle is a terrible place for Baker West, he says. It's because Seattle is too close to the Northern Lights. You know, magnetic storms. The radio signal would be lucky to reach Vancouver Island, he says, let alone Moscow. And listen, Senator, this Louis McKesson just quit VOA. No kiddin'! He just quit about this. It makes Louis sick, he says. The pinko who is the head of MIT is still gung-ho on Seattle.'

* * *

Raymond Kaplan on Valentine's Day in Manhattan.

He made his appointment with Roy Cohn at Senator McCarthy's office in the Waldorf Astoria on Park Avenue. Kaplan rode the elevator to McCarthy's floor and discovered the space wasn't an office at all. It was an apartment. Men and women stood around in a huge living room under framed photographs of children and old people. Coats and hats were piled on chairs and settees. The people who were sitting on the dozen Louis XV armchairs were rereading their subpoenas and wiggling their feet. Kaplan walked over to a stack of out-of-date magazines and began thumbing through a *Look*. Kaplan eavesdropped on two semi-whispering men. They both had comb-overs and were sweating so heavily their skin glistened under those pitiful strands of hair. *We moderns would wonder why these guys didn't just shave their heads bald.*

'It's the Internal Security Subcommittee that investigates Reds,' one murmured. 'The way I hear it is the Senate gave McCarthy the Senate Committee on Government Operations because it's a nothing committee. They figured he'd just disappear into the woodwork.' The man stopped talking and glanced around to see if anyone was eavesdropping. 'McCarthy is stupid like the pope is Jewish. He realized that the Senate Committee on Government Operations is the umbrella over the Senate Permanent Subcommittee on Investigations. The dirty so-and-sos gave McCarthy exactly what he wanted. Now he can hunt down Reds to his heart's content.'

Neither guy shaved his head because baldness is freaky. . . . The only bald men in America in 1953 are Mr. Clean and the Broadway actor Yul Brynner.

'So, Roy Cohn is chief counsel?'

'Yea. And Jack Kennedy's kid brother, Robert, is the assistant counsel.'

At that moment, two guys came out of a door laughing and horsing around. One was tall. The other short. Elmer Fudd and Bugs Bunny. Both had bushy heads of hair. 'See you tomorrow, come Cohn or Schine,' one of the comb-over guys whispered.

The short guy saw Kaplan. 'You Raymond Kaplan?'

'Yes.'

'Roy Cohn. This is my associate David Schine.'

Cohn carried himself younger than his twenty-six years. Kaplan thought it was too bad Cohn talked through his nose. The Schine guy was six feet tall and resembled an elongated five-year-old. (He was born in 1927 and was twenty-six.) Schine started jiggling up and down like he had to pee. Cohn turned to Schine. 'What is it now?'

'Roy, you said you'd help me find my notebook!'

'What? Right now? Can't you see I'm talking to Mr. Kaplan?'

Schine stuck his lower lip out in a pout. He reached down and pulled up a *Look* magazine and hit Cohn on the head with it. Cohn went into the body position of a brawler and then snatched up a *Time* magazine and began hitting Schine. They carried on this way with complete indifference to how it appeared.

'Mr. Cohn,' Kaplan said, interrupting the horseplay. 'I brought the memo I told you about.'

'Just read it out loud, Mr. Kaplan,' Cohn said, now swatting Schine's ears with two rolled-up *Time* magazines.

'The letter is written by Jerome B. Wiesner, Associate Director, Research Laboratory of Electronics, Massachusetts Institute of Technology. It is dated two years ago—December 26, 1951.' Kaplan stopped. He waited for Cohn and Bugs to stop horsing around. They finally did. Kaplan read the letter. They still wanted the Baker station in Seattle.

'My God,' Cohn said, dropping his rolled-up magazines to the floor. 'They've been squirreling around for two years. What on earth is the problem? How well do you know this Wiesner? You think he's a Red?' Kaplan couldn't answer right away. The thought had never crossed his mind. Cohn gave a scowl of impatience and snapped, 'Are you?'

David Schine's upper body swayed toward Kaplan as if Schine was contemplating beating him now with a rolled-up magazine.

* * *

Roy Cohn at a pay phone.

'Can I speak to Jean, please. I'm returning her call. Thanks.'

He waits. She picks up: 'Hi, Roy. Is Joe with you?'

'No.'

'We had another fight and he stormed out.'

'Don't worry. You know Joe is Joe and he's nuts about you. You'll be married by summer.'

'Small hope, Roy.'

'I betcha a quarter.'

'A quarter on what?'

'I bet you twenty-five cents that you'll be Mrs. McCarthy by summer's end.'

'You're on, buster.'

* * *

Flushing, Queens.

Raymond Kaplan went home after meeting with Roy Cohn and found his wife at the range cooking. They gave each other a peck. 'David Two is staying for dinner,' she told him. His son David's best friend was also named David. The two boys were in David One's bedroom playing cowboys or something. Kaplan walked by the door. His son had a cowboy pistol and so did the other David. They were shooting each other.

'Bang!' David One howled to David Two.

The boys noticed Kaplan in the doorway so they both hammed it up, each boy clutching his stomach, saying 'I'm a goner!' as they fell to the carpet on their faces.

'Boys! Where did you learn how to play dead like that?' Raymond asked.

Both boys looked up from the floor in surprise.

'From TV.'

'*The Lone Ranger!*'

'*Dragnet,* too!'

Raymond Kaplan walked into his son's room, gently kicking aside some toys. 'Well, boys, that's not the way men die when they're shot in their bellies or chests.'

'It isn't?'

'No one dies falling forward unless they are shot in the back. When you're shot in the stomach, the force of the bullet knocks you to your back.' He walked to his son's bed and faced the two boys. 'Shoot me.'

Both boys jumped up and started yelling 'Bang!'

Ray flung out his arms and fell to the bed on his back and stared dead-eyed at the ceiling.

'I shot you in the head, Mr. Kaplan,' David Two howled. 'I shot you in the head.'

Kaplan heard his wife coming down the hall. He whipped upward to sit on the edge of the bed. He put his finger to his lips and gave each David a stare. His wife walked in the room. 'What are you boys doing?' she said, staring at her husband.

* * *

In early 1953, Uncle Sugar ordered Howard Hunt to pack up from Mexico and relocate his family to the Balkans, those dreary Slavic lands north of Greece. War was in the air because of a border dispute between Italy and Tito's Yugoslavia.

During WWII, Neville Chamberlain, that disgraceful Limey, had called Yugoslavia 'a far away country between people of whom we know nothing.' Ten years down the road, ignorance still held sway.

Yugoslavia's capital, Belgrade, was a dreary city of metal buildings and empty sidewalks. Here Hunt had coordinated all acts of espionage with British MI6 agents—each one a stuffy Eric Ambler walk-on as far as Hunt was concerned.

Hunt would write that he took to drinking with a Brit spy with the unfortunate name of Crouchback. 'You are diminutive for an American, old man. Do you know John Hamilton?'

'John Hamilton? No.'

'John Hamilton was ridiculously tall. You see, old man, I was there when John Hamilton parachuted in.' Crouchback gave a chuckle. 'He blew off course and almost slammed into a grove of wolf trees. After that, I called him Lumberjack. He was huge, old man. Tall. Almost seven feet. The Lumberjack and Tito got to be fast friends. The Lumberjack would disappear for weeks at a time and return with crates of guns. Good guns. American guns. Winchesters. Whereas old Fitzroy MacLean only brought Tito old Spanish guns that still used flint. You know Fitzroy MacLean, old man?'

'No.'

'Who do you know, old man? Fitzroy MacLean. Eton. He's the real *old boy* and all that. Fitzroy MacLean parachuted into Bosnia around '42 or '43. Tito loved Fitzroy MacLean almost as much as he loved the Lumberjack. In those days, Tito was living in a cave with a big entrance that was hidden behind a waterfall. It was a huge space that Tito fixed up. He had an electric generator and a goddamn chandelier hanging from the ceiling. A snooker table. He'd raided King Peter's palace so he had wine and caviar and tinned foie gras. I get an appetite just thinking about it. How about you, old man?'

'Am I hungry?'

'Yes.'

'No. Not really.'

'Well, okay. It's only three. It's too early to starve. Where was I, old man? Yes. I remember. During the day, Tito and Fitzroy and the Lumberjack would creep about in the wood bushwhacking Jerry and the spigs—that's the Germans and the Blackshirts.'

'I know,' Hunt said.

'So, Tito and Fitzroy and the Lumberjack pop off the enemy all day and then stay up all night drinking King Peter's wine and playing snooker and debating politics until they'd start talking about women. Just like you and me, old man.'

'We haven't talked about women.'

'Yet, old man. We haven't talked about women *yet*. Tito and Fitzroy and the Lumberjack had a competition among themselves to see who could deflower a Muslim girl first. The cave was in Bosnia, you see, old man. Your Lumberjack won.'

'He's not my Lumberjack.'

'Oh, he would be if you had seen him, old man. The Lumberjack was from Hollywood. An actor. I'm sure John Hamilton wasn't his real name.'

'I've been to Hollywood.'

'You don't say, old man? Are you an actor?'

'No. A writer.'

'Sorry, old man.'

'Don't be.'

'I'm still sorry. Have I seen any pictures that you wrote the stories for?'

'No,' Hunt said sadly.

'So how can you write for Hollywood, old man, if they don't film your stories?'

'For every fifty screenplays that get written and paid for, only two are actually filmed.' Hunt changed the subject. 'So, were you living in that cave with Tito and Fitzroy MacLean and the Hollywood Lumberjack?'

'No, old man,' Crouchback said. It was his turn to be sad. 'I was stuck on the Dalmatian coast with Duane Hudson and his Chetniks. What a blasted waste, old man! The Chetniks were the only Serbs who loved only Serbs. Tito's partisans were all inconclusioned. I mean, all in-in.'

'They were all inclusive?'

'Yes. Inclusive. Well, that's why you're a writer, old man. They were all inclusive. They'd give a gun to a Croat. A Jew. A Muslim. As well as Bulgars and Montenegrins and White Russians. Tito didn't give a toot as long as you could bloody shoot.' Crouchback signaled the bartender. 'More libations, old man.' Then he turned to Hunt. 'Ask me how we all knew Jerry had left Belgrade.'

'When Radio Belgrade stopped playing "Lili Marlene."'

Crouchback was crestfallen.

'It was the same all over Europe,' Hunt said, and paused and then said, '*old man.*'

Crouchback wasn't fazed in the least. 'You know it was your Lumberjack who convinced Tito that Stalin was no good. The Lumberjack kept saying, *Your dick, Tito, is bigger than Stalin's.* So far those words have stuck, what ten years later, old man? There is Stalin and the Iron Curtain and then Yugoslavia. Stalin tells Tito to not speak to Mao and Tito shrugs and talks to Mao. You know NATO was going to ask Tito to join, and then that border deal in Trieste dropped foul on everything.'

* * *

Pittsburgh. Jane Spock's memories ate her—her memories of life in Manhattan. She'd gaze into a corner of whatever room she was in and recall that Benjamin Spock had been the only man in Manhattan who enjoyed shopping with his wife. Shopping for women's clothes. He encouraged Jane to dress in the latest fashion. He was a heterosexual man who actually read *Vogue,* so he knew what he was talking about. He never told her this, but her flamboyant, but good taste, attire made her appear exotic. She was no longer plain. He dressed her to emphasize her knockout figure.

Now in Pittsburgh, Jane dressed like everyone else's wife. The women of Pittsburgh made Mamie Eisenhower's pink couture seem positively Parisian.

Back in Manhattan, Benjamin Spock dressed like a dandy himself. As a couple, they radiated social success. Now Benjamin dressed like a Pittsburghian too. Now he'd only page through *Vogue* if it was a magazine in a dentist's waiting room and if he felt like perusing the brassiere advertisements.

* * *

In Russian, the title of *The Catcher in the Rye* was Над пропастъю во ржи (*Over the Abyss in the Rye*).

* * *

Flushing, Queens.

It was Thursday, March 5, 7:30 p.m.

Ray Kaplan wasn't home yet. David was supposed to be in bed asleep, but he had the radio beside his bed on softly, twirling the dials, fishing for his new favorite song. He found it.

'TV Is the Thing This Year.'

David listened to it. 'TV Is the Thing This Year'—a novelty song played on all the stations, sung by Dinah Washington. She was twenty-eight and black and a great R&B singer.

A bouncy organ begins playing for two bars, and then Dinah begins singing with only drums accenting the lyrics:

If you wanna have fun come home with me
You can stay all night and play with my TV

David didn't know that Dinah Washington was only a stage name. The black singer had been born Ruth Lee Jones in Tuscaloosa, Alabama. She grew up on the South Side of Chicago. She sang gospel music until she got the devil in her and began singing straight R&B. It was said that she always wore a mink even in August. It was said she carried a .38 pistol with her. 'TV Is the Thing This Year' was on every juke in every roadhouse whose patrons dug race music.

Radio was great, but now it's out of date
TV is the thing this year

David heard his mother walking into the bathroom down the hall. He heard the door shut. A pipe started rattling. The sound of the shower. He hurried into the living room and turned on the television—a B&W set that cost $75.* David knew his mother couldn't hear the sound over the shower. David knew by experience that he could watch for two minutes before she finished. It was worth it. All of David's friends were allowed to stay up until eight or eight thirty. David turned on the TV. He turned the dial and found *The Lone Ranger.* The masked man in the white hat was pushing his way through the swinging doors of a saloon. The bar was crowded. A man with a headband with a feather and regular cowboy clothes was playing the piano. He must be a half-breed.

'Time to face the music, Ratman!' the Lone Ranger shouted.

The half-breed yelled, 'Lemme finish this song.'

'You're under arrest, Ratman!'

Ratman played the piano one-handed while reaching with his free hand to his holster. Then Ratman jumped up and spun toward the Lone Ranger, who was already in the middle of drawing his own gun. Shots rang out. The half-breed fell dead on his belly—he was not blown backward the way Dad said he should.

David now hears a police siren. Not on TV, from the street. It blares up to the house. A pair of car doors slam. A few seconds later, the doorbell buzzes. David punches off the television. The boy runs to the front door and opens it.

Two policemen stand there and then peer down at him.

David slams the door and tears to the bathroom door and pounds. The shower is running. His mother doesn't answer. She can't hear. Her son does something that he is never supposed to do. He opens the bathroom door. He gets his mother. He tells her that the police are at the door. She puts on a bathrobe and runs to the hallway in bare feet.

The cops tell her that her husband is dead.

She faints to the floor and her robe spills open.

---

* His dad said that was expensive.

* * *

Raymond Kaplan died in Cambridge, Massachusetts, earlier that evening. The man was run over by a truck on a side street near the Massachusetts Institute of Technology. It had been unseasonably warm that day and there was no ice on the sidewalks that could have caused the man to slip.

The sun was going down. The truck driver, Henry Burke (forty), said Kaplan dashed in front of him as he drove slowly by the Massachusetts Institute of Technology. An MIT professor named Frederick Adams was driving with his wife behind the ten-ton trailer truck. He saw Kaplan walk out of a building at MIT and then hesitate a moment on the sidewalk when he saw the truck, and then dash into the road just in time to be struck and flattened. The newspapers reported that Mrs. Adams didn't see the accident; she only heard her husband exclaim, 'Someone has run right in front of that truck!'

The police impounded Kaplan's briefcase. The police just told Mrs. Kaplan that a truck had hit her husband. Kaplan's body was shipped back to Flushing aboard a hearse that drove all through the night to make the Jewish funeral the next day, Friday. As Kaplan's family was leaving that funeral, reporters were swarming outside. 'Mrs. Kaplan, what do you think about your husband's suicide note?'

The grief etched in Lillian Kaplan's face was replaced by confusion. Then she became wide-eyed and gasped for air and fainted.

* * *

No one in the U.S.A. knows that on this very day in the U.S.S.R. Joseph Stalin will die. Since 1922, he has been the first general secretary of the Communist Party of the Soviet Union. Since 1941, he has also been premier of the Soviet Union. He is now seventy-four years old. He lies on his deathbed. He had a stroke two days before. His eyes—they open. You can almost hear them open. A lizard sound. Stalin pops his eyes open and slowly peers at each personage in the room. He peers at his son; his daughters; everyone's worthless marital partners; their brats. Next Stalin peers at the politicos. The doctor. A girl taking notes—a secretary—ah, in her case Stalin is too preoccupied with dying to even entertain a thought about fucking her. Stalin eyes each person in the room and ends by narrowing his brow at his three-year-old granddaughter, Yekaterina, standing there with her hand in her mouth, *his* daughter Svetlana standing behind *her* daughter. Svetlana will describe that moment like this:

> 'Papa suddenly opened his eyes and cast a glance over everyone in the room. It was a terrible glance.... Then something incomprehensible and awesome happened. Papa suddenly lifted his left hand as though he was pointing to something above and bringing down a curse on us all. The next moment after a final effort the spirit wrenched itself free of the flesh.'

* * *

The police had found a note in Raymond Kaplan's pocket.

> Dearest Lil and David:
>
> I have done nothing at my job which I did not think was in the best interest of the country or of which I am ashamed. And the interest of my country is to fight Communism hard. I am much too upset to go into the intricate details of the decision which led to the selection of Washington and North Carolina as sites for the Baker East and West stations....
>
> This is not an easy thing to do, but I think it is the only way. You see once the dogs are set on you, everything you have done since the beginning of time is suspect. It will not be good or possible to be continuously harried and harassed for everything that I do in a job.
>
> I have never done anything that I consider wrong, but I can't take the pressure upon my shoulders anymore. This is sincere, believe me darling, even though the mess has made me too upset to write coherently. I love you and David beyond life itself. You are innocent victims of 'unfortunate circumstances.'
>
> You and darling David should not be made to bear any more than... this act will make you do, if I don't I am afraid you too, through absolutely no fault of your own, will be continuously hounded for the rest of your lives. This way you may have a chance to live in some future happiness. I cannot tell you any more.

Good-bye my darling—I wish I could think clearly enough to express my feelings as I really do—I am sorry.

My deepest love to all—I can say no more now.

Raymond.

Don't forget the insurance. I have annual leave coming which you may get paid for. I owe the Government $100 for travel advances. They owe me $18.

Some more is in the green case.

* * *

Claire Douglas still hadn't heard from Jerry Salinger in New Hampshire.

On a whim, Claire married a man who was a student at a business school. She will have the marriage annulled by the end of 1953.

Jerry Salinger had been previously married as well. Their marriage lasted about as long as Claire's would. Even William Burroughs had a similar war experience; before he met Joan, he married a European so the woman could gain citizenship.

* * *

The month of April.

William Burroughs was again searching for *yagé* in Central America, in Colombia. He had the good fortune that the citizens he encountered mistook him for a representative of the Texaco Oil Company. Burroughs enjoyed free lodging and transportation on his psychedelic quest. He subsequently heard that Texaco had surveyed the area several years before and they found no oil and pulled up stakes.

Up in the States, Burroughs's first book was published under the pseudonym William Lee (his mother's maiden name) as an 'Ace Double Book' paperback.

Burroughs didn't give a fig that he was earning less than a penny royalty on each book because he'd already accepted a thousand dollar advance. Burroughs didn't know how his book was being reviewed in the motherland. In the April 5 issue of *The New Yorker,* Eudora Welty published a book review—not of *Junkie,* of course. She reviewed J. D. Salinger's new *Nine Stories.* The grande dame of southern letters wrote, 'Mr. Salinger's work deals with innocence, and starts with innocence.... There is not a trace of sentimentality about his work.... It might be said that what Mr. Salinger has written about so far is the absence of love. Owing to that absence comes the spoliation of innocence, or else the triumph in death of innocence over the outrage and corruption that lie in wait for it.'

'William Lee's' *Junkie* possessed no form of innocence. The seething humor of the narration was so dry it is easy for a reader to miss the artistry necessary to create such a quick read. That said, 'William Lee's' *Junkie* garnished zero serious literary attention—no writer the caliber of Eudora Welty reviewed *Junkie.* In fact, it appears that *no* newspaper reviewed the paperback in 1953. Before the publisher of *Junkie* published the text, he felt that the country wasn't ready for the unrepentant narration of a drug abuser, so 'William Lee's' book was bound back-to-back/upside-down with the memoir *Narcotic Agent* by Maurice Helbrant. *Narcotic Agent*'s cover showed a blonde in a slip being handcuffed. *Narcotic Agent* was a condensed version of the memoirs of a Federal Bureau of Narcotics agent, which had been first published in 1941.

The two books worked well as a complement. The following is a combination of both authors' narrations of childhood memories:

> I went to a progressive school with the future solid citizens, the lawyers, doctors and businessmen of a large Midwest town. I was timid with the other children and afraid of physical violence. One aggressive little lesbian would pull my hair whenever she saw me. I would like to shove her face in right now, but she fell off a horse and broke her neck years ago. When I tacked a dead mouse to the classroom blackboard, I was expelled. That suited me. [I then became a] rewind boy in the projection room of the old Manhattan Theatre in Brooklyn. I was paid only a dollar a week, but my sister and I were able to see all the pictures free. The projector operator was a young fellow called Happy. He was a morphine addict. One night, the film stopped suddenly and I turned to see Happy crumpled up on the floor. His heart had stopped from an overdose of morphine. This was

the first time I had ever seen death. You can never tell what goes on in a kid's mind. The word *morphine* took on a terrible fascination in my mind. I decided that instead of becoming a scientist, I would be a detective, terror of the underworld.

In one of the nine stories in Salinger's *Nine Stories,* a shell-shocked WWII vet tells a young girl who is a stranger to him a fantastic story about fish that eat bananas and are thus called Banana Fish. Salinger himself had once been a shell-shocked WWII vet. In this story, Salinger's bananas are no more phallic symbols than the bananas the United Fruit Company harvested in the banana republic of Guatemala.

A banana was just a banana.

Salinger's shell-shocked vet also kisses the little girl's feet, a literary reference, no doubt, to *Crime and Punishment* when Raskolnikov kisses the feet of Sonia the harlot. In Salinger's story, the war vet returns to his hotel room to pull a loaded gun from his suitcase and shoot himself because he is appalled by adult heterosexuality.

He shoots himself in the right temple of his forehead.

* * *

When President Kennedy was shot for the second time in his head, a third of his skull exploded and showered wet brain pieces everywhere.

There will be controversy concerning these bullets. The first bullet could have been fired from a number of sites, including the Texas School Book Depository. There will be conflicting evidence that suggests one bullet entered at the front of Kennedy's head (hence the brief suspicion that the limo driver Greer shot Kennedy). That bullet could have come from the so-called Grassy Knoll. Kennedy was buried three days after his killing. There was no forensic evidence kept of what was left of Kennedy's skull. Not that it would have necessarily done any good. The technology in 1963 was absurdly primitive by modern CSI standards.[*]

---

[*] At least the technology portrayed on CSI television shows.

Chapter 9

Opa-Locka Airport, Florida, 1953–1954

Jackson Pollock was only forty-one years old and already over the hill by 1953. He had become famous on August 8, 1949, when *Life* magazine did a four-page spread asking, 'Is He the Greatest Living Painter in the United States?'

Originally, *Life* magazine had wanted to feature Willem de Kooning. During this time, the movie star Gary Cooper was fifty-two and was still handsome, yet Willem de Kooning was a younger forty-nine and he was even more handsome. And de Kooning's paintings were beautiful splotches of gorgeous color with even more gorgeous brushstrokes. The more abstract they were, the more they appeared to reference reality. The thing that queered it for de Kooning was when *Life* realized that the God of American Painting had to be American-born and de Kooning had been born in Rotterdam. Next in the contemporary art world lineage was Mark Rothko, but he was born in the Balkans, that sorry place where Howard Hunt remained cooling his heels.

That left Jackson Pollock. He was born in Cody, Wyoming, and Cody was named after Buffalo Bill. You couldn't get more American-born than that. In 1948, Pollock's paintings lurked at the utter brink of art moderne. Any reference to reality, let alone naturalism, in Pollock's work was nil. His paintings were pure globs and streaks and splashes of paint.

Jackson Pollock's nickname was 'Jack the Dripper.'

Life decided that Pollock was America's version of Picasso. Yet, Pablo Picasso had his Blue Period, his Rose Period, his Cubist shams. After ten years of dripping, how could Pollock develop? The hayseed public of 1953 still considered Pollock famous, but the shark jaws in Manhattan's art circle projected zero generosity toward this balding alcoholic artist. Pollock's first great supporter, the then forty-four-year-old art critic Clement Greenberg, had just told Pollock, 'You've lost your stuff. You had a good run, but now it's over.'

* * *

Frank O'Hara was a Navy veteran of the Pacific theater who worked the front desk at the Museum of Modern Art in 1953. Frank O'Hara looked younger than twenty-seven. He would always look younger than twenty-seven. Frank O'Hara still believed in Jackson Pollock. His painting depicted something O'Hara could only call 'the efflux of the soul.' For O'Hara, Pollock's paintings implied Questions, not Answers. Pollock's paintings left one with the impression that perhaps the soul was not a Thing, but a Question.

O'Hara supported Jackson Pollock's aboriginal abandonment of his multicolored dab-and-dip style. O'Hara loved Pollock's new black and white splatters. After work one day, O'Hara kept an appointment to view Pollock's newest painting at the Ninth Street Gallery.

'How big is it?' O'Hara asked over the phone. He was told it was 86¾ inches by 58⅛ inches. O'Hara whistled. 'Not bad. A very tall and very wide door.' (The joke in Paris was that if the painting is big, it must have been painted by an American.) O'Hara asked, 'Does it have a number?' (Pollock often numbered his paintings rather than give them a concrete name so the viewer didn't try to see unintentional imagery in the paintholic chaos.) O'Hara was told that this new one was titled with a name, 'The Deep.'

O'Hara saw the painting. To describe it simply: 'The Deep' was a white-gray cloud with a part in the middle revealing dark colors. There were a few splatters of yellow. Red.

O'Hara looked upon 'The Deep' and almost fainted. He would later say in exaggerated gay fluctuation, 'I nearly swoooned.'

To his mind this was American Chiaroscuro. It was not a Painting, but the Remains of an Event. This was a depiction of American Glamour encroached by a Flood of Innocence. This Ambiguous Ambiguity. This was Pollock's final Homage to those whose art he had Appropriated—Navajo sand paintings, Matisse, Soutine. It was like the End of Painting.

A Curtain being Shut.

O'Hara felt this way, yet when he was asked at parties 'What did you think of the painting?,' O'Hara would hem and haw and end up saying something disjointed: 'The cathedral, the fetish, the all-seeing eye.' He had no idea what he meant. 'I guess what I mean is this is a depiction of America as a *vast something.*' Then he'd ask, 'Who said that? Walt Whitman probably.'

'Probably. It sounds too abstract for Frost.'

'Ford? John Ford?'

'Frost, I said. Robert Frost.'

'No, I mean John Ford, the cowboy director. Jackson is a cowboy born in Cody, Wyoming. In American epics, that encrustation of myth always has a sense of inelegance. Otherwise, the artist is assumed to be European. An insincere Italian. An insincere Brit. But how can an American paint after Manifest Destiny is over? That's what Pollock's newest painting is.' O'Hara would pause and sip his drink. 'It's like that comment that Hans Hofmann made about Pollock. That Pollock was crummy because he didn't paint from nature—and Pollock thumped his chest and said, *I am nature.*'

★ ★ ★

The Balkans again. Crouchback asked Howard Hunt out of the blue, 'Tell me, old man, what's the most rank place in the United States?'

Without hesitating, Hunt said, 'The Ozarks.'

'The Lumberjack said Yuba City, California.'

Hunt shrugged. 'You say banana and I say pea-anah.'

Crouchback frowned. Hunt was speaking too American for the Brit. 'Well, the Ozarks and Yuba City are paradises compared to these Balkans.'

'What's wrong with the Balkans?'

'Look around you, old man. The Balkans are ugly and arduous. Ugly and arduous forests. Ugly and arduous mountains. Ugly and arduous buildings. Ugly and arduous women. Ugly and arduous babies. Ugly and arduous food. The people here have a word for this land—*vukojebina.*' Crouchback stopped talking. This crummy Brit was going to make Hunt ask what *vukojebina* meant. Hunt wasn't going to.

'Aren't you going to ask me what *vukojebina* means, old man?'

'No.'

The Brit gave a quick frown and tugged at his collar and then said, 'It's a word Serbs use to describe most of this country. It literally means "wolf fuck." The kind of landscape where wolves breed.'

Hunt just had to repeat that term. 'Wolf fuck,' he said.

'Right, old man. Why would anyone want to rule this godforsaken *vukojebina*, old man, why?'

'Ours is not to reason why—'

'Yes yes. *Do or die.* The American creed. Tell me, old man, is it a requirement that all CIA officers are also card-carrying Republicans?'

'What?'

'You in the CIA all appear to be conservative God-fearing Negro haters.'

'Actually most CIA officers are knee-jerk liberals.'

'Really, old man? In the CIA?'

'Yes. I'm one of the few conservative God-fearing Negro haters who works for the Company.'

'So, old man, do Americans beat their wives—I mean all Americans, not just Secret Service officers?'

'Some. Do you beat your wife?'

'No. I'm a homosexual, old man. Do you beat your wife?'

'No. Not that I recall.'

'I give you three weeks in Sarajevo and you'll start slapping her plenty. Two months and you'll use your fists.' Crouchback slapped his fist into the palm of his other hand. 'Oh, you think I'm kidding, old man? The reason you should start beating her now is because when you finally leave this bloody *vukojebina,* you'll want to burn your clothes. If you don't start beating your wife now she'll disobey you and not burn her wardrobe like you'll tell her to.'

Hunt would write that at this point he was totally confused. 'Why will I want to burn my clothes?'

'Because it is impossible to wash that piquant Yugo smell out of them, old man. Your trousers and shirts will be of no use to you anymore.'

'What is the *Yugo smell*?'

'Cabbage, old man, rank cabbage. Cucumbers soaked in vinegar. I tell you that I helped the Lumberjack douse his suitcase with kerosene and we placed a small lit candle on it and gambled how long it would take for the candle to burn down, igniting the suitcase. I said two minutes. The Lumberjack said eight. He won. Then, he explained why he won...'

The Brit stopped talking. He wanted Hunt to ask him what the Lumberjack said. Hunt didn't say anything. Crouchback looked pained. 'The Lumberjack said that the suitcase was American, but the candle was European. Europe burns slower than America. I mean that's what he said to me, old man.'

★ ★ ★

East Coast, U.S.A.

John Kennedy's younger brother and lawyer, Robert, was serving as assistant counsel to Roy Cohn. Robert Kennedy didn't hunt Communists. He went after original prey. Possessing zero fear and 110 percent ambition, Robert Kennedy went after three hundred Greek shipping families who still traded with Red China. We were at war with North Korea and Red China gave material aid to our enemies.

One of those targeted Greek shippers was Aristotle Onassis, age forty-seven. Aristotle Onassis was of abbreviated height like Roy Cohn, but the Greek was a much more robust man. Aristotle Onassis was also one of the richest men in the world. During Prohibition, Onassis's boats sailed Irish whiskey to Joe Kennedy. Now, Aristotle Onassis slaughtered underage whales in the Atlantic, a violation of international law. Aristotle Onassis was now in secret negotiations with Saudi Arabia to transport oil to Red China aboard tankers flying the Saudi flag. Kennedy would indict Onassis. American customs would be ready to seize any Onassis ships that came to port.

★ ★ ★

It was spring of '53. Jacqueline Bouvier was almost twenty-four years old. She was a Roman Catholic with black hair. She was as virgin as the day she was born. Her voice was audible, although she seldom spoke a few decibels above a whisper. She spoke like a geisha. She spoke in girlish soupçon. Jacqueline Bouvier had been dating Jack Kennedy for a good year now. Joe Kennedy had hounded his son, as well as his protégé Joe McCarthy: 'You're both near forty years old. If you don't get married, voters will assume that you're queer.'

★ ★ ★

Jack phoned Jacqueline. He didn't call her to ask her to marry him. He requested that she bring her sister Lee on a double date with him and Ngô Dinh Diem, 'the future premier of Viet-Nam.' Kennedy also said, 'This is the important part. You told me Lee can tell a *tính tù* after five minutes.'

'What's a *tính tù*?' Jacqueline asked in a coquette whisper.

'That's Vietnamese for *pansy.*'

'What make you think this Ngô Dinh Diem is that way?'

'He is fifty-one or fifty-two and has never been married. He has no illegitimate kids. He never dates. Yet, he doesn't hang around in the *tính tù* circle in Hanoi.'

'How do you know?'

'That's what the CIA tells me.'

'Why is it important to know?'

'I'm going to climb out on a limb for this Oriental. I need to know what could embarrass me.'

That Friday, Jacqueline and her younger sister, Lee, met Jack, who was escorting a slight, but very beautiful Asian man in the lobby of Les Trois Mousquetaires at 820 Connecticut Avenue. This was Ngô Dinh Diem. He looked twenty years younger than fifty. Ngô Dinh Diem wore a very light gray, almost white, shirt made of raw silk. A gray cashmere jacket. Jacqueline didn't notice his gray trousers, his coat and shirt were both so exquisite. Jacqueline introduced herself in French. Ngô Dinh Diem answered her back in French. Flawless French. French-French. Jacqueline listened to him talk one, two, three sentences, and decided this was the most luminous French she'd ever heard spoken by a man, any man, Frenchman or not. Ngô Dinh Diem had a trace of an accent, yet Jacqueline's ears didn't read it as Asian. It was almost the way they spoke in Marseille with the difference that Ngô Dinh Diem softened all the dental consonants. There were times when his speech almost felt like singing. The maître d' recognized Jack. 'Good evening, Senator Kennedy.' They were led past a wall-length mirror. Of course, Jacqueline and Lee glanced at themselves. Jacqueline was surprised to see Ngô Dinh Diem inspect his image as well.

Remember, this is 1953. You and I are familiar with walking into restaurants, even classy restaurants, and hearing music over a sophisticated sound system. That technology did not exist sixty years ago. A radio may serenade diners at the local greasy spoon. Nightclubs may have jukeboxes and live music. Yet, high-class restaurants were silent save for the murmur of patrons and the pizzicato of silverware clicking on plates.

Here inside Les Trois Mousquetaires there was tinny accordion music playing. With clarinet and banjo. Kennedy looked around for the musicians.

'Muzak,' the maître d' said.

'Muzak?' Kennedy repeated.

'Elevator music.'

Kennedy nodded. 'Ah. The newest fad. Do you know that President Eisenhower even has elevator music piped into the West Wing?'

'The Muzak company is creating music for restaurants now. We're the first in Washington. How does it sound, Senator Kennedy?'

'Sounds very . . . modern.'

The maître d' stopped and snapped his fingers and a young, compact dark-skinned man walked up. Their *navigateur.* He appeared more Foreign Legion than Les Trois Mousquetaires. They followed him. The restaurant had a high ceiling and brighter lighting than was normal in an establishment of its caliber. Except at the bar. To the right of the bar was an alcove of tables, each one hidden behind a large marble urn stuffed with floral arrangements. Those were the tables where senators and congressmen took their mistresses. Not on a Friday or Saturday night of course. *Post* columnist Drew Pearson was sitting at the bar nursing a Singapore Sling.

The Kennedy party approached their table—white linen tablecloth, plates, Brancusi salt and pepper shakers, linen napkins folded into discrete teepees. Lee walked ahead of Ngô Dinh Diem and gave him a glance over her shoulder. She allowed him to seat her, swooping in a stoop into her seat to give the Asian time to gaze upon the hidden depths of her décolleté. Once seated, the menu *porteuse* arrived. The menus he handed them were ridiculously wide and tall. Jacqueline fished out a cigarette. The *sèche garçon* materialized with his lighter, '*Ah, mademoiselle!*'

She held her hand up and said, '*Pardon.*'

The maître d' rushed up pinching a fresh package of Boyard. Jacqueline returned her L&M cigarette to its box and handed the maître d' Black Jack's Zippo lighter.* Then she placed the maître d's Boyard between her lips. He flicked her Zippo at the end of the cigarette.

It was lit.

Lee spoke to Ngô Dinh Diem in English. If her sister Jacqueline spoke in a Little Red Riding Hood voice, Lee was Goldilocks. Lee explained to Ngô Dinh Diem that Mademoiselle Bouvier believed it was bad luck to light her cigarettes with anything other than her father's Zippo.

'*Père,*' said Ngô Dinh Diem with a nod and a smile. 'It was a gift from your father.'

Jacqueline had her smoking arm elbow down on the table. She answered in puckish English. 'No. I stole it.'

'She was ten when she swiped it,' Lee added, also in English.

The four made rather stilted small talk in English since Lee's French was only passable, and Jack's atrocious. Lee said what she would order first, '*soufflé de saumon.*'

'Is *saumon* salmon?' Jack Kennedy asked.

'*Oui.*'

Jacqueline's delicate voice said, 'I'm going to order *coquilles St. Jacques à la provençale.*'

'Excuse me,' Diem said softly in English, almost in a whisper. 'In Viet-Nam this is an unlucky month for shellfish. Spring is lucky for scallops and mussels.'

'What would you recommend?' Jacqueline asked in French.

'But I have never eaten here before,' he answered in French with a small helpless wave of his hands.

'What catches your fancy?' she asked, again in French.

'Swordfish with wine, tomatoes, and herbs,' he answered (*'thon à la provençale'*).

Jack Kennedy was frowning at his menu. 'I tell you, I'm going to have a fat lobster.'

The four then all made monkey talk about the main course. Then

---

* 'Black Jack' is the nickname of Jacqueline's father, John Vernou Bouvier III.

the appetizers. Jack and Lee wanted vichyssoise. Jackie felt impish and asked for *soupe à l'oignon*.

'What's that, Jackie?' Jack Kennedy asked.

'Onion soup.'

'Good God. Feeling romantic, I see.'

'Jacks, let's get some pâté,' Lee said to Jacqueline.

'*Pâté de veau et porc avec gibier?*'

'With duck?' Lee said.

'Yes,' Jacqueline said in English. 'How about with pheasant and partridge too?'

'Don't you think that's too gamy?' Lee asked in English.

'Only if we add hare.'

Jack Kennedy asked, 'Is that a joke like, *Waiter, there is a hair in my soup*?'

'Hare as in *bunny*, Jack,' Jacqueline answered.

Ngô Dinh Diem was having difficulty with the word *Jack*. He would never ask the Occidentals for clarification, but he spoke about it afterward with his brother Nhu on a flight back to Saigon: 'Jack Kennedy was *Jack Kennedy* and was also *John Kennedy*. *Jacqueline* is a variation on *Jack*, and the future Kennedy wife was also called *Jackie*. Yet the sister called her sister Jacqueline *Jack* just as all three called Kennedy *Jack*. It wasn't until the end of the dinner that I perceived an S sound at the end of Kennedy's future wife's name. Her sister was calling her *Jacks*.'

Nhu shook his head gravely. 'In Viet Nam, names are not so confusing.'

At Les Trois Mousquetaires, the waiter appeared at the table. He announced that his name was Frisco.

'As in San Francisco?' Lee asked.

'*Oui*.'

Like all the waiters at Les Trois Mousquetaires, he wore a black tuxedo and had black hair and a *Mona Lisa* moustache. If this was Hollywood, one would say the waiters all came from central casting.

Jack said, 'I'd like hom-ard lah Amereeca.'

'The gentleman means *homard a l'Américaine*,' Jacqueline said. Then she touched Ngô Dinh Diem on the cuff and said, 'Your French is so beautiful. Will you order for all of us?'

'Of course,' Ngô Dinh Diem said in English. Diem placed their order.

The texture of his French transformed. He spoke slowly at first. He spoke precisely. The waiter gave an almost imperceptible scowl of impatience. Diem first ordered for Jack. The waiter scribbled jagged lines on his pad. Diem read the menu a bit and without looking up said what Jacqueline wanted in four sentences. At the end of each one, Diem raised the tenor of his voice, almost as if each sentence was a question. Jacqueline realized this was extremely subtle intimidation. Diem was implying that the waiter couldn't actually be counted on to fulfill the order. Yet Diem spoke lightly as if the order was of no consequence. Then he began to tell the waiter what Lee required. With each sentence, he drew out the first few syllables of the first word, so the waiter was unable to guess what Diem was ordering and thus had to pay close attention to what was said. As Diem progressed to the hors d'oeuvres, the waiter interrupted and asked Diem in French, 'What does the *Oriental* want for his main course?'

'*Ultérieurement,*' Diem whispered like a snake.

The waiter stood stone-faced and wrote. Then Diem told him what he wanted. He spoke in a form of impenetrable contempt, subtle contempt, a contempt that was subliminal. This is what *he* wanted to eat. No. It was this is what he *expected* to eat. Although the waiter was only a waiter, not a cook, Diem's voice threatened that the waiter would be held responsible for the perfection of the dish.

Next, the sommelier arrived at the table. He too was from central casting. The four diners all fussed about the wine, finally choosing a Pouilly-Fumé and a Pouilly-Fuissé and for later, a Côtes du Rhône. Then they people-watched. Richard Nixon was there. He ate like a dockhand with a knife in his left hand and the fork in his right. Lee started asking *National Geographic*–style questions about Viet-Nam. Diem answered as if Lee was the most intelligent woman on the planet. Later, a young man who looked vaguely like Liberace walked behind Ngô Dinh Diem, and stared at Lee and shook his head mouthing a big 'No.'

The dinner was eaten French style. Both Diem and Jacqueline set the pace. Appetizers and the main course are eaten quickly with little talking. (Wine and coffee and dessert can last all night if you wish.) The table was filled with different kinds of tarts and crêpes. Something at the bar caught

Diem's eye. Jacqueline eyed that direction. A very tall fat man was no longer anchoring the end of the bar. His absence revealed a faded brown photograph hanging on the wall.

'Do you know photography?' Diem turned to Jacqueline and asked in French.

'I know paintings,' she replied.

'Will you come with me?'

'Of course.'

Diem nodded at Jack Kennedy and Lee and escorted Jacqueline Bouvier to the photograph at the bar.

It was a photograph of a woman in a white Victorian dress leaping in the air above a great stone stairway leading down to a garden. Beside it was another photograph of a man in a tux with a Duchampian *Mona Lisa* moustache driving a go-cart from the British side, his passenger a woman with a determined jaw wearing a white Victorian dress just like the jumping woman's.

'Lartigue,' Diem said. 'Jacques Henri Lartigue.'

'The driver?' Jacqueline whispered.

Diem appeared as if he was repressing a smile. 'The photographer.'

'Oh, the photographer. Yes. I've heard of him.' She was lying.

'Photography was invented in Paris. Lartigue was the first and greatest photographer.'

'Do you take photographs?' Jacqueline asked without thinking. If she had thought about the question, she wouldn't have asked it because the last thing she could imagine this Vietnamese mandarin doing was being a shutterbug.

To her surprise and delight, he nodded. 'Since I was a small boy.'

'What kind of photographs do you take?'

'I take photographs of still things. Things that are not moving. Very still things.'

'Oh.'

'Lartigue took photographs of things that were moving. Racing. He loved automobiles. These long racing cars that are just boxes with engines in them. He took photographs of the first airplanes. He took photographs of dogs being thrown in the air. Women running in their long black dresses. The stillest photograph he took was of a girl in a straw hat being helped out of the fuselage of a racing car with a huge steering wheel.'

⋆ ⋆ ⋆

Les Trois Mousquetaires. The meal is over. The bill is presented in a leather sheath.

Jack Kennedy didn't ignore it. He was oblivious to it.

Jacks and Lee knew the drill. They rose to go to the powder room. Ngô Dinh Diem sat and assumed as the guest it was he who was supposed to pay for the meal.

⋆ ⋆ ⋆

Jacks and Jack and Lee and Diem standing on the sidewalk.

'Pretty good,' Jack says.

'Very good,' says Diem.

Lee remarks, 'It reminds me of—what was that restaurant we love to go to in Paris, Jacks?'

'Le Grand Véfour,' Jacqueline says.

Diem appears a little taken aback. Jacqueline notices. 'You have an opinion on Le Grand Véfour, Diem?'

The Asian shakes his head. 'It's been so long since I ate there.'

'Well, I'm going to Paris next week,' Jacqueline says. 'I'm going to go to Le Grand Véfour and order *thon à la provençale.*'

⋆ ⋆ ⋆

The next morning. Jacqueline was eating a breakfast of eggs, grits, toast, potatoes, bacon. She was not eating for two. Jacqueline was the first one to say that she ate like a horse. The woman never gained weight. Some slanderers whispered that she possessed a 'helper' like the opera singer Maria Callas—a tapeworm.

That was just gossip.

The bell rang at the apartment she was subletting from her father. She went to the door. It was Ngô Dinh Diem. He was dressed immaculately.

He was almost embossed. It seemed to be his usual state. He held a flat package wrapped in butcher paper that was roughly the size of the Lartigue photographs. Her first thought was that he had bought the photograph from Les Trois Mousquetaires and was giving it to her as a gift.

'I want to ask you a favor,' he said softly as she welcomed him in.

'Come again?'

'I want to ask you a favor.' As he said that for the second time Jacqueline saw there was an address written on the other side of the package. Diem took roughly three paragraphs of talk to ask her to hand-deliver the package to the address written on it.

It was an address in Paris—a convent in Noisy-le-Grand. The package was for one Soeur Angelique. Jacqueline didn't want to pry. Diem knew that. 'I don't want this package to go through postal services,' he said.

'I understand. They'll damage it,' Jacqueline whispered.

He made no comment. Instead, Diem asked if she was staying with family or friends or at a hotel.

'I'm staying at a nunnery,' Jacqueline said straight-faced.

Diem's face didn't move, but his eyes widened.

'I'm just kidding. I'm staying at the Grand Hotel.' Then Jacqueline said, 'I'm not going to get into trouble for this? You didn't steal it, right?'

'Steal what?'

'The Lartigue.'

He understood immediately. 'No no no. This is a photograph for Soeur Angelique. I took it myself. I have known Soeur Angelique for most of my life. I knew her before she took the veil.'

Diem left. Jacqueline put the package on the floor of the coat closet. She wouldn't tell Jack about it. *I have a secret.* She went back to the closet and took the package out. She used her fingers to tap it carefully. One side was wood and the other glass. It was a framed photograph surely.

He didn't want to send it through official channels?

It must be pornographic.

She opened the package.

Lee telephoned her sister. 'You've had Diem's package for twenty-four hours.'

'I've had Diem's package for twenty-four hours.'

'You've opened it.'

'I have not.'

'Don't give me that, Jacks. I know when you're lying before you even speak.'

'I didn't open the package. I gave Diem my word.'

'You never gave him your word. You said yourself that he never said, *Do not open the package.*'

'Okay. I opened it. It's one of the Lartigue photographs.'

'No, it isn't.'

'What? Oh, course it is.'

'You told me that he assured you it was not a Lartigue photograph.'

'I'm just saying that. I didn't open the package. But I'll open it now.'

On the phone: the sound of ripping paper.

'Okay. I've opened it.'

'And—?'

'It's a photograph. Diem must have taken it himself. It's a photograph of sticks of bamboo.'

'No!'

'Yes. Sticks of bamboo. What's so surprising about that?'

'I'm coming over.'

'What?'

'I'm going to see these sticks of bamboo for myself.'

'Jack is coming over.'

'So what?'

'He's taking me out.'

'No, he isn't.'

'Yes. He is.'

'No. You're lying.'

'I'm not lying.'

'Jacks, I saw Jack today. He was on the way to the airport. He's going to meet his father at their house in Florida.'

'Oh.'

'I'm coming over.'

'I won't be here.'

'Yes, you will.'

* * *

Howard Hunt was called back to Washington from the Balkans to learn of Eisenhower and Nixon's new diplomatic desire: to overthrow the government of Guatemala.

'Doesn't it bother those boys that Colonel Jacobo Árbenz Guzmán is the fairly elected president of Guatemala?' Dorothy asked her husband over the phone.

'United Fruit Company wants the colonel departed,' Hunt said. The United Fruit Company was, among other entities, the future Chiquita Banana. Most of the population of Guatemala were illiterate peasants bound by a medieval agrarian caste system put in place since 1899 by United Fruit. 'Árbenz instituted land reforms that cut into United Fruit's profits. Árbenz fits the profile to turn Red. Communists had made inroads into the Guatemala government.'

'You're right. I read that three seats in Guatemala's fifty-eight-seat congress are Red.'

'Four seats are Red,' Hunt corrected.

'Well, it sounds necessary, but how does United Fruit hold sway over Eisenhower?'

'Dulles Number One is a United Fruit trustee. Dulles Number Two is a United Fruit lawyer. Ann Whitman's husband is United Fruit's top public relations officer.'

(Allen Dulles was the pipe-smoking head of the CIA. His brother John Foster Dulles was secretary of state. Ann Whitman was Eisenhower's Girl Friday.)

'Honey, do you think you'll change your mind?'

'Change my mind about what?'

'Being just another United Fruit lapdog.'

'Honey, my hatred of Communism is bigger than my pride.'

Howard Hunt said those words and he meant them.

* * *

Howard Hunt began strategizing the secret invasion of Guatemala from an airfield situated outside of Miami. Hunt managed to fly up to frozen D.C. every other weekend or so to see his daughters and Dot, who was having what were discreetly called 'female problems' with her third pregnancy.

Hunt thrived living the Pretend Bachelor life down in Florida. Field headquarters was a two-story barracks at the Opa-Locka Airport outside of Miami. Opa-Locka was where Amelia Earhart took off on her attempt to circumnavigate the globe sixteen years earlier. When Hunt had a few drinks, he would coax the listeners forward and then reveal in a whisper that the 'circumnavigation nonsense was just cover. Amelia was scouting Jap islands for the State Department. A Jap Zero shot her down.'

Hunt was an expert at Black Propaganda, lies that got civilians killed. Hunt invented propaganda by graffiti. He used shortwave radio to direct right-wing Guatemalan students to scrawl the numeral 32 on buildings and billboards in the dead of night. The number 32 was a reference to Article 32 of the Guatemalan constitution banning international political parties such as Communism.

Propaganda by Graffiti was Postliteracy before its time.

Hunt's students also attached stickers to the houses of anyone remotely leftist that read: 'A Communist lives here.' Hunt had some CIA stunt pilots bomb Guatemalan towns with empty Coke bottles, objects that made an unnerving whistle as they rained down from the clouds.

In CIA lingo, Hunt's top-secret operation was named Operation Success.

★ ★ ★

The date: September 11, 1953.

A studio on Cahuenga Boulevard in Hollywood.

Cameras were about to film the first episode for the third season of *I Love Lucy.* The show hadn't yet started and Desi Arnaz walked out. He appeared very casual in a way that showed that he was in fact nervous as hell. 'Now before we start the show, some of you in the audience may have heard rumors that the House Un-American Activities Committee has questioned Lucy about her registration twenty years earlier in the Communist Party.' He paused to let that sink in. 'Lucy told them that she hadn't known what she was doing.' He paused and almost rolled his eyes signifying *You know how dizzy Lucy is*... 'Lucy only joined to make her elderly grandfather happy. Lucy never went to meetings or whatever it is that Communists do. After her dear grandfather died, Lucy forgot all about it.' He took a step toward the audience. 'I'm here to tell you that the only thing red about Lucy is her hair!'

★ ★ ★

TV is the thing this year, oh yes
TV is the thing this year
Radio was great but now it's out of date
TV is the thing this year

★ ★ ★

Seven days before, Lucy, age forty-two, had been subpoenaed to appear before the House Un-American Activities Committee for secret 'closed door' testimony in room 512 at 7046 Hollywood Boulevard. It was a nondescript eight-story office building. Desi had given her a pill to take.

'What is it?'

'Something that will calm you down.'

She took it.

She walked into room 512. She was feeling good about her body. She'd lost the weight she gained when she was pregnant. There were three men in this room, but they only glanced at her.

A single chair was behind a table facing the three men. Their table was about ten feet away. There would be nothing intimate about the forthcoming interrogation. Lucy noticed a gray-haired *American Gothic* woman sitting at a stenography contraption.

A very large man light on his feet waltzed up and said, 'I'm William A. Wheeler.' He began the session by asking her to state her full name.

'Lucille Desiree Ball Arnaz.'

Laughter. Lucy glanced around. *Who was laughing at her?*

'Where were you born?'

'Jamestown, New York.' *Laughter.* 'By the Pennsylvania border—' *Laughter.* '... near Lake Erie.' *Laughter.*

'You are presently a resident of Los Angeles County?'

He asked that. Lucy bird-eyed the room again. They had a laugh track piped in here?

'Yes.' *Laughter.*

'And your profession?'

'Actress—' *Laughter.* 'Television actress now.'

Lucy looked around the room in controlled panic. Canned laughter here? *I Love Lucy* was filmed before a live audience, yet the soundmen still peppered the audience responses with prominent chuckles and guffaws. It was intelligently done. Not like the *Abbott and Costello Show,* where every little thing generated artificial laughter: Open a door. *Laughs.* Turn on a light. *Belly laughs.* Light a cigarette. *Screams of hilarity!*

Lucy decided the laughter was only in her head. The sounds were the result of the pill Desi gave her.

'I asked, *How long have you been engaged as an actress?*'

'Since 1933, I guess; 1932 or 1933.' *Silence.*

'What is your educational background?'

'Just school, high school.' *Light laughter.*

'You have been employed in motion-picture work since you left school?'

'No; I was in New York working.' *Silence.*

'Excuse me, Mrs. Ball, uh, Mrs. Arnaz,' Wheeler said. 'Didn't your mother send you to New York because you were romantically seeing Johnny DeVito, the son of the gangster Sobo DeVito?'

'She wanted to send me to a convent, sir,' Lucy said.

Sounds of guffawing, har-de-har har.

'Grandpa Hunt'—*applause*—'convinced my mother I'd be serving God better by doing something I was good at.' *Sounds of hilarity.*

'But the John Murray Anderson School for the Dramatic Arts threw you out, didn't they? Didn't they say you were no good?'

'Yes, they did, sir.' *Sniggers.* 'Grandpa Hunt insisted I repack my suitcase and go back to New York City and prove them wrong.' *Peals of mirth.*

'But you returned home shortly after, didn't you?'

'Yes, sir. Because I had rheumatoid arthritis.' *The audience going, 'Awwww . . .'* 'It lasted for two years. With Grandpa Hunt's help, I headed straight back to New York City. I was the Chesterfield Cigarette girl for a while.' *Applause.* 'And then got work on Broadway.' *Applause.*

'Didn't you get fired by Florenz Ziegfeld as well as the Shubert brothers?' *Gasps!*

'Yes.' Her voice broke. *A chuckle.*

'Did they fire you because you were a Communist?'

'No. Of course not.' *Two chuckles.*

'Why were you fired?'

'Because I was no good.' *Roars of mirth!*

'So, you moved to Hollywood?'

'I moved to Hollywood to act in movies.' *A giggle.*

'How long have you been a resident here?'

'Since 1933.' *Nothing.*

'Did you ever reside at 1344 North Ogden Drive?'

'Yes. We rented it.' *Still nothing.*

'When did you first register to vote?'

'I guess the first time I ever did was in 1936.'

'I would like to hand you a photostatic copy of a voter's registration and ask you if that is your signature.'

One of his younger men walked the document over to Lucy. She studied it.

'That looks like my handwriting.'

'You will note that the party that you intended to affiliate with at that time was the Communist Party. Would you go into detail and explain the background, the reason you registered to vote as a person who intended to affiliate with the Communist Party?'

> Inside Lucy's head: 'God. I've got to hold it together. I've got to watch my tongue. I am a forty-two-year-old-woman. I have the greatest TV show in the country. It could all get taken away. I will never get a second chance.'

'It was our grandfather, Fred Hunt,' Lucy said with resignation. 'We just did it to please him. My father died when I was tiny, before my brother was born. Grandpa Hunt is the only father we *ever* knew. I never intended to actually vote [Communist]. My grandfather was a socialist as far back as Eugene V. Debs. My grandfather was in sympathy with the workingman. He took the *Daily Worker.*' *The sound of gentle booing comes from outside the room.*

'He considered the Communist Party a workingman's party?'

'I never heard my grandfather use the word *Communist.* He always talked about the *workingman.*'

> Inside Lucy's head: 'Christ! We were never able to keep a maid even

> though we paid the highest prices in the neighborhood. Grandpa would walk out into the kitchen and ask the maid, *How much are you getting?* They would answer, *Oh, $20 or $25 a week,* or whatever they were being paid. And Grandpa would say, *That is not a working wage. What are you doing here?* They would quit.'

Lucy wiped her forehead with a handkerchief. 'He was just a fanatic on bettering the world. It was vital to him that the world must be right twenty-four hours a day for the workingman. I have said many times, *Thank goodness, he is interested in the* Daily Worker *instead of getting drunk with the men on the corner or being interested in women.*'

Sudden sounds of women shrieking with laughter.

Lucy continued: 'Sometimes it got a little ridiculous because my position in the so-called capitalist world was pretty good'—*a few yuks*—'and it was a little hard to reconcile the two.' *A snicker.* 'We didn't argue [politics] with him because he had had a couple of strokes'—*sounds of audience sympathy*—'if he got overly excited, why, he would have another one.'

> Lucy's position in the 'so-called capitalist world': Desilu filmed *I Love Lucy* on movie film instead of broadcasting live. CBS thought these kids were fools to do that. Desilu owned the rights to each show after the initial broadcast, but who would ever want to see an episode of a television show once you already saw it? Television shows were ephemeral, like leaves fluttering down from trees in late September.

'Do you know whether or not any meetings of the Communist Party were ever held in your home at 1344 North Ogden Drive?'

'No, I know nothing of that.' *Silence.*

'I would like to read a portion of an affidavit submitted by Rena M. Vale. I would like to read a portion of page one hundred twenty-seven—' Wheeler reads a document where Rena M. Vale claims she attended a Communist Party new member class held in Lucy's apartment.

'Do you have any knowledge of any meetings held in your home, Miss Ball?'

'None whatsoever.'

'Are you acquainted with Rena Vale?'

'I never heard the name before in my life.' *Silence.*

'Do you know whether or not your grandfather, Fred Hunt, held meetings at the home?'

'Not to our knowledge ever, and he was always with someone. He had had two strokes and we had a nurse who lived there at the time.' *Silence.*

'Are you familiar with the words or the phrase *criminal syndicalism?*'

'No, but it is pretty. What does it mean?' *Silence.*

'Criminal syndicalism?'

'What does it mean?' *Silence.*

'According to the voter's registration for the year 1936, the reverse part of it, you signed petition one-six-four-F. This particular petition was for the repeal of the Criminal Syndicalism Act in California.'

'What does it mean?' *Silence.*

Inside Lucy: 'Syndication. Syndication. Desi and I own the syndication rights to *I Love Lucy*. There are so many hours of television to fill. There will always be so many hours to fill. Each year there are more and more stations in every city, in every town. Everyone needs a TV show to watch. Every new TV show is a risk. *I Love Lucy* is not a risk. People will rewatch episodes that they've already seen. *I Love Lucy* has a life bigger than a half hour at nine o'clock every Monday night.'*

'The Communists were taken to court and tried for criminal syndicalism, and you signed this petition to take the Criminal Syndicalism Act off the statutes of the State of California.'

'May I see the signature?'

'Unfortunately, they have been destroyed, those particular petitions.' He lowered his head and read some papers. Then he raised his chin. 'Do you have anything in addition you would like to add for the record?'

Inside Lucy: 'Yes! I am a woman who is forty-two years old and I will not let anyone take *I Love Lucy* from me!'

---

* Lucy invented reruns. Each episode of her show would continue to make her millions for the rest of her life.

'Yes, I would, Your Honor. I want to assure you that I have never done anything for Communists. Nothing in the world could ever change my mind.' She raised her handkerchief as if she was going to dry her eyes, but they were not wet. 'I was always opposed to how my grandfather felt about the way this country should be run.'

Inside Lucy: 'Communism is for kids. Not women who are forty-two.'

'...Things were just fine the way they were. It sounds a little weak and silly and corny now, but at the time, it was very important [to make Grandpa Hunt happy] because we knew we weren't going to have him with us very long. In those days [being Communist] was not a big, terrible thing to do. It was almost as terrible to be a Republican in those days...'

Inside Lucy: 'Republicans. Communists. They're all the same. Everybody wants what they don't have. When you're a woman who is forty-two all you have right now is all you will ever have.'

'...I have never been political-minded in my life. I certainly will do anything in the world to prove that I made a bad mistake by trying to appease an old man by pretending to be interested in the Communist Party...'

Inside Lucy: 'I would believe in hell if it was a hell just for Communists and Republicans. Let them all lie atop of each other in snot and slime and spend eternity cleaning that stuff off their money, their dollars or rubles.'

'...I voted for Richard Nixon for the Senate in 'forty-eight. I voted for Nixon and Eisenhower last election.' *Out of nowhere, a sudden burst of laughter that transforms into a cachinnatory explosion of hilarity.*

'I have no further questions. Thank you for your cooperation.'

'Can we go off the record?' Lucy asked. *Sniggers.*

The woman at the machine looked at the fat man. The fat man nodded.

'Am I cleared?' Lucy asked. *Tee-hee-hee.*

'Cleared? You were never charged. Rest assured that this testimony will remain sealed.'

'Thank you very much, Mr. Wheeler.'

Animal applause!
Animal applause!
Animal applause!

★ ★ ★

Hollywood. That Sunday, Lucille Ball was listening to Walter Winchell's Sunday evening broadcast. 'Take note of this. A top television comedienne has been confronted with her membership in the Communist Party.' Lucy wondered who he was talking about. Could it be Imogene Coca? Then the next morning, two guys in trench coats and fedoras were prowling around among the orange trees outside Lucy's house. She had scheduled a dinner party that night. Six couples were coming. Each called that morning canceling with sorry excuses.

★ ★ ★

If you don't get married, people will assume that you're a queer. In the middle of September, John Kennedy married the former Jacqueline Bouvier in Newport, Rhode Island. The plan was that Jacqueline's father (a semi-notorious philanderer), Black Jack Bouvier (now divorced from Jacqueline's mother), would walk her down the aisle. The morning of the wedding, Black Jack (or Black Orchid as he was sometimes called) stank of whiskey and couldn't walk so Jacqueline's stepfather, an Auchincloss, did the honors.

★ ★ ★

'TV is the thing this year . . .'

In the Desilu studio in Hollywood.

After Desi proclaimed, 'The only thing red about Lucy is her hair!' the studio audience went crazy with applause. The next day after the show, Lucy held a press conference wearing pink toreador slacks with a matching pink hair ribbon. She had a cigarette in one hand and a full highball glass like the one Joan Vollmer had balanced on her head when she was playing William Tell Mexican style with her husband.

(William Burroughs was describing the shooting of his wife this way: 'I felt like Joan's brain drew the bullet toward it.' Burroughs still had no idea what devil made him say, 'It's about time for our William Tell act. Put a glass on your head, Joan.')

Desi was there at Lucy's press conference. He told the reporters that he was 'kicked out of Cuba by the Communists when the revolution hit there.'

That was a white lie.

In 1933 Cuba, Fulgencio Batista, a sergeant in the army, led a military coup that overturned the government. Batista put Desi's father in jail for one year, and then exiled the family from Sugar Island. Batista was still in power. Sometimes behind the scenes, sometimes in the dictator's seat. Sometimes he had the support of Cuba's Communist Party. Other times not.

Anyway, on Sunday, September 13, Walter Winchell said on his radio broadcast that the HUAC and J. Edgar Hoover cleared Lucy one hundred percent. 'Mr. Lincoln is drying his eyes for making her go through this.'

We can assume Winchell meant President Lincoln.

⋆ ⋆ ⋆

Picture us standing at the Kennedy newlyweds' bedroom door. We won't open it. Merely listen. We hear nothing in particular. Keep in mind that the British poet Philip Larkin will one day say that 'Sexual intercourse began in 1963—between the end of the *Chatterley* ban and the Beatles' first LP.' Fifty-nine-year-old Alfred Kinsey's *Sexual Behavior in the Human Female* had finally been published in the beginning of the summer. This is the companion volume to *Sexual Behavior in the Human Male,* published in 1948. Both volumes purport to whisk away the veil of innocence covering American sexuality. Kinsey's commonplace statistics proclaimed 60 percent of men and 30 percent of women engaged in sex before marriage. Senator Jack Kennedy (age thirty-six) is an accredited member of his gender's 60 percent. It is very likely that his wife is a member of her gender's 70 percent virgins. In 'TV Is the Thing This Year,' Dinah Washington sings about the joy that Jacqueline Kennedy could experience with Jack.

Now he turned my dial to channel one
I knew that this was gonna be fun
He turned my dial to channel two
That station thrilled me through and through

Except, not.

Jack's girlfriends would go on record as describing the senator as a 'fornicating whirlwind.' His ego was huge, but pleasing a woman was never his concern. Jack would be called a 'jack rabbit.'

Jack never saw himself as suffering from 'premature ejaculation.'

He just saw no reason to exert himself.

* * *

One of the most surprising revelations in *Sexual Behavior in the Human Female* was the percentage of reputable American heterosexual couples who engaged in acts previously known only to traveling salesmen and contortionists, acts with pseudoscientific terms:

Nocturnal bidding
Polyfidelitistic
Cunniformlingucss
Nymphoanapestic
Ophelia emissions

* * *

Earlier, after the wedding ceremony and before the newlyweds were going to leave for their honeymoon, Jacqueline's new sister-in-law, Ethel, whispered in her ear: 'Remember. You don't get fireworks with marriage. Just children!'

* * *

On September 29, Senator McCarthy married Jeannie Kerr at St. Matthew's Cathedral in Washington. Roy Cohn was one of the ushers. Jean slipped him a quarter encased in plastic.

* * *

The following letter to the editor concerning the suicide of Raymond

Kaplan was printed in the *Washington Post* two days before Thanksgiving on November 24, 1953.

Voice at Seattle

On November 18, the Navy opened its great new world-spanning radio transmitter near Seattle, Wash.

Only eight months ago, Senator Joseph McCarthy and his aides charged Voice of America personnel with aiding the Communist cause and wasting millions of dollars by choosing a site near Seattle for the great proposed VOA transmitter, Baker West. Choosing to ignore the fact that a majority of the best radio engineers in America, civilian and military, consider the Pacific Northwest an excellent location for a globe girdling radio transmitter, the senator gave the American public the impression that there would be an almost total loss of money to the taxpayer, and Soviet Russia would be aided if a Voice of America transmitter was built near Seattle.

The late Raymond Kaplan, a capable young Voice of America engineer and Air Force reserve officer, was so appalled at the distortion of truth that he saw no hope for men in his position. He committed suicide, leaving a note in which he said, 'once the dogs are set on you' there is no escape.

The opening of the Navy transmitter is a sadly late vindication of the judgment of Raymond Kaplan and his associates.

SPECTATOR
Washington

In fact, it had taken a quarter of a billion dollars in *modern* funds to build what was the most powerful transmitter in the world—ten massive antenna cables, all more than a mile long, spanning the Jim Creek valley, a wilderness prowled by cougar and bear. The whole works was nicknamed 'Big Jim.' The Navy could now communicate instantaneously with all its ships anywhere on Earth. Big Jim used as much electricity as a city of sixty thousand. The forty-odd technicians up in the foothills had to park their cars in special grounded parking stations or else, after they stepped out of their automobiles, they would conflagrate from the inside out, their bones burning first.

The electricity was that powerful.

* * *

A month before Jacqueline Bouvier became Jacqueline Kennedy, she flew to Paris. On the cab ride to her hotel, the black Peugeot ahead of them rolled up to a curb as a figure in a duster jumped out gripping an old-fashioned tommy gun. He started blasting away at the windows of a café and then spun back to the Peugeot. Her driver began babbling that the shooting was part of the Café Wars. A civil war was happening in the North African French colony of Algeria and two rival factions were killing each other in the Algerian expatriate community by assassinating each other in cafés. Jacqueline was later disappointed that she thought in clichés when she realized that her first mental utterance was 'That was just like a movie.'

* * *

Christmastime, Manhattan, 1953.

William Burroughs was staying with Allen Ginsberg at his apartment off Tompkins Square Park. Ginsberg was trying to live the straight life. He had 'girlfriends' who were actually girls, not boys in drag.

As for Dorothy Hunt, she made her husband vow that if their child was a boy he would be named Howard Jr. and his middle name would be Saint John. The husband agreed.

In New York, Ginsberg and Burroughs fucked now and then. Burroughs would take the subordinate position. His dry voice would go squeaky. He would say over and over, 'This is so good. You are so beautiful. This is so good.'

Now that Dot was pregnant she refused to fornicate with her husband. This had been the story with Lisa and Kevan. She would spread her hands over her belly in a gesture saying, 'Do I really have to explain myself?' Hunt asked Joe Darwin to send him a copy of Kinsey, both volumes.

As for William Burroughs—as a sexual creature, there is something tender yet repulsive about knowing how he transformed his sardonic nature during sex.

In Mexico, the Kinsey volume arrived at Howard Hunt's office. He opened it and discovered that 68 percent of wives had sex during pregnancy. He didn't know how to handle this. He and Dorothy didn't talk about sex. No couples did. (He was sure of that.) Then one night Hunt got drunk and told her about what he had read in Kinsey. He stood there naked on the bedroom floor pointing his erection at her. Dot's eyes suddenly teared up. She looked down into the bed. Then raised her head and gave this stark holler: 'If we fuck, Howard, the baby could be born with polio.'

* * *

The year *Sexual Behavior in the Human Male* had been published (1948), William Burroughs and Joan were living in South Texas where they practiced heterosexual sex as well as farming cotton and marijuana. One Texas day, Bill and Joan were driving through the town of Beeville with the kids. Bill pulled to the roadside. He and Joan would often do outrageous things like the thing they were going to do. It was beyond lust. It was beyond anything that appeared in Kinsey.

Joan got out of the car and hiked up her skirt.

Burroughs got out too and slid off his trousers and folded them.

The pair then got in the dirt beside the road and fornicated with abandon. Burroughs took the bottom as all gentlemen do in such circumstances.

Julie and Bill Jr. waited in the back seat.

Dr. Spock had nothing to say about this.

Alfred Kinsey had nothing to say about this.

A Texas sheriff voiced his opinion—

Burroughs and Joan thought they were hidden from the lazy traffic. They weren't. A sheriff's car rolled up. Joan and William were jailed overnight. They were fined $173 (over $2,000 in modern currency).

Nobody took their kids away from them.

* * *

In Paris, Jacqueline had brought Diem's package with her to drop off at the nunnery. She had indeed opened Diem's package back in Washington, D.C. What was inside was a photograph more surprising than pornography. The package had wrapped in it a very spare and strange photograph of an animal's dissected heart lying on slate, along with a handwritten line in liquid French that translated to:

the heart's gravity tugs.

Or:
the tug of the gravity of the heart.

Or:
the tug of the heart's gravity.

Chapter 10

Suddenly, California, 1954

Seattle, Washington.

The new year of 1954. Buster Hendrix is eleven years old. Fourteen years from now, he will release the song 'All Along the Watch Tower.' Buster's parents are now divorced. Lucille Hendrix lives over the Rainier Brewery on Hanford and Ninth Avenue South. Buster and his half brother, Leon, live with his father, Al, on South Jackson Street.

Al pumps gas for money. Neither father nor his sons clean the house. When Buster and Leon get rowdy, their dad whips them with a belt. If that doesn't make the boys settle, he sends them to their mother's place on Hanford and Ninth Avenue South. The boys prefer their mother to their father, anyway.

Buster and Leon are always on the lookout for green cars. Welfare workers drive green cars. Welfare can take the boys away to foster care. Buster and Leon often show up for dinner at the houses of neighbors.

Buster Hendrix in a grocery store: He walks to where the bread-in-plastic is stacked. He carefully considers a loaf and opens the packing—slips out two slices of bread, shoves them in a pocket. He'll use the same method on the sliced ham. Buster then leaves the grocery and passes a hamburger joint where he helps himself to some of these new plastic packages full of mustard or ketchup.

Buster listening to the *Your Hit Parade* Top Ten on the radio. He pretends to play guitar using a broom. He digs Dean Martin. The boy will blow across the top of a Pepsi bottle whenever Martin is singing on the radio.

When Buster feels pressured, he lapses into a stutter.

Buster's father gets the two boys up at four a.m. The sleepy kids walk to the Wonder Bread Bakery and get day-old doughnuts for free. The pair continue walking and eating doughnuts and reach the 'industrial district.' Catch a bus. Ride twenty miles south of Seattle to a farm where the boys pick strawberries. Pickers are paid a piece rate. The boys pick enough for lunch—hamburgers made out of horsemeat—ten cents apiece.

Buster is good at art. He draws pictures of flying saucers. Some are constructed like two plates placed atop each other. Some are like the saucer that burrows into the suburban ground in *Invaders from Mars.* Others have a bubble chamber on the top. Still others are shaped like mushroom bulbs.

* * *

William Burroughs's parents moved to Palm Beach, Florida, with William Burroughs Jr. The boy's father, William Sr., visited once. The man's fingers were jaundice yellow from nicotine. The thing that most impressed his son, William Jr., was that Pop ate meat with his fork turned upside-down European style.

William Burroughs had sought out a warm climate just like his parents. Burroughs now lived in Tangier, on the Mediterranean coast of Morocco. His neighborhood was a massive conglomeration of small stucco buildings built upon ancient small stucco buildings. Burroughs lived a few blocks from the writer Paul Bowles. The two knew each other, but were not close. Just as Burroughs was gay and had once been married to a woman, Paul Bowles was also gay and *still* married to a woman. It never occurred to Paul Bowles to attempt to shoot a glass William Tell style perched on the crown of his wife's head.

Burroughs was not impressed with the antics of Salinger's Holden Caulfield. Burroughs was particularly enamored of a Bowles story that takes place in the Caribbean, 'Pages from Cold Point.' It is a wonderfully calm and sordid tale about a widower who allows himself to be seduced by his devious sixteen-year-old son. After a series of such incestuous sexual liaisons, the boy then successfully blackmails the father into allowing the boy to be financially independent.

J. D. Salinger's faux naiveté U.S.A. seems ingenuous when compared to 'Pages from Cold Point.' Such perverse Bowles-like events certainly occurred all through the Western Hemisphere in the 1950s, but such things were never spoke of, let alone written about.

* * *

Washington Post columnist Drew Pearson had been born in the nineteenth century and had been a capital muckraker since the 1930s. Pearson appeared as himself in the 1951 flying-saucer-on-the-White-House-lawn classic *The Day the Earth Stood Still.*

Pearson was now staunchly anti-HUAC. He was the only man in Washington who hated McCarthy as much as Lester Callaway Hunt, Democratic senator of Wyoming (and no relation to Everette Howard Hunt). After Pearson wrote something particularly nasty about McCarthy, the senator from Wisconsin unscrewed one of the ceiling lights in the Senate hallway and waited in the shadows. When Pearson came jaunting down that very hallway, McCarthy popped out and pushed Pearson into a wall. McCarthy then shot his right knee up into Pearson's balls. McCarthy's knee felt Pearson's scrotum squish against his patella. When McCarthy had been a young man in Wisconsin, he boxed. In the boxing ring, the moment the bell rang, McCarthy would charge out of his corner and without pause or consideration begin pummeling the other guy. If the other guy was better, McCarthy refused to back down. Someone commented, 'That McCarthy. He either wins or drops.'

Pearson had been needling 'the Roy Boy' G. David Schine during the summer. 'Roy Boy' was a draft dodger. 'Roy Boy' claimed he was 4-F because of a slipped disc. Pearson got the Army to reopen G. David Schine's file. 'Roy Boy' was reexamined. Then G. David Schine was conscripted into the Army. Cohn instantly put pressure on Army brass to give preferential treatment to Schine. The Army ignored Cohn. '*Cohn practically fawns over that Schine boy. Cohn won't be happy until the kid is declared a general and works from the penthouse of the Waldorf.*' One story goes that Cohn threatened to have his committee investigate the Army. Cohn and McCarthy's story is that the Army used Private Schine as hostage to stop any investigation. These commotions between McCarthy/Cohn and the Army became public and were unseemly.

The Senate began hearings on the matter at the beginning of spring 1954. These were the notorious Army-McCarthy hearings. Until this moment, none of McCarthy's tribunals had been public like various interrogations conducted by the HUAC. In addition, the Army-McCarthy hearings would be televised. Until now, citizens only read in newspapers what McCarthy had done or said. For the next thirty-six days, the Army-McCarthy hearings were broadcast live on ABC and DuMont during the daytime and captured a 68 percent share of the viewing audience.

Housewives were the majority, but every tavern that had a television kept the Army-McCarthy hearings running. Every barbershop had the hearings broadcasting from the radio. Most viewers and listeners had a favorable impression of McCarthy before TV.

This sentiment changed.

★ ★ ★

As if to celebrate the unifying omnipotence of television, Swanson frozen foods introduced the TV dinner to America. For ninety-eight cents consumers could sup on either Salisbury steak or meat loaf or fried chicken or turkey. Each meat was accompanied by mashed potatoes and green peas, all stored in a distinctive aluminum tray with ridged compartments for each food. It took about thirty minutes to heat them up in an oven at 425°F (218°C). The TV one would eat in front of was very expensive because a recession was occurring. A new car was just shy of $1,700. A new television set was $800. *Honey, do we get a new car this year or wait and get a television instead?*

★ ★ ★

Jane Spock watched Joe McCarthy on television and thought the man both crude and a bully. He was a blowhard. He was an intellectual buffoon. Articulate arguing was a debating tactic beyond McCarthy's skill. McCarthy's verbal weapons were slander and insult—'Even a little child knows more than you do, General!'

★ ★ ★

Two American birth-control pioneers, Gregory Pincus and Dr. John Rock, began testing ovulation-inhibition formulas from Syntex (Carl Djerassi) and a company named Searle. Pincus and Rock chose Searle's norethynodrel over Djerassi's norethisterone.

Pincus worked as a consultant for Searle. No one raised a red flag over 'conflict of interest.'

Djerassi insisted to Syntex that now they needed to affiliate themselves with a monster pharmaceutical company. He told them the answer was

Parke-Davis in Detroit. In the early twentieth century, Parke-Davis had successfully manufactured stress-reduction products that contained cocaine. Then in 1914—in February—the *New York Times* reported:

NEGRO COCAINE 'FIENDS' ARE A NEW SOUTHERN MENACE.

Parke-Davis diversified.

They then marketed the first widely available epilepsy treatment, Dilantin.

In our 1950s, they were among the few firms allowed to manufacture the Salk polio vaccine.

⋆ ⋆ ⋆

Washington, D.C. Jacks brought sister Lee to one of the Army-McCarthy hearings—Roy Cohn's first day giving testimony.

Two skinny sisters wearing Chanels. Jacqueline smoking furiously the whole morning. 'So, who is that?' Lee whispers to her sister.

'Roy Cohn. Sitting beside him—'

'Oh, you can't miss McCarthy. Gosh, he has a five o'clock shadow and it's only ten in the morning.'

—the two women have the voices of hand puppets—

Jacks said, 'McCarthy has a ten o'clock shadow. A two o'clock shadow. A beard like a rabbi at five.'

'And that guy over there—the bulldog with a red crew cut whispering to McCarthy?'

'He's a moonshine lawyer named Ray Jenkins. He's the committee's lawyer. That means he presents both sides of the case with each witness. He is both prosecutor and lawyer for the defense.'

'How does that work?'

'The other day Jenkins was questioning this general and asking the general in a manner sweet as pie to tell the terrible things Cohn said to try to give his Roy Boy an easy picnic. So the general recites all the terrible things Cohn did. Then Jenkins turns around and wipes his face and when he looks back it's like he's a different person. His voice goes lower and he starts getting the general to say that everyone in Washington phones him up for special favors when their brother or friend or a constituent gets drafted.'

'So, Cohn didn't do anything that a congressman from Podunk County, West Virginia, wouldn't do?'

'Exactly,' Jacks said.

'Still, why not have two lawyers, one who's a protagonist and the other an antagonist?'

'Because that would be jake and nothing in D.C. is remotely jake.'

'Hmmm. So who's that old gent whispering to the fat guy?'

'Joseph N. Welch of Hale and Dorr. Brahmin lawyers. He's representing the Army.'

'I read about Welch. He works at a stand-up desk like Ernest Hemingway.'

'Notice anything about every man's shirt?'

'Uh. No. Wait. They're all blue. Everyone is wearing a blue shirt!'

'On television, a blue shirt looks like a really clean white shirt.'

'Oh. I don't get— Oh, I see. In black and white, blue looks white.'

Someone pounded a gavel. People spoke non sequiturs into their microphones. Suddenly Roy Cohn was ready to testify.

'He's such a shrimp!' Jacks whispered to her sister Lee.

* * *

Culture.

Detroit?

The Motor City had a decent symphony orchestra led by a French conductor born in the nineteenth century as well as an art museum where the French sculptor Auguste Rodin's *The Thinker* sat naked on a pedestal outside the front door thinking French thoughts.

A vernacular culture of jazz and blues also flourished in an Afro neighborhood named Black Bottom. Yet tunes and thinking were camouflage for the truest ethnology of Detroit—

Automobile Culture.

A man's circle of friends could never include men who worked for a different auto company from his. General Motors executives only socialized with other General Motors executives. The same with Ford and Chrysler. This put physicians as well as Wayne University professors on an unofficial social registry as every gathering given by a motor executive had to have at least several participants who had nothing to do with the auto industry. (Of course, these participants brought their wives with them.) One day at Wayne, a fellow professor came up to Carl Djerassi—'I've described you to my Ann Arbor crowd. Bob McNamara wants to invite you to join our book group.'

'What's a book group? Who's Bob McNamara?'

'He works at the Ford Motor Company.'

'What's a book group?'

'A group of husbands and their wives who all read the same book and get together once a month to discuss it.'

'Discuss the same book month after month?' Djerassi asked in a voice both dead of tone and filled with bored incredulousness.

'No. A new book every month. The other guys in the group are Ford people who want to keep their credentials as intellectuals.' The professor touched Djerassi's arm. Djerassi frowned at this touching. 'We don't just talk about books,' the professor went on. 'Most of their wives are good-looking and the booze is top-shelf.'

Djerassi stared at the man's hand. 'So, what's this Bob McNamara like?'

'Bob is like a city divided by a river,' the professor answered.

'All cities are divided by rivers.'

'One half of Bob is pure work. And Bob's approach to work is pure tangibles. When Bob McNamara went to work at Ford, we were losing nine million dollars a year. GM was Oz. Now we're on the incline and GM is downward ho.'

'What did this McNamara do to change things?'

'His strengths are statistics and facts. He does not believe in surprises. He does not believe that a car should be fun. He believes a car should be utilitarian and serve its purpose—to drive you safely from one place to another. He doesn't care about grilles and fins—why should anyone else? He has nothing but contempt for convertible buyers—why pay more for a car that doesn't have a roof?'

'Sounds like Bob has the same kind of aesthetic they have in the U.S.S.R.'

The professor raised his index finger to his mouth in a *shhh* gesture. 'He does. But don't say that to his face.' Then the professor added, 'I'm sure he makes love to his wife, Margy, by the clock. Three minutes for foreplay. Two minutes for . . .' He stopped. He was suddenly disturbed. 'I shouldn't joke. Margy has polio.' Then he added, 'Not that it shows.'

'So, what's Bob's other half?' asked Djerassi.

'His wife?'

'You said Bob was a city divided by a river.'

'I did?'

'So, what's the book this Bob McNamara wants us to read?'

'*The Rebel* by Albert Camus.'

* * *

Many years from now, journalist Bob Stone will describe Robert Strange* McNamara as a 'Puritan in Babylon; living the private life of a Puritan, but competing with other Babylonians.'

In Detroit, Djerassi had a hard time picturing this Bob McNamara riding a motorcycle like the punk Marlon Brando played in a movie that came out last year called *The Wild One.* In that movie, Brando played the president of the Black Rebels Motorcycle Club (Black Rebels being a metaphorical color, not referring to skin pigment). When a chick asks Brando, 'What are you rebelling against?' he answers, 'What you got?'

* * *

On April 6, American senator John Kennedy gave a speech in D.C. titled 'The Truth about Indochina': 'Mr. President, the time has come for the American people to be told the blunt truth about Indochina,' he said, addressing Eisenhower directly. Kennedy was a shrewd politician and he followed his opening with a French kiss: 'I am reluctant to make any statement which may be misinterpreted as unappreciative of the gallant French struggle at Diên Biên Phu . . . *but*—'

Diên Biên Phu was a flat valley in north-by-northwest Viet-Nam surrounded by steep hills coated by coniferous forests similar to the lush palette of the Wisconsin Dells. It was here that the French intended to stop the Viet Minh from circuiting men and supplies from northern Viet-Nam (aka Cochin China) through Laos into southern Viet-Nam.

---

* His mother's maiden name.

The French landed nine hundred parachutists into Diên Biên Phu. They were commanded by a fifty-one-year-old Colonel Christian de Castries, who had received his military training at the renowned Saumur Cavalry School.

There were no horses at Diên Biên Phu.

Second step: Christian de Castries named the five main military positions at Diên Biên Phu after his mistresses, Anne-Marie, Beatrice, Gabrielle, Isabelle, and Huguette (an old-fashioned name in 1950s France similar to old-fashioned American names like Gladys or Mildred today). It was at Huguette that Castries had a landing strip built for supply planes. By March of 1954, sixteen thousand French were now positioned in Diên Biên Phu. Castries saw to it that none of his troops was denied heterosexual carnal joy as he authorized two *bordels mobiles de campagne* (mobile field brothels) to operate at Anne-Marie and Beatrice (third step).

★ ★ ★

Kennedy was barely familiar with the leader of the Viet Minh, Ho Chi Minh. A scene played out when the French first landed in Diên Biên Phu: Ho Chi Minh held out an empty rice bowl and used a pair of chopsticks to tap the bottom of the bowl, saying, '*Ma vuong.*' ['The enemy.'] He raised the chopsticks and used their tips to circle the rim of the bowl and said, '*Danh tù.*' ['Us.']

★ ★ ★

As Kennedy progressed in his speech, he emphasized that the conflict in Viet-Nam was a colonial war. The blunt truth was the Vietnamese were so oppressed by their French masters that they could not think clearly about the dangers of Communism.

There was much that Kennedy knew, but didn't say—the French colony was a puppet monarchy ruled by a false emperor named Bảo Đại; there was the intense presence of Corsican gangsters; the French government bought and distributed the highlander tribes' only cash crop, opium (similar to the U.S.A.'s encouragement of the poppy farmers of Afghanistan in 1980). All Kennedy actually said was that the French must give the Vietnamese more 'freedoms.'. He did not say that 'For America to send additional aid to the French was like throwing money out the window.' Kennedy ended his speech by quoting Thomas Jefferson, always a sure source of dignified American platitudes.

* * *

Ann Arbor was a college town fifty minutes west of Detroit. Carl and Norma Djerassi pulled up to the McNamara abode, a large two-story house with a large yard in a neighborhood of other large houses, the neighborhood surrounded by block after block of compact University of Michigan professor and student housing. It was abnormal that an important bigwig at Ford would pick Ann Arbor to reside. Ford people lived in the ritzy suburb of Bloomfield Hills, a few miles north of Detroit.

Djerassi and his wife, Norma, walked up the four steps to Bob McNamara's porch and pressed the doorbell at the same time as a very tall man opened the door. He wore slacks and a starched white shirt open at the collar and old-fashioned wire glasses from the 1930s. His black hair was buttered back across the crown of his skull. The first thing he said was, 'You are twenty minutes late.' He was peering at Carl when he said that.

'We got lost,' Norma Djerassi said.

'Didn't you follow my directions?'

'Your directions?' Carl said. He sounded exasperated. 'Your directions were screwy.'

'They were not screwy. They were accurate.'

'You told us to take Geddes Avenue and make a left on Observatory and then make a right on Washtenaw.'

'I told you to go south-by-southeast on Washtenaw.'

'There is no such direction as south-by-southeast. You are either driving south or you are driving southeast.'

Norma butted in: 'Driving north on Washtenaw—Washtenaw turns into East Huron Street without announcing itself. Carl drove for ten blocks before I realized we were no longer on Washtenaw.'

'So, you two backtracked?'

'I backtracked,' Carl said.

'I made him stop at a service station and ask directions to East Stadium Boulevard,' Norma said.

'Then I found Iroquois Place,' Carl said. 'But there was no Frieze Avenue.'

'Iroquois?' McNamara said. 'I told you Cherokee Road.'

'Look. Right here,' Carl said, holding up his notes. 'See? I distinctly wrote *Iroquois.* You must have confused Cherokees with Iroquois. Fortunately, Iroquois Place practically collides with Cherokee Road.'

'No. You are wrong, Professor. I told you *Cherokee.* You must have written *Iroquois* without thinking.'

'Cherokees have nothing to do with Iroquois. Cherokees live in the South and Iroquois in the Northeast.'

'Cherokees had everything to do with the Iroquois. Cherokees spoke Iroquoian as did the Mohawk tribe and of course the Iroquois tribe.'

'There was no such tribe as the Iroquois. The Iroquois were an association of tribes—Mohawks, Oneidas and Onondagas and Cayugas and Senecas. They all lived in the Northeast.'

'But still the Cherokee spoke Iroquois,' McNamara said in a mock southern drawl.

'I hope you discuss *The Rebel* with as much fervor as you defend south-by-southeast and redskins,' Norma said, trying to laugh and sound pleasant.

McNamara turned and walked into his house. The Djerassis followed. There was a small tiled front hallway that lay beneath a stairway that led up to the second floor. To the left was a small bathroom as well as another door leading to the family room. (Or maybe the McNamaras called it a 'rec room.') Anyway, the door was open and the Djerassi husband and wife could see the McNamara family clutter inside—lots of kids' toys strewn on the carpet. Carl Djerassi frowned. He had no respect for parents who didn't make their children put their toys away.

To the right, the living room where six couples sat in chairs and on the couch. The men had crew cuts. The wives all wore poodle dresses and each woman wore glasses. In the 1950s, you can't imagine how ugly women's glasses were.

McNamara did not introduce anyone to the Djerassis. After a brief uncomfortable moment, everyone had an impromptu moment of introductions. Djerassi was suspicious of them all. Albert Camus's book *The Rebel* (the publishers lopping off the word *Man*) was an unusual choice for such suburban goys. *L'Homme révolté* had been published three years earlier in Paris and had only now been translated into English. Even more than Marlon Brando or James Dean, Albert Camus, with his perpetual Bogart cigarette hanging off his lip, was the avatar of Caucasian cool.

One of the wives spoke first. 'I myself liked the book.'

Another wife: 'I thought it was interesting to go from the rebellion of the slave to the rebellion against God.'

'Yes. You're right,' said the first wife.

The wives got to talk for a while, then the husbands began speaking—

'I think being a rebel is arrogant,' said one.

'Why on earth?' asked a wife.

'To go against the grain is counterproductive.'

'But the squeaky wheel gets oiled.'

'The squeaky wheel gets hammered down,' said another husband.

His wife corrected him. 'I think you mean that the nail that sticks up gets hammered down.'

'But what if you are a slave?' asked another wife. 'You have an obligation to rebel.'

'Even slaves can be arrogant,' Djerassi said. 'Arrogance is not a disease.'

McNamara took interest. Djerassi continued, 'Early in life I had to choose between honest arrogance and hypocritical humility. I chose honest arrogance and have seen no occasion to change.'

'That sounds like a quote,' said a wife.

'Pride goeth before a fall,' said another wife.

'Pride goeth before destruction, and a haughty spirit before a fall,' Djerassi said, correcting the woman's quote. 'Proverbs sixteen: eighteen.'

'How do you know the Bible so well?' asked the corrected wife.

'Jews wrote the Bible.'

'All of the Old Testament and most of the New,' McNamara said. 'The Book of Revelation was written in the second century by a Greek gentile with two interchangeable names, John the Presbyter and John the Humble.'

'Bob tries to be Bob the Humble,' his wife said, steering the conversation away from Semitism. 'He tries to be humble and when he is, he is very proud of the fact.'

'There is false modesty, but not false pride,' McNamara said.

The wife who misquoted the Bible said, 'Virgil talked about subduing the arrogant.'

McNamara corrected her this time. 'Virgil was talking about the power of Rome to subdue foreign arrogance with its even greater imperial arrogance.'

⋆ ⋆ ⋆

Imperial arrogance—

Bob McNamara's past—there he was in 1945 over in the Pacific theater working side by side with Curtis LeMay on an island off Japan planning the firebombing of sixty-seven Japanese cities. One single night alone, McNamara and LeMay's airmen killed one hundred thousand men and women and children in Tokyo, citizens either burned alive or suffocating in the great Air Suck caused by the firestorms. 'Thank God, we won the war,' LeMay once told McNamara. 'If we'd lost the war, we'd have all been prosecuted as war criminals.'

⋆ ⋆ ⋆

A month after Kennedy's Viet-Nam speech, the final French radio message came out of Diên Biên Phu on the seventh of May:

> 'The enemy has overrun us. We are blowing up everything. Vive la France!'

John Kennedy heard the news and held his head in his hands for a moment and then raised his head and said, 'This is the French equivalent of Custer's last stand at Little Big Horn.'

⋆ ⋆ ⋆

Ann Arbor, 1954. Margy McNamara poured sherry for everyone, saying, 'Virgil said that Rome would show mercy to those who have submitted to the foreign arrogance.'

'You can rebel against the arrogance of reason,' said a verbally battered wife. 'You can rebel against the arrogance of husbands.'

'But you cannot rebel against arrogance itself because humble rebels don't have the stuff of true rebellion,' Djerassi said. 'I think Ernest Hemingway called that stuff *cojones.*'

'Camus was talking about the *rebel man,*' said McNamara. 'Women are not capable of rebellion.'

'But Bob,' his wife said, 'women can rebel against *cajones.*'

'That's what wives do,' chirped a wife.

Djerassi corrected McNamara's wife. '*Cojones.*'

'That's what I said.'

'No. You said *cajones.* That's Spanish for *chest of drawers.*'

'We've gotten sidetracked from Camus's *The Rebel,*' McNamara said.

'As you wish,' Djerassi said with a smile. 'Camus's theory of rebellion also includes metaphysical rebellion. Every wife in America owns many *cajones*, but not *cojones,* and thus they should rebel against God for giving them that lack.'

'And since Hemingway was brought up,' said McNamara, 'I think it's important to mention that Jake Barnes had a war injury in *The Sun Also Rises,* but it wasn't that his *cojones* were shot off. His *cojones* were intact. It was that other part connected to the *cojones* that was missin'.'

'What do you mean, Bob? Oh wait. Oh, Bob! That's disgusting.'

'Bob, is that true?'

'I read it in *Look.* Hemingway said that himself in *Look.*'

'It is interesting that Camus doesn't talk about *cojones* at all,' said Djerassi.

Several wives simultaneously uttered the words 'Thank God.'

★ ★ ★

Washington, D.C. Jacqueline Bouvier tells her sister Lee in a soft, secretive voice the details of Diem's photograph: 'It was a very stark and troubling photograph, but very beautiful at the same time. Very modern. The object in the photograph was shot as it lay across a white surface. On that white surface was an abstract shape that looked like a withered plum. It was moist, and a single strand of dark liquid ran in a line down the painting. The dripping object appeared anatomical. I have a friend who is a zoologist at the Smithsonian—Nickel Edwuz, you remember him? I showed Nickel the photograph. He said it looked like a heart. Anyway, we brought the photograph to the Smithsonian. Nickel was right. It was a photo of a heart. A fish heart. It was the heart of a blue panchax—a fish only found in Indochina. There was calligraphy on the white surface the wet heart was sitting on: *Gravité du coeur.* Gravity of the heart.'

⋆ ⋆ ⋆

Ann Arbor. The men rose from their chairs and walked into McNamara's office single-file.

The women rose and meandered with the cups and cookie dishes into the kitchen.

Not a word was spoken to instigate these actions. Everyone acted like a demi-puppet.

Among the men in his office, McNamara pulled a bottle of the Good Stuff out of a bottom drawer of his desk and opened it and provided shot glasses. Carl Djerassi glanced around, giving a slight frown at the impersonality of the room. Books stacked on a shelf. Several framed Ford Executive Awards. A bare bulb sticking out of the ceiling. A framed picture of an old man and woman on the desk. Djerassi realized that he had never met someone as arrogant as McNamara. Yet, a smart guy never forgot that Detroit was now near the pinnacle of American political and economic power. Education in Detroit was small potatoes. The tallest building in Detroit was the Penobscot Building. It was forty-seven stories tall. Robert McNamara was forty-seven stories tall. Robert McNamara would be Djerassi's entry into the world of Power and Business. Perhaps his and McNamara's mutual arrogance would even spawn a détente. McNamara would work in Detroit for the rest of his life while Djerassi planned to split as soon as he found and/or captured a Golden Fleece.

Djerassi heard someone say, 'Anyone see the Stanley Cup?'

Someone else: 'Ha! The Red Wings sure slashed the Canucks.'

'How can Ted Williams fracture his collarbone in the first game of spring training after flying thirty-nine combat missions without injury in Korea?'

'Ask his barber.'

'Did you see the Tigers crush the Orioles three to zero?'

'Zero! Zero! Zero!'

'What sweetness the zero taught us!'

Djerassi had nothing to add to this conversation.

* * *

None of the French soldiers at Diên Biên Phu was allowed to read Camus's new book, *L'Homme révolté*, should he want to.

The Rebel Man.

Yet, the book wouldn't have done the French soldiers any good strategically speaking even if they had been allowed to read it.

* * *

Ann Arbor. In the McNamara kitchen, Margy McNamara began washing the tea frou-frous in the sink. Norma Djerassi leaned over and said softly into Margy's ear, 'Men live uneasily with or under the threat of genius in women.'

* * *

At the end of March in Washington, D.C., Dorothy Hunt gave birth to a long-awaited son: Howard Saint John Hunt. His godfather was William F. Buckley Jr.

Howard Saint John Hunt was born with a clubfoot. When Dorothy was told, she saw the deformity as a godly rebuke.

During this time in the U.S.A., you could count the citizens on one hand who knew the fact that every year one hundred thousand babies were born with a clubfoot. Every year in the U.S.A.

Clubfoot.

Say the word aloud, *clubfoot.* It sounds like a medieval affliction. Or a *Frankenstein* thing.

Harelip. Hunchback. Clubfoot.

The Latin term for the affliction is *talipes equinovarus.* Ankle plus foot. When you were old enough to walk your clubfoot would turn inward—your Achilles tendon splayed—and it would appear that you were walking on your ankle. Dr. Spock had nothing to say about the clubfoot in *The Common Sense Book of Baby and Child Care.* The image of a shuffling Igor from *Frankenstein* was lodged in father Howard Hunt's mind. Doctors assured Hunt that when his son was five or six the deformed foot could be 'corrected' with surgery.

Hunt dealt with Saint John's clubfoot by burying himself in his work—using the airwaves as a weapon against the Communists in a more vicious fashion than the White Propaganda of the Voice of America. Hunt thrived on Black Propaganda.

During May, Hunt supervised the sending of—via shortwave radio—fake news announcements in Spanish to Guatemala: '*¡Combatientes un gran espada sin limita cruzan ambos el partidario del comunista!*' ('Anti-Communist fighters are streaming across both borders!') The Hunt News also reported the lie that Guatemalan citizens were spontaneously rising up against the government and Árbenz had fled the country to Moscow. Hunt had a female disc jockey with a *castellano* accent address the wives of Guatemala: '*Tiene un atractivo comunista, pequeña piscina y un patio privado para teyer el sol. Además, hay un bar comunista podrá relajarse, ver televisión, jugar juegos, leer, etc., desayuno y refrescos están disponibles. Usted comunista hacer su proprio té y café, e incluso puede usar comunista.*' The English translation:

> 'Should your husband be a Communist or have sympathy for the Communists cease conjugal relations. Force him to sleep elsewhere. Force him to sleep alone. Accept no caress or kisses from him until he embraces democratic values.'

Hunt's next scheme, Operation Washtub, involved planting a phony Soviet arms cache in neighboring Nicaragua that would reflect poorly on Árbenz. Then, Hunt discovered that a Swedish ship loaded with Czechoslovak weaponry arrived in a Guatemala port. He alerted Eisenhower's people and the president went on the radio to announce this was definite proof of Árbenz's Soviet links. Árbenz, in turn, produced the excuse that the Czechs were the only ones to sell Guatemala needed artillery for their armed forces. Árbenz didn't mention that the Czechs had shipped his government barely functional German weaponry captured during World War II.

Howard Hunt could taste the forthcoming invasion of Guatemala. He woke up with a hard-on every morning. Then in June, Uncle Sugar pulled Hunt off Operation Success. At first, Hunt was too startled to be enraged. Hunt was told he was being given a promotion. Hunt would go to Japan to be in charge of the entire CIA operation in North Asia—China, Korea, Taiwan, Hong Kong, the Philippines, and Japan itself. His cover was as

Department of the Army civilian adviser to General Matthew Ridgeway's Far East Command. Hunt didn't want to go. He had bad memories of the Japanese. 'For my money,' he was known to say, 'I think we stopped dropping atom bombs too soon.'

* * *

Washington, D.C. The Army-McCarthy hearings. The cigarette smoke is thick in the gallery, thickest over the heads of Jacqueline (Jacks) Kennedy and her sister Lee. They watch Roy whisper in Joe's ear and the fat man whisper in Joe's other ear. Jacks whispers to her sister, 'I'm pregnant.'

'You sure?'

'Pretty.'

"That's so great.' Lee hugs her sister while they bounce up and down in their seats. Suddenly, everyone in the audience seems to clear their throats at once as if they're about to become a Greek chorus. Now Roy Cohn is standing trying to ram through the point that Chief of Staff Robert Stevens was good friends with David Schine because of a photograph of Stevens smiling at Schine as if the lad was his own son. The strategy of this implication is unclear, but it turns out that Stevens was actually smiling at a third person in the camera's range—a colonel named Bradley. Only Colonel Bradley had been cut out of the picture.

We moderns can see this as scissors before Photoshop.

Next Welch is asking, if Bradley and Stevens were in fact *not* smiling at each other, why did Bradley have a look of pleasure on his face?

'Colonel Bradley had a good steak dinner afterward,' Cohn answers. 'Maybe he was anticipating it.'

Welch snaps back, "If Bradley is feeling good about a steak dinner, Schine must be considering a whole haunch of beef.' Everyone in the audience laughs. When Jacks laughs, it emits from high in her throat behind her tonsils. It's like the laugh of a child. Now Joe W. asks a rhetorical question: 'Who had reproduced the photo? A pixie, perhaps.'

Senator Joe yells, 'Will the counsel, for my benefit, define—I think he might be an expert on this—what a pixie is?'

Joe Welch gives a viper smile. 'Yes. I should say, Mr. Senator, that a pixie is a close relative of a fairy.'

* * *

Pause. The modern assumption is that the affections between Roy Cohn and G. David Schine included carnal participation, and that those two boys and probably McCarthy himself were as gay as the son of Lester Callaway Hunt of Wyoming, a boy who was arrested the year before for soliciting sex from a male undercover Washington police officer—a crime that has been kept hush-hush. The actual evidence concerning Roy Cohn and G. David Schine indicates their relationship, whatever the intentions, was likely never consummated. During at least two-thirds of the twentieth century, sexual repression was strong in America. Many clandestine relationships between men and men, and women and women, and men and women, were definitely consummated, while an equal number of such relationships were, alas, not.

* * *

Jacks whispers to her sister, 'I'll be back. I'm going to the ladies' room.' The older sister stands and shimmies down the aisle of knees and shoes and leaves the auditorium. Lee sits and listens to the bickering. She watches everyone whisper something to someone else. Everyone is scowling. The hearings break for lunch. Lee realizes that her sister has never returned.

Lee left the auditorium to search for Jacks. She found the ladies' room. Lee heard her sister before she saw her. Jacks was quietly weeping in a locked stall. The attendant was a tiny old black woman.

'My sister,' Lee said.

'She been there for half an hour.'

Lee knocked gently on the stall door. 'Jacks. It's me.'

Lee intuitively knew what had happened. Her sister had miscarried.

* * *

'You've done enough. Have you no sense of decency, sir? At long last, have you left no sense of decency?' Those are the words of the most famous sound bite of the McCarthy hearings. They will be spoken by sixty-three-year-old Joseph Welch, born in the nineteenth century. Those will be the twenty words that bring down McCarthy on June 9, 1954.

Some believe Joseph Welch staged events so he could speak those very words on TV—

'You've-done-enough-have-you-no-decency?'

'Wait a minute, Mr. Welch.'

'What now, Ed?'

'Don't rush the words.'

'Okay.' Pause. 'You've done enough.' Pause. 'Have you no decency?'

'Wait, let's add some syllables.' Pause. 'You've done enough, sir. Have you left no sense of decency—.'

'No. I'll say it this way.' Pause. 'You've done enough. Have you no sense of decency, sir? At last, have you left no sense of decency—.'

'At *long* last, have you no sense of decency—'

'At long last, have you left no sense of decency—.'

'Let's try it from the top.'

'You've done enough. Have you no sense of decency, sir? At long last, have you left no sense of decency?'

'Don't just say words. Say them as if Fred Fisher is your firstborn.'

'Okay. Here goes—'

'Wait. So tell me again. Who is Fred Fisher?'

'A kid who works for the firm in Boston. He's what, thirty-two? Thirty-three, maybe. He worked for the Army Signal Corps during the war. Then he went to Harvard. Started working for Hale and Dorr in 'fifty-one. I was gonna bring him down to Washington, but the kid told me that he was a member of the Lawyers Guild. I had to tell him, *Sorry, son. The Lawyers Guild is as pink as Pepsodent. We can't take any chances.*'

'So you've baited the trap?'

'Yeah. McCarthy has the papers about the kid. Tomorrow I'll bait Cohn and that will surely send fire up McCarthy's ass, asshole that he is.'

'What about the deal you made with Cohn?'

'It won't matter. Joe's so predictable. He'll barge ahead and babble.'

'Okay. One more time, Mr. Welch.'

'You've done enough. Have you no sense of decency, sir? At long last, have you left no sense of decency?'

* * *

We are live now. Senator McCarthy is responding to Mr. Welch's *decency* jab: 'How can you talk about any *sense of decency*? I have heard you and everyone else talk so much about laying the truth upon the table, but then I heard the completely phony Mr. Welch saying, *before sundown* you must get these people *out of government*. I want you to have it very clear, very clear that you were not so serious about that when you tried to recommend this man for this Committee.'

Mr. Welch said, 'Mr. McCarthy, I will not discuss this with you further. You have sat within six feet of me and could have asked me about Fred Fisher. You have seen fit to bring it out! If there is a God in heaven, he will see to it that attacking Fred Fisher will do neither you nor your cause any good.' Then Mr. Welch said, 'I will not discuss it further.' He looked at Cohn. 'I will not ask Mr. Cohn any more questions.'

There was a beat of silence before applause roared through the room.

If the spectators had held roses, they would have pelted Mr. Welch with them. Someone did shout 'Bravo!' A recess was declared. McCarthy walked out. Everyone acted as if he had screwed up. How? He looked at a woman he didn't know and said, 'What did I do? What did I do?'

Mr. Welch stood in the hallway weeping crocodile tears.

Several days later, the hearings were recessed indefinitely. The technical term was *sine die,* Latin for 'without day'; in legalese it means the court will not assign a date for a future meeting.

★ ★ ★

A week or so afterward, Senator Lester Callaway Hunt of Wyoming sits in his office in the Senate Building on a Sunday afternoon. Like those of all the offices in the Senate the ceiling is high enough that an elephant could comfortably stand even in a Democrat's office. Every office has a chandelier. In Hunt's office, the unnecessarily long floor-to-ceiling red drapes are shut, although they are rippling from the spring breeze blowing in the window. The senator's radio is on. The Washington Senators are playing the Baltimore Orioles. The sportscaster has a brusque, low-key, unflappable voice. His critics say listening to him is like listening to an undertaker.

> 'New ball thrown into play... Cairo on the mound... Anastasia the hitter... The pitch... Ball three... Three and oh.'

Senator Hunt was born in the nineteenth century. Senator Hunt is holding a hunting rifle in his lap. He is holding an eighteen-inch-barrel Winchester that his father gave him fifty years ago when Lester was a boy. Eleven days earlier Senator Lester Callaway Hunt had announced that he was retiring from the Senate because of health issues. His kidneys.

> 'Bullock walks off second... Fiddler on first... They're ready for anything... One out, last of the ninth... The pitch... A swing from Anastasia... A drive hit out toward the right-field corner—'

Senator Hunt now wipes the sweat from his forehead with a handkerchief and then leaves the cloth pressed against his brow. He now raises the rifle stock backward and presses the barrel against the handkerchief.

The office is quiet. The street is quiet.

Just the radio:

> 'Winslow is going back... Back goes Winslow... Winslow makes a one-handed catch against the bullpen—'

Senator Hunt is not leaning his forehead against the barrel of an eighteen-inchWinchester rifle because of his kidneys or any aspect of his health.

> 'Sardanapalus is up... Cairo is winding... The pitch... Smack... A grounder... It's rolling—between Fiddler's legs... Winslow gets it... Tosses to Fiddler at first... Sardanapalus beats the ball... Safe.'

As revealed before: Hunt's twenty-year-old son had been arrested for soliciting oral sex from an undercover officer.

> 'Pearl up next... Cairo is winding... Sardanapalus is going! Polo at second. Cairo spins, throws. The throw is wild...'

Hunt kept his son's homosexual arrest undercover until last week.

> 'Sardanapalus is safe... Sardanapalus stole second... What a felon... The throw got past Polo... Sardanapalus has done it... Cairo would've

thrown him out, but Polo couldn't handle the bad throw... Sardanapalus now has a career blast of two hundred fifty-eight stolen bases.'

The Republicans found out about the queer Hunt son. They blackmailed Senator Hunt into resigning or they'd go public about his pink prodigy.

'Nova at the plate... Cairo pitches.'

The day before, Senator McCarthy had threatened to go after a senator 'from the west' about an issue involving corruption. Senator Hunt had skimmed a few thousand dollars where he shouldn't have. It was unnecessary pilfering. It was legislative chump change. What was he thinking?

'Nova swings... Crack! Pop fly—'

Washington pedestrians outside hear the blast of Lester Callaway Hunt's Winchester.

'Where's Winslow? Sardanapalus rushing to third... They're waving him in... They're waving him in... Winslow scoops up the ball... Throws... They're waving Sardinia in... The throw to the plate is perfect... Sardinia, uh, Sardanapalus is doornail dead—'

Senator Hunt's *Life had stood—a Loaded Gun.** After the ambulance and body bag, the *New York Times* will claim Senator Hunt was despondent over his health.

'Wait... We have an argument... I think Sardanapalus was out! We have an argument... We have rhubarb... No... Sardanapalus is safe—'

---

* A line from Emily Dickinson.

Chapter 11

The American Embassy in Tokyo, Japan, 1954

In early June, Howard Hunt's 'revolutionaries' begin invading Guatemala. They fail to take the country. Yet, by June 27, President Árbenz understands his regime will never be free of ruthless American interference and he abdicates. After he flees his country, one hundred fifty thousand Guatemalans are rounded up and killed by U.S.-backed 'authorities,' while another fifty thousand civilians 'disappear.'

Howard Hunt's Operation Success was a . . .

The Hunts themselves lived in the Ochanomizu (Tea Water) District of Tokyo, a neighborhood of old families, noble families. The Hunts lived in a neo-traditional Japanese house built by Frank Lloyd Wright. It had rice-paper walls. Their nanny, 成田国際空港, overlooked care of the girls and took complete care of Saint John the infant—feeding, cleaning, guarding him as he napped. The woman always carried Saint John. The baby's feet were to never touch the floor. When Saint John remembered this many years later he never knew if this had been a Japanese custom or because of his clubfoot.

Two years after Saint John's birth, Yukio Mishima's (born 1925) fifth novel, *The Temple of the Golden Pavilion,* will be published. The book's protagonists are a man with a clubfoot and his psychotic friend who stutters. After Saint John learns the rudiments of speech, he too will begin to stutter.

* * *

Rhodes, an island in the Mediterranean.

The crew aboard the Voice of America's ship, the *Courier,* were like characters in a situation comedy. There were Mack, Rooney, Zink,

Spocket, and Hydupe. The *Courier* also had a Greek cook named Pavlos. He supplied the *Courier* with beer and had the foresight to hide the cases in the cooler behind a single layer of cans of Coca-Cola. Once when shore patrol pulled a surprise inspection, the officer left with the words, 'I guess you guys really like your soda pop!'

Once, Zink and Mack were short of beer funds. They straightened up their uniforms and walked into a bar called Bufos Skilos. The pair walked with authority through the tavern as if they were inspecting it. Deep frowns played upon their mugs, fooling the bartender into thinking they were about to declare Bufos Skilos off limits to VOA sailors. The barkeep then treated the pair to ouzo on the house along with some B-girls. Word spread from tavern to bar, and the pair were offered free liquor in every watering hole along the waterfront.

Yes, the *Courier* crew were treated as beloved conquerors among the islanders, who were mostly Greek Orthodox—secret pagans as polytheistic as Herman Melville's nineteenth-century tattooed cannibals out in the Pacific.

A popular drinking joke on Rhodes went, 'On the day Christ was born, certain sailors off the coast of Illyria heard a wailing from the woods and terrible voices howling, *The god Pan is dead!*'

* * *

Oedipus and Odysseus were Grecian wanderers and so was Aristotle Onassis. He loved nothing more than cruising the Mediterranean and its adjoining seas with intriguing passengers he could lavish with generosity. He was a *planaomai*—a man of wealth and taste who goes to seek knowledge and pleasure. A man without a fixed itinerary. He was also a bit of the *phoitaõ*, a word that meant both the wanderings of the gods and those of mortals who are mad. Onassis had a beautiful rich man's yacht. When he sailed into port at Rhodes, he stared dumbfounded at the *Courier.* The ship resonated deep inside him.

When the Mediterranean air became damp above the *Courier,* the air surrounding the antennas ionized into plasma and ignited as St. Elmo's fire. Blue fireballs could streak from an antenna to any ungrounded items poking out of the ship. It was Pavlos the cook who named this blue buzzing light 'twigerty.' Anyone aboard the *Courier* as well as passing ships could also be hit with twigerty. Islanders witnessing these snakes of electricity assumed the devil was involved. Sometimes the air was so electric that Mack and Spocket and Hydupe juggled fluorescent balls of light with their bare hands. At one such display, the Greek Orthodox archbishop of the Dodecanese Islands and his entourage, which included the *parslowch* (governor of the Dodecanese) and a troop of Greek Boy Scouts, were aboard the *Courier,* and at the sight of sailors handling blue balls of electricity, all the Greeks dropped to their knees and gesticulated the sign of the cross, crying, 'God have mercy upon us.'

Aristotle Onassis boarded the *Courier* at dawn, and turned his head back and forth in childlike awe. The possibilities of this boat thrilled him tremendously. Onassis recognized that the boat had been reoutfitted from a tanker. He heard of a Canadian convoy escort, just eleven years old, for sale in Italy. Onassis now had a vision of buying and refurbishing that ship into a yacht that would make Odysseus gnash his teeth in jealous rage.

* * *

Howard Hunt in Japan.

He accomplishes little at first. Hunt shuts down some of his predecessor's useless money holes. Hunt floats small helium balloons into North Korea promising a five-thousand-dollar reward and resettlement in the West to any North Korean pilot who will fly a MIG-15 into South Korea. The only plane that comes is a 'rust-bucket with wings, some kind of Yak trainer.'

Howard Hunt talking to Joe Darwin in the United States on the transpacific phone: 'The other evening Dot and I returned home and found the entire household staff watching TV. I was about to chew them out for watching without asking permission when I saw that they were all weeping. Even the men . . .' It seemed that the Americans had forced Tokyo television to broadcast Japanese army footage. Japanese civilians watching footage of Japanese soldiers killing Chinese peasants. Defiling Yankee corpses. Japanese soldiers forcing Japanese civilians to kill their children before advancing Australian troops arrived.

World War II remained alive in everyone's mind in 1954 as 9/11 is still alive in 2013. During World War II, Leslie Fiedler had served in the

Pacific in the Navy, stationed aboard a ship that floated offshore from Iwo Jima. His job was to interrogate Jap prisoners. The poor saps had all been indoctrinated by their superiors to kill themselves before being captured. Half the prisoners Fiedler saw were too shot up to commit hara-kiri. The waters surrounding Iwo Jima were littered with severed arms and legs and hands. Japanese prisoners without legs insisted on pulling themselves up the net from the PT boats to the ship. They couldn't lose face. Before Fiedler's interrogation, the prisoners had to strip to have their bodies shaved for lice. The Japs would see Fiedler coming forth with a razor and assume he was going to castrate them. The prisoners would lose control of their bladders, unintentionally peeing all over Fiedler.

One day on the beach, Fiedler found a Japanese helmet with half a skull and a brain mashed inside.

* * *

Ann Arbor.

Another Sunday of Robert McNamara's book group. McNamara himself chose this month's title, *The Divine Comedy* by Dante. In addition to actually reading the book, he gave each member, husband and wife, the same assignment—to use an Italian dictionary and retranslate the first three lines of the poem.

'As I told you last month, the first three lines of Dante in Italian are: *Nel mezzo del cammin di nostra vita / mi ritrovai per una selva oscura, / ché la diritta via era smarrita.*'

'Of course, Bob, technically speaking, Dante didn't write the poem in Italian because Italy as a geographical/political unit didn't yet exist.' Carl Djerassi made that comment.

McNamara said, 'Of course, Carl. But the words Dante used existed then and exist now. Every word is in the Italian dictionaries I got everyone.'

No one said anything.

'Who wants to go first?' McNamara said, leaning back on his chair.

Still no one responded. McNamara's wife, Margy, raised half her arm as if it was a flipper while scrunching up her shoulders. 'Okay,' she said in an usually squeaky voice. 'Here goes—'

'Midway in human life's allotted span,
I awoke obscured in a great forest,
Perplexed by paths with the straight way at strife.'

No one said anything.

'Well, honey. Interesting,' Bob said. 'Anyone else?'

The wife of another Ford man raised her hand.

'Okay, Mrs. Eyezbrands, you have the stage.'

The woman cleared her throat and read:

'Midway life's journey I was made aware
That I was lost in a forest dark,
My right way being blotted by distance.'

'*Blotted by distance*,' someone repeated. 'That's nice.'

McNamara looked around the gathering to see if there were any other comments. 'Well, I think anyone who translates Dante has to be mindful of his metaphors, which you two lovely women were not. Now *Nel mezzo* means *in the middle. Del cammin* means *of the path. Di nostra vita* means *of our life.* So our life span—our *allotted span*, as my wife puts it, is definitely a *path*.'

'Thus it's a metaphor,' Djerassi said.

'I prefer to think of it as figurative language,' McNamara said. 'Then, *mi ritrovai—I found myself—per una selva oscura—in a dark wood.* So, I think it's clear that the *path* and the *dark wood* are both figurative rather than literal.'

'In other words, *path* and the *dark wood* are metaphors,' Djerassi said, and then recited the rest of the lines: '*Ché la diritta via era smarrita—for the straight way was lost.*' Then Djerassi said, 'That isn't figurative at all. *For the straight way was lost*—does that mean that life's path is a *straight way* until you get lost in the forest like some Goldilocks?'

'Translating is not an exact science,' McNamara said. 'For my translation, I chose to keep the spirit of the figurative language, but be more exact.'

'Lay it on us, Bob,' Djerassi said.

'Okay,' McNamara said.

'In the middle of the journey through life
I found myself lost in a dark wood
Miles away from the right road.'

'The story of your life, Bob,' Djerassi almost said. He bit his tongue. He said nothing.

Then McNamara said, 'So Carl, read us your translation of Mr. Dante.'

'Okay.'

* * *

Alger Hiss was released early from Lewisburg Federal Penitentiary, in November. This was the month Hiss was born in. November was the month when things went bad for him at his trial. November would be the month he died in.

A red convertible came to pick Hiss up at the prison. As Hiss walked toward the red convertible, those convicts still on the inside opened the windows behind the bars and cheered. The red convertible was driven by Hiss's longtime law school and New Deal friend Chester Lane. Hiss's son Tony was in the back seat with Posey—she had the day off from the Doubleday bookstore on Fifth Avenue where she was paid thirty-seven dollars a week.

Hiss heard a whirling noise in the sky. He looked up.

A police helicopter hovered.

'They followed us all the way from New York!' Posey said, reaching out of the convertible and grabbing Alger's shirt, all the while staring up into the sky with glazed paranoia.

Alger hated seeing his wife's face distorted by emotion. Posey was now fifty-one years old. She'd always possessed a strange beauty that had nothing to do with youth or age. Her beauty was austere. Posey could have played the part of Marilyn Monroe's best friend in a motion picture because Posey's beauty did not diminish that of another woman. Posey was a woman who required an educated male eye to appreciate her. Let Monroe seduce the bellboys and millionaires. Posey attracted the poets and sophisticates.

That said, Alger had never been remotely sophisticated. He had met Posey in the late 1920s when she was already married as Mrs. Priscilla

Hobson. In 1929, Alger heard she had divorced. He wrote her from Boston. She answered and invited Alger to come spend a Manhattan weekend with her. Alger ran to a Cambridge drugstore and bought a diaphragm for Posey. When Alger handed it to her in New York City, she bunched up in laugher. She educated the young man that diaphragms were not *one size fits all.*

The red convertible headed back to the city. Tony was in the back seat behind his dad, who sat on the passenger side. Posey was sitting behind the driver, craning her neck, peering up at the helicopter following them. It was really too cold to have the ragtop down, but a Red Convertible Celebration when one gets out of Lewisburg Federal Penitentiary was a Red Convertible Celebration. Alger tried to start a conversation with his son—'It's good to be going home, Tony.'

'It's good to have you back, Alger,' his son answered.

The son of Alger Hiss had never been required to call his progenitor 'Dad' or 'Pop' or any other patriarchal label. When Tony first learned to speak, he had called his father 'Alger.' Such familiarity was unheard of in 1954.

Tony also called his mother 'Posey.'

Dr. Spock had written nothing about what a child should call his parents. The unwritten assumption was that either *Mom* or *Dad* would do. A child calling his parents by their first names was beyond Dr. Spock's view of the world.

'Alger, I've read all the Freddy the Pig books.'

'Gosh, Tony. That's great. That series began long before you were born.'

'I like the first books,' Tony said sadly.

'But don't the new books have Martians in them?'

'There's too much social tension in them,' Posey yelled, her head craned back watching the helicopter. 'Freddy and the other talking animals were more carefree during the New Deal.'

Tony leaned forward in his seat and whispered to his father, 'The Martians try to trick the animals into rioting.' He leaned back, then leaned forward. 'Alger, is rioting wrong?'

Alger started to answer, but couldn't. He had spent the last forty-four months in a federal penitentiary. Rioting had never crossed his mind. (The riot at Attica State loomed a decade and a half into the future.)

Suddenly, Posey leaned forward and began pounding the back of the front seat, howling, 'Keep calm, Chester! Keep calm!'

Chester had been calm as a clam.

'Keep calm, Chester! Keep calm!' Posey stared back up at the helicopter. The truth was that Posey had always been a little nuts. 'Keep calm, Chester! Keep calm!' In the 1920s, Posey was analyzed by a woman who had studied with Freud. This woman kept flying squirrels as uncaged pets in her house.

'Keep calm, Chester! Keep calm!'

* * *

A final image of Leslie Fiedler during World War II. He is sitting on a black coral beach listening to 'Orphan Ann' on the radio, a female deejay whose broadcasts were intended to discourage American troops. History would misname Orphan Ann as Tokyo Rose.*

> 'Hello, you wandering boneheads in the Pacific. Orphan Ann here. I'm the little sunbeam whose throat you'd like to cut. How's tricks? We're ready for a vicious assault on your morale, seventy-five minutes of music and news for our friends—I mean our enemies—in the South Pacific. Before our first musical blow at your morale, 'Hey Pop I Don't Want to Go to Work' by Rudy Vallee and his Connecticut Yankees, I have to share this health alert. You know that I wish each one of you little boneheads could spend the night with Orphan Ann, but it would be no use. Your officers won't tell you this, but those Atabrine pills they give you every day to prevent malaria have a terrible, terrible side effect. They make it so you can never make love with a woman again. I know that you know exactly what I mean. The pump won't work. It's as if vandals stole the handle. So, keep those yellow pills under your tongue and spit them out first chance when no one is watching. Okay, now for Rudy Val— Wait! Wait! [Muffled noise.] Here is a special emergency message. Honolulu has

---

* There never was a 'Tokyo Rose.'

been alive with rumors all day that you boneheads have dropped a secret bomb on the city of Hiroshima. As usual, the truth is the exact opposite. The Japanese are the ones with the top-secret weapon. The new Tokyo Death Ray has wiped out three hundred American airplanes as they flew over the skies of Hiroshima to attack. Three hundred airplanes! Just think of all the widows and orphans back home in Toledo and Cheboygan!'

Chapter 12

Detroit, Michigan, 1955

Alfred Hitchcock's 1951 movie *Strangers on a Train* ends with an out-of-control merry-go-round spinning madly. Where would one get the dizziest—on the outer rim or nearest the axis?

January 1, 1955, is the axis of the 1950s.

* * *

Claire Douglas is living in J. D. Salinger's New Hampshire cabin. This winter they decide to marry in June. Salinger has a short story called 'Franny' in the January 29 issue of *The New Yorker.* He tells Claire that 'Franny' is his wedding present to her. This story concerns the spiritual crisis of a college girl named Franny at Yale, during a football weekend she's sharing with her shallow boyfriend.

Franny looks like Claire.

Franny has a blue suitcase like Claire does.

Claire and Salinger find themselves driving through the New Hampshire sleet with their two witnesses in the back seat searching for a justice of the peace.

* * *

After the wedding, Jerry Salinger grew a Genghis Khan beard.

Beards were in the air.

Norman Mailer began sporting a goatee that no one had the courage to tell him looked ridiculous.

Even Jackson Pollock had a beard. Last summer in the Hamptons, Pollock was drunk and wrestling with the equally drunk painter Willem de Kooning because MoMA's Frank O'Hara had just written that the 'American art kingdom was divided between Pollock and de Kooning.' According to O'Hara, Pollock was the age's Ingres and de Kooning its

Delacroix. As de Kooning and Pollock wrestled, de Kooning recalled that his theory of art was simple. The Dutchman loved following drunks around in Manhattan as they weaved down the sidewalk. Each drunk stumbled in unique fashion. This was the theory of de Kooning's line. This explained de Kooning's paintings. For all de Kooning's shadowing of drunks, he had never considered the consequences of two drunk men wrestling.

Pollock and de Kooning both tumbled into a rut in the sand.

Pollock landed first and de Kooning fell on Pollock, snapping Jack the Dripper's right ankle.

Frank O'Hara was also a poet. He wrote poems about both artists.

> I have my beautiful de Kooning to aspire to. I think it has an orange bed in it, more than the ear can hold.

Jackson Pollock had to wear a full leg cast all summer. He lay around his house in the Hamptons feeling sorry for himself. He stopped shaving. O'Hara's poem continues:

> I am tired today but I am not too tired. I am not tired at all. There is the Pollock, white, harm will not fall, his perfect hand.

When Jackson Pollock dies, he will still be sprouting a beard.

* * *

Finally, Joe McCarthy stopped shaving one February weekend. He intended to grow a modest beard because now whenever Senator McCarthy rose to speak, his colleagues all walked away or formed little clusters in the aisle talking among themselves. If McCarthy buttonholed a colleague in the hallway, they would always interrupt him. 'Let me finish,' Joe would say. The other would always smile and reply, 'I thought you *were* finished. It's always hard to tell.' McCarthy had a vision that a beard would give him a rebirth of dignity. 'Look what it did for Abraham Lincoln.' By Sunday, his stubble gave him the visage of a mean drunk.

He went out to the barbershop and treated himself to a good razor shave.

* * *

Jack Kennedy was bedridden on his belly. He had a bad back from Addison's disease and if the forthcoming operation didn't kill him then the steroids and the problems in his gut likely would. Jacqueline went out to shop for some lobster for dinner. She didn't trust the cook to choose right. She returned home to Georgetown to find her husband distressed in bed. The servants had all disappeared. 'I couldn't reach any books,' he said. 'All I could find was this map of the United States.'

The U.S.A. had forty-eight states in 1955.

'Forty-eight states,' he said. 'There are forty-eight states. Why? If Russia dropped the bomb and a thousand years from now men from Mars landed and studied a map of the United States what would they think?'

'That the Russians were very bad,' Jacqueline said.

'No. I mean the map is narration. All these big states in the West . . .'

His wife interrupted with her whispering voice—'And little slivers in New England.'

'Look at Rhode Island. What is Rhode Island? It isn't even an island. You'd look at its boundaries and think there must be something of incredible value in that little land. Gold. Silver. Uranium.'

'The Pilgrims came from the Netherlands, which is a dinky country. Holland and the Netherlands. Dinky. Powerless.'

'Yet the Dutch owned the East Indies. Cape Town. Manhattan,' Jack said.

'But for how long?'

'For as long as Rhode Island ruled America.'

'Look at the Mississippi River. Why didn't any state try to claim both sides of it?'

'And Florida. It's a peninsula like Italy, but why don't Georgia and Alabama take their fair share of the Gulf of Mexico?'

'It's as if Greece owned the French Riviera and the Italian coast as well.'

'How did Alabama get a little pinch of coastline?'

'There's a story there. One stubborn Alabaman finally said *no* to the Floridians. Maybe he just wanted a little square of land on the coast no bigger than Rhode Island, but the Alabama legislature forced him to give them his little sliver of land.'

'And what's with Michigan? That part that comes off the top of Wisconsin should be Wisconsin's.'

'Or a separate state. The forty-ninth state.'

'And why isn't New Orleans in Mississippi?'

'New Orleans is in Mississippi.'

'It's *on* the Mississippi, but not *in* Mississippi.'

'I see. You're right.'

'What would you say has the most right angles? Utah?'

'No. Wyoming.'

'What's that all about? Utah should be a perfect square.'

'A circle! Why is no state a circle? Or an oval?'

'Men don't think in circles. They think in squares. Or complications.'

'Women think in circles. If a woman ran America from the jump, Utah would be a perfect bull's-eye. Or shaped like a heart.'

Her husband got a faraway gaze in his eye.

'What is it, Jack?'

'Valentines,' he said. 'The heart. I dreamt about the heart again.'

'You mean Shelley's heart?'

'No, it was Joe's heart. Joe Junior.' He started to sweat, as Joe was his long-dead older brother. 'It was like the dream I had the night before Eisenhower's heart attack. This motorboat came up. I couldn't see the driver. I mean I saw them, but I couldn't take them in. Just like in the Eisenhower dream he handed me an urn. I opened it up and there was a leather black thing inside. *Shelley's heart again?* I asked. He answered me without speaking. I knew it was Joe's heart.'

* * *

In 1822, the great Romantic poet Percy Bysshe Shelley was lost at sea off the coast of Italy. When his body washed ashore, it was burnt in a bonfire. As the poet's corpse popped open from the heat, one of his friends (not Lord Byron) reached into the flames to grab Shelley's heart from his gaping chest.

The poet's heart was later given to his wife, Mary (the author of *Frankenstein*). She kept the heart until her death. She was fifty-three. In 1889, Percy's heart was buried with his and Mary's only surviving son, Percy Florence, who died at the comfortable nineteenth-century age of seventy, living more than twice as long as his father, who died at twenty-nine.

★ ★ ★

'Jack, wake up, darling.'

Jack Kennedy wasn't actually sleeping. He lifted his head.

'I know what your dream meant.'

'The dream about Joe's heart?'

'Yes. After you dreamt about Shelley's heart, Eisenhower didn't die from his heart attack. That dream was only a signal like your dream of Joe's heart. I think it means that Joe died for you so you could go on. It means you're going to make it through the operation.'

'Is that how Freud would interpret the dream?'

'That's how Madame Bouvier, fortune-telling gypsy, interprets the dream. Now go back to sleep. You need your rest. You're going to live forever.'

★ ★ ★

Seattle, Washington.

Buster Hendrix was now in sixth grade. His school had an equal number of Negro and Caucasian and Asian students. Buster still lived in his father's house while his pop lived in taverns like the Shady Spot Tavern on 23rd Street or the Mt. Baker Tavern on 25th and Jackson. The sun set and Buster's house was usually dark—the power bill hadn't been paid. Buster's aunt and uncle then let the boy live with them. His dad began taking in boarders—one was a woman who loved the blues. She had maybe a hundred seventy-eights, including Muddy Waters. Howlin' Wolf. Black men who played electric guitars. Buster would spend afternoon after afternoon at his father's house, listening to her records.

She played them on a record player she wound up like an alarm clock. A record player that didn't need electricity.

This woman didn't own a single Dean Martin LP.

★ ★ ★

Leslie Fiedler's *An End to Innocence: Essays on Culture and Politics* was published. The title essay concerned Alger Hiss, who still insisted that he had been railroaded; he had never been a spy.

Fiedler didn't believe Hiss. Not at all. Fiedler wrote that conclusive evidence proved Hiss was a Soviet spy. This made the left wing's illusion of spiritual innocence invalid. The Left had believed that it was romantic to spy for Russia. 'After all, look at Hiss; his deep social conscience; his love of the worker; all stoked higher by his ultra-earnest wife, Posey, a woman who could not even let a casual visitor call the day *fine* without reminding them of the plight of the American sharecropper.' Furthermore, the Left wanted to believe that even *if* Hiss was a spy, he was only naive. Last year Anaïs Nin presented the world with her novel *A Spy in the House of Love.* The Left believed that Alger Hiss had been a spy *for* the House of Love.

Fiedler argued, *No, no, no! Stalin's government loved nothing.*

Fiedler insisted that the 'liberal principle in the U.S.A. was no guarantee against Evil. American liberalism has been reluctant to leave the garden of its illusion, but it can dally no longer: the age of innocence is dead.'

Dead like the god Pan was dead.

* * *

Whittaker Chambers hated Fiedler's essay. Chambers felt it was 'hosing out the Augean Stables inside the liberal mind by disposing of the duality of both Hiss and himself.' Chambers's mention of the Augean Stables was a reference to Hercules, that Greek strongman who changed the course of two rivers to wash out the manure-jammed stables of a herd of immortal cattle. This classical reference to the cleansing of cow shit appealed to Texans like Senator Lyndon Baines Johnson or that Senator 'Son of the Dairy State' Joe McCarthy. Senator Richard Nixon from California was flat-out enthusiastic over Fiedler's essay, but not because of a love of cows. Nixon wrote the author, 'So much has been written and said about this case, which has completely missed the real points involved, that it was a pleasure for one who was so close to it, as I was, to read the objective analysis which you presented.'

Which seems preferable—to be praised by Richard Nixon and scorned by Whittaker Chambers, or vice versa?

* * *

Georgetown. Jacqueline—Jacks—was sipping iced tea with her sister Lee in the backyard.

'Lee, I have our neighbors scoped out. I haven't met them yet. They're Mary and Cord Meyer.'

Lee repeated their names to get the feel of them. 'Mary Meyer. Cord Meyer. Cord is a peculiar name. Doesn't it make you think of a vacuum cleaner or a church organ?'

'Cord? Oh. Cord is a vacuum cleaner, definitely. And Mary was once Mary Pinchot. A Pinchot girl. Her father was Amos Pinchot the politician—Teddy Roosevelt and whatnot. Amos climbed into a bath-tub filled with hot water in the 'thirties or 'forties, I forget which, and sliced his wrists open.' Jacks held out her arms, her own wrist turned upward.

'Goodness.'

'Dad was discovered in time. There was talk of Dad getting a lobotomy like you-know-who, but nothing came of the talk.'

'What of Cord's family?'

'His blue-blood father had a breakdown and spent some time in a padded sanctuary.'

'Enough with the crazy dads, Jacks!'

'Cord's nickname is Cyclops on account of a Japanese hand grenade blowing out an eye on Guam or Okinawa. He had a twin brother who died on Guam or Okinawa. After the war, Cord worked with the UN to save the world from nuclear weapons. He met Jack in 1945 at a UN press conference in San Francisco.'

'He did? Did Jack ever mention him?'

'No. But gossip says that Jack couldn't stand Cord and vice versa. After San Francisco, Cord became a spy.'

'CIA?'

'CIA.'

'What do you say when you meet him?'

'What do you mean?'

'I mean if he says he's a plumber, do you wink or just nod your head and say, *Interesting*—'

'Only spies in the field have cover stories. Cord works in the K Building. Or maybe the L Building.'

'What are the K and L Buildings?'

'Buildings on K and L Streets, dope. CIA buildings. Buildings where the spies are.'

'Oh.'

'Lee, no one in Georgetown ever asks what the K and L Buildings are, just as no one ever asks what Cord does in Washington. Everyone in Georgetown is in the know. And no spy in Cord's position explains himself because that would suggest that commoners have a right to know.'

'What if you pretend that you don't know he's a spy?'

'Lee, we have to assume everyone in Georgetown is a spy. Last year Cord almost lost his job. Someone accused him of being a Red.'

'Who?'

'No one knows.'

'Oh. The old *guilty until proven innocent.*'

'*Punished until proven innocent.*'

'Enough about Cord. What's his wife like?'

'I hear she loves dancing to the Big Bopper—'

'I heard that James Angleton loves Elvis Presley.'

'No.'

'Yes.'

'So back to Meyer. Mary has an interest in art—weird modern art. She has three boys, Quentin, Michael, and Mark.'

'Will Jack try to fuck her?'

'No. She's too old for Jack.'

'How old?'

'She's probably nine, ten years older than myself.'

At that, a large golden retriever trotted into the Kennedy backyard. Jacqueline and Lee made baby talk to the dog and coaxed him over. Jacqueline read his dog tags. 'His name is Matisse. He belongs to the Meyers.'

'Well, let's bring him back home!'

Jacks took the dog by the collar and the two sisters led the dog out of their backyard and through a small plot of grass and bushes into the Meyers' backyard proper. A plumpish woman was lying on a blanket on the grass. She was sunning herself. Her legs were spread. In the nineteenth century, one would have said, 'She was naked as a robin.' In the twentieth century, the ornithological reference changed for some unknown reason and now both Jacks and Lee would report later, 'Mary Meyer was naked as a jay.'

* * *

Georgetown. Mary Meyer had been raised in a nudist household. She didn't apologize for her nakedness or explain it. 'Oh, you've brought Matisse back. Sorry. He does wander the neighborhood.'

'That's okay. I'm Jacqueline Kennedy, your new neighbor.'

'I know.'

'And this is my sister Lee.'

'I didn't know that,' Mary said. 'Want to join me?'

The sisters turned to each other. 'I think it's not warm enough for me to sunbathe,' Jacqueline said. 'Can I take a rain check?'

The irony of 'rain check' was funny, but not funny enough to laugh at, but then it became funny that they were not laughing and the three women laughed.

'You know you laugh like Marilyn Monroe,' Mary said to Jacqueline. She paused a beat and added, 'You talk like her as well.'

* * *

Saigon. Fifty-four-year-old Ngô Đình Diệm had just been appointed by the French as the premier of South Viet-Nam. His right-hand man was younger brother Ngô Đình Nhu. Because Diem remained single, Nhu's wife, Madame Nhu, was considered South Viet-Nam's unofficial first lady. Diem and the Nhus controlled only one Saigon block, the block that the Gia Long Palace perched on. The real power still lay in the figurehead 'emperor' Bảo Đại, a man who danced whenever the French government clapped. The French allowed Saigon to be clandestinely controlled by the Binh Xuyen gangsters (50 percent), as well as various Vietnamese cults (15 percent) and Corsican businessmen and gangsters (35 percent).

General Duong Van Minh changed this situation.

Duong Van Minh was a Vietnamese educated at the École Militaire in

Paris. He was on the dark side of thirty. The French nicknamed Minh l'Éléphantesque and the Americans Big Minh and the Vietnamese Úi Tiền Đầy (*Fat Boy*), as Minh was six feet tall (a foot taller than 99 percent of the Vietnamese) and weighed close to two hundred pounds (mostly muscle). He had dentures, as Tojo's troops pried out his teeth back in '43. Big Minh's hands were so massive that he escaped from a Viet Minh prison camp by strangling his guard with a single paw at the end of an outstretched arm.

★ ★ ★

In the story 'Franny'—Salinger's wedding gift to Claire—Franny walks into a restroom and sits in a stall and weeps. The story says she's weeping because of the shallowness of her boyfriend. Many critics assumed Franny was crying because she was pregnant.

No. Salinger insisted no.

Salinger, himself, had a Catholic view of pregnancy—when the woman's belly could no longer be concealed, it became a lump advertising Original Sin.

While Salinger's view was typical of that of most men in the U.S.A., Norman Mailer was a member of a small male minority who adored their pregnant lovers and/or wives. Adele and he had careful carnal relations almost to the day of delivery. 'Norman was never disgusted by my big belly,' Adele would say. 'He was always telling me how beautiful I looked. I was the Madonna. Norman would get as excited as I did when the baby moved inside me.'

Neither Norman nor Adele was worried about sexual intercourse giving their baby polio.

★ ★ ★

Saigon.

Big Minh planned to rid Saigon of the Binh Xuyen with 'Operation Rung Sat'—Rung Sat being the yellow silt/saltwater mangrove swamps that surround the Saigon River as it empties into the South China Sea. Big Minh's gangster counterpart was fifty-one-year-old Le Van Vien—nicknamed Le

Vien Bay (*Bay* for *skull* in Vietnamese). Le Vien Bay was the Al Capone of Saigon. He divvied up his Binh Xuyen gang into five fiefdoms: Gambling, Opium, Protection, Harlots, and Governmental Thievery. Each fiefdom had a separate chief. Khan Thanh Quang (only twenty-eight) oversaw the illicit women rackets. Big Minh and his men lured nearly thirty of Khan Thanh Quang's men to a small hotel off Ho Pac Street on the pretext of the men 'interviewing' a group of prospective European harlots. In groups of two and three, Caucasian women escorted each Binh Xuyen member separately into a room where much to his surprise his throat was slit by one of Big Minh's men, the dead or dying one's body then dropped through the shaft of the dumbwaiter down to the basement. Big Minh's men had just started their butchery when Brother Nhu showed up. He wanted to personally kill some Binh Xuyen. He fulfilled his desire by cutting throats and then reaching his fingers inside each wound to pull down the tongue and use his knife to sever it from the jaw.

Later, Big Minh had the tongueless bodies dumped in the basement of a building owned by the gambling supervisor, Tru Tol Fuk. Big Minh's intention was this act would spread mistrust followed by paranoid discord throughout the Binh Xuyen. Brother Nhu had an interesting addition to this plan. He 'fermented' his collection of twenty-five-plus severed tongues in an aquarium filled with yellow swamp water brought from the Rung Sat. The tongues were then placed in a single waterproof suitcase that resembled the suitcases each chief used to send Le Vien Bay his tribute cash. The tongue suitcase was stored in a warm oven for an hour. Next, a boy who was a mute (Nhu's perverse touch) delivered the warm suitcase to Le Vien Bay at his penthouse near Gia Long Palace. The kid signaled Le Vien Bay's guards that he was carrying tribute from the harlot prince, Khan Thanh Quang. It was common knowledge that Le Vien Bay enjoyed opening his tribute suitcases himself. The mute boy was allowed to present his package to Le Vien Bay, who rubbed his hands together before opening it.

The suitcase was filled with severed black tongues.

Each tongue was wagging.

Le Vien Bay smashed the suitcase shut, not noticing that the tongues swarmed with mosquito larva. Le Vien Bay then lost his cool.

Other Binh Xuyen chiefs believed that the black tongues were punishment for someone who had 'talked.' Khan Thanh Quang? Tru Tol Fuk? Le Vien Bay himself? Each Binh Xuyen gang began killing the members of other gangs, then Big Minh's soldiers killed any survivors.

The killings happened so quickly that the French had no time to protect the Binh Xuyen. Word got to the French that Big Minh was turning his sights on them. Thus, on May 8, Secretary of State John Foster Dulles flew to Paris to meet with French premier Edgar Faure. The pair signed a treaty stating that the French would withdraw from Viet-Nam (Cochin China) and the U.S.A.'s 'military advisers' would back Premier Diem. The moment the French troops left, Brother Nhu informed the remaining French Corsicans they would be killed if they didn't flee Saigon in twenty-four hours. Ngô Dinh Nhu detested the French. He would tolerate the newly arriving Americans because they seemed a silly people easy to manipulate.

* * *

Manhattan.

The Mailers were living in a top duplex in a four-story building on East 55th Street between First and Second Avenues. It was furnished in Danish modern and Adele's paintings covered the walls. Mailer had described her work in a letter as 'very modern. You won't be able to make head or tail of them, just color and gobs of pigment . . . really weird . . .'

In 1955, everyone threw parties. The Mailers were throwing a marijuana party at their duplex.

Montgomery Clift was invited. Both Norman and Adele were casual friends with the Hollywood star. When the couple lived in a loft downtown, Montgomery Clift once showed up in blue jeans and helped them spackle the walls.

A few months ago, up on 55th Street, their buzzer spoke in the middle of the night.

It was Montgomery Clift blind drunk.

Montgomery Clift was now thirty-four years old and nearing the end of a three-year Lost Weekend where he had made last year's *Indiscretions of an American Wife*—a stinker not worth the celluloid it was coiled on. On the other hand, when an actor had made *A Place in the Sun* and

From Here to Eternity, his legacy was permanent. Monty would always be an actor's actor.

Montgomery Clift showed up at the party.

The bash was in full swing when he arrived. Norman Mailer was lying on the floor in a living room smoked with primo Early Girl. The writer's big head was lying by the hi-fi speaker, Dave Brubeck's *Jazz Goes to College* spinning on the turntable. Although Brubeck wouldn't write 'Blue Rondo à la Turk' or 'Take Five' for four years, *Jazz Goes to College* contained 'Balcony Rock' and 'Le Souk.' It was semi-cool jazz for white intellectuals.

Brubeck was born the same year as Clift, 1920. Monty Clift and Adele were lying on a stairway. The steps were covered by a white rug.

Norman didn't care about those two. Monty was mostly queer. Besides, the year before, the Mailers went down to Mexico City to visit Mailer's first wife and his daughter. They participated in what would come to be known as wife-swapping.

So, we're with Adele and Monty on that white stairway. The lamp above the hi-fi is on, but everywhere else is dark. All the windows are open. You can see traffic and the lit apartment windows across the street. You can hear the traffic.

Adele stares into Monty's face, that perfect, beautiful face hanging in the dark before her like a tragic saint. Monty flickered the muscles around his eyes signifying deep desire for her, then deep pain—religious pain—poetic suffering, a troubling idea, a Marxist frown followed by the pure joy of inspiration.

Montgomery Clift moved his face closer.

Adele didn't move her face. Monty would have to kiss her first.

Their noses were almost touching. She half-shut her eyes. Nothing happened. She tipped her head very slightly to the right. She felt the warmth of his breath. The damn hi-fi was up so loud she couldn't hear anything but taxis honking and Paul Desmond's saxophone.

Wait. Now the slightest of pressures.

Monty's lips were against hers. Or were they? Their lips were barely touching.

A little movement.

Tentative shadow kisses.

His nose was to the left of her nose. She felt like she was being kissed by a little boy. She reciprocated in the same fashion. She could be as much a child as he could.

Or was Monty kissing her the way he thought a woman would kiss a man? Was Monty imagining Adele was a man? Was Monty imagining that he himself was a woman? Was this a fag kiss? Adele pushed her head forward and mashed and mashed and mashed their lips.

Monty reached up and held her face, stopping her forward motion. She opened her eyes. He wasn't pulling his head away from hers. He was just stopping her. Controlling her head. Their lips were barely touching. She shut her eyes again. She tried to press her face forward but he was keeping her at bay. Their lips were still touching. Now Monty was moving his. It was as if he was trying to speak.

He was speaking. Syllables. Moving his tongue against his teeth.

A diphthong.

Then Monty gently bit her lower lip. Bit her in the pout. And lowered his hands from her face, resting them in her lap. She thrust her tongue out and in between his lips, but now he was clenching his teeth.

She put her right hand around the back of his head and pulled his jaw into hers. She thrust her tongue through his lips against his teeth.

The bastard wouldn't part his teeth.

The woman pressed with all her might, but she got nowhere. She ran her tongue along his teeth, but this made her think of dentists. She pulled back and muttered, 'Damn you.'

'What a thing to say, Adele.'

Then Monty reached behind her head with one hand and pushed her forward, sucking her entire lower lip between his teeth.

She opened her mouth. She felt his tongue dip into her mouth and flick itself down the middle of her tongue and then escape.

She had a vision. This is *wide-screen kissing.*

She stuck her tongue between his lips and he let it poke inside his mouth. He tasted of gin and Lucky Strikes.

For Adele, this was a paradise of osculation.

She flicked her tongue across the top of Monty's tongue. He curled his tongue up to the bottom of hers and pushed it against the roof of his mouth. It was hard like cartilage.

He let her tongue go.

The pair mushed their embouchures together.

They kissed in gentle sucks like fish.

They sucked each other's puckers like bottles of pop.

Adele came up for air and rubbed her cheek along Monty's. She returned to his lips. Adele remembered some woman's magazine said you use thirty-four facial muscles when you kiss.

She moved her mouth away from his and over to the side of his head and nibbled on his earlobe.

He took her head in his hands and tilted it until his mouth was behind her ear. He slowly licked the under-mushroom of her ear. He moved her head once more and mushed lips. She tasted a sweaty and meaty taste. What had he been tasting behind her ear?

Kissing this man had the euphoric tendencies of reefer.

They kept their lips connected and changed positions on the stairs. Siamese kissers. They now stretched their legs down the stairs. Adele reached over and gripped the stair railing and then leaned her weight into Monty's body. She was dimly aware of voices. A crowd. She glanced up. The record was over. She and Monty found themselves taking turns whispering like quiet animals while Norman wobbled to his legs and turned the Dave Brubeck record over and placed the needle on it.

Scratch-scratching then music again.

Adele was now determined not to come up for air until side two had finished spinning.

Chapter 13

Cody, Wyoming, 1955–1956

September in Pittsburgh. Jane Spock began taking the latest thing in tranquilizers, Miltown, so named after a location in New Jersey that was spelled M-i-l-l-t-o-w-n. Miltown with one L was the most modern of modern antidepressants. Those white aspirin-sized tablets were the forerunner of all modern benzodiazepines such as Alepam and Medopam and Murelax and Noripam and Ox-Pam and Purata and Serax—and finally—Serepax.

Users nicknamed Miltown 'Brain Candy.'

Miltown was to 1955 America what LSD will be to the Summer of Love in 1967.

Even TV comedian Milton Berle started calling himself 'Miltown Berle.'

Jane washed her Miltown down with a martini. If anyone pointed out that Miltown and alcohol don't mix, she'd just shrug and say, 'My doctor said it was okee-dokee.'

* * *

Detroit. Robert McNamara's nemesis at Ford had the name of Crusoe (like the desert island castaway, Robinson). When McNamara was in his early thirties at the end of the 1940s, he had been Crusoe's assistant at Ford. Crusoe was middle-aged and short and stocky and had learned the auto industry by the seat of his pants. McNamara was a whiz kid from Harvard Business School. Soon, another old-timer named Beech, who was Crusoe's rival, glommed on to McNamara, that young man wearing grandfather's glasses and buttering back his hair.

McNamara let himself be Beeched.

Yet, McNamara found himself working with Crusoe on that man's baby, a car called the Thunderbird. Crusoe intended it to be the ultimate young man's car. It would be a two-seater. That prompted McNamara to argue, 'Four-seaters always have a better profit margin.'

'But that violates the whole principle of the Thunderbird,' Crusoe wailed. In the end, both two- and four-seaters were made. McNamara's four-seater outsold the two-seater three to one.

By 1955, Crusoe felt the time was ripe for Ford to destroy General Motors. GM ruled the market for mid-priced cars. Crusoe had his designers work in secret and they came up with a car that Crusoe was convinced would capture the zeitgeist of the '50s as they rolled forward into 1960. Crusoe sold the president of Ford, Henry Ford II, on his idea. McNamara in his starched white skirt and skinny tie and glasses and buttered hair thought Crusoe's car was folly. The younger man believed the way to crush GM would be to rule the market for both expensive and cheap autos. Crusoe knew McNamara was his enemy and kept the younger man out of the loop of his top-secret car. McNamara took the quiet position of a samurai.* McNamara knew those executives who followed Crusoe vis-à-vis Henry Ford II would destroy themselves with Crusoe's folly.

Henry Ford II had insisted that the very name of this car must be magic. He hired a research group to come up with suggestions. They first told him that the name of his new car should be short so it would display well on dealer signs. It should have two or at most three syllables to give it cadence. It should start with either the letter C, S, J, or F, letters that would be snazzy stamped on the hood in metallic calligraphic doodads. The name should not suggest double entendres—no jokes about the name like Milton Berle. Finally, and most important, the name should be an American one. Suggestions were: Altair, Ariel, Arrow, Dar, Jupiter, Mars, Ovation, Phoenix, Rover, and finally, Zip & Zoom.

Henry Ford II did not want a comic-book name. He wanted a name with poetry. Henry Ford II was not a poet so he turned to an established American member of that clan born in the nineteenth century, sixty-seven-year-old Marianne Moore.

She submitted a list. Henry Ford II rejected her poetic suggestions.

Finally, Henry settled on a name himself. He may not have been a poet, but he was a member of the Ford bloodline. He found inspiration in his heredity. Seven years earlier, Henry Ford II had named his first son Edsel Ford II, named after Henry's own father, Edsel Ford.

---

* ...with buttered hair instead of a topknot.

★ ★ ★

California. James Dean died in a car crash on September 30. He was twenty-four years old. He had been driving a Porsche 550 Spyder.

This car hadn't been made in Detroit, of course. It was manufactured in West Germany.

The Diet of Worms.

★ ★ ★

Cornish, New Hampshire. Reporters try to invade the Salinger home. Men in fedoras with binoculars can be seen climbing the Salingers' trees—all because the writer has become a notorious media recluse. Salinger is the Greta Garbo of letters. Cornish old-timers resent this newcomer's notoriety. Local cranks begin mailing obscene notes and pictures to the Salinger home.

Cornish, New Hampshire = Yoknapatawpha County, Mississippi.

★ ★ ★

Autumn in New York. Joan Didion is a woman three years younger than James Dean. She is the California-born soon-to-be associate features editor of *Vogue* magazine. It is a brisk Friday evening. Joan takes a cab down to a party on Bank Street in Greenwich Village. During this time, J. D. Salinger's 'Raise High the Roof Beam, Carpenters' has just been published in *The New Yorker.* Salinger's constituency is the types at this ground-floor party—vacant girls who 'do something interesting' for *Mademoiselle* as well as a few tweedy grad students from Princeton. Everyone here is the *young at heart.* Didion is buttonholed by a Sarah Lawrence student who prattles on about Salinger's 'Zen nature.' Because of Salinger, every coed had now pondered that essential Zen koan, 'What is the sound of one hand clapping?' Didion tells the girl, 'I remember a date once asking *What is the sound of one hand clapping?*' She pauses for the punch line. 'I slapped him.'

The girl is confused. 'Because he was being fresh?'

Didion circles away, sipping her glass of vapid unidentifiable white wine. She will later realize that Salinger flattered the essential triviality in all these young Democrats. Salinger was self-help advice disguised as fiction. It was Double Your Energy and Live without Fatigue for Sarah Lawrence girls. To Didion, J. D. Salinger had become a middle-class American guru. Maybe he would start a religion like that science-fiction writer had back in California. What was it called? Sciencetology?

At least J. D. Salinger wrote fine sentences.

Sentence by sentence, Didion felt Salinger could be as good as it gets. The problem was that J. D. Salinger loved his Glass family more than God could possibly love any of us.

* * *

Georgetown. The road that passed the Kennedy property and the Meyers' curved sharply at the intersection. The Meyers' dog, Matisse, was crossing the road at that very intersection and a green car barreled around the blind curve and hit the dog.

A dog is a pet and pets are thought not to be sentient and the car keeps going.

There are three Meyer boys. Quentin is ten, Michael is eight, and the baby of the family is Mark. Quentin is smart and Mark is mystical like Prince Myshkin in *The Idiot*. Michael was the all-American popular kid. Perhaps a future politician.

It is Michael who finds Matisse's body.

Grief hurls itself at him. It is incomprehensible that Matisse is dead. This spot in the road now becomes a magnet of death.

* * *

On October 23, 1955, a referendum is held in South Viet-Nam to determine the country's leadership, a contest between Emperor Bảo Đại and Ngô Dinh Diem. CIA agent Joseph Darwin is in Saigon, talking on the phone: 'Hey, Hunt. This line is secure. Yeah, I'm in Saigon. Listen to me—what a town of weasels. I suggested to old slant-eyes Diem that he provide two ballot papers for the election—red for himself and green for Bảo Đại. Why? I'll tell you. The Vietnamese are the most superstitious people on earth. Red signifies good luck while green indicates bad. But ole Diem didn't bother with ballots at all. He announced that he won the election with ninety percent of the vote. As a result, he is staying in Gia Long Palace with his brother Nhu and the Dragon Lady.'

★ ★ ★

The Dragon Lady was Madame Nhu. Perhaps the term *Dragon Lady* seems both misogynistic and racist, but the term's origin was not.

The Dragon Lady was from a popular 1930s–1940s daily comic strip, *Terry and the Pirates,* which spun out the adventures of a white soldier of fortune in Indochina. During the war, Terry and the Dragon Lady helped the Chinese defeat the Japs.

Madame Nhu, Viet-Nam's very real Dragon Lady, was born in 1924 to a wealthy Hanoi family. Her mother was the cousin of Emperor Bảo Đại. Madame Nhu grew up a tomboy. The girl was raised speaking perfect French. She played piano. She took ballet lessons. As a teenager, her eye fell upon one of her mother's licit lovers, Ngô Dinh Nhu. He was fourteen years older than her. When the girl turned eighteen, she married the thirty-two-year-old. Nhu was Roman Catholic. His new wife converted from Mahayana Buddhism. After the wedding, the teenager was captured by the Viet Minh. According to legend, the Viet Minh believed the girl's piano was really a radio for contacting the French.

Now in the present, Madame Nhu evolved a fiery tongue. Have pity on husband Nhu and brother-in-law Diem. Madame Nhu had screaming fits if she did not get her way. She threw objects at men who made her angry. She adored power. 'I am not afraid of death,' she told a female reporter from Paris. 'I adore power. In the next life, I will have an opportunity to be even more powerful than I am today.'

★ ★ ★

Bad Girls in America who were unmarried knew you could never teach a man what to do properly in bed until after marriage.

Jacqueline Kennedy had been a Good Girl.

Sometimes near the end of husband Jack's sixty seconds of in-and-out,

Jacqueline might give an innocent quiver or gasp and it reminded her husband of the joke, *Honey, are you okay? You moved.* Yet, Jack felt Jackie was innocent the way a good Catholic wife should be. When Jackie said, 'Honey, I'm with child,' Jack was relieved.

He was off the hook for at least a year and a half.

Then Jacqueline had her second miscarriage. Jack's sister-in-law, Ethel, said that Jacqueline was too refined to bear a child. See Carl Djerassi down in Mexico City a few years previously; a flashback here has nothing to do with Jacqueline Kennedy and everything to do with Jacqueline Kennedy. Carl Djerassi was talking about norethisterone on the telephone with a colleague from the north who told Djerassi, 'Basing your career on a drug to prevent recurrent miscarriage would be a mistake.'

'Why?' Djerassi barked.

'Miscarriage has no pizzazz. No one talks about it. It's shameful. It almost always happens at home or in a public bathroom so there are no medical records.'

Djerassi pondered this. 'You are a fool, yet you are probably right.'

⋆ ⋆ ⋆

Detroit, 1955. Crusoe had a heart attack days before Halloween. It would incapacitate him for the next two years. Robert McNamara took over the helm of the Edsel. Much was at stake at the Ford Motor Company over the success of the Edsel. History will repeat itself for McNamara in 1961—he will take over the management of Eisenhower's meddling in Viet-Nam.

⋆ ⋆ ⋆

New Hampshire. Salinger's first baby, Margaret, was born in December of 1955. The birth was successful, yet Margaret was sickly and her father was in a Christian Science phase. No medicine. No doctors. Who or what Salinger invoked when he used prayer as the substitute for medical healing is unknown.

As for Margaret's mother, Claire Salinger sank into a bleak postpartum depression. Her eyes were often as blank as those of fish on ice in the grocery. Dr. Spock advised mothers if they were feeling blue after childbirth that they go to the beauty parlor or a movie.

* * *

One of Jackson Pollock's old friends from Cody, Perry Olive, came to visit the painter at his digs on the eastern end of Long Island, New York. One day the two were walking through a snowless inland field at sunset. It was cold. The two came to a corral containing three white mares. Perry climbed the fence. 'Come on, Jackson!'

Jackson stayed where he was. He watched Perry approach one horse and murmur something in its ear. Next Perry's body did a Peter Pan flip and he was sitting on the bare back of that horse. Perry began singing to the horse—kind of nonsense *la la la la la*. Perry sat straight upright with his hands at his crotch where he communicated with the horse with his fingers. Perry and the horse began cantering in the corral. The corral seemed about the size of the ice-skating rink at Rockefeller Center. Perry rode the mare faster and faster. He wasn't trying to show off. The mare liked letting go. Jackson Pollock watched Perry and the horse. The moon appeared in a rent in the clouds and Perry glanced down at Pollock. In the pale light it appeared as if his friend was weeping.

Again, Jackson Pollock was born in Cody, Wyoming. Throughout his life, Jackson would go through constant cowboy phases. He'd dress like a cowboy. He'd twang up his voice. After he became famous, some people would say, 'Pollock is a cowpoke painter. His paintings are the result of lariats made of paint.' Yet, the truth of the matter was that Jackson Pollock was only a cowboy in his mind.

Jackson Pollock had never ridden a horse in his life.

Jackson Pollock was a man who could get behind the wheel of a car in Manhattan and drive uptown at seventy miles per hour, ignoring the lights, dodging traffic, running other cars off the street onto the sidewalk, ignoring the pedestrians leaping out of his car's path, yet riding a horse, even one saddled up, terrified him.

Perry rode two of the mares and tried to ride the third, but she threw him—*she didn't want no western rider.*

It was after midnight when Perry and Jackson tried to find their way home by moonlight. Jackson never spoke. Perry didn't feel like talking. The latter left Long Island the next day.

★ ★ ★

Los Angeles, California, New Year's Eve.

Howard Hughes was fifty years old and in 1955 allegedly the richest man in the world. Hughes was only *somewhat* reclusive compared to how the man would disintegrate into the Shadow as the years progressed. In 1955, Hughes lived in a bungalow at the Beverly Hills Hotel. He appeared in public, but always under his terms.

Howard Hughes was only as handsome as he needed to be. He had dark hair and a Clark Gable moustache.

For this New Year's Eve, Hughes planned to party with three beautiful women simultaneously, keeping each consort unaware of the others. Hughes had contrived a ten p.m. date with minor actress Jean Peters in the Crystal Room of the Beverly Hills Hotel. Jean was a little over the hill. She was a twenty-nine-year-old with light brown hair with red highlights and sultry lips and a good figure. Hughes planned a second ten p.m. date with movie star Susan Hayward in the Polo Lounge in the Beverly Hills Hotel. She was thirty-eight and not over the hill because she was a serious actress with one Academy Award nomination in her past. Hughes's third date was hidden in a bungalow that he rented for the night. She was fifteen years old.

Hughes planned to spend the evening hopping from one woman to another. This was madness! How would the man accomplish the subterfuge?

Howard Hughes walked into the Polo Lounge and spoke to the head waiter, Roberto. Hughes handed Roberto an off-white pebbled cloth envelope containing a one-hundred-dollar bill and five twenties and ten tens. The hundred was for Roberto, the rest as tips or bribes as the head waiter saw fit. Hughes then checked to make sure his corner table was secure. It stood on the very edge of the outdoor seating. The air was filled with lemon from the lemon trees and cigarette smoke.

The Polo Lounge was already crowded. An occasional girl or woman in a dry bathing suit strolling among the tables.

Hughes then hurried to the Crystal Room. It was huge. Roundish. A dancing floor. A bandstand. A small lemon tree on each table. He raised his head to the ceiling and saw the immense space was covered with nets containing red and white and blue balloons. Hughes found the maître d' and gave a him a dirty white envelope containing two thousand dollars.

Then Hughes walked to the front of the hotel and smoked a cigarette. After a few minutes, a young waiter with a pencil-thin moustache walked out. 'Happy New Year, Mr. Hughes,' he said. Hughes nodded. A taxi pulled up among many taxis and Jean Peters got out. Jean Peters was fifteen minutes late—punctual in her unpredictability.

Susan Hayward was always thirty minutes late.

'Get me when Miss Hayward arrives,' Hughes whispered into the ear of the man with the pencil-thin moustache.

Howard Hughes helped Jean remove her coat and draped it in the coat-check closet of the Crystal Room. Jean was wearing an emerald-green evening dress. Her décolleté was generous. Hughes kissed her cheek. 'You look smashing,' he said.

'You got dressed up too,' she said.

Hughes smiled. He'd been to the barber. He'd taken a bath. He was wearing a Rhumsfeld British tuxedo. Hughes and Jean made chitchat standing until they were led to the corner table. Then a secondary waiter came for their drink order. Jean had a daiquiri. Hughes ordered a gimlet. He knew according to his instructions that the first gimlet would be a virgin.

'Your lip is quivering. What's wrong?' he asked.

'They're making me do another western.'

First, she had been the female star of *Apache*. Burt Lancaster was her lover. They both wore Apache red-face. Next Jean was in *Broken Lance,* a semi-biblical, pseudo-Shakespearian tale about the family intrigues of a cattle baron played by Spencer Tracy. Jean herself played a 'governor's daughter' who was in love with Tracy's 'half-breed' son, Robert Wagner. There were only two female parts in the movie. Jean was window dressing. The Mexican Katy Jurado stole the picture. Now, she—

A new waiter hurried up to the table.

'Telephone, Mr. Hughes. It is Paris.'

'Excuse me,' Hughes said to Jean and walked with purpose from the table. He then hurried through the lobby and rushed down a hallway into the Polo Lounge. He sat in his chair as Susan Hayward entered the restaurant. She was wearing a silver Grecian sheath dress. They kissed on the lips. She slid her hand quickly across his pants where his cock was. They sat down. She caught someone else's waiter and asked for a bottle of Gordon's and a satchel of ice.

'I am so sick of playing an alcoholic, you won't believe it,' she said.

'That alcoholic is going to get you an Oscar.'

'I pray you're right, Howard. I really do.'

'But Lillian Roth was yesterday. Get ready for Genghis Khan. Get ready for John Wayne.'

'I'm ready,' she said.

'Get ready for Cinemascope.'

'I'm ready.'

'Get ready for Mormons.'

She frowned. 'I hear they're blowing up A-bombs in Utah.'

'They are, but I'll get them to stop for the filming.'

'Isn't that dangerous?'

'What?'

'The radioactivifization.'

'You mean the radioactivity?'

'Yeah.'

'It only lasts for a day or two. I'll make sure Dick brings a Geiger counter. I'll get a gold-plated one for you.'

At that moment, a waiter came up. 'Mr. Hughes. You have a call.'

Hughes made a big show of studying the face of his watch. 'From?'

The waiter lowered his voice, 'Washington, sir.'

'Sorry,' Hughes said and touched Susan Hayward's arm and then walked purposefully through the Polo Lounge, giving quick smiles to people at the tables who said, 'Hey, Howard. Happy New Year.'

Howard rushed down the hallway and through the foyer and into the Crystal Room. Jean Peters was paging through the menu.

'Sorry,' Howard said.

'Saving the world again?' she asked.

'TWA,' Howard said. 'Nixon is breaking our balls.' He picked up the menu. 'What are you getting?'

'Lobster.'

'What kind of lobster?'

'The kind with shells.'

'I mean lobster Newburg?'

'I have to watch my weight. A steamed lobster and cocktail sauce.'

'Just that?'

'Yeah, just that. You know, Howard, that's what TV dinners need.'

'Lobster?'

'Yeah, lobster.'

The waiter came up again. 'Telephone, Mr. Hughes.'

'Oh, Christ,' Hughes said.

The waiter said in sotto voce, 'It's Vice President Nixon.'

Howard rolled his eyes and touched Jean's shoulder.

He hurried back into the Polo Lounge. Susan Hayward was smoking and talking to a young trim man in a bathing suit. The young man was sitting in Howard's chair. The young man glanced up and then inspected Susan.

'Beat it,' Howard said. The young man raised his head again. 'I'm Howard Hughes.' The young man smiled at Susan Hayward as he stood up and said, 'See you.'

Howard made sure he was standing ramrod tall. He was taller than the kid in the swimsuit. Hughes noticed two menus on the table. Both were closed.

'Save the world again?'

'Saved the world again. What are you having?'

'I thought I'd wait for you.'

She opened up the menu and began to read. Howard opened his menu too. Then he looked around. The Polo Lounge was very crowded now. The talk was excited. The drunken level of the chatter was escalating. Howard sipped his Virgin Mary. He frowned. The fool had put alcohol in it. Hughes could match Susan drink for drink and Susan kept track of the drinks, but Howard was drinking double tonight. He didn't want to slip up.

They chatted about the menu. Howard asked what Susan thought about each item. At first, she liked the attention. Then she got irritated. Howard said, 'You know the foodstuffs of Salt Lake City are not renowned. I think I'll get the Polo Lounge to ship seafood up to you in dry ice.'

'Will that work?' she asked.

'It works for shipping dead people.'

Then the waiter came up. He oozed with apologeticness. 'It's Washington again. They have your answer.'

Howard just said to Susan, 'Forgive me. You don't know how important this is. Order me lobster, okay?'

'Lobster what?' she called out.

'Just lobster and butter. And another Bloody Mary.'

Hughes hurried back into the Crystal Room. He believed that he could pull this off. He saw Desi Arnaz and Lucille Ball sitting at a table with Bogart and Bacall. He was vaguely aware that Desi and Lucy were a big deal in America. Howard Hughes had no interest in television. He imagined that he would live a full life and then die without ever watching the idiot box.

Idiot box. That's what he called it.

He'd never seen *I Love Lucy.* He didn't realize the shenanigans he was engaged in were pure situation comedy.

Situation comedy was how the suits in New York described *I Love Lucy. The Honeymooners. December Bride. Ethel and Albert.*

Hughes sat down and began lecturing Jean Peters. 'You have to understand about westerns. People who go to them don't care whether they're good or bad. It's like going to a baseball game. The difference between a good and bad western is infinitesimal. People go to a western for American comfort.'

'By why don't you produce westerns, Howard?'

'I made *The Outlaw.*'

'That was about Jane Russell's tits, not cowboys.'

'*Hell's Angels* was a western.'

'What the hell, Howard?'

'It was. The cowboys were riding airplanes instead of horses.'

The waiter came. He looked worried.

Hughes carried off his back-and-forth for three more rounds, including a trip to the john where he ran to the bungalow and playfully tore the clothes off his fifteen-year-old nymphet who was dressed as Little Bo Peep and then told her to get dressed as Jane Russell. But it was not even midnight when Susan Hayward followed Hughes into the Crystal Room. A band had set up and was playing crooner tunes without the crooner.

'Jesus Christ, Howard.'

'Susan Hayward?'

'Are you having New Year's Eve dinner with this S.O.B.?'

'Yes.'

'I am too.'

'What?

'Over in the Polo Lounge. He gets all these phone calls, right?'

Jean nodded.

'He runs between us both,' Susan said, pantomiming with her fingers someone rushing to-and-fro.

'Howard!'

'Yeah. Howard!'

'It's just I couldn't decide which of you would be the most delicious dinner companion. Susan, sit down. Here, Susan, have my chair. I'll get another.'

Howard believed he possessed the genius of a general at war. He was going to pull this off. These two women would eat together, and what—the French have a word for it. *Meang-a-twah?* Marmalade. Margarine. Who gives a goat's ass what the term was? And Howard made this mental leap: How could his fifteen-year-old fit into this fling? Howard was, in fact, a genius of sorts. He could hold all this in his mind. But Susan plucked a live lobster out of a waiter's tray and pulled the bands off its claws and threw it in Howard's lap as Jean Peters rushed away from the table to get her coat.

Susan hated to be part of scenes like this. She walked away.

Howard Hughes ended up with just the kid in the bungalow that night.

Chapter 14

Bloomingdale's (Asylum), Westchester County, New York, 1956

See Jane Spock in Pittsburgh. She was getting more and more out of control. She said inappropriate things at parties. She asked single young women or even teenage girls questions about sex. More and more, Jane was left without supervision as Benjamin was always gone from home giving lectures and talks and signing autographs. Dr. Spock was almost as famous as Frank Sinatra. A poll stated that Dr. Spock was the second most respected American male besides President Eisenhower.

Jane refused to let her husband travel by air. He had to travel by train.

Strangers on a train.

Strangers in Pittsburgh.

Strangers in the Spock bedroom.

As sacred as marriage was during the 1950s, there were two simple ways of ending a marriage short of murder.

A Mexican divorce. Or one in Reno.

Reno, Nevada. Upstate. High desert. It was a cowboy town. There were no fancy hotels. Just good honest craps and blackjack and roulette joints. Even the grocery stores had slot machines. It only took six weeks to establish residency in Reno plus two weeks of paperwork to procure an uncontested divorce, an act nicknamed 'Reno-Vated.' You couldn't get unhitched that quick without a lot of hoopla anywhere else in the U.S.A.

Dr. Spock considered a Reno divorce and then he didn't. He couldn't possibly leave Pittsburgh for eight weeks. There was one other method of dealing with a troublesome spouse and Dr. Spock did it.

He stuck Jane in an asylum.

* * *

Allen Ginsberg's scandalous 685-line vociferation of free verse, *Howl,* begins with this line:

I saw the best minds of my generation destroyed by madness...

* * *

Jane Spock found herself a prisoner in the most sophisticated bughouse in America: the New York Hospital Westchester Division, located about twenty minutes north of New York City. The New York Hospital–Westchester Division was called Bloomingdale's because it was built on land that the blue-blood Bloomingdale family had sold to the state. Bloomingdale's was called 'a country club nuthouse.' Perhaps. It was still a place surrounded by tall spiked fences and privets.

Jane Spock roiled with indignation at her confinement. After all, she was the one who introduced Freudian psychoanalysis to her husband. And twenty-five years later, Ben had the *gall* to stick *her* in an asylum! Back during the Depression, Jane had taken a job working for a doctor who was researching the relation between emotions and contagious diseases. Jane's job entailed conducting and recording the actual interviews with patients. Jane wanted to better understand her subjects so Jane voluntarily went into psychoanalysis herself. At first, that drilling into her unconscious was thrilling. Then Jane began returning to the apartment upset, fried by the process. Jane became so troubled and edgy that Dr. Spock began seeing a head doctor himself so he could understand what Jane was going through.

* * *

A propeller airplane landed one morning at the Reno-Tahoe Airport. A six-foot-three male playwright named Arthur Miller stepped off the airplane. He was forty years old. A hatch opened on the side of the plane and a black man in a one-piece uniform began handing suitcases and miscellaneous baggage to passengers. Miller was handed a valise, sorry-looking because of its slight volume. Miller saw a green Chevrolet waiting for him. The novelist Saul Bellow was standing between the open driver's door and the front seat, resting his chin on his arms, which were resting on the top of the door. Bellow was almost forty-one and had a kind of harmless turtle face. Bellow was also quite a bit shorter than Miller. Both writers were in Reno to get divorces.

'That all you brought?' Bellow asked. Miller nodded.

'Rookie,' Bellow said with just a hint of a grin. Bellow knew the Reno drill. Miller was meeting him in Reno because the two shared the same editor at Viking, who had sent a telegram to Bellow asking for a recommendation for a place for Miller to cool his heels to establish Nevada residency so he could get his divorce. Bellow said that the cabin next to his was vacant. The editor thought the two writers would get along. They were both Jewish. One wrote plays, the other novels, so perhaps they wouldn't be competitive. Both forty-year-olds were at similar levels of success in their careers. Miller was America's premier dramatist next to Tennessee Williams. Miller had written the Pulitzer Prize–winning play *Death of a Salesman* in 1949. Four years later, *The Crucible* opened. As for Bellow, his third novel, *The Adventures of Augie March,* was almost a best seller, but more important, it won him the National Book Award for 1954. As a novelist, Bellow was a bigger deal than Norman Mailer was in 1956.

Miller put his grip into the back seat, and then got in on the shotgun side up front.

'Why do we not want to stay in Reno?' Miller asked.

'Imagine Fourteenth Street rolled up in a ball and dropped in the desert,' Bellow answered. 'That's Reno.' He started the car. The engine rattled. 'As it is, we have to come in once a week for groceries and liquor and laundry, and that is more than enough.'

They drove. 'Besides, there are only two hotels in Reno—the Mapes and the Riverside. No one stays there but tourists. Too expensive.'

Miller noticed that the neon signs in Reno were all lit even at high noon.

'I thought you're from Chicago,' Miller asked. 'How do you know about Fourteenth Street?'

'I taught at Bard,' Bellow said. 'You don't want to hear the rest of it.' He pulled over to Jackpot Market. 'Let's get groceries.'

'We'll live in separate cabins?' Miller asked even though he knew the answer. Bellow affirmed. Miller asked that question so he could take his own shopping cart; they weren't sharing a refrigerator. The two men moseyed down a few aisles together and then separated. Miller's wheel squeaked. They were the only men in the store. They ended up at the checkout at the same time. A few women with their own grocery carts had been trailing them both, taking note of what the men were buying.

Miller filled his cart with a few T-bone steaks, a carton of eggs. Hot dogs. Hot dog buns. Belgian biscuits. And a can of Folgers. A carton of milk and some margarine.

Bellow had a jar of Skippy and a jar of applesauce and a stack of eight different TV dinners along with two rolls of toilet paper and a tube of Ipana toothpaste.

Bellow glanced at Miller's cart.

'Not a whisper of bad breath,' Miller said, quoting Ipana's slogan.

'Better get some salt, sweet-breath. Some ketchup too.' Bellow didn't say anything about toilet paper. 'You drink coffee with crème?'

Miller nodded.

'Better get Mocha Mix,' Bellow advised. 'Milk won't keep for a week.'

'Sure it will.'

'Okay. Suit yourself.'

Miller wheeled his cart away with salt and ketchup and toothpaste and only one roll of toilet paper. Miller had a box of cigarettes in his valise.

The two paid for their groceries. There was a slot machine by the door, but neither man went near it. They got in Bellow's car. It was warm, but not stuffy. Bellow drove down a street and made a turn into a short alley lined with garbage cans. He stopped the car and kept the motor running and got out. He banged on a screen door and called out a word. It almost sounded Asian. Inside, it looked like a kitchen, that of a restaurant. An Asian man in a white paper hat appeared. It appeared that he knew Bellow, who handed the Asian some money. The Asian disappeared and returned with a white bag, such as one you would get from a bakery. Bellow nodded and then circled the hood and got into the car. He put the bag in the back seat with a careless motion. Miller wasn't going to ask. Bellow volunteered nothing and just drove to the Jackpot Laundromat.

Miller tagged along inside this time.

Bellow walked to a still machine filled with clothes and then lugged his wet clothes into a laundry basket. All Bellow's whites were pinkish.

Miller opened the door to the only available dryer. Bellow shook his head and said, 'Come on,' as he headed for the door. Miller held the door and Bellow lugged the wet laundry to his trunk. He balanced the basket on his knee and unlocked the trunk one-handed. He put the basket down over the spare and then rumpled up the clothes. Then he shut the trunk.

They stopped at Jackpot Liquor Store. A real cowboy stood using his hat to catch silver dollars spilling out of his slot machine. Bellow went to the counter and bought gin. Miller bought Scotch.

'It's like we're going into the jungle,' Miller said.

Bellow answered: 'Mistah Kurtz, he dead.'

* * *

Back in 1933, Dr. Spock had just turned thirty and had begun sessions with the thirty-seven-year-old psychiatrist Dr. Bertram Lewin, the founder of the *Psychoanalytic Quarterly.* At first, Dr. Spock mostly talked about his mother. Spock said, 'My mother was born in 1877. My mother was a nineteenth-century Victorian child. As an adult, my mother's judgments were severe. My mother terrified me. I was the oldest living child.... My mother turned me into a mama's boy, really.... My mother made me wear my winter underwear until the middle of spring.... When I was six or seven, my mother tried to teach me to read, but I would confuse f-i-s-h with b-i-r-d. Mother would lose patience and grab me by the hair and shake until my teeth rattled, hissing, *Benny, how can you be sssso sssstupid?'*

* * *

In 1956, Jacqueline Kennedy was pregnant again, this during a year when 4,210,000 babies will be born. Note that when pregnant mothers first skimmed *Dr. Spock's Common Sense Book of Etc., Etc.,* they never skipped a chapter because of gender specificity. No woman knew whether she was having a girl or a boy. The first experiments with sonograms will not happen until 1959. All pregnant women back then existed in a state of Not Knowing, that universal situation since Eve was first with child.

* * *

Nevada. Miller and Bellow left town under a towering sign. Miller turned and read out the back window: WELCOME TO RENO THE BIGGEST LITTLE CITY IN THE WORLD.

Bellow drove toward Pyramid Lake, forty miles north. Bellow turned on his radio. The disc jockey said that the number of divorces in Reno had surpassed Las Vegas and rang a cowbell. Then fiddles and banjo music played.

'I hope you like hillbilly music,' Bellow said. 'There be no swing in Reno.'

Miller just gave a good-natured grunt.

They drove. The landscape was a dull ripple. Rocks. Mountains. All looked fake.

'They shoot giant-bug science-fiction movies out here,' Bellow said.

'Getting any work done?' Miller asked.

'Yeah. Nothing to do but work.'

They mostly stayed silent. The radio was playing a cowboy polka. Then Miller noticed a peculiar house in the scrub. It stood on stilts.

'Are there floods out here?'

'No,' Bellow said.

* * *

They drove through the scrub and over a ridge. Pyramid Lake appeared. Miller had glanced at a road map on the airplane. He figured Pyramid Lake was maybe twenty-five miles long and five to ten miles wide.

'Pyramid Lake,' Bellow said. 'You can think of this as your own Walden Pond.'

Miller grunted.

'This is Pyramid Road,' Bellow said.

They were on the west shore of the lake.

'Why is the road so far from the shore?' Miller asked.

Bellow answered, 'Quicksand. The Injuns take the signs down and hope the fishermen will get swallowed up.'

On the radio, the disc jockey bragged once again that Reno surpassed Las Vegas in number of divorces. Bellow turned the radio off.

They passed a single phone booth.

'Phone booth,' Bellow said. 'You'll get to know it well.'

'The cabins don't have phones, I take it.'

'Nope.'

They drove ten minutes more. Miller saw two cabins coming up, beyond a shabby motel where no cars were parked.

'Shut down,' Bellow said. Miller didn't know what he meant at first. Then he did. 'Just the three owners live there. All old ladies. They got a phone.' Bellow pulled the car between twin cabins. 'The drill is this: If there is an emergency, someone calls the motel. One of the old ladies comes out and lets you know. You run down to the pay phone and call your party.'

Bellow stopped the engine. It went *tick tick tick*, then a quiet rushed into the car that was so sudden that Bellow's and Miller's breathing seemed embarrassing.

Miller opened his door and stepped out. It was quiet enough to hear the swishing of his trousers. Bellow got out as well. He slammed his car door just as Miller was pressing his door closed delicately to preserve the quiet.

Bellow pointed to the nearest cabin. Miller understood that this cabin was Miller's.

It was still too quiet for either man to speak.

There was another cabin kitty-corner from Miller's, obviously Bellow's. Miller lugged his groceries toward his cabin door. It was unlocked. In fact, the door didn't even have a lock. Inside, it was small and stuffy. At least it seemed clean. The furniture was all metal, painted Army green. Miller went to the refrigerator. It ran on gas. He opened it. The light was burned out, but it was cold inside. He filled the fridge. He stepped back to study the result. Miller's groceries were pathetic in their meagerity. They would have looked even worse if the light had worked. Miller then heard the banging of a typewriter coming from Bellow's place.

Show-off.

* * *

The next morning at Pyramid Lake, Nevada.

Miller found a radio and was listening to the news while having a smoke with his coffee. Then he heard human vocalizing. He turned off the radio. It was a man howling in the distance. Miller ran out of his bungalow and cast his vision across Pyramid Road. There was some guy standing on a hill over there. They were facing west so Miller couldn't see the guy's face. Even then, Miller just knew it was Bellow. He was just howling. Miller couldn't make out any words. Bellow wasn't howling in rage or pain, but he wasn't cheering either.

Miller went back into his cabin and turned the news back on.

★ ★ ★

Every morning Saul Bellow walks across Pyramid Road and up the hill and howls his heart out for about an hour. Miller doesn't ask him why. Bellow volunteers nothing. Both become apostles of this Pyramid Lake commorancy. The two type separately, but often in sync, until sunset. The two hit bad patches at the same time and walk outside to have solitary smokes. They're like coeds whose bodies synchronize their periods.

It's so quiet outside that when either one has something to say, they whisper. Sometimes during these quiet and fallow moments, Bellow says, 'Wanna go for a drive?'

They drive. They talk louder now that they're driving. Bellow always turns the radio on. Chatter is okay. He doesn't want a discussion.

They never see another car, going or coming.

They drive past the house on stilts.

'See the hole in the ground under the house?'

Miller looks. 'Yeah.'

'The guy keeps a silver mine down there. He needs money, he goes down and digs up some silver.'

Another time they were passing the stilt house and Bellow pulled to the shoulder. He turned off the radio and the car. 'Listen,' he said.

Miller heard a distant piano playing 'Chopsticks.' It played once. Then again. Then again again.

Bellow started up the car. 'He has a grand piano up there. "Chopsticks" is all he knows how to play.'

There were crazier things. The two saw people shapes in the vast distance that disappeared as if they had fallen into a pit.

'People live in holes out there,' Bellow said. 'Mostly guys on the lam from the law.'

The two don't talk of anything personal. One time they drove into a town on the southeastern side of the lake called Nixon. Bellow began talking.

'Now it comes,' Miller thought. 'He's going to tell me the story of his divorce and the story of his new woman that he plans to marry.'

'I know you were a Trotskyite,' Bellow said.

That utterance surprised Miller. 'How can you tell?' Miller said. 'I might have been for Stalin. Edmund Wilson was. In 'forty he was still writing that the U.S.S.R. was the moral light at the top of the world.'

'Don't kid a kidder. All you New York Jews were for Trotsky. Trotsky girls were all fly-around dames. Me, I was all of twenty-five and I was down in Mexico. A European lady I knew arranged for me to meet the Old Man at his villa.'

'You met Trotsky? I am impressed.'

'I got there just after he'd been attacked,' Bellow said. 'I rode in the ambulance to the hospital. They took him in a room and tried to stitch him up. He had bandages on his head like a dunce cap. His cheeks and his nose and his moustache, even his teeth were streaked orange and black with blood and iodine. His eyes were open and rolled to the ceiling. I looked up too, wondering what he was looking at. I looked back down and realized he was dead.'

'Pennies on a dead man's eyes,' Miller said. He couldn't think of anything else to say.

'That was just it. They couldn't get his eyes shut. They tried everything. For the casket, they laid pigs' eyelids over his eyes. A makeup girl from Warner Brothers flew down to make it look right.'

* * *

Pittsburgh.

Dr. Spock sat in his living room fretting. How was he going to pay for Bloomingdale's? He had just started a company called Spock Projects Inc. He wrote for *Ladies' Home Journal*. He wrote stories about disciplining one's children for *American Weekly*. He still needed more money.

Damn! Dr. Spock couldn't even eat hamburgers anymore as he had a disorder of the esophagus that made swallowing painful at best and often impossible. It was a disorder with a Walt Disney name, 'nutcracker esophagus.'

Spock's phone rang. Spock's editor, Robert F. de Graff, was calling. He wanted Spock to write two additional books. Spock said, 'I will write them if you double the royalties on *Baby and Child Care*.' Robert F. de Graff, born in the nineteenth century, said, 'Sure.'

Nutcracker esophagus was treated by taking Miltown.

A secondary gripe Spock had was the placement of advertisements for baby products in his book. 'I want you to take them out on the next reprint.' Robert F. de Graff, born in the nineteenth century, said, 'No, Benny. They stay.'

* * *

Reno. This is Miller's first supply run into town with Bellow. Again, the latter drives. Something is bugging him, but neither man talks. The two bring their laundry baskets into Jackpot Laundromat. There are women inside. A few bored children. A cowboy standing holding his open hat beneath a slot machine, but nothing is coming out. Bellow and Miller put their laundry in separate machines and drop coins in to turn them on and then drive to the grocery store. This time Miller gets two rolls of toilet paper. He skips fresh meat and gets hot dogs and TV dinners.

A woman comes up and says, 'I can tell by your baskets. You need a woman's touch.'

'What do we need?' Miller asks with a smile.

She starts to say something. Then she puts a finger in her mouth. 'Just a minute. Don't go anywhere.'

She darts down an aisle. She returns with two small tins the size of sardine cans. She give one to each man. 'Here's to Nevada,' she says. 'The leave-it state.'

The men didn't answer. They didn't understand. They were busy examining what she had handed them.

'Leave your money here. Leave your wedding ring. Leave your atom bombs.'

She had handed them tins of rattlesnake meat.

* * *

Later in the car. Bellow said, 'Rattlesnake. That's what Pound is.'

'Pound? Ezra Pound.'

'Yeah. That S.O.B. John Steinbeck wants me to sign a petition to free Pound from the loony bin.'

'Pound is a kike killer by proxy on the radio.'

'Yeah. Screw Steinbeck. Screw Pound.'

Bellow stopped the car at a newsstand. Inside, Miller began snooping around in the bins of magazines. He picked up a *Swank* magazine. Then shook his head. Bellow came up. 'Come on, Tiger. You got seven weeks to go. They don't sell *Playboy* in this burg.' Miller said nothing. Bellow said, 'I got a stack in my cabin you can use.' Without a pause, Bellow added, 'They came with the place. A bunch of old cowboys were staying there before. They even left the issue that has Marilyn Monroe naked.'

★ ★ ★

The two men returned to the Laundromat only to find a short guy with curly hair taking photographs of the washing machine where Miller's laundry is twirling on the final cycle.

'Get away from there!' Miller shouted.

The photographer spun around, alarmed.

'You Hollywood shutterbugs will stop at nothing. You wanna see my underwear, I'll hold it up.'

'No no no,' the guy said. He had an accent and was holding a Leica. 'I have a Guggenheim,' the guy said.

★ ★ ★

On the drive back Bellow said, 'I know that next to Tennessee you're America's foremost playwright, but *Hollywood Reporter* takes photographs of your laundry?'

Miller was still pissed off. 'I don't know.' He rubbed his forehead. 'You just never know these days.'

'He said he had a Guggenheim. Maybe he takes photographs of laundry and then paints pictures of the spinning clothes, sort of like Homemaker Abstract Expressionism.'

They get back to the cabins and Bellow asks Miller over to sit in front of his cabin to have a drink. Miller bought a fifth of Scotch in town, but goes into his cabin to get his almost empty Scotch. Bellow is out front with a fresh gin and tonic.

'Lemme ask you something kind of personal,' Bellow asks. 'When you were with your wife in bed, before the divorce, when it was bad but you were still fornicating, did you ever pretend she was someone else?'

'What do you mean?' Miller asks even though he damn well knew what Bellow meant.

'You know. Pretend you were screwing someone else.'

'Sometimes.'

'Who?'

'You first.'

'Me?'

'Yeah.'

'Mary McCarthy. You know who she is?'

'Sure.'

'You ever see her?'

'Yeah.'

'In the flesh?'

'Yeah.'

'Then you know. She's elegant like a sweet in Rumpelmayer's window. She wears makeup like porcelain. She's witty. She's a sadist. You should see her after she's written a hatchet piece and she glows as if fat Ed[mund Wilson] had just made her orgasm. And so there I am—I am big fat Ed[mund Wilson]. The only way we can do it is if she sits on top of me facing away. So she's bouncing up and down like she's riding a horse and I watch that pucker between the cheeks of her ass and then I raise my head and Mary McCarthy is peering over her shoulder with a kind of smirk.'

Bellow stopped talking and took a breath.

Bellow doesn't tell Miller this, but Mary McCarthy was the head of the judges that awarded Bellow the National Book Award.

Then Bellow asks, 'Who do you pretend you're screwing?'

'Marilyn Monroe,' Miller answered.

Bellow looked over. 'In your dreams, friend.' Bellow shakes his head. He is disappointed how common Miller's fantasy was.

* * *

Dr. Spock's father, Benjamin Ives Spock, died in 1931 at age fifty-eight. In modern terms, that's akin to death at seventy-eight. Dr. Spock's psychoanalyst, Dr. Bertram Lewin, asked his analysand about his dreams. Ben Spock answered that he dreamt exclusively about his dead father. Although that father spent more than half his life in the twentieth century, the man was a distant and imposing nineteenth-century-style patriarch. 'The giant Cyclopes in my dreams were father figures,' Ben said. Lewin then said, 'Freud said that the most basic rivalry is what the boy, the son, feels toward his father. This is all unconscious, mind you.' Dr. Lewin speculated that as a boy Benny had been more fearful of his father than his mother, even though his father had never displayed anger toward his son.

'That sounds absurd,' Spock said.

'No, no, no, it's not absurd,' Dr. Lewin responded. 'I see it all the time with children and their fathers. When the father has no part in disciplining the child, the boy inflates his father's hidden anger in his mind. It balloons into a huge fearful monster. And the child lives in fear of Daddy.'

* * *

Lake Pyramid, Nevada. One morning Bellow walked down from the hill where he had been howling and saw a truck parked beside the cabins. There was a camera set up. Arthur Miller was talking to a guy holding up a microphone. The two were finished by the time Bellow got down. Miller was already back in his cabin. The two guys were carting their camera back into the truck. In 1956, news cameras were huge, as awkward as refrigerators.

'What's happening?' Bellow asked.

'We had to interview this Miller guy.'

'Why? What's he done?'

'He's going to marry Marilyn Monroe.'

Bellow made him repeat it.

'Walter Winchell broke the story.'

The truck drives away. Typing begins coming from Miller's cabin. Bellow goes into his cabin. Typing starts. Then stops. Bellow goes into the closet that is filled with *Playboys*—him searching for the one with Marilyn Monroe.

The sun is going down. Miller has stopped typing for about an hour. Bellow stands in front of his cabin.

'Come on out, Miller. You can't hide in there forever.'

Miller comes out.

'What's this I hear about you shtupping Marilyn Monroe?'

Miller grins.

'Oh, don't act coy like a girl. You're proud as shit. Does she have sweet tits?'

Miller closed his eyes, then opened them. 'Yes. Marilyn has sweet tits.'

'What's she like?'

'What's she like? She's a girl. She's like an orphan. She was an orphan. She goes to a party and can always tell the ones who had been orphans too. She can always tell adults who've been orphans like her. It's a lonely look in their eyes.'

'I don't think you can be an orphan like you were as a child.'

'What do you mean?'

'Childhood is temporary, but once you're an orphan you are always an orphan.'

'Marilyn says that orphans have their childhoods stolen.' Miller turned away from Bellow and said, 'Marilyn is a born Freudian. She doesn't believe in accidents of speech.'

'She believes in Freudian slips?'

'Yeah. And she has no common sense. I don't mean that she has no common sense because of Freudian slips, I mean she's in a state of naiveté. She believes she can tame a rabid dog. It's perceptive naiveté.'

'But what is she like in bed? She's famous!'

'Marilyn says the famous are like balloons in the sky. *Look at their freedom! Shoot them down!* You know sometimes she's like a woman combing her hair with a pistol. I met her before she was famous.' Bellow said nothing. 'Back in 'fifty-one, I took the *Super Chief* from New York to Hollywood. I was going out for a script, but it was a vacation from my wife, the kids, everything. Elia [Kazan] took me to the movie studio. Marilyn was shooting a scene. It was one of her first pictures. *As Young As You Feel.* She was wearing this black veil and had to walk across the room and she walked one foot in front of another. Those hips. That backside. I was a goner. The next night they threw a party for me—you know, famous young playwright here from New Yawk. She was there. We danced together. We talked. I told her she should act on the stage. No one had ever taken her seriously before. I left the next day. Actually, right after the party I went and got my suitcase and waited eight hours at the train station.'

'Why?'

'Because I would have called her. I would have taken a taxi over to her place. We did write to each other—her in Hollywood and me in Brooklyn. I remember writing to her saying that if she needed someone to *look up to* she should go after Abraham Lincoln. Then she came to New York last year.'

'That's when it started?'

'Seeing each other?'

'Sleeping with each other.'

'Yes. But sleeping is not really what we are doing.'

'So what is she like?'

'I've been trying to tell you that.'

'Come on, smarty-pants. What is Marilyn Monroe like in bed?'

Miller didn't say anything.

'Come on. Man to man.'

'Sweet enough to eat.'

'Come on. *Mano a mano.*'

'Her fingernails are always filthy,' Miller said.

'In bed?'

'Yeah. Sure. All the time. Lint. Grime. Grease.'

'Grease? How does a woman get grease under her nails?'

Miller gave an earnest shrug. 'My God, I don't know. But if it is possible to get grease under her nails, Marilyn will find a way.'

* * *

Paris, France. In the lobby of Cinémathèque, one of the three cineastes says, 'I read that Dean is sick of being Jerry's straight man.'

Someone else, perhaps Godard: 'I read that one of their spats went, Jerry Lewis: *Dean, I love you.* Dean Martin: *You can talk about love all you want, but to me you're nothing but a dollar sign.*'

'But who knows? The newspapers say the breakup is official. Yet the pair are shooting a new movie called *Pardners.*'

'What is a *pardner*?'

'I don't know. It is a western.'

'Ah. I get it. It is how *américain* cowboys pronounce *partner*. You know the dubbed shit we see here—the cowboys are all calling each other *Monsieur* this and *Monsieur* that.'

'Monsieur Jesse James.'

'Monsieur Billy the Kid.'

'In the original *américain* version,' Jacques Rivette says, 'it's *pardner, hombre, desperado*.'

Jacques Rivette will one day direct his own movies like Truffaut and Godard, but he will never be as popular or as important. Rivette's first film will be two hours and forty minutes long. Rivette's second film will be four and a half hours long. Rivette's third film will be twelve and a half hours long.

* * *

One of J. D. Salinger's tropes in his *New Yorker* stories was that madness was the chief temptation of modern life, especially for the young. Tell that to Jane Spock. There is conflicting testimony whether or not she received electroconvulsive therapy. In 1956 lingo, this was called shock treatment. Zap job. Getting steady with Reddy.

The room where Jane would have gotten the juice likely smelled like a gas station garage. All zap rooms smell the same.* Jane would have been instructed to remove her shoes and hose. She would then climb onto the table and fit her back and limbs into a shallow body-shaped indentation. A nurse would take off Jane's Princess Oyster watch. Then Jane's wrists and ankles would have been clamped to the table. The nurse would smear graphite salve on Jane's temples. Jane may have joked, 'Smells like suntan lotion.' Then the nurse would put the headphones on Jane's head, and ask her to open her mouth and bite down on a piece of rubber hose. Then a technician would switch on the juice. There's no way to describe what one's mind and body go through.

---

* No one ever identified the source of the filling-station ambience.

I sing the body electric.

Jane Spock's body would have shot upward, only the wrist clamps and ankle straps keeping her from hitting the ceiling. She would start peeing in her pants.

* * *

I saw the best minds of my generation destroyed by madness . . .

One of Allen Ginsberg's patriarchal poets and sponsors was Dr. William Carlos Williams. This man had been so beaten down by the controversy surrounding his appointment to the Library of Congress that he committed himself to a small asylum in New Jersey called Hillside Hospital. Williams swallowed all the pills the doctors and nurses and wards asked him to take. He was released in just two months.

* * *

Pyramid Lake, Nevada. This is what Walter Winchell announced on the radio: 'America's best-known blond moving-picture star is now the darling of the left-wing intelligentsia, several of whom are listed as Red fronters. Playwright Arthur Miller, reportedly next husband of Marilyn Monroe, will get his marital freedom in two weeks. Next stop trouble. The House Un-American Activities Committee subpoena for Arthur Miller will check into his entire inner circle, which also happens to be the inner circle of Miss Monroe, all former Communist sympathizers.'

Miller getting a subpoena.

Miller has befriended more than a few Nevada cowboys, yet he is immune to western mythology. He can't think of a single Jewish cowboy. One of the Nevada folk tells him that a Jew cowboy is one who sells horses to be made into Hanukkah candles. This is the truth, not a joke. The only cowboys left in Nevada catch wild horses that are then butchered into dog food. Now that the news is out that Miller is a Red, the dramatist worries that his good standing in the cowboy community will evaporate. Miller might even get a shellacking. Then one cowboy offers to fly Miller to the man's vast Texas ranch to hide out and ignore the subpoena. It turns out this cowboy had once served under the writer Dashiell Hammett in the Aleutians, that finger of islands off Alaska. The cowboy never forgave what HUAC did to Dash.

Cowboys have a code and they live by it.

* * *

Saigon.

Madame Nhu, Diem's sister-in-law, was a schizophrenic bluestocking. The woman took it upon herself to police the morality in Saigon. She instituted morality laws outlawing abortion, adultery, divorce, birth control, dancing, beauty pageants, boxing, and cockfights. She was called Queen Bee behind her back. She also wore risqué décolleté gowns, unfitting for such a prude. One afternoon when her brother-in-law Diem was taking a studious photograph of a dead beetle belly-up on a large white mushroom the size of a dinner plate, Madame Nhu entered the room dressed in only a pale blue scarf wrapped around her hair. She revealed raised and remarkably pointy breasts. A young boy's buttocks.

'You must take photographs of my classic flesh,' she commanded her brother-in-law, the president.

Diem had no desire to do so. Madame Nhu picked up a jar of developer with both hands and raised it above her head and threw it against the wall. It smashed in a splash.

'Calm down,' Diem said. 'Stand over here.'

She did. The wall behind her was white and empty. Diem took one, two, three photos—never asking her to move or smile.

'This is silly,' she finally said.

The woman had a blue silk scarf tying up her hair that she untied and then began playing with it. It was semitransparent. Madame Nhu took it upon herself to press the scarf against her breasts. Under her breasts. She posed like a seasoned trollop. Diem knew that no matter how much Camus he read, he would never understand Nhu's wife. His poor brother couldn't even divorce the woman because she had seen to it that divorce was now illegal.

* * *

Rumor has it that before Miller's divorce was finalized on June 11, he heard from the chairman of HUAC, Francis Walter, who said if Marilyn Monroe would pose for a photograph with him, he'd waive Miller's hearing.

'Do you want her nude or wearing clothes?' Miller asked. Walter sputtered. Miller told Walter where he could stuff his whatnot. Miller then tracked down the federal process server hunting for him through Reno.

'Give me the fugging papers,' Miller told him.

The guy did. Miller's subpoena was printed on pink onionskin. Was this a bureaucratic coincidence—pink? Pinko.

* * *

In Seattle, Buster Hendrix finally got his first guitar. A piece of junk, really. Barely functional. A wooden 'cowboy' acoustic guitar that only had one string. The E string. Lord, one string or not, Buster worshipped that guitar. By tuning the single string between slack and tight, he could pluck out one and a half octaves. He could play simple melodies. By changing the tautness of the string while plucking it, Buster made weird tonal blends that sounded Japanese.

* * *

Bloomingdale's, New York State. Jane Spock inside the madhouse:

> *Daddy!* My first analyst in Manhattan—I only talked to him about my father. When I was a young girl, Father contracted syphilis. Father died a raving lunatic in a padded cell in some asylum—a Vincent Price kind of place; dark stone; bars on the windows; the whole place reeking of disinfectant.
>
> So here I am inside the prestigious Bloomingdale's. There are rubber rooms here. Also two gymnasiums and a dozen tennis courts and even a golf course. There are two nurses for each patient. Did I tell you about Miss Eustace?
>
> I was surprised to find there were no stairs inside Bloomingdale's. No steps anywhere. Just inclines. (So patients cannot trip.) A nurse, a horse-faced blonde, escorted me to my room. My room was small,

smaller than a motel room. The horsey nurse unpacked my suitcase and stacked everything on empty shelves along one wall. There is no closet in my room. The nurse never turned her back to me.

The only substantial piece of furniture is my bed. My bed is narrow and very high. There are no stairs inside Bloomingdale's, yet if one was to fall out of my bed, you would break your arm. Or worse. Off to the side of the room is my bathroom. There is no bathroom door, just a curtain. There is a Japanese toilet—a metal hole in the floor. A ceramic alcove with a shower nozzle. A metal sink with very tiny faucets. The water flow dawdles. If one were to get hold of a razor and cut one's wrists, the water flow would do nothing to accelerate the bleeding. The bars of soap are only as big as matchbooks.

There is no garbage receptacle in my room, only a brown grocery bag with the top folded down. Every day a woman takes the bag away and leaves an empty one. She takes the empty bag and folds it closed and then sticks an index card with my room number on it at the fold and staples the whole thing shut. I assume a doctor will go through my garbage in the morning.

There is no radio in the room. No clock. At least my window opens. There is a metal screen that is securely bolted across the front of my window.

None of the nurses ever turns their back to patients. At bedtime, the nurses all wait until everyone is in their room, then the doors locked from the outside. Did I tell you about Miss Eustace?

There is one pair of twins in Bloomingdale's. The Miller twins—Margaret and May. I've been told that once one could tell them apart because Margaret Miller was crazier than her sister. Then May became just as bad. Now no one can tell which sister is which.

Bloomingdale's has a freelance Swiss psychiatric nurse with an amazingly high reputation. Her wages I hear are astronomical. Her name is Miss Eustace. She believes in God. Miss Eustace knows judo. I wanted to provoke Miss Eustace so I began refusing food. On the third day of my fast, Miss Eustace force-fed me by tube.

* * *

Connecticut. When Henry Luce first began publishing *Time* in 1923, he wanted his magazine to 'appeal to every man and woman in America.' Some thirty years down the road, even Norman Mailer read *Time*. The Mailers were now living in Connecticut and had *Time* delivered weekly to the mailbox of what Adele always described as their 'large white saltbox [house] with five bedrooms.' *Time* was published every Monday. The February 20 issue had a cover story on the governor of Ohio and inside a story on 'Art: The Wild Ones.' The latter article began, 'Advance-guard painting in America is hell-bent for outer space. It has rocketed right out of the realms of common sense and common experience. That does not necessarily make it bad. But it does leave the vast bulk of onlookers earthbound, with mouths agape and eyes reflecting a mixture of puzzlement, vexation, contempt.' Mailer kept reading. The story claimed 'the bright young proconsul of the advance guard' was Jackson Pollock, aka 'Jack the Dripper.' Pollock was now forty-four years old—eleven years older than Mailer. Mailer had no idea that the art world already considered Pollock a has-been. *Time* magazine certainly didn't say so. Later that day, Mailer asked his wife, Adele, for a big canvas and some enamel paint.

'I want to paint a Jackson Pollock.'

Pollock's trademark style was a cultural cliché so no one in their right mind would try to imitate him. But Mailer did. He had cans of enamel and stood on a stool and poured paint on the canvas. Black and blue and red.

'There's nothing to this,' Mailer said.

He was wrong. When Pollock was at his most masterful, he painted the way Balanchine danced. Pollock arced his body. Pollock flung paint from wooden sticks. Pollock understood gravity and paint, and adjusted his wrist from the floor accordingly as he circled the canvas flinging paint. Splattering. Dribbling. Pollock kept his head cocked. His elbows bent. One arm extended dripping paint. The kineticness of his body created a painting. What was up? The bottom of the painting? The side? The paint swirled and boomeranged. Pollock created arabesques inside arabesques. Know that Pollock was not a prisoner to spontaneity. If necessary, he'd retouch the drips and splatters with his brush.

Mailer was clueless about Pollock's technique. When push came to Mailer's shove, the writer agreed with *New York Times* art critic Howard

Devree, who recently proclaimed that Pollock's paintings looked like 'depictions of baked macaroni.'

Adele watched her husband painting and suggested that he should pee on the canvas like Pollock supposedly did.

Mailer didn't unzip. He finished his imitation Pollock and then told his wife that now he was going to do a Picasso. He'd paint a nude of her by memory. Mailer finished that painting in ten minutes. Then he took his pants off. Adele helped him make a plaster cast of his scrotum and his angry erection.

* * *

Back in Manhattan. Ruth Kligman was a painter who worked in a small gallery.

It was a Monday night roughly two or three weeks after the *Time* magazine with the Jackson Pollock article had appeared when Ruth walked into the Cedar Tavern in Greenwich Village. It stood on the east side of University Place between East 11th and 12th Streets. The Cedar Tavern was the watering hole for famous action painters such as de Kooning and Kline and Motherwell and Aristodemis Kaldis.

Also, Jackson Pollock.

The Cedar Tavern had become a bohemian tourist attraction with the tourists coming to see Pollock the Action Painter in his natural habitat. Everyone seemed to know that every Monday Pollock drove into Manhattan from Long Island for a session with his psychiatrist. The paint flinger then stopped at the Cedar for a bout of liquid happiness.

To Ruth, the Cedar was small and crummy. There was a long bar along the north wall. The walls were painted pea-soup green and the lighting was jaundice yellow. No tourist realized that the action painters hung out here because it was an anti-Parisian café. It was American faux working class. Ruth was meeting some artist friends here and they hadn't arrived. The woman sat in the booth and nursed a stinger. Then the noisy bar sucked into a hush—

Jackson Pollock had just walked in.

Ruth didn't think he looked like much. He was bald on top. He had a bongo beard that emphasized the fat under his chin. Pollock's eyes immediately zeroed in on Ruth. He saw her as a meaty woman. Pollock ordered a drink at the bar and strode directly to her booth and sat down without an invitation and began drumming his nicotine-yellow fingers on the table as the pair made chitchat. Ruth had a throaty Bad Girl voice. Pollock talked through his nose, but his nasal voice was articulate. Ruth was articulate as well.

Still, they left separately.

It took two weeks for Ruth to connect with Jackson Pollock again. But now here they were in Ruth's bedroom, the full moon visible through the window facing Jane Street. Ruth was naked and so was Pollock, taking turns chugging from a bottle of cheap merlot. Ruth had a sloppy voluptuousness about her. Jackson Pollock looked sloppy naked, but back then men could get away with pudge.

Ruth had been raving to Pollock about his black and white paintings of the past two years.

'I painted those on cotton duck with basting syringes,' Pollock said.

'Some of them remind me of Basho.'

'Bash-oh? Who dat?'

'A Japanese monk who dipped his long hair in an inkwell and then shook his head over a sheet of rice paper and—'

'Then *wa-lah,*' Pollock interrupted.

'Yeah, a painting.'

'No,' Pollock said. 'A Basho.'

'Anyhow, your paintings with blue and pink and black show that black is a real color.'

'Who first said "black is a real color?" Greenberg?'

'Matisse. Greenberg said your black and white paintings were controlled chaos.'

'They were chaos controlled,' Pollock said.

'What's the difference—semantics?'

'No.' Pollock reached out his hand, the pointer finger curled against his thumb, and then like a kid playing marbles, he thwacked her nipple.

'Hey!' she said.

'Before God created the world, there was chaos. He created the world by controlling that chaos.'

Then he squinted as if he was seeing her room for the very first time—

the vanity; an ironing board propped against the wall; the novels by Henry Miller and Anaïs Nin stacked on the floor. Pollock suddenly shouted, 'I see a red door and I want it painted black!'

The door to Ruth's closet was firehouse red. Pollock jumped naked out of bed and ran to the closet door and opened it. There were dresses hanging inside and a shoe rack attached to the back of the door. The back of the door was natural wood. 'Do you have any black paint? Black enamel?' Pollock asked.

'Maybe,' Ruth said. She hopped out of the bed naked and knelt and stuck half her body under the bed. Her buttocks were hoisted to the ceiling and Pollock appraised them with pleasure. She slid a sea chest out from under the bed.

'My utilities,' she said.

Pollock disconnected the shoe holder from the back of the door and laid it on the bed. He did this as delicately as you could expect a man to do it. He glanced down at Ruth's open utility chest and saw a hammer, a few nails. A wrench. Some steel wool.

'For mice?' Pollock said.

'Foremice?' she asked, pronouncing the two words as one.

'*For mice*, I said. The steel wool?'

She was confused and then she was not. 'Yeah. Mouse holes. Here's something! Here's some black enamel. And a paintbrush.'

'I don't want a paintbrush,' Pollock said. 'You have a baster?'

'You mean like for a turkey?'

'Yeah.'

'Lemme check.' Ruth got up and ran into the kitchen. Pollock ran after her. He found that he wanted to watch everything this naked woman did. He realized that he was following her with the open bottle of merlot. What else to do but take a swig?

'Yeah. I got one.' Ruth pulled a plastic baster out of a drawer. The syringe was clear plastic and the squeezer was a rubber yellow bulb.

He took the baster and handed her the merlot. They both ran back into the bedroom.

'You got a screwdriver in that chest?'

She looked. 'No.'

'Okay.' Pollock opened the red closet door and stood inside it saying,

'I'm too excited to think reasonably.' He carefully slid the fingers of his left hand into the hinged side of the door. 'I have more finger room if I pull it out this way,' he remarked. She wasn't sure what he meant. He gripped the open side of the door with his right hand. 'I only started three paintings this year. I didn't finish one of them.' Then Pollock gave a tremendous grunt and ripped the door toward the right, yanking it and the screws out of the doorframe. There was clutter on the floor that he kicked out of the way with his bare foot before he leaned the door, red side out, against the wall.

'Sorry I had to tear it out, but maybe once I get started I'll want to turn it lengthwise or upside down.' He tried to open the enamel can. The top was stuck. 'Greenberg goes after me because I'm not doing *easel painting.*' Pollock got the top unstuck and opened the enamel and removed the yellow squeezer from the top of the baster and used that end to stir the paint. 'Look, Picasso never stopped doing easel paintings. Picasso is God over all of us.'

'You love Picasso?' Ruth asked.

'I dream of Picasso every night,' Pollock said. 'I dream he's hanging outside my window upside-down like a bat.'

Pollock put the yellow bulb back on the baster and stuck the inhaling end into the enamel while pinching the yellow squeezer tight. He then released the yellow squeezer and black enamel propelled itself up into the syringe as if the paint was alive and eager to get started. Pollock moved to the detached red door and quickly jerked his arm to squirt a black arc.

'Clement Greenberg said my black paintings were figurative.' Pollock sneered. 'I was dealing myself out of the mainstream of action painting.' Pollock stepped back and quickly squirted a blob at maybe ten o'clock inside the circle. 'I was never in the mainstream of action painting.' Pollock then said, 'I *am* action painting,' as he squashed the black blob of paint with his thumb. 'You paint an oval with some doodad inside it and it instantly reads as a head. But is this a head? No. It's a circle with some paint inside the boundaries.'

Ruth laughed.

'I started painting this way to show up all those kids who think it's simple to splash out a Pollock.'

Ruth said, 'I read Greenberg saying the danger of your recent work is that it is too close to decoration like wallpaper.'

Pollock stopped studying the red door and snaked his head in different directions to scrutinize the room. Next, he ran out into the hallway. Ruth had a kitchen and a bathroom and the room where her TV was plugged in. She heard Pollock hurrying into all of them before he returned to the bedroom and began squirting a zigzagging swirl of paint on the red door.

'What were you doing?' Ruth asked, raising the merlot to her mouth.

'Looking to see if any of your rooms have wallpaper. I want to do those walls next.'

'I have no wallpaper.'

'I know that. So this red door is it.' He gave a squirt of the syringe to the top of the door. Then he used a finger to give the blob a flagellum.*

'That reminds me of your black sperm painting.'

Pollock spun around. 'My what?'

'Your black sperm painting. That painting with all those little black squiggle shapes swirling through the air. They looked like little black sperm.'

'My sperm is not black,' Pollock said, turning back to the wall.

'Prove it.'

'I'll need help.'

'I'm Miss Handy-Dandy.' Ruth turned Pollock back around and then knelt and put his penis between her lips. It was already slightly swelled. It crossed her mind that he should paint the red door using his phallus. This idea stayed in her head for only a moment. As Pollock stood above her and digested with his awareness what her lips were doing, he mused using his pecker as a paintbrush and immediately rejected this amusement. Black enamel was murder to get off one's fingers. The last thing a guy wanted to do is be scrubbing his genitals with turpentine to get rid of all that black enamel.

Pollock said, 'Follow my hands, baby. I'm going to turn us around.' They maneuvered together so now Pollock was facing the red door while Ruth bobbed below him.

'I'm really going now, baby,' Pollock said, aiming the baster. 'I want to see this red door black as night. I wanna see the moon blotted out from the sky.'

---

* The tail of a sperm.

Before Pollock squirted the baster, he heard a noise from outside. *Clop clop clop.* 'Ruth! Hear that? Hoofbeats!'

Pollock stepped backward, pulling his erection out from between Ruth's lips. He rushed to the bedroom window where a streetlight stood illuminating his naked body as if he were an exhibitionist. Pollock focused down three stories to Jane Street.

Where was the horse?

And then Pollock saw it. Down on the street walked a horse. It was brown. Pollock had no idea what breed it was. Ruth was now standing naked beside him. A policeman was riding the horse. He had his holsters and a billy club around his waist and was wearing the style of helmet that Pollock had only seen polo players wear.

'Cossack!' Ruth spat out.

Pollock thought she was nicknaming his penis.

Pollock gaped at this horse and tears poured from his eyes. There was nothing more beautiful than this sight. Ruth saw that Pollock was crying and turned away. And then looked back. Ruth Kligman was incredibly touched. Men wept in the Torah. Men wept in the Old Testament. Men did not weep in Manhattan. This was not an age where men did anything other than lead with their chins and their dicks. Jackson Pollock's tears were this man baring his soul against this American decade of the 1950s.

She shoved Pollock onto her bed.

Ruth was a modern girl who kept condoms in her nightstand. She wished that scientists would invent a pill or something that would defuse a guy's little critters before they left his testicles.

'Why you frownin', baby?' Pollock said.

She didn't answer and slid the condom on him and blotted out the mechanics of birth control like the moon with their rutting. Before Pollock left before dawn, he showed her his spunk sack.

'Ick,' she said. 'Get that thing away from me.'

'See? White as snow.'

'What?'

'Not a single *noir* sperm in evidence.'

Chapter 15

Long Island, New York, 1956

Dr. Spock was the keynote speaker at a pediatrician convention held in Dallas, Texas, so he was forced to skip his weekend visit to Jane at Bloomingdale's. The Texan in charge of the convention picked Dr. Spock up at Love Field and drove him to his hotel, the Adolphus. They were walking through the lobby when the Texan said, 'I've got an actual Texas oil tycoon who is dying to meet you. His name is H. L. Hunt.'

'Achel Hunt?'

'Yeah. H. L. Hunt.'

'What kind of name is Achel?'

'What? Oh, I see. No, his name is the initials H and L. Like D.A. for district attorney. Or L and M cigarettes.'

'What does H and L stand for?' Spock asked.

'Damned if I know. Everyone calls him Hunt. The point is that Hunt really wants to meet you. It's about his kids. Two of them are nuts. Like bedbug nuts. Wait, here he is now. I'll introduce you.'

A very tall and paunchy older man was sitting on a couch in the lobby. He stood up and was even taller. He had the stance of a man born in the nineteenth century. He had that Texan larger-than-life visage.

'Come hither and sit down,' Hunt said, lowering himself to the couch. He patted the large empty space beside him. Spock sat down.

'Do you play cards, Docker Spock?' he asked.

Spock shook his head.

'That's too bad,' Hunt said. He said it as if Dr. Spock had said one of his children had died. 'Hunt doesn't fiddle-faddle, Docker Spock. Hunt has two children who have problems with their sanity.'

'I'm sorry to hear that.'

Hunt raised himself from the couch, and then dropped to his knees on the floor.

'Hunt's first problem is his son, Hassie. The other is Hunt's daughter, Haroldina. They have different mothers. What is the odds of that?'

'Both having problems with their sanity?' asked Spock.

The kneeling man nodded, and then said, 'Come down hither with Hunt.'

Spock resisted and then found himself kneeling on the floor. He believed that Hunt was going to ask him to join in prayer. Instead, Hunt lowered his chest toward the floor and supported himself with his hands.

'Docker Spock, you ever creep around like a baby?'

'No,' Dr. Spock said.

'It's invigorating. You don't know anything about babies until you've crept a bit.'

Hunt started crawling from couch to couch. There were well-dressed Texans in the room. They all ignored Hunt as if they'd seen his act before. Spock raised himself and sat back down on the couch.

'There are some who believe that instability of the mind can be inherited,' Spock said to Hunt.

'Hunt is not crazy,' the big man on his knees said over his shoulder.

My God, what a huge ass that man has! 'Such things can skip a generation,' Spock said.

'Hunt's father was not crazy,' the crawling man said, now heading back toward Spock. 'Neither was Hunt's mother. They were different for sure. Hunt's father fought for Jefferson Davis in the War between the States and Hunt's mother was a nurse for the Yankees in Illinois. But they were not crazy.'

Hunt turned around and began crawling toward the other couch. 'Hunt's stock come from the Huguenots. That's as pure bred as a white man can be in this country.'

'How many other children does Hunt have?' Spock asked.

'Altogether?'

'Yes.'

'Thirteen. Fifteen if you include Hunt's kids who are crazy.'

'All from one mother?'

'Three. Hunt's first wife died two years ago.'

'How old are Hassie and—' Spock gulped before pronouncing the name. 'Haroldina.'

'Hassie is in his early thirties and Haroldina in her late twenties.'

Spock thought a moment. 'Is Hunt's first name Harold?'

'Haroldson. And what's Docker Spock's first name?'

'Benjamin,' Spock answered. 'But I would never name a daughter Benjamina.'

'Does Docker Spock have any daughters?' Hunt asked from the floor.

'No.'

'So how the hell can Docker Spock know what he would name a daughter?' Hunt stood up without waiting for an answer. 'That is great. Just five minutes of crawling a day keeps a man fit.'

He walked toward Dr. Spock's couch and plopped down.

'Hassie and Haroldina are both far too old for the purview of a simple pediatrician,' Dr. Spock said.

'No, that's just it,' Hunt said, wagging a fat finger at Hunt. 'When Hassie and Haroldina were kids, they seemed like kids—they had their share of punishments when they were brats. Yet the signs were there. The adult Haroldina hears voices that tell her to do things. She heard voices as a child. Hell's woods, all kids hear voices when they were kids, right?'

Dr. Spock was about to give a detailed answer and then he said, 'Sure.'

'Only Haroldina never outgrew hearing voices,' Hunt said. 'Hassie would have fits as a kid and roll around in the dirt. When he was twenty-three and had already made five or eight million dollars from his own wells, he would suddenly jump out of a moving car and roll around in the spillage near the pumps. Roll in the oil.'

Dr. Spock thought a moment. 'Is Hunt saying that both Haroldina and Hassie never outgrew childhood fantasies and impulses?'

'You are the docker. You tell me.'

'Spock is a pediatrician,' Dr. Spock said.

'When Hassie was a teenager he began to speak of himself in the third person. You see how easy it is, don't you?'

'Spock says *Yes* to Hunt,' Dr. Spock said. Half of Spock was offended at being deceived by Hunt's 'royal we' nonsense. The other half appreciated Hunt's humor.

'You should have some sense of mental hygiene, Docker Spock, since you caged your own wife up in Bloomingdale's.'

Dr. Spock leapt up from the couch and turned in a circle and sat down again, closer to Hunt. Spock projected a low voice through clenched teeth. 'How did you know that?'

Hunt leaned closer to Dr. Spock and said softly, 'I'm the richest man in the world and I'm a Texan.'

Dr. Spock backed away and whispered as fiercely as it is possible to whisper, 'My wife is none of your business.'

Hunt moved his head closer to Dr. Spock's. 'Don't get riled. I want to make a donation to you to study this problem.'

'What problem?'

'How to recognize insanity in children so the parents can cure it before it starts.'

Dr. Spock thought for a moment. 'I think that it could be counter-productive if modern parents begin thinking normal childhood behaviors are the possible symptoms of schizophrenia.'

'There are plenty of bad seeds out there, Docker Spock. I'm not talking about them.'

Spock was about to say, *What the hell are you talking about?* Instead he asked, 'Where's your daughter now?'

'Home, staying quiet with her husband.'

'And your son?'

'My doctors gave him a lobotomy.' Hunt went silent for a moment. 'I think he is happy now.'

* * *

Jane Spock in the 'bat house'—Bloomingdale's:

> I try to keep up my appearance, but I've lost so much weight. Soon I stopped caring.
>
> I remember women's magazines. I remember advertisements for women's beauty products. We can't read women's magazines here. We can't watch TV. It's easy to neglect your appearance.
>
> I see Benny every weekend. Visitor's Day. Benny's whole round-trip is more than eight hours of driving. He doesn't bring the boys. He won't bring the boys. Depending on how I am feeling, I will either dress up or deliberately wear a ratty housedress.

I observe myself nagging Ben. 'Why can't you make more money like other men do?' 'Why can't we move back to Manhattan?'

'Well, why can't we?'

Ben comes and primarily talks with my psychiatrist. She is a handsome woman named Mrs. Penny. Her husband, Mr. Penny, is deceased. So, Ben and Mrs. Penny talk and walk the grounds. I know that Ben knows the secret of psychoanalysis—it never ends. You talk and talk and talk and then you die. Ben has always expected my psychiatrist to solve all of my problems for me. He has never asked me a personal psychological question during our entire marriage.

Ben believes in mental hygiene.

What is Benjamin talking to Mrs. Penny about? Is Ben trying to mash her in the foliage? Feel underneath her stethoscope?

I have always been so independent. Back in the twenties, I protested fiercely against Temperance. Excuse me, Prohibition. I was a good speaker. They got me a truck and a microphone. I would give intelligent arguments defending the freedom of citizens to enjoy booze. I gave my speeches outside the New York Public Library on Fifth and 42nd Street. Or else we'd drive downtown to Wall Street and preach against the Bear Market and the alligator spread.

Temperance. No one wets their whistle at Bloomingdale's. God, I miss alcohol. Brandy. Vodka. I have loved the numbing joy of Miltown. God, I miss all that. Miss Eustace makes me swallow chlorpromazine pills. They make my blood feel like liquid lead.

I have become a lead head.

* * *

Dr. Spock was talking to one of the few intellectuals in Texas, a man who laughed when Spock told him about H. L. Hunt. 'Did you get it about his wives?'

'Get what?' Dr. Spock asked.

'That he married all of them at once.'

Spock was confused for a moment. 'As in bigamy?'

'We don't call it that in Dallas. We just call it Hunt's Way.'

'He had three wives simultaneously?'

'Well, actually, he had kids with two wives simultaneously and kids with another woman who he married after his first wife died.'

'I'm speechless,' Dr. Spock said.

'Well, we've all heard it from Hunt: *I'm not a Christian. I do not have to go by Christian ethics.*'

★ ★ ★

New York City? Long Island?

Jackson Pollock woke up on the floor. He was confused. Was he down on the floor painting? Where was the light? You can't paint in the dark. Pollock attempted to stand erect and his equilibrium spun him and he stayed on his knees. He envisioned an evolutionary chart in his mind—monkey walking erect and turning into Fred Flintstone who turns into Jackson Pollock who walks erect for two steps—

And then crashes down to the floor.

A rushing realization about his paintings crashed into his head as well. Pollock began crawling on the floor in the dark. Jackson Pollock realized that the last vertical painting that he had painted was in 1946. Ever since then, he had painted horizontally on the floor. There was no up or down to these paintings as they were being created.

His drip painting.

Each painting wasn't even like a map laid flat. Pollock never knew what was the top of the painting (north) and what was the bottom (south) until he was finished.

He crawled on the floor in a widening gyre. He realized that to display these paintings vertically on a wall was an abomination. All of his paintings in all those apartments of millionaires and in all those museums had to be ripped from the wall and displayed on the carpet.

My God, how could he have been so stupid?

Jackson Pollock was tired of crawling on his hands and knees. He tried standing again and couldn't. He just gave in to gravity and lay completely on the floor and curled into a fetal position and went back to sleep.

★ ★ ★

Hollywood, May 12, Saturday night. The actress Elizabeth Taylor phoned Montgomery Clift around six thirty.

Taylor was twenty-four years old. Clift was thirty-five going on thirty-six. Elizabeth had once been in love with Clift. His beauty was like a sunspot interfering with radio signals. Liz soon realized this man had a complex sex life consisting of mostly other men and several mother figures. She now felt as if Clift was her brother. About half the time, Clift seemed like her younger brother.

'Hi. It's Liz. There's a shindig at our digs. Food. Come over.'

'Man, Liz. I'm beat. I'm staying home. I gave the chauffeur the night off.'

'Oh, come on. Don't poop out. You know how to drive.'

'Okay. Monkey's uncle.'

Clift drove up into the hills on a road that looped and curled like a fling of white paint on a Jackson Pollock painting. It took ten minutes to reach Liz's digs—a ranch house that sat on a precipice. (Kiss it good-bye when the big tremors came.) A few people were inside. The men were all excited about Brooklyn Dodgers pitcher Carl Erskine's second no-hitter against the New York Giants. Clift's buddy Kevin McCarthy was one of those guys—'We shudda been there, Monty!' McCarthy was forty-two.* He was the star of a picture that had been playing in theaters since winter, *Invasion of the Body Snatchers.* It was making money, but not even Bosley Crowther at the *New York Times* had bothered to go see it. No one imagined that one day *Invasion of the Body Snatchers* would be judged seminal cinema of the 1950s.

Montgomery Clift was sullen, but he and McCarthy did their gag dialogue: 'Think of the marvelous thing that has happened,' Monty said in a deliberate monotone. 'Seeds drifting through space for years, took root by chance in a farmer's field, to offer us an untroubled world. There's no need for love.'

McCarthy said (hamming it up): 'No emotions? Then you have no feelings, only the instinct to survive? You can't love or be loved, right?'

Monty said, 'You say it as if it were terrible. Believe me, it isn't.' Monty spoke as if he was speaking to a small child. 'You've been in love before,

---

* Kevin McCarthy was the writer Mary McCarthy's kid brother.

Kevin. It didn't last.' Pause. 'It never does.' Pause. 'Love, desire, ambition, faith—without them life's so simple, believe me.'

Eight people started clapping. The ninth joined the group applause in a tentative fashion, not recognizing that this routine was dialogue from *Invasion of the Body Snatchers.* Eight people in the room knew that the pods in the movie represented Americans brainwashed by fear. Everyone in, say, Iowa, knew that the pods represented Communism.

Liz made her entrance dressed in white and covered in silver and diamonds, making pigeon kisses with everyone. She flopped beside Monty, who began bitching to Liz about how *Raintree County* was going. It was their second picture together. Clift thought his work was shit. Liz pooh-poohed him.

Dinner was served—Mexican served Mexico City style with sophistication and no melted cheese.

Monty had a glass or two of wine.

A woman was chattering about her shrink. 'So Rosalind told me that when man walked erect civilization began. Freud said that when man was on all fours all he saw of a woman eye-level were her genitals. From her rear. Now standing erect he could see that whole woman. And she him.' Monty looked at the clock. It was ten thirty. 'But Rosalind said that civilization lost an essential understanding of genitals. So Bobby and I strip and I crawl on the floor and he follows me on his hands and knees, looking straight ahead into my little oyster.'

'Well, you know what they say,' someone said. 'The world is your oyster.'

'With nothing inside it,' added Montgomery Clift, standing up. 'I'm goin' to drive home. I have to get up early for church tomorrow.'

Everyone looked at him. The woman who had been talking downed a goblet of chardonnay.

'Was the sun still up when you came here, Monty?' Liz asked.

'Yeah.'

'Well, there are no streetlights on the road down to Sunset. So drive careful.'

Kevin McCarthy said, 'I'm pretty bushed too.'

'You have a big day at church tomorrow as well?' Liz said.

'Catechism,' Kevin said. He turned to Montgomery Clift. 'Just follow my car down. We'll be like the Donner Party.'

Everyone said their good-byes. Kevin got into his DeSoto. Monty, a Nash. They drove down the hill, Kevin in the lead. Kevin turned on his radio. Fats Domino sang 'Blueberry Hill.' Kevin laughed. 'Yeah, Blueberry Hill in Hollywood. Yeah.'

The road was nothing but a downhill corkscrew.

Monty kept losing sight of McCarthy's rear lights. He sped up.

McCarthy behind the wheel—Monty's headlights glaring into his rear-view mirror. *Shit, he's gonna rear-end me.* Bad enough for the car—but McCarthy could see Monty unintentionally bumping McCarthy's car off the road and down a cliff.

McCarthy sped up.

Monty sped up so he could see McCarthy's lights and follow them.

McCarthy sped up even faster. Monty too.

Then Monty's headlights disappeared and McCarthy heard a crash.

He braked for a moment. He was hoping to see Monty's headlights. Nothing. McCarthy jumped out of his car and ran up the hill. Clouds of dust. The smell of burning.

There was Monty's car bisected up through the hood by a pole.

The engine was running and smoking. All the windows were spider-webbed, even the back. McCarthy didn't see any fire, but the smell of burning got stronger. McCarthy went to the Nash. He couldn't get the driver's door opened. He didn't see anything. He ran around to the shotgun side. That door was crumpled too. He ran back to the driver's side and used his elbow to clear the glass away. Monty's body had somehow rolled under the dashboard. McCarthy reached in for the key to turn off the engine.

Kevin McCarthy ran from Monty's wreck back to his car. He made a U-turn and barreled back up the hill. He rushed into the house. 'Oh shit fuck Monty is dead Monty is dead.'

Some people thought he was joking. Not Liz. Someone picked up the telephone and called for an ambulance. Liz jumped into a car—a Jaguar—and swerved down the driveway to the road down the hill.

Elizabeth Taylor was driving too fast. She made the hairpin curves. She suddenly worried that maybe she had passed Monty's wreck. Then, there it was. She stopped in the middle of the road, her engine running, the lights shining on the crushed wreckage. The hood was sliced up to the windshield by a pole. She tried the doors. They wouldn't open. She climbed up the trunk and inspected the back window. She climbed off the trunk and saw a large rock gleaming in her headlights. She picked it up and lunged it through the back window. It was safety glass and it crumpled even more inward. She got her fingers under the edges and pulled it toward her and made a space big enough to crawl through. She squirmed into the back seat, and then over the front seats. She bellied into the shotgun seat and reached down. She felt Monty's head.

He was moaning—a constant wordless alarm.

She pulled him up by his shoulders and the thing that used to be his head—and still was unfortunately—and she laid it on her lap.

His head was gushing blood. Her white dress was totally wet and in the weird light, it appeared bluish.

Monty as a blue blood.

It took Kevin and the others twenty minutes to get the driver's door open. Soon the paparazzi vultures had arrived and were taking photographs. Someone at the hospital must have tipped them off about the emergency call. Where was the damn ambulance? Liz Taylor sat with the pulverized pulp of Monty's head in her lap. His eyes had disappeared into the red boils of his swollen cheeks and eyelids. His pouring blood was soaking the car, soaking her dress, soaking the entire world with blood. Who could have believed that Montgomery Clift had so much blood in him? And all the flashbulbs going off— Flash! Flash! A few seconds of darkness and someone else taking another picture. In the distance of the flash and darkness and flash again, Monty's face seemed to get bigger and bigger. Finally, Kevin McCarthy convinced one of the paparazzi to drive him to the nearest hospital so he could lead the ambulance to the wreck. By the time McCarthy returned with the ambulance, there was a cop car by the wreck. Monty was gone. The original ambulance that had been lost in the hills finally found the wreck and sped Monty to Cedars of Lebanon Hospital.

* * *

Nevada. Arthur Miller at the pay phone listening to Monroe.

'Logan said I was vulgar. I was vulgar. He wants me to do things I don't feel. *Just walk across the room. Forget the motivation.* I swing my behind and he says I am vulgar. But I felt like swinging my behind. My character would swing her behind. He says just don't swing your behind so much. What's too much? I want to quit, Arturo. I want to quit.'

In public, Marilyn called Arthur 'Papa.' In private, 'Arturo.'

'Oh, Arturo! I just want to be your girl. I want to be your wife. I want to live in Connecticut or Long Island, and be there for you at the end of the day when you're done writing. Maybe I'll make a movie now and then, but only a really really really good movie. I just want to be your wife.'

Miller can't believe he is hearing such dialogue from Marilyn. He had left his first wife because of adamant domesticity. Miller doesn't know why Bellow is leaving his wife and son because the man has never mentioned it, but Bellow's motive is the same as Miller's—the domesticity of an American wife is like a hook dug into the back of both men's necks. They feel so strongly about this perhaps because neither man has ever seen *I Love Lucy* and other televised propaganda for domesticity. Neither writer has a TV set at home. There are no TVs at Pyramid Lake—neither Miller nor Bellow even noticed. Neither Miller nor Bellow is aware that married couples on TV sleep in separate beds.

Not now. You'll wake the baby!

Yet, here Marilyn Monroe is speaking of pure domesticity to Miller.

Not now. You'll wake the baby!

You know what making love with Marilyn Monroe is like? Arthur could tell you. It is desperate passion. It lasts long. It's quick. Nothing matters. Monroe fucks as if this is the last fuck either of you will experience before the world ends. Everything depends on this moment. There is a desperate clarity about it. Sometimes there is finesse. Sometimes a clumsy gesture. None of it is important. The only important thing is that you and she are together wrestling naked in the hurricane in the eye of God. To hear Marilyn talk about being a housewife makes Arthur Miller gasp for air in this phone booth about ten miles as the bird flies from a town named Nixon.

Nixon, Nevada.

Miller slides down the side of the phone booth. He has fainted.

* * *

For the record, Richard Nixon's wife, Pat, was born Thelma Catherine Ryan in Ely, Nevada, a town located in the middle east of the state, a quick drive across the border into Utah.

★ ★ ★

In Saigon, Nhu, with brother Diem's tacit approval, began torturing and often killing suspected Communists. Nhu had already sent one hundred thousand Vietnamese to prison camps in the wetlands or to Côn Son Island several hundred miles east of the southern tip of the Viet-Nam archipelago. It was on Côn Son Island that the most horrifying concentration camp was erected, thousands of political prisoners of both sexes squashed inside individual 'tiger cages.' They were more like human birdcages. They were so small that circulation was cut off in prisoners' legs. The most common cause of death was slow-mo gangrene.

Ngô Dinh Diem had no feeling about all this pain his brother had created. Ngô Dinh Diem now understood the black heart of rage that beat in Nhu's chest. His brother had explained to him about the dry drowning he experienced in Paris. 'That act was against God,' Nhu said. 'It was against even the devil. Pain should be real. Injury should leave wounds. God allows pain and physical misery to accomplish his wishes. God allows the devil to burn the flesh of sinners. Dry drowning is different. It is an unholy kind of hurting. It would sicken even the devil.'

Diem nodded his head. He understood.

★ ★ ★

On June 1, Jack Kennedy gave a speech to a gathering of the Conference on Viet-Nam in Washington. The gist of his talk was that Viet-Nam was the 'cornerstone of the Free World in southeast Asia.' Viet-Nam was 'the finger in the dike.' It will be forever unknown why Kennedy intellectually nosedived into his absurd support of Ngô Dinh Diem and family. To be fair, even President Eisenhower and his Republicans sanctioned Diem's cancellation of the Unification of Viet-Nam elections.

★ ★ ★

Monty's face.

Before Montgomery Clift drove to Liz's, he had a perfect profile. A perfect nose. A perfect Omaha nose of a man born in Nebraska. Imagine Montgomery Clift turned his face to look at you. Like most actors' faces, the features are more beautiful in B&W than in color. Yet either way, real-life 3-D or B&W or Technicolor—what a beautiful face he had. Montgomery Clift was a method actor and believed in complex physiognomy. Women in the audience saw what Elizabeth Taylor saw: Clift was a young man needing mothering. A young man who wore his heart on his sleeve while possessing complicated secrets.

Montgomery Clift even looked younger than he was. If you knew nothing about Montgomery Clift—the drugs, the sexual ambiguity with an older woman, so on and so forth—photos of Monty reveal a callowness that is deeper than the mere callowness of youth.

Some modern critics said that Clift's face reflected the new modern self-doubt about traditional masculinity. You might say sixty years later that Montgomery Clift had the face of a gay man of the 1950s, a time when the liberal heterosexual assumption was that such males possessed sociological doubts about their masculinity whether they were fey or musclemen.

Go rent *Red River.* Montgomery Clift was twenty-seven, and the movie's star, John Wayne, had just turned forty-one. You can catch glimpses of Clift smirking at Wayne. This is no queer smirk of self-doubt.

Rent *I Confess.* Montgomery Clift plays a priest. Monty also had the face of the ultimate priest as viewed by the non Catholic majority, a face capturing twenty centuries of Catholic deception and misery. What I mean by that is that Montgomery Clift wasn't a modern priest, but one from a time when priests tortured and burnt other priests as heretics. Clift is the priest waiting for his pyre to be set on fire in the town of Worms, West Germany.

The beauty of Montgomery Clift's face precluded him from doing comedy.

Now think about the fact that all these different faces were the singular face that smashed into his steering wheel going sixty miles an hour down a hill in the dark. The accident Picassofied Monty's features. The impact broke his nose and crushed one of his sinus cavities. A tooth propelled itself into and through his lip before shattering at the root. The nervous circuitry on the left side of Montgomery Clift's face was permanently damaged.

Turn the other cheek.

Half of *Raintree County* had been filmed. Monty was in almost every scene. The producer made plans to erase Monty from the picture and reshoot. Elizabeth Taylor begged the man, Dore Schary, not to replace Monty. 'I'm afraid he'll kill himself.'

Eight weeks later, eight weeks of wiring and plastic surgery and gaining nourishment by sucking soup through a straw, Monty was discharged. A few weeks after that Elizabeth Taylor divorced her husband. A few weeks went by—she married someone else. Taylor and Clift resumed filming *Raintree County.* Monty's face wasn't that bad. The makeup people were good. But Monty was in so much pain. He drank. He took pills. He probably had over two hundred and fifty different kinds of painkillers in his dressing room. His face would get worse as time went on.

* * *

If there was an actor whose face was the antithesis of Montgomery Clift's, it was Jerry Lewis. Lewis had an average face that he distorted into that of an idiot, an idiot man-child who was too much a loser to even be a respectable goofball. A man with no nuance. No secrets. A schmo audiences in the 1950s identified with for some unfathomable reason. A reflection, perhaps, that beauty and intelligence are not democratic.

Picture two guys in Manhattan in August 1956. Two guys at the Y sitting in a steam room together. They're in their midtwenties. Their stomachs are flat, but neither is a Charles Atlas. Nautilus machines haven't been invented yet. No one takes steroids.

'I saw *Pardners* last night,' one says.

'Martin and Lewis?'

'Yup.'

'By yourself or with a date?'

'Took my kid brother.'

'How was it?'

'A tired jape. A horse opera with no fat lady and a lame horse.'

'You practice that answer?'

'Hey, I'm a writer, remember?'

'There's no writing on the pages of *Vogue.*'

'Screw you,' says the guy who writes for *Vogue*.

The other waves his hand. 'So tell me about *Pardners*.'

'Dean's a goofball and Jerry balls the blonde.'

'No, really; come on.'

'Jerry plays a millionaire's son. A real pussy. Comes west. Dean Martin is the real thing—a real cowboy. They try to save a ranch from an evil banker.'

'So, what else is new?'

'One funny moment—Jerry tries to roll a cigarette. The tobacco spills all over. He sneezes. He lolls his tongue out to lick the paper and looks like a dog.'

'You ever roll a cigarette?'

'Nope.'

'Think you could do it?'

'Tell me how, smart guy.'

'Pretend I got a sheet of rolling paper in the palm of my hand.'

'You have a sheet of rolling paper in the palm of your hand.'

'Hold it crease-down between your thumb and fuck finger. Curl up your pointer and press down on the crease. Use your Arab hand to pinch tobacco in the paper. Spread it evenly. Let a bit hang off over each end.'

'Both ends?'

'Yup. Both ends. Then remove your pointer. Position your middle fingers so they form a straight line. Move both thumbs under the paper. Begin rolling up the paper with your thumbs until you reach the edge with the glue.'

'Got it.'

'Lick it. Use your thumbs to seal the paper. Pinch off any tobacco at the ends. Squeeze the end you want to stick in your mouth. Light the other end. Smoke it like John Wayne.'

'Now that John Wayne! He was a cowboy one hundred percent.'

'You know that chick I'm dating?'

'The one down the hall at *Vogue*?'

'Yeah, Joan.'

'Joan from California?'

'Joan from California. Her name is Joan Didion.'

'How old is she?'

'Twenty-one. Twenty-two. She's got the hots for John Wayne.'

'You get into her pants yet?'

'Not quite. I thought I would after our conversation about John Wayne. She was telling me how much California girls love the way John Wayne says, *Let's ride. Saddle up. Forward ho. A man's gotta do what a man's gotta do.* When John Wayne sees a girl and says, *Hello there,* he speaks with Sexual Authority.'

'She said that?'

'She said that. *John Wayne speaks with Sexual Authority.*'

'What did you say?'

'I took a breath and said, *Well, hello there.* Just like that.'

'What did she do?'

'She looked disappointed. She said, *Try again.*'

'And you said—'

'*Republic is a beautiful word.*'

'Huh?'

'*Republic is a beautiful word.* John Wayne said that in a movie once. I think he said it to a señorita in a cantina in *Flame of Barbary Coast.*'

'What did Joan do when you said that?'

'She kissed me. Sorta. She wasn't really into it. Then she said she had to go.'

'Well, John Wayne looks like a man. A man's man.'

'And what do I look like?'

'A guy who works at *Vogue.*'

'You mean a guy who works at a woman's fashion magazine.'

'Yeah. A guy who works at a woman's fashion magazine.'

'I always thought I looked a bit like Montgomery Clift.'

'Dream on.'

* * *

It was now Arthur Miller's last week in Reno. He heard a woman's voice coming from Saul Bellow's place. She was Sondra Tschacbasov, soon to be Bellow's second wife. She had long hair and bangs. She was obviously very bohemian. Very Greenwich Village.

It was time for the final trip to Reno for groceries—final for Miller. For some reason Bellow planned to keep on working in the desert even though he had established residency in Reno.

So this was the situation: Arthur Miller drove Bellow's car to Reno with Sondra on the shotgun side.

'So I hear you're a Red, Arthur,' she said.

He looked at her. Scrutinized her. He took her head in with a glance and then shot his eyes to her apple breasts realizing that she witnessed this. Boobs. He was a boob man. Yet, Miller didn't raise his gaze. He lowered his eyes instead. He caressed her blouse with his sight. He scanned her skirt. Her long legs. Her ankles. Her shoes. Then Miller shot his eyes up smack into her face and she immediately glanced away.

Victory!

Then she shot her eyes back at him. Her eyes were huge. They were the color of translucent peas. The front of her hair was cut in bangs a good two inches above her eyebrows. Her nose was working-class, which is to say that it was neither aquiline nor pug. Her lips were ample. Her smile would always seem reluctant. Hers were lips that were made to pout. Hers were lips that were made to suck—

Oh, forget that thought.

'Your heroism has been clipped to your lapel like a delegate's badge at a liberal convention,' she said to Miller as she stared at his larynx.

'What? That's a snotty thing to say.' He raised his gaze.

'You said it about Saul.'

'What? When?'

'In 1945. *The New Republic*.'

'I've forgotten.'

'Saul hasn't forgotten.'

Miller drove for a bit.

'Saul never said anything to me about it.'

'He's biding his time . . .' Arthur felt her movement toward him. He smelled her breath as she stuck her pointer into his ribs, saying, 'Until he can stick it to you!'

'Stop it!'

Sondra Tschacbasov tickled Miller as you would a little boy. She was laughing hysterically. Miller swerved off the road, but swerved back on.

Miller turned on the radio.

First, they drove to the Laundromat. Miller put his colors in one machine and his whites in another.

'You don't have very much,' Sondra said. 'Can I throw Saul's things in with yours?'

Miller was surprised, but he said, 'Sure.' Sondra piled everything—colors and whites—into the machine containing Miller's whites. He doesn't say anything. So much for the feminine touch.

At Jackpot Market, things were even stranger. The two rolled their individual shopping carts down different aisles. Miller got his TV dinners. Sondra wheeled a shopping cart filled with two different kinds of deodorant and packages of chocolate doughnuts and a dozen onions and a carton of Kleenex. Miller thought of many things to say.

Rib her about the onions and Kleenex.

In the end, he just glanced at her tits saying nothing.

At the Laundromat, they separated Bellow's things from Miller's.

'Aren't you curious about Saul's howling?' Sondra asked.

Miller didn't answer.

'Reichian,' she said.

Ah. Wilhelm Reich. Age fifty-nine. Born in the nineteenth century like Freud. Reich had even once been a student of Freud. Reich invented origami. No. Orgonomy! That's it. Orgone for short. Orgasms. Everything human was tied into the orgasm. He built boxes you'd sit in to get spontaneous orgasms. Reich made magnetic boxes that you could hold in your hands and use them to move clouds in the sky. Cloud rustlers? No. Cloud busters. Reich was in prison, wasn't he? Just another crank like Lee Strasberg. Screaming was a part of both of their processes. (Know that Arthur Janov would not develop the Primal Scream until 1967.)

* * *

Saigon. Ngô Dinh Diem received a package from France. It contained negatives that had been sent to him at great cost. Diem went into his modest darkroom. The negatives were dirty, but after cleaning there were no scratches. He printed each one simply. There were seven in all. After the prints dried, he selected one and then telephoned his brother, who was in another room in Gia Long Palace.

'Come down to my darkroom, Nhu,' he said. 'I have something to show you.'

'I'll come presently.'

* * *

Diem methodically put his chemicals away and emptied the containers of bath. Nhu came into the room wearing a black silk bathrobe.

'Is it late?' Diem asked.

'It is three in the morning,' Nhu answered.

'Oh.'

'What did you want to show me?'

'This.'

Nhu studied the photograph. The man's lower face seemed to crumple and then inflate as he started a high-pitched cackle that increased in volume until Nhu sounded like some screaming jungle bird. He did a little dance as he laughed and then dropped to his ass right there on the floor shaking in mirth. Finally, he rolled over and staggered to his feet. He looked completely exhausted. He'd even wet his pajamas.

'This was not the reaction I had expected,' Diem said.

'Why did you show me this?' Nhu asked, struggling to keep a straight face.

'The French did this. I wanted to show you that the French can be on the devil's side and thus be a part of God's Plan for Humanity.'

'Oh. Of course,' Nhu said and began laughing again.

* * *

Japan. Howard Hunt got word that he and his family would soon leave Tokyo for South America. Howard Hunt was being restationed in Uruguay, a South American country located on the Atlantic coast, a country squeezed between Argentina to the west and Brazil to the north. Uruguay had now become a hot spot almost as important as Mexico City because both Argentina and Brazil had evicted the Russian embassies. The KGB now concentrated on infiltrating Uruguay.

Hunt first flew to Washington to bone up on the new assignment. Next Hunt flew down to Havana, Cuba, where all the Latin American CIA station chiefs were there for a meeting.

Havana was a city rich in patriarchal mythology for Hunt. In 1926, Hunt's father was a Miami Beach lawyer with a partner who was a card sharp with a dedication to liquor and Lolitas. One weekend, Hunt's father went into the office and found the office safe open and five thousand dollars in cash missing. Hunt's dad made some phone calls. He discovered his partner had taken the night boat to Havana. Hunt's father unwrapped his Army Colt .45 and chartered a sea plane to fly to Havana, where he found his partner in Sloppy Joe's Bar—the original Sloppy Joe's run by José Abeal on the corner of Zulueta and Ánimas. Hunt's father strode to the bar and raised his Army Colt .45 to the back of his partner's neck and cocked the trigger. The partner started flabbergasting and reached into his pocket and handed Hunt Sr. almost five thousand dollars, having spent some greenbacks on shots of rum.

Howard Hunt told this story to everybody.

Hunt was now thirty-seven, as old as his father had been when he came to Havana to get his money back. Hunt took a room at the Aldama Palace on Gomez Corner. All the Cubans wore gray check suits, gray felt shoes. On the street, empty taxis and ox carts full of melons.

Grab a catfish sandwich with onions and red sauce for twenty cents. Cuba Libres thirty cents. Waiters gathered at every doorway, talking among themselves.

Perros de Presa Canarios barking from several blocks away—catch hounds from the Canary Islands, hounds the size of lambs, hounds bred for working livestock.

Hunt's meetings were alternately boring and alarming. Some chiefs said they'd heard good things about the Castro brothers and Ernesto 'Che' Guevara. These were the same guys who visited Havana's taverns where naked Cuban girls performed 'acts' with male donkeys.

Howard Hunt wasn't a prude.

In fact, after seeing nothing but porcelain Japanese girls as well as his wife for more than two years, Cuban women were exotic.

Cuban women women women everywhere Cuban women.

Fifteen years from now, Dorothy Hunt will swallow her Catholic tenets and prepare to divorce Howard because of his relentless pursuit of Cuban tail. It is speculation to assume Hunt's obsession began here at the CIA Latin America Section leaders meeting in 1956, but an intelligent speculation nevertheless. Hunt discovered that every sultry Dolores del Rio Latin femme fatale myth was truly multiplied by three. Viva Cuban women! It was their jungle blood. Things you would be too ashamed to do with a white woman were honest fun with Cuban females.

Gentlemen don't talk.

Before Hunt left Cuba, he saw a For Your Eyes Only confidential report. A platoon of Batista's army had met a small group of rebels and slaughtered them all. The report stated that among the dead were the Castro brothers.

Good riddance.

* * *

Summer on Long Island.

Long Island was 118 miles in length and twenty in width. This is about the same length as the Big Island in the state of Hawaii while being four times skinnier.

Jackson Pollock lived in an inland village called Springs. It was closer to the North Fork than the Hamptons on the South Fork.

Pollock hadn't fucked Ruth since spring. Then in June, Ruth had moved ten, twenty miles south of Pollock to teach at the Abraham Rattner School of Art in Sag Harbor, a town on the north edge of the South Fork.

Pollock heard.

The painter drove over to Ruth's house. They rekindled their carnal knowledge. The day after the Fourth of July, they had an all-night romp in Jackson's barn and his studio, his wife, Lee, up in the house asleep. It was the next morning—Ruth and Jackson walking toward Jackson's car, a 1950 Oldsmobile 88 convertible. In sunlight, the car was asparagus green. They walked and Lee was standing on the back porch. She was a woman enraged. She screamed, 'Get that woman off my property before I call the police.'

That broke Pollock and Kligman up.

My property.

* * *

On June 29, Arthur Miller and Marilyn Monroe get a marriage license in Westchester County, New York. (Jane Spock is in her madhouse maybe twenty miles away.) Cars filled with paparazzi race after Miller and Marilyn. One paparazzi is a girl from France—Mara Scherbatoff of *Paris Match*.

(One of Jane Spock's fellow inmates is an old woman named Haberglass.

She had been born in Wisconsin and occasionally becomes convinced she is Marie Antoinette.)

Mara Scherbatoff of *Paris Match* speaks good English.

(Old woman Haberglass will only speak French to the staff, including Miss Eustace. Without asking Miss Eustace if she speaks French, Jane Spock begins translating Haberglass for the benefit of Miss Eustace.)

Mara Scherbatoff hitches a ride with a male American photographer.

It's a green Chevrolet.

The green car.

So many green cars on Long Island.

The green Chevrolet races after Miller and Marilyn's along with all the other drag-racing paparazzi.

('*C'étaient des fous, mais ils avaient cette petite flame qui ne s'éteint pas.*' 'What did Mrs. Haberglass say?' 'I think she said, *We're all mad, but we have a little flame which does not go out.*')

Miller and Marilyn hear the crash. Marilyn turns and sees a huge tree shaking, the green Chevrolet crashed into the trunk. Mara has been hurled onto the blacktop.

('*Tout ce que nous connaissons de grand nous vient des névrosés. Ce sont eux et non pas d'autres qui ont fondé les religions et compose les chefs d'oeuvres.*' 'What is she saying this time?' '*Everything great in the world is done by neurotics. They alone founded our religions and make great movies.*')

Miller and Marilyn drive away, outdistancing all the reporters. As for Mara Scherbatoff:

She's dead.

* * *

On Long Island, Jackson Pollock's wife, Lee Krasner, takes a boat to Europe to contemplate divorce. Ruth moves in with Pollock. They go to Long Island highbrow art parties and all the women cluster around Pollock. Ruth is ignored. She is a few extra pounds heavy. She has dark ratty hair. She is nobody's Audrey Hepburn.

She is jealous of Pollock.

Ruth takes the train back to Manhattan in the middle of the week. On Friday, August 10, she has a date with a 'Jewish comedian.'

'So, the rabbi goes to his first Jackson Pollock show. He looks around and goes up to the artist, saying, *I don't get your paintings.* Pollock says, *I paint what I feel inside me.* The rabbi looks concerned and says, *Have you ever tried Alka-Seltzer?*'

'Oh, that's so dumb.' Ruth squeals and still laughs hysterically.

'Jackson Pollock starts painting pictures that are just one color. Gold. His Jewish shrink goes to the show and says, *Jackson, I didn't know you had a gilt complex.*'

'I don't get it.'

'Gilt complex. G-i-l-t, not g-u-i-l-t.' Pause. 'Okay. Last one. So, Lee Krasner goes to Europe to think about divorcing Jackson Pollock. De Kooning says to Jackson, *To keep your wife, you should paint nudes like I do.* So Jackson Pollock tries to get a college girl to pose for him. A Catholic college girl won't pose nude. A Baptist college girl won't pose nude. But a nice Jewish girl poses nude. He paints his nude of her. He finishes. The nice Jewish girl gets dressed. He pays her the modeling fee. Now you know as well as I do there is no such thing as a nice Jewish girl. She looks Jackson Pollock in the eye and starts French kissing him. Suddenly they hear a car door slam. Out a window, Jackson Pollock sees Lee Krasner getting out of a taxi with her suitcase. *It's my wife!* He howls at the Jewish model. *Quick! Take all your clothes off!*'

* * *

Ruth Kligman rode the Long Island Railroad back to Jackson Pollock and the East Hampton station that Saturday, August 11. She brought a friend with her, Edith Metzger. She was maybe twenty-five.

No one will remember what she looked like.

Edith was a receptionist in a beauty salon where Ruth got her hair done. Ruth loved beauty parlors. She'd never had kids so Ruth knew nothing about Dr. Spock's recommendation of beauty parlors as a method of getting rid of postpartum depression. No. Ruth just loved the ritual of them. 'I loved getting set and sitting under the dryer reading *Vogue* or movie magazines and putting mascara on while still under the dryer, because somehow the heat from the dryer made the mascara work better and my eyelashes would be thicker and longer.'

Ruth became friends with Edith.

Edith was screwing the boss of the beauty parlor. The boss was married. Edith was Jewish. She had the sour karma of being born in Germany in 1931.

★ ★ ★

Saigon. Ngô Dinh Diem was well read. He finished in one sitting Albert Camus's new novel, *La Chute*. The novel was told in the form of a monologue spoken by a French patron in a bar in Amsterdam called Mexico City. A single line in that book shook Diem to his core, and *shook* is not used as a metaphoric verb. Diem's torso started shaking. It was hard for him to breathe. The narrator of *La Chute* spoke this line:

For more than thirty years, I had been in love exclusively with myself.

Diem realized that was his character exactly. He had allowed Soeur Angelique to love him. He used Soeur Angelique as a mirror of his own intense love of himself. Nothing else in the Camus novel matched that epiphany. Camus had been born in Algeria and Diem understood that this book was said to be his response to the French brutality in putting down the revolution for independence in that North African country.

Diem didn't see this. There was no mention of Algeria in *La Chute*. He recalled for a moment the photograph he had shown his brother Nhu—a B&W photo of two Arab men's heads nestled together. One head was fourth-fifths facing forward. The other head was in profile, the nose fitting perfectly into the contours of the first head's cheek. These Arab heads had been severed from their bodies. One could see the cut perfectly in the head that was in profile. The result of the severing was curious. One would think that the man's throat would be visible, resembling a cut pipe that had been severed. No. The human remains inside the neck were curled together in layers like pages of a burnt newspaper. There was no visible throat pipe. The hair of the man in profile was cut to the skull. The full-faced man may have been bald. He did have a slight beard while his companion was clean-shaven. The eyes of the full-faced man were open, but drowsy. The single visible eye of the man in profile seemed drowsy as well. Both men's mouths were open. Their lips were lips. The full-faced man only had two teeth on his upper gums, with the space of the missing tooth between. Something had been stuffed in that man's mouth—the same sort of thing that had been stuffed in the profile man's mouth.

Dangling out of each mouth was a severed penis.

The penis in the mouth of the full-faced man hung out of his lower lip and down his chin. Behind it, you can see the pouch of a severed scrotum. It reminded Diem of a large toad. The penis of the man in profile was also in profile. That penis was the same thickness of the full-faced man's. Both penises had been circumcised. The heads posed a narrative question. Had the men been castrated, maybe castrated together, and then had their members stuffed in their mouths, and then perhaps a moment later or longer, had their heads split from their bodies? Probably not. Far easier for the French to shoot the men in the chest, and then remove the heads and genitals in any order, and then pose them for the camera. Perhaps the genitals were even mixed up—the penis of the full-faced man nesting in the mouth of the man in profile and vice versa.

Of course, none of this mattered. Diem recalled how the writer Ernest Hemingway shot rhinoceroses and tigers and then cut off the animals' heads to have the head taxidermied to hang on his wall.

None of it mattered really, except politically.

For more than thirty years, I had been in love exclusively with myself.

* * *

New York State. Bloomingdale's.

After six months in the asylum, Jane Spock was released. Jane was packing her suitcase and Miss Eustace stood watching. Jane asked Miss Eustace to do her a favor. 'Can you turn your back to me?'

Miss Eustace smiled. She took out a cigarette. 'Want one?' she asked.

Jane shook her head. Certain patients were allowed to smoke—certainly not the women who would try to put the cigarette out on their own arms or someone else's. But none of the patients who could smoke were allowed to light their own cigarettes. Miss Eustace handed Jane a Zippo.

'Light me up, will you?' she said to Jane.

Jane flicked the flame. She lit Miss Eustace's cigarette.

Then Miss Eustace very slowly turned. She held her cigarette in the hand of her bent right arm and held her elbow with her left hand. She walked slowly to the wall. She was wearing a very white blouse. She wasn't wearing a slip. Just a very thick brassiere.

* * *

Pittsburgh, Pennsylvania. Sunday night, July 1. Jane Spock was home and watching *The Ed Sullivan Show* with her husband, Ben, for the first time in six months. The theme of tonight's show was an appreciation of film director John Huston and his new film, *Moby Dick*.

Everyone in America knew *Moby-Dick* was a doorstopper of a nineteenth-century novel about the hunting of a mythic white whale by a man with a peg leg. What adult had time to read it? Kids in college and high school were a different story.

The author of *Moby-Dick,* Herman Melville (1819–1891), had only recently been 'invented' by Pulitzer Prize–winning biographer and critic Carl Van Doren shortly after the institution of Prohibition in 1919, a year when America was celebrating the centenary of a dull poet who was the beloved of the suffragettes, James Russell Lowell (1819–1891). Columbia University professor Carl Van Doren wanted to find a hard-drinking contemporary of Lowell to promote and came up with Herman Melville, a forgotten has-been. Melville's big book, *Moby-Dick,* had been a notable failure of the mid-nineteenth century. Van Doren elevated the unknown Melville to the American literary pantheon in his book *The American Novel*. Interest in Melville simmered through the Depression and the war. Soon academics presented a Melville for everyone: Melville as modernist; Melville as Byronic Nietzschean battling the genteel love novels of the feminine writers of his time; the enduring myth that Melville failed because his antebellum reading audience was too provincial to recognize his genius.

The American reading public had failed Melville, not the other way around.

Melville mania crested when a biography of the man written by Newton

Arvin won the National Book Award in 1951. John Huston had the folly to try filming Herman Melville's great doorstopper, *Moby-Dick,* with a script by future 1960s science-fiction superstar Ray Bradbury.

John Huston's *Moby Dick* would open that week.

★ ★ ★

Over in Paris, disciples of the Cinémathèque had concocted a concept known as the *auteur theory*, which stated the director of a motion picture is the 'author' of the movie, not the actors or producer or cameraman. Ed Sullivan was actually on the vanguard of film appreciation with his centerpiece on Huston, son of the ham actor Walter. Ed Sullivan highlighted Huston's memorable motion pictures such as *The Maltese Falcon* and *The Treasure of the Sierra Madre* and *The African Queen*, but featured clips from the yet-to-be-released *Moby Dick*. Folk singer Burl Ives appeared and sang an old whaling tune, 'Blow Ye Winds,' and Gregory Peck, who played Captain Ahab, came on the stage and read from the book.

This was Ed Sullivan on CBS on Sunday, the first of July.

Over on NBC was a new show conceived to compete with Ed Sullivan, *The Steve Allen Show*, hosted by jazz aficionado and composer Steve Allen (age thirty-four). On Sunday, the first of July, *The Steve Allen Show* had Elvis Presley as a guest. He wore a tuxedo and sang 'Hound Dog' eye to eye with a basset hound that wore a small top hat.

Elvis Presley creamed Herman Melville in the ratings

★ ★ ★

The chief movie reviewer (the term *film critic* wasn't yet a term) for the *New York Times* was one Bosley Crowther. Several days before his fifty-first birthday he reviewed the new John Huston film. His review began: 'Herman Melville's famous story of a man's dark obsession to kill a whale, told with tremendous range and rhetoric in his great novel, *Moby Dick,* has been put on the screen by John Huston in a rolling and thundering color film that is herewith devoutly recommended as one of the great motion pictures of our times.' Crowther's review ended with: 'This is the third time Melville's story has been put upon the screen.

There is no need for another, because it cannot be done better, more beautifully or excitingly again.'

* * *

In June, Arthur Miller testified before the HUAC. They wanted him to name names that had already been named by others. As the writer Elizabeth Hardwick will point out, the committee wanted to make Miller an example of 'good civic obedience.' She will also write, 'Betrayal was now the norm of good citizenship.' In modern America, one's 'private conscience' was a 'niggling absurdity.' Then there was Miller, sitting stoic and refusing to fink on anyone. At one point in the hearing an exasperated House member whines, 'Why do you write so morbidly, so sadly, Mr. Miller? Why don't you use that magnificent talent of yours in the cause of anti-Communism?'

* * *

Out east. Georgetown.

Jacqueline Kennedy is fond of Mary Meyer. Mary is like an older sister. Or Jacqueline's fantasy of how an older sister would treat her—which wasn't the way Jacqueline treated Lee. Jacqueline and Mary often talk of art. Jacqueline has gone off on a tear in her elfish voice about Jackson Pollock—'A monkey with a palette and paintbrush could paint more intelligently.'

'Look, Jacks,' Mary says. 'Pollock said that the modern painter cannot express his age of the airplane, the atom bomb, the radio, in the old forms of the Renaissance or of any other past culture. Each age finds its own technique.'

Jacqueline thinks about this. 'Sort of like every dog will have his day.'

* * *

It's August 1956. Night. A green car. An angry man behind the wheel. The car this angry man is driving is a new Lincoln. The driver is Ed Sullivan. The sponsor of *The Ed Sullivan Show* is Lincoln-Mercury, so this is why Sullivan drives a Lincoln instead of a Cadillac. The traffic is light, yet Sullivan drives hunched down, both hands on the wheel life-or-death style, barking at his twenty-three-year-old son-in-law slouched on the shotgun side. 'Goddamn Ed Murrow. Goddamn Ed Murrow. That nincompoop still won't invite me to the goddamn Correspondents Roundup shew. That guy will invite Eric Sevareid, but not me.'

'But you're the host of a variety show.'

'I was a Broadway columnist for the *New York Daily News* for a hundred years and Murrow never invited me. I tell you, son, his snub eats at me and eats at me.'

'So... Let's change the subject. I can't believe you're having Elvis on the show.'

Sullivan and his son-in-law were cruising down the twisty Naugatuck Valley in Connecticut.

'I'm having Elvis on the show. Three times.'

'You were so disgusted with his dry humping on Milton Berle.'

'I wasn't disgusted. I'm not a prude like your mother. Elvis didn't seem like family entertainment. The worst part was when his bass cello player rode his instrument like a hobby horse and slapped both the sides.'

In the oncoming lane comes a crummy three-year old green Pontiac. The driver is a young man, an overworked X-ray technician. He keeps nodding off at the wheel.

'So you've changed your mind?'

'I've changed my mind.'

'How much are you buying Elvis for?'

'Fifty thousand dollars.'

Sullivan's son-in-law whistles. 'That's a lot of smackers for dry humping!'

The green Pontiac drifts into Sullivan's lane and smashes into Sullivan's Lincoln.

This is happening three months after Montgomery Clift's car crash—

Edward Sullivan flying through the Lincoln's windshield headfirst. The ambulance comes. In the end, there isn't a mark on Sullivan's Great Stone Face. But he'll still be stuck in a hospital for months.

* * *

The wreckage doesn't stop here. It was late Saturday morning, August 11, 1956. Still on the East Coast. Long Island. Jackson Pollock picked up Ruth and Edith at the East Hampton train station. Neither of the girls had luggage. Pollock drove his convertible—again, a green automobile—to a place called Cavagnaro's, where he had a Piels and the girls had coffee. He then drove them to his spread in Springs.

Jackson spent the day drinking gin.

Edith had a breakdown with Ruth and told her how the Nazis had destroyed her father. Edith took a picture of Ruth in a black one-piece bathing suit sitting in Jackson Pollock's lap. Later around five or six, Jackson made everybody a steak.

At sundown, Jackson said, 'Come on, girls. We're going to Levy's party.'

'Who's Levy?'

'I dunno. He's having a party in Eats Hampton. I think he's a lawyer.'

'A divorce lawyer?'

'You wish.'

'Shouldn't we get dressed up?'

'Nah. It's casual.'

'Jackson, are you sure you're okay to drive?'

'Sure I'm sure. Sure I'm sure I'm sure I'm sure. Get in the car.'

The women piled into Jackson's green convertible. Jackson was wearing a black shirt and gray slacks. He took his shoes off and threw them in the back seat. His socks were the color of peanut shells. Jackson started the car and drove. About thirty seconds into the drive it was apparent something was wrong. Not that Pollock was driving erratically. He began driving slower and slower. Soon, a turtle with a limp could move faster. Pollock was driving in the middle of the road. Finally, he stopped his green convertible.

"I'm fine,' he told the girls. 'I need to stop for a moment.'

The 1950s had passed the halfway mark. This hot summer was the second summer past the halfway point. Jackson Pollock had been speeding through the late 1940s, flinging paint on the canvas, but now he wanted to sit in his car in the middle of the road.

A police car stopped. One cop inside. He got out. He was young. 'Good evening, Mr. Pollock,' the cop said. 'Is everything okay?'

'Everything is fine. I'm just talking to the ladies. How's it hanging?'

'Everything's okay, Mr. Pollock. How about you? Need any help?'

'No, thank you. We're on our way visiting friends in Eats Hampton.'

The cop drove away.

Pollock started his green convertible. He drove for about thirty seconds south when he started to fall asleep at the wheel. Both women were now furious. 'Turn this car around. Let's go home.' Pollock drove into the gravel parking lot of the Cottage Inn planning to turn the car around. Edith jumped out. 'I'm going to call a cab,' she said.

'No you're not!' Pollock said. He told her that the Cottage Inn was a Negro tavern. There were a few black guys slouching in the parking lot eyeing this white guy with the two white chicks and a green convertible. It was a Saturday night. The door of the Cottage Inn opened and you could see the jukebox actually jumping up and down on the floor. It was spinning Dorothea O'Faye singing 'I'm Sighin' for My Scion Who's a Yale Man.'

Jackson Pollock started singing along. Ruth coaxed Edith back in the car. Jackson Pollock stomped the gas and headed north, pedal to the metal. He was speeding home at maybe sixty miles an hour.

Edith began howling, 'Let me out! Stop the car!' She stood up and flipped into the back seat. She then stood again, screaming, 'Stop stop stop stop stop!'

Pollock began laughing and with his ridiculous beatnik beard he resembled a Spanish clown. The green convertible raced down Springs-Fireplace Road. The green convertible passed Pussy's Pond. The green convertible was speeding dead center toward a pair of trees.

The trees were elms.

Walt Whitman had grown up on Long Island. The seeds for these elms had been planted when Walt was a boy. Another poet, Allen Ginsberg, wrote a poem in 1953 titled 'The Green Automobile.'

* * *

The summer of 1956 is an election summer. Eisenhower's people wanted Eisenhower to dump Richard Nixon from the ticket. Eisenhower agreed. He wanted the forty-six-year-old deputy secretary of defense Robert Anderson to be his running mate. Eisenhower threw Nixon a bone: 'Why don't you switch jobs with Anderson, Dick?'

Nixon wasn't having any of it.

In the end, Eisenhower thought that he would look bad dumping Nixon midstream.

* * *

In New York City, Norman Mailer wrote a column in the hip newspaper he cofounded, *The Village Voice,* saying that he wanted Ernest Hemingway for president. This piece was not a goof, yet of course it was. Mailer claimed that the public was tired of professional politicians, which was how Eisenhower the War Hero had been elected. The same stature would hold true, according to Mailer, in regard to Hemingway. Then Mailer wrote a curious line that he does not elaborate. It is repeated here in the same spirit: 'This country could stand a man for president, since for all too many years our lives have been guided by men who were essentially women, which indeed is good for neither men nor women.'

* * *

Recall Richard Nixon's younger brother, Big Don. He opens his second Nixon's restaurant, in Fullerton, California. On September 4, the Nixon patriarch, Francis A. Nixon, dies at seventy-seven. Richard Nixon will one day give a speech and say, 'I remember my old man. I think that they would have called him sort of a little man, a common man. He didn't consider himself that way. You know what he was? He was a streetcar motorman first, and then he was a farmer, and then he had a lemon ranch. It was the poorest lemon ranch in California, I can assure you. He sold it before they found oil on it.' Nixon will pause for the laughs. None come. 'And then he was a grocer. But he was a great man, because he did his job, and every job counts up to the hilt, regardless of what happens.'

This will be all delusion on Dick's part. In reality, his father, Frank Nixon, was a sour butcher who'd wear the same beef-blood-soaked shirt for a week as he'd try to fuck the housewives who came to buy groceries in his high-priced grocery store. As a father, he once tried to drown Dick when the kid was only six or seven, tried to drown Dick in an irrigation canal in Yorba Linda, California. In an old interview Nixon had once said,

'There were times when I was tempted to run away from home and all that sort of thing. I never did.'

* * *

Carl Djerassi was now thirty-three and had found a cheap way to run away from Detroit. Like many East Coast and West Coast intellectuals, Djerassi had picked up Aldous Huxley's skinny book *The Doors of Perception*. This was Huxley's chronicle of a single ingesting of mescaline, a natural psychedelic derivative of peyote, which was in turn a small desert cactus lacking spines. Huxley believed that the experience of turning your brain wild, into an indescribable rapture of the senses, gave you accesses to the visionary life that was natural to William Blake and Swedenborg and Bach.

How can a slender intellectual ever put himself in the place of a robust partygoer, or share the feeling of one who stands at the limits of an athletic workaholic?

Djerassi was fascinated with testing the boundaries of his mind with mescaline, or as Djerassi the chemist would name it, 3, 4, 5-trimethoxyphenethylamine.

One Saturday in Detroit, Djerassi and two other professors ingested mescaline sulfate at a suburban pizza party. The wives did not partake. Their husbands were no beatniks. Their husbands were psychic adventurers like Huxley.

Nothing happened to the trio at first.

The pizza did not spin.

The pizza did not change colors.

The pizza did not transform into someone's face.

Djerassi, for one, spent several hours waiting. Then Djerassi began floating around his backyard. Everyone below him started giggling. He saw his guests and their wives as 'a gaggle of Falstaffs.'

Djerassi touched down on the lawn.

The guests all devoured a new meal of ham and pickles and chutney and pie. Toward the end of the evening, inside the house, Djerassi split himself apart like an amoeba and sat in a corner coldly contemplating his other self there across the room. Later, Djerassi was standing in his bathroom about to brush his teeth before bed and began a jag of giggling at his reflection in the mirror.

This seemed to him a splendid way to finish an evening exploring the limits of endomorphy.

* * *

The year before, Norman Mailer and his girl, Adele Morales, were in New Orleans. One thing led to another, and the couple found themselves in the French Quarter attending a peyote party. In a kitchen, a blonde was stirring a chili pot filled with the cactus brew. It even smelled hallucinogenic. For some reason, this young woman was wearing a nurse's uniform.

Adele found herself alone with the nurse. She sipped a ladle of liquid cactus. Her tongue began prickling up. A black guy suddenly appeared. He handed her a slice of orange, saying, 'Suck on it. That will cut the bitterness.'

The guy's name was Ray. He talked her through waves of nausea. She didn't puke. Norman appeared. Ray and Norman and Adele left the party to go hear Max Roach and Charlie Parker.

In those days, Roach and Parker were considered mere practitioners of bop—music said to have a 'hole in its head.' Roach and Parker had not yet achieved the status of the Gods of Bebop, the Gods of Cool.

The three travelers took chairs at the edge of the stage. Neither Adele nor Norman was interested in the effects on each other's head. The only information they shared was that once nausea passed 'I now feel ecstatic.'

Mailer had a tin ear, but prided himself on possessing exquisite taste. Roach and Parker began dueling solos on 'Salt Peanuts.' Mailer nodded his head as if he understood what he was hearing.

Adele would write that she felt like Max Roach was 'having sex with me from the stage.'

The married couple ditched their black companion and drove back to their hotel. The street weaved. The car weaved. Then the street started undulating. The Mailers abandoned it on a side street and made it back to the hotel on foot. Their room was situated beside a blinking red neon 'HOTEL' sign. They shut the shades. The red blinking bled through the shades. The two lay together on the bed. Adele wasn't sure if her eyes were open or shut. She saw pregnant women whose bellies exploded into flowers. Norman told her he saw Aztecs cutting open the bellies of women on pyramids.

* * *

As for Carl Djerassi, one year later, he didn't 'come down' from the mescaline he took late Saturday afternoon until late afternoon on Sunday. Djerassi was lying in bed that night with his wife, trying to describe what his journey had been like.

'I shed layers of my personality,' he said. 'I shed them like the layers of an onion.'

His wife said rather coldly, 'You've obviously never peeled an onion.'

'What do you mean?'

'When you finish peeling there's nothing left.'

Later, the pair would go through a bitter divorce. The bitterest of divorces.

* * *

Jack Kennedy's wife, Jacqueline, was pregnant again and staying at the Hammersmith Farm outside Newport, owned by her mother and her stepfather, an Auchincloss

Jack was not there with his wife.

Jack was not even in America.

* * *

It's night on the Riviera—*The Tender Is the Night* Riviera. Offshore, a titanic yacht is moored. In a dining room that can sit forty people, forty people wearing tuxedos and jewelry and smoking with cigarette holders are being entertained by Frank Sinatra. This is a private concert. Frank Sinatra has had a five-year reign of masterpiece LPs.* In fact, Sinatra has invented the concept of the LP, that is, a disc that is not just a collection of miscellaneous songs, but a collection of songs meant to be played in the order in which they appear on each side of the disc. He has recorded *In the Wee Small Hours,* containing mostly desolate songs of heartbreak. Also, *Songs for Young Lovers* (the antidote to the previous record). In

* LP = Long Playing record; a thin vinyl disc played on a record player at 33.3 rotations per minute.

Sinatra's future are *Come Fly with Me, No One Cares, Nice 'n' Easy*—a run of masterpieces equal to T. S. Eliot's *The Waste Land*, 'The Hollow Men,' 'Ash Wednesday.' Sinatra was Sugar Ray Robinson returning from retirement to deck Rocky Castellani and Bobo Olson. Sinatra was Alfred Hitchcock's *Strangers on a Train* through *Rear Window* through *Vertigo* through *North by Northwest*.

Here on the Riviera, Sinatra has just finished his first set of fifteen songs. He is wearing a tux. He lights a Lucky Strike. 'I'd like to take a breather here and say hello,' Sinatra says. 'I've been having a lot of fun doing the show. I'd like to pause to have a smoke and wet my whistle, but first, ladies and gentlemen, let me honor a young man at the piano. Speedy Henderin.'

The applause is civilized.

'I'd like to get a loud round of applause for our host, Aristotle Onassis.'

The lights are dim. There is a single spotlight that swings white light across the forty guests and lands on Onassis. He's hunched next to a champagne bucket. He is a reticent man, but he is not shy. He quickly stands and bows in four directions.

'Ari has spent more than four million dollars to create this yacht. As you know it is named after his daughter. The *Christina* is the most elegant and advanced private yacht afloat in the world. Let's give Ari another hand for the *Christina*.'

More applause.

'And our most honored statesman guest is Sir Winston Churchill.' The spotlight seeks Churchill out. 'And Sir Winston's bird,' Sinatra says. 'And when I say *bird* I don't mean *broad*. Sir Winston always brings his bird Toby in a birdcage. What kind of bird is Toby, Sir Winston? What? Oh. Okay. Sir Winston has identified Toby as a parakeet. Lemme tell you that in the neighborhood I grew up in a *parakeet* is someone who sings and that isn't healthy.' He draws his finger across his throat. 'For all of you of foreign disposition, parakeets are people who fink to the cops....

'And I'd also like to say hello to King Farouk.'

Applause.

'And I'd like to introduce the legendary Maria Callas and her husband...Mr. Callas.'

Applause. Most people in the audience know that Maria and Ari are semi-clandestine lovers. The opera diva's husband is furious at Sinatra's mention. The fury is, as they say, *written on his face.* The man is Giovanni Battista Meneghini. A middle-aged woman gets out of her seat and hurries to the stage. She raises her hand and beckons Sinatra to lean over.

'She's left the ship,' the woman whispers. Sinatra smells the gin on her breath. '*They* had a big fight.' She then steps away and gives him a poignant look as if Sinatra should know what this tiff concerned and whether it was Giovanni and Maria who had the big fight or Aristotle and Maria.

'Well, no, madam,' Sinatra says in mock indignation. 'I most certainly will not slip into your cabin after the show.' He waits a beat. 'What island did you say your room was?' The moment the joke sinks in, Sinatra quickly says, 'And last but not least, let's have a warm hand for the Democratic senator from Massachusetts, Jack Kennedy . . .'

Kennedy's name is greeted with relieved laughter.

* * *

Jack Kennedy is a guest on the *Christina.* He is taking a vacation alone without his pregnant wife, Jacqueline. So far, it has been a lousy summer. Jack Kennedy had almost been the Democratic vice presidential candidate to Adlai Stevenson. No one had heard of Kennedy, yet on the first vote he came only thirty-eight votes shy of being the vice presidential candidate. That shook the delegates. Another vote was called for. On that vote, the party warhorse, fifty-three-year-old Senator Estes Kefauver, a man who made his reputation going after gamblers and the publishers of comic books, won the nomination.

Kennedy gave a gracious concession speech:

> . . . And therefore, ladies and gentlemen, recognizing that this Convention has selected a man
>
> who has campaigned in all parts of the country,
>
> who has worked untiringly for the Party,
>
> who will serve as an admirable running mate to Governor [Adlai] Stevenson,
>
> I hope that this Convention will make Estes Kefauver's nomination unanimous.
>
> Thank you.

That speech cost Kennedy. God forbid that Adlai Stevenson actually wins. If so, that guarantees that Stevenson will run for reelection in 1960. If he loses, Jack Kennedy's first shot at the presidency will be in 1964. If Stevenson wins, then Estes Kefauver will be the Democratic nominee that year. Jack could be the vice-presidential candidate, but what a sorry situation that would be. Kennedy would not be able to run for the presidency until he was in his fifties, and Jack Kennedy does not expect to live into middle age because of Addison's disease.

Immediately after the convention, Kennedy's brain was consumed by entitlement and libido.

Jack Kennedy wanted what he wanted.

Jack Kennedy was a member of the leisure class. Jack Kennedy made plans to go to the Riviera. Jack Kennedy was a statesman. On the Riviera, he'd talk to Winston Churchill aboard the yacht belonging to Greek shipping tycoon Aristotle Onassis. Kennedy had met Churchill during the war; Kennedy would now pick the old Brit's brain.

Jack Kennedy also was experiencing a respite from his back problems. This made him an even more energetic cocksman than usual. And Jacqueline, of course, would never do even for mandatory intercourse.

* * *

Jacqueline begged Jack not to leave for Europe. Her husband left without looking back. He now found himself engaging on a daily basis in quick carnal hoopla with several European women, including a particularly young bird named Pooh, who referred to herself in the third person just as Hunt the creeping Texan had done, saying such things as 'Pooh would like some champagne now.'

Or 'Pooh would like to go swimming.'

Or 'Pooh would like to suck your Catholic cock.'

* * *

'So, this is the *cock*tail hour for me,' Sinatra says. 'We're going down the line and we're gonna get a little ouzo tonight. You know, I feel sorry for people who don't drink because when you get up in the morning that's the best you're going to feel all day. Do you know that most Greeks drink five glasses of ouzo every day? That is why dead Greeks burn for a week when you cremate them.'

Sinatra sips his milky brew.

'This is good, let me tell you. And ouzo is fitting because I'm going to sing a saloon song. Do you all know what a saloon song is? Those are the songs that the singer sings in a bistro somewhere at two o'clock in the morning when everyone is gassed...Numbsville...Now this particular song concerns a young man who's fallen off the wagon; who's been sopping up booze since before breakfast. He's a young man who's fractured...stoned...he's mulled. He has a lot of trouble. Obviously, its source is a girl. *Cherchez la femme.* Which means in French *Why don't you share the broad with me?* Imagine that this lad finds himself aboard the *Christina.* You know the *Christina* is nine-tenths as long as a football field? It has eighteen staterooms, all named after Ari's favorite Greek islands. You know, Naxos and Corfu and Lesbo.

'Anyone here sleeping in Lesbo?

'Ha! A woman, it figures!

'That reminds me: There were three deserted Greek islands. On one, two Italian men and one Italian woman were stranded. On another, two French men and one French woman were stranded. On the third, two Greek men and one Greek woman. A month later, on the first island, one Italian man had killed the other for the Italian woman. On the next island, the two French men and the French woman were living happily together in a ménage à trois. On the final island, the two Greek men were sleeping with each other and the Greek woman was cleaning and cooking for them.'

Sinatra waits for the voluminous laughter to subside.

* * *

Jacqueline Kennedy by herself, pregnant and lying in the sun smoking in the U.S.A. She's smoking these new modern cigarettes. Salems. No, they are not named after the Pilgrim witch-burning town. The name comes from the town where they are rolled, Winston-Salem, North Carolina. Jacqueline lights one with her father's lighter. But it finally fails to produce a flame. She searches her pockets for matches, but can't find any. Jacqueline goes back to the house, to the kitchen, to the stove to turn on a burner to light her Salem from that ring of fire. She pokes around a gazebo and finds a candle in a lantern. She takes it to the stove and then she returns to the beach with her eternal flame.

Her *almost* eternal flame.

Jacqueline imagines her and her Salem cigarette are having a tête-à-tête.

Jacqueline listens to the cigarette by inhaling and she replies by exhaling a little cloud of smoke through her nose.

Cigarette, the word is French.

It is a slender word. It is feminine. *Cigare* is fatter and masculine.

Jacqueline believes that cigarettes are sharp medicines that kill germs, prevent disease.

Jacqueline believes *Qui fume prie.* Smoking is prayer.

Jacqueline is a lazy woman at heart. Smoking kills time.

When Jacqueline was very private, she would exhale a smoke ring. She still got a thrill out of that. Blowing the smoke through the pucker of her lips. Nuns, of course, told her when she was a teenager that blowing smoke rings was the most obscene action a virgin could make.

★ ★ ★

In the hills above Monte Carlo, Maria Callas was riding as a passenger in a silver Ferrari puttering along, driven by her second sometimes lover, the existential writer Albert Camus. This summer, the man was Almost Famous. Next year, Camus will become Definitively Famous after winning the Nobel Prize.

'The ancient Greeks had limits,' Camus said in French as he drove toward the sun in lazy fashion. 'Modern man does not.'

'You're driving like an old woman,' Callas complained. 'This is a Ferrari.'

'You want me to drive like a modern man. No! I'm driving like a Greek.'

'A Greek old woman,' Callas said with a snort.

'I'm driving like an ancient Greek. I have limits. Modern man does not. First came the atom bomb, then the hydrogen bomb. Next, there will be the nitrogen bomb. Each bomb does not just double the power of the previous bomb, but it expands in monumental increments. The hydrogen bomb blows up one hundred times more than the atom bomb, and the nitrogen bomb will blow up ten thousand times more than the hydrogen bomb. And so on.'

'Faster, Al, faster. Drive like this car is powered by the hydrogen bomb.'

'Ha! to the hydrogen bomb. The iridium bomb will be a thousand times stronger. Then will come the barium bomb.'

'But man can't blow up the universe,' Callas said. Then she added, 'A woman could, but a man never.' Then she screamed, 'Look out, Albert! Even old women must watch where they are driving. I will light your cigarette for you.'

'Thank you.'

'There?'

'There!' Then Camus said, 'At the dawn of Greek thought Heraclitus was already imagining that justice sets limits for the physical universe itself:

> The sun will not overstep his measures; if he does, the Erinyes, the handmaids of justice, will find him out.

'But there will be no end to the strength of the bombs man can build. Man has the power to end his own history. The Greeks never said that the limit could not be overstepped. They said it existed and that whoever dared to exceed it was mercilessly struck down.'

—Camus said this from the passenger's seat in the Ferrari as Maria Callas forced him to let her drive—

Callas spoke: 'Al, my love, I do not think that fellow who invented the atom bomb was struck down.' She frowned. 'What was his name? Orphenheimer?'

'Oppenheimer. His name *is* Oppenheimer.'

'Well, Opperheimer wasn't struck down after he invented the atom bomb. And he wasn't struck after he invented the hydrogen bomb.'

'We will be struck down if you don't let up on the gas.'

'You old woman, Al! I am barely pressing it. Want to see me really stomp the gas?'

'No, my dear. Please don't. And anyway, Op-*pen*-heimer didn't invent the hydrogen bomb.'

'Sure?'

'Positive. A Polish-born Jew named Stanislaw Ulam did, along with an American named Teller.'

'Teller what?'

'Teller, Teller, Teller. I can't summon his first name at the moment. He was American. John Wilkes Teller. Houdini Teller. Someone whose last name is Teller.'

'But Ulam and Teller weren't struck down.'

'Not yet. Watch out for that truck, Maria!'

'I am watching for all trucks.'

'Well, watch better, Maria,' Camus said, slouching as low as he could in his seat. 'Anyway, the men of whom we speak were not struck down because of the sublime beauty of the cloud of mushrooms.'

'You mean the mushroom cloud?'

'Yes. Exactly. They say it is as beautiful as the Mediterranean sun. But then there is tragedy in the heart of it.'

'In the heart of what?'

'The sun. And the cloud of mushrooms.'

⋆ ⋆ ⋆

Jacqueline Kennedy had once eavesdropped on a conversation by three American intellectuals. One asked, 'How is man different from the animals?' The second answered, 'He has a soul.' The other said, 'He has reason.' Then Jacqueline piped up in a voice that was almost shrill, 'Man is different from the animals because he is the only one who smokes.'

Jacqueline now hummed the opening of *Don Juan*. She knew enough Italian to sing one of the lines: 'Life without tobacco is not worthy of being lived.'

Jacqueline imagined and imagines that this is a perfect moment—celebrating the smoke of life. She sucks the smoke deep, deeper into her lungs. Her body is a Renaissance tower. Her baby is there down in the basement. The cigarette smoke fogs down the tower and forms a gentle cloud over that baby.

The breath of life.

Her wonderful baby is sharing this delicious cigarette.

⋆ ⋆ ⋆

Onboard the *Christina.*

Frank Sinatra: 'Now our young man wanders on the deck of Aristotle Onassis's great yacht. He passes the Olympic-sized swimming pool and it's full of dames in new bikini bathing suits. Our young man doesn't even look because as I've told you his problems stem from a broad. This is very difficult to defeat... Communists you can defeat, but a dame is a different matter.... You see, his broad flew the coop with another guy and all the bread.... Our young man takes an elevator down to the lower decks of the *Christina.* He walks past the fully operating hospital operation room. He considers getting his heart removed, but he finds out the chief surgeon is getting steamed in the spa. So, our boy goes into the library. As you may know, the *Christina*'s library is only filled with history books as Mr. Onassis doesn't believe in fiction. You know a famous American, Henry Ford, felt the completely opposite way. He said, *History is bunk.* Anyway, there's a library full of first editions of very old books. Books so old they're written in languages that everyone has forgotten how to read. Our lad sees all these books about Odysseus. *Who the hell is Odysseus?* he asks out loud. The librarian hears him and says, *Maybe you know him as Ulysses.* Our lad says, *Why is Mr. Onassis so interested in the Civil War?*'

There is no laughter.

'Come on, folks. Ulysses S. Grant. You know Ulysses, he invented the Trojan horse, which is an enormous prophylactic.'

There is laughter.

'So why are there three names for the same characters in mythology? Why is the king of the gods Zeus in Greece and Jupiter in Italy and Eisenhower in the U.S.A.? Why is Aphrodite the goddess of love in Greece and Venus in Italy and Ava Gardner in Hollywood? Does anybody know the god of laughter?' Pause. 'No one? The god of laughter is Gelos in Greece and Risus in Rome and Jerry Lewis in...' He pauses. 'In Vegas!'

* * *

On August 23, 1956, Jacqueline Kennedy's belly exploded with pain and she was rushed to the hospital to give birth to a stillborn daughter. She and Jack had planned to name the child Arabella if she was a girl. This tragedy was in all the newspapers. The *Washington Post*'s headline:

Sen. Kennedy on Mediterranean Trip
Unaware His Wife Has Lost Baby.

* * *

Aboard Aristotle Onassis's yacht, the *Christina,* floating off Côte d'Azur.

Frank Sinatra takes another sip of ouzo. 'Our lad wanders into Ari's bar. I trust you've all been to Ari's bar. It has twenty-five barstools and each one is covered with whale skin.' Sinatra turns to his pianist, 'Speedy, whales have skin, right, not just blubber?'

Speedy—a young man who looks like he should be delivering telegrams—says, 'I think they have hides like cows.'

Frank shrugs. 'Well, Ari's twenty-five barstools are each covered with the whale skin pulled from the most intimate part of a whale. Well, wait a minute. The Greeks call it όσχεο. The Romans say *scroto.* The Dodgers calls them *balls.* Now I ask you, there are twenty-five seats at the bar. Where did Onassis find one whale in the Mediterranean to snip snip snip, let alone twenty-five? I took my kids to see the new Disney cartoon *Pinocchio.* Now I know why in that scene where the whale swallows Pinocchio, the whale's voice was as high as Maria Callas singing.'

Only a few dare laugh, but their laughs are exaggerated and malevolent.

'Do you know the great book *Moby-Dick*? Any of you actually read *Moby-Dick*? I have a copy right here. I can pass it around . . . Did you know that the author Herman Melville was Italian? Yes. That's the great secret. The second great secret is that the Mediterranean is full of whales. Well, *Moby-Dick* starts with the sentence "Call me Ishmael." It turns out that the parents of our young heartbroken kid on the *Christina* named their son after the hero of *Moby-Dick*—only he likes to be called *Ish.* Now Ish goes into Ari's bar and sits on the only white barstool in the joint. And this seat made out of whale balls comforts Ish in a strange way because he's just had his own όσχεο twisted up by a dame. Now let me be honest with you good people. The only reason I read *Moby-Dick* is because Nancy my daughter had to read it in high school. She comes home one day saying, *This is the sickest, biggest piece of puke in all history.* I said, *What are you talking about, this is an American classic.* She opened the book and holds it open to a certain page and says, *Read this! These guys are jerkin' off a whale!* And sure enough, she was right. Ishmael is down in the hull of the ship with the other guys squeezing whale spunk. He goes:

'"I bathed my hands among those soft, gentle globules of infiltrated tissues, wove almost within the hour; as they richly broke to my fingers, and discharged all their opulence, like fully ripe grapes their wine; as I snuffed up that uncontaminated aroma . . . like the smell of spring violets. . . ."

'Yes, ladies and gentlemen! Whale spunk smells like spring violets!

'"Squeeze! squeeze! squeeze! all the morning long; I squeezed that sperm till I myself almost melted into it; I squeezed that sperm till a strange sort of insanity came over me; and I found myself unwittingly squeezing my co laborers' hands in it, mistaking their hands for the gentle globules. Such an abounding, affectionate, friendly, loving feeling did this avocation beget; that at last I was continually squeezing their hands, and looking up into their eyes sentimentally . . . I could keep squeezing that sperm for ever! . . . I saw long rows of angels in paradise, each with his hands in a jar of spermaceti. . . ."

'Now, before I get too carried away, it behooves me to return to that young man sitting down on that whale scrotum stool down in Aristotle Onassis's bar. [Sinatra begins singing.] It's quarter to three. There's no one in this blubber-room, but you and me . . . [speaking] no no no . . . I'll sing it straight. *Uh-um.* [Singing.] It's quarter to three. There's no one in the joint except you and me. Set 'em up, Joe—(that's Joe Kennedy)—'

Sinatra nodded at Jack.

'—here's a little story I want you to know . . .'

* * *

After the show, Aristotle Onassis scolds Frank Sinatra. 'You know, your speech. Rome was an infection. They were unimaginative people who substituted what they lacked in artistic genius with a genius for war. Rome copied Greece, but lost the flavor of the original. Not only that, they copied the last years of Greece, its decadence and mistakes. Rome ignored the strong vigorous grace of the great writers Homer and Plato. It was not life that Rome copied from Greece but puerile and overintellectualized abstractions.'

Sinatra laughed. 'That's one way to look at it.'

* * *

Aristotle Onassis next found Jack Kennedy standing on the deck with Pooh. Ari walked by. 'Why the long face my friend?'

'My wife. The baby was born . . . stillborn. The baby was born dead.'

'How terrible. You must return immediately. Let me arrange it.'

'Wait, Ari. Why? Why ruin a lovely time?'

'Pooh doesn't think that Jack should leave,' Pooh said.

'Jack, do you want to be president someday?'

'Yes, Ari. I want to be president someday.'

'And Pooh will be the first lady,' Pooh said.

'Jack, you absolutely have to return to America.'

'Are you kicking me off?'

'Jack, I'm a Greek. What kind of host would kick a United States senator off his boat?'

* * *

Back in 1935, Elvis Aaron Presley's twin brother, Jesse Garon Presley, had been stillborn.

Chapter 16

Memphis, Tennessee, 1956

William Burroughs wrote to Allen Ginsberg from Tangier:

> Every Arab in Tangier has the Jihad Jitters.
> Jihad means the wholesale slaughter by every Moslem of every infidel.

Burroughs told how on any given day, all the stores suddenly shut down. Dozens of children then paraded down the twisting streets, avenues narrow as alleys. Each kid carried a little Moroccan flag, which is composed of a field of red with a green star.

Then there is a lull, followed by a crowd of thousands of Arab adults now storming down the streets. Burroughs got caught in such a riot one day and ran over to the nearest police headquarters to hide out. A hundred Arabs were soon outside the door howling in rage at the cops. 'When the sun finally sets, imagine 20,000 teenagers swarming through the streets vociferating, *Fuera Français!* ['Out with the French!'].

Burroughs found this Moroccan moment 'beautiful.' He made the flip comment that the police themselves 'drive around in jeeps machine-gunning each other.'

* * *

Jewish egghead Leslie Fiedler came up with a theory on the level of the Jihad Jitters called the Good Good Boy and the Good Bad Boy in American culture. Fiedler's Good Good Boy does what his mother pretends she wants him to do and be. The boy obeys and conforms. The Good Good Boy is the juvenile remnant of the traditional antistatic European youth. It was a fourteen-year-old Good Good Boy named Bobby Franks that the two nineteen-year-old male psychopaths Leopold and Loeb killed and buggered back in 1924.

Yet, according to Fiedler, it is the Good Bad Boy that mother loves best.

The Good Bad Boy does exactly what he wants to do. He will deceive his mother. Break her heart—but nothing so bad that she can't forgive him.

It is the Good Bad Boy that is America's vision of itself.

Fiedler believed Americans are crude in our beginnings and endowed with an intuitive sense of moral justice. The Good Good Girls love Good Bad Boys because they refuse to be 'sissies.'

That said, Leopold and Loeb had been Bad Bad Boys.

Fiedler goes on to suggest that Elvis Presley is America's premier Good Bad Boy.

* * *

September 9, 1956, 8:00 PST. Buster Hendrix is at his aunt and uncle's house. The living room. Red carpet. Red leather chair where his uncle sits in the shadows. He is all black but the whites of his eyes. Smoking a pipe. His wife is high yellow. Six cousins, four through nine, belly-down on the floor or sitting with Mama on the couch. The TV is a small Pye television, Model V 110, sitting on a cheap wooden stand. It looks like a cross between a typewriter case and an aquarium. Buster stands at the edge of the living room. He is too wired to sit. On the television, the *really big shew* starts on CBS. Abstract black and white shapes appear on the screen. To Buster's eyes, these shapes are like some secret writing. Surely on other planets, the spacemen are watching the same show at this same moment. This is a *really big shew* of universal import. Roman trumpets blare and the announcer announces, 'Good evening, ladies and gentlemen, your Lincoln dealer and your Mercury dealer present *The Ed Sullivan Show,* America's number one TV variety show starring the nationally syndicated columnist of the *New York Daily News* Ed Sullivan. And tonight it stars Elvis Presley and the Vagabonds. And now here is our host, Charles Laughton.'

'What? Where's Ed?' the uncle says.

'He's still in the hospital from his car crash.'

Charles Laughton—possessing girth like Alfred Hitchcock—struts quickly out onto the stage.

'Who's that?' several kids ask.

'The Hunchback of Notre Dame,' says Buster's aunt.

'Hello. How do you do, ladies and gentlemen?' are his first British words. 'Tonight as always my friend Ed Sullivan has arranged for some wonderfully talented guests to entertain you. I'm very happy indeed to have the pleasant job of presenting them to you.' The fat man gives a little 'hop' as he introduces the Amin Brothers, two young Greeks who perform circuslike acrobatics. Buster almost forgets why he is watching *The Ed Sullivan Show* tonight. There is no TV at home, remember. The novelty of watching the one brother standing on his head on the upraised foot of his older sibling entrances Buster. Next is a white Broadway singer named Dorothy Sarnoff who sings a song from *The King and I.* She is wearing a formal gown with opera gloves. Next, a comedy polka band. Now Buster feels restless. Next, Laughton appears in a totally black room with four picture frames hanging on the black wall behind him—three have a shiny circular object inside them. The first frame has a very small image of what Buster recognizes as the cover of Elvis Presley's first album.

'You're all wondering what these objects are behind me,' Laughton drawls. 'I'm going to tell you. They're gold records. These gold records, three of them, have been awarded to a singing star that you're going to meet in a moment. I'm talking about Elvis Presley... The very first opportunity Ed Sullivan will award these gold records to him personally, but now away to Hollywood to meet *Elvin* Presley.'*

* * *

In Tangier, William Burroughs imagined the Jihad riots as a musical:

> The [National Political Party] hates me.
> The guides all berate me,
> I'm nobody's sweetheart now.
> I got the Jihad jitters,
> I mean scared of those critters,
> They's a-coming for to disembowel me now...

---

* Laughton mispronounced Elvis's name!

Burroughs was particularly delighted that at the red-hot climax of each riot the Arabs began fits of laughter.

* * *

The Ed Sullivan Show. The scene changes. A black set with several abstract guitar shapes. Elvis strides forward out of the darkness wearing a plaid sport coat and a polka-dotted shirt. Even in B&W, you can tell this jacket is louder than loud.

Buster hears girls screaming, but they will never appear on the screen. Four of Buster's cousins are girls and they all say, 'Eeeeeewe'—a protective racial response in front of their black parents. Elvis speaks: 'Ladies and gentlemen. This is probably the greatest honor that I've ever had in my life. There is not much I can say, except do what makes you feel good. We want to thank you from the bottom of our heart. And now "Don't Be Cruel."' A band begins playing. Elvis sings. Elvis groans. The girls on the set scream. The shot changes. Buster sees the four Jordanaires, Elvis's white backup singers. They are also wearing plaid jackets. They stand onstage shortest to tallest. The Jordanaires are tapping their feet in a synchronized left/right, left/right. It looks like these young men are marching. *I don't want no other lover, baby it's just you I'm thinking of.*

'Those Jordanaires are all goofy-looking kids,' Buster's uncle says.

Girls' screams inside the Pye television (Model V 110). The shots alternate from simple close-ups of Elvis from the breast up to shots of Elvis from his belly/acoustic guitar up.

Buster finds that he is playing an invisible guitar. The girls in the TV are still screaming like crazy. Buster pretends that they are screaming for him. The song is finished too quick, too quick. Elvis takes a bow. 'Thank you very much. Thank you, ladies. And now, friends, we'd like to introduce you to a brand-new song. It is completely different from anything we've ever done. And this is the title from our brand-new Twentieth Century Fox movie and my new RCA Victor *escape*—release.'

Buster is oblivious to the Freudian slip Elvis just made: escape/release. So many years later, this Freudian slip means what?

Elvis begins singing, 'Love me tender. Love me sweet.'

A girl's song. Buster notices that Elvis's sideburns are level with his earlobes. Buster thinks Elvis's pompadour is amazing—a bird could nest in it. There is a single spotlight on Elvis. The shadow of Elvis's chin plays across his right shoulder. Elvis sings and the camera backs up slowly and stops. The set is now completely dark except for Elvis in his ridiculous coat.

The camera returns to Charles Laughton. 'Well, well, well-well-well, ladies and gentlemen—Elvis Presley. And Mr. Presley, if you are watching this in Hollywood, and I may address myself to you—it has been many a year since any young performer has captured such a wide, and, as we heard tonight, devoted audience.'

* * *

Buster is one of 60 million people that science will determine are watching the *Ed Sullivan* 'Elvis' show tonight. This means that 59,999,999 people and Buster are now watching the white couple Conney and Mack tap dance to 'Tea for Two'; 59,999,999 people and Buster watch a commercial for a Lincoln-Mercury automobile, watch Charles Laughton tell a mock children's story titled 'Little Girl and Wolf' that ends with Little Red Riding Hood pulling an automatic out of her basket and shooting the wolf in her grandmother's bed dead. Laughton says: 'Moral: It's not so easy to fool little girls nowadays as it used to be.'

Only the cool intellectuals who are watching *Ed Sullivan*—all two dozen of them—get that Laughton was making some obscure connection between Elvis as Wolf and Little Red Riding Hood. *Will the chick shoot Elvis? No, man, no. She'll hop into bed with him!*

Now comes a thirty-one-year-old female singer from Jamaica named Amru Sani.

'High yellow,' Buster's aunt says.

Amru Sani is wearing an Indian sari and sings 'I'm in the Mood for Love.' Next, Carl Ballantine, a white magician/comedian pushing forty, does card tricks. Now 'Toby the Dog': an undistinguished-looking Scottie trots out alone onstage toward a champagne bottle and flips it into the air with his paw so it lands on the cork. Charles Laughton appears to say, 'Now let's go out to Hollywood, to see that man again, Elvis Presley.'

* * *

Morocco. William Burroughs wrote to Allen Ginsberg that he thought the whole Muslim uproar in Tangier was a 'cheap baboon trick.' Burroughs's wildlife notes:

> When a baboon is attacked by a stronger baboon, the weaker baboon redirects the attack on an even weaker baboon.

* * *

The Ed Sullivan Show. Elvis appears in his loud jacket, three of the Jordanaires standing behind him. 'Go man go,' Elvis says. 'Ready teddy to rock and roll...' Buster immediately begins playing his ethereal guitar that no one can see. On TV, Elvis shakes his head and lowers his head to his chest. The camera angle changes. Buster now sees the view from over the drummer's shoulder.

'That's D. J. Fontana,' a cousin calls out. 'He's twenty-five years old!'

Buster trembles as D. J. Fontana rolls his sticks on his snare. To his left Buster can see Bill Black slapping his stand-up bass. Next the guitarist, Scotty Moore. Next is a close-up of Elvis from his chest up. 'Got a flat top-catch and a dungaree doll,' he sings and swings his gaze into being cross-eyed and raises his hand to his ear and the girls inside the TV scream on cue. Now Buster is scat-singing imaginary guitar solos over Elvis's singing. Buster goes, 'Doodle-dee-doodle-dalah we bop chachung!' Buster's voice breaks. Buster doesn't care. Buster is enthralled. Now a long shot of Elvis facing the camera and he's singing about the 'sock hop ball.' Elvis is energetically shaking his buttocks behind him.

Scotty is playing a solo. It lasts for seven seconds. Buster does not breathe. Buster hears with sonic clarity Scotty piercing the Ray Butts EchoSonic amplifier. Scotty is doing country finger-picking alternating with Duke Ellington chords. Buster pretends it is he, this thirteen-year-old kid, who is playing those riffs on his ghost guitar.

His imperceptible guitar. *His fingers! My fingers! Wait!* Buster is now working his thumb and all the remaining fingers on his left hand. He is matching Scotty note for note. Meanwhile, Elvis has become a pure animal. Now the camera is behind the drummer again. Elvis is jumping up and down, sporadically fake strumming his prop acoustic guitar. Scotty's and Buster's solos are over and a nanosecond before Elvis starts singing again he studies something above his head off-screen.

'What's up there?' Buster's uncle says.

The camera does not show. Now a long shot of the band. Buster finally notices a nice little square amp between the drums and the piano.

* * *

One night during the Jihad Jitters, Burroughs was walking home. Three Arab men followed the American. One of them pulled out a dagger that was one foot long. Burroughs spun around and yanked out his six-inch switchblade. He lowered his torso into 'a classic Commando Tactic Knife Fighter's Crouch,' holding his left hand out to parry.

Burroughs scared the Arabs silly. The trio fled. Burroughs did not yell or say anything. Soon the three return laughing to Burroughs and beg him for money.

As turbulent as the Jihad Jitters were, William Burroughs wrote Allen Ginsberg that Tangier was as safe as any town he had ever lived in. Tangier was even incomparably safer than Mexico City. Burroughs wrote in capital letters:

ARABS ARE NOT VIOLENT.

* * *

Back to *Ed Sullivan*: The second Presley set has concluded. The camera is a close-up of Elvis. 'Ah, Mr. Sullivan. We know that somewhere out there you are looking in, and ah, all the boys and myself, and everybody out here, are looking forward to seeing you back on television.' He pauses. 'Friends, as a great philosopher once said, *You ain't nothing but a hound dog . . .*'

Buster begins baying like a dog. Then begins scat-singing, working off Scotty's arpeggios—*dee dop dodee pop gaga-doleep bop deddle-deddle fresopintop-per* . . . 'You ain't nothin' but a hound dog cryin' all the time—' *dee dop dodee pop gaga-doleep bop deddle-deddle fresopintopper* . . .'You ain't never caught a rabbit—' Buster's aunt: 'That boy's grammar! He should be ashamed!'

dee dop dodee pop gaga-doleep bop deddle-deddle fresopintopper...'And you ain't no friend of mine!'

Buster twists and pirouettes and crashes over a tall standing lamp.

dee dop dodee pop gaga-doleep bop deddle-deddle fresopintopper...

Elvis immediately stops singing the song. Buster is on his back on the red carpet staring at the ceiling and hears Charles Laughton's voice say, 'What did somebody say? Music hath charms to sooth the savage breast...' What just happened? Buster believes the irrational—that he caused Elvis to stop singing 'Hound Dog' after the first verse.

* * *

Christmas, 1956. Howard Hughes gave a loan to Donald Nixon for $205,000—$1.6 million today—sending the funds to Don's mother, Hannah, who had put up the family property in Whittier as security.

This loan will never be paid back.

After Donald's loan, the 'troubles' for Hughes's airline, TWA, ceased. An antitrust suit against Hughes Tool was also aborted.

* * *

'We've come to the end of the show, ladies and gentlemen,' Charles Laughton said several seconds before *The Ed Sullivan Show* concluding theme song cued up. 'Before I say another word I would like to remind you that this is Civil Defense Week—' This was 1956. Every American—both young and old—participated in a dry-run preparation of what to do when the Russian atomic bombs started to drop. Laughton continued: 'And all of you are urged to acquaint yourself with the Civil Defense system in your community and to cooperate with your local Civil Defense authorities.' Now is the moment when Buster finally noticed that Laughton had a folded white handkerchief in the other chest pocket of his suit. 'I hope you've enjoyed meeting all our guests. I've very much enjoyed acting as your host. The next Sunday as you know, Ed Sully-van will be back so you won't have any more of this kind of nonsense.'

* * *

After Charles Laughton's death in 1962, his wife, Elsa Lanchester (she played the Bride of Frankenstein), will out her husband—Laughton only engaged in sex with men.

Theirs was a most peculiar marriage.

As for the loins of Elvis Presley—the singer had probably slept with more than one hundred girls by now. A boy could lose count. Elvis and his girl usually went back to his room to munch on candy bars and watch TV until the station went off the air for the night. Then they would talk until dawn, then have simple sex. Elvis's favorite method of birth control was rubbers. His second, luck.

'Elvis had an innocence at that time,' more than one girl would remember. 'I'm sure it didn't last. But what he really wanted was to have a relationship, to have company...'

If Carl Djerassi could have appeared in Elvis's room, he could have informed the couple in the bed that 'the only animal other than humans that has *sex for fun* is the Pygmy Chimp Bonobo. Humans are willing to have sex 365 days of the year. In all other species copulation is seasonally controlled and related to the optimal time for fertilization and rearing of offspring.' Djerassi would tell how 'every 24 hours there are 100 million acts of intercourse by humans in the world.'

How many of those acts in the 1950s were attributed to or inspired by Elvis Presley is known only to God.

Chapter 17

The American Embassy, Montevideo, Uruguay, 1956–1957

It is December 18, 1956. Michael Meyer is nine years old. This is the day he will die. He will be run down by an automobile. Like everyone who has been hit by a car (and this writer has had that experience), one has no premonition that a Pontiac or Oldsmobile is destined to strike you at seven in the morning or at high noon or, in Michael's case, six p.m.—you are destined to be at the wrong place at the wrong time. What happened to Michael happened because of television. It's unthinkable to picture modern parents not possessing at least one television for their children. In 1956, the Meyer household still lacked a TV. The Rack family across the road had an Admiral ten-inch portable. The plastic cabinet was 'Chevy Turquoise' and white. It usually sat on the kitchen counter. Michael and his brother Quentin would go across the road every afternoon after school to watch television with Bobby and Cindy Rack, each kid sitting on a barstool in the kitchen like adults at a tavern. There were great things on television for kids during the late afternoon—*Felix the Cat, Sherlock Holmes, Billy Bounce and Wilti* (Wilti was a rabbit that lived in Billy's hat).

The Meyers ate dinner each night at six. In the 1950s, all across America citizens had dinner at six. Men never worked late. Even if the breadwinner worked for the CIA, he got home in time for dinner. The Rack family was rare. The Racks ate like Europeans, their dinner late at seven thirty or even eight, thus the Meyer boys would lose track of time watching TV in the Racks' kitchen where no mother was stirring a pot at the stove. Some nights the boys did not get back home until six thirty. Their mother told them if they ever returned home a half hour late again, she would forbid them the pleasures of the Rack television.

As the autumn progressed into December, the sun—of course—sank earlier each afternoon. It was dark by five thirty p.m. As the clock ticked toward six, Quentin and Michael were peering intently into the face of the Racks' 'Chevy Turquoise' Admiral ten-inch portable television, jiggling their legs, desperately hoping that Flash Gordon would escape from the Martian Claymen, men who had been turned into clay by the evil Queen of Mars, a woman who was now under the influence of the faux Asiatic, Ming the Merciless. The boys were waiting until the very last minute to return home.

Flash Gordon did escape from the Claymen—although the last image of the show was a cliffhanger of Flash's pointy rocket exploding in the Martian sky.

The boys had ninety seconds to run across the street to their house for dinner at six.

* * *

McClean. An old man behind the wheel of a Studebaker plowed into the small body of nine-year-old Michael Meyer. The driver jumped out of the car and stood on the road terrified. Petrifaction is not an uncommon response after you run someone over. Quentin was on his knees howling over his nine-year-old brother. The driver paid no attention to the hysterical brother. Instead, he stood in the road screaming along with Quentin. What should he have done? He should have rushed to Quentin and told him to go get help. Then the man should have taken off his coat and wrapped it around the little boy he had run down.

People in America rarely act like people do in the movies. People in America are often not particularly heroic. Perhaps this hysterical old man was a blessing in disguise. Mary heard his howling in the night and ran down to the spot in the road. She went to Michael and she knew her nine-year-old son was dead. She still told Quentin to run to the house and call an ambulance. She then spent most of the next forty-five minutes trying to comfort the ridiculous man who had killed Michael, her son.

* * *

Just after Christmas, Howard Hunt sailed his family aboard an Argentine liner to Uruguay, to the capital city on the Atlantic coast, Montevideo.

Montevideo. The name sounds prematurely modern, as the word *video* was barely a noun in 1957, let alone a verb or way of life. In Spanish *Montevideo* means 'Eastern Point,' designating this city's position near the mouth of the Rio de la Plata as it empties into the Atlantic.

Hunt's daughters began crying as they sailed up the Plata to Montevideo. 'Daddy, the river is full of garbage. The beach is full of garbage.' The city of Montevideo itself had a depressingly stagnant Ohio-ish architectural sense about it, with unimaginative brick or concrete buildings and stray pages from newspapers in Spanish blowing down the streets.

Norman Mailer will describe the Hunts' auspicious arrival in Montevideo this way:

> Hunt and his wife, Dorothy, came in like F. Scott Fitzgerald and Zelda. Twenty-two pieces of luggage, all monogrammed with an E.H.H., no less. Plus untold furniture and cartons.

Thirty-four years from 1957, Norman Mailer will continue his astounding and cluttered career by writing a 1,310-page novel about the CIA titled *Harlot's Ghost*. A sixth of the novel will be set in Montevideo, Hunt figuring prominently as a character in Mailer's novel just as Hunt does in this novel that you are reading. Why will Mailer write about Hunt? Mailer will say in an interview that Hunt had airs and vanities that made him a marvelous character. In his novel, Mailer will confidently describe Hunt's 'rigorous' work schedule in Montevideo—Hunt 'is off every weekend at some large *estancia* in the pampas hunting for *perdiz* and working his American charm on very rich landowners.' Mailer describes the study in Hunt's house in the suburb of Carasco—its walls adorned with framed photos of Hunt in a 'Chinese dugout with a sniper's gun. Hunt on a ski lift in Austria. Hunt with brace of pheasants in Mexico. Hunt with antelope horns in Wyoming.' Mailer's description of Saint John's father living with Hemingwayesqe macho gusto is accurate according to what his son told me. What is most spooky is Mailer's accurate description of Hunt's snobbery—his constant bragging of his lineage (all lies). Finally, Mailer mentions that Hunt writes novels in his 'spare time.'

* * *

Norman Mailer never wrote about Big Don Nixon. Big Don opened his third Nixon's in Anaheim, adjacent to Disneyland (which was two years old).

★ ★ ★

In 1957, Lawrence Welk was a well-watched ABC television bandleader as well as a fluent accordionist. Even in 1957, Lawrence Welk was perhaps the squarest man in America.

★ ★ ★

In Montevideo, Uruguay, Howard Hunt soon discovered the American ambassador's wife was a flamboyant drunk who often kicked off her heels and did pirouettes at dinner parties. The ambassador himself was a bald fool with a stammer. By this point, Saint John had learned the rudiments of speech and he talked with a stutter.

For the first time in his life, Howard Hunt found himself picking up Dr. Spock and reading. He read what Dr. Spock had to say about stuttering—this affliction usually occurring when the child is between two and three years old. Dr. Spock said that the child's emotional state has much to do with stuttering. If you try to make your left-handed kid use his right, this can cause stuttering—

Wait a minute! Buster Hendrix was left-handed. His father would flat-out beat Buster to force him to use his right hand. Yet, Buster never began stuttering.

—Dr. Spock said stuttering can occur when a parent becomes stricter in discipline; when a newborn sibling is brought into the house; when a father is called into the Army. When a child becomes two, he concentrates on verbal skills. He attempts to speak in longer sentences in order to express ideas that are more complex. The kid may start a sentence two or three times struggling to find the right words. If the parents are worn out by their two-year-old's constant talking, they may just say 'Uh-huh' in absentminded fashion while they go about their business, frustrating the young speaker because he or she cannot hold their audience. This frustration manifests in stuttering—

During this time, Buster finally got strings for his acoustic guitar. Guitars have six strings. Each string is a different width. Guitars are usually strung with the fattest string on the top, down to the thinnest string on the bottom, this being so the guitar can be played with the right hand. Buster had to restring his guitar vice versa to play it left-handed. He'd stand with the neck of the guitar over his right shoulder. If his father came into the room Buster would quickly twirl the guitar so its neck was over his left shoulder—he'd begin playing it with his right hand. This was how the young man began to play ambidextrously.

—Dr. Spock stressed that stuttering is not a physical affliction. For example, under your child's tongue is a fold of skin that runs from the middle of the underside of the tongue to the floor of the mouth. This is called the frenum. Everyone has a frenum beneath their tongue. We may stutter and the frenum of our tongues may be short, but the frenum has nothing to do with stuttering. Dr. Spock warned in no uncertain terms that parents are never to consider cutting their stuttering child's frenum.

★ ★ ★

Margaret Salinger was eighteen months old and could speak roughly six distinct words and dozens of syllables of baby talk. She was too young to stutter. That winter, her father had been 'summoned to Rome' to attend a *New Yorker* social function in Manhattan. Father and mother and child checked into their Manhattan hotel room. Jerry Salinger left the hotel for some reason or another.

This was Claire Salinger's first trip to Manhattan since the baby was born, her first escape from the intense isolation of Cornish.

Cornish Cornish Cornish.

Cornish day.

Cornish night.

Snow in Cornish.

Cornish yokels. Cornish hillbillies.

Now Claire had arrived in the center of the world, New York City. Skyscrapers. Crowds. This was the real world. She would hold Margaret in her arms and look out the window of their second-floor hotel room, look down on Fifth Avenue, look down and see an army of men wearing their fedoras. All those hats. All those people.

Claire Salinger bundled up her daughter and left the room and ran down the streets of Manhattan, ducking her head not to knock the hats off of any runty pedestrians. Slamming the baby headfirst in a snowdrift, Claire scrambled into a deli and found the pay phone and called the only person she knew in New York. A cousin. A second cousin actually—a male who took a cab uptown and picked up the distraught mother. He got her a sublet and a nurse for Margaret. He kept Jerry Salinger away. The second cousin made sure Claire saw a psychiatrist three times a week—a Freudian, of course.

* * *

In Uruguay, Saint John and his sisters were watched by an Irish Catholic nanny inherited from the embassy by the name of Stella McGoey. She was a stern brittle woman. 'She wouldn't let us do anything fun,' the adult Saint John will say (now without a stutter). 'We just had to sit and color. My parents hosted many embassy functions. Everybody dressed up nice. Perfume in the air. People standing around with martinis and Bloody Marys. We kids were supposed to stay at the other end of the house and color in our coloring books. Sometimes I would escape and run to my mother with Stella McGoey chasing me, clawing at my clothes. I'm running down halls. I'm running up stairs and down stairs, daring Stella to catch me. I would just burst into the middle of this cocktail party to get to my mother, *Mama! Mama!* Stella would drag me away. It was all real embarrassing for my parents, I'm sure. I just didn't want to be in the back of the house with my sisters coloring.'

* * *

March 16, 1957. New York City. Norman Mailer's wife, Adele, gifted him with her first and his second daughter, Danielle.

The year 1957 will prove to be the Biggest Bang of the Baby Big Bang—the numerical height of births in the U.S.A. There will be 4.3 million babies born, including David Bowman, the author you are reading. In the

Arab calendar, 1957 was 1370. Saudi Arabia was not experiencing a baby boom in 1370 but Osama bin Laden was born six days before Danielle Mailer—the tenth of March.*

★ ★ ★

At the first of the year, Joe McCarthy began reading Dr. Spock reverently. Jean pulled some strings with Cardinal Spellman, and the McCarthys adopted a five-week-old girl from the New York Foundling Home. The couple named her Tierney Elizabeth after Joe's mother.

Joe McCarthy was crazy about Tierney.

He was determined to be the perfect father. He read Dr. Spock constantly, drunk or sober—usually drunk. By morning, he would have forgotten what he had read and have to read those pages again.

Dr. Spock was an enthusiast of fathers actively participating in the raising of their children. McCarthy agreed. He would make a point to be the one to change his daughter at least once a day. Not Jean or the nanny. Him. Usually in the morning. He even gave her a bottle now and then.

Joe knew his political career was over. Investments were the answer. Uranium was the ticket. Jean said that uranium was to 1950s America what oil had been to John D. Rockefeller's America in 1870. Joe's good friend from Green Bay, Skeet Olson, had a uranium mining company. Last year, McCarthy invested all his cash with Skeet. McCarthy still had not made a profit yet, but he was sure the Geiger counter of good fortune would start clicking at any moment and he'd buy a ranch for Jean and Tierney in Arizona.

But on Valentine's Day, Skeet's company folded. Skeet fled to South America.

The McCarthys were broke.

Joe still had enough money to buy Canadian whiskey, though. He still hit the bottle nursed the bottle sucked the bottle drank shots tossed 'em back.

★ ★ ★

* David Bowman was born on December 8.

It was the spring and McCarthy was on the twelfth floor of the Bethesda Naval Hospital. He had hepatitis and cirrhosis and delirium tremens. Surgeons had to cut growths off his leg. Jean told reporters that he was in an oxygen tent.

He was really in an iron lung.

Joe McCarthy was stuck inside a mechanical tube the size of a small water heater. Only his head stuck out of the front of the thing.

McCarthy knew he was dying.

He wasn't worried how he would be judged after death. He had not been a bad man. He'd been an ambitious man. There is a difference. The only ones he hurt deserved to be hurt.

* * *

Montevideo.

Howard Hunt threw a party because there were a number of interesting Americans in town. He was nursing a Scotch with a Texan named H. L. Hunt. The first Hunt was thirty-eight. The second Hunt was sixty-eight.

'I hear that you are one of the richest men in the world,' Hunt the Younger said. 'What brings you to South America?'

'Business and pleasure,' was the elder Hunt's answer. 'Oil and oil.'

It took a moment for Howard Hunt to get the joke. Then he said, 'I hear you come from Huguenot stock. Me too.'

The elder Hunt was taller than the younger Hunt. The elder Hunt put his hand on Howard Hunt's shoulder. 'You know what the most evil thing about Communism is, cousin? It is its ravishment of private property together with its liquidation of the owners.'

Howard Hunt gave an enormous smile. He hadn't heard, or, more important, *given,* a good tirade against Communism in days.

The oilman went on: 'You know that only a small number of the people the Communists conquer are exempt from outright slavery.'

Howard Hunt almost started bopping up and down, he was so happy. 'Confidential statistics say it is about three percent to five percent.'

'That's right, son,' H. L. Hunt said. 'Back in Texas I sponsor radio shows that tell Americans what is up with the Communists.' He then bellied closer to Howard Hunt. 'The nearest parallel to modern Communism is probably the fifth century, when savage tribes from northern Europe swooped down upon the civilized people along the Mediterranean coast who had gone weak with decadency.'

Howard Hunt tried to think that through. Was H. L. Hunt equating wop degradation to Nordicism?

'Look,' Hunt the Elder said. 'I'll tell you the business about the big money in the U.S.A. It turns pink through a conspiracy that begins when nurses are placed with babies who will inherit wealth. It goes on with governesses and tutors. Then mistaken playmates or mistaken classmates or mistaken teachers skillfully continuing the conspiracy. It continues through planned marriages and, for those not available for marriages, lovers. The Mistaken'—Hunt emphasized that word—'will certainly not overlook the proper approach to deceive the senile.'

Howard Hunt was now at a loss for words. He had no idea what this odd old oilman was talking about.

* * *

Hunt with Hunt in Uruguay.

Howard Hunt said to H. L. Hunt, 'America has never been the same since McCarthy left the Senate.'

'McCarthy, a good man even if he is a Catholic,' H. L. Hunt the oilman said. 'I once hired his Hasidic boy Cohn to do some legal work.'

'What kind of legal work?'

'Family business. Wills and heredity. Keeping track of my family.' Then the oilman Hunt dropped to his knees. 'Come on, cousin. Let's creep a bit.'

* * *

The late 1950s were golden years for Madison Avenue in Manhattan. Television and advertising. Advertising and television. Then, as now, no one really knew the actual degree to which advertising helped a new or old product. There were occasional masterpieces of advertising on TV, just like on radio. Now and then word spread about a fantastic billboard that drivers would travel out of their way to view.

Mostly a belief in advertising was and is always based on faith, like prayer.

In Manhattan, a certain two guys at Ogilvy & Mather on Madison

Avenue stopped after work for some suds at O'Paddy's on the corner of East 49th Street. They did not look rushed. They were obviously bachelors not required to rush home to the family. One of the Ogilvy & Mather guys was named Lamb and the other one Smith.

'How was D.C.?' Lamb asked Smith.

'Lousy with heat.'

'I heard you lost the Heritage account.'

'I lost the Heritage account.'

They were silent.

'Sorry.'

'Yeah. Thanks.'

They were silent again.

'So there's this story going around town down there. It's about how McCarthy died.'

'Yeah?'

'So McCarthy is lying on his hospital bed. The priest gives him last rites, *unum sanctum onomatopoeia*. Etcetera, etcetera. Then McCarthy pops his eyes open and peers at everyone in the room—the priest; his so-called wife and their rug rat; Everett Dirksen; Roy Cohn; the Kennedy boys; even Eisenhower—'

'Eisenhower was there?'

'Yeah. With Mamie. Anyway, McCarthy looks at everyone and then shoots up his left hand into the air and curses everyone and then drops dead.'

'Really? What did he say?'

Smith told him.

'No!'

'Yeah.'

'My God. To his own wife?'

'To the president of the United States.'

'Man oh man! Barkeep, another round.'

Chapter 18

Black Mountain, North Carolina, 1957–1958

On May 8, Ngô Dinh Diem arrived by air in Washington, D.C. He would stay in America for ten days. At a meeting with Jacqueline Kennedy, Diem asked, 'Did you open the package?'

'Of course not,' Jacqueline lied. Like many American women, she was a master of guilt-free indignation that was itself a second lie.

Premier Diem apologized.

'I accept,' Jacqueline said. Then she told him that she had gone to the nunnery and rung the bell beside a blank door. She waited. She rang the bell again. She could not hear the bell ringing. She waited on faith. Finally, a small Judas window in the door opened. The small slot was maybe four feet from the ground. Jacqueline had to stoop to peer into the spectacled eyes of what appeared to be a very old Asian woman.

'I have a package for Soeur Angelique,' Jacqueline announced in French.

The eyes peered at Jacqueline, studying her face. The nun then said, 'Leave it outside the door and go away.'

Jacqueline did as she was requested. Then she stopped at a café down the street. An hour later, a red Citroën zoomed up and the driver darted out of the car to pick up the package and then drive away. She couldn't tell if the driver had been a man or a woman. If it had been a woman, she was not a nun, because the driver was wearing slacks.

Jacqueline finished the story, and she and Ngô Dinh Diem sat in silence. They had been sitting in the tearoom at the Carlyle Hotel in Manhattan where the Kennedys kept a suite. 'Thank you,' Ngô Dinh Diem said. And then he told her the story of Soeur Angelique.

★ ★ ★

Summer. The Millers—Arthur and Marilyn—were living out on the eastern end of Long Island. Marilyn Monroe was pregnant. Suddenly, she grabbed her stomach and fainted. An ambulance came. It raced toward Manhattan, a two-and-a-half-hour drive. The woman had a miscarriage. An ectopic pregnancy. She was talking with Miller: 'Should I do my next picture? Stay home and try to have a baby again? I know I'd make a kook of a mother.'

'I think you should do the picture,' Miller said. 'You're a movie star.'

* * *

Joe K. Darwin sent Hunt a package in Montevideo. Before Hunt opened it, he picked up the telephone.

'Darwin.'

'This line still secure?'

'Hi, Hunt. Yes. This line remains secure.'

'What's in the envelope?'

'Listen to me: Better sit down. It's a photograph of something hotter than Brigitte Bardot's rear end.'

'Who's Brigitte Bardot?'

'Oh, my brother, my brother. Listen to me. I feel you are lost at the bottom of the world. You don't know Brigitte Bardot? Then you likely won't know the Edsel.'

'Ed Sill, who's he?'

'What?'

'Ed Sill.'

'No. Ed-sel. E-d-s-e-1. It is an automobile. It is a Ford. It's the hottest car in America.'

'Never heard of it.'

'For months there's been an endless stream of ads about the Edsel in magazines and newspapers and on TV. The ads are all the same. They only reveal the Edsel's hood ornament with the come-on *The Edsel Is Coming.*'

'So no one knows what the car actually looks like?'

'Listen to me: Not until September the fourth. But I work for Central Intelligence. I have photographs and blueprints. Listen to me: Open the envelope.'

'Okay. Gimme a minute. Okay. There.' Silence.

'Say something, Hunt. Pretty modern-looking, huh?'

'Yeah. Pretty modern-looking.'

Then Darwin said, 'I see the best minds of my generation driving an Edsel.'

* * *

The August before the Edsel's unveiling, the Freudian that Claire Salinger was seeing in Manhattan persuaded her to return with Margaret to her husband in Cornish, New Hampshire. She did, but she had conditions. (1) Margaret would be allowed to have friends her age. (2) Claire would take Margaret to the doctor on a regular basis. J.D. agreed to these terms.

* * *

Seattle. Ruby Chow's closes at two a.m. They have turned the sign off. This Chinese restaurant occupies the ground floor of a refurbished mansion several blocks outside the perimeters of Chinatown. Ruby Chow's was snazzy. No chop suey hash house. Traditional Cantonese cuisine. Inside, they were cleaning up. The restaurant was decorated with large color photographs of the owner and cook, Ping Chow (in his early thirties), wearing traditional bodhisattva opera costumes.

Chinese opera.

Chinese opera is filled with song and speeches and costumes and acrobatics and sometimes characters even spit fire. Ping Chow had been a star in the Chinese opera until the Japanese invaded China. Now, as his houseboys clean the restaurant, he always spins different recordings of Chinese opera on the hi-fi. Somehow, his choices always end up metaphorically being about his wife, Ruby Chow, the woman the restaurant is named for and one of the most powerful behind-the-scenes Chinatown residents who has nothing to do with the Tongs.

A Chinese opera about Ruby would begin with a demon spitting flames, a personification of the Chinese Exclusion Act of 1882 signed into law by President Arthur. Then flags flip past signaling the passage of time to 1920 when Ruby is born on the Seattle docks. This is not unusual as the Chinese did not go to hospitals. Ruby's father dies in 1932, the nadir of the Great Depression. Ruby's widowed mother sells lottery tickets. Ruby's brothers beg for leftovers at the back doors of restaurants. At this moment inside Ruby's in 1957, Asian urchins rap on the back door for handouts that they are, of course, always given. Back in the opera, Ruby grows up. The Chinese Exclusion Act of 1882 starts screaming. Although the Chinese Exclusion Act of 1882 has been modified through the years, it's still on the books in principle.

Ruby moves from Seattle to Manhattan. She gets married. To whom? She has two sons. What happens to the husband? He's an acrobat and somersaults offstage and is never heard of again. Ruby is now a waitress at the Howdy Club, a discreet gay bar in the West Village in Manhattan. She discovers she has an affinity for gay men. Then she spies Ping Chow. A man who loves women. A man who is one of the stars of the Chinese opera company. They've become stranded in New York as the Japs have just bombed Pearl Harbor.

Ping is so handsome.

Ping and Ruby become lovers.

Ping joins the American Army and is honorably discharged one year afterward because the Asian still cannot speak or understand English. (A condition that has not changed after fifteen years.) Ping and Ruby move to Seattle. Suddenly, the devil explodes into a ball of fire and somersaults off the stage as the Chinese Exclusion Act of 1882 is finally repealed because China has become our ally against the Japs.

In Seattle, Ping cooks in a Chinese clip joint. Ruby is a waitress. She gets along with Caucasian customers. She tells them what to order. She builds up a regular white clientele. A scenery change. Ruby and Ping save enough to buy a mansion that had been converted into a hash house on Broadway and Jefferson. A black neighborhood. The Chows open Ruby Chow's in 1948. Ruby Chow's is the first Chinese restaurant located outside of Chinatown.

Chinatown old-timers laugh. Chinatown old-timers place bets on how quickly the restaurant will fold.

Ruby Chow's thrives.

The few celebrities who come to Seattle always eat at least once, often several times, at Ruby Chow's. There is an exclusive and secret gay club in town. They ask if Ruby has a problem hosting their annual banquet. 'As long as you pay with American money,' she says with a wink. Ruby also gets involved in civics, which means she becomes a politico. She wants the Chinese to get a fair shake. She wants the internal Chinese sexism against daughters stopped. She wants the Chinese of Seattle to become enlightened about the American Constitution. The Bill of Rights. She wants, in turn, to demystify Chinese culture for white people.

Here comes another dragon. The mayor of Seattle. He wants to rename the neighborhood below Yesler Way from 'Chinatown' to 'International Center.' This name is antiseptic. It sounds like French and Brazilian immigrants might live there now. No. It's only international as far as Asians go. Filipinos live there with the Chinese. So do the seven thousand Japanese who had been relocated to internment camps during the war. Ruby lobbies to keep Chinatown's name Chinatown. *Chinatown* is a direct translation of *Tang Yin Fow.* The name Chinatown is not racially noxious.

Ruby fails in her efforts to keep Chinatown *Chinatown*.

Ruby Chow is just Chinese-centric. Many years from now Chow apologists will point out that being Chinese-centric was not being racist. That's a mistake über-liberals make. Ruby Chow is unapologetically Chinese-centric, but only for those who are National Chinese. Communist China has ceased being China. Ruby has a very hush-hush relationship with a Chinese-American CIA man. Ruby Chow must keep Communist influence out of Seattle, out of Chinatown.

⋆ ⋆ ⋆

On September 4, the Ford Motor Company of Detroit revealed the Edsel to America like a supine and naked Brigitte Bardot. Americans who knew how to drive mobbed the dealerships. Even those who didn't know how to drive wanted to see the Edsel.

One of the names for this car that the poet Marianne Moore had suggested was Utopian Turtletop.

Every Ford executive (other than Robert McNamara) was thrilled at the crowds at the dealers until the sales figures revealed what McNamara knew they would: no one was actually *buying* the Edsel; the crowds were just looking.

Another name Moore suggested was Andante con Moto.

Then there were the rumors that the Edsel's celebrated hood ornament flew off the car at speeds over seventy mph.

Moore's other suggestions were the Mongoose Civique or the Pastelogram or the Intelligent Bullet. Finally, the Bullet Cloisonné.

The Edsel looked as if it would become a magnificent failure.

⋆ ⋆ ⋆

It is a cultural irony that Jack Kerouac's motor log classic *On the Road* was published contemporaneously with the Year of the Edsel. Kerouac himself and his friend Allen Ginsberg were self-proclaimed *beats*—*beat* being a combination of criminal slang and the word *beatific.* Neither of the pair was actually called a beat*nik* until after October 4, when the U.S.S.R. successfully launched a satellite into space called Sputnik. In fact, it was named Sputnik 1, implying that more Sputniks would follow. Sputnik itself was the size of a beach ball with four long antennas extending from its rear.

Back in the U.S.A., the suffix *-nik* was added to one-syllable English words for modern ironic effect. Fans of Kerouac were *beatniks.* So were guys who had beards and girls who wore berets. Smokers were *cigniks.* Dave Brubeck fans were *jazzniks.* Those who knew the sound of one hand clapping were *zenniks.* Several multisyllabic words were also *nik*ed such as Nabokov's readers, *Lolita-niks.*

Those who drove Edsels were not called *Edselniks*, however. They were called the short and simpler:

Edniks.

⋆ ⋆ ⋆

This is what the dapper Vietnamese Ngô Dinh Diem told Jacqueline Kennedy about Soeur Angelique:

> I met her in university. She was the daughter of one of my professors. She was shy. I was shy. We liked to read the same books. She was my heart. We kept our relationship secret. We did this not because we were doing something shameful. It was just that things between us were very intense. Her father found out about me. He sent Soeur Angelique to France. I thought that he forced her into a convent, but I later heard from Soeur Angelique herself that it was her choice.

I have never opened my heart up like that to a woman since Soeur Angelique's terrible parting.

Diem's romance with Soeur Angelique had gone deep into the man in a profoundly literary manner. The two had often sat in cafés sipping French coffee and talking of their childhoods and their dreams. Soon they realized they had nothing more to speak to each other about. That was a moment of delicious liberation. They knew each other's soul now and they could stop talking and sit silently sipping French coffee. Diem loved this girl terribly and he didn't know what to do next. Then Diem unfortunately made an offhand comment to Soeur Angelique that they should run away together to Paris. He wasn't serious. But Soeur Angelique gasped. She shot her hand over her lips. She stood and ran away. The next morning, Diem couldn't find Soeur Angelique anywhere. He learned that she had taken a midnight flight to Paris. Alone.

It was her intention that when she disembarked, she would take the vows and become a nun.

Diem heard that news and his heart took flight. He had never read the American text *The Awakening,* by Kate Chopin, yet he was mimicking the feelings of her novel's protagonist. Diem remembered every motion of Soeur Angelique's body. The sound of her speaking voice. Ngô Dinh Diem remembered the smell of their coffee that they drank together. Ngô Dinh Diem's memories were the strongest things he had ever felt in his life up to that point. Ngô Dinh Diem was content to now divide his life into two portions. The first, his quest to lead Viet-Nam. The second, to remember every moment that he encountered Soeur Angelique. Memory evoked more passion than the experience itself. He began taking photographs for Soeur Angelique and sending them to his once beloved's nunnery in Paris. Diem's photographs were ambiguous, filled with arcane symbolism that even Diem did not understand. Ten years ago, Diem came upon a French doctor who had just amputated an injured soldier's leg. The doctor gave Diem the leg as graveyard humor, saying, 'Some photograph this will make.' Diem later placed the piece of leg on a soft gray sheet of rice paper and photographed it. He sent the result to Soeur Angelique. She would understand the beauty in such a photograph.

Diem's photograph caused international problems.

The nunnery contacted the Paris post office, which then contacted the postal office in Viet-Nam. The nunnery would no longer accept packages from Ngô Dinh Diem.

★ ★ ★

On November 27, a daughter named Caroline was born to Jack and Jacqueline Kennedy. Three weeks later, Jack went on a bachelor vacation to Cuba.

★ ★ ★

Ex-con Alger Hiss did not think of himself as a jailbird. A condition of his parole in 1954 was that he could not make any public appearances for sixteen months. He used this time to write a memoir of his experience in the American gulag of Pennsylvania. Knopf bought the book and intended to publish *In the Court of Public Opinion* in the summer of 1957. Knopf 'smelled' best seller and printed sixty thousand copies.

Just before publication, Hiss spoke at Princeton, where the entire campus was cluttered with papier-mâché pumpkins and typewriters. By all accounts, Hiss's speech was so dull it anesthetized an entire auditorium of listeners.

When Hiss's memoir was finally available in bookstores it was not a best seller.

The left-leaning (and goofy-looking) iconoclast I. F. Stone dismissed *In the Court of Public Opinion* as 'Time-Life Dostoevski.' Hiss's prose displayed zero emotion.

Alger Hiss abandoned the literary life to become a salesman for Feathercombs, a backless comb made of looped piano wire for women. Hiss wasn't particularly simpatico to feminine coiffures, yet the man could always get his foot in the office of a department store buyer or beauty salon once the boss heard 'Alger Hiss is here.'

★ ★ ★

During this time in Texas, a sixteen-year-old girl named K. K. Connally was sure she was pregnant. K.K.'s father, John Connally, was a big-deal lawyer in Fort Worth. He represented one of the two richest men in Texas, Sid Richardson, who was also one of the ten richest men in the world. K.K.'s father was traveling to Washington, D.C., on an errand for Mr. Richardson. K.K.'s father usually brought Mom with him. Before her parents left for Washington, the lesbian who taught gymnastics at Arlington High School had telephoned John Connally to say that she thought Kathleen had morning sickness. K.K. had to argue with Dad and Mom that everything was okay; she and Bobby Hale had not fooled around. Bobby Hale was eighteen and a senior at Arlington. John Connally would later write, 'We were living in a 1950s world: Elvis and hula-hoops and backyard bomb shelters, penny loafers, 3-D movies, and McCarthyism.' He will offer these as excuses for him and his wife not knowing how to 'manage' their daughter's budding sexuality.

K.K. learned about the New England poet/saint Emily Dickinson in English class. Emily Dickinson always wore a white dress. K.K. didn't have a white dress, but she took one of her mother's and returned to her high school's football field. She loitered until the team quit practice and the arc lights were turned off. K.K. put on her mother's white dress and then began to roll the length of the grassy field. When she reached the goalpost, she rolled back across the field to the other end zone. She rolled toward the opposite goal again. She rolled back and forth across the football field that way. The girl began to find that she could not breathe. She was hyperventilating. She had heard that rolling like she was would make the thing, that thing, fall out of her—that is, if she was pregnant. She collapsed and woke up in a hospital. She checked herself out and went to Bobby Hale's home. Bobby had a twin brother named Billy. The boys' father, I. B. Hale, had been a beloved Texas Christian University linebacker during the Depression. He now was chief of security for General Dynamics, a defense-industry contactor that built ships and submarines and tanks.

* * *

Leslie Fiedler turned forty on March 8, 1957. The essayist recalled Goethe's advice: 'Be careful what you wish for in your youth, for you will get it in your middle age.' Fiedler had amended that statement to: 'Be careful what you wish for in your youth for the *young* will get it in your middle age.'

He wrote that sentence in the previous month's *Encounter* magazine in his essay 'The Un-Angry Young Men.'

Fiedler was writing of the U.S.A.'s 'postwar' generation—citizens born in 1940 or after, the ones who would later be referred to as baby boomers. 'We ended their innocence before they knew they possessed it; and they passed directly from grade school to middle age.' Fiedler's own high-school-aged son complained that Fiedler's generation had robbed his of the 'possibilities of revolt.' Any act of revolution would be 'an empty piece of mimicry.' Fiedler believed that the only book that was youth's own was still *The Catcher in the Rye*—Fiedler discounting *On the Road* by not mentioning it. Fiedler physically described these Un-Angry Young Men by describing callow youth playing bongo drums with their shirts unbuttoned in Washington Square Park. Fiedler then claimed that 'adults' allow the American young to indulge in cultural violence by watching movies and TV because there was no real violence in American culture (i.e., the labor protests of the '20s and '30s, strikebreakers, D-Day, Iwo Jima). He briefly mentioned lynching down South, but his unspoken attitude was that the South was not really part of America. In the end, Fiedler believed that the relation of un-angry young men and women of 1957 to their elders was that of pupil to teacher. Today's kids no longer just 'chucked it' and went to live in a garret in Paris like the Lost Generation. Fiedler acknowledges only one new thing in the air—jazz: 'The first cultural snobbism of the very newest young tends to be based on taste in jazz—*Do you dig Bird?*'

Fiedler was so square he followed that sentence with an explanation, assuming his readers were not hip enough to understand his reference: 'this is to say, *Do you like the music of Charlie Parker?*'*

* * *

The Manhattan painter Willem de Kooning was fifty-four years old, a card-carrying member of Leslie Fiedler's generation.

All over America, fifty-four *was* middle-aged. Yet, Willem de Kooning was still robust. He resembled a modern fifty-four-year-old man from our

---

* Not like the book you are reading, which assumes that you are hip as a whip.

time. Even if Viagra had existed sixty years ago, Willem de Kooning would have had no need of it to engage in carnal delight with Ruth Kligman.

Yes, the late Jackson Pollock's Ruth Kligman.

She was now all of twenty-eight years old and had become de Kooning's girlfriend. The pair had waited a respectable one year after Jackson Pollock's death to begin their carnal coupling.

The critic who first put both Pollock and de Kooning on the map, Clement Greenberg, was now forty-nine. He was 80 percent bald with an ample gut. He turned on Pollock and now that Pollock was dead, Greenberg had begun chipping away at de Kooning. Recently Greenberg proclaimed:

> de Kooning hankers after *terribilità* prompted by a similar kind of culture and by a similar nostalgia for tradition.

At first reading, that may sound like a compliment. It wasn't.

* * *

Fort Worth, Texas. On March 16, K. K. Connally stole her mom's station wagon and drove with Bobby Hale to Ardmore, Oklahoma, to get married by a justice of the peace. The newlyweds spent three days driving to Tallahassee, that Florida town as landlocked from the Gulf as Fort Worth. K.K. and Bobby took a small apartment in a boardinghouse. Bobby quickly got a job at a factory that made boats. K.K. began sneaking out of the rooming house late at night and slipping into the front seat of her mom's station wagon to listen to the radio. She listened to talking, not music. Mostly she listened to the radio preacher Oral Roberts.

* * *

March 1958. Willem de Kooning and Ruth Kligman traveled to Havana, that so-called Cuban capital of sordidness, to sightsee and cleanse themselves of Eisenhower's antiseptic America. The pair got in at midnight. The streets were crowded with laughing gringas and gringos who were being stoically observed by slouching Cuban men wearing white suits and sinister expressions. After, de Kooning and Ruth checked into their hotel,

Risa Chico.* The couple was too exhausted to do anything but order *bogavante* from room service and then go to bed.

Roosters began crowing before the sun was up. Our two Manhattanites covered their heads with pillows. At sunrise, the pair gave in to the poultry and went down to the street intending to stroll through ante meridiem Havana. De Kooning was wearing white slacks and a light gray shirt and white shoes, and looked casually affluent. Ruth wore beach pajamas that were white with red polka dots.

The two Americans were delighted with the drunken architecture of Havana. The city was part Mexico and part Montparnasse and part Cairo. The buildings were the color of children's suckers—lime green, pink, crimson. The two were following a green wall. Across the street, old women were sitting on stools fanning themselves in the shade. The sidewalk on the Americans' side was too narrow for the couple to walk side-by-side, so de Kooning followed Ruth. He enjoyed the rolling of her rear end beneath the legs of her red polka-dotted beach pajamas. De Kooning was reminded of a word that Hemingway used. A Spanish word, a Spanish term.

Guardaespaldas.

A *guardaespaldas* was the 'man' who followed you to protect you from being shot in the back. Another foreign word abruptly flashed on and off in de Kooning's brain: *terribilità*. This was a word Hemingway never used.

Ruth had been chatting away and when de Kooning wasn't responding, she glanced over her shoulder. 'What's wrong, honey?'

'Nothin'.'

'Liar. You're scowling.'

'It's the sun.'

'You're scowling at the sun?'

'Yeah, I'm scowling at the sun.'

Ruth turned to face him and poked him in his ribs. 'You are not. You're thinking about that crapbird Greenberg again. Admit it!'

De Kooning shook his head. 'Okay. Yeah.' Ruth turned around and continued walking. Up ahead in the green wall was an arched doorway where red theater curtains covered the entrance instead of a door.

---

* The Laughing Boy.

De Kooning shouted, '*Terribilità!* What kind of word is *terribilità*? The last artist who was *terribilità* was Michelangelo, and he used naked men as models for his female nudes.'

In front of the pair, down the street, that red curtain—a man's head poked out sideways from the curtain, and both de Kooning and Ruth called out, 'Proust!'

The man gave a loud hiccup and his head disappeared back inside.

He had indeed resembled a Cuban Proust. His hair was elaborate and old-fashioned, parted in the middle like the dead French writer. The Cuban also had a Proust moustache.

De Kooning and Ruth passed the red curtains and continued up the street a bit until it forked in three directions. De Kooning turned to estimate the distance they had already walked. At that moment, the Cuban Proust exited from his red curtain and headed in the direction that the Americans had come from. The man was now wearing a small white boating cap. He was dressed in a black coat and white shirt and black pants that were so short they revealed the man's white socks and a sliver of the flesh of his ankles. His dark loafers were so old they were reptilian.

The Cuban Proust was walking very carefully.

'Ruth!' de Kooning said. 'He is drunk. Let's follow.'

Ruth turned. 'How can you tell? He's not staggering. Because of the hiccup?'

'No. He's moving as if he's walking on a wire.'

The Cuban Proust was indeed conspicuous by his desire to be inconspicuous. Ruth and de Kooning followed the drunk Cuban Proust on that narrow sidewalk, staying about thirty paces behind. Suddenly, the Cuban fell to his side into the street. It was almost like he expected a bed to appear and break his fall.

None of the old women moved.

De Kooning and Ruth ran over and helped the Cuban up. He didn't smell of drink, but his eyes were glazed. His boating hat was still on his head. He was a lanky Cuban and raised his boating hat and said, '*Gracias.*'

A red convertible raced down the narrow street. Its radio was turned up quite loud.

'Is that Elvis Presley?' Ruth asked de Kooning.

'Driving the car?'

'On the radio.'

'Quick, Ruth. He's getting away.'

'Elvis?'

'Our drunk Cuban.'

The man had turned a corner. The Americans reached that corner and saw the drunk Cuban continuing his way down the street, walking a bit more carelessly in his white socks and reptile shoes. The street zigzagged with no cross streets. On this street, young Cuban women sat on crates fanning themselves. The drunk Cuban raised his boating hat at each as he continued down the street.

'Floozies?' Ruth asked de Kooning.

'Beats me,' was his answer.

The Cuban Proust started swaying as if he was walking across the deck of a boat sailing on rough seas. Up the street was a theater whose façade was missing. The two Americans could see many tiers and balconies inside. The stage held a pile of rubble. Little handcarts were lined up in front of this theater. As de Kooning and Ruth walked closer they saw a group of Cuban men inside the shell of the theater gesticulating around a prone man. He appeared to be so dedicated to alcohol that he could not propel himself upward with his feet. His companions were not paying attention to their carts.

One cart was stacked with fish and ice. On another cart sat a four-tiered green cake on a silver platter. The drunk Cuban Proust weaved over to that cart and in one motion picked up the cake on its platter with both hands and continued lurching forward.

It never dawned on de Kooning or Ruth to call out or say anything.

* * *

Fiedler concluded his essay 'The Un-Angry Young Men' with this idea: 'One feels sometimes that homosexuality is the purest and truest protest of the latest generation, not a burden merely, an affliction to be borne, but a politics to be flaunted.' He mentioned Truman Capote and Carson McCullers and James Baldwin. Homosexuality is 'the last possible protest against bourgeois security and the home in the suburbs in a world where adultery is old hat.' He ended 'The Un-Angry Young Men' by writing that generations don't make books or motion pictures or songs or plays, men and women do. 'When a young writer arises who can treat this matter in all its fresh absurdity . . . I . . . will be leaning from a window to cheer him on and to shake down on his head the torn scraps of all surviving copies of this article.'

Fiedler was a smart man, but he was oblivious to Negro rhythm and blues. He forgot that abstract expressionism didn't die with Jackson Pollock.

Mescaline and other psychedelic drugs did not appear on his radar at all.

★ ★ ★

Tallahassee, Florida, April 28, 1959.

K.K. got a shotgun.

Bobby Hale passed the police lie-detector test.

The Connallys buried their oldest child, Kathleen, aka K.K., a suicide, under Fort Worth soil.

★ ★ ★

Havana, Cuba. Ruth Kligman and Wilhelm de Kooning followed the drunk Cuban Proust with the green cake down through the labyrinth of Havana.

'Now that cake is full of *terribilità*!' de Kooning said.

'That cake is full of grandeur,' Ruth said.

'That's what *terribilità* means,' de Kooning said. 'Grandeur.'

'Oh gee. No kidding? Can you beat that,' Ruth said, mocking him because she obviously knew the definition of *terribilità*.

Up ahead a man pushing a wheelbarrow was heading toward the Cuban drunk and the two Americans. The man's wheelbarrow contained a half dozen pyramids of green or yellow banana bunches. The drunk carrying his green cake swerved to his right to go around the man with the wheelbarrow, who also swerved in the same direction to get around the drunk.

'So maybe my skin is too thin, you think?' de Kooning said.

'It's all your Luciferian pride,' Ruth said.

'Greenberg said that I aspire to grandeur. What's wrong with that?'

The man with the wheelbarrow was not smiling. He then pushed his wheelbarrow of bananas forward in the opposite direction as the Cuban with the cake shifted in that direction as well.

'Honey,' Ruth said, '*Greenbird* didn't say that you *aspire* to *terribilità*. He said that you *hanker* after *terribilità*.'

The Cuban with the wheelbarrow set it down and held his chin, thinking. Then he pointed stage left.

'What's wrong with *hankering*?' de Kooning asked. 'It's an English word that comes from the Dutch.'

'Honey,' Ruth said. 'One *hankers* for green cake, not artistic grandeur.'

The Cuban with the green cake stood for a moment. Then he pointed stage right with his right arm. The man with the wheelbarrow gave a large smile. The two men lurched forward in their separate directions and passed each other with no difficulty.

The Proustian Cuban then held his green cake with outstretched arms. He was heading toward an old red Cadillac parked up ahead. Neither de Kooning nor Ruth recognized the age of the Cadillac except it was too old to have fins. The drunk Cuban used his left hand to slide the green cake in one motion onto the red hood and push it along that hood and then up the windshield that was slanted at maybe a forty-five-degree angle. The man continued sliding the green cake along the top of the red Cadillac and down the back window, then across the trunk. The cake still looked intact and none the worse for its tilted traveling. The drunk Cuban pushed the cake off the trunk in a fluid, one-handed motion, catching the cake's platter with his free hand. Then he put his right hand under the cake as well and continued down the street, momentarily limping.

The drunk's white socks had rolled below his ankles.

De Kooning spoke. 'Well, the thing that Greenbird said that is really insulting is that I am trying to *forestall* the future. Forestall the future of what? Painting?'

They passed an old Cuban woman sitting at a sewing machine on a stool, mending a burlap sack.

Ruth said, 'Greenbird is implying that you're scared about the future of painting.'

The street was now surrounded on both sides by four-storied yellow stucco apartment buildings with elaborate balconies. Several motor scooters raced by, each one driven by a man with a hysterical woman behind him, clinging to his waist. These women were either screaming or laughing; the Doppler effect made it hard to tell which.

Now the Cuban drunk stopped before an immensely tall and narrow mega-shutter that was constructed by a hodgepodge of smaller square and rectangular shutters. It resembled a sculpture created by that Dutch Neo-Plasticist Piet Mondrian,* if he had worked with wood instead of paint and canvas. The drunk Cuban faced that shuttered wall and began talking. Enough of the slots were missing on each piece of shutter that it was likely the drunk Cuban could see whomever he was speaking to.

De Kooning said, 'So an artist must keep rejecting the past, instead of honoring it? Look at Greenberg himself. His acclaim is rooted in the past. There was Jackson, me. Then he rejects us and roots through Greenwich Village like a truffle hog searching for a new painter.'

The drunk Cuban finished his conversation and turned forward and proceeded down the street. Suddenly, the man's legs appeared to give out. Almost! He shot out his right arm to steady him against another panel of broken shutters. The cake stayed secure in the crook of his left arm. Next, the Cuban began lurching forward while de Kooning and Ruth passed the monster shutter. They both glanced through a series of broken slats and saw the head of a green parrot in profile.

The sidewalk was now made of orange- and plum-colored tiles. The street itself turned into packed dirt. The buildings appeared to have more curlicues on them. Florida deco.

'Greenberg,' de Kooning said to Ruth. 'He's a—what's the word for Bela Lugosi?'

All at once maybe four or five radios began blaring different stations of Cuban deejays proclaiming things in excited Spanish.

'Greenberg is like a movie star?' Ruth yelled.

'No. He's like a Dracula. A thing that sucks blood,' de Kooning hollered back.

The two Americans were now passing a green building the same color as the frosting on the cake.

'You mean a vampire,' said Ruth.

---

* 1872–1944.

'A what?'

'A vampire!'

'Yes! Greenberg is a vampire!'

'Greenberg is the *Picture of Dorian Gray*!'

'Didn't Proust write that?'

'No! Wilde did!'

'Billy Wilder?'

'No, *Wilde,* not *Wilder!* Oscar Wilde!'

The sidewalk had widened into a tiled plaza that surrounded a marble bust sitting on a stubby Greek pedestal. The bust was slightly larger than life and depicted an officious-looking man with a moustache and a frown. The bust was maybe a foot higher than the top of the drunken Cuban's head. That fellow stopped with his cake and stared up at the marble face. He tilted his head as he studied the face and he suddenly lost his balance and almost dropped his green cake. Then the drunk Cuban stood straighter and raised his arms. He attempted to balance the green cake on the top of the marble head of the man with the moustache.

It was not working.

De Kooning hurried over and said, 'Let me help.'

Now that de Kooning was closer, he saw green frosting all over the Cuban Proust's nose. The cake was intact so obviously the drunk must have bumped the cake against his upturned face. As the two men both raised their arms and tried to steady the cake, de Kooning called out to Ruth, 'You know what Stevens or was it Swan said about me? They said the more I abstracted the painting the more personal and narrative my paintings became.'

'Yes! They said that was the secret of your art.'

'They called my paintings the painterly versions of soliloquies.'

'Yes. *As perfect in their own way as any words uttered by Hamlet or Lear.*'

'Do you think Stevens or Swan—whoever said it—meant King Lear or Edward Lear the limerickist?'

Ruth laughed.

Just as it appeared that the cake could actually balance on the marble head, five or six shouting men ran up the street. De Kooning lowered his arms and saw they were the Cubans with the handcarts from the ruined theater. They circled the pedestal and began yelling at the drunk Cuban, who dropped his arms to his sides in resignation. The cake balanced on the marble head for a moment and then plopped through the air and splattered on the tiles. The body of the cake beneath the green frosting was golden. Now one of the Cubans began beating his fist against his opposite palm as he yelled at the drunk Cuban. De Kooning could tell from his gestures that the man expected payment from the drunk for the stolen and now ruined green cake. De Kooning knelt and scooped up a hunk of cake with his bare hand. He ate it. It was good cake. It had been made with sweet liqueur. There were vague hints of banana. The Dutchman gouged out another piece and reached up to offer it to Ruth. The men had all stopped shouting and were watching de Kooning, who scooped up a third handful of cake and offered it to the man who had been beating his palm. He nodded at de Kooning and took it. He did not say '*Gracias,*' but he did actually eat the cake. Then his companions knelt and began gouging out pieces of cake. While this went on, the drunk edged up the sidewalk toward a curling wrought-iron stairway that suggested French Quarter architecture from New Orleans. The circular stairway led up the face of a four-story pink stucco apartment building. The drunk began stepping carefully up the winding stairs. The men all watched him as they scooped up pieces of green cake.

These circular stairs did not lead to any opening in the side of the building. The circular stairway stopped several feet short of the balustrade on the roof. When the drunk Cuban reached the top of the circular stairway he stopped and stood still.

At that moment, a small black dog with white spots trotted up and distracted everyone as it lunged for pieces of cake. Then abruptly the drunk was falling through the air and landed on the dirt street. His reptile shoes flew off his feet upon landing while his fallen body created a brown cloud of dust.

No one moved. Everyone crouched or stood with their handfuls of cake.

The drunk lay for a long while. Then he suddenly sat up and shook his head. Then he stood and brushed the dust off his trousers and continued weaving up the sidewalk with only white socks on his feet.

* * *

It was the month of June and Mary Meyer was at Gus Bundy's divorce ranch in Nevada. She spent the summer in the desert waiting to become a resident of Nevada for a quick no-contest divorce. An opera singer was staying at the ranch. A male opera singer.

The two had an Affair.

This is what illicit lovers did in the 1950s—had Affairs.

Mary Meyer established Nevada residency. Her husband, Cord, intellectually agreed with this divorce, but he was bitter. Cord gave her physical custody of Quentin and Mark, now twelve and eight, but demanded the right to control their education. She returned to Washington, D.C., to take painting lessons.

There were a handful of women artists in Washington. Adlai Stevenson dated an artist. Dean Acheson's wife painted. So did Estes Kefauver's better half. Still, most Washingtonians felt about art like President Truman had felt: 'So-called modern art is merely the vaporing of half-baked, lazy people.'

* * *

In 1958, filmmaker John Huston met with Jean-Paul Sartre in Paris. The Frenchman had written a ninety-five-page synopsis of a movie based on the life of Sigmund Freud. In 1958, Mary Meyer conducted an Affair with Ken Noland—a thirty-something Color Field* artist. No one today remembers Noland's work. All he is remembered for is a moment that occurs several years hence in Manhattan. In 1958, Donald Nixon filed for bankruptcy. There has been a recession going on in 1958 that is being blamed for the Edsel fiasco, a disaster that will never be blamed on Robert McNamara. In fact, the 1958 recession created McNamara's kind of 'no-frills' American climate. This year he developed his personal vision of the 'zeitgeist' auto of the 1950s, the Ford Falcon, an inexpensive auto. The only accessories offered would be a heater and a radio.

* * *

---

* Color Field paintings were abstract, but not as 'expressionistic' (i.e., 'messy') as, say, a Jackson Pollock.

Arthur Miller and Marilyn Monroe had bought an old saltbox house in Connecticut just as Norman Mailer had. The combined fame of Arthur Miller with Marilyn Monroe allowed them to contact the greatest architect in America, Frank Lloyd Wright, to see if he could remodel the abode. Wright was an old man in his early nineties. It had been twenty-four years since he had designed the Japanese house that Howard Hunt and his family had lived in. The renowned architect agreed to design a 'dream house' for Arthur Miller and Marilyn Monroe for a one-hundred-thousand-dollar fee (over a million dollars in modern money). Miller and Monroe drove to Manhattan to pick Wright up. The old man was wearing a cape and a 'gaucho hat.' He slept on the ride to Connecticut. The old man then inspected the site with a flashlight.

Like many Americans, Frank Lloyd Wright spoke through his nose. He sounded like W. C. Fields.

In the end, the Millers paid for Frank Lloyd Wright's extremely expensive blueprints and filed them away. The house Wright designed was a modernist Xanadu with a circular living room with a domed ceiling sixty feet in diameter supported by fieldstone columns, each seven feet thick, along with a seventy-foot swimming pool gouged into the hillside. The Millers did not want to dwell in Connecticut living on the faux-Hollywood set of *Citizen Marilyn*.

⋆ ⋆ ⋆

Over in Bridgewater, Norman Mailer could not believe that Arthur Miller had not yet asked him over for a drink so the novelist could meet Marilyn Monroe. Mailer had met Miller at a party or two back in the city. The still clean-shaven Miller had not been overtly hostile to Mailer or Mailer's new ridiculous goatee, yet Miller acted like an aloof WASP. He would talk only about his new hobby, gardening. It was like he was an intellectual Mr. Greenjeans.

Norman Mailer was working hard on turning his novel *The Deer Park* into a Broadway play. That was Arthur Miller's territory. Mailer was not intimidated. Anyone could write a play.

Mailer had forgotten the first time he had met Miller.

The playwright always remembered.

It was back in Motherless Brooklyn right after the war, 1947. It was the year of Arthur Miller's *All My Sons.* Miller was living on Pierpont Street. One afternoon there was a screaming argument going on down the hall. It sounded like some man was going to kill some woman. Miller cautiously opened his apartment door and followed the voices of rage down the hall. He came to the stairwell and surveyed downward. Mailer was below, sitting on the steps in uniform. From Miller's elevated angle, Mailer looked even shorter than he actually was. Arthur Miller recognized the woman the soldier was arguing with as a fellow tenant on his floor. Miller returned to his apartment. Later, Mailer approached Miller on the street. Mailer was twenty-four and Miller was thirty-two. 'My name is Norman Mailer,' the young man said. 'I'm a writer too.' *The Naked and the Dead* will not be published until 1948. 'I just saw *All My Sons,*' Mailer said.

'What did you think?'

'I could write a play like that.'

Miller looked down at this kid and laughed.

* * *

Seattle. Buster Hendrix was fifteen years old and his mother died of a ruptured spleen. It was said that his father would not let Buster and Leon go inside the funeral home to view her body. He made the kids wait in the truck. When their father returned, he gave each boy a healthy snort of Seagram's 7.

* * *

Connecticut. The telephone call finally came from Miller to Mailer: 'Why don't you and your wife come over to Roxbury for a drink? We live at the intersection of Tophet Road and Gold Mine.'

The Mailers sped to the Millers' in Norman's cramped red Triumph sports car. Its engine was more a cough than a purr. Arthur Miller heard the car pull into his driveway and strolled out to his porch like the owner of a plantation to greet his white-trash relatives. Miller was lanky—six feet three inches tall. Mailer climbed out of the Triumph hating Miller on sight because of those six feet three inches. Mailer hated Miller's height even more because Mailer's own legs felt stubby from driving his cramped

Triumph. And there was Arthur Miller wearing a crisp Hathaway shirt. Mailer was wearing his cleanest dirty shirt because Adele had neglected the laundry. (At least she had ironed the shirt before Mailer put it on.) Of course, Norman Mailer's final hate of Arthur Miller was because Miller was shtupping Marilyn Monroe and Mailer was not.

Arthur Miller waved the couple in through the front door and offered them a drink.

'Sure,' Adele said.

Mailer nodded affirmatively without smiling.

Miller's house was Danish modern (like Mailer's apartment had been), but more like a 'Danish modern beatnik pad' in Mailer's eyes. Miller made Norman and Adele Old Fashioneds with too much bitters and not enough rye. The playwright then took a church key and popped open a can of Piels for himself.

The house felt empty. There was a vacuum cleaner standing upright in the middle of the room. It was plugged in. It was dark green and appeared abandoned.

'Marilyn likes to vacuum the house,' Miller said.

'Tophet is such a peculiar name for a street,' Adele said, her salvo at Small Talk.

'It's funny about names,' Miller said. 'My father's name was Isidore—I-s-i-d-o-r-e. Tophet—T-o-p-h-e-t—is from the Bible. The Old Testament. It's another name for hell, a place where the wicked are tormented for eternity.'

Mailer wasn't really listening. What he heard was, *My father's name is another name for hell.*

Miller continued. 'In Hebrew it's *ha-tōpheth*—a valley outside of Jerusalem where the Canaanites sacrificed children to Moloch by burning them alive.'

Mailer thought that was impressive, a father naming his son after Moloch. Mailer remembered seeing that fag beatnik poet Allen Ginsberg riffing on Moloch on the Jack Paar show:

> Moloch! Moloch! Robot hamburger stands! Invincible suburbs! blind capitalists! spaghetti strap nations!

Mailer thought of Miller's *Death of a Salesman.* The protagonist, Willy Loman. 'No wonder Willy was such a *low man,*' Mailer said, making his weak pun.

'You know, Norm, I never considered Willy's last name as some sort of play of *low man on the totem pole.* I remember that I was watching *The Testament of Dr. Mabuse* on TV. You know, Fritz Lang.'

Mailer was not a cineaste. He couldn't place the kraut name Fritz Lang. Miller was obviously a Jew enthralled with the Germans.

'So, in *The Testament of Dr. Mabuse* there is this detective whose boss is named Lohmann.' Miller spelled it. 'The detective is being tortured or something by the bad guys and he's on the telephone begging, *Lohmann? Help me, for Christ's sake! Lohmann?* Next thing the detective is in a padded cell strapped in a straitjacket muttering, *Lohmann? Lohmann? Lohmann?* Loman was just a terrified cry for help to someone who will never come.' Miller sipped his beer. 'A soul's black addiction.' He sipped again. 'That's what Brecht called it.'

Krauts.

Norman Mailer began jiggling his foot with impatience. Miller got up to replenish their drinks.

'Marilyn has been called to the coast,' Miller said over his shoulder, walking into the kitchen.

Mailer stood up and looked at his watch and said, 'We gotta go.'

* * *

Mailer lead-footed his Triumph down Hell Road, screaming, 'That bastard! That bastard! That bastard!'

That Moloch.

* * *

Manhattan. Alger Hiss and Posey squabbled all the time now. Or rather, Posey bitched. Alger put his hands together and flapped them, as if he was pantomiming a bird. He was, in fact, pantomiming a flying squirrel. Back in the 1920s, the female psychiatrist who had analyzed Posey had once studied with Freud and also kept uncaged flying squirrels inside her office.

Another Manhattan couple: Willem de Kooning and Ruth Kligman. They had vicious squabbles and they weren't even married. 'Why don't you go to the grave with your Jackson Pollock!' de Kooning would yell.

Ruth would scream back, 'I spent two months with Jackson, and still you are jealous?'

'I am not jealous! You know what Frank [O'Hara] calls you?'

'I'm sure that I don't know nor care what that little queer says.'

'He calls you Oldsmobile Eighty-Eight Girl.'

'To hell with Frank O'Hara.'

'Frank calls you Death Car Chick.'

* * *

Word got around in Connecticut. When Adele met the writer William Styron's 'matronly wife' at the supermarket, she told Adele: 'Marilyn was hiding upstairs the whole time. She chickened out. She didn't want to meet your husband.'

* * *

Seattle. Buster goes to Bob Summerrise's World of Music to spin forty-fives of blues and R&B.

Buster with his buddy Parnell sneaking into a theater to see Little Richard. They get backstage. Little Richard recognizes them as the kids dancing in their seats in the front row.

Buster flunks music in school.

Buster pretends he is playing Elmore James licks on an invisible guitar. Buster practices a duckwalk clutching his invisible guitar. Buster is fifteen years old. His need, his desire, for an electric guitar burns stronger than even the boy's teenage hormones.

* * *

For much of that summer the Millers moved south-by-southeast, living out on eastern Long Island—surrounded by fields, no ocean. Marilyn was pregnant for two months and miscarried. Then an ectopic pregnancy.

Tubal. Cut out of her. Down in Midland, Texas, twelve-year-old George W. Bush was racing his mother, Barbara, to the hospital. She had just miscarried. She sat shotgun holding a jar in her lap that contained the juicy remains of the fetus. It was difficult for her son, George W., to keep his eyes on the road. That thing in the jar—

★ ★ ★

Seattle. Restaurateur Ruby Chow becomes the first Asian woman in Seattle to wrap her long hair into a clump above her head in that distinctive new hairdo called a beehive, a hairdo just concocted that summer by a beautician in Elmhurst, Illinois, for a magazine contest. Ruby Chow was five feet tall and now with her beehive (or B-52 as it was also called), Ruby Chow stood five feet eleven.

Chapter 19

Aboard the *Chola Srivijaya* Bound for San Francisco, 1959

In 1959, Ed Sullivan had as much cultural brawn as Ben-Hur. Sullivan's *rilly big shew*[*] was a Sunday institution across the U.S.A. Yet, Sullivan still ate his liver over that ten-year snub by Ed Murrow. As the puppeteer Señor Wences said over and over, 'Revenge is a dish best served cold.'

On January 8, 1959, Fidel Castro and his troops rolled into Havana. Castro now ruled Cuba. Several days later, Sullivan jumped a flight to Havana. The Black Irishman was accompanied by his favorite cameraman 'Andy-roo' Laszlo. The pair used stealth and shady contacts to reach Castro in the bush. Sullivan interviewed the leader of this *revolución* in a hut filled with sweaty Cuban men possessing both beards and rifles.

Ed Sullivan was fifty-seven years old and wore a suit. Fidel Alejandro Castro Ruz was thirty-two years old and wore filthy combat fatigues. Sullivan was clean-shaven. Castro had his Hasidic-Arabic-Lincolnesque beard.

'Are you the George Washington of Cuba?' Sullivan asked.

By nightfall, Sullivan and Laszlo returned to Havana. The capital was chaos and panic. It was like Madrid 1937. It foretold the Fall of Saigon in 1975. In Havana, the Batista supporters who hadn't been shot or jailed were scrambling to escape the city aboard boats or airplanes. On Sullivan's tear to the airport he ran into the actor George Raft, sixty-three years old. Raft had become a star in 1932 as the original *Scarface* (Al Pacino was waiting to be born eight years later). Raft was remembered now in 1959, if at all, for his portrayal of gangsters. Raft would stand with his gat in his pocket, mindlessly flipping a coin. Raft was a gangster of few words, but when he spoke it was in a dry staccato. For most of the 1950s, he was down in Havana as part owner of the Capri Casino. Raft's partner was Meyer Lansky ('Hyman Roth' in *The Godfather Part II*).

---

* Sullivanese for 'really big show.'

Castro's 'Fidelistas' had shut down every casino in Havana and taken over the banks. Millions that belonged to the Corleones was now in the revolutionaries' pockets. Raft was now broke and had been abandoned by his gangsters. Ed Sullivan slipped Raft pin money and saw to it that Raft flew with him back to New York City.

The two settled into their seats.

'Can you read yet?' Ed asked.

'No,' Raft said. He was illiterate. (Or 'postliterate' as we moderns say.)

'Helluva mess in Cuba,' Ed said.

'Helluva mess,' Raft repeated.

'You got out by the skin of your teeth!'

'Helluva mess.'

'Come be on my *shew.*'

'Can I tango again?'

Instead of answering that question, Sullivan asked one of his own. 'How much did you lose to the revolution, George?'

Raft began to unbutton his Hathaway. 'My shirt, Ed. I lost my shirt.'

* * *

Across the country in Seattle. Buster Hendrix was old enough to be in eleventh grade at Garfield High School. Garfield was integrated—50 percent white, 20 percent Asian; 30 percent black.

Buster was a kid who liked to wear ink-black peg pants. A black-and-white-striped shirt with the collar up.

The kid had a black girlfriend who spoke with a southern accent. Buster had to go to her father and formally ask if he could take the daughter out for a date.

* * *

On Sunday, January 11, the Castro footage appeared on *The Ed Sullivan Show.* A quick clip of Castro was shown at the beginning—'Are you the George Washington of Cuba?' Then commercials. Next, Victor Julian's poodles appeared wearing clothing for a Poodle Fashion Show.

Next, six minutes of Castro.

Ed Sullivan referred to Castro and his men (including Che Guevara) as 'revolutionary youngsters.' Sullivan asked Fidel if he played football in high school. Sullivan meant Green Bay Packers football and Castro thought he meant *soccer* and answered, 'Yes.'

'Did it help you win the revolution?' Sullivan asked.

* * *

Other highlights of that Sunday's *Ed Sullivan Show* were Professor Backwards, who mastered the art of 'controlled dyslexia' and talked backward, making jokes about psychiatrists.

(Freudians? !esruoc fO)

Then a pair of men or women in ape suits juggled with two men not wearing ape suits. A few weeks after these monkeyshines, Prime Minister Fidel Castro came to America to tour. He was met by enthusiastic American viewers of *The Ed Sullivan Show* at most of his stops. Castro's popularity was also bolstered by Desi Arnaz's Cuban ethnicity. After all, Cubans were friendly fellows with great senses of humor who murdered English expressions with their funny accents.

Several months after Castro's visit, the marriage of the Cuban Desi Arnaz and the gringa Lucille Ball began to go belly-up and the pair filed for divorce. The cause—the Cuban masculine temper; the Cuban libido for women and rum.

Castro was having his own problems with Americans. Eisenhower would not give Cuba aid even after Castro turned down the Russians, who would. Eisenhower had authorized Dulles to begin preparations for a secret CIA-sponsored military takeover of Cuba.

Howard Hunt got a phone call down in Uruguay. He took a plane back to Washington.

* * *

Ernest Hemingway lived a large part of each year in Cuba. Hemingway had been born in the last year of the nineteenth century and his reputation has gone up and down, and will likely to continue oscillating for the next hundred years.

When the writer Joan Didion was a college girl, she taught herself prose style by retyping *The Sun Also Rises.*

The Sun Also Rises was Hemingway's second novel. That book was and remains perfect. Some of us reread it every seven years or so. Whatever one's opinion is of Hemingway's macho animal-killing ways, the narrator of *The Sun Also Rises* had a terrible war wound to his genitals. His balls were intact while the man's penis itself was injured and lost. That was an ironic narrative stance for a writer to use to describe and make judgments on machismo.

In 1959, Hemingway lived in both Cuba and Idaho and kept an apartment at the Knickerbocker Club in Manhattan—Fifth Avenue and 62nd Street (southeast corner).

Papa (as he wanted his intimates to call him) was in Manhattan the winter of '59. *Papa* was also, you may recall, Marilyn Monroe's public pet name for Arthur Miller.

One Saturday night, thirty-two-year-old George Plimpton was up at Hemingway's apartment. Plimpton was tall and thin with a dry blue-blood voice, yet there was something Eleanor Roosevelt about his face. Plimpton was the editor of the literary magazine *The Paris Review.*

Plimpton walked into Hemingway's apartment and saw the great man was already entertaining a Spanish bullfighter as well as A. E. Hotchner—born in 1920 and remembered by us moderns as the man who partnered with Paul Newman to manufacture Newman's Own food products such as Newman's Own Pasta Sauce and Newman's Own Lemonade. In 1959, Hotchner functioned as Hemingway's chronicler. Very old literates would say that 'Hotchner was Papa's Boswell.'

There was a woman present as well. Her last name was Hearst as in William Hearst, aka *Citizen Kane.*

Hotchner said 'Hi' to Plimpton and left the room, probably heading for the can. Plimpton said, 'Say, Ernest, when we figure out where we're going shall we invite Norman Mailer to come meet us?'

Hemingway furrowed his brow. 'Mailer. Norman Mailer? Sure. Why not?'

Plimpton telephoned Mailer. 'Hey, it's me. George.'

'George?'

'Plimpton, Norman. George Plimpton.'

'Of course, George. I'm pulling your leg.'

'Are you doing anything tonight?'

'What you got planned?'

'Well, I'm here with Ernest Hemingway and we're going to go out someplace and wondering if you'd like to join us—it's me and Ernest and Hotchner and Antonio Ordóñez the bullfighter and—'

'Heck yes.'

'Well just stay by the phone and I'll call you when we decide where we're going and you can meet us there.'

'Okee-dokee,' Mailer said in a southern accent.

'And no head butting with Papa, okay?'

Mailer grunted.

Plimpton hung up. Hotchner returned to the living room. 'Who ya jawin', George?'

'Norman Mailer.'

'What! Why?'

'I thought he could join us.'

Hotchner shook his head at Hemingway. 'That's a terrible idea. Mailer's ego is the size of marlin and he has the moral sense of an eel. Papa doesn't need Mailer's company.'

Hemingway gave a perplexed shrug. Plimpton shrugged as well. The bullfighter and the Hearst woman had no opinion. Plimpton certainly wasn't going to call Mailer back to tell him there was a change of plans. The five left Hemingway's and took a cab to Sardi's on West 44th Street. It was eight p.m. and the columnist Walter Winchell was only now finishing up lunch.

* * *

In his uptown apartment, Norman Mailer was bare-chested and opened his wardrobe to survey his duds. He put on a bullfighting shirt. He poured himself a third Scotch. He rubbed his hands. For more than a decade, Mailer had ruled the macho roost of Ernest Hemingway. No one had exactly acknowledged that, but it was true. Mailer decided that he would show up and be gracious to the old man. He might even call him Papa. No. He would call him 'Pappy.' He'd use his theatrical Texas accent. He had no intention of acquiescing to the old man.

Back before the war—Mailer was at Harvard and Hemingway was his idol. Hemingway was maybe forty back then. Mailer was sixteen, seventeen, eighteen. Hemingway drank gin while he wrote. Norman drank gin while he wrote. Norman was short. Hemingway was pugnacity personified. Mailer was a bantamweight. Mailer liked to box undergraduates who were taller than he.

More recently, Mailer wrote poems about Hemingway. Bad poems. Around the time that he wrote the Hemingway-for-president piece, Mailer sent his third novel, *The Deer Park,* to Hemingway in Cuba with a note. A couple of months later the package came back from Cuba with '*domicilio desconocido*' stamped on it.

'That tough rump roast over-the-hill has-been ignored my package!'

Mailer was ignorant of how sloppy the mail was in Cuba. His package never reached Hemingway. In fact, Hemingway had been passing through Manhattan that year and bought *The Deer Park* at Scribner's bookstore for eighty-five cents (out of his own pocket). Someone later at a café asked Hemingway what he thought of Mailer's *Deer.*

'Mailer really blows the whistle on himself,' Hemingway said.

Hemingway began to say more but the waiter came with drinks at the same time that a drunk German blonde slapped another drunk blonde from Finland. That was a significant distraction and everyone present forgot about *The Deer Park.*

Meanwhile, Norman Mailer is sitting in his apartment and staring at his telephone waiting for Plimpton's call so Mailer can meet Hemingway.

Experience tells us that staring at a phone is not going to make it ring. Mailer usually believed that. Then he reconsidered. *That's how losers feel.* Could he will the phone to ring? He had just finished a portion of a novel that he called *The Time of Her Time,* in which the narrator uses only his penis and his Nietzschean Will to Power to make a 'frigid' woman have an orgasm for the first time in her life.

Mailer directed that kind of intensity to staring down the phone. He stared and stared. He wasn't thinking of Plimpton. He was willing the phone to ring of its own accord.

Operators all over the city were suddenly nerved up! They couldn't put it into words, but they became aware that something was being radiated over the telephone lines that was not mere telephone calls. Men slid into phone booths and then changed their minds and slipped out.

And of course, Norman Mailer's phone rang at that moment, its little bell tinkling against itself.

Mailer took a deep breath. He was not going to reach out and answer right away. He would let it ring a second time. It did. Norman reached for the receiver, but yanked his hand back as if his fingers had been burned.

Mailer would wait for eight rings.

Did he have the cojones to wait for eight rings? The phone rang a fourth time. He had the cojones.

Wait. Mailer felt anxious doubt.

The phone rang a fifth time.

What if Plimpton just hangs up?

Mailer reached for the phone and then he didn't. It rang again. Mailer bit his thumb and turned away from the ringing. Then he realized his mistake and spun around—

He had to keep his will focused on the telephone.

It rang for the seventh time. Mailer took a breath. Now he could answer. Wait once more. In a moment of Triumph of the Will, Mailer let the telephone ring again.

Norman Mailer picked up his telephone on the ninth ring, almost regretting not pushing fate and waiting for the eleventh or twelfth ring.

'Hello, George,' Mailer said. 'Where shall I meet you guys?'

There was a pause. Then a voice slurred, 'Hello? Hello? Norman, that you?'

Who? It was Monty. Montgomery Clift. 'Monty, I can't talk. I'm expecting a call.'

'Can't you talk for just a minute?'

'No, Monty. I'm hanging up.'

Mailer hung up the phone.

It rang. Mailer picked up the receiver. 'Hello?'

'I just wanna tell you something.'

'Monty! I'm hanging up. Don't phone again.' He was about to slam the phone down and then he said, 'Monty, where are you?'

'Christopher Street.'

'Take a cab uptown.'

Monty mumbled something. 'You sure? You sure?' Mailer repeated his instructions. 'Okay, Norman. I'm coming.'

Mailer slammed down the phone.

What if Plimpton had phoned just now? Well, he'd get a busy signal and phone again. Mailer realized the mistake he made. Mailer now used his brain to visualize Plimpton and willed him to pick up the telephone and dial Mailer's number. Then the image of Plimpton turned into one of Eleanor Roosevelt. Shit. Mailer switched the images of their faces back and forth until they formed a third, translucent face.

* * *

In 1959, Buster Hendrix finally got an electric guitar. His dad bought it for him. Or that's what Al said twenty years hence. Maybe Ernestine Benson bought the electric guitar. Some would say that Benson bought the electric guitar, but Al Hendrix made her return it. Then Al bought Buster an electric guitar himself.

Buster's father wanted his kid to start mowing lawns to earn money to pay him back.

At any rate, Buster's first electric guitar was a Supro Ozark. It was white plastic with a black headstock. The white was known in the music store business as 'mother-of-toilet-seat finish.'

The Supro Ozark still had a crisp, sharp tone.

Buster restrung his Supro Ozark for his left hand. He didn't have an amp. He had to find other guitarists who'd be generous enough to let him plug in. The first song he learned how to play was 'Tall Cool One.' His hero was guitarist Duane Eddy, already an old man at twenty-one years old. Buster's first gig was in the basement of the Temple De Hirsch Sinai synagogue. Buster was subbing for a missing guitarist in a band that was maybe called the White Eagles or the Panthers or the Hip Doodles.

Buster played wild and loud.

During the first break, he was fired.

Al was now against the guitar. Buster worried that his father would destroy it. After all, when his dad was drunk and ugly, he would slap and sometimes outright slug his son.

Buster's next band was named the Velvetones. They had a piano player. They also had a kid who blew tenor sax. The Velvetones had one-two-three-four guitarists. The guys played sock hops at the Yesler Terrace Neighborhood House. They got a steady gig at Birdland at Madison and

22nd Street, smack on the border between Blacktown and the cracker north end. Birdland always had a black and white clientele. It was a bottle club. Minors were welcome from eight p.m. until eleven. Buster would hang out there to check out the other bands. He persuaded a guy named Dave Lewis to allow Hendrix to solo on his Supro Ozark for ten minutes while Lewis's band was on break. Dave Lewis said, 'Sure.'

* * *

George Plimpton sat at a table at Sardi's across from Ernest Hemingway and felt guilty. He stood and excused himself and headed toward the john. He made a quick dodge right to a row of phone booths. He would call Norman Mailer. Plimpton put a dime in the coin slot.

Do you all know or remember how a rotary phone works?

Plimpton put his pointer in one of the ten different holes in the black plastic rotary dial marked with a number as well as three sequential letters of the alphabet. Plimpton used his pointer to dial the rotary clockwise until his finger reached the finger stop. Then Plimpton removed his pointer and the rotary quickly returned counterclockwise to its original location.

Plimpton used the two seconds of this action to formalize his decision to tell Mailer that Hotchner queered the deal.

Plimpton dialed a second digit.

In 1959, New York City only had one North American Numbering Plan. That meant you could place a call anywhere in Manhattan without first dialing what would later be called the area code.

Plimpton dialed a third digit. Dialing gave a caller time to rethink the nature of the call.

What else should I say to Norman? He'd tell Mailer where they were. He'd tell Mailer to show up and pretend he had another dinner date at Sardi's.

Plimpton dialed the fourth digit.

In *The Time of Her Time,* Mailer's narrator finally achieves his sexual goal to make a so-called frigid woman orgasm through strenuous fornication that climaxes when he turns the woman over on her belly—

George Plimpton dialed the next-to-last digit.

—Mailer's narrator then begins sodomizing the woman and then turns her around to resume missionary-position in-and-out.

Time stands still in George Plimpton's phone booth, his finger dialing the rotary.

His finger...

If George Plimpton had no arms, he could dial the phone with his nose. With his tongue (as unsanitary as that would be). Plimpton may or may not have known this, but Norman Mailer would dial a telephone with his erect penis if he had to.

Mailer was a self-proclaimed Phallic Narcissist who believed the only true female orgasms were vaginal ones created by the motion of a grand phallus.

Let other men diddle and nibble.

At this moment, George Plimpton almost slaps his forehead—'Wait a minute! What am I doing? To hell with Norman Mailer.'

It didn't dawn on Plimpton that he was being mind-controlled by Mailer. Plimpton knew nothing about mind control. He didn't believe in hypnotism. He knew nothing about Project MK-ULTRA, nothing about Nixon's interest in mind control. Plimpton had no interest in Nietzsche's Triumph of the Will nonsense. George Plimpton just hung the pay phone up.

The next time he saw Norman Mailer he would tell a lame lie about getting a busy signal.

* * *

Seattle. Buster Hendrix at Birdland. The skinny kid jumped onstage with an electric guitar.

He started tapping his foot fairly fast. He was wearing Stacys. Buster gave a shrug and then began noodling on that Supro Ozark. He'd strum a few fast chords, then snakes of notes. The mouths of some snakes are blue inside. Sky blue. That was Buster's notes. No one on the dance floor or at the bar could dance to it. The audience thought his wrong notes were the right notes and the right notes wrong. They were like white children in the suburbs of Seattle who think there is only one language in the world: English. And Buster Hendrix's guitar was speaking in baby talk.

Buster's guitar was speaking in Dr. Seuss. Buster was a prodigy. Buster was an idiot savant. Buster was doing tonal bebop riffraff. Buster was playing nonsense. It had no testosterone. Buster played with a femininity that masked itself as grace.

The same God that made Jackson Pollock suddenly start flinging paint on canvas in 1948 was striking again through the spiny fingers of this black kid.

Buster was playing Coonskin—that being an art term a white art critic named Rosenberg used to describe Jackson Pollock as a painter. 'Coonskin' referred to the wild warriors of 1776 New England, those trappers wearing coonskin hats, leaping from the trees to shoot at those goose-stepping British Redcoats—professional soldiers, professional soldiers all shot down by amateurs because the Redcoats couldn't even see the forest through the trees, let alone the Americans hiding behind the tree trunks.

Young Buster saw the forest.

The white critic named Rosenberg had pointed out that 'The Coonskinners win, but their method can hardly be considered a contribution to military culture.'

That's untrue. That's just something to write. That's being carried away with metaphor. That's forgetting metaphors are always at least one step removed from the object at hand.

There was logic in Buster's abstract accidentals. We moderns have digested Chaos Theory and now know that there is no such thing as a random act. Young Hendrix was creating an electric squall that only a sonic weatherman could read, yet it could be read.

Buster was playing post–rock 'n' roll even though he was not aware that rock 'n' roll was dead. Buddy Holly had just died on February 3 in a plane crash in Iowa. Elvis was in the Army. Little Richard had given away twenty-five Cadillacs after a religious vision in Australia compelled him to become a Seventh Day Adventist. Jerry Lee Lewis had disgraced himself by marrying his thirteen-year-old cousin. Chuck Berry was on trial for fornicating with fourteen-year-old Apache jailbait in St. Louis.* Be assured that Buster's playing was beyond Buddy and Elvis and Little anybody—beyond rock 'n' roll itself.

Here was a riff in a simple rhythm.

A blues four-step.

4/4 time.

---

* Writer Peter Guralnick was *only* sixteen years old during this time.

He syncopated in 3/4 time.

He played some sequences in 5/16.

He made notes climb up his neck until they squealed higher than birds. Trapped mice.

Then notes bending downward. The notes poured out slow like cubes of Jell-O. The notes were wiggling green, raspberry, lemon.

Buster played in bone time. Nursery rhymes. Kid stuff. The last oasis. The sound of an Oriental woman having a climax. How'd this Negro kid know that? The sound of Marilyn Monroe's nylons swishing against each other as she wiggled down a row of seats at the symphony, at the matinee, at the boxing match, at the donkey show in Mexico City. Then violent chords predating heavy-metal chords, which duplicated the sound of Ed Gein up in Joseph McCarthy's home state of Wisconsin skinning dead Wisconsin women and inspiring the creation of Norman Bates.

* * *

Manhattan. Norman Mailer sat before his phone and stared and tried not to drink the Scotch too fast. Mailer didn't write science fiction, but a writer named Ray Bradbury did. He wrote his still well-known collection of short stories about Mars, *The Martian Chronicles,* back in 1950. Back in 1959, we all expected that Americans would land on Mars long before the twenty-first century began. A man recently died in 2006, a man who conducted isolation experiments on himself to experience the effect of a long desolate trip to Mars by spending days, then months in total isolation in various caves in Switzerland. He had no clocks or calendars. He slept when he wanted to. When he came out of the cave of his longest isolation he was told he'd been in for ninety-three days. He was dumbfounded. He thought he'd only been in for forty-four days. Something similar happened to the mind of Norman Mailer. A combination of Scotch nullifying the man's nervousness and impatience made Mailer believe he had only wasted two hours waiting for George Plimpton to call. Instead, Mailer was floored when he heard Montgomery Clift calling his name from the street. He opened the shades. The sun was about to rise.

'Come on! Get some breakfast with me!' Clift yelled.

* * *

April. Ocean liner in the Pacific. The *Chola Srivijaya*. Two days out from Hong Kong. Final port, San Francisco. There are wealthy Asians onboard. Some loaded Englishmen too. A few Australians. All up in first class. The idle rich. They could afford jet fare, but enjoy the quaint lethargy of a cruise. Down in second class, a few American geologists and mining engineers. Third class is four dozen Chinese adults and even more children. Third class is much cheaper than a plane ticket.

The *Chola Srivijaya*'s nautical staff are Anglo-Saxons. The *Chola Srivijaya*'s waiters are mostly undercover Red Chinese eavesdropping for Mao. The *Chola Srivijaya* will dock in California a little under three weeks from now.

First class. Eleven a.m. The portside ballroom. The floor has just been mopped. Fresh white linens on each table. The champagne buckets bone empty. A luxurious young Asian woman in pajamas and her dignified older husband (also Asian)—the man wearing slacks and an armless T-shirt—stand facing each other.

Note that the man's T-shirt is very clean.

The skin of the man's underarms is smooth.

The man places his right hand on the back of his wife's shoulder. She mirrors this gesture to him with her left arm. Their free arms are raised with their palms at chest level. The man grasps the woman's hand.

'Not so tight,' a young man says. He utters that instruction in Sam Yup Cantonese, the dialect of Shanghai, as he uses his foot to maneuver a white cloth to dry some wet spots on the ballroom floor. He is eighteen years old, wearing an impeccably pressed white shirt with black trousers and a sport coat. He ironed each piece of clothing himself. He has ironed his own clothes every day since he was thirteen.

He is also myopic, wearing thick glasses called Tojos, although the boy is Chinese, and Tojo of course wasn't.

The young man is tall for a Chinese teenager—five feet seven inches. He weighs 135 pounds.

He dries the spot and kicks the cloth under a table and nods to the corner of the ballroom where an Asian man in cook's garb places the arm of a record player on a spinning record. Latin music begins sounding—

violin, sax, piano, maraca, bongos. No singing. Without knowing the record, you intuit the rhythm—*cha cha chaaah*.

The couple begins dancing. They're doing the Cha-Cha, a dance with ambiguous beginnings in the 1920s voodoo fields of Haiti, and then fortifying itself in Havana. The Cha-Cha is the dance Howard Hunt did with the Cuban harlots. Once on *I Love Lucy*, Ricky tried to teach the Cha-Cha to his wife, Lucy. Of course, Lucy had two left feet. Lucy cha-chaing—spastic female indignity.

Aboard the *Chola Srivijaya*, the Asian teenager shadows the dancing couple, saying, 'Step to the left. Now, slightly backward.' The boy now directs his comments to the man. 'Left foot! Left foot! Back now with your right. Rock up with your left. Good. Good. Step forward with your right. Close your feet together. Don't stop. Step forward with your left. Rock your right foot. Step left with your right. Step left with your left. No no no and no. This way!'

He cuts in and dances with the man—

'Follow my steps.'

Readers! Have you ever heard the Sam Cooke song, 'Everybody Loves to Cha Cha Cha'?

> Took my baby to the hop . . . she hit me with the news . . . she said she couldn't do the cha cha cha . . .

The Asian boy leads the man in this left/forward plus back/right along the floor in a pattern that from the ceiling would be that of a New Mexican swastika. There is a kind of homoerotic/classic Greek beauty about these two males dancing.

> I told her . . . they'd play some other dance but we sat there for an hour and a half and we never got a chance . . .

The Asian boy cha-chas exquisitely. Short quick steps. Polished wingtips. A few years ago, this youth won the prestigious Crown Colony Cha-Cha Championship. In the back pocket of his pants with their creases sharp as knives rests an actual switchblade along with a small deck of cards that contain silhouettes of male shoeprints depicting dance steps for fifty ballroom dances.

> Every song they played was the cha cha cha . . . 'Tom Dooley' cha cha cha; 'Tea For Two' cha cha cha . . .

'Now you lead and I follow,' the teenager instructs. 'No no. Feel the music. Feel it in your hips. That's right. Now step to the left. Good. Now rock up on your heel. Right foot! Right foot! There! There!' He reaches out to the woman in the pajamas and maneuvers her into his former position in front of her husband. Did I tell you her pajamas were sea blue?

> I told her not to worry . . . Baby, if you let me take you by the hand I'm gonna teach this dance to you . . .

After forty-five minutes, the record player is clicked off. The pajama'd courtesan and her husband thank the boy. The woman turns to leave. Her husband slips a Hong Kong pound note into the boy's pocket. Then he follows his wife with his arms extended holding an invisible woman and dancing the Cha-Cha.

> After we practiced it for a little while she was cha cha chaing better than me . . .

Now another woman enters the portside ballroom in first class; an Anglo-Saxon wearing a gown she wore the night before. The gown is wilted, but the woman seems full of pep. 'Harry won't come,' she pouts in a South African accent. 'Show me how to lead.'

Without smiling or expressing himself in any way with his lips, eighteen-year-old Lee Jun Fan assumes the woman's position, and gives her the same right foot/left foot instructions that he gave to his first students. Without music. Then the record player is put on. She smiles at the boy as if they had just slept together.

They haven't.

There is a scratch in the second song on the record. Each time the second song is played, she tilts her head back and shouts 'Hoopla!' in sync with that crackling scratch. After forty-five minutes she tips the boy a U.S. dollar and leaves.

* * *

Later that day, down in third class, 8:00 p.m. In a darkened room a projector is running a movie for about twenty kids sitting on the floor. The movie is B&W. Up on the screen swarm Asian kids. An older kid is beating them. The younger kids fight back. They do not use their fists. It looks like they're slapping each other. On the soundtrack, these kids squeal in Cantonese. At the bottom of the screen subtitles in Mandarin appear. The Cha-Cha instructor is standing at the back of the audience, behind even the projectionist and whirring projector. The young man watches the movie with an expression that alternates between a smirk and a frown. The movie was made ten years ago when the young man performed as a child actor. He, himself, is that eight-year-old B&W kid on the screen now beating on a fat old man with a stalk of celery as if the vegetable stalk was a Samurai sword.

Last image of our Cha-Cha instructor—

The middle of the night.

The youth is roaming the cabin corridor. He walks with purpose although he frequently bumps into walls. His eyes are closed.

A sleepwalker.

This youth has had the condition of unconscious perambulation since he was three. He bumps into a fire extinguisher that isn't hidden in some cubbyhole as in first class, but is out in the open, hooked on a wall. He bumps the fire extinguisher and at the same time the ship sharply tilts, a combination that perturbs the fire extinguisher, causing it to leap from the wall. The youth doesn't open his eyes, but he whips his left hand up to block the fire extinguisher from striking his head while his right hand palms the fire extinguisher, and with one sweeping arc of his arm returns the apparatus to its hook on the wall.

The sleepwalker continues down the corridor.

This young man's Cantonese name is Lee Jun Fan. His parents were former stars of the Chinese opera. They had both known Ping Chow. In early 1940, Lee Jun Fan's parents were touring America when his mother got pregnant. By the time she began showing, the opera company was in San Francisco. She stayed behind and gave birth to Lee Jun Fan on the 27th of November, 1940. Everyone returned to Hong Kong. Nine months later: Pearl Harbor. Eighteen days after that, Hong Kong fell to the Japs on Christmas Day.

A bad time would be had by all.

After Japan's Oppenheimer surrender, the child Lee Jun Fan went on to star in eleven movies. Lee Jun Fan also learned how to ballroom dance. Lee Jun Fan also trained in a martial art called Gung Fu. The boy and his father never got along. Lee Jun Fan became a teen. The boy and his father still never got along. Lee Jun Fan was a rapidly learning Gung Fu student. The boy was also a hood, instigating brawls against the kids from England. This kid knew his way around the Hong Kong jail. This kid skipped Hong Kong high school as often as Buster Hendrix in Seattle. Lee Jun Fan's mother explained to her son that if he returned to America before his nineteenth birthday he could claim American citizenship.

Lee Jun Fan made plans to sail for California.

His father slipped him fifteen American dollars and his mother slipped him one hundred. (The boy and his father never really got along.)

Lee Jun Fan was about to leave the house with his bags. His father called him back. Lee Jun Fan walked toward his father, but the man waved his son away. 'Get out of here.' It has been said that uttering those words was a Chinese tradition to ensure that one's son would be forced to return to Hong Kong for his father's eventual funeral.

The cooks onboard the *Chola Srivijaya* were Hong Kong Chinese. A baker recognized the lad from the movies. They talked. The baker learned Lee Jun Fan could dance England style. Next thing, Lee Jun Fan was giving dance lessons to rich passengers every morning in the portside first class lounge. Lee Jun Fan still slept in third class. He was paid nothing by the ship and split his tips with the Chinese baker. Lee Jun Fan was allowed to dine in first class, however. Much better food. And he was allowed to dance recreationally with Asian and sometimes white women in the first class portside lounge until two in the morning.

Sometimes during recreational dancing, a woman would slip her hand into Lee Jun Fan's pants. That made him uncomfortable. Her fingers might discover that Lee Jun Fan possessed only a single ball; his right testicle had never descended. We violate his privacy because this is perhaps his deepest hidden shame. And his only shame. Three weeks more at sea, then the *Chola Srivijaya* docks in San Francisco. Several weeks after that, Lee Jun Fan makes his way to Seattle to live with a benefactor and attend an American high school to get a diploma that will allow him to attend American college. His high school in Seattle is Edison Technical on 1701 Broadway. This is roughly one mile from where Buster Hendrix cuts class at Garfield High School over on 23rd Street.

* * *

Manhattan. Willem de Kooning spent the last spring of the 1950s possessed by the adoration of vulgarity. Relentless vulgarity. De Kooning loved the melodrama of vulgarity and the vulgarity of melodrama. De Kooning admired Weegee's photographs of transvestites in handcuffs sitting in the backs of paddy wagons. The painter's favorite book became that Mickey Spillane paperback where private eye Mike Hammer shoots a naked murderess in the belly and she gasps out, *How could you do it?* and Hammer replies, *It was easy.* De Kooning watched noir TV every Wednesday night—'There are eight million stories in the Naked City . . .'

When summer rolled into town, Willem de Kooning and Ruth Kligman flew to Italy. From the moment the Alitalia plane touched down at Ciampino Aeroporto, it was apparent that Rome was an eruption of classical vulgarity. Rome was the original Naked City. This city would not purify de Kooning's desire for lowbrow delight. All those narrow Roman streets, the scooters, the little Italian cars, the noise. Italians everywhere were talking of *psychology, psychological* this and that, but the Italians did not use the Italian term, *psicologico.* Instead, they spoke the German word, *psychologisch*. 'What's the big deal, Willem? Freud wrote in German.'

'So did Hitler.'

'Hitler/Freud—two sides of the same coin. Besides, it's like how Americans use French for sex—*Ménage à trois. Fellatio.*'

'*Fellatio* is Italian, Ruth.'

* * *

Willem de Kooning and Ruth went everywhere, always trailed by half a dozen newspaper photographers chewing candy, perched on their scooters popping flash photos.

All those Italian Weegees.

Willem de Kooning was a celebrity in Rome, you see. He was the Great American Painter. Every public touch he and Ruth shared was photographed. Every bite of food. These cameramen were paparazzi, of course, but that word wouldn't enter the international vocabulary until the following year, the second year of the 1960s, when an Italian film being shot that summer in Rome by Federico Fellini will be released to movie theaters. It is to be titled *La Dolce Vita.*

It will change world cinema forever.

* * *

Lee Jun Fan went up to Seattle to board with Ping and Ruby Chow on the corner of Broadway and Jefferson. Lee Jun Fan was given a shoebox room in the attic. Lee Jun Fan was to be a waiter at the restaurant. He proved to be a belligerent waiter. Lee Jun Fan may have been a petite acrobatic marvel, but he was also the epitome of arrogance. See Ruby Chow with her gigantic beehive towering over Lee Jun Fan. The Chows apparently tolerated Lee's antagonism out of Ping's deep loyalty to Lee's father (who didn't care for his son any more than Ruby and her big hair did).

Chapter 20

Alaska, 1959

Seattle: Lee Jun Fan transformed. He knew not the cause. Lee Jun Fan began to reject frivolity. First, he stopped dancing. He lived only for Gung Fu. What older Gung Fu students had taken weeks to digest in Hong Kong, Lee Jun Fan mastered after only one hour in Seattle. The teenager began giving public Gung Fu demonstrations after school and before work at street fairs and in parking lots.

Lee would tell the gathered audience that he was going to demonstrate a fighting technique invented centuries ago by a diminutive Buddhist nun, a secret fighting technique previously only revealed to the Chinese. (Lee Jun Fan never mentioned this, but his mother had German ancestors. In Hong Kong, various Gung Fu students jealous of Lee had exposed his mixed blood, yet Lee's teacher refused to dismiss the youth from class. Lee was too good.) There in some Seattle parking lot, Lee Jun Fan, wearing black pajamas like a Viet Cong, would demonstrate moves that resembled the choreographical gestures of Martha Graham (not that any working-class Caucasian citizen gathered around this strange 'Oriental' had heard of Martha Graham). Lee's quicker moves resembled t'ai chi movements accelerated by amphetamines. In 1959, no Occidental American had witnessed t'ai chi (Supreme Ultimate Fist 太极拳) let alone Fu Jow Pai (Black Tiger Gung Fu 黑虎拳) or Choy Gar (Rat Gung Fu 蔡家). Or Gouquan, Shequan, and Mei Haw Auan (Dog Fist 狗拳, Snake Fist 蛇拳, and Plum Blossom Fist 梅花拳). Each one of these disciplines had its own version of Zui Quan (Drunken Fist 醉拳). Modern pulp writer Ian Fleming, now seven books into his James Bond series, gave his hero 007 the abilities learned in Jujitsu—how to flip attackers over his shoulder. Few Americans other than veterans who'd been to Japan knew the difference between Judo (Gentle Way 柔道) and Karate (空手). Thus, Lee Jun Fan's posturings often seemed like Asian Foolishness (蔡家太极拳).

Fifteen minutes into his demonstration, the Caucasian audience began its inevitable heckling. Lee always wore his glasses so he could see the crowd. He'd then point at some male and say, 'You look like you know how to fight.' This white man was always taller and outweighed the young Asian. Lee would encourage the fellow to step forward. He would. Then Lee would dare the Caucasian to punch him. The chosen guy always reacted with surprise. He glanced at his buddies. Looked back at Lee with an evil smile—*Here it comes, you little skinny slant-eyes—Kapow!*—guy shooting out a one-fisted roundhouse that Lee would easily deflect with one hand himself, instantly responding with a strange snaking punch of his own at the end of his other arm, a punch that always stopped not more than the width of a feather from the Caucasian hombre's face. The guy would try a few more cowboy movie punches that Lee would deflect with Gung Fu arm and foot responses. Lee Jun Fan rarely hurt any of his white male guinea pigs. He only ended the demonstration by razzing the crown of some knucklehead's skull with his knuckle à la Moe to Curly in *The Three Stooges.*

★ ★ ★

Seattle, several blocks south. Buster Hendrix had a new high school band, the Rocking Kings. The band would do Hank Ballard's country hit 'The Twist,' only slower. Their drummer was named Exkano. They would play 'The Twist' with Exkano doing what he called a 'slop beat.' It was a shuffle, not a twist. The similarities between both those dances and Lee Jun Fan's Cha-Cha were the swiveling of the pelvis.

Meanwhile, Buster's father was getting worked up about Buster spending so much time with that damn electric guitar.

Buster feared for his Supro Ozark's safety.

Buster began storing the guitar at the back of the stage at Birdland. Hiding it, actually. Then one Friday afternoon he went to Birdland. The Rocking Kings had a gig. He needed his guitar, but it had gone missing.

Buster told everyone he had 'forgotten' his guitar at Birdland and someone had obviously swiped it. He could not admit that he had feared that his own father would destroy that guitar. In modern terms, we'd say Buster Hendrix had Stockholm syndrome with his father.

* * *

One summer day in Cuba, Ernest Hemingway went fishing for marlin aboard his boat, the *Pilar*, with Castro and his cabinet as honored guests. Castro hooked the biggest catch of the day. As the *Pilar* headed back to port, Castro put his arm around Hemingway's broad shoulders—picture Castro with his black Hasidic/Islamic beard buddying up with Hemingway with his scruffy Santa Claus beard. Castro told the Nobel Prize winner, 'I have never read anything like *The Old Man and the Sea*. Your greatest quality as an intellectual is the way you present your monologues. When asked what I like best about your writing, I say your monologues. We cannot really call your books novels or fiction. I learned history reading you. *A Farewell to Arms* is history. What is a man without history? *For Whom the Bell Tolls* is history. *For Whom the Bell Tolls* has had a significant influence on my life personally. I remembered the point where the entire plot developed in *For Whom the Bell Tolls*—a small patrol of Fascists draws near to an area where combat is taking place while a man with a machine gun watches the Fascists from a distance. At the precise right moment, the machine gunner cuts the Fascists to pieces. You showed me how one man, well placed, could stop an army and that was how I deployed my men over and over during the revolution—one soldier killing dozens of Batistas.'

* * *

New Hampshire. At a town council meeting, Richard Pavlick was complaining about the flag: 'You all know that Alaska became the forty-ninth state five months ago in January. Here it is June already, for Pete's sake, and all that's flyin' are old forty-eight-star flags.'

'Mr. Pavlick, you know very well that Hawaii will become the fiftieth state any day now.'

'But it hasn't happened yet. Those flags that are flyin' are invalid. It's like waitin' to give a child an immunization to Spanish flu until a double immunization for Spanish flu and typhus is available, yet all around us children are dropping dead of the Spanish flu.'

The room was silent as everyone tried to figure out what Pavlick had just said. Finally Finley the bartender at Shake's Place spoke. 'Now see here, Pavlick. I read in the newspaper that—'

'What newspaper, Finley?'

'The *Manchester Union Leader.*'

'That rag? Who believes anything the *Manchester Union Leader* says?'

Several citizens piped up, 'I do!'

'Listen, Pavlick, the government announced that according to law, when a state is added to the Union, we have one year to update the flag.'

'Very good, Mr. Finley. Are you satisfied, Mr. Pavlick?'

'Why even fly the damn flag then? Why not hang the maple leaf flag? Or the hammer and sickle?'

After the meeting, a dozen people gathered to talk—not about the flag of the United States of America, but about newspaper reports that told how the actor who played Superman on TV had shot himself in Hollywood.

★ ★ ★

Viet-Nam. Ngô Dinh Diem now derisively referred to the Viet Minh as the Viet Cong. The first 'official' American deaths that occurred in Viet-Nam happened on July 8, 1959, at a Vietnamese infantry base camp at Bien Hoa, twenty miles as the black stork flies north of Saigon. There are eight Americans at Bien Hoa, members of the U.S. Military Assistance Advisory Group. The sun finally goes down around eight thirty and the jungle is saturated with an instant darkness pocked by stars. No moon. Six Americans decide to watch a movie in the stucco mess hall. Their last names are Ovnand and Buis as well as a captain from Iowa with the name of Boston and a man named Heller. The names of the other two will not be recorded by *Time* magazine. The movie they see is two years old, *The Tattered Dress* staring Jeff Chandler (then thirty-nine) and Jeanne Crain (thirty-two). Each American takes a chair and positions himself in a half ring around the screen. Two Vietnamese soldiers stand guard outside the door smoking and rolling dice.

The opening credits of the movie roll. Everyone makes themselves comfortable. No one really knows what this movie is about. After the credits, a woman—a wife—rushes to her husband in a tattered dress. She's obviously been raped. All of the men are sucked into the movie. Back in America, there is no organized feminist specific objection to rape. Religious men are against it for biblical reasons. Most guys don't think about rape much, but in a movie rape has a quasi-erotic context. The raped woman's husband appears to go and shoot the guy who attacked his wife. The guy is arrested. Now comes the hero, Jeff Chandler. He is a John Wayne–style hero type who has never really made the leap to eternal star. (He never will. Jeff Chandler is forgotten today.) Jeff Chandler plays the lawyer who will defend the husband for shooting his wife's rapist. Now comes the actress Jeanne Crain. She's cute, but not beautiful. She's known as 'Hollywood's Number One Party Girl.' She plays Chandler's proper wife.

All while this movie has been running Viet Cong guerrillas have been quietly circling the stucco mess hall.

The two Vietnamese guards outside the front are garroted.

A Viet Cong peeks through the door. All that is visible are the images from the black-and-white film. The rest of the room is impenetrably dark. There are no silhouettes of sitting soldiers.

At the back of the mess hall, two Viet Cong stick the muzzles of their French MAT submachine guns in through the open windows. *Time* magazine will not call the Viet Cong the Viet Cong. *Time* will refer to them as *terrorists.* Meanwhile in the movie, Jeff Chandler and Jeanne Crain go to Nevada to defend the playboy. Several soldiers, only seconds from death, probably wonder if this is going to be a courtroom drama like *Anatomy of a Murder.* The movie is running on a sixteen-millimeter projector. In these days, movies are stored on reels, maybe six reels per movie. In a movie theater, a projectionist operates two movie projectors and the transformation from one reel to anther is almost transparent to the audience. In this makeshift movie theater in Bien Hoa, when one reel is finished, the projector must be stopped and the lights turned on so the reel can be changed.

The first reel is over.

Ovnand stops the projector and pulls on the lights. The Viet Cong let their French MAT submachine guns rip. Ovnand and Buis are torn apart. Boston is wounded. Heller dodges bullets and leaps to pull off the lights. The room goes black. A Viet Cong at the door raises his arm to throw a bomb into the mess hall, but it explodes too soon. This confuses the remaining Viet Cong and they all slip into the jungle, carrying the body of their blown-apart comrade with them. Over the next several years, 58,217 more Americans like Ovnand and Buis and Boston will be killed and wounded. In 1961, forty-two-year-old Jeff Chandler will die in a botched surgery to repair a spinal disc herniation. That same year, thirty-six-year-old Jeanne Crain will enter semiretirement after starring in an Italian movie, *Nefertiti, Regina del Nilo,* costarring Vincent Price.

* * *

On Friday, the 18th of September, Marilyn Monroe flew out to Los Angeles to be part of a Hollywood toast to the premier of the U.S.S.R., Nikita Khrushchev. That night, after the luncheon, Marilyn telephoned her husband.

'How did it go, honey?'

'Okay. A lot of talking and speeches and translations in Russian and English. Khrushchev stood up and hollered in Russian that he wasn't allowed to visit Disneyland.'

'Why can't he visit Disneyland?'

'He said it was because we launched rockets from Disneyland.'

'What?'

She repeated the sentence.

'He was joking, honey.'

'Oh. No. Well, maybe. He was real steamed up about Disneyland though. There was even someone at the luncheon dressed in a Mickey Mouse costume. Mr. Khrushchev asked me who the mouse in the costume was and I told him, *Mighty Mouse.* He didn't know I was lying. And anyway, Frank Sinatra and I decided that tomorrow morning we'll take Khrushchev to Disneyland as *our* guests.'

'Will you really?'

'Sure. Why not? We'll do it in secret.'

'Was Skouras at the luncheon?'

'Of course. He made a speech.'

Spyros Skouras was the president of Twentieth Century Fox. Skouras once suggested to Arthur Miller that the playwright should thank the House Un-American Activities Committee for 'helping him find his way *back* to America.'

'What did Skouras say?' Miller asked.

'He told that old boring story of how he and his brothers came to America with a few carpets and now he's the president of Twentieth Century Fox. Khrushchev then said that he was a bastard son of a coal miner and now he's the boss of Russia.'

'Did Khrushchev really say he was a *bastard son*?'

'Yeah-yeah. At least I think so. But then I don't speak Russian.'

'Marilyn, did the translator say *bastard son*?'

'Oh Arturo. I don't know. Whatever was said it put Skouras in his place.' She paused and then said, 'Khrushchev was just like me—the odd man out.'

* * *

Willem de Kooning and Ruth Kligman in Rome.

The pair are running down a sunlit hill chasing a flock of wild geese. At night, de Kooning and Ruth are walking down the Spanish Steps.

'Look,' Ruth said. 'Down there.'

'Look at what?'

'That pillar. It's moving.'

'No, it isn't. Are you crazy? Oh wow! It is moving!'

'It's not a pillar. It's the Leaning Tower of Pisa!'

The Americans were following someone costumed in what was surely a seven foot-tall replica of the Leaning Tower of Pisa. The person inside the costume was staggering down the Spanish Steps, a woman in a black evening dress walking beside screaming in Italian, 'Carlos! Carlos! Stand straight. You'll fall over.'

'I am standing straight!' the man shouted back in Italian. And saying that, he tipped over and rolled down about a dozen steps.

'My God, another drunk!' de Kooning said to Ruth. 'Let's wait for him to get up—'

'—and follow him.' Ruth knew her man.

Except the Leaning Tower never stood. There were many people walking up and down the steps, but none stopped or even paid attention to the man in the costume, his loafers and black pants sticking out from the circular bottom of the costume. The woman tried to help this Carlos to stand by pulling his arm, but he couldn't or wouldn't cooperate, and he ended up pulling her down on top of his costume's round façade. De Kooning and Ruth rushed down the steps to offer assistance.

* * *

Los Angeles, California. Khrushchev had snuck out of his American hotels three times before—twice in Manhattan, once in Kansas, and now yet again this morning at the Ambassador Hotel. The premier of Russia strode out of an employee door in the alley at seven a.m. dressed in a blue bellboy costume. The fat man was followed by a thin and dark Russian suited up and carrying a second black suitcoat over his arm—Khrushchev's bodyguard and translator. A taxicab pulled up. The two Russians crawled in the back seat on either side of Marilyn Monroe—Frank Sinatra sitting up front shotgun beside the cabby. The cab sped off. Sinatra made small talk. Monroe smiled. She was in her Good Sport mode. Khrushchev took off his bellboy coat and the bodyguard reached across Monroe's lap to help the premier into a black jacket that had a few medals on the lapel. Then Khrushchev removed his bellboy bow tie and his bodyguard attached a clip-on tie to Khrushchev's white collar. The cab drove forty-five minutes south to Anaheim. On the ride, Monroe pulled out a notebook. On four pages, Monroe's friend Natalie Wood, an actress who had been born Наталья Николаевна Захаренко in San Francisco, had written phonetic dialogue for Marilyn to speak to Khrushchev. The first line was 'New-pluska pon qeck Dostoevski compulra?' *What is your favorite book by Dostoevski?* With an excited smile, Marilyn Monroe asked Nikita Khrushchev that question.

* * *

At last, Disneyland. The two Russians and the sexiest woman in America and the most masculine crooner in America got out of the taxi at Disney's gates. Sinatra sauntered over to a souvenir stand to buy everyone Donald Duck sunglasses. Marilyn purchased two Mickey Mouse ear caps. She put one on her head and the other on the bald crown of Nikita Khrushchev. The Russian smiled like a little boy.

Sinatra laughed and paid everyone's entrance fee and bought enough tickets for twenty rides times four. First, the quartet came to 'Main Street U.S.A.' Khrushchev studied every architectural aspect as if this truly represented the sociological reality of a typical American small town. On street level, Disneyland appeared to be moderately crowded, yet if one flew above in a whirlybird, you would have seen that the entire amusement park was deserted save for fifty people who basically walked in circles around the two Americans and the two Russians to give the illusion that the amusement park was crowded. These 'walkers' were American agents working together with Russian agents to keep Khrushchev *Khrushchev-fied,* so to speak. Up in our whirlybird, we moderns may think Disneyland was primitive, yet by contemporary 1950s standards, the place was more than a mere glorified amusement park. Many exhibits had not yet been built, but there were monorails and submarine rides, and a replica of the Swiss mountain called the Matterhorn had just opened. Down below, the first ride Khrushchev went on would prove to be the only one he rode. It was called Mr. Toad's Wild Ride—the toad in question a character from the Disney 1949 animated picture *The Wind in the Willows,* which was in turn based on a famous novel for the children of 1908. Mr. Toad's Wild Ride began when go-carts designed like a miniature 1905 Waverley Coupe rolled down a chute. There was room for two riders in each Khrushchev shoved Sinatra and the Russian bodyguard in the first. Then Khrushchev and Monroe, both wearing mouse ear caps, climbed into the next. Then their car sped up crashing through a fake wall into the interior of a mansion's library where an automated cartoon badger balanced atop a teetering ladder almost dropped a stack of books as the pair's car sped through the room and through a fake fireplace. Marilyn Monroe acted as if Mr. Toad's Wild Ride was thrilling. She could be a good sport without even trying. She permitted Khrushchev to put his left arm around her back, but then wiggled and screamed as they raced down the streets of turn-of-the-century London so that Khrushchev was unable to get a good grip down her blouse or up her skirt. Everything with Khrushchev was dealable until the cart entered hell, the last portion of the ride.

No joke.

The two descended into a simulation of hell where little comic devils hopped out of the darkness on either side of their cart. Suddenly, Khrushchev bolted upward in panic. The Russian premier tried to throw his bulk over Marilyn Monroe in order to flee the still-moving 1905 Waverley Coupe.

* * *

Christmas Eve was on Thursday this year. A week earlier in a Hollywood studio an elaborate bathtub was constructed. Filming started on Thursday and Friday, broke for the weekend, and then continued Monday, Tuesday, and Wednesday. When this scene was edited it would only last forty-five seconds. All that happened for thirty-five seconds were shots of a seemingly naked woman taking a shower in a bathtub encased by a tile wall and a semitransparent shower curtain. The actress taking the shower had a very striking body. Most men in the United States would pay triple the twenty-five-cent ticket price to watch this actress, Janet Leigh, take a shower. Of course, the shower scene would occur in Alfred Hitchcock's *Psycho.* Leigh (age thirty-two) wore a moleskin body suit to hide her breasts and pelvis as the scene was filmed. Janet Leigh would appear in most of the seventy-eight separate images that make up the most famous film montage in history. A nude model was used for the other images. Her name was Marli Renfro. She was a twenty-one-year-old stripper and 'glamour model' who had previously appeared in such magazines as *Modern Man* and *Ace* and *Escapade.* Miss Renfro was paid five hundred dollars for her uncredited posing in the shower. Miss Renfro was almost nude save for a feminine version of the codpiece. The bit of film with the longest duration of this redhead's body was less than half a second long.

Psycho will open in June next year and will still be playing in Manhattan during the fall. Renfro will appear naked on the cover of the September 1960 issue of *Playboy.* Norman Mailer, who will be going through an excruciatingly difficult time psychically speaking, will take his wife to the DeMille Theatre to see *Psycho.* Norman Mailer will merge with Norman Bates. Several weeks after seeing the film, Mailer will find himself carving up a woman with a knife.

* * *

First New Year's Eve again!

Good-bye, 1959.

Seattle. Buster Hendrix now has a guitar as beautiful as a girl. He has named the white Danelectro Silvertone guitar that his comrades in the Rocking Kings chipped in to buy Betty Jean.

Betty Jean was only available in the Sears catalog. Betty Jean came with an amp. Betty Jean cost $49.93, just four dollars down.

Betty Jean was relatively cheap because the pickup casting was made of a lipstick tube. The rest was masonite and aluminum and Brazilian rosewood. The body of a Danelectro Silvertone was a classic piece of what guitar historians now call Atomic Deco.

More important, a Danelectro Silvertone looked cool.

When one strummed a Danelectro Silvertone, it sounded like the future.

Buster Hendrix painted his Betty Jean Silvertone fire-truck red, and then painted her name on it.

Betty Jean.

* * *

Rome. Ruth Kligman and de Kooning are guests at a New Year's Eve party at some millionaire's villa. They do not know the host, some Italian film producer named Gucci or Giuseppe. No one here at the party knows what time it is—you were stopped at the door if you were wearing a watch. The heart of the party is in a large two-tiered library. The books look old and seem all in Italian. All the furniture, if there was furniture, has been removed.

Ruth and de Kooning lean on the second tier's balcony. At some point, two very tall redheads enter the room wrapped together in what appears to be some sort of white sheet.

'Botticelli's nieces,' de Kooning remarks.

The two women begin spinning in opposite directions, unspooling an impossibly long sheet between them. As the portion of the sheet covering their bodies decreases, it becomes apparent they are naked beneath their portion of fabric. They both stop when only a single layer of sheet covers each one.

The host, a small fat man dressed the way a movie producer should dress, stands at the railing of the second tier and through cupped hands yells, 'Before you is Rome's first drive-in movie theater!'

At that moment, half a dozen young women in Roman tunics pedal into the library scrunched in the seats of little metal children's cars that look like miniature Renaults. These women pedal hunched over, their elbows raised higher than their ears, and line up before the unwound sheet. They then pull their legs out of the children's cars and sit there with legs splayed wide as a movie projector is rolled in.

'The film you are about to see is still in progress,' the host shouts. 'The sound has not yet been dubbed. It will be done in the new year. I will not tell you who has made this picture or who stars in it, but I will tell you that it is a masterpiece.' He then claps his hands. 'Continue with the party.'

The lights dim. The projector starts. The film begins screening across the white sheet. The film is black-and-white. Music begins playing from a phonograph player—some electric Roman circus music again. People begin talking. De Kooning and Ruth watch the movie—

A helicopter flies past a statue of an open-armed Christ giving a benediction to the Roman skyline. The helicopter flies over a penthouse roof where women in bikinis are sunning themselves. All have unshaved armpits.

'Is that legal to film ladies' underarm hair?' Ruth asks de Kooning. He replies by gesturing a Roman shrug.

Now in the movie naked men in Asian masks are dancing inside a nightclub. A young and beautiful Italian man smokes. He has a most amazing pompadour that is not really a pompadour.

A woman hides a black eye beneath sunglasses at night. She drives the beautiful Italian man through Rome in a Cadillac convertible.

'Beautiful, isn't she?' a man says to de Kooning.

'The car or the woman?' de Kooning asks.

* * *

Ruth wanted to mingle. De Kooning walked down to the library's floor and wandered behind the two women with the sheet. The light of the movie bled through the sheet. De Kooning now watched the handsome Italian dancing cheek-to-cheek with a woman who could only be Nordic—

The woman is a blonde. The woman is wearing a black strapless dress. The blonde possesses the most amazing breasts of any living woman de Kooning has ever seen. The blonde possesses the cartoon breasts of de Kooning's *Woman* paintings.

Now a bearded satyr jumps into the nightclub. He is waving his arms up and down. The blonde and he bounce up and down together. She kicks her shoes off. She twirls.

Is this dancing?

In a long shot, de Kooning saw another woman, a lovely woman with dark hair who is so drunk she kneels on the dance floor. De Kooning reflected that he himself had been to more than a few Manhattan bacchanals but never an affair strewn with such *Satyricon* delight. Then de Kooning was sidetracked by a group of Americans complaining about Rome—

'The modern part of Rome is like San Diego without the ocean.'

'I was surprised at how dinky the Colosseum is.'

'It's certainly no Wrigley Field.'

'I want you to know that I am not an American artist,' de Kooning announced. He was not sure which bodies he was addressing. 'I am a New York artist. A painter from Manhattan. Sensible people throughout the world have all returned to the cities. I have more in common with Romans than I do with an American who grows corn in Idaho.'

'They grow potatoes in Idaho,' an American woman said.

De Kooning turned and watched the movie playing on the sheet.

—the woman with the amazing breasts is wading into Trevi Fountain. The handsome man follows.

Some Italian partygoers finally recognized de Kooning and surrounded him, wanting to hear gossip about the art world.

'All classic art is fear and trembling,' de Kooning proclaimed. 'Raphael is languid trembling. Cezanne wobbled more than he trembled . . . Great art makes me anxious. It is like when you are too nervous to even care whether the chair you are sitting on is comfortable or not.'

The movie was still going on. Or maybe it was a different movie? De Kooning saw a middle-aged man slumped at a table with a bullet hole in his temple. De Kooning watched for a while. More scenes inside nightclubs. More scenes inside convertibles driving down Roman streets at night.

At yet another party, the handsome man is riding a drunken woman as if she is a donkey. Another drunk woman is covered in feathers. A group of partygoers leave the party and walk on a beach toward the ocean. The sky is overcast. Maybe it is dawn? What is happening is that fishermen have dragged a vast aquatic body onto the beach.

Whatever the fishy thing is, it possesses a huge single eye that doesn't blink.

It is big like a whale. It is dead.

'This continent is dead,' de Kooning said. 'Europe is dead.'

Further down the beach—the handsome man with the pompadour that isn't a pompadour sees a young girl waving at him. There is an inlet of water separating them. She is trying to signal him. Is she a stranger? Her gestures appear incomprehensible to the man.

Is she a young woman or just a child? Whatever she is, there is something of a pure essence about her. The handsome Italian man walks away. *Why doesn't he just walk into the water like he did at Trevi Fountain?*

The sheet goes black. The film has finished.

'I need some air,' de Kooning announced.

De Kooning was stricken with claustrophobia. He entered other rooms full of people. None of these rooms had windows. Some fat Italian man asked de Kooning in broken English, 'You be drunk?' Before de Kooning can answer, the man said, 'I sure am!'

De Kooning found himself stumbling up a narrow stairway, a passageway like something found inside a boat. He passed a single porthole. The sun was up outside. Why didn't someone announce the New Year?

1960!

De Kooning opened the porthole. The air was refreshing and cold. He could just about fit his Dutch head out the opening. He saw nothing outside but the Roman dawn. He looked down and could only see the sloping walls of this building.

'Some say that the light of the atom bomb will change painting forever,' he yelled out the window. 'When we see that initial great flash, our eyes will melt out of our faces in ecstasy.'

De Kooning suddenly remembered when he first sailed to America as a stowaway aboard a steamer. He looked through a porthole smaller than this Roman window and saw a depressing flatland that resembled Holland without windmills. He had sailed into Newport News off the coast of Virginia.

The last masterpiece. De Kooning suddenly wondered when he had painted his last masterpiece. A few years ago? Ruth had walked into the studio and looked at it—it was a big painting—and she said, 'Zowie.'

De Kooning named it *Ruth's Zowie.*

Ruth's Zowie was about line. Lines. Boxes. Mailboxes. Billboards. Shapes on a map. A map of the United States. No. A map of New England. The big blue space Massachusetts. A yellow splotch for Rhode Island and a yellow gash for Connecticut. Above, the pink wilderness of Vermont and New Hampshire. A green border to keep them out. Who? The citizens of New Hampshire.

The critics who raved about *Ruth's Zowie* said *Ruth's Zowie* was an irresolvable dialectic. They said *Ruth's Zowie* was a perpetual dialectic of counter-energies and counter-brushstrokes.

Now here in Rome, in de Kooning's mind's eye *Ruth's Zowie* was timid. That blue Massachusetts shape should have been split. The right side made darker. Much darker. Almost pure black. The black of the sea below the plankton. The place where the whales sleep balanced upside down on their noses. It struck de Kooning that humans saw white as cold. Snow. Ice. Astronomers postulated that if you were to study the Earth from the moon, both poles would be white with ice.

Earth was green and blue and white.

Yet, the cold at the bottom of the sea was colder than white ice. There was a cold that was beyond mere freezing. It was the Black Cold. The Black Cold was too savage for the European mind. The Black Cold was an untamed wilderness.

When your lover saw the painting of the Black Cold, she did not yell 'Zowie.'

She felt an awe beyond language.

The Black Cold was a coldness and a blackness expressing the Indifference of God.

It was time. De Kooning saw this clearly. It was time for him and Ruth to go home. To return to the U.S.A. To Manhattan. De Kooning felt this in his Dutch bones. De Kooning would return to the land of Coca-Cola and paint another masterpiece.

* * *

Detroit U.S.A. When the economics of this year have been totaled in Detroit, the best-selling car will be Robert McNamara's Ford Falcon. As a final automotive note—Nikita Khrushchev escaped from his 1905 Waverley Coupe in Mr. Toad's Wild Ride at Disneyland because as he and Marilyn Monroe rode through hell the Russian saw a vision of Joseph Stalin in the fake flames.

* * *

New Year's Eve in Seattle. Young Buster Hendrix crossed the border of 1959 into 1960 still remaining in a virgin's condition, but now at least he has Betty Jean.

Finally, forget huge tail fins and elaborate grilles—America will end the decade with just the basics in their cars: a heater and a radio. As for the frenzy of the bed, it is wise to remember what a woman* told Leslie Fiedler while they were arguing about Marilyn Monroe's Reign of Eros in the 1950s:

> Monroe was unthreatening.
> Through her, America pretended to want sex,
> but America didn't really want it at all.

---

* Molly Haskell.

Book Two

1960–1963

Chapter 1

Reno, Nevada, 1960

In 1960, Manhattan copywriter Donald DeLillo is a young man of twenty-three. Donald DeLillo works at Ogilvy & Mather. Many of his older peers in the advertising milieu such as Lamb and Smith see their work as the equivalent of selling used cars—Lamb and Smith must con suckers into buying lemons.

DeLillo's trousers are cut from different cloth.

Each morning before DeLillo leaves for work, he peers into the bathroom mirror and says several times, 'I am an extremely handsome young man.'

He speaks that sentence every morning and he believes the sentence he speaks.

'I am an extremely handsome young man.'

When Don DeLillo arrives at work, he experiences his day as beautiful toiling. When he is handed a prototype of a shampoo, he pours the shampoo in his hands.

Is it beautiful?

Golden shampoos are.

Blue dandruff shampoos look medicinal like a laxative.

Both shampoos are worthy.

A beautiful-looking shampoo will in turn make your hair beautiful. Medicinal shampoo will make you beautiful by making your hair healthy.

'This shampoo will make me an extremely handsome young man.'

* * *

On January 4, the first Monday after the holiday, DeLillo hears that Albert Camus has died in a car crash. That French intellectual supreme was forty-six years old. Camus's *The Stranger* and *The Plague* were the first serious novels that DeLillo had read as a teenager when he worked a summer job parking cars at Coney Island. DeLillo had time on his hands. Listening to the radio slowed time down. Reading books was different. Reading made the time valuable. At night, DeLillo began dating girls, older girls who had read Camus too. Girls who had read Camus in English, but still called the books by their French titles, *L'Étranger* and *La Peste.*

At Ogilvy & Mather, only a handful of admen know who Camus was. At the very least, Lamb and Smith had read *The Rebel* because familiarity with French existentialism was a great ticket to convince a Vassar girl to take off her blouse. At lunch, Lamb tells DeLillo that Camus must have been driving a sports car like James Dean and Smith postulates that Camus was probably driving drunk like Jackson Pollock. DeLillo considers this. 'Hello, boys,' a woman's voice says. Everyone looks up. It's Phyllis Robinson—the chief copywriter at Doyle Dane Bernbach—and her signature cigarette holder. 'Hello, Mrs. Robinson,' everyone says. She smiles and says, 'I couldn't help overhearing you fellows chat. I want to tell you that I know someone who knows someone who knows someone who had actually driven Camus around the U.S.A. when he visited here after the war. Camus was always the passenger and Camus was always telling the driver to *Slow down. Slow down.*'

⋆ ⋆ ⋆

New Hampshire. The last time this state voted Democratic was back in World War II, so no matter who the 1960 Republican candidate was, he would win New Hampshire's four electoral college votes guaranteed. Who would be on the Republican ticket? President Eisenhower had contempt for Nixon. Eisenhower wanted his secretary of the Treasury to run instead, Robert Anderson (age fifty). He declined. Anderson would subsequently become a forgotten political crony performing backroom diplomatic missions for LBJ as well as lobbying for Sun Myung Moon before becoming an alcoholic swindler sentenced to prison for tax evasion, finally dying in 1989 of throat cancer.

⋆ ⋆ ⋆

Washington pulled Howard Hunt's leash. He was told that the CIA brass had decided to depose Fidel Castro with an army of Cuban refugees and

Hunt was picked to plan the invasion because of his smashing success in Guadalajara. Hunt's handlers sent him to Havana to scout things out. Hunt checked into the Hotel Vedado. It had unreliable air-conditioning and green lizards flicking along its walls. Loudspeakers outside on the street blared Castro propaganda all day. Hunt found the sidewalks filled with uniformed *barbudos* (bearded ones), Czech-made burp guns casually slung over their shoulders. They shuffled through the patios of all confiscated property, especially ex-syndicate funhouses. Hunt found that even Sloppy Joe's was empty and the bartenders sullen. He visited a sporting house above the Mercedes-Benz dealer. The rooms were crammed shoulder-to-shoulder with harlots. There was no money in Cuba. Everyone was either a harlot or a pimp. Yet, there were few customers. Hunt enjoyed a bevy of Cuban women simultaneously. Thereafter, he wondered if that had been what the French called an orgy. He then realized it couldn't be, as he was the only male participant.

Sometime before midnight, the loudspeakers would stop. They would start up again at seven a.m. Around eight, military jeeps rushed up to various buildings around his hotel, uniformed *barbudos* jumping out with machine guns poised. They'd run into the buildings and drag out men and women in handcuffs. Children would appear at the upper windows howling, 'Mama! Papa!'

Howard Hunt flew back to Tampa. Then he hopped a plane to the capital to speak to Eisenhower's people *mano a mano*. He told a room full of Eisenhower's State Department men in their gray flannel suits, 'This is how the island should be taken—first, assassinate Castro. Next, bomb the radio and television stations. The hope of a popular uprising in Cuba is a delusion. The people will only come around after the real revolutionaries have wiped out the Communists.'

The State Department dullards rejected Hunt's ideas although they would come up with nothing better. Hunt flew back down to Miami, where the Cuban exiles told him that all they wanted was money as they would overthrow Castro themselves. Hunt had to explain that Castro's Cuba was far better protected than Batista's had been. The United States could not even directly give money to the Cuban refugees because of something called the Neutrality Act.

Hunt moved into a safe house in Coral Gables. The CIA ordered

Hunt to secretly organize a paramilitary parachute battalion to drop into Cuba. He did. That is, he organized a jumpers training camp in Retalhuleu, Guatemala.

Mexico City was where Hunt decided to work out the logistics for the invasion. Hunt moved his wife and kids up from Uruguay to the neighborhood of Lomas de Chapultepec. Stella McGoey came along as well.

* * *

Soon, the whole Cuban invasion was falling apart before it could even begin. One important exile, Pedro Martínez Fraga, was unhappy with his low rank and declined to call a meeting with other exiles in Mexico. Another important exile, Ricardo Lorié, had a dedication to Batista as well as a dedication to alcohol. 'Nino' Díaz and José Ignacio Rasco were okay, but Sánchez Arango was a Marxist opportunist who misappropriated half a million dollars that the Castroniks had seized from the bank accounts of wealthy Batistaniks who had fled the country.

The Mexican contact Roberto Varona was a phony and a lowbrow with a terrible temper like Eisenhower.

Hunt found Colonel Martín Elena, the exiled 'head' of military affairs, a 'humorless martinet' who had no rapport with anyone, especially the paramilitarists.

Fraga distrusted Rasco who distrusted Varona and everyone distrusted Elena.

Next, Mexicans started following the Cubans. The safe house was compromised. Hunt wanted to shut down the Mexican operation and run things from Florida. Eisenhower finally heard about the operation directly and was enraged. The invasion of Cuba must appear to be completely a Cuban operation.

Hunt moved his family again up to Miami. Dot hated Miami. She took the kids farther north to Washington, D.C. Hunt conducted his paramilitary exercises without a wife. Thank God, he had a Cuban mistress. He also had a two-bedroom house on Poinciana Avenue in Coconut Grove.

Bernard Barker was assigned to be Hunt's Tonto. Barker was a Cuban-American pilot who'd been shot down over Germany. He survived Stalag Luft One. He returned to Cuba. The CIA convinced Barker to join the Havana police force as a mole. Yet, when Barker wanted to renew his American passport, the American consulate in Havana refused because Barker had joined a uniformed force of a foreign country (the Havana police force). The CIA failed to contact the consulate to clear things up. That now left Bernard in Cuban limbo without a passport to anywhere else.

It was Barker whom Hunt would spend the night with at the Watergate in 1972, both locked in a restaurant and hiding in a closet.

* * *

New York City. Phyllis Robinson sends DeLillo a copy of a month-old *Le Monde Diplomatique.* He pages through the yellowed French text reading of Camus's death. The man himself would have called his death '*une mort imbécile*.' Camus died in the passenger seat of a Facel Vega on a road named Nationale 5 in the countryside of Burgundy. No other *automobiliste* was involved besides the Facel Vega's driver, Michel Gallimard. Pedestrians who witnessed the crash attested that the Facel Vega suddenly zigzagged off the road and smashed into a single tree (like Jackson Pollock's car had done in Long Island), and then bounced against another tree.

Camus's neck snapped.

Camus died instantly like men on the gallows do if they are noosed up correctly. Michel Gallimard's wife and daughter had been in the back seat of the Facel Vega and fortune saw to it that this pair was not harmed. Michel Gallimard himself had used up his good fortune and took five days to die. A family dog had also been traveling in the Facel Vega. She ran from the wreckage into the forest and was never found. Before his death, Camus had been often quoted as saying, 'There is nothing more absurd than to die in a car accident.'

DeLillo spoke out loud, 'You were the world's second most famous existentialist, so you would know about that.'

Jean-Paul Sartre was still more famous than Camus in America. Sartre was still working on his screenplay for John Huston about Sigmund Freud discovering the Oedipus complex.

* * *

The Democratic National Convention was held in Los Angeles in mid-July. Kennedy won the nomination and as part of his political maneuvering, he publicly chose Lyndon Johnson of Texas to be his running mate.

Jack did not truly want Lyndon.

Jack and his advisers were dead sure that Lyndon would not accept.

Lyndon accepted the nomination nevertheless.

* * *

July 14 in Reno, Nevada.

The temperature is just 97 degrees. Dry heat.

A modest parade is rolling down Maple Street. None of us was there, but we can see the parade on newsreel footage. We'll see there are no tall buildings in Reno. The newsreel camera was perched maybe five or six stories high. Here comes a limousine convertible. Two in the front seat.

—A man drives as always.

—Can't tell who's sitting shotgun.

A man and a woman sit in the back, both dressed in white. The man wears horn-rims, the woman sporty sunglasses. The man's hairline is receding. The woman's blond hair is perfect.

This limousine convertible is eerie in its transhistorical familiarity—it reminds one of that limousine ride a week before Thanksgiving in Dallas, Texas, 1963. We're at the same elevated window as if we stood in the sixth-floor window of the Texas School Book Depository, the president's limousine cruising by below.

In Reno 1960, the back-seat couple wave to the thin crowd. The man in white is playwright Arthur Miller. The woman is white is his actress wife, Marilyn Monroe. Miller and Monroe are here to make a picture. *The Misfits.* Miller's screenplay. The making of *The Misfits* will become the prototype for every novel or film about a disastrous film shoot.

* * *

Arthur Miller's script has an art-house plot, which means it has no plot to speak of. It concerns the relationships between three modern Cowboys and a Woman. One of the modern Cowboys is a Pilot. Each of the four is an American Misfit.

They do not fit in. They do not seek status.

The Cowboys have not read *The Organization Man* and the Woman doesn't buy her beauty products from Avon Ladies.

Marilyn Monroe plays the Woman, divorcée Roslyn Taber. Her Cowboys are over-the-hill Gay Langland; a Mediterranean named Guido—he's the pilot; and a damaged rodeo rider, Perce Howland. The three male leads will be played, respectively, by Clark Gable (fifty-nine) and Eli Wallach (forty-four) and Montgomery Clift (thirty-nine). The climax of *The Misfits* occurs at the end of the movie when the three men make plans to rope some wild mustangs in a salt flat forty miles south of Reno. Guido will get into his airplane and terrify the horses from the air, while Langland and Howland lasso the fleeing mustangs. Roslyn tags along. She hasn't asked until then what the Cowboys are going to do with the horses they capture. Langland informs her that the mustangs will be sold to a dog-food company.

Yes. Dog food.

Miller's script is not about the Death of the Mythic American Cowboy. The Mythos of Cowboys is already dead before the story even begins.

The Misfits is the American Cowboy's Postmortem.

* * *

Director John Huston, foolhardy enough to have filmed *Moby Dick*, has agreed to helm *The Misfits.* He has a taste for the droll and unseemly. In the end, he will prove to be the ultimate Misfit of them all.

Marilyn Monroe had always thought of John Huston as a father figure. Marilyn trusted Huston. He directed the actress in her first dramatic role, *The Asphalt Jungle.* She was in the movie for all of five minutes lying on a couch. Last month, Huston phoned Monroe and told her he signed on to direct *The Misfits* 'because I am deeply concerned about the *bourgeoisization* of America.' He told her this over transatlantic phone cable calling from his castle in Ireland. 'America is going through a reactionary phase with no social consciousness, don't you think?'

'Yes!' Monroe shouted. 'America needs a Robespierre.' She added, 'I have just finished reading Thomas Paine's *Rights of Man.*'

'Hmmm,' Huston said. 'I recommend that you read Norman Mailer's *The Deer Park.*'

Long pause. 'No. No. No. I didn't like Norman Mailer's *Deer Park* at all,' Monroe said. 'He's too impressed by power, in my opinion.'

★ ★ ★

Arthur Miller originally wrote *The Misfits* as a Valentine for Monroe. At the beginning of the film, Roslyn Taber has come to Reno to finalize a divorce from her husband. Irony is a bugger. Since February, Monroe's marriage to Arthur Miller had been belly-up as a result of *Let's Make Love,* Monroe's last picture. *Let's Make Love* was what Monroe did with her co-star, the French actor born in Italy Yves Montand (thirty-eight), who was married to French actress Simone Signoret. It was almost beside the point that the script to *Let's Make Love* was a stinker. Yet, Monroe convinced her cuckolded husband to do rewrites even though a Hollywood writer's strike was going on. It was another open Hollywood secret that Arthur Miller was a scab.

The Millers agreed to be silent about their failed marriage to get funding for *The Misfits.*

★ ★ ★

Director John Huston arrived in Reno on July 17. Filming began the next day. Of course, school had been long out since June. A grade-school boy named Budworth Taylor hung around the set. Buddy for short. By the second day, Huston befriended the lad. By the fourth day of the shoot, Huston's Cadillac would glide by Buddy's house each morning and the chauffeur would give a short honk—

short like a short bird call.

The boy ran out and jumped in the back seat beside Huston.

'Where are we goin' today, Mr. Huston?'

The things Buddy saw and will see!

For example, Marilyn Monroe doing a dreamy dance and then wrapping her arms around a tree, moving her pelvis up and down.

Buddy had never seen a Marilyn Monroe movie. His parents forbade it.

Although the kid himself was too young to describe the Marilyn Monroe he witnessed in the flesh, Buddy was perched on the cusp of puberty and knew that Marilyn Monroe was more than *pretty.* After the boy grows up he will see the Monroe in his memory as writers had described and will describe her—

Marilyn was a waif figure of saucy pathos.

Marilyn was *la femme éternelle.*

Marilyn had fits of giggling like a geisha.

There was a miracle in her face.

Marilyn's face was like a curl of smoke.

There was a ghost sitting on her chest.

If Marilyn had to make a mistake, she wanted it to be a new one. Marilyn wanted to make new mistakes.

Marilyn walked like a rope unwinding.

Marilyn's poise had true innocence. Un-self-conscious spontaneity. Marilyn could only be understood from that point of divine beauty.

Marilyn had an untidy divinity like a banana split or a melting Mars bar.

* * *

The Republican National Convention was held in Chicago at the end of July. Richard Nixon won the nomination and chose fifty-eight-year-old Henry Cabot Lodge Jr. as his candidate for vice president. Lodge had been named after his grandfather, a rather intense warmongering Republican senator who served under the reigns of Teddy Roosevelt and Woodrow Wilson. The modern Henry Cabot Lodge Jr. had once been a Republican senator from Kennedy's home state of Massachusetts. In fact, eight years earlier in 1952, Lodge lost reelection to Kennedy in an upset. Why Nixon thought Lodge would beat fellow native son Kennedy in Massachusetts in 1960 is still a mystery.

* * *

Reno. From the first day of shooting, Marilyn Monroe was late getting to the set—a few hours late at first. Soon she missed whole stretches of the day. The sun might even be setting when she arrived.

Marilyn Monroe suffered from the terrors of insomnia, the terrors being more potent than the insomnia itself. She ingested barbiturates. They failed her. Maybe, just maybe, Marilyn Monroe could fall blessedly asleep by six a.m. Soon, Miller would find Marilyn lying naked in their sixth-floor suite in the Mapes Hotel, her butt up in bed, some scared quack trying to find a vein to inject yet another shot of Amytal.

★ ★ ★

Marilyn Monroe had begun to detest her husband's script and by extension her husband himself. 'Arturo could have written me anything and he comes up with this. If that's what Grumpo thinks of me, well I'm not for him and he's not for me. When I married that man, I fantasized that I could get away from Marilyn Monroe through him. Here I find myself back doing the same shtick. I can't stand it. I can't face doing another scene as *Marilyn Monroe.*' She said those words on the telephone to her drama coach Paula Strasberg. 'You have to come out here, Paula, and rescue me.'

★ ★ ★

Clark Gable showed up in Reno on August 12. He did not hate the script to *The Misfits.* He just did not get it. He was being paid seven hundred fifty thousand dollars to play that aging cowboy Gay Langland. Gable had only starred in five westerns in a career of sixty-nine movies—three of them filmed in the 1950s. Even so, Gable knew the genre upside down. It was in every American's blood.

Why wasn't *The Misfits* a shoot-'em-up?

Miller explained to Gable that *The Misfits* was an Eastern western. When Miller said that, he meant Eastern as a synonym for Asia. Zen cowboys. Gable thought Miller meant East Coast.

As a heterosexual love object, Clark Gable still had poise, yet he was unmistakably Old. This older man/younger woman arrangement has continued to be played out in movies for fifty years since *The Misfits* and will probably be played out for fifty years to come. Marilyn Monroe felt marvelous playing a love scene with Clark Gable. It was destiny. When

Marilyn was seven and Gable was thirty-two, the little girl kept a photo of this movie star in her bedroom.

* * *

One day the temperature in Reno was 100 degrees. The next day 105 degrees. Then 102 degrees. Dry heat. Dry heat. Dry heat. Then the temperature dipped to 95 degrees.

John Huston's fifty-fourth birthday occurred on August 5. John Huston was born in Missouri in a town named Nevada.

Nevada, Missouri.

Here in Reno, Nevada, the temperature on August 5 was 105 degrees. Dry heat. No one threw John a birthday party.

By August 5, Marilyn Monroe was raging, 'John Huston treats me like an idiot. This is just a movie about cowboys and horses. They don't need me at all. They want to put my name on the marquee so the movie will make money.'

John Huston knew that he treated Marilyn like an idiot. Huston was Old School. He hated it when a Method actor came up to ask, 'How should I play this scene? What is my motivation?'

John's usual answer was, 'Just do it, kid.'

* * *

Georgetown. Jacqueline Kennedy reminded her husband that it was imperative that he get the votes of America's substantial population of mothers and mothers-to-be. In 1960, more than 4,200,000 babies would be born, only down one hundred thousand from the Baby Banner Year of 1957. 'You have to get Dr. Spock to film a commercial for you, Jack.'

Kennedy's people contacted Dr. Spock. The Pediatrician Supreme was happy to help. He showed up at the Kennedys' Georgetown house. Dr. Spock was not comfortable reading a prepared speech, so he was filmed having coffee with Jacqueline and chatting.

'Just do it, kid.'

The line that was pulled from that conversation was Mrs. Kennedy saying, 'Dr. Spock is for my husband and I am for Dr. Spock,' in her soft voice with a slight lisp.

* * *

Marilyn Monroe's drama coach Paula Strasberg (fifty-one) finally showed up on the Reno set of *The Misfits* to rescue the actress. Ten years before in *All About Eve,* Monroe played a dumb blonde who was a graduate of the 'Copacabana* School of Dramatic Art.' In real life, Marilyn was a student of the Method, a school you never graduated from (much like Freudian analysis). Drama guru Lee Strasberg devised the Method. Lee was Paula's fifty-eight-year-old husband. The Method was his Silly Putty duplication of the theories of an old Russian, Konstantin Sergeievich Stanislavski, a cohort of Chekhov. Konstantin Sergeievich Stanislavski believed an actor should burrow himself into the psychological truth of a character. A primitive example: if an actress such as Marilyn Monroe was going to cry in a scene, she must summon up the essence of weeping. Strasberg made the technique personal—Marilyn should summon up the personal memory of a particular moment when she cried and use that memory to weep on cue.

* * *

Monty Clift's bed arrived at the Mapes Hotel before his actual body did. Like Marilyn, Clift was often afflicted by insomnia so he had his own bed shipped from Manhattan. In similar fashion several years from now, President Jack Kennedy will have his special orthopedic mattress shipped from Washington, D.C., to the Texas Hotel in Fort Worth, on the 21st of November 1963. The hotel will be instructed to remove only one mattress from the two-mattress bed and replace it with the presidential mattress. Instead, those Texas fools will deliberately remove both mattresses and just put the single orthopedic mattress in the middle of the double-mattress bed frame. Where is Jackie supposed to sleep? On their Final Night

---

* A Manhattan nightclub.

together as husband and wife, Jack and Jacqueline sleep in separate beds in separate hotel rooms.

* * *

How did Arthur Miller sleep? By August, he and Marilyn weren't even sleeping in the same room, let alone the same bed. Marilyn slept solo in their suite in the Mapes Hotel while Arthur bedded down in a mouse hole down the hall where he could rewrite the script, making Huston's daily changes.

At least, Miller could type in peace.

He also felt compelled to write to Saul Bellow to report from the stomping grounds where they had first met. Miller typed, 'These are the darkest days imaginable. Like a sap, I believed that I could win my wife's love back by writing her the first and greatest dramatic role for her, but—' Miller stopped typing and whipped the paper out of his Underwood and inserted a clean sheet to type again: 'Everyone is mesmerized by Marilyn's fabulous acting. She's never reached this level. Every time she plays Roslyn, everyone's heart breaks.'

* * *

John Huston's skull and his pillow were strangers at the Mapes Hotel as well, but not because of insomnia. Huston stayed up all night playing craps at the casino at the Mapes. John Huston loved the theater of rolling dice across a green felt craps table—the angular felt diamond texture on the inner wall of the tables. Huston loved craps's arcane and Byzantine rules.

Amateurs would stoop over a craps table and squint at each of the sections—how many chips are on Come, on Don't Pass Bar, on Pass Line, on Field. John Huston was like a great Russian chess player before a chessboard. The American would glance at the middle of a craps table—somewhere right of the word *Come*—and take in the whole pattern of chips/bets.

Why is it called craps?

The game's origins were in a medieval France dice game called *crapaud*—French for *toad*. Players would crouch on the floor like a toad and roll the dice. It has been suggested that because Joan of Arc thought her soldiers looked undignified squatting and hunched when they gambled she commanded that they stand upright like dignified men and roll their dice across a long ridged table.

Huston just called craps Playing Dice.

John Huston loved the one-handed rolling of the dice itself. Someone calculated a hot table had 102 rolls per hour. Huston loved the movements of the stickman, moving the dice with his delicate wood hoe so human touch would never jinx a shooter's dice. As written before, Huston could glance at a craps table in action and intuit all the possibilities, put even money on what players nicknamed Yo-leven, *yes;* even money On the Hop with a Hard Four, *no;* Hard Way with Centerfield Nine, *no.* Do a flat bet on Jimmy Hix, *possibly.*

John Huston played craps by the seat of his pants.

Huston would roll the dice all night in his Italian-made white safari suit, wearing a bow tie on his Chinese silk shirt. There was always cognac in Huston's cognac glass; a lit cigar always between his fingers or his teeth.

He survived the daylight hours by taking catnaps on the set.

Clark Gable was fifty-nine, and spied the fifty-four-year-old John Huston and his women at the craps table one night. Gable told the guests at his table, 'If Huston keeps that lifestyle up he'll be dead in a few years.'

In the end, John Huston will outlive Gable by twenty-seven years.

★ ★ ★

The King of Hollywood Damaged Goods, Montgomery Clift, showed up in Reno on August 12. Monty was coming from Hemingway's Idaho, where the actor had been studying for his part by riding with real cowboys at an actual rodeo. When Buddy and Mr. Huston arrived at the Reno set on Monday, Monty had a wide white bandage over his nose. In Idaho, he got his snout horned by a bull. 'Don't worry,' Mr. Huston said. 'We'll use it in the picture.'

Monty Clift's broken nose could have been a disaster in a different picture with a different director. Thankfully, a busted nose wasn't as severe an insult to Clift's face as four years ago when his features smashed through a car windshield while following Kevin McCarthy down that Hollywood hill in the dark—

Small world—Kevin McCarthy had already filmed his single scene for *The Misfits.* McCarthy played Raymond Taber, the husband Marilyn Monroe's Roslyn Taber was divorcing. Thank God Montgomery Clift had still been in Idaho, for Clift now hated his former friend. McCarthy was poison. Clift believed McCarthy had used Clift to get himself bigger parts.

As for the injury to Monty's nose—*The Misfits'* insurance company didn't want to insure this actor to begin with, as he reportedly remained an emotional mess taking Nembutal and Doriden and Luminal and Seconal, not to mention all that liquor. Yet Huston believed Monty was the only actor who could play the part. Huston threw his weight and forced the insurance company's hand. As if to thank Huston, Clift will stay clean and sober during the shoot, except for one night in September…

* * *

Paula Strasberg arrived in Reno.

Enter the *Spider.*

No matter what the temperature, Paula Strasberg strutted onto *The Misfits* set dressed completely in black. A black sack dress. A black caftan. A black palmetto fan.

The crew nicknamed her the Spider.

The woman had a chubby odd-shaped face. Buddy thought she would be perfect playing a witch on *The Twilight Zone.* Or a woman who ate children.

The Spider would huddle with Monroe in the star's trailer. Or else sit alone in the back of the Spider's air-conditioned limousine.

The Spider could have shared Marilyn's air-conditioned limousine, but the Spider demanded one of her own; she told Marilyn the budget of the movie shouldn't be her concern; Marilyn was being paid three hundred thousand dollars to do this picture while the Spider was being paid almost twice as much.

Outside, the August sun beat the top of the Spider's limousine with hammers of heat.

When Marilyn Monroe finally arrived on the set and the day's filming finally began, the Spider would crawl out of her limo and sit in an umbrella chair behind John Huston. Marilyn would only take acting directions from the Spider. The woman in black had created a notebook for Marilyn. In one scene, the Spider wrote this advice:

You are the limbs of a tree.

Perhaps this was the advice Marilyn used in a hump-the-tree free-form dance she did in front of an elm, a scene that would be extensively cut on a demand from the censors. Suffice it to say, John Huston never told Humphrey Bogart or Katharine Hepburn 'You are the limbs of a tree.'

Huston finally forbade Paula Strasberg to speak to Marilyn. 'It isn't as if Marilyn doesn't know how to speak plain English and needs an interpreter.' Then Huston added, 'While you're at it, don't speak to me either.'

* * *

Buddy had seen Montgomery Clift in a western once. Today in Reno, Clift is shooting his very first scene. His character, Perce Howland, is standing in a real phone booth in a real parking lot off North Virginia Street. The temperature is 104 degrees. A dry blaze. Perce Howland talks for more than ten minutes to his 'mother' on the phone and the camera never cuts. Some of his lines are, 'No, ma. I'm okay. My face isn't hurt. My face is fine... You would too recognize me.'

The other costar, Clark Gable, is watching the performance and says to John Huston, 'That fag is really good.'

Buddy knows what a fag is.

* * *

Monty fell off the Sober Pony only once in Reno. He got plastered at a lesbian bar near the Truckee River. The sun had been down for hours and it was still 100 degrees. The heat was muggy. Clift's keeper found him and lugged the drunken actor back to his room at the Mapes and tucked him in. Around five in the morning, Montgomery Clift was sleepwalking naked down the halls among the apparently nonplussed tourists.

On another bad night at the Mapes, Marilyn Monroe was so strung out on poison that she was riding up and down in the elevators completely naked.

Sleep elevating.

★ ★ ★

Dear Saul,

If this movie isn't a success, it will be the biggest flop in history.

★ ★ ★

That night in the casino, John Huston counted six women in green dresses at the craps table. Six did not come up at Pass or Don't Pass. Huston made a Come bet and lost. He saw a set of twins at the table.

Both women.

Both skinny in nearly identical green dresses. When the first twin was a shooter, Huston gambled she was a loser and put five hundred on Don't Pass. She rolled Little Joe from Kokomo (a four). Huston found himself the loser. When the second sister was the shooter, Huston gambled Pass. She crapped out. Huston, of course, lost again. Huston noted the best shooters were left-handed. Huston favored his right, but when he was the shooter he rolled southpaw and crapped out. If he tried to put a little English on his fist, the dice either flew off the table or did a pathetic Mellenberg Roll barely bouncing past the middle of the table.

Huston lost twenty thousand dollars that night.

Huston headed to his room and walked past a guy wearing a panama hat who was actually flipping a gold coin George Raft style in his right paw. The man raised his left paw and pointed at Huston and said, 'You're not leaving Reno until your tab is paid.'

★ ★ ★

On Friday, August 26, Marilyn Monroe overdosed on sleeping pills and was flown to Los Angeles. Arthur Miller sat beside her in the ambulance.

The driver had a tape recorder going. He was going to sell its contents to *Hollywood Confidential*.

'Don't shit me, Grumpo,' Marilyn howled. 'Everyone treats me like a joke including you, Grumpo. But I'm the joke that makes everybody money. I'm Miss None. I've always been Miss None. Miss None. That's what I register in hotels as because I can never remember my alias. Don't shit me. You know when I christened that submarine last year? The workers voted me their favorite actress and the admiral said that that made me a Communist. I feel sorry for the Creature from the Black Lagoon! You know, Arturo—Arturo, Arturo, Arturo—you thought I was beautiful and innocent, you were Abraham Lincoln. Then you saw I was beautiful, but a monster too, and you were a Nazi. Don't shit me. When was the last time you told someone a joke? Don't shit me. You have no sense of humor. When was the last time we screwed in the daylight? Don't shit me! I feel sorry for the Creature from the Black Lagoon!'

Marilyn Monroe was admitted to Los Angeles Westside Hospital where she was treated for barbiturate dependency. A Hollywood rumor then self-ignited that Marilyn was back in town for additional bedding with Yves Montand. Another rumor—Marilyn-in-the-hospital was just a cover for John Huston's desperate attempt to raise scratch to pay off his Reno craps table debts at the Mapes.

Chapter 2

Hilldale, Somewhere in the U.S.A., 1960

New York City. When Willem de Kooning heard gossip that Pablo Picasso liked sitting naked in his living room in the South of France watching French wrestling shows on French television, the Dutch-born American artist began watching *American* wrestling on his TV.

Ruth could not abide.

'Ruth, look at this guy, Bruno Bullwinkle.'

'I thought Bullwinkle was a moose.'

'Look at him. His gut. His jowls. He is a moose.'

'I mean a cartoon moose.'

'Bruno is like a cartoon. He's like a painting. He's *Woman 1* and *Woman 3* and *Woman 5*.'

'Honey. *Woman 1* and *Woman 3* and *Woman 5* were almost ten years ago.'

'Seven years ago.'

'Fine. I'm leaving you with your Bullwinkle and going down to the Cedar.'

* * *

In those days, eight out of ten Americans owned a television. Citizens everywhere in the U.S.A. could tell the difference between entertainment on television and televised Real Life such as *Candid Camera* or *Queen for a Day*. For *Election 1960,* Richard Nixon was scheduled to debate John F. Kennedy four times on television. Network TV. Not as entertainment, of course.

This was to be Real Life.

This first debate was to concern Domestic Affairs.

Foreign Affairs were Nixon's version of machismo. Nixon scorned Domestic Affairs. Just say the word: *Doe-mes-stick*. Women's work. The heart of the feminine. That was why Nixon couldn't wait for the last debate—Foreign Affairs.

Man's work.

The day of the first debate, September 26. Kennedy showed up at the Chicago studio with a healthy tan, wearing a great suit. Nixon had just been released from the hospital and was pale as a vampire. Nixon refused makeup. The debate was preempting the western *Cheyenne* and the Mark Twain-ish Mississippi riverboat drama *Riverboat.* It was also preempting *To Tell the Truth.*

Kennedy had the opening statement. 'We discuss tonight domestic issues, but I would not want that to be—any implication to be given that this does not involve directly our struggle with Mr. Khrushchev for survival.' Zingo! Kennedy proclaimed this debate was about Foreign Affairs from the jump. The debate now followed Kennedy's terms. Nixon ended up agreeing with everything Kennedy said.

Kennedy looked like a suave detective.

Nixon looked like a cheap grifter. A vampire grifter.

* * *

Caroline Kennedy was almost three years old. She was at Grandpa's house with her mother and her aunts and some other women. They were all in the kitchen. The TV was on. It was almost nine thirty. She never got to stay up this late. She knew that *Ben Casey* and Boris Karloff were on this late.

Her uncles and the other men were in the big room watching TV as well.

Caroline's father was in a place called Chicago. He was going to be on TV tonight. It had something to do with the 'lection.

He was going to fight someone called Mr. Nixon.

It was time for the program.

There was Daddy. He was sitting in a tiny desk.

Next to him was a man sitting at a big desk. Then another man in a tiny desk like her father.

The man in the big desk started talking.

Then her father started talking.

He was inside the TV. He was on the TV screen. She had never seen her father do such a thing before.

Then the man in the big desk made her father stand up and walk to a music stand.

Oh my. Daddy's going to start singing.

Then it was just her father's head on the TV. He kept talking. She followed his sentences but it was adult talk. She recognized the name *Mr. Khrushchev.* That was a bad man who looked like Fred Mertz on *I Love Lucy.* When would her father start singing? He said the word *freedom.* She recognized that word. It meant going to bed at any time you wanted, not when your parents told you to.

Then her father was still on the TV, but he was smaller. Caroline could see Daddy now from the pants up, standing at the music stand, but still not singing. Daddy was talking about farmers. Caroline knew what farmers were, of course. When would Daddy start singing? She loved it when he sang, 'Mares eat oats and does eat oats and little lambs eat ivy...' She noticed that both her daddy and Mr. Nixon had one eye that was lower than their other eye. 'A kid'll eat ivy too, wouldn't you?'

Now Mr. Nixon got up to the music stand. He also just talked without singing. He talked about schools and hospitals and highways and old people. Suddenly Caroline's daddy was on the screen. He was writing something at his little desk. Was he cheating? Now there were four or five men on the television.

Each was sitting facing away from the camera. One by one they swiveled in their chairs and said:

'I'm Sander Vanocur, NBC News.'

'I'm Charles Warren, Mutual News.'

'I'm Stuart Novins, CBS News.'

'Bob Fleming, ABC News.'

Caroline was suddenly chilled. This was like the picnic last summer when her cousin stole a piece of pie from the pie table. Her uncles and aunts stood in front of Caroline and all her cousins to question them to find out who took the pie.

A man was asking her father a question as Daddy stood at the music stand. She couldn't follow his answer except it concerned a party. A birthday party? Caroline's birthday was on November 27. She had memorized that. She didn't know exactly when November 27 was, but for as long as she could remember it had always occurred after Thanksgiving.

Mr. Nixon was now answering a question. He said that he was hungry—'after my trip abroad to Hungary I made some recommendations.' Her daddy then talked. He mentioned Africa. Caroline knew that was the place where Negroes were from. Then another man said something to her daddy and he talked about farmers. Then Mr. Nixon talked about farmers too.

Then another man sitting in the chair. The camera only showed the back of his head. His hair was very short as well. He asked Mr. Nixon a question. He mentioned President Eisenhower. That's all she understood.

What the man with the back of his head toward the camera actually said was: 'Now, Vice President Nixon, Republican campaign slogans—you'll see them on signs around the country as you did last week—say *It's experience that counts*—that appears over a picture of yourself. On August 24th, President Eisenhower was asked to give one example of a major idea of yours that he adopted. His reply was, and I'm quoting: *If you give me a week I might think of one. I don't remember.* I'm wondering, sir, if you can clarify which version is correct—the one on the billboards or the one put out by President Eisenhower?'

Caroline didn't understand Mr. Nixon's answer—he said something about furniture, about the *cabinet.* Next her daddy said something about Abraham Lincoln. Then one of the sitting men asked her father a question about 'a Bill.'

Who was Bill?

Her father talked about teachers. Mr. Nixon then talked about money. Two new sitting men appeared. She couldn't see one's face but for some reason from the back one guy reminded her of Perry Mason. Nixon talked. Another back of two men's heads. One was wearing glasses. Both men had longer hair than the first men. Their hair was black and it went below their ears on their neck.

Caroline was almost three years old and television was mysterious. Television was never boring. Caroline wondered why there hadn't been any commercials yet. Her daddy was talking about men named Bill and rules and 'the floor' of someplace.

Next thing she knew, everyone was done talking.

Caroline had not been listening to her mother and her aunts, but now she did. They all said the debate was a draw. They all said Nixon seemed awful good. Years from now Caroline would read descriptions of how bad Nixon looked physically that night. He was 'jowly.' He had a 'five o'clock shadow.' No one mentioned how both Nixon and her dad,

JFK, had the same slanting squint. At any rate, that was the reporting of eyewitnesses at the studio and the televisions in most households were not sophisticated enough to capture Nixon's five o'clock shadow, let alone any shadow on his soul.

⋆ ⋆ ⋆

The last shooting of scenes for *The Misfits* gets played out in between and during the Nixon-Kennedy debates. Everyone said Kennedy won the first one. Nixon the second. The third was a tie. One more to come. The fact was that unless Kennedy somehow screwed the pooch for the fourth debate, he would have won them all by showing that he had presidential stamina.

Miller would have vague kaleidoscope memories of the debates. Everyone in Reno drank whiskey and watched. (Everyone except Marilyn. She was up having quiet fits in her room.) Arthur Miller thought Nixon was wearing his brother's suit coat. Nixon was a 'foxy self-pitier.' Arthur Miller was for Kennedy because they had read some of the same books.

⋆ ⋆ ⋆

John Huston was shooting *The Misfits* in chronological order, an unusual technique. The movie was also being filmed in black-and-white. The latter did not seem wise vis-à-vis the box office. Who wants to go to an old-fashioned B&W movie when there is Technicolor and Trucolor and Polycolor all shot in Cinemascope? But Huston was working with United Artists, nicknamed the 'Greenwich Village of Hollywood.' They made 'arty' films. A B&W movie was a retro-modern artistic choice. Even Alfred Hitchcock's movie about (among other things) Janet Leigh taking a shower had been filmed in B&W.*

⋆ ⋆ ⋆

* Hitchcock's longtime editor George Tomasini was working on *The Misfits.*

The last big scene of *The Misfits* was the horse hunt, filmed in the salt flats near Dayton (forty miles south of Reno, a little east of Carson City). In this scene, Clark Gable intended to let himself be dragged by a horse.

It was autumn in Reno—windy and cold and dusty. Veterinarians stood beside Huston on the shoot. When one horse looked exhausted, the vets sent in a substitute. The first horse had a white spot on its black rump, so someone painted a white spot on the rump of the next black horse and the horse after that.

The scene was shot over and over. Buddy heard a woman suddenly howl at Mr. Huston. 'He's not young! He's not as well as you think!' Buddy thought she was talking about a horse, but she was Clark Gable's fifth wife and she was fearful about her husband's health.

Buddy saw that the hollering woman was pregnant.

After this scene was shot, location filming in Reno was finished. One of the nine photographers who were on the set took a farewell photograph of Monroe and Miller standing side by side in the doorway of their hotel. The couple who appear in the painting *American Gothic* look more cheerful. Like Ms. Gothic, Monroe is stage right, half her face leaning on the doorframe. Black dress. Blond hair. She is completely wrung out.

Miller stands stage left. He's half a head taller than his wife. He is wearing dark clothes. Pencils poke out of his pocket. Glare is smeared across his glasses so one can barely make out his eyes. His mouth has no expression. His hair is uncombed. A shadow hides his receding hairline. Miller's hands are hanging limply at his sides. Miller is a geek zombie. Miller is a dead man standing.

* * *

The night before, Huston threw a joint birthday party for Monty Clift and Arthur Miller at some roadside casino. Miller had turned forty-five. Monty was forty. Miller put his arm around Monty's shoulder and said, 'The day I turned forty my wife threw me out of the house for sleeping with Marilyn Monroe.'

'Do I want worse or better luck?' Monty asked.

Chapter 3

Watergate Towne, District of Columbia, 1960

The heart of Joseph Nye Welch, a man born in the nineteenth century, will pump for sixteen days short of seventy years before it stops its incessant beating on October 6, 1960. Joseph Nye Welch became a dead man in Hyannis, Massachusetts, inside a house that stood a mile from the Kennedy compound.

On that same day, October 6, Clark Gable sent a telegram to Huston saying he would come to the studio in Hollywood to shoot several necessary scenes, but would agree to no more changes to the script.

★ ★ ★

Washington, D.C. Back in February, the Italian company Società Generale Immobiliare had purchased ten acres on the old Chesapeake and Ohio Canal after ferreting out that the U.S. federal government planned to lay a major highway through the neighborhood known as Foggy Bottom. The land cost $10 million ($114 million in modern funds). When the highway plan went public that summer, it tripled the land's value. Now on October 21, Società Generale Immobiliare makes a public announcement of their intentions to build a city within a city in Foggy Bottom, a massive complex that will combine office and residential space with shopping and entertainment facilities. More important, the structure is to be designed curvilinearly, that is, with rounded corners.

Pause from the twenty-first century for a moment. Architectural computers are so advanced that an architect can crumple a piece of paper and create the blueprints for a one-hundred-story building built in that exact chaotic shape. In 1960, buildings with curved corners are as wild as architecture can get. Still, Società Generale Immobiliare fully intends to construct one of the foremost modern buildings of the twentieth century in stodgy Washington, D.C.

Much of the funding for the project comes from the Vatican. Privately, Pope John XXIII referred to the project as Vatican West.

The Roman architect is fifty-three-year-old Luigi Moretti.

Società Generale Immobiliare is selling Moretti to the Americans as the 'Frank Lloyd Wright of Italy.' A more accurate description would be that Luigi Moretti was a cheap Italian knockoff of Albert Speer.*

Moretti was never Mussolini's favorite architect, but Moretti had been declared the Fascist era's most *Roman* architect. Moretti would brag, 'I'm obstinately Roman, well beyond that of the registry office.'

So was Mussolini, aka Il Duce.

Around the cusp of 1940, Moretti designed Fascist government buildings as well as gymnasiums for Fascists in the City of Muscle (as Rome was called). Following the complete liberation of Italy in April '45, Moretti was arrested by the Americans and charged with 'trying to found a new fascist political party.' Yet, Italian Fascist blood was thicker than olive oil. After the war, Moretti's associates saw to it that he was freed.

Now steer back to Rome, 1959. See Willem de Kooning wearing what he believed to be a Leaning Tower of Pisa costume made of lightweight papier-mâché. The drunken Italian couple had insisted that de Kooning and Ruth take the 'tower' and attend an architectural costume party at the Casanova. When the American couple reached the party, they saw dozens wearing costumes of sleek-looking piazzas and towers. The pair of Americans also saw the partygoers in their costumes raise their right arms out of the armholes of their buildings to give and return the Roman Fascist salute. It turned out this was a party celebrating long-dead Mussolini and his still-living favorite architects. De Kooning was not wearing the Leaning Tower of Pisa, but rather the Cella (Chapel) Foro Mussolini. Luigi Moretti was also in attendance, wearing a scaled-down replica of a twirling staircase around the perimeter of his body, representing the *scalinata* that Moretti had designed for Mussolini to use to reach his private theater box at the Casa del Balilla. Somehow, it seems fitting that Moretti has designed an American project that after it is constructed will be given the simple name of:

Watergate.

---

* Hitler's architect, convicted during the 1946 Nuremberg trials to confinement in Spandau Prison in Berlin, where Speer still lingers in 1960.

★ ★ ★

Reno, Nevada. John Huston's last trip to the casino. The gangster in the hat followed Huston's every move. Huston himself was deep in thought considering the Gambler's Fallacy—that one's first roll of the dice can somehow influence the second roll of the dice. And so on.

In mathematics, there is no such thing as luck.

Huston would not partake of the Gambler's Fallacy tonight. Huston would not look for signs. He would look for what we moderns would call *anti-signs.* Huston surveyed the players at the table. He saw three women with the same number of large baubles on their necklaces, five. Huston saw three separate men each wearing horn-rims. He saw a man with an eye patch smoking two cigarettes at once. Huston calculated the different numbers between 1 and 12 one could come up with by attaching a mystical value to baubles or eye patches.

There was a single figure that had nothing going for it: 5. Huston bet that numeral on the Hop.* He won. He doubled his Hop. He knew what he was doing. He was not following a pattern. He had just put the Gambler's Fallacy on its head.

We have all heard time and time again that a gambler has an equal chance of rolling seven sixes as of rolling six sixes and one five. Thus if it doesn't matter what number one bets, why not bet the same number over and over? According to the mathematics of logic, if a pattern appears it is not actually a pattern.

It is not luck, as luck does not exist.

Huston gambled like a statistician. The moment he felt superstitious, he stepped away from the craps table for a few minutes. Then he went to the table and bet on 5 again. He played this way all night. He finished at six a.m. John Huston had made his money back, plus nearly a thousand in pocket cash. Before he left the Mapes, Huston walked up to the gangster in the hat and slipped a ten-dollar tip in the man's pocket.

★ ★ ★

---

* A single roll bet on any combination of the two dice.

Montana. Leslie Fiedler and a buddy decided to drive to Ketchum, Idaho, to meet Ernest Hemingway. Fiedler knew Hemingway's hunting partner Dr. Saviers. Fiedler figured that would be enough of an introduction. The two Montanans drove all night and reached Ketchum before nine o'clock in the morning. It was a small town surrounded by mountains. They drove out to Hemingway's cabin and parked. They knocked on a door at the back porch. A voice called out, 'Come on in.' They walked into a kitchen. The first thing Fiedler saw was bags of leftover Halloween candy. The *TV Guide* was open on the kitchen table. And there was the old man, Hemingway. He was sixty-one. Back in 1960, you were old if you were sixty-one. It was like being seventy-five today. Fiedler prepared for a bone-crunching handshake with Papa, but the man's grip was timid. He found Hemingway in shaky shape, but at one point Hemingway managed to smile at Fiedler, who would one day write: '[I saw] suddenly, beautifully, [Hemingway was] twelve years old. A tough, cocky, gentle boy still...'

* * *

The Misfits still did not have an ending. A month ago, Marilyn had told her husband, 'Ros and Gay should just break up.' Then Marilyn poked her husband in the chest and said, 'When the Chinese commit suicide, they always hang themselves in the doorway of their offenders.'

The night she told her husband that, Arthur Miller hunched in his dingy little room in the Mapes Hotel and typed this letter to Saul Bellow:

> The trope of the script is that Roslyn is such a life force that she can't bear to see anything killed, not even a rabbit eating from Gay's garden, a garden she civilized him into growing and nurturing. She loses it when she discovers the mustangs will be killed for dog food.
>
> With sudden despair, I realize this trope doesn't hold water.
>
> Roslyn is no vegetarian. Where does Roslyn think meat comes from? She adores Gay's dog [Peaches]. She never connects [Peaches] to horsemeat dog food.
>
> The better masculine attribute expressing my theme would be a plot concerning Roslyn's association with aristocratic Hemingway big game hunter types—pseudo he-men who fly to Africa to shoot

beautiful elephants and tigers. These men kill not for financial need or some gourmet greed. They kill merely for the sport of the bloodshed.

Miller heard an abrupt thump at his door and jumped up. He opened it a crack and peeked out.

Marilyn was not hanging there Chinese style.

Miller had been told that the tongues of suicides turn bright blue. He had also been told that in Africa there was a poisonous snake whose inner mouth was colored bright blue. Miller's typewriter was blue. Miller shut the door. He walked to his typewriter and whipped out the letter to Bellow and crumpled it up. Then he sat down and typed the new end to *The Misfits.*

★ ★ ★

Idaho.

'Fiedler?' Hemingway said, repeating Leslie Fiedler's name. 'Do you believe that sh-sh-sh-shit you wrote about Huck Finn?'

'Yes.'

He glanced around the room. 'I don't believe what you say but I will defen-dish…'

He could not complete the sentence—*but I will defend your right to say it.*

Fiedler was grateful that Hemingway knew something of his work. To Fiedler, Hemingway seemed like a fictional character. It was as if Fiedler's book of literary criticism, *Love and Death in the American Novel,* had been a novel itself.

He and Hemingway sat for long periods in silence. The conversation took place in dribs and drabs. 'Tell Norman Mailer I never got his book,' Hemingway said. 'He complained about that in *Advertisements for Myself.* He's like one of those students who telephone me in the middle of the night to get something they can hang me with and get their precious PhDs.'

Fiedler was uncomfortable. He was too proud to see Hemingway as the last living greatest writer of the twentieth century. He was too petty in an American highbrow way to forgive Hemingway for his crummy books while exalting him for *The Sun Also Rises.*

A Frenchman could do this.

And we all, even you who are female, must acknowledge Hemingway's mastery of the clipped sentence. As mentioned previously, Joan Didion learned how to write by retyping *The Sun Also Rises.* And of course, Hemingway's use of repetition and compression was what he sucked from Gertrude Stein after she befriended him in Paris. As for Hemingway's macho posturing—the hunting and shooting of magnificent mammals—Fidel Castro could forgive him that. 'It is true that Hemingway liked big game hunting,' Castro would say in a speech. 'His grandson presented me with a book about his grandfather and big game hunting in Africa. I asked him, *How do the environmentalists feel about this?* His grandson said to me, *Well, these are new times, we cannot redesign Hemingway to fit into these times because in his day he criticized the hunting of men in the massacres of war.* At that time there was no awareness about the need to protect nature, so many men were killing animals; there were no environmentalists.'

★ ★ ★

Idaho. It was nine thirty in the morning in Idaho when Hemingway broke out a bottle of wine imported from the Pyrenees. Hemingway said that he did not want to talk about literature or politics, but that was all he ended up talking about. 'Norman Mailer is so articulate,' Hemingway said. Hemingway also mentioned Vance Bourjaily, a writer like a young colt or a young middleweight whom everyone was talking about in 1960. Yet, by next year, there would be nothing more said about the man.

Then Fiedler squinted at the open *TV Guide.* It was turned to Saturday Night Fights. They talked boxing. Fiedler noted Hemingway's teeth—yellow. Widely spaced. He smiled like a little boy. That was when Fiedler had his vision of Ernest Hemingway as a beautiful twelve-year-old boy. Fiedler had heard Gertrude Stein on the radio telling that when Hemingway was twenty-three he cried out, 'I'm too young to be a father!' Fiedler heard Hemingway now mentally crying out, 'I'm too young to be an Old Man!'

★ ★ ★

John Huston sent Clark Gable the new end to the script. Gable changed his mind about acting in another change to the script. This end, this last scene of the movie, was number 269, and it was filmed inside a Hollywood studio.

★ ★ ★

Miller knew that he could not renounce the script of *The Misfits.*

The movie will end with Ros and Gay driving away from Reno.

Ros and Gay will not drive into any sunset. That would be corny. They drive off into the black desert night. The last lines in *The Misfits* are spoken by Gay:

> How do you find your way back in the dark?
>
> Just head for that big star straight on. The highway is under it. It will take us back home.

★ ★ ★

That scene was a wrap.

The Misfits was forty days over schedule, and cost $4 million, half a million over budget. *The Misfits* was the most expensive black-and-white picture ever made between *The Great Train Robbery* in 1903 and 1960.

★ ★ ★

Los Angeles. Clark saw a rough cut of *The Misfits* and thought it was the best work he had done in his life. The next day, Clark Gable was stricken by a heart attack. It did not immediately kill him like the heart attack that got Joseph Nye Welch. Gable did end up in critical condition, but he was awake. President Eisenhower even phoned the actor in the hospital to tell him, 'Listen, I just had one. You'll get through it. Just have a positive attitude.'

★ ★ ★

Election Day—November 8, 1960.

After Richard Nixon and Pat voted, Pat took the girls to Beverly Hills to have their hair done. A separate car—a black Cadillac—sped Nixon and his military attaché Major Don Hughes and his Secret Service agent back toward the Ambassador Hotel. Abruptly Nixon commanded, 'Pull over.' The driver was confused. 'Pull over. Pull over.' The driver pulled to the curb. A horn honked two cars up. A guy in an idling white convertible (the top down) had his arm raised. 'Come on, boys,' Nixon reportedly said, or something similar in faux masculine fashion, and the three men scrambled out, leaving their driver behind, the two men following Nixon to the convertible with the engine running. Nixon directed Hughes and the Secret Service agent into the back seat. He walked to the driver's door. 'Scoot over, John,' Nixon said.

The Vice President of the United States of America got behind the wheel. The rest of the vice president's motorcade entourage now sped down the street. Nixon whipped a U-turn with savoir faire and headed back the way they had come. The passengers asked where they were going. Nixon laughed and said, 'For a drive.'

Nixon gripped the wheel with both hands at ten-past-ten position (or ten-to-two as a Communist would see it). His right fist was much larger than his left as he had slugged someone the day before. Nixon had a temper. Word was he beat Pat. Yet, he had not hit her the day before. Instead, Nixon had slugged a campaign worker. A man.

Nixon stopped the car in La Habra, at a little white house with an orange grove as its front yard. It was Nixon's mother's house. Hannah Nixon. 'Just a minute, boys,' Nixon said and jumped out of the car. The boys waited.

Ten minutes later, Nixon came back smiling at the remains of a joke. Don and the Secret Service agent assumed Nixon would now drive them back to the Ambassador. Instead, Nixon continued south. He introduced them to the fourth passenger. He was a Los Angeles cop named DiBetta. He worked the bunco squad. The two passengers in the back seat discussed the origin of bunco, which is a fake card game. 'It's probably a derivative of *banca,* the Tijuana term for three-card monte.'

'I've never been to Tijuana,' Hughes remarked.

'That's it, boys,' Nixon declared. 'We're driving to Tee-wana.'

'What?'

'Boss, you serious?'

'Tee-wana, Tee-wana, Tee-wana. Hey senior, you wanna buy my seester?'

It's hard for us moderns to see Richard Nixon as anything other than a cartoon face. However, he looked handsome with intensity at eight thirty in the morning on November 8, 1960, after he made the decision to drive 141 miles south to the Mexican border town of Tijuana. Among the other passengers, Donald Hughes looked like an extra in a movie set in Washington, D.C. The Secret Service agent had a hatchet face. His name was Sherwood.

It was a long, often desolate, roll south.

In Raymond Chandler's *The Long Goodbye,* Philip Marlowe's drinking buddy Terry Lennox shows up at Marlowe's pad in Los Angeles and asks the 'shamus' to drive him down to Tijuana where he can catch a plane. Marlowe says, 'Sure.' He also says that he cannot be privy to any information that Lennox has committed a crime or has 'essential knowledge that such a crime has been committed.'

Marlowe drives Lennox down to Tijuana in five sentences.

> I drove fast but not fast enough to get ragged. We hardly spoke on the way down. We didn't stop to eat either. There wasn't that much time.
>
> The border people had nothing to say to us.

Nixon's drive is just killing time, not melodrama. As in *The Long Goodbye,* there is nothing to describe about the drive from Los Angeles to Tijuana. The closer to the border one got, the more the landscape became nothing but Paleozoic boredom and arid nothingness.

'How do you think we'll do, Don?' Nixon asked, the wind in the convertible blowing his hair like a movie star.

'The Anderson story hurt,' Don said—a reference to columnist Jack Anderson breaking a story about Howard Hughes's loan to Donald Nixon.

'I'd like to cut out Anderson's heart and take a hammer and beat it into mush,' Nixon said, yelling to be heard. 'At least I didn't make the campaign a battle against Catholics.' He said that and bit his lip. 'Being a Quaker,' Nixon said, 'I understand belonging to a minority religion.'

'Are Quakers Protestants, Mr. Vice President?' Sherwood hollered.

'No, they're Jews,' Hughes yelled even louder.

Nixon whipped his head around and Hughes burst out laughing. Then Jack Sherwood started laughing. Sherwood identified himself as a papist. Hughes was Catholic too. Nixon yelled a monologue about how a priest had first alerted him to Alger Hiss. 'His name was Father John Cronin. He did work with the unions, which were all run by Communists in the forties.'

'So what faith do you follow, DiBetta?' Nixon asked.

DiBetta identified himself as a Scientologist.

'What's that?'

DiBetta tried to explain. No one understood.

'Give us an example of this El Ron Hubbard's philosophy,' Nixon commanded.

'Well, okay. He has this to say about failure. He uses the example of driving an Edsel into a wall. He says, *One does not intend to run his Edsel into the wall and yet runs it into the wall. That is a failure.* Then he says, *One intends to run his Edsel into the wall and does run the Edsel into the wall. That was a win. Then one intends not to run his Edsel into the wall and does not run it into the wall.*'

'That is a win,' Nixon shouted.

DiBetta seemed very happy. 'Yeah, yeah, right, Mr. Vice President. I mean, Mr. President.'

'So what happens if you intend to run the Edsel into the wall but do not run your Edsel into the wall?' Nixon asked.

'Well, that is a failure.'

'If it's an Edsel, it certainly is.' Nixon laughed.

Nixon stopped for gas in Oceanside. Hughes took this moment to walk beside Nixon as he headed toward the restroom. Hughes said, 'We have to at least tell Cabot Lodge where we are.'

Nixon said, 'Just a minute.' He went into the one-room can and shut the door. It is very likely that he locked the door. He stayed in a while. The faucet was running. Nixon came out of the bathroom gingerly wiping his right hand with a towel. 'It still hurts like the dickens,' Nixon said.

'I tell you we should have someone take a look at it.'

Nixon said no. 'Then news vultures will find out that I slugged a cripple.'

Nixon put on a smile and asked his entourage if anyone wanted a Coca-Cola. Sherwood said, 'No thank you, Mr. Vice President.'

Nixon then asked everyone to call him 'Mr. President.' He wanted to get familiar with the sound of it. Sherwood will remember that Nixon asked them, 'Calling me Mr. President won't give me bad luck?' Hughes will remember Nixon saying the same thing, but as a statement, not a question. DiBetta then started a conversation about the Catholicism of Joe McCarthy and Joe Kennedy. Nixon confirmed that McCarthy got wheelbarrows full of support from JFK's father. 'McCarthy even dated two of Kennedy's sisters.'

Everyone got into the convertible—Nixon behind the wheel—and continued south. The weather was fine. Hughes subsequently said that at that moment he understood Nixon's motive for this drive. The campaign was finally over. He needed to clear his head to be ready to accept the result of the election.

This man could be the next president of the United States.

Hughes could not tell whether Nixon wanted to embrace the thrill of that as a possibility or just forget about the government of the United States of America for a while.

They yelled at each other about what they wanted to do down in Tijuana. A bullfight was on the agenda. DiBetta joked about girls. He knew a place where a girl picked up the spare change thrown to the stage with the lips of her vagina. Nixon did not believe that was anatomically possible. DiBetta turned and squinted at the two passengers in the back seat. Their eyes told him to let it go.

He turned. He saw the highway sign for La Jolla.

* * *

Dr. Seuss lived in La Jolla.

The writer Raymond Chandler had lived in La Jolla and had died the year before in 1959. Chandler's first six Philip Marlowe novels were all set in Los Angeles. His last Philip Marlowe novel, *Playback* (1958), took place in a city a short drive north of San Diego named Esmeralda—La Jolla fictionalized. Howard Hunt had once sent Raymond Chandler a snide letter complaining that the writer had 'cannibalized' his Philip Marlowe short stories to write his Philip Marlowe novels. Chandler wrote Hunt back:

> Dear Mr. Hunt... I am the copyright owner of my short stories and I can use my material in any way I see fit... There is no moral

or ethical issue involved... You must pardon me if I find it a little ludicrous that you should object.

★ ★ ★

Inside Richard Nixon's convertible heading for Mexico. Nixon raised his head at the highway signs and sang out, 'Sandy egg oh!'

Nixon told his companions that at the border they would have to stop to get car insurance for Mexico, a scam against gringos that had been going on since the days of Pancho Villa. 'Let me take care of it,' DiBetta said. He walked to a guard booth. DiBetta was thirty-four years old. On the short side. But barrel-chested. He was Leslie Fiedler without Fiedler's biblical whiskers. The Mexican knew DiBetta. The two talked. Then DiBetta walked back to the convertible. 'Let's go.' Nixon drove them across the border, passing under a sign that said, TIJUANA—THE MOST VISITED CITY IN THE WORLD. They drove for about fifteen seconds and DiBetta said, 'Stop for this man, Mr. President.'

A Mexican policeman was waving his arms. The car stopped and he climbed into the back seat.

'This is Lieutenant Clamesto,' DiBetta said. 'He's all the insurance we need.'

Clamesto was wearing a fat .45-caliber automatic pistol. He told them there were no bullfights today. He asked them if they wanted to meet the greatest bullfighter in Tijuana. The gringoniks said 'Sure!' with enthusiasm. They drove down the main street of Tijuana.

Tijuana was as far from the original Aztec gods Huitzilopochtli and Quetzalcoatl as it was from Minnesota or Sheboygan. It had the ambience of a small town. The architecture was more Grand Rapids than red tiles à la *Under the Volcano.* A writer would say, 'The streets were filled with black blooded volcanic uncertain people.' The streets were also filled with taxicabs. A sweet acrid dust layered everything. In the center of Tijuana was a Woolworth's. Nixon was instructed to double-park in front of the Woolworth's. In the crowd was another cop. He was not wearing a holster, but he gripped a long billy club ringed with the bent tops of carpenter's nails.

'I will watch your car,' he said.

The four gringoniks followed Clamesto down a snaking alley. They came to a stucco wall with an iron door. Clamesto banged on it. Nothing happened. Then the door rattled and squeaked open. A woman with a scarf over her head like a gypsy stuck her head out. Clamesto spoke to her. They walked in.

They were inside a patio where every surface was piled with bougainvilleas. Bumblebees the size of gumballs buzzed everywhere. The woman led the men to a small man who sat in a wheelchair. Clamesto talked to him in Spanish. The crippled man listened and then wheeled himself into an archway of his hacienda. The gringos followed and saw a magnificent stucco room the size of a ballroom. The light was dim, but not too dim to eclipse the dozens of bullfight posters on the walls. The man in the wheelchair was Silverio Eloy Zotlouco, aka Amillita Soldado, the best bullfighter in Mexico thirty years ago. On the wall was a particular photograph of Silverio Eloy Zotlouco with Ernest Hemingway. The old bullfighter told the gringos in Spanish that Hemingway came all the way from Cuba to Tijuana to see him. Hemingway had proclaimed Silverio Eloy Zotlouco the only bullfighter of consequence outside of Spain. Silverio Eloy Zotlouco's quaint stature had added to his appeal—that such a small man could master a bull!

Hughes excused himself and asked if there was a phone he could use. Hughes then told Nixon that he was going to call the FBI and tell them where they were.

'Do you have to?' Nixon asked.

'For the good of the country—yes.'

Hughes was gone for ten minutes. When he returned, Silverio Eloy Zotlouco was still telling stories. After fifteen minutes more of this, the only one who wasn't overcome by sleepy boredom was Nixon himself. The vice president patiently examined the dried ears of bulls Silverio Eloy Zotlouco had been given after each fight. Although thirty years had passed, Silverio Eloy Zotlouco remembered each bull he danced with. The sound of its snorting. How it smelled.

A woman came out with mescal and shot glasses. Hughes said, 'Now boys. Let's not get too carried away. Just a little medicine and we'll be traveling.'

The gringos walked back to Main Street. Suddenly it seemed as if there were dozens of kids and adults trying to sell them things. Gum. Trinkets.

Sherwood bought a small Tijuana Bible as a souvenir. They passed by the Woolworth's. The windows were exactly like all the Woolworth's with the exception of the torso mannequins, which were dressed in Spanish-cut blouses. The white convertible was still present. The cop with the billy club leaned against the passenger side. At that moment, there was confusion at the Tijuana Woolworth's, a commotion. Police cars squealed up. The gringos were all confused.

A Mexican in a suit runs up to Nixon and begins jabbering in Spanish. This is Tijuana's mayor, Xicoténcatl Leyva Alemán. It seems that J. Edgar Hoover called Tijuana and it is Mayor Xicoténcatl's intention to take Nixon out to lunch. Then the cops all talk together. Nixon and the other gringos except Hughes are shooed into Nixon's white convertible. Nixon wants to drive, but a Mexican cop already sits behind the wheel. He zips the car away. No one knows what is going on.

The Mexican drives them to a restaurant called Old Heidelberg. None of the gringos notices the incredulousness of supping in a German restaurant in Tijuana instead of a Mexican restaurant.

Everyone walks into Old Heidelberg and is seated at an elaborate table. The place is very fancy in a Germanic style, yet it is empty save for a few European-looking barflies. The gringos sit at the table for fifteen minutes. Then a Mexican in a suit runs in and ushers everyone up. Nixon's crew all follows the Mexican to their convertible outside. Hughes tells DiBetta to drive. They have a police escort. Nixon asks Mayor Xicoténcatl, 'What's going on, senior?' The mayor tells Nixon that his police have just stopped a *del lejano oriente* (an 'Oriental') with a gun. But it was all a big mistake. 'He was waiting in an alley to shoot you because he thought you were someone else.'

'Who else could I possibly be other than the vice president of the United States?'

'The gunman is Cuban-Chinese,' DiBetta says as if that answers everything. DiBetta must now talk with Nixon for fifteen goddamn minutes assuring him that there is no Cold War intrigue among Tijuana's Cuban-Chinese. Finally Nixon gives up. 'Let me tell a joke,' Nixon says and then asks, 'What's the word for *Chinese food* in China?'

No one knows.

Nixon gives the answer, 'Food.'

* * *

The American border guard was surprised to see Richard Nixon on the Tijuana side of the border, but he still Acted by the Book.

'Are you all citizens of the United States?'

'I am,' Nixon said, 'but I don't know about the other sons-of-a-bitches.'

Hughes said, 'We're all Americans here.'

They headed north up the Pacific Coast Highway.

In *The Long Goodbye,* Chandler described Marlowe's drive north out of Tijuana on the Pacific Coast Highway in greater detail than the gumshoe's drive south. 'It's one of the dullest drives in [California]. . . . The road north is as monotonous as a sailor's chantey. You go through a town, down a hill, along a stretch of beach, through a town, down a hill, along a stretch of beach.'

For Nixon and the boys it was already three o'clock when they left Tijuana. When they reached the El Toro Marine Corps Air Station, they stopped. Hughes rushed Nixon out of the car. A bunch of Marines who had been waiting were ushered over to pose with the possible next president. Nixon was handed a football to hold. Nixon expressed confusion.

'We stopped to play touch football,' Hughes said.

'But we didn't stop to play touch football,' Nixon said.

'We stopped to play touch football,' Hughes repeated.

Nixon and his crew returned to the Pacific Coast Highway. Twenty minutes later, Nixon made the driver stop at the mission in San Juan Capistrano. Nixon told everyone to wait in the car a minute. No one waited. They all followed Nixon, keeping a discreet distance. They saw Nixon walk to the front of the church and suddenly disappear in front of the first pew. Everyone ran to the spot. They found Nixon on his knees praying. Everyone quickly hurried away. Nixon got up. They returned to the car. Before they entered the highway, Nixon commanded the car to stop. 'Soon I'll be the president of the United States.' He left the car and walked to a roadside stand and bought a pineapple milk shake.

They drove all the way back to Los Angeles in silence. Nixon paged through the Tijuana Bible that Sherwood had bought. It was a pornographic comic book. There were pretty good drawings of Blondie and

Dagwood. That is, drawings of Blondie and Dagwood humping like barnyard animals. There was something so sexy about Blondie that peering at her tits and bush was almost as exciting as seeing Ava Gardner's tits and bush in a stag photograph.

As for Dagwood, think submarine sandwich.

The car reached the Ambassador Hotel at six o'clock. It was already nine o'clock on the East Coast. The polls were closed. There was a mob of reporters outside the Ambassador. They wanted to know where Nixon had been. *Nixon has some 'splaining to do.* Nixon told the party that the trip to Mexico was spontaneous. 'We just started driving and Tijuana is where we wound up.'

* * *

After Clark Gable's heart attack, the actor held on for ten more days. On Wednesday, November 16, the actor died.

> How do you find your way back in the dark? Just head for that big star straight on. The highway is under it. It will take us back home.

* * *

Richard Pavlick was now seventy-three years old. Richard Pavlick was as enraged at American politics as a man can be. The election! Kennedy won!

Joe Kennedy, now seventy-two, bought the election for his son-of-a-bitch son Jack.

That is what Pavlick believed and history confirms Pavlick's take. Jack would be reported bragging to Ben Bradlee that the election cost his father $13 million. In modern terms that means that the presidency can be bought for $500 million—small change in our modern billionaire's world.

Pavlick began giving all his possessions away. He owned only crap utensils, threadbare linen, stuff that not even Goodwill would want, but the citizens of New Hampshire were like hillbillies and the townsfolk picked Pavlick's shack clean.

'Go on, Frankie Lee,' Pavlick said. 'Take that candelabra.'

'What about your 1946 Woody station wagon?'

'You keep the goddamn away from my Woody. I'm keeping that station wagon. I'm driving the hell out of here.'

'Where are you going?'

'I'm not going to tell you, Frankie Lee. But when I get there you'll know.'

Chapter 4

The Great Lakes, 1960–1961

Norman Mailer's Big Party. It was November 1960.

Norman Mailer now lived on the Upper West Side in a sublet that Mailer's friend Doc Humes had told him about.

The Big Party. Adele was wearing a black cut-velvet dress. It was an expensive black dress. Norman was wearing a bullfighter's shirt that he picked up in Mexico.

Dread. Adele was experiencing dread. At a later date, she would describe her feelings in the same language William Burroughs used describing the daylong dread he felt before shooting his wife in her forehead.

There were many people at the party like bees inside a hive. Dozens were party crashers off the street. The thing Adele would remember later was how people smelled; 1960 had been a year of not bathing.

The Big Party. People smoking grass. More people making out or passed out.

Adele found a friend in the bathroom and told that friend that she could not stand the craziness anymore. 'I want to kill myself!'

'Ditch Norman, Adele.'

'How? I have no money? What about the kids? Norman is nuttier than ever.'

Adele left the bathroom and found Allen Ginsberg standing in the middle of the room in a boxer's stance in front of Norman Podhoretz, a thirty-year-old intellectual who was toying with writing an essay titled 'My Negro Problem—And Ours.' At this exact moment, Podhoretz was convinced that Ginsberg was going to slug him because Podhoretz had just told Ginsberg, 'Kerouac and Burroughs are second-rate talent and you shouldn't associate with them!' (Ginsberg had shouted back, 'You big dumb fuckhead!') Podhoretz was now warning the participants of Mailer's Big Party, 'Ginsberg is going to punch me. Watch out!'

Norman Mailer, pugilist supreme, came over and led Ginsberg away.

A little later, a retired boxer named Roger Donoghue (age thirty) picked up a table as long as the neck of a giraffe, a table covered with bottles of booze, and heaved the thing up into the air. Donoghue had been told that Mailer's Big Party was a celebration of his birthday.

Mailer then held up a photograph of himself getting arrested outside Birdland in the Village. 'Anyone who wants to see it, try and take it from me!' Donoghue stepped over the toppled gin bottles and left the apartment to take the elevator down to the street. Mailer followed and ran down the stairs and met the ex-boxer on the street. Mailer tried to pick a fight. Donoghue had trained Marlon Brando to box in *On the Waterfront*. Donoghue, himself, came up with Brando's immortal line, 'I cudda been a contender.'

Donoghue popped Mailer once in the eye.

A moment later, Mailer ran into George Plimpton standing on the sidewalk and hit the editor of *The Paris Review* across the face with a rolled-up *New York Times* as he screamed, 'I told you to bring influential people with money to my party!' Down the line, Plimpton would claim that he gave Mailer a 'good stiff left jab.' A witness would report, 'Mailer was kicking George in the leg like a little dog chases a pony.'

Around three o'clock a.m. there were only about twenty people at the Big Party. Mailer herded everyone into the living room and said, 'I want you all to line up in two groups. All of those who are for me stand over by the couch. All of you who are against me stand by the buffet.'

No one moved. He began shoving people into groups. He shoved Adele into the line of those who were against him.

He put his arm around their maid/nanny Nettie Marie Biddle and said, 'She is the only one who has never betrayed me.'

* * *

At four in the morning, everyone had left Mailer's place but a guy named Lester Blackiston, a beat boxer and a hanger-on. Also, a nameless black male party crasher. Adele was alone with these two personages. Norman was out on the street. Then suddenly Norman was back. He had a black eye. His bullfighter shirt was torn and stained with blood. Norman was so drunk Adele did not believe that he knew where he was. He charged into the apartment looking for someone to hurt.

Adele was instantly enraged. She held her arms out like she was holding a cape. 'Aja toro Aja. Come on you little faggot, where's your cojones, did your ugly whore of a mistress cut them off, you son of a bitch!'

Mailer charged his wife holding out a filthy penknife he had found somewhere. For a moment, he saw Adele as a black-and-white Janet Leigh. They both had luscious big breasts. But Mailer didn't have a butcher knife like Tony Perkins. Just a penknife. Then again, perhaps a 'penknife' does not sound like much, but Norman Mailer drove that small piercing sharp blade deep enough in Adele's chest to nearly puncture her heart. Then he spun her around and stabbed her once in the back.

As Mailer inflicted this violence he was not accompanied by screeching Bernard Herrmann violins like the shower scene in *Psycho,* but Mailer's ears were roaring as if he had a double case of tinnitus.

Adele was now on the floor. Unable to move. Blood pouring out of her.

The black guy yelled, 'My God, man. What have you done? We gotta get her to a hospital.'

Mailer started kicking his bleeding wife.

In another room, Mailer's two little girls were sleeping. They had slept through the entire Big Party. They had slept through the stabbing of their mother by their father.

Adele lay on the floor and reflected on her and Norman watching *Psycho.* She remembered after the stabbing the camera rolls up to Janet Leigh's big open eyeball as her character tries to peer her way out of death. Adele kept her own eye open and moving. No fish-eyed death peer for her.

The black man tried to lift Adele Mailer up. Mailer shoved him away. Mailer and the black guy started wrestling on the floor. Finally, the black guy cold-cocked Mailer and lifted Adele up by her armpits and quickly dragged her to the elevator.

Down in the lobby—a few drunk guests. Someone saw Adele and the blood, and ran into the phone booth and called for an ambulance. The black guy left Adele in the lobby and split without haste. *These crazy white people.* Who knew how the evening would end up—these drunks believing that he was the one who stabbed the white woman?

Doc and Anna Lou Humes lived below the Mailers. They had been to the party and left around one. They would later state that Adele had been brought down the stairwell lying on a thin mattress held by two white men they had never seen before. At any rate, Anna Lou Humes said that she called their family doctor.

The doctor came. He glanced at the bleeding woman and commanded Humes to call an ambulance.

Someone started yelling in Adele's ear. 'You fell on a broken bottle. You fell on a broken glass.'

In the aftermath, Mailer would say, 'I'm not going to hide behind a woman's skirt and claim it was broken glass.'

The police came. Everyone who could disappeared. The cops knew a knife wound when they saw one. 'Who did this, Mrs. Mailer? Who did this?' Then the ambulance. Nettie, their maid, rode with Adele. She had hustled the children to a friend's apartment on the floor above the Mailers' sublet.

'I'm going to die,' Adele Mailer said.

'Don't talk like that,' Nettie said.

If you have ever been stabbed, you know there is often a humble regret as you realize that your body cannot be controlled by your will.* You follow that regret with a regret of the things that you neglected to finish or accomplish in your life. Many people who have been stabbed then begin regretting some of the things that they did do.

* * *

New Hampshire. Richard Pavlick took off in his 1946 Woody station wagon one December morning as the relentless snow fell. The man drove down the plowed farm roads to the plowed interstate to stalk Jack Kennedy. It will be unclear the number of places Pavlick stalked Kennedy. The lone assassin on the road is an American trope. Think of John Hinckley Jr. traveling by bus to stalk Jimmy Carter and Jodie Foster and then ending up spontaneously shooting President Reagan out of dumb luck. John Hinckley Jr. was influenced by repeated viewings of the movie *Taxi Driver,* a movie about Manhattan loner Travis Bickle, who spontaneously tries to assassinate a presidential candidate who comes to the city. Bickle

---

* Christian Scientists who are stabbed will go through a different thought process.

instead ends up shooting a pimp out of frustration. The screenwriter of *Taxi Driver,* Paul Schrader, created Travis Bickle after reading Arthur Bremer's *An Assassin's Diary,* published after its alleged author had stalked presidential candidate George Wallace around the country in 1972 and finally shot the presidential candidate five times at a rally in a shopping center in Laurel, Maryland. The FBI discovered Bremer's diary several days after this shooting. According to its pages, Bremer originally wanted to shoot President Nixon, but Nixon's security was too good. So Bremer chose Wallace instead. Bremer described in his journal stalking Wallace as he crossed the Great Lakes. 'Call me Ishmael,' Bremer wrote.

★ ★ ★

Manhattan. The ambulance rushed Adele Mailer down to University Hospital on East 20th Street. The two-inch blade of the penknife had nearly killed her. She was in intensive care swamped by pain, part of her consciousness floating around the ceiling looking down at her body. Adele thought that she appeared glorious down there, laid out on the hospital bed like a pre-Raphaelite painting of Ophelia drifting down the lazy river.

It wasn't until Monday afternoon that the doctors let the police question Adele. After the cops left, Adele's husband himself talked his way into her hospital room.

'I wrote you a poem,' he said. '*So long as you use a knife, there's some love left,*' he read.

Adele started screaming. Mailer hurried out of her room. The cops were waiting in the lobby and arrested him. Their intention was to drag him to Bellevue. 'I'm not crazy,' Mailer screamed. He told the cops that Adele had cancer and he had to 'relieve' her of the tumors with that knife. He told the police this using his terrible fake Texas and alternately southern accent.

Mailer next had an opportunity to tell a judge that it was important that he not be sent to a mental hospital. He used his normal tone of voice to say, 'Otherwise my work in the future will be considered that of a disordered mind. My pride is that I can explore areas of experience that other men are afraid of. I insist that I am sane.'

Sometime during this ruckus, television reporter Mike Wallace interviewed Norman on CBS. Mailer talked about how the knife was a symbol of manhood to juvenile delinquents. He suggested that the city institute jousting tournaments in the city parks. Mike Wallace commented on Mailer's black eye. 'Yeah. I got into quite a scrap Saturday night.'

* * *

Norman's mother visited Adele in the hospital. Mother Mailer wanted Adele to assure her that she was not going to send Norman to jail. 'How could *you* have let this happen to America's number one novelist?'

Norman Mailer.

Norman Bates.

Norman Bates had a mother fixation, too.

Next, the examining psychiatrist from Bellevue came to see Adele. He said Norman was a paranoid schizophrenic with suicidal and violent tendencies. He recommended shock treatments. He brought the necessary papers with him. Adele had the authority to sign them. She said that she would think about it. Suddenly all the big-shot intellectuals who'd fled out of the lobby when Adele was bleeding were cramming into Adele's hospital room, saying, 'What a tragedy. America's greatest novelist. Don't give him shock treatments. It would destroy his talent. What a tragedy for Norman. What a tragedy for Norman.'

What a tragedy for Norman Bates.

* * *

Jackie's pet name for JFK was 'Bunny.'

She gave birth to Bunny's son on November 25—the Friday after Thanksgiving. She yet again gave birth prematurely. She underwent yet another cesarean delivery. John F. Kennedy Jr. was born alive. The newborn weighed six pounds.

* * *

December 1960. Seattle. The Rocking Kings became Thomas and the Tom Cats. Buster liked playing at the club called the Castle. The audience was mostly white. It was an officially integrated club.

Buster discovered feedback. If you cut the core of a speaker and put a towel in it and then stuck toothpicks in the woofer, you would get your guitar to give an electric moan. You could manipulate the toothpicks and make the sound more shredded. Make the feedback shriek. Blare up into itself. If Buster manipulated the toothpicks *and* his guitar simultaneously, he created a whole new form of music.

Animal music.

He bet the elephants at the Seattle Zoo would dig it!

★ ★ ★

Washington, D.C., December 7, 1960. The president-elect's brother Robert made a morning telephone call to Robert McNamara in Detroit. Several hours later, the Kennedy brothers' brother-in-law, Sargent Shriver, flew to Detroit to meet with Robert McNamara. The next day, McNamara himself was flown to the capital and was driven down a Georgetown alley that paralleled N Street. The limo stopped. McNamara was led through a snow-covered backyard to the kitchen door of a good-sized house. The kitchen was crowded with men, including the president-elect. All the men talked both to and at McNamara. Among the things McNamara said back was a question to John F. Kennedy, 'Did you really write *Profiles in Courage*?'

John F. Kennedy affirmed that he had.*

That night McNamara returned to Ann Arbor. It was snowing in Michigan worse than D.C. Robert McNamara spent most of a whiteout weekend sitting in his anonymous office in the house brooding. On Tuesday, December 13, Robert McNamara was again in Washington, D.C., being driven to Kennedy's kitchen where McNamara handed the president-elect a letter that stated that McNamara would accept the job of secretary of defense provided he could run the department as he thought fit.

And McNamara would not have to go to parties.

Kennedy accepted the letter. Little did Robert McNamara imagine that one year from now he would live for White House parties. The man would even stand before a full-length mirror practicing this new dance

---

* History will prove that Kennedy was lying.

called the twist to appraise himself honestly and be sure that he did not look ridiculous shaking his hips.

* * *

McNamara had never said good-bye to Carl Djerassi. No telephone call. No letter. Nothing. That shook Djerassi. Not that he felt let down as much as he saw how ruthless arrogance could be. He realized that arrogance should in fact be that ruthless.

* * *

Florida. Howard Hunt went Christmas shopping, but purchased presents in a perfunctory manner. He felt no holiday cheer. He was sick of his paramilitaristic masculine exile. His troops were accusing each other of being Batisteros. Or socialists. It appeared that the exiles with the most military experience had, in fact, been in Batista's army.

Hunt felt disgust for the whole group.

Hunt found them Shallow Thinkers and Opportunists.

Besides, they all owed their lives to the CIA.

When Howard Hunt had been in Guatemala at the camp he felt things were being run in a professional military manner. Everyone wore khaki 'uniforms.' They went through drills as tough as those at any Marine Corps base. Soon Hunt heard whispers of dissension. Most of the trainees had been civilians. They could deal with weapon handling and singing the old Cuban national anthem every morning, but they wanted the rest of camp life to be more informal. Various Cuban exile leaders also said, 'To have Cubans under the orders of foreigners is humiliating. We cannot accept it.' Then Raymond Sardiñas said the leaders were too old and out of touch. Power plays were already going on to determine who would lead Cuba once they successfully killed Castro.

'Jesus H. Christ,' Hunt would rave out loud to himself. 'Every last son-of-a-bitch should rise above their machismo and just concentrate on the Mission.' Hunt even heard word that ballsy independent anti-Castro saboteurs intended to infiltrate Cuba through the country's metaphorical anus—a little-known U.S. military base at the southern port of Guantánamo Bay.

* * *

Howard Hunt finally went north to Washington, D.C., for Christmas. Dot told him her mother was dying. She berated her husband about finishing with this mission. He told Dot he had no idea when the Cuban invasion was going to take place. Eisenhower's people did not care about Hunt's private problems. They kept postponing the invasion.

One night, Dot did not have time or was too exhausted to cook him dinner. Hunt's daughter Kevan told him she made him dinner. He smiled. Kevan prepared a TV dinner. Hunt started laughing and crying at the same time. TV dinners were all he ate down in Florida.

On December 11, Jack Kennedy and his family, including his new baby John, were relaxing for the holidays at his father's mansion in Palm Beach, Florida. Richard Pavlick had reached Palm Beach as well. His Woody was parked at the Royal Poinciana Way motel. In the payload was a bushel basket full of dynamite sticks with blasting caps and several tins filled with gasoline.

Pavlick adored Florida. It made his rage against Joe Kennedy float outside his New Hampshire body. Florida was warm in a way that was incomprehensible to Pavlick's very anatomy. Do not forget that Pavlick had been born in New Hampshire. He had lived in New Hampshire his entire life. It was warm in New Hampshire in the summer, sure. But this was the first time his biological clock had experienced such warmth in December.

It was a good day to die.

He drove his ramshackle Woody down the posh streets of Palm Beach. Back in the parking lot of the Royal Poinciana Way motel Pavlick had wired seven sticks of dynamite to an ignition switch that rested beside the right cheek of his butt. It sat within easy reach of his right hand.

Pavlick steered lazily with his left paw.

Pavlick pulled down Royal Poinciana Way, the street where Joe Kennedy's Mediterranean-style mansion, La Guerida, was located. Richard Pavlick idled his station wagon twenty feet from the massive gates of the estate. The Secret Service agents either did not see him or saw him but did not think it was worth investigating.

Pavlick could not see much from Royal Poinciana Way as La Guerida was built on a downward slope of a hill. The president-elect's limousine was parked waiting on the street. Today was Sunday. Jack Kennedy would go to church. Richard Pavlick planned to ram his Buick into Kennedy's limo and then press the detonation button kamikaze style.

Kamikaze is a Japanese word meaning 'divine wind.'

Richard Pavlick's dynamite would be a divine wind indeed. One rich father shouldn't get away with buying the office of the presidency of the United States. You just couldn't. That was an American Abomination. Pavlick squinted into his rearview mirror and imagined what it would be like to see Abraham Lincoln sitting in the back seat.

It should be said that Richard Pavlick had formulated suicide bombing forty years before it became the technique of choice for Shiite terrorists. Yet, Richard Pavlick was not going to kill Kennedy to be the instrument of an Angry God. Richard Pavlick was going to kill John Kennedy for the personal glory of Richard Pavlick of New Hampshire U.S.A., just as Jaime Ramón Mercader del Río Hernández killed Trotsky for the personal glory of Jaime Ramón Mercader del Río Hernández of Barcelona, Spain.

Suddenly Jack Kennedy was walking out of his father's compound. Pavlick released the brake. Jack Kennedy was walking with his three year-old daughter, Caroline. Then a woman appeared holding Kennedy's three week-old son. Pavlick immediately assumed the woman was Jacqueline, but in actuality, she was the nanny. Everyone got into the limousine.

Children.

A child and a baby.

This moment was the saving grace and triumph of that previous decade, the 1950s. Even an insane New Hampshire psychopath could not bear to assassinate the president if it meant killing his children. The limousine drove President-elect Kennedy, his young daughter, his infant son, and his nanny to a Catholic church.

Pavlick drove the other way.

Pavlick spends four more days in Palm Beach waiting for the right moment to blow up Jack Kennedy. One would expect that even an inexperienced kamikaze assassin from New Hampshire would shark the streets of Palm Beach cautiously so as to not break any traffic laws, but on December 15, patrolman Lester Free stops Pavlick for crossing over the dividing line. The latter notices the bushel basket of dynamite in Pavlick's station wagon. Pavlick is arrested. The Secret Service fakes reports that they knew all about Pavlick and he was arrested because the Secret Service gave patrolman Lester Free the suspect Pavlick's license plate number. The local newspapers call Pavlick a 'Modern Ignacy Hryniewiecki,' referring to a prominent member of the Nihilist movement who assassinated Tsar Alexander II in Saint Petersburg with a suicide bomb in 1881. Pavlick hears this and is incensed, as he believes the papers are calling him a Communist. Pavlick's anger abates somewhat after his lawyer explains that historically the Nihilists predated Marxism. Next, because the popular and scandalous 1956 novel *Peyton Place* was set in a fictional small town in New Hampshire, the national newspapers began calling Pavlick 'the would-be assassin from Peyton Place.' Pavlick did not read fiction so he didn't understand the reference.

* * *

Seattle. This is that dead zone between Christmas and New Year's. The Tom Cats are driving home from a gig far from Seattle. They had borrowed someone's brother's 1949 Studebaker. It is so old they even argue about what color it is. It is night and it is snowing—Seattle doesn't get much snow in winter, but there is already half a foot on the ground.

The Studebaker slips and rolls off the road.

Everyone is okay.

The Tom Cats huddle inside the car waiting for sunrise. At dawn, most of the Cats wake up to see that Buster is already out of the car making snow angels in a flat field.

* * *

January 20, 1961. Inauguration Day. Washington, D.C., digging itself out of a blizzard. Excited weathermen on all the channels state that this is the coldest day in the capital's history. The cold does not appear to faze Jack Kennedy. At age forty-three, he is the youngest elected president in American history. Also the first Roman Catholic president. Finally, Jack Kennedy is the first twentieth-century president who has actually been born in the twentieth century. At his inauguration, Kennedy takes his top hat off to give his inaugural address bareheaded.

Simultaneously, Marilyn Monroe is in Ciudad Juárez in Mexico. There was a popular song that went, 'It's a sin for you to get a Mexican divorce.' Monroe wanted to procure a quiet Mexican divorce from Arthur Miller and not overshadow the inauguration in the press. When the news broke, it instantly became global. *Nedelya,* a Russian magazine, said, 'Monroe found in Arthur Miller what she lacked. She exploited him without pity. He wrote scripts for her movies and made her a real actress. Marilyn paid him back. She left him. Another broken life on her climb to the stars.' The Communists in Russia were official prudes and bluestockings. Yet, the Bolsheviks themselves had instituted no-fault divorce back in 1917. If one subtracted the travel time, dissolving a marriage in Moscow was even quicker than a Mexican divorce.

* * *

The Misfits opened on the 1st of February. Bosley Crowther in the *New York Times:* '[Monroe/Gable/Clift] are amusing people to be with, for a little while, anyhow. But they are shallow and inconsequential, and that is the dang-busted trouble with this movie...'

* * *

The last time Arthur Miller had seen John Huston was at the Clift/Gable birthday party in Reno. Huston took a puff on his cigar and told his screenwriter, 'Marilyn acts like she's never understood why she was funny.'

Miller arched an eyebrow.

'And that was precisely what made her so funny,' Huston said. 'She's a natural comedian.'

Miller bit his lip. He thought Huston was now criticizing the humorless stance of his script. It was at that moment that he had a terrific epiphany about Marilyn Monroe. Apropos of nothing, he said to John Huston, 'Marilyn is hardly able to spell. What could she do besides be a movie star?' Then he said, '*The Misfits* script is brilliant. If it fails it is because in this country sex and seriousness cannot exist in the same modern woman. Goddammit, John Huston, this American illness is not about to end either.'

'Maybe that's what you should call your next script,' John Huston said.

'What?'

'*American Illness.*'

* * *

Buddy had a small part in *The Misfits.*

Buddy was small for his age, like most actors. For the scene, he is dressed like a kid in the first grade. He sits on a bar next to Clark Gable, who holds a pint glass filled with dark liquid. Buddy and Clark Gable are in a crowded tavern watching Marilyn Monroe swat a paddleball back and forth with her paddle. She swats that little rubber ball straight up as the crowd counts off her paddles.

Buddy cannot take his eyes off her behind. She sticks it out with each stroke of the paddle. Her behind is bigger than most. Buddy is not quite sure why this woman's behind pleases him, but it does.

Marilyn now swats the ball in the boy's direction. She is not wearing a brassiere. She keeps bending forward low.

Buddy's whole body feels good. Clark Gable is making a barely perceptible purr. They could both watch Marilyn Monroe swat that rubber ball with that wooden paddle all day.

John Huston keeps the cameras rolling and rolling. When the filming stops, Buddy realizes that he is drenched in sweat. Schoolboys never sweat! At least, not this much.

* * *

In February, the poet Sylvia Plath had a miscarriage, a desolate experience she had in common with Marilyn Monroe and Jacqueline Kennedy. Plath was twenty-eight. She was married to the British poet Ted Hughes, two years older than his wife. After Sylvia left the hospital, she wrote a poem about her immediate condition post-miscarriage.

In the poem, Sylvia recounts how she finds the red 'Get Well Soon' tulips on the bed table too excitable. The room is white. The room is winter. Sylvia is teaching herself peacefulness by lying quiet. Sylvia is propped between the pillow and the sheet cuff. Why can't she shut her eyes? 'Stupid pupil, it has to take everything in.' The nurses in their white caps. They stick her with needles to get her to sleep. Sylvia squints at a photo of her husband and his smile is a little hook snagging her skin.

The drugs the nurses give feel great. The drugs they give make her too sensitive. Sylvia can hear the red tulips breathing through the white paper they are wrapped in. The paper is white like swaddling. The vivid tulips are eating this woman's oxygen. The vivid tulips remove Sylvia's face. She can hear them. Sylvia can hear the noise they make. Red engines. Tulips should be in cages. The tulips yawn like some great African cat.

Sylvia now becomes aware of her heart. It closes and then opens again like a red tulip. It undulates this way because her heart loves her. Now Sylvia sucks the inside of her mouth. This sucking tastes salty like salt water. This wet taste comes from a country as far away as health.

Sylvia doesn't think lower than her heart. Sylvia doesn't think about her loins. What do the noisy tulips have to do with experiencing a miscarriage? Suddenly Sylvia Plath bolts up in bed and howls, 'I have nothing to do with explosions.' The nurses come running. 'I have nothing to do with explosions.'

Time for the hooks.

* * *

In March, Lee Jun Fan began attending the University of Washington in Seattle as a freshman. Lee took courses in theater, speech, and Chinese philosophy. He also rode buses south to Northern California and north to Canada to seek out displaced Gung Fu masters. He was following the actions of Hollywood gunslingers in westerns seeking out quick-draw masters in the wilderness. He also proceeded to Americanize his body. Most Gung Fu masters back in Hong Kong lacked any Spartan physique. They even had potbellies. Lee Jun Fan took a different direction and adapted Charles Atlas's muscle-bound techniques to bulk up, getting to the point that he could do push-ups holding himself with only one finger—the pointer—on each hand.

* * *

Springtime in Seattle. Buster Hendrix had dropped out of high school and was earning twenty dollars a month doing this and that. Buster's father rarely showed up at home. Buster was feeding himself and Leon on the generosity of the black high school kids who worked in a burger joint down the street. At the end of the day—midnight—they would give Buster a big garbage bag full of the cooked hamburgers they had to throw away.

Those were some beautiful nights—eating hamburgers on a roof with Mary, who had snuck out of her house.

She was loving high school. She loved to read. One night, eating old burgers, she was all excited about *The House of the Seven Gables.*

'It's 1961, Buster. I want to be a modern female. Shall we never, never get rid of the Past? That's in *The House of the Seven Gables.* Here. I have to read you this, okay?'

'Okay. These hamburgers are good tonight.'

'*Shall we never, never get rid of this Past?* That's what Hawthorne wrote in the book. Past is a capitalized word. The Present is also. *The Past lies upon the Present like a giant's dead body.*'

'The Jolly Green Giant?'

'No, dummy. A giant like Jack-and-the-Beanstalk's giant. Listen to this: *The Past lies upon the Present like a giant's dead body. And the young must waste all their strength in dragging about the corpse of the old giant who died a long time ago and only needs to be decently buried.*'

'What hole would be big enough—the Grand Canyon?'

'The giant is not that big. You think slavery is over? We're all slaves to bygone times.'

'Bygone? What are those?'

'The past, dummy! We're all slaves to the past. We read dead men's books! We laugh at dead men's jokes. We listen to the songs of dead men.'

'I don't.'

'Most white people do. Beethoven. Handel. That crap. We cry at dead men's pathos!'

'Pay what?'

'P-a-t-h-o-s. Feeling sorry for yourself. You feel sorry for yourself all the time.'

'I do not. I'm not sorry eating these hamburgers. There is no pathos between those buns!'

She laughed. 'Okay. That's a good one. We're sick of dead men's diseases with which dead doctors kill their patients! We worship God according to dead men's religion. We must be dead ourselves before we can begin to have our proper influence on our own world, which will then be no longer our world, but the world of another generation, with which we shall have no shadow of a right to interfere.'

'Shadow of what?'

'The Shadow knows, stupid.' She did a sinister laugh like Lamont Cranston. 'Man, don't you read any books?'

'I read lots of books.'

'Name one.'

'I forget.'

'You know how to read, don't you?'

'Yeah. Of course. Words. I can't read music. I don't have to. Words on the page aren't that important either.'

* * *

Washington, D.C. President Kennedy did not want to invade Cuba with Howard Hunt's motley 'army.'

'The whole damn thing has been foisted on us by Eisenhower,' McNamara said.

'It's Eisenhower's damn shit and now it's on the soles of my shoes as well,' Kennedy complained.

'To get back at us, Nixon saw to it that the invasion would be made public knowledge,' Robert Kennedy said. 'If we abort it, we look like pussies to the Bear.'

'As it is, the Red Chinese are calling us a Paper Tiger,' McNamara said.

'All I know,' Kennedy said, 'is that our balls must always be bigger than Ivan's.'

* * *

On April 12, President Kennedy held a press conference in Washington, D.C., during which he declared that the United States military would not invade Cuba. Howard Hunt was in town and heard Kennedy's words and smiled, taking in that speech as a CIA man would hear it. What a superb effort in misdirection. Hunt had already gotten the green light to set his men loose on Castro.

The invasion would begin on April 14. A Friday. For the entire weekend, no one knew how the invasion was going. Not President Kennedy. Not E. Howard Hunt. There were no satellites orbiting a hundred miles above Cuba that could take a photo of a single corn flake sitting on a turtle's shell.

Everyone just assumed the best.

Officious pageboys brought reports that all the troops had landed on the beaches of the Bay of Sows while the brigade's six airplanes bombed and destroyed the entire Cuban air force. Castro had been killed. Communism in Cuba was no more. The Cubans in the barrio in Miami got word of these 'reports' and went crazy with joy.

Hunt spent all weekend drinking rotgut coffee and following Radio Havana.

No news.

* * *

All this time in Washington, D.C., President Kennedy was closeted with his advisers arguing out the Cuba invasion. The assumption now was that the Cuban invasion was A.S.U.—All Screwed Up. Robert McNamara was attentive to the various ranting, but was unmoved in his interior. The invasion of Cuba was a CIA action. The Cuba Invasion was the CIA's Edsel.

* * *

Howard Hunt went home to take a shower. On impulse, he went to a closet and lugged out his trumpet case. He had not opened it in maybe ten years. The brass was still polished. He took his mouthpiece out of its compartment and cleaned the inside with a Q-tip and stuck it in the open end of the leadpipe of his trumpet. He fingered the three valves. They needed oil, but he would make do. He blew. His embouchure—the contortions of his lips that blew air into the horn—was shot, but the notes were in tune. Hunt started noodling the blues.

The Cuba blues.

Then he shot the trumpet down with his arms and then whipped it back to his lips and blew 'Reveille.' Then a bit of John Philip Sousa. *America. America. America.* There were no blues in America.

Then Hunt was aware of a sonic disturbance. The telephone ringing. Hunt's first thought was that it was a neighbor complaining. 'Yeah,' he declared into the mouthpiece of the telephone.

'Señor Hunt?'

'Yeah.'

'It's Felíx Thersites Ameijeiras.'

Hunt had to think a moment. Felíx Thersites Ameijeiras was a minor lead with the brigade. 'Where are you?' Hunt demanded.

'Havana.'

Hunt was stunned with joy. 'Havana! That's wonderful!'

'It's not what you think, Señor Hunt,' Felíx Thersites Ameijeiras said. 'There is a man with me who wants to talk with you.'

'Who wants to talk with me?'

'Castro.'

'Castro?'

'Here.' The sound of the phone changing hands. 'Hello, Señor Hunt,' a male voice said in English.

'Who is this?' Hunt demanded in Spanish.

The voice answered back in English. The voice insisted that he was Fidel Castro. Hunt answered in Spanish that he didn't believe him. 'Put Felíx back on the line.'

'Maybe I will, Señor Hunt. Maybe I won't. I wanted to tell you personally that your mercenaries failed. They tried to storm the beaches of the Bay of Sows and were overcome by the wilderness.'

'What wilderness?' Hunt spat out in Spanish.

'The marshes beyond Playa Girón.' (English.) 'Then the Barman Wood beyond the marshes. On the west side of the Bay of Sows, they ran aground in Zapata Swamp. By Sunday morning the Cuban air force began bombing your men and sank your ships.'

'You have no airplanes. We destroyed the Cuban air force on Friday.' (Spanish.)

'You destroyed what-do-you-call-it? You destroyed crap.' (English.) 'I instructed my pilots to put crap planes on the runways and camouflage our Soviet jets. I outfoxed you, Señor Hunt.'

'I don't believe a word you are saying.'

'You will when none of your men return.'

'What do you want?'

'I want to tell you what corrupt pigs your mercenaries are. The Cuban army is an army of farmers and good true men. A hundred Cuban soldiers were slain by your mercenaries, yet we still captured one thousand of those war criminals.'

Hunt said nothing. He just brooded.

(In English.) 'Tell me, Señor Hunt, what would your government do if one thousand Cubans invaded your country? Say we sailed up the Mississippi and invaded Nebraska—'

'The Mississippi doesn't go to Nebraska,' Hunt said in English.

'Don't quibble. You would kill as many Cubans as you could and then beat the prisoners before sending them to prison for life for being war criminals. But this is not how we will treat your mercenaries even though it is hard for us to be humane. We have seen over one hundred fifty beloved *compañeros* killed, yet not a single Cuban soldier has struck a prisoner with the butt of his rifle. We have cared for the wounded.'

'What are you going to do with my men?' (Spanish.)

(In English.) 'Perhaps you know that on a certain occasion the Spanish people in Cuba exchanged Napoleon's prisoners of war for hundreds of pigs. Your mercenaries failed your invasion of the Bay of Sows, yet we will not trade pork for pork. We will return your war criminals unharmed in exchange for tractors and bulldozers. I will be talking with Kennedy shortly. I just wanted a word with the man who planned this invasion.'

'Why?' (Spanish.)

'Because I know that you are—there is only a Cuban word for it—a *petrolero.*'

'An oil driller?'

'Yes. In slang. You are attracted to black Cuban women.'

'How do you know that?'

'Certain Soviet comrades informed me. What I want to suggest to you is that every time you find yourself about to have a carnal encounter with a Cuban woman see my face implanted over hers and remember your impotence in the Bay of Sows.'

Hunt spit out in Spanish, '*Me cago en la revolución, me cago en Fidel, me cago en Cuba, y me cago en la mierda.*'—'I shit on the Revolution. I shit on Fidel. I shit on Cuba. And I shit on shit itself.'

'*Me cago en nada,*'—'I shit on nothing'—Castro said and hung up the telephone.

* * *

This song swept Cuba:

Fidel, Fidel, ¿Que tiene Fidel
Que los americanos no pueden con él?
Fidel, Fidel, what does he have
That the Americans can't deal with him?

* * *

Hunt held the phone as he was consumed with a biblical rage of grief. Hunt stood gnashing his teeth in a horrible grimace, his cheeks pulled up into the bottoms of his eyes in a reptile squint, his lips peeled back from his teeth in a rapid snarl. The tendons on his neck were the width of celery stalks. Both his ears were flushed red.

Cuba was E. Howard Hunt's Outer Dark.

Hunt started jabbering to himself: 'Castro teareth me in his wrath, Castro gnashed upon me with his teeth, mine enemy sharpeneth his eyes upon me!'

Hunt began to hiss and gnash his teeth with such fury that fillings popped out of the crevices they had once filled. Gold bits now lay in the trough between the man's gums and the insides of his cheeks. Bits of gold lodged under Hunt's swollen tongue. He squeezed his jaw shut tighter and tighter. When Hunt could squeeze no more he began rubbing the occlusals of his top and lower teeth back and forth like some out-of-control oral/dental machine, filing the cusps and grooves into a surface as smooth as a rim of porcelain.

Hunt spit blood. He swallowed blood. Hunt bit through his lower lip and felt the blood pouring down his chin. The sound in Hunt's ears had disintegrated into a mammal bay as pathetic as a horse led to slaughter. And this sound shocked Hunt in such totality that the man fainted into an epileptic fit of grief. Hunt lay upon his shoulders, thrusting his pelvis up while stamping his feet, left to right, left to right. Then Hunt raised his hands to his head to commence yanking out his hair.

* * *

Desi Arnaz donated $50,000 ($400,000 today) to ransom the Bay of Sows prisoners back. Arnaz also saw to it that these veterans of the debacle appeared on *The Ed Sullivan Show*. Premier Khrushchev's response to the U.S. and Cuban machismo maneuvering was to begin erecting the Berlin Wall.

* * *

Seattle. During these events, Buster Hendrix stole a book from Larson's department store. Its title caught his eye, *Flying Saucers: A Modern Myth of Things Seen in the Sky.* A guy whose first name was Carl and last name was Jung had written it. Jung! Buster liked that name.

Jung—Jungle—Jungle Gym.

Buster stuffed the book under his peacoat. It was too warm to wear a peacoat and the clerks at Larson's were fools. Buster hurried unmolested out of the store and took the book to Roosevelt Park. Buster hoped it had pictures of flying saucers. It didn't. He began reading it. Or trying to read it. He gave up.

Buster had no idea that Carl Jung was still alive and had been the younger disciple of Sigmund Freud. In fact, these two Europeans came to America together in 1909 and stayed in Manhattan. Once they were settled in their hotel, the older man felt a stark fear that Jung would soon turn against him. Freud and Jung took a trip to Coney Island, where they looked at themselves in a fun-house mirror and Freud found himself wetting his pants. Freud stayed incontinent for the entire American trip. When the two returned to Europe, Jung announced that he was no longer interested in unraveling the Oedipus complex. The younger man became interested in vibes and destiny and the mental ozone of a woman or a man. Jung had spent the last fifty years formulating what old moderns today call New Age Thinking and young moderns call Neo Burning Man Tribalism.

Furthermore, the relationship between Freud and Jung was similar to that of Richard Nixon and John Kennedy. Jung was nineteen years younger than Freud while Kennedy was four years younger than his counterpart. Several weeks after Kennedy's Cuban humiliation, Nixon will claim in a memoir, Kennedy asked the elder statesman to the White House.

Nixon entered the Oval Office finding Kennedy looking extremely beat. Kennedy said, 'It really is true that foreign affairs is the only important issue for the president to handle, isn't it?' Nixon will then quote Kennedy as saying, 'I mean who gives a shit if the minimum wage is $1.15 or $1.25 in comparison to something like this.'

We should read Nixon's vision of history with skepticism. Nixon was destined to be an unreliable narrator.

* * *

Seattle. Sometime during this period, Lee Jun Fan had one of those F. Scott Fitzgerald–style three a.m. Dark Nights of the Soul. He dreamed that the Angel who had wrestled with Jacob in Genesis appeared to battle Lee using the techniques of Gung Fu.

Lee Jun Fan faces the Angel. Lee is dressed in black slacks and a black shirt and black t'ai chi slippers. The Angel is dressed in all white. The Angel is glorious. The Angel is Caucasian.

Both Lee and the Angel shuck their shirts.

The Angel's chest is hairy. He possesses two immense wings and gives them a flap. They are man-sized wings shaped like those of a great swan. Then the Angel cracks his knuckles and then turns away from Lee. His wings start below his shoulders and appear attached to his spine. Below these wings, the Angel's back is hairy. The Angel starts rapidly shaking his head as if he is shaking water out of his ears.

Lee turns from the Angel. His bare chest and stomach reveal a hairless physique more glorious than the Angel's.

Both the Angel and Lee now move like ballet dancers warming up, practicing Gung Fu punches and kicks.

Lee's bones crack.

The Angel's bones are silent.

Lee walks away from the Angel moving like a cat. The Angel follows. Lee peers over his shoulder at the Angel.

Lee stops.

The two face each other for a second time. The Angel walks toward Lee with his wings tightly closed and his hands in fists with arms bent at his hips like a pose in a daguerreotype of a Victorian gentleman boxer.

Lee keeps his arms down and his hands at his sides. If he had wings, they would be shaped like those of a hawk and he would commence with warning flaps.

The Angel makes the first move. His great white wings flap open as he gives a terrifying scream and kicks at the mortal once, twice, many times.

Lee deflects each of the kicks.

Then Lee kicks at the Angel, backing him up. The Angel closes his wings as he spins and kicks Lee's head.

Lee is on the ground. The Angel silently gloats above him, giving several triumphant flaps of his great wings.

Lee slowly rises from the ground with each arm poised as if he were wearing a cowboy holster holding a gun on either hip.

Lee rushes the Angel and the Angel punches Lee once with his fist and once with his elbow and then spins and flips Lee over his shoulder.

Lee lies on his back again.

The Angel spreads his wings and punches at Lee, who is still on the ground. Lee stays on his back and deflects the blows. Lee then leaps up. He stands still for a moment and blows on his hand as if to remove some feathers before rushing the Angel with both a scream and a kick that the Angel easily deflects, before punching Lee once in the chest and once more in the belly, before giving a final kick to Lee's head.

Each of the Angel's blows sounds like a bullwhip cracking.

The Angel looks down at Lee on the ground again and flaps his wings while wagging his finger.

Lee rises, but not with the speed and grace of the first knockdown. Lee snorts and begins running in place.

Drums from somewhere begin beating.

A trumpet plays.

The bare-chested Angel smiles.

The two throw punches at each other, but both stop short.

A noise warps up through the beating drums that resembles the sound of a long carpenter's saw being flapped up and down like a steel bird's wing.

The Angel throws a kick and a punch that Lee easily deflects. The Angel kicks at Lee with his left foot and misses. The Angel kicks with his right foot and misses. The Angel spins in a circle kicking at Lee's head, but the mortal moves out of range as quickly as an arrowtooth eel.

The Angel kicks dead air.

Stray white feathers are now drifting through the air as if there had just been a furious pillow fight.

Lee bounces up and down in place like Cassius Clay in the ring.

The Angel throws yet another impotent punch. The Angel does a spinning kick with each foot. Lee deflects both with a slight smile.

The Angel always hollers with his blows. Lee stays silent. The Angel kicks again and again and then stops to silently appraise Lee.

Lee breaks this stillness by springing forward to kick the Angel's face twice. The Angel only manages to deflect Lee's third kick.

Now the Angel is standing still and confident, as if only then does it dawn on him that he is divine. His opponent is not. The Angel gives a single flap of rage with his wings. The disturbance in the air would have surely knocked Lee to the ground if he hadn't been bouncing in place. The Angel peers at Lee's feet dancing back and forth until Lee leaps and kicks the Angel in the mouth.

Lee kicks the Angel a second time. And a third time. Now it is the Angel who is on the ground.

The Angel springs back to his feet. The two throw punches and kicks that each successfully deflects.

The Angel stays silent. Lee now makes high-pitched *whoops* that sound almost feminine, yet with a single springing kick Lee sends the Angel to the ground, his wings wide open. The Angel leaps to his feet and gives four or five furious flaps of his wings as he kicks and punches at Lee.

Some blows connect. Most do not.

The two now spar with each other as if they are fencers.

Lee punches the Angel in his chest and belly giving two mock Apache hollers, each punch skin-to-skin sounding like a bullwhip snapping across the surface of a kettledrum.

The air is thick with white feathers.

Lee now goes nose-to-nose in the Angel's body space, throwing punches, most of which are deflected, but Lee's right fist hurls into the Angel's chest and his left into the Angel's stomach and Lee smiles in savage delight.

Lee now bobs up and down fast in front of the Angel. The Angel stands swaying slightly. Then the Angel starts hopping up and down looking like a kid. The Angel throws a series of impotent kicks that Lee easily deflects before slugging the Angel with a right and a left and then another right followed by a second left. Lee gives a call with each punch that sounds like a crow caw.

The Angel is ass-down again, his wings crumpled behind him.

Lee bounces up and down above.

The Angel now squints at Lee. His vision must be blurry. He shakes his head. He tries getting up. He loses his footing. The Angel keeps his arms stiff, fists poised ready, yet he is so wobbly his body language says, 'Don't hurt me anymore.'

Lee is no sucker. The Angel suddenly throws a kick that Lee ducks and the Angel's own momentum topples him yet again to the ground.

And again, the Angel jumps up.

The Angel throws punches through the air thick with feathers. Lee deflects each blow until he punches the Angel in return. Then again and again. Each blow connects. Lee kicks. Each kick sounds like a wet towel striking a rock.

The Angel is ass-down on the ground, wings in shreds, leaning against a brick wall.

Lee does his Cassius Clay bouncing, peering down at the Angel.

The Angel tries to stand and can't. He touches the socket of his hip as if it has been injured.

The Angel limps to his feet.

He tries to kick and falls prone on the ground.

He struggles to his knees. He struggles to his feet. This is the fourth time the Angel has been on the ground too injured to bounce back up.

Lee could have finished the Angel off four times, but hasn't. Lee is toying with the Angel?

The Angel finally makes it to his feet.

Lee looks down at his own feet and looks up into the Angel's face and shakes his head. The Angel rushes forward and Lee easily gets him in a headlock, belly to belly, his arm above the Angel's injured wings.

The Angel is impotently flailing his fists into Lee's back, punches that are so weak that they sound like the wet hands of a drunk trying to applaud.

The Angel finally speaks. 'Let me go. The day breaketh.'

'I will not let thee go, except thou bless me,' the Asian man says.

The Angel asks, 'What is thy name?'

Lee Jun Fan tells the Angel his name.

The Angel replies, 'Thy name shall be called no more Lee Jun Fan, but Bruce Lee, for as a prince hast thou power with God and with men, and hast prevailed.'

Bruce Lee asks for the Angel's name, but the Angel will not tell him.

Chapter 5

The Island of Dr. Moreau, Somewhere off the Southern Coast of the United States, 1961–1962

The 2nd of May. Eighteen-year-old Buster Hendrix slouched shotgun in the front seat of a Bullet Bird* speeding out of town. Our youth was ignorant on where the car was heading. Buster did not even know very well the Chinese kid who was driving. Or the black kid and the white kid in the back seat. Buster's job was to keep cool tunes on the radio. The Chinese kid had piloted them as far south as Tukwila when a squad car spooked up its siren and the Bullet Bird pulled over.

Even a child younger than Buster could steal a car in Seattle. The citizens possessed a careless innocence that seems prehistoric fifty years on. Ninety percent of Seattleites, even citizens living in bad neighborhoods, barred their back doors at night yet kept their front doors unlocked. An even greater percentage of Seattleites left their car keys in the ignition and left the car doors unlocked. Even good teenagers felt tempted to joyride. And now there was Buster, cuffed and jammed in the back seat of the police car whining, 'I didn't know that Bullet Bird was stolen. Honest injun, Offisa Pup.'

'Whaddya call me?' the white cop shot back.

'Nothin'. I didn't call you nothing.'

Buster sat for a day in jail. The jailer let him keep his book—*Flying Saucers: A Modern Myth*. The lad knew how to read it now. The day after he had stolen the book, Buster Hendrix walked into the library on 4th Street. Buster prowled the stacks until he found a black librarian shelving books. He asked her if she could explain *Flying Saucers: A Modern Myth*. The librarian was busy and the kid was an urchin, but an urchin with charm. She asked him his name.

---

* Slang for a Ford Thunderbird.

He was about to say *Buster*, but instead said, 'Jimi Marshall Hendrix.'

'Lower your voice, Jimi Marshall Hendrix. This is a library.'

'Okay. So what's your name?'

'Miss Bluegoose. Don't you dare laugh.'

'I won't, ma'am. I mean, Miss Bluegoose.'

She paged through the book he had presented.

'Okay, Jimi. Let's sit down over here. A famous Swiss psychiatrist wrote this book. He says he doesn't know whether flying saucers are real or not, but probably not.'

'So what's up in the sky?'

'Projections of our unconscious mind.'

'What's that?'

'Well, you know the images you see when you're sleeping? That's from your unconscious. Sometimes we have dreams even though we're awake.'

'Huh. That's interesting. Maybe I'm dreaming you, Miss Bluegoose.'

She was in her thirties. Her skin was so obsidian it was as if her flesh had been painted on. The whites of her eyes and her teeth were startling. Younger children and old grandmothers believed Miss Bluegoose was a Voudon saint. The librarian now told Jimi Marshall Hendrix, 'In the past, when people experienced troubled times, angels appeared in the sky. Today we see flying saucers.'

'Why?'

'Because we're all so worried about the atom bomb.'

Jimi shook his head. 'I don't buy it.'

'Do you believe in werewolves, Jimi?'

'You mean like *The Wolf Man*?'

'Yes. Do you believe men who've been bitten by a werewolf turn into werewolves themselves on the night of a full moon?'

Jimi laughed. 'That's cracked.'

'Well, a long time ago in Paris they had a revolution where all the rich white folks got their heads sliced off by the guillotine. But just before that revolution, everyone—rich people and the poor—were nervous. They knew trouble was in the air. During this time, the police of Paris got reports every night about werewolves lurking in the streets.'

'Really?'

'That's what Carl Jung says.' She pronounced it 'Young.'

'Who's he?'

'He wrote the book you gave me.'

'His name is Carl Jung.'

'Jung is pronounced *young*, not *jung* like *jungle.*'

'That's crazy. No wonder you believe in werewolves.'

'Now I don't believe in werewolves, young man. I believe in that Carl Jung who is pointing out in his book that when society gets nervous people see monsters in the dark and angels in the sky.'

⋆ ⋆ ⋆

A few blocks south in Seattle, Bruce Lee had saved almost three thousand dollars, more than enough to buy a decent car. Ping Chow told the young man he should get a Studebaker Silver Hawk.

'The Silver Hawk has as much pep as a Cadillac, but not as expensive.' Ping Chow spoke to the boy in Cantonese, but spoke English when he referred to *pep.* There was no Chinese equivalent for that word.

'How less expensive?' Lee asked Ping Chow in English.

'These cars do not succumb to cheapness,' Ping Chow answered in Chinese. 'Come. I'll drive you to Wok Sam's.'

The two took Ruby's Edsel—Chow grumbling how the Edsel was a woman's car. 'The grille of the Edsel looks like a toilet seat.'

Chow drove the Edsel to the car lots near Rooster Park. Wok Sam's Studebaker lot was like the Pontiac and Ford lots—rows of gleaming cars the colors of toothpaste; pennants snapping above in the wind. Wok Sam himself was a slender man wearing sunglasses and a shirt like a priest's.

'Is he a priest?' Lee muttered to Chow.

'Of course not.'

'What's with the collar?'

'That's a polo neck.'

Lee had no idea what a polo neck was. How did Ping Chow know these things?

Wok Sam also wore a meager Fu Manchu goatee. He had high Mandarin cheekbones and spoke Cantonese to Ping Chow. Bruce Lee was sure Wok Sam possessed Asian eyes and was in fact Asian, but Lee had never seen an Asian wearing sunglasses before.

Wok Sam and Ping Chow were discussing six-cylinders and horsepower as well as torque and bore stroke. It was as if Bruce Lee were an artist who could not be bothered with mechanical issues.

Suddenly Wok Sam reached out and poked Lee's chest. 'Ping tells me you desire a Silver Hawk.'

Lee answered by saying, 'Ping has told me that I *want* a Silver Hawk.'

'Come over here. Look at this car.'

The car was branded on the trunk with raised chrome stating, *Silver Hawk*. The car was sleek. It looked like a miniature Cadillac. A strip of chrome circled the car midway at the doors. Above the chrome, the car was white. Below, it was blue.

'Look at that empennage,' Wok Sam said in English.

'What is *empennage*?' Lee asked.

'Caudal fins,' Wok Sam answered.

Lee almost shrugged, but instead just stayed quiet.

'Caudal fins,' Wok Sam repeated. 'Tail fins. This car has beautiful tail fins—not gaudy and obstreperous like a Caddy.' Then Wok Sam spoke to Lee in a tone of voice that suggested Wok Sam was cutting off an objection from Lee before he could raise it. 'Caudal fins serve a purpose. They stabilize the car against wind. That's why the car is named Silver Hawk.'

'I thought the fins of the car were designed like a shark's.'

Wok Sam's mouth frowned. 'Don't you know anything about evolution? Birds evolved from fish. This car is both bird and fish. The tail end is like a shark's and on the opposite end of a shark are his teeth—'

'You're speaking of a shark, not a car,' Bruce Lee said.

'Yes.'

'I just needed clarification.'

'And when the shark bites, the waves become scarlet billows, but as the song goes—when Mack the Knife uses his switchblade there is never a trace of blood.' Wok Sam waved his right arm, saying, 'This is the car Mack the Knife would drive.' He paused to let Bruce Lee take that in, then said, 'Everything in life is somewhere else, and you get there in a car and this car—Mack the Knife's car—is a car that all the traffic will respect.' Then Wok Sam moved closer to the center of the car. 'Come here. Come here. Look at that dashboard. Look at the seating space. There is room for you to take Jenny Diver and Polly Peachum and Lucy Brown for what you young people call a *spin*.'

Bruce Lee's first impulse was to laugh as if he actually understood what Wok Sam was talking about. He followed his second impulse, which was to say, 'You mean to say the Silver Hawk is a car to fornicate with round-eyes in?'

'What's wrong with being round?' Wok Sam retorted. 'Look at that steering wheel. It's round. The tires are round as well. There's nothing wrong with that which is round.' He said that and then shot out his arms to yank off his sunglasses, revealing a pair of eyes that bulged completely out of his eyelids. His eyes were indeed round, but he was an Asian. Was this affliction some kind of disease? Then Lee realized the man's eyes were not moving. They observed nothing. Wok Sam was blind. Wok Sam returned his sunglasses to his nose. 'For you, Bruce Lee, you can take Sukey Tawdry on a drive in this car.'

Finally, Lee laughed. Buying a car from a blind man was splendid dharma.

It would be nice if Bruce Lee and Buster Hendrix had met before now, but they had not. Lee was twenty and Hendrix was eighteen. Buster Hendrix's various bands played in Lee's neighborhood, but Bruce Lee had perfected the steps to the Argentine and Uruguayan and American and Finnish style of the tango, thus he had no interest in a reductive dance like the twist. Yet, Bruce Lee was striving to simplify his style of Gung Fu by eliminating decorative and other needless movements. Unfortunately, he never made the connection between a simplified Gung Fu and the simplicity of Chubby Checker's twist.

As for Buster Hendrix, he hung out with a handful of Asian kids, but Hendrix was completely unphysical. It is doubtful that even if he had met Bruce Lee, the two would have had anything to say to each other.

Bruce Lee loved driving his Silver Hawk. Two lunchtime customers at Ruby Chow's were actual Chinese working on the police force. They summoned Lee over to their table.

'We hear that you have a new automobile.'

Bruce Lee did not particularly respect police officers, but he tolerated these two. 'Yes. Want to see it?'

'Yes. Yes.'

The two police officers followed Bruce Lee to the corner of Nash Street just as Lee's Silver Hawk swerved out of its parking spot into the street and peeled away. Bruce Lee sprang into the air as if he could fly and began sprinting after his car up the street. The two cops started running as well, then stopped and looked at each other. They turned and ran to their squad car and drove after Bruce Lee. They pulled along beside the running man and commanded, 'Hop in!'

Lee did. He sat in the back seat. He was a man who had just sprinted several blocks, yet his breathing was casual.

'There it is!' Lee said in a voice that betrayed excitement.

Bruce Lee's Silver Hawk was driving on a bridge above the street. The cop car missed the entrance and wheeled a circle and then raced up the on-ramp. On the elevated highway, the Silver Hawk was eight or nine cars ahead of them. Then a second police car pulled the first car over. The drivers of the second police car were Occidentals, their windows already rolled down. 'This isn't Chinatown,' the one riding shotgun called out to the other car.

Bruce Lee rolled down the back window. 'Someone just stole my car.'

The two white cops talked to each other. Then the one sitting shotgun said, 'All right, then.'

Lee's police car raced back onto the road.

'We've lost 'em,' the cop behind the wheel said. They cruised Japan Town and Snow Land and Sweet Cheeks. Then they spied the Studebaker racing up the hills toward Big Jim Creek.

* * *

The black kid driving the Silver Hawk and sitting beside Buster Hendrix said, 'Let's go get electrified at Big Jim.'

'What's that?' Buster asked.

'The biggest radio transistor in the world.'

A black girl in the back seat said, 'There's so much electricity in the air your teeth start to play the radio.'

Buster shrugged, 'Sure. As long as we can get good stations.'

Next thing they knew a police car was wheeling behind them. Buster found himself dragged out of the car and then handcuffed and pushed facedown on the hood.

'I didn't know the car was stolen,' Buster began whining.

The cops had told Bruce Lee to stay in the police car. He now stared out the window at the four black kids handcuffed around his Silver Hawk. He did not pay any particular attention to the runty kid facedown on the hood. Bruce Lee did not feel anger at any of these kids. He knew the necessity of the young breaking laws. He just wanted his Studebaker back. Bruce Lee, of course, had no idea that he and the black boy named Buster Hendrix were simultaneously punching out a historical moment by honing their individual skills in Gung Fu and Electric Guitar in such a way that their combined efforts were a clarification of what painter Jackson Pollock had said more than ten years earlier:

> 'The New' needs new techniques. The modern painter cannot express this age with the airplane, the atom bomb, the radio, in the old forms of the Renaissance or of any other past culture.

'Liquid, flowing...'—Pollock's swirls, a Hendrix guitar lick, Bruce Lee's Drunken Fist—

Fluid American modernity.

Form out of chaos.

A Gung Fu Asian truism was:

Do not mistake chaos for fluidity.

* * *

As for Buster Hendrix, he spent eight days in juvenile—six kids to a cell, Buster the punk. The youngster was surprised to see the policeman he had called Offisa Pup come to visit him outside the bars of the cell—that is, the cop who arrested him the first time in the Bullet Bird came to Buster's cell.

'So James Marshall Hendrix,' the police 'offisa' said, 'when I do my duty, my duty is did. Transgression. Apprehension. Retribution. Yet, I feel peculiar responsibility for y', I do.'

'You do?'

'I do.'

'Can you get me out?'

'Out?'

'Out of jail.'

'Why?'

'Because I'm innocent.'

'Innocent my eye. You're facing five years in the coop, that is if there's somewhere to send y'. Walla Walla and Presque D' Lam will not take colored boys and neither will Kerosene Acres. The only place to fit you is Coconino and that is crammed with adult colored who will chew you another, son.'

'Another what?'

'Sphincter. Poop chute. Gol-dingit, I detected something earnest about y'character and an earnest character must not be denied. The state will allow you to skip the pokey if you allow your person to be conscripted into the armed forces.'

'You mean the military?'

'Affirmative.'

The young man reflected. 'I want to fly. I want to join that Air Force.'

'The Air Force only takes fodder who have graduated from college.'

'I still don't want to join the Army.'

'Use your noodle. Y'been apprehended one and one times in a car that was snatched. Join the Army's Airborne Division.'

'I'll get to fly planes?'

'Certainly not. But you will get to jump out of them.'

'With a parachute?'

'If you behave yourself, yes.'

There was silence for five minutes.

'Okay, Offisa Pup,' James Marshall Hendrix muttered.

'Whaddya call me?'

'Offi-sir. I called you Offi-sir.'

'You bet you did. And what's with this Buster nonsense?'

'What do you mean?'

'Why does person after person call you Buster?'

'That's my name.'

'Your name, my eye. Did your papa name you Buster?'

'Nope.'

'Your mama?'

'Uh-uh.'

'Who then?'

'It's a nickname.'

'Well, it's a foolish nickname. You join the Army and insist every black soldier and white soldier refer to y'as James Marshall Hendrix.'

'Okay.'

'Okay? Say, Yes, *Officer.*'

'Yes, Offisa.'

'Your dilemma is solved, James Marshall Hendrix. Fancy me packing a mind like this around all these years and never any sign of a headache. How uncanny. S'long, James Marshall Hendrix, s'long.'

Thus, James Marshall Hendrix 'voluntarily' enlisted in the 101st Airborne Division on May 31, 1961, and would never be called Buster again. His stint would be for three years. If he qualified, he would be transferred to the Army Reserve, adding another three years to his obligation. He would be out of the Army in 1967.

As it will turn out, six years from now in 1967, both Bruce Lee and James Marshall Hendrix—now known as Jimi Hendrix—will pass each other on the backlot of a TV studio in Burbank. Hendrix will be there to appear as a guest star on a show about a fake rock group called *The Monkees.* Bruce Lee will be on the set to continue his role as the costar of the television series *The Green Hornet.* Lee plays a masked chauffeur fluent in Oriental martial arts named Kato—a masked chauffeur who drives exclusively for a masked round-eyes millionaire who fights crime in the city by pretending to be a criminal himself named the Green Hornet.

Bruce Lee and Jimi Hendrix will glance at each other and there will occur a mutual glimmer of recognition. Their mouths will open, but neither will say anything and they'll just continue on their separate ways.

Incidentally, Bruce Lee always believed the Gung Fu truism stated previously possessed more truth if stated in reverse:

Do not mistake fluidity for chaos.

* * *

On the last day of May 1961, James Marshall Hendrix arrived in Fort Ord, California. Boot camp. It was named after Edward Otho Cresap Ord, who saw action against the Seminoles and the Confederacy and died eighteen years after the war in Havana of yellow fever.

James Marshall Hendrix at Fort Ord—the young black man weighed 155 pounds and was five feet ten inches tall.

The Army cut off his conk.

James Marshall Hendrix was homesick.

All the grunts at Fort Ord figured they'd be going to Laos. A few cats in the know said Viet-Nam.

★ ★ ★

Idaho. On July 2, a Sunday. The summer thus far: Ernest Hemingway had been hospitalized for high blood pressure. He was convinced he was being followed by the FBI or worse. *The Ed Sullivan Show* was long over when the writer sat on the floor of his Idaho cabin. He didn't feel right in the head. The wooden floor was bubbling like pancake mix on a skillet. There were heads watching him from the ceiling. He pressed the double barrels of his favorite Boss & Co. deep in the palate of his mouth.

Ernest Hemingway pulled the trigger, missing his sixty-second birthday by nineteen days.

Whenever Leslie Fiedler was at a bar or a smoker after this suicide, he had to tell the same story. It always took Fiedler the third or fourth drink for him to tell it. He starts by complaining about middlebrow Jews who feel closer to gentile Jake Barnes than to Hasidic Robert Cohn. In 1961, probably two-thirds of Americans have no idea who Jake Barnes and Robert Cohn are. But absolutely everyone Fiedler talks to knows Barnes and Cohn from *The Sun Also Rises.* Cohn is the obnoxious Jew. Barnes is the damaged goy narrator. Fiedler believed people admired Hemingway for the wrong reasons.

Hemingway himself was not a bull. Hemingway was a steer. (If that doesn't immediately resonate, think of aficionado Jake Barnes's war wound.)

Fiedler then recalled how Hemingway read *TV Guide.* Fiedler recalled how Hemingway and Mary drove Fiedler and Seymour Betsky into town to pick up the car. Hemingway had to go to the bank. He walked up to the glass doors and they would not open. Nobody realized that it was Saturday. (No bank was open on Saturday in 1961.) 'Shit,' Hemingway said.

Fiedler would then stop telling the story by saying this and repeating the word *shit*. He finally got sick of telling this story and would write the encounter out of his system in an essay titled 'An Almost Imaginary Interview: Hemingway in Ketchum.' Fiedler would write down everything that he said about the encounter and how he felt, including this sentence: 'I loved Hemingway for his weakness without ceasing to despise him for his strength.'

* * *

'Hunt? It's Joe. Joe Darwin. Listen to me: You remember Frank Olson... Sure you do. He's the guy who took a brody out of the Hotel Pennsylvania in New York City back in '53... Edgar tested lysergic acid diethylamide on him... I can't spell it. *Lysergic acid diethylamide* is un-spell-able... What's it do? Listen to me—lysergic acid diethylamide makes you swan dive from the window of your thirteenth-floor hotel room... Of course not! Edgar didn't personally shove it down Olson's throat. Edgar just saw to it that a few years later your pal at MIT was slipped a little lysergic acid diethylamide and then jumped in front of a truck... Calm down! I'm being facetious. Listen to me, guess who was given lysergic acid diethylamide last week?... Bingo! Papa used a shotgun because there is nothing to jump off of or in front of in Potatoland.'

* * *

Fort Ord, California. On July 14, 1961, James Marshall Hendrix scored the lowest points in marksmanship among thirty-six soldiers in his platoon. In the summer of 1961, Private First Class James Marshall Hendrix was still a teenager and was not even remotely a warrior, let alone even a foot soldier. You could never imagine Private First Class James Marshall Hendrix chillin' with Achilles. If the former had been at Troy, the first chance he got he would have stolen a rowboat or a raft and tried to sail back home to Macedonia. Yet, remember that 1961 is the cusp of the American Assumption of Military Obligation. Since the Japs bombed Pearl Harbor, every young man had to assume that he would be drafted. The U.S.A. had been a military culture for twenty years. To cope, Private First

Class James Marshall Hendrix kept a small box of crayons on his person and drew pictures of flying saucers whenever he could.

★ ★ ★

Despite everything, Cold War warrior Howard Hunt's three-night/two-day novel spun out of his typewriter as fast as he could stick the paper in the roller. He wrote several Steve Bentley thrillers—one with the self-promoting title of *Steve Bentley's Calypso Caper*—again reflecting his inspiration of Spanish women. Another Bentley was called *Angel Eyes* and concerned the search for a secret tape recording that endangers a politician's career. Conceivably Richard Nixon's lifelong secretary, Rose Mary Woods, could have picked that one up in an airport to read on the plane. Under the pen name Gordon Davis, Hunt wrote *House Dick* about six-foot, hundred-and-eighty-four-pound Pete Novak, house detective for the Hotel Tilden in Washington, D.C.

★ ★ ★

On Halloween, James Marshall Hendrix was sent to Fort Campbell, Kentucky, located on the Tennessee and Kentucky border, sixty miles south by southeast of Nashville. Fort Campbell was more than one hundred thousand acres of runways and barracks as well as the top-secret location of an extensive underground nuclear weapons storage and modification facility. There at Fort Campbell, James Marshall Hendrix jumped out of a tower that was thirty-four feet high. He jumped with a parachute. James Marshall Hendrix's first time ever as passenger in an airplane was also the time he had to jump out of one. He sat scrunched there with twenty-five other first-time jumpers. They all looked a little stricken. But not Hendrix. A heavy drone consumed the sonic space in the airplane. A motorized drone. The sound of massive propellers beating the air. Hendrix was entranced by this sound. It was one of the sounds he had been searching for with his guitar. Hendrix did not want to jump when it was his turn. Again, not because he was scared, but because of the drone. His squad leader pushed him out of the airplane and Hendrix was airborne through the silence of air, the silence of slicing through the sky toward the crowd on the ground. It never dawned on Hendrix to open his parachute so it automatically opened on its own accord. (Novice jumpers all had timers in their chutes.) Although Hendrix was hearing true silence, in his sonic imagination he was replaying the drone of the plane.

★ ★ ★

Mary Meyer first fucked Jack Kennedy on January 22, 1962.

No one documented or remembers what form of birth control was used.

Several years earlier, birth-control pills were tested on psychotic white women and poor Latino women in Puerto Rico, Haiti, and Mexico. (Obviously Mary Meyer was not a woman in any of those categories.) At the beginning of 1962, oral contraception was only legal for married women. Searle's norethynodrel initially outsold Syntex's norethisterone; however, by the time of Altamont in 1969 (the so-called '60s' end), norethynodrel was found to cause thrombosis (blood clots) and its popularity plummeted.

★ ★ ★

In early February 1962, Drew Pearson's column 'Washington Merry-Go-Round' reported on a Twist Party at the White House. 'The big story social Washington has been buzzing about has not been [the capture of] U-2 pilot Powers, or astronaut Colonel Glenn [orbiting the earth], or the proposed summit meeting [with Khrushchev], but rather who leaked the news about the big White House Twist Party when even the Secretary of Defense [Robert McNamara]—to the amazement of his generals—twisted and when the president himself danced until 4:30 [a.m.].'

Pearson informed his readers that because the Twist Party took place on a Friday night, fish was served.* (This unidentified fish was 'poached in a creamy sauce of white wine.') Pearson also mentioned that Jackie Kennedy was trying to poach the chef at the French embassy for the White House. Pearson told that the female guests were wearing such 'a

* This is and will be a Catholic dietary requirement until Pope Paul VI's *Paenitemini* in 1966.

dazzling array of pink and cream-colored beauty, it [made] you think of having too much ice cream.' Three musical groups performed—the Air Force Singers, Lester Lanin's Strollers, and an unnamed 'U.S. Marine combo.' The latter was surely the group that performed twists for the ice-cream-cone guests. George Plimpton was there—without Hemingway, of course—or Norman Mailer, for that matter. Jackie's brother-in-law was present, Prince Radziwill, along with Jackie's sister, Princess Radziwill. In 1962, the Radziwills were the epitome of the Jet Set, a now antiquated term describing the languid European rich coming to and fro. The term *Jet Set* had been coined by a columnist who wrote under the pen name Cholly Knickerbocker, aka Igor Cassini. His brother Oleg was now twisting at the White House Twist Party. He was the first lady's personal fashion designer. According to one fashion columnist, Oleg possessed 'luxuriant silver-gray hair, a neatly clipped moustache, and the look of a handsome ladies' man.' For two years, this 'wise cracking bon vivant' had been pushing a line of garb called the American Look. Last year, after the first lady had been severely criticized for wearing nothing but European couture, the Eurocentric Jacqueline Kennedy made a public relations move and dressed often in Oleg's American Look line of fashion. Oleg had been born in France, but now loved lunches consisting of a hamburger with a cup of tea. He described his American Look dresses and smocks as 'geared to the American woman's way of life. They are functional, easy to get in and out of, since no woman today has the time to fuss with difficult clothes or a staff of servants to help them.' Most of the women at the White House Twist Party wore Oleg's ice-cream-colored sheaths, but his fashion line in Washington was renamed the 'Jackie Kennedy Look.' Imagine these Washington women as they twist the night away to such songs as 'Let's Twist Again' and 'Percolator Twist' and the Isley Brothers' original version of 'Twist and Shout,' and of course, this one playing over and over, 'Twistin' U.S.A.'

When the twist was first mentioned at the beginning of this book—Richard Nixon twisting with Joan Crawford—the specifics of its choreography were not described. In a nutshell, to *do the twist,* a dancer would duplicate the imaginary action of stubbing out a cigarette with the toe of their shoe while drying off their behind with an imaginary beach towel. In the late '60s, paparazzi photographs of Jacqueline Kennedy sunbathing nude will reveal that the first lady had a modest postérieur. When she twisted in 1962, if she pretended to stub out a cigarette with her toe, it was an L&M.

If cigarettes are sublime as modern author Richard Klein contends, the ridiculous (which always follows the sublime) comes by postulating that if the cartoon character Fred Flintstone was doing the twist he would have stubbed out a Winston with his bare toes (cavemen didn't wear shoes). Mr. Flintstone is mentioned now because as incredible as it may seem to you, during the Kennedy era, Winston cigarettes ran a cartoon television commercial where Fred Flintstone walked with great enthusiasm into a Stone Age smoke shop and sang about the joy of Winstons with the proprietor.

Winston tastes good;
Like a cigarette should...

* * *

This book's moral points for the last time to the White House Twist Party, to the secretary of defense, Robert McNamara, now forty-five, stubbing out a cigarette while wiggling his rump. Watch as McNamara twists with the boss's wife, the first lady. McNamara is a handsome middle-aged man. McNamara's longish banker's haircut still remains buttered straight back with a prominent part starting over his left eye.

This 'twisting' makes McNamara happy. It makes him aware of his good fortune. He loves his position in the Kennedy administration. He loves what Kennedy calls the New Frontier. McNamara could never have done this twist at a Ford Motor Company party in Detroit.

The last thing on McNamara's mind right now is Viet-Nam. Only fifty-two American advisers will die there this year. What is on Robert McNamara's mind are the pro and con reasons to destroy the world with nuclear weapons in a war with the U.S.S.R.

McNamara continues to love his wife and love his kids, but McNamara is seldom home. He lets his wife, Margy, steer the domestic ship. Three or four nights a week, McNamara sleeps on a cot in the secretary of defense's office at the Pentagon, an office on the third floor, an office located in what is called the E-Ring, the 'Power Corridor' overlooking the Potomac. See old sleepyhead McNamara prone with his buttered head upon a pillow, lying docile below his desk where a globe sits, a globe that is turned as are all the other globes in generals' offices with the Arctic Circle shifted downward as if it was located at the equator. Everyone in the Pentagon considers the strategic possibilities of the Arctic Circle because when the time comes to let the Minuteman missiles rip, the most direct air path to Moscow is up and over the North Pole. This is nicknamed the Santa Claus Route.

McNamara so seldom sleeps at home that he has begun having dreams where the president of the United Sates visits the McNamara household in Georgetown and as McNamara presents his children to the president, he forgets their names.

* * *

On March 24, President Kennedy was in Palm Desert, California, staying at Bing Crosby's mansion. The president was traveling solo. No Jacqueline. No kids. The president had originally planned to stay at Frank Sinatra's place, but canceled at the last minute. The president's brother-in-law Peter called Sinatra to say the president was rejecting Sinatra's hospitality because of rumors of the singer's connection to 'Organized Crime.' When this phone call came, Sinatra's workers had already finished constructing a concrete landing pad for Kennedy's presidential helicopter as well as other security structures as per the Secret Service's request. Sinatra was so enraged at the president's snub that the singer stripped and took a sledgehammer and began smashing up the helicopter landing pad in his backyard.

Bing Crosby was not a volatile man in the same manner as Sinatra. Crosby and President Kennedy spend a pleasant evening together in Crosby's living room, the president listening attentively to Crosby's show-biz stories about Jerry Lewis. Crosby then leaves his own house and drives west to stay in his mansion in Hollywood. At some point in that sojourn, unbeknownst to Crosby, his car passes a Los Angeles taxicab heading east that carries a sole passenger, Marilyn Monroe. The latter, of course, also has no idea that her cab has passed Crosby. Once the cab arrives in Palm

Desert, she is only dimly aware that she is about to fuck President Kennedy for the first time in a location provided by Bing Crosby.

Note that Peter's line to Frank Sinatra about 'Organized Crime' was a lie in terms of being a motive for the president to renege on Sinatra's hospitality. Bobby had pointed out to his older brother that Frank Sinatra would never vacate his own house so the president of the United States could fornicate with Marilyn Monroe. The sober Kennedy biographer Michael O'Brien will claim that this meeting on March 24, 1962, will be the only time President Kennedy and Marilyn Monroe will actually 'sleep together' in biblical fashion.

* * *

Washington, D.C. Howard Hunt began writing White Propaganda for a respectable series of travel guides that unbeknownst to the public were published by the CIA. Hunt's pseudonymous 'other,' Robert Dietrich, had yet another Steve Bentley D.C. potboiler, *Curtains for a Lover,* published as well. This was not a thriller concerning interior decorating. *Curtains* was and is slang for 'death.' The paperback contained passages crammed with sour visions of contemporary Washington, D.C.:

> It was a part of town . . . where Cocaine and Horse are peddled in the shadows; where muggers lurk in dark alleys . . . And against all that one lone colored policeman for every five city blocks. One reason why Washington has, per capita, more rape, more crimes of violence, more liquor, more perversion and more crooked politicians than any other city in the country. Our fair city, I thought, and grimaced.

* * *

In 1962, the IRS and the SSA and the CIA did not have computer technology. There were only ten thousand computers in the United States. Even with those limitations, every American had at least one permanent file kept on them by at least one government agency. After James Marshall Hendrix's dad or his fiancée mailed the serviceman at Fort

Campbell his red Danelectro Silvertone aka Betty Jean, Sergeant First Class Louis Hoekstra added this text to James Marshall Hendrix's permanent record:

> Pvt Hendrix plays a musical instrument during his off-duty hours, or so he says. This is one of his faults, because his mind apparently cannot function while performing duties and thinking about his guitar.

One afternoon in the barracks, James Marshall Hendrix was noodling on Betty Jean when another black private, twenty-year-old Otis Pilgrim (not his real name), walked by the open window and heard guitar lines that seemed a combination of Beethoven and John Lee Hooker. Pilgrim knew about Beethoven. He'd been classically trained and could play the piano, the violin, the trumpet, and the trombone. Pilgrim's heart was now exclusively into the electric bass guitar.

Pilgrim went into Hendrix's barracks and introduced himself. They spoke in code to each other—Albert-King-Slim-Harpo-Jimmy-Reed. Music was (and still is) the secret communication of youth. In 1962, a kid from Florida could be in a bus station in Seattle sitting next to a kid from Albuquerque, and if they dug the same music or books or movies, they achieved instant simpatico.

People who did not speak their lingo were Squares.

Sergeant First Class Louis Hoekstra wrote this on James Marshall Hendrix's permanent record:

> At times Hendrix isn't even able to carry on an intelligent conversation, paying little attention to having been spoken to. At one point, it was thought perhaps Hendrix was taking dope and was sent to be examined by a medical officer with negative results.

★ ★ ★

Jimi Hendrix and Otis Pilgrim became fast friends. They formed a five-piece band with other soldiers called the Kasuals. They played covers of King Curtis and Booker T. & the MG's on weekends at nearby Negro clubs like the Pink Poodle. James Marshall Hendrix began singing. He did not like his voice, but he was the only one in the group who could sing more or less in key.

Hendrix also kept pawning his electric guitar for cash. Every three weekends, he would show up at the Pink Poodle without Betty Jean as she was still in hock.

Staff Sergeant James C. Spears added this note to Private Hendrix's permanent file:

> Pvt Hendrix fails to pay just debts. He owes a laundry bill of approximately $80.00 and has made no effort whatsover to pay it. When Pvt Hendrix was questioned by the 1st Sgt and myself concerning this matter, he said that he had given the money to a buddy in the infantry who intended to pay this debt for him. It was later proven he had lied about this. To this date the laundry bill is still delinquent.

★ ★ ★

Roman architect Luigi Moretti flew to Washington, D.C., to defend his design of Watergate Towne at a committee meeting of the Federal Commission of Fine Arts. Imagine if private eye Steve Bentley had manifested from the pages of Howard Hunt/Robert Dietrich and had accompanied the Italian architect to that meeting—

> I walked with my newfound Roman pal, Luigi Moretti, to the Federal Commission of Fine Arts on F Street NW, seven long blocks east of the White House. This was a high-class federal neighborhood of federal granite and federal pillars. This Commission has given Luigi and the Società Generale Immobiliare nothing but grief since they submitted the design of Watergate Towne—or as the *Washington Post* calls it, 'Antipasto on the Potomac.' I'd never seen Luigi so steamed as he was when he read that slur.
>
> 'I try to do magnificence with Foggy Bottom,' Luigi ranted in broken English. 'The Commission shovels me nothing but grief. And what is Foggy Bottom to preserve? I go and see junk. Piles of rotten tires. No boats. No wharfs. Just bums in the bushes.'
>
> I could propel Luigi an earful about Foggy Bottom, but that would

be like pouring gasoline into a volcano. Those in the know referred to Foggy Bottom as *Little Appalachia* on account of all the hillbilly folk who lived in wooden crates scattered below the dead saplings, folks who made their bucks peddling reefer to the deaf college-age pseudo-beatniks who attended Croesus Prototokos University for the Deaf. The only other establishments in Foggy Boom were hamburger hideaways and fleabags where nervous out-of-towners took their tomatoes and paid for rooms by the quarter hour. (Out-of-towners screwed quickly, I guess.)

Luigi and I trudged into the National Building Museum, and were directed to an antechamber where Luigi was instructed to stand at a podium before the elevated benches of the Federal Commission of Fine Arts officials. There were eleven of them—all fat and elderly with white hair. As they poked questions at Luigi, the ones with men's voices turned out to be women and vice versa for the codgers.

'Signor Moretti, Watergate Towne's so-called curve-linear design is at variance with most commercial architecture in Washington, D.C.'

'Curvilinear,' Luigi Moretti said.

'What's that? Speak up!'

'Curvilinear.'

'That's what I said.'

'You said curve linear. The architectural term is *curvilinear.*'

'You say poe-tay-toe and I say tomato, Signor Moretti. Circular architecture doesn't play in Washington, D.C.'

'Are you telling me, ma'am, that Washington, D.C., is a capital of squares?'

'Are you making a joke at Mrs. Linkwater's expense, Mr. Moretti?'

'No, Your Honor. At my own expense, I am sure.'

'Let me talk, Ed. Look Moretti—*Mr.* Moretti—your plans for Watergate Towne have no gardens. No playgrounds. No windows until the top, sixteenth floor. This is an imposing building. It is designed like an armory.'

'Let me add another point—Signor Moretti, the tower will obscure views of the Washington Monument and the Lincoln Memorial.'

'Also, Mr. Moretti, I think that—'

'Can I speak?'

'What's that, Mr. Moretti?'

'Can I speak to answer some of the committee's points?'

'Of course, Signor Moretti. Answer away.'

'You complain about no windows until the top floor. The Washington Monument has no windows until the top floor.'

'But the Washington Monument is in the tradition of an obelisk.'

'Yes! Right! It *is* an obelisk. The obelisk was designed during the Twelfth Dynasty in 1962 B.C. during the reign of—'

'What's that you say, Mr. Moretti—1962? This year? Don't be ridiculous, Mr. Moretti. Why, Cleopatra had an obelisk in her backyard thousands of years ago.'

'I said 1962 *Bee Cee.* Before Christ—'

'Oh. Before Christ.'

'Can I continue?'

'Yes, Signor Moretti.'

'Obelisks were built by the pharaohs of Egypt—although the word *obelisk* is a Greek term first used by Herodotus.'

'Excuse me. And Herodotus was Greek?'

'He was an ancient Greek. And democracy as you know was invented by the Greeks, not the Egyptians.'

'What's your point, Moretti?'

'That you Americans keep the body of the father of your country, George Washington, under an Egyptian obelisk and the body of President Abraham Lincoln inside a massive statue of himself as if he were Ramesses the Second. Is Washington, D.C., a modern city of the twentieth century or—'

'Just a minute. You're getting out of hand, Signor Moretti—'

'I want to hear this, Tim. *Or what,* Mr. Moretti? Finish your sentence— *Or what*?'

'Is Washington, D.C., a modern city or a city of slaves and pharaohs?'

* * *

Arthur Miller opened the newest issue of *Life* and saw a color photograph of his ex-wife swimming nude in a scene from her new movie. It depressed him. Everything always came down to Marilyn Monroe getting naked. He repeated his tired tirade to himself: 'Marilyn is proof that sexuality and seriousness cannot coexist in America's psyche. Sex and seriousness are mutually rejecting opposites. In the end, Marilyn has to swim naked in a pool in order to make a picture.'

He recalled a conversation that he had with somebody or other. It was a woman. She made a joke of a newspaper interview where Marilyn Monroe said she read Dostoevski. Oh. Now Miller remembered. It was with Diana Trilling. 'America refuses to believe that any one with Marilyn Monroe's sexual powers has a need to read Dostoevski. America believes if you have the sexual advantages of a Marilyn Monroe, why on earth wouldn't she spend her day making love? Why would she waste a moment on Dostoevski?'

A week later, Arthur Miller heard the movie his ex-wife was making was canceled. Someone showed Miller an ad posted in *Variety* 'thanking' Marilyn for having cost the film crew their jobs in a rotten economy.

* * *

Fort Campbell, Kentucky. Jimi Hendrix constantly tried to sneak off work detail. Staff Sergeant James C. Spears added these comments to Private Hendrix's permanent record:

> Approximately 1 month ago, five other men were on detail in the billets with Pvt Hendrix. When he was found to be missing, SP4 Mattox and Pvt Stroble began to look for him and later found him in the latrine masturbating.

Another time, Private Hendrix wandered off with his electric guitar. He did not have an amp, he just wanted to noodle on the strings. Hendrix got lost in the woods—easy to do as Fort Campbell was one hundred thousand acres. Hendrix came to the end of the trees and found himself on the edge of a slight cliff. A huge field spread below him—little trees sprouting up between discarded military vehicles—jeeps, trucks, whatnot.

Hendrix started noodling on his guitar and then it happened. The ground burst upward in one massive bubble of green. The earth was convulsing maybe twenty feet into the air before returning to the level of its previous topography while the trees continued upward, shooting out of the skin of the ground with their roots intact. They flew eye level with Hendrix before crashing back to the ground.

This was the first time in his life that Hendrix had been below the Mason-Dixon Line. He assumed this was a natural phenomenon down south, some kind of Dixie earthquake. Hendrix picked his guitar up and continued noodling.

Later, the guitarist strolled back to the barracks to find an uproar of confusion. Every soldier who was outside was being screamed at by a sergeant to return to their barracks. Hendrix strolled into his and got chewed out by his platoon leader for having disappeared. Hendrix took it and then strolled to his bunk to continue noodling his guitar. While he played, his outer ear picked up on the chatter swirling around him.

Apparently, an H-bomb had accidentally gone off underground in a storage facility.

The next day, people in weird radioactive suits came. All the soldiers had to strip to their skivvies so one of the spacemen could run a Geiger counter along each soldier's body. The Geiger counter made a noise when the spaceman passed it over Hendrix. The spaceman conversed with another spaceman. Then they talked to their commander. Then they ignored Hendrix and went to another soldier in his skivvies. Apparently, the camp was all clear for signs of radioactivity. Hendrix forgot about the Geiger counter.

'Hey, Hendrix,' his platoon leader said the next day. 'So you made the Geiger counter go haywire.'

'What do you mean?'

'I mean you weren't radioactive, but you made the thing register things that it wasn't built to register.'

'What's that mean exactly?'

'You are one strange coon.'

* * *

New York City. Phil Ochs, a twenty-one-year-old folk singer on Bleecker Street, was working on a new song. He was half singing, half talking these words, 'Sailing over to Viet-Nam, southeast Asian Birmingham . . .'

He liked the off-rhyme of *Viet-Nam* to *Birmingham*. He liked tying Viet-Nam to the worst racist city in the South. 'Training a million Vietnamese to fight for the wrong government and the American way . . .'

Yes we burned out the jungles far and wide
Made sure those red apes had no place left to hide

* * *

Saigon. Brother Nhu spent most of his time filtering money out of the country. He was pleased that his wife acted as the first lady of the country. In May, she was the hostess of a public unveiling of a statue of the two legendary Trung sisters—they being the legendary Vietnamese sisters who led an attack against the invading Han Dynasty troops. The statue was seventy-five feet high. Those in the audience with opera glasses could see that each sister had the same face even though the Trungs had not been twins. Each Trung sister had the face of Madame Nhu.

The same time as the Trung sisters statue was unveiled, Madame Nhu started the Women's Solidarity Movement. This was Madame Nhu's paramilitary organization—Catholic Vietnamese women with guns.

* * *

Fort Campbell, Kentucky. In May 1962, Otis Pilgrim clued James Hendrix in to a music contest with a thousand-dollar prize up at George's Bar in Indianapolis. The two drove Otis's '55 Plymouth to get there. Otis's '55 Plymouth could not drive in reverse, but the trip to Indianapolis was a straight-ahead five-hour trip solid north across the edge of Kentucky into the center of the Hoosier State. The two planned on finding a drummer and a singer in Indianapolis and then splitting the prize money with the two.

Pilgrim and Hendrix spent Friday night in a cheap hotel. They ran out of money. They lived in the car. Someone connected them with a band called the Presidents. Otis convinced the Presidents to be his and Hendrix's backup band. The Presidents were skeptical at first until they heard Hendrix play. The guitarist, Baby Boo Young, recognized Hendrix as an artist. The song they played at George's Bar was a hit for the Shirelles, 'Soldier Boy.'

Soldier boy
Oh, my little soldier boy
I'll be true to you

It was decided that Hendrix would sing it. But the gender specificness bugged him, so he sang the more genderless-specific lyrics to Elvis Presley's 'Soldier Boy':

> Soldier boy why feel blue
> Don't you believe that she will be true?

Hendrix sang the lyrics of Presley's song to the melody of the one that the Shirelles sang. As Hendrix sang and played, this young guitarist's fingers were so long that he could bend the strings in such a way that listeners had the illusion they were hearing both Soldier Boys simultaneously.

It was brilliantly weird.

Of course, Indianapolis being Indianapolis, the threshold of normalcy, Otis and Hendrix did not win the contest, but Hendrix made an important musical connection with Baby Boo Young.

* * *

Fort Campbell, Kentucky. Private James Marshall Hendrix's permanent record finally caught up with him:

> I recommend without hesitancy that Hendrix be eliminated from the service under the provisions of AR 635-208 as expeditiously as possible.

On May 31, 1962, Private First Class Hendrix had a complete medical exam and was discharged from the United States Army. He planned to head back to Seattle with the four hundred dollars he had in his pocket. When his bus reached Clarksville, Tennessee, Hendrix got off the bus and walked into a black jazz club to wet his whistle. It was crowded inside. His heart expanded. He never knew that his heart could be so big. He bought drinks for everyone. Four hours later, his four hundred dollars was gone.

He made it back to Fort Campbell. He snuck into the Army base through a gap in the back fence. He found Betty Jean under a bunk in an empty barracks.

He had felt no shame when he sold her.

Hendrix felt no guilt now, stealing her from the soldier who bought her with legal tender.

* * *

'Eduardo' Hunt will teach his son Saint John the difference between the bossa nova and the mambo, but like most teenagers of the time, Saint John will love the blues. In the early 1960s, white boys from Britain exposed white teenagers on both sides of the Atlantic to this African-American musical idiom. Saint John in particular will like the frog-voiced Chester Arthur Burnett, aka Howlin' Wolf, who had been born in 1910 in Mississippi. Shortly after Saint John's father's Watergate night, Howlin' Wolf will write a song, 'Watergate Blues':

> Guard walked his beat. Checking all the doors. Found a little bit of tape. Now the whole world know.

Frank Wills, an African-American, is the security guard in the song. He noticed the first taping of the basement door right away. He opened the door and looked around and stripped the tape off the lock. Wills walked to the security office to call his superiors. (Remember, he did not have a cell phone—no one in 1972 did.) Wills was told to go check the stairwell and every hallway. On his way back to the garage, Wills bumped into a woman he knew. It was lunch hour for the graveyard shift. The two went to the Howard Johnson's twenty-four-hour restaurant and got takeout. While Frank was gone, the 'Plumbers' all entered the garage. They saw the tape was missing. Etc. Etc. Meanwhile, Frank and the young woman were having hamburgers and milk shakes. If Frank had been wearing a calendar watch, the 16 would have changed to 17—it was after midnight. Frank's girl went back to work. Frank went to the garage-level door. He saw the new piece of tape on the door. He called the police this time.

> Don't do us wrong; if you do, make no mistake, cuz we'll blow the whistle on you just like we did at Watergate.

* * *

William Burroughs finally had *Naked Lunch,* his second novel, published by Grove Press. At the International Writers Conference in Edinburgh, Mary McCarthy was quoted as saying that William Burroughs's *Naked Lunch* was one of the 'outstanding novels of the age.' What she actually said was that it was 'one of the interesting novels she had read that year that was not like anyone else's.' She never said that it was one of the outstanding novels of the year, let alone of the age. Elizabeth Hardwick did not want to write an essay saying *Naked Lunch* was not a masterpiece because that would be unfair to Burroughs. But she gave it a try. She began her essay by attempting to summarize the plot. She was frank that the book's most recurring images either involved feces or the auto ejaculations of men who are hanged. 'Yet what saves *The Naked Lunch* is [its] humor. Burroughs's humor is peculiarly American, at once broad and sly.' Hardwick compared *Naked Lunch* to nineteenth-century American vaudeville. Without mentioning Officer Pup, she cited the current hipster stance that the police are the enemy.

Leslie Fiedler, on the other hand, hated *Naked Lunch*. He called Burroughs an extraordinarily naive man, naive artistically. Fiedler insulted him for 'just now discovering Wilhelm Reich.' Fiedler did not italicize the *now,* but he should have to emphasize his *hipper than thou* stance. Burroughs's constant image of 'the meaningless orgasm of the hanged man' is not an 'authentic cosmic vision of the end of man, total death.' Burroughs possesses a 'stupidity monumental enough to be called holy.' Burroughs sees the 'disaffiliated bourgeois young [readers] can believe that their own affectless lives, their endless flirtation with failure... are neither specific and particular disasters... but symptoms of more general cosmic catastrophe.' Fiedler ends his piece by saying William Burroughs has transformed his humanity to become an alien creature. *Naked Lunch* is a traditional genre:

Naked Lunch is science fiction.

* * *

The French auteur du cinéma, Jean-Luc Godard, was in the U.S.A. that spring shooting footage for an as-yet-unnamed documentary about America. Godard traveled solo. He loaded his 16mm Beaulieu camera himself with B&W film and shot away. Godard was in California and then in New York City on May 19 when President Kennedy publicly celebrated his birthday at Madison Square Garden. Godard had no idea what his own cinematic intentions were. The footage he shot was blurry and underlit and as a work of *cinéma vérité* (truthful cinema), it was more *vérité* than it was *cinéma*.

Godard had captured shots in California of Frank Sinatra in an armless T-shirt swinging a sledgehammer at what looks like a driveway in the desert. A voice-over—an American speaking—says, 'That's the pad Sinatra built for Kennedy to land his helicopter on. Then Peter phoned to say that his brother-in-law, the president, was going to stay with Bing Crosby instead. Both of the brothers are worried about bad publicity over Sinatra's alleged mob connections. Frank screamed, *Crosby's a Republican, you putz!* and hung up and then came out here with his sledgehammer.' A male voice with a French accent asks, 'Can you tell me where we are?'

'You don't know where you are, for christsake?'

'It's for the camera.'

'Oh. We're in Palm Springs. [Pause.] California. In California.'

Jump cut. Stunted Joshua trees. Next, the Empire State Building. Next, a big hospital room. We see an old man in a hospital 'lounging suit' sitting in a wheelchair. President Kennedy is in the room. (The man in the wheelchair is never identified, but it is Kennedy's seventy-three-year-old father, Joe, recovering from a stroke.) On the soundtrack:

'It's not your birthday. Your birthday isn't for ten days.'

'Ten days, Dad. It's an early birthday party.'

'How old are you?'

'I'll be forty-five years old, Dad. Forty five.'

'No. No, no, no. How old are you *now?*'

'I'm forty-four, Dad.'

'That's how old I thought you were.'

(The soundtrack was doctored. Joe was so discombobulated by his stroke that he could not speak save for shouting the word *no*.)

The camera pulls back to reveal four other old men in wheelchairs and a young male paraplegic in a cot. Kennedy chats with all of them, but the sound is too muffled to make out what anyone is saying, although Kennedy's Cape Cod accent is discernible.

Now a silent shot of the Seagram Building on Park Avenue and 52nd. The Four Seasons Restaurant swamps the ground floor. The camera spins. A limousine pulls up. President Kennedy jumps out. A crowd on the other side of the street is standing behind police sawhorses. The film is silent. Kennedy runs across the street and starts shaking hands. Godard (presumably) runs with his camera across the street trailing the president. The sound suddenly kicks in. Kennedy stands with a young white man who asks, 'How is your back, Mr. President?'

'It's fine,' President Kennedy says. 'Thanks for asking.'

Inside the Four Seasons—the sights and sounds of people eating crabmeat from seashells instead of plates. President Kennedy goes from table to table glad-handing. Another long shot of the now empty and silent restaurant as President Kennedy sits by himself at a corner table eating crab from *his* seashell.

Now we're outside Madison Square Garden. Streetlights are lit. The sound of chanting. Traffic. A group of black protesters holding signs:

NEW YORK CONGRESS OF RACIAL EQUALITY ASKS PRESIDENT KENNEDY TO HONOR HIS PLEDGE TO END HOUSING DISCRIMINATION.

Inside Madison Square Garden. The dull roar of the crowd. An Italian woman talking. A man's voice saying, 'It can hold twenty thousand people. Boxers fight here. This is where the circus comes to town.' The Italian woman speaks. She keeps using the word *acustica*.

Acoustics.

A shot of the opera singer Maria Callas saying a single word with emphasis, '*Acustica!*'

Shots of people sitting. Clouds of cigarette smoke. Cigar smoke. A whole sling of talking. 'Where's Jackie?' *I can't believe Jackie's not here.* 'Sinatra was 'sposed to sing, but word is he's pissed at Kennedy.' *'Bout what?* 'Frank doesn't need a reason to get pissed.' *Last week's plunge was the greatest since June 1950?* 'I bet it was U.S. Steel getting back at Kennedy for screwing with 'em.'

Silent shots of Ella Fitzgerald climbing out of the back seat of a dark Cadillac and being led through the crowd outside Madison Square Garden.

Remember all this footage is in black-and-white.

Now, a backstage shot of a disheveled and harried man smoking a cigarette talking to Maria Callas. 'So after the "Star Spangled Banner," there'll be Jack Benny and Ella Fitzgerald and some dancers. And then Jimmy Durante.' Maria Callas's expression is blank. 'Then some soldiers and Peggy Lee and Bobby Darin.' He pauses. 'And then you.'

It is apparent that Maria Callas does not know who any of these people are.

Now, a silent profile shot of Jimmy Durante dancing while holding a beat-up fedora like a giant seashell to his ear. A jump cut to Maria Callas on the stage. She's wearing a dark chiffon gown, her hair in a bouffant. The sound kicks in. Callas is singing the 'Seguidilla' from *Carmen*. To speak frankly, the 'Seguidilla' is Carmen's 'let's fuck' invitation to Don José near the end of the first act. There is no way to tell whether the poverty of the sound is due to the *acustica* of Madison Square Garden or Godard's cheap equipment.

A shot of the front row. A black hipster voice saying, 'Yeah, man. Those cats paid one thousand dollars for those seats.'

Repeated shots of twelve thousand people in the audience giving Maria Callas a standing ovation. Callas walks offstage and the handheld camera follows. Coming toward Callas is Marilyn Monroe walking in tiny steps like a geisha. Monroe is wearing a white mink coat. The camera isn't an X-ray, but know ahead of time that beneath Monroe's mink is a skintight nude-colored dress that is as thick as a coat of Dutch Boy paint.

Maria Callas is thirty-eight years old and Marilyn Monroe is thirty-five.

The two women consider each other. The film goes silent as the footage now moves in excruciating slow motion, the camera moving from Monroe's face—she looks like a woman experiencing a psychedelic hallucination—then sliding between the two. Next, the camera spins back to catch Callas's face looking at Monroe—the opera diva's expression appearing to oscillate at a thousand vibrations per second between a stare of predatory hate and astonishing terror.

The two women finally pass each other.

Jump cut. Callas in her dressing room. On the soundtrack, a distant crowd screaming and singing 'Happy Birthday.'

Jump cut. Camera angle toward the stage from the Seats Where Noses Bleed. At this distance, Marilyn Monroe appears naked onstage. We can hear her singing. This whole shindig at Madison Square Garden that we have been watching was produced by Richard Adler, a popular Broadway lyricist (*The Pajama Game*). Now, he writes jingles for commercials. Monroe is now singing a little coda that Adler wrote lyrics for (to be sung to the melody of 'Thanks for the Memory'):

Thanks, Mr. President
For all the things you've done,
The battles that you've won,
The way you deal with U.S. Steel,
And our problems by the ton
We thank you so much.

A jump cut to the interior of a fancy town house. A party is taking place. Bobby Kennedy is dancing close with Marilyn Monroe. The camera focuses on her buttocks. Then the camera swings up and reveals Bobby's wife, Ethel, staring, her face absolutely without expression. We realize that Ethel is as transfixed on Monroe's buttocks as the camera once was. The camera returns to derriere level. Marilyn's ass is a sanitized posterior. You forget her buttocks are for sitting down. It doesn't dawn on you for a moment that Marilyn Monroe must actually possess an anus. No. Just these twin delightful pear shapes. On the soundtrack, the sound of bowling pins being knocked down. A male voice says, 'Her dress is like flesh with sequins sewn on.' (Those in the know recognize the voice of Adlai Stevenson.) Another male voice (Arthur Schlesinger): 'Talking to Marilyn is like talking to someone under water.'

A long shot of Maria Callas standing by herself in an alcove at the party. She is not even holding a drink. Jimmy Durante walks by, glances at her, and continues. Callas looks completely lost—a state familiar among famous women. They are so used to being fawned over, they have forgotten how to mingle and start a conversation that is not about themselves.

* * *

Down south. Jimi Hendrix now wore his post-Army hair in a Little Richard conk, also referred to in coiffure circles as a 'marcel.' Hendrix had also gotten into playing surf guitar on his new Epiphone Wilshire guitar that Otis Pilgrim, now honorably discharged from the Army, helped him secure from a Clarksville music store.

Hendrix had bought Betty Jean back from the pawnshop for the very last time.

Hendrix seldom slept with his Epiphone Wilshire as he was constantly gobbling amphetamines so he could stay up all night practicing, because Baby Boo Young had come down from Indianapolis and he and Pilgrim and Hendrix formed a band. They called themselves the King Kasuals. They moved to Nashville. The three scored an apartment above Joyce's House of Glamour. Soon their pad was decorated in Bachelor Spartan. On warm Friday afternoons, the three guys would slouch near the windows of Joyce's House of Glamour to watch Aretha Franklin getting her hair done.

Guitarists were, as they say, a dozen to a dime in Nashville. Good pickers could play their guitars backward and frontward, play them between their legs and behind their backs, and even play them with their teeth. Hendrix could do these things, especially with his teeth.

Hendrix continued playing weird licks that approximated the drone of the transport plane he had jumped out of at Fort Campbell. These sonic visions were inappropriate when Hendrix soloed on 'Green Onions' or 'Poison Ivy.' The crowd would throw ice and lemons at Hendrix.

Otis Pilgrim bequeathed Hendrix the nickname 'Marbles,' as in 'lost his marbles.'

Then Pilgrim had the brilliant idea of Hendrix opening solo for the King Kasuals in a show called 'Jimi Hendrix & His Magic Guitar.' Jimi could play his Epiphone Wilshire upside down or on his back producing feedback and bending the strings into pretzels. He could do whatever he wanted. The music was sideshow freaky, but Jimi got the avant-garde bug out of his system for when he came out with the King Kasuals to play 'Green Onions' and 'Poison Ivy.'

During this time, Otis got some kind of small monkey and named him Monkey. This simian would sit for hours in the apartment above Joyce's House of Glamour watching Jimi Hendrix's monstrously long fingers as he noodled up and down the fretboard of his Epiphone Wilshire guitar. Hendrix grew fond of Monkey's attention. He went to the music store and bought the monkey a Maccaferri 'Islander' plastic ukulele. Jimi removed three strings but left the G. He taught Monkey to bend notes on that single G string. Then Hendrix added the C string. Then the E and A. Hendrix taught Monkey the basic chords to simple songs such as 'My Dog Has Fleas.'

Hendrix added Monkey to his opening act, 'Jimi Hendrix & Monkey & Their Magic Guitars.'

There was one big problem with Monkey—Pilgrim had never toilet-trained him. Neither had Jimi. Their landlord threw a fit. A white stripper named Rosalie offered to buy Monkey. She intended to add the monkey and his ukulele to her own act. Pilgrim jumped at the chance. He, as well as Jimi, were simple men in their comparative considerations of man and beast. In the end, Monkey was just a monkey. Both men instantly forgot about him and his fate by the next morning.

The apartment soon stopped reeking of monkey poop.

Hendrix returned to playing as Jimi Hendrix & His Magic Guitar solo.

★ ★ ★

Manhattan. *Vogue*'s editor-in-chief Jessica Daves killed the Monroe spread after the star's suicide. To run the photos would be American Bad Taste. Yet, the next week Daves was fired for something or other. Her replacement, Diana Vreeland, saw elegance, grace, and playfulness in the Monroe photos. They were the perfect epilogue for Monroe's career. The issue ran as planned.

The most haunting photo showed Marilyn posed in a black Jackie Kennedy wig.

One of Jackie's sisters-in-law from the Kennedy side had just revealed (out of spite) that Jackie herself sometimes wore a wig so Jackie was a Jackie impersonator just like Monroe.

Jacqueline, the woman, had always detested Monroe. If someone dared say to Jacqueline's face, 'You talk like Marilyn Monroe,' Jacqueline would reply in a cold breeze of voice, 'I talk like myself. That woman talks like me.' Jacqueline Kennedy was not present in Manhattan the night Monroe sang for Jack Kennedy, wearing that infamous slinky buttocks-provoking gown. Instead, Jacqueline took the children to a horse show in Virginia. She did not concern herself with the other women Jack fucked, such as Mary Meyer. Jacqueline herself was even friends with Mary Meyer. She respected Jack's taste in Mary Meyer as a mistress.

But Marilyn Monroe was nothing less than a PWT cunt.

Particularly galling was Monroe's voice. When it went into that little-girl whisper, Monroe did inflect words exactly like Jacqueline. The first lady believed in her heart that Marilyn Monroe was mocking her.

* * *

Albert Camus had been dead for two years longer than Marilyn Monroe. Three years before Camus's death, that writer met with Charles de Gaulle in a dark café in Paris in March of 1957. The air was a fog of Gauloises and Gitanes. De Gaulle was 'officially' in retirement. Camus had never loved de Gaulle. In fact, when Camus was editing a radical French newspaper with an English name, *Combat,* Camus saw to it that de Gaulle's military rank was always written with a disrespectful lowercase *g,* instead of *Général de Gaulle* as every other French newspaper printed the name. But neither did Camus hate de Gaulle. Now the two were discussing the situation in the French colony of Camus's birth, Algeria. De Gaulle said, 'North Africa is lost to France. Frenchmen are discouraged. They lack self-confidence.'

Camus took a drag on his cigarette and then said, 'I suggest giving French citizenship to all Algerians regardless whether they are Moslem.'

De Gaulle swatted his hand in the air. 'Right, and we'll have fifty coloreds in the Chamber of Deputies.' De Gaulle took a sip of brandy. 'Algeria is lost and all Frenchmen are discouraged. France lacks self-confidence.'

Camus said, 'No! The French are not discouraged. The French are furious. French fury is behind every apartment and house in Paris.'

'French fury?' De Gaulle sneered. 'I'm sixty-five years old* and I've never seen a Frenchman try to kill another Frenchman except myself.'

Now it is August 22, 1962. President de Gaulle is seventy-one. He is driving in a Citroën DS along with his wife in Paris. It is a regular 1961 Citroën DS with no bulletproof armor attached to the body. The car has regular safety glass in the windows and the windshield, not bulletproof glass.

The car turns on to Rue du Bonheur and is raked by machine-gun fire.

---

* De Gaulle was lying about his age! He was sixty-six years old.

The laps of both de Gaulle and his wife are immediately filled with bits of safety glass. De Gaulle has been fired upon in several wars and estimates there are three to four gunmen firing at his Citroën DS. De Gaulle's driver floors it straight ahead. Two of the car's back tires blow, yet the Citroën keeps going at a steady clip out of range of the gunfire. Both de Gaulles escape without injury.

One hundred eighty-seven spent shell casings will be found on Rue du Bonheur.

* * *

New York City. The painter Ken Noland was mentioned earlier as the painter who had a brief fling with Mary Meyer in 1958. Here is the moment that Noland is remembered for today—

Greenwich Village.

Willem de Kooning is posing for a Swiss-born photographer named Robert Frank on a dark Manhattan street downtown with a few blurry lights in the background. De Kooning himself is illuminated by either an unseen streetlight or a flash.

After the picture is taken, Robert Frank and de Kooning go their separate ways.

De Kooning walks over to the Cedar Tavern. Know ahead of time what happens next will be said to have occurred at an artist's bar called Dillons in order to drum up some mythology for that now-forgotten joint. As it was—

De Kooning struts into the Cedar Tavern and sees Clement Greenberg sitting next to Ken Noland.

Clement Greenberg is getting ready to proclaim that Kenneth Noland is the Rightful Successor to Jackson Pollock and Willem de Kooning. Noland is in his thirties. After the war, Noland studied at Black Mountain College in North Carolina, the proudly 'experimental' education nexus of art and liberal education U.S.A. style whose notable alumni and teachers included painter Robert Rauschenberg and poet Robert Creeley and choreographer Merce Cunningham as well as his companion, the musician John Cage. There at Black Mountain, Noland learned to incorporate the geometric Dutch Neo-Plasticism of Piet Mondrian into an American Plasticism that contained a geometrical purity similar to the Shell gasoline station sign.

Clement Greenberg (or possibly his critical competitor Jed Perl) once wrote something like: 'During our long slough through the 1950s, Noland's work became the antithesis of the paintings of Pollock and de Kooning. Noland did not dabble with chaotic splashes or swabs of color. Noland's Color Field/Neo-Plastic paintings were always geometric. Pollock and de Kooning's Abstract Expressionism was all Sturm und Drang. Noland's Color Field/Neo-Plasticism clarified the joy of all that is chromatic and ovoid.'

There inside the Cedar Tavern, Noland's face itself is Neo-Plastic, but not ovoid. His skin covers but cannot hide the hard angles of his skull. Noland leads with his chin. Noland always has a cigarette dangling off his lip. Central casting would never pick him to play an artist. Noland would be cast as a private dick or an Air Force pilot. In fact, during the war, Noland was a glider pilot/cryptographer stationed in the exotic hot spots of Cairo and Istanbul. Here inside the Cedar Tavern, Clement Greenberg is a good ten years older than Kenneth Noland. Greenberg is at the maximum of great weight before he will eventually slim down. The trim Kenneth Noland is sucking up to the fat man, but this younger man is shameless. Sucking up has been and always will be the nature of the beast that is the Manhattan Art Scene.

Noland senses hostility in the air. He squints over Greenberg's shoulder and sees de Kooning strutting toward them.

Uh-oh.

'Greenbird,' de Kooning grunts.

Greenberg turns. Noland sees de Kooning poke Greenberg in the belly, saying, 'Hey, fat boy. I hear you were talking at the Guggenheim and you said I was washed up.'

'Yeah,' Greenberg says, his voice getting high-pitched as it always does when he gets nervous. 'I said that. And I meant it. You haven't done a good picture since 1950.'

Noland is as alert as he has ever been since the war. He does not want to queer things with Greenberg, but de Kooning has tremendous sway in the art world.

Noland does not want to do or say anything rash.

De Kooning takes in what Greenberg said and retorts, 'And you haven't written a truthful word since 1949, you crap hack!'

At that, Clement Greenberg throws a sloppy punch. Noland thinks, *Shit! The first blow!* Yet, Greenberg misses and the momentum of his fist pulls the fat man off his barstool belly-down onto the floor.

Noland does not move. You do not mess with a fellow's play.

Greenberg raises himself on his hands and knees into a doggy crouch. A crowd of young male artists surround de Kooning and Greenberg. One punk says, 'Kick him in the nuts, de Kooning! Kick him in the nuts!'

Noland takes the cigarette out of his mouth. He stays on his barstool, but the toes of his shoes are poised ready to spring his body up and forward to rescue Greenberg if necessary. De Kooning peers down at Greenberg and then squats to reach under Greenberg's armpits. De Kooning then lifts the fat man to his feet. Greenberg stands steady peering at de Kooning, who says in a deliberately exaggerated Dutch accent, 'You wouldn't recognize *terribilità* if it punched you in the nose.'

Like a sucker, Greenberg blocks his nose with an arched arm, allowing de Kooning to project a classic roundhouse punch to Greenberg's stage-right kidney. This propels the greatest art critic of the age backward, Greenberg's head knocking into a table, spilling drinks and food into the laps of several women who are sitting there.

'Make him pay! Make him pay, de Kooning,' the young men begin yelling.

The Dutchman has already turned and walked out of the bar. To Noland's eye Greenberg earned his tit for tat. Noland stands up and pushes his way through the young punks. He leans down to help Greenberg to his feet and someone puts his hand on Noland's shoulder—

* * *

Georgetown, 8:05 p.m., Monday, October 8.

A man named Roswell Gilpatric sits in a darkened car parked in front of Robert McNamara's house. McNamara's downstairs lights are all on. From his car, Gilpatric can see a good thirty well-heeled men and women sitting inside listening to some lit-wig jabber about the Bhagavad Gita. Roswell Gilpatric is listening to his car radio broadcast Game 4 of the World Series.

—the San Francisco Giants versus the Yankees in the Bronx—

Roswell Gilpatric is deputy secretary of defense and is semi-comfortable with his boss's highfalutin literacy. McNamara is ten years Gilpatric's junior and was probably raised on a better class of books than Gilpatric was. If McNamara says the Bhagavad Gita is a great book then the Bhagavad Gita is a great book. Roswell Gilpatric's only objection tonight is that their enemies at the Pentagon could smear his boss as a left-leaning non-conformist by McNamara ignoring the World Series to host a shindig on Bombay literature.

—it's the bottom of the sixth, two to zip, the Giants catcher Tom Haller just stroked a two-run homer off pitcher Whitey Ford in the second—

Eventually, the Yankees score two runs. The night wears on. On the seat beside Roswell Gilpatric sits an envelope containing a slew of photographs that have the potential to ignite World War III.

Seventh inning. Hear the announcer *going crazy* as the bat of Giants second baseman Chuck Hiller has smacked a grand slam.

—'Looky there! Looky looky looky! Holy cow!

'Call your sons! Call your daughters!

'Chuck Hiller has just hit a grand slam.

'Were my eyes deceiving me or did that baseball have a tail of flame like a comet?

'Holy cow! Holy Toledo! This is the first grand slam for the National League in World Series history.

'Holy roller holy roller coaster! There are 66,607 Yankee fans in attendance at Yankee Stadium and they are all standing and cheering for the Giants' second baseman Chuck Hiller.

'Holy cow! Here comes Jim Davenport into home plate. Home is holy! Jim Davenport is holy. Holy grand slam! Holy slam! Holy cow! Holy slam cow grand cow holy holy holy.

'Today there are no bums in baseball. Everyone is holy. Every bat is holy. Every baseball. Grand slam the skyscrapers in Manhattan are shaking! Holy New York City! Holy San Francisco!

'Here comes peppy Matty Alou into home. Matty Alou is holy. Matty Alou is peppy.

'Here comes Ernest Ferrell Bowman into home. Bowman is holy.

'And now a hero's holy hero, the holiest man in Yankee Stadium, Chuck Hiller. His second holy season with the Giants. Chuck Hiller is holy. Holy Chuck Hiller's mother! Holy his father too! Holy is Chuck Hiller's wife! If he ain't married yet, holy his girl.

'Holy the crack of Chuck Hiller's bat. Holy the grand slam. Today every pop fly is holy. Every grounder is holy. Every strike-out is holy.

'Baseball is holy. Baseball is holy.

'Oh my gosh, whew! One thousand times whew!'

★ ★ ★

The Cedar Tavern. Six disheveled young men are all ass-down on the bar floor. One has a bloody nose. Another is rocking back and forth holding his belly.

Kenneth Noland stands and does not appear to have a scratch, although you could say there is blood in his eye. He reaches out his right arm and helps Clement Greenberg to his feet. The art critic shakes his head and then wags a finger at the beaten youths: 'I'll remember you. I'll remember every pig apple one of you.'

Noland leads Greenberg toward the door. The fat man stops and spins around, calling out, 'None of you will ever paint in this town again!'

Chapter 6

Chinatown, Los Angeles, California, 1962

Roswell Gilpatric's very name is a delicious utterance that would bode well as a character's name in a work of fiction, although if Roswell Gilpatric were a character in a Howard Hunt spy novel his name would be spelled *Roswell Gilpatrick,* as the lowercase *k* gives his name masculine closure. Roswell Gilpatric (no *k*) is and will continue to be a major character in the history of the 1960s, yet for unaddressed reasons his presence will be slowly erased by historians year after year after year. The man was born in Brooklyn in 1906 as Roswell Leavitt Gilpatric. In less than three weeks he will be fifty-six years old. Five years from now, Roswell Leavitt Gilpatric will fornicate with Jacqueline Kennedy in, among other places, tourist accommodations near the great palaces of Angkor Wat in Cambodia. That future fornication, however, has nothing to do with the so-called Cuban Missile Crisis.

Roswell Gilpatric will live to be eighty-nine years old. He will always remember his part in what the Russians named the October Crisis.

> You know 2001 is the true first year of the twenty-first century? Yes. There was no Year Zero between Christ's conception and Christ's birth. The first year of the nineteenth century started in 1801 and the first year of the twentieth century began in 1901. And so it goes. I am honored to have made it as far into the future as I have. What do I remember clearest about 1962? My answer will surprise you. Foremost, is a particular Pepsi commercial on television. Yes! The slogan on this Pepsi commercial summed up what it was like working in the Kennedy White House. My wife and I had one of the first color sets in Georgetown, but this commercial was intentionally filmed in B&W . . . What's that? Yes, intentionally filmed in B&W like *The Misfits.*
>
> The commercial starts with a neon sign blinking on and off

announcing FOUNTAIN. A male voice says, 'Have you noticed something new at the soda fountains today? People who think young say, *Pepsi, please.*' As he speaks, B&W images appear of handsome men and women in their early twenties sipping Pepsi.

These images continue as a young woman starts singing a bouncy tune, 'The lively crowd today agrees those who think young say, *Pepsi, please.*'

'They choose the right one, the modern light one.'*

'Now it's Pepsi, Pepsi, for those who think young.'

When Bob's guests—Mr. McNamara's guests—finally left his house, they didn't look particularly young as they did look hoity-toity, stepping off the front porch in Brooks Brothers and mink. I had never read the Bhagavad Gita then—and still haven't—but the Bhagavad Gita appeared to put Bob in the perfect apocalyptic frame of mind to look through the photographs I brought with me of U-2 surveillance images of Russian offensive nuclear missiles being assembled in Cuba. 'Holy cow,' McNamara said. 'Holy cow. Holy cow. Oh no—shit shit shit shit. Excuse me, Ros.' I told him that no excuses were necessary—'*Shit shit shit* is an appropriate response.' Kennedy had not seen the photos yet. We decided we would both show them to him in the morning.

I remember that the goddamn rain started in the middle of the night, the rain that would postpone Game 5 of the World Series. It was six a.m. when Bob and I showed President Kennedy the surveillance photographs. The president was sitting on a stool wearing just his blue pajama bottoms while Dr. Janet was placing leeches on his back to bleed the man to cure his adrenal insufficiency. 'You'll have to turn away, Dr. Janet, these pictures are classified,' Kennedy told her. She rolled her eyes. Her actual name was Dr. Janet Travell. She was sixty years old. The president gave her the dignity of flirtation, but she was the only woman who could touch his naked body so often in so many ways that had nothing to do with the hand gestures of Eros.

Bob established that these were pictures of MRBMs and likely

---

* On this line, the melody quotes 'Makin' Whoopee.'

IRBMs—medium range and intermediate range ballistic missiles. This meant the Russians could destroy New York City and Buenos Aires from the vantage point of Cuba. The thing I remember is Dr. Janet leaving the room with a container full of fat leeches and Kennedy screaming in rage that we were going to wipe out Cuba with our own MRBMs and IRBMs. Bob calmed him down. Thereafter, for the rest of the day—for an entire week to be exact—about twenty civilians in the know and God knows how many generals shouted and whispered to each other day after day about the pros and cons of destroying the world with H-bombs and A-bombs and missiles. Fallout. Black Snow. Black Death.

Any man who passed the boundary from the twentieth century to the twenty-first became a modern man regardless of how old he was. I am now aware and confess to you moderns that there was not a single black man among those stuffed shirts who argued so passionately about the fate of the world. Not a single Asian. No Cherokees. Of course, there were no women present, save for Dr. Janet. There must have been one or two Jews who argued about the End of the World, although I can't think of who was who right now.

Right off the bat, Bob pointed out that the addition of twenty to forty missiles in Cuba did not significantly change the U.S.-Soviet Balance of Power. I told the president, 'There's no reason to risk nuclear war over missiles that do no long-term harm to American security.' Then Bob said more to himself than to the president, 'Nietzsche says you must be proud of your enemy.' At that Kennedy yelled, 'I sure as shit am not proud of Khrushchev. Are you, Bob?' Bob looked all contrite. Then Bob—Jack's brother Bob—said, 'My brother's chances of being reelected for a second term are worse than zilch if he lets the Soviet Union surreptitiously install atomic missiles ninety miles off Florida.'

Then Jack's brother Bob floated a balloon: 'Can the CIA fake a Cuban attack on the U.S. base in Guantánamo Bay to justify hauling U.S. troops to Cuba?' That idea was shot down, thank God. Then the president met with the chiefs of staff. The head chief was General

Taylor. He's long dead now but I think he was sixty-one years old at the time. The two Kennedy brothers loved him. They thought of him as an uncle. Robert Kennedy even named his fourth son after the General, Matthew Maxwell Taylor Kennedy. General Taylor was all for cautious thinking before we bombed the pants off the Cubans. Then Curtis 'Bombs Away' LeMay pounded the table with a fist and yelled, 'We should invade Cuba now! The Russians won't touch Berlin—they're too chicken. If they try something, we'll fling a few Minutemen their way.' LeMay was just getting started. 'The so-called peace we've had since Eisenhower left office has been a false one and, besides, that great Chinese warlord General Sun Tzu said, *You should love peace as a means to new wars—and the short peace more than the long.*' McNamara says as rebuttal, 'Sun Tzu was never a warlord and Nietzsche said that.' LeMay insisted that Bob was mistaken. Kennedy dropped his head into his hands and said 'Nietzsche schmietzsche, I will not authorize a sneak attack on Cuba and be the Tojo of the 1960s.' LeMay countered back with: 'You'd prefer being the Chamberlain of the 1960s instead?' Oh my! That was a double-sworded barb as it not only referred to Chamberlain appeasing Hitler in Munich—but Kennedy's father, Joe, was the ambassador to England at the time, and supported 'Peace in Our Time.' LeMay was implying, 'Like father, like son.'

I remember that Game 5 of the World Series was finally played. José Pagán from Puerto Rico drove in two runs for San Francisco—a single in the third and a homer in the fifth. The score was tied 2–2 in the eighth. Then Yankee Tom Tresh walloped a three-run homer, and that was all she wrote.

The day after the game, additional U-2 photographs were thoroughly analyzed. The Cuban missiles were more formidable than we first thought. They could hit anywhere in America save San Francisco and the Pacific Northwest, a region where a terrific storm was threatening to rain out Game 6 of the World Series. Kennedy's death technicians also estimated that if the U.S. attacked Cuba, we would kill one hundred thousand innocent civilians. General Curtis LeMay heard this and phoned Kennedy to shout, 'There is no such thing as innocent civilians!'

Anyway, the public never knew anything about the missiles until the next Monday. By that point, on my suggestion, McNamara had convinced Kennedy that a blockade of Cuba was the way to go. The day before Kennedy's Monday speech, I told McNamara to tell the president to say that we were establishing a *quarantine* on Cuba instead of a *blockade*. 'In international language, a blockade is an act of war. A quarantine is not.'

It was my job to know those things. While Bob was commanding the Ford Motor Company, I served as the undersecretary of the Air Force. Kennedy wanted a man experienced in military matters to watch Bob's back.

I remember Kennedy on national television revealing the missiles in Cuba to the public. He said the Russian missiles were 'in flagrant and deliberate defiance of the Rico Pact of 1947' as if the Rico Pact of 1947 would mean something to the average American. *Oh, honey! Those lousy commies can't get away with violating the Rico Pact!* Anyway, Rico sounds like it has something to do with gangsters, doesn't it? Wasn't Edward G. Robinson named Rico in *Little Caesar*? 'Oh mama, is this the end of your Rico?'* At any rate, Kennedy said that the U.S. was going to *quarantine* the island.

The next morning, the *Washington Post* had a headline that said, KENNEDY ORDERS CUBA BLOCKADE AS REDS BUILD A-BASES ON ISLAND. Two other articles called the action a *quarantine*. By the end of the October Crisis, twenty-seven articles will call it *quarantine*; twenty-eight articles will call it both *quarantine* and *blockade* interchangeably; and ninety-three articles will call the action a *blockade*.

The rain in San Francisco didn't stop for what seemed like forty days and forty nights and when the deluge was finally finished, Game 6 of the World Series was played and the home team outpitched the Yankees. The World Series was tied with three wins apiece.

The most dramatic moment of this whole Cuban Missile Crisis came the day after the president's speech. This is the scene they always film for the movies. Bob and I couldn't get any straight answers from

---

* The actual quote is 'Mother of Mercy! Is this the end of Rico?'

the Navy on exactly how they are going to implement this *quarantine.* The president made it clear that no orders would be followed that did not originate with him. There were not going to be any Bay of Sows screw-ups. Together, Bob and I stormed down the halls of the Pentagon and burst into the Navy's command center, which was called the Flag Plot. It was a massive conference room with a fifteen-foot ceiling and armed Marines standing guard. A plastic nautical map of Cuban waters covered one wall with three-dimensional red markers representing U.S. warships that were moved to different positions by guys with long rakes exactly like the kind stickmen use on craps tables. The man in charge of the Flag Plot was named Anderson. He was a punk actually. The first thing he said was, 'What do you want?' as if we had no business being in the Flag Plot.

'We want to know how you're enforcing the blockade,' Bob said.

'We're enforcing it.'

'How? Exactly what are you doing?'

'Sir, you are not authorized to ask such questions.'

'I'm the goddamn secretary of defense. You tell me what you are doing.'

Anderson protests. 'Don't swear at me.' Ha! A sailor who's sensitive to curse words? McNamara stood firm. Anderson got out a red book that contained text swear-to-God written at the time of the War of 1812.

'We go by the book. First, we require the boat to stop.'

'How do you do this?'

'Do what?'

'Communicate with the ship.'

'With flags.'

'What about radio?'

'We also communicate by radio.'

'Do you have sailors on standby on each boat who can speak Russian?' I asked.

Anderson didn't know. He was turning red.

'What's step two?' Bob asked.

'If the boat keeps coming we fire once across their bow. Then we fire at their propellers.'

'Boy,' Bob said, 'we are the width of a single matchbook close to a nuclear war with the Soviet Union. Your ships will absolutely not be firing at some Russian ship's propeller.'

Anderson started yelling and yelling. McNamara told me to 'Straighten him out.' But I pointed up at the map. There were eight American warships surrounding the waters of Cuba, but another American warship farther away in the Atlantic. 'What's that ship doing?' I asked Anderson. He wouldn't tell me. Then McNamara goes to a Marine guard and swear-to-God demands his pistol and Bob McNamara gets it and he strides up to Anderson with the pistol and pokes the barrel of the gun to the bridge of Anderson's nose. 'I am the secretary of defense. I am authorizing myself to blow your brains out if you don't tell me what the sons-of-bitches on that boat are doing.' Anderson actually starts pissing his pants and says, 'It's hunting a Russian submarine.'

Well, what it was doing we found out later was dropping depth charges on a Soviet submarine to force it to the surface.

That next morning, the Soviet news agency TASS released a telegram from Khrushchev to President Kennedy that said, 'You are acting like a pirate. Your demands are arbitrary. This blockade is an act of aggression. Our ships have been instructed to ignore it. *Nyet nyet nyet blah blah blah*.' Khrushchev said that and yet twenty Russian ships had turned around in the middle of the Atlantic and headed back to port. Then they turned around and began heading for Cuba again. The next day or maybe the day after that, Khrushchev sent a second message saying if the United States will say that we'll never invade Cuba or support any other forces that might try, 'then the necessity of the presence of our military specialists in Cuba will disappear.' Kennedy agreed in a flash. You know how the President of the United States of America sent Khrushchev this response? The Hot Line hadn't been thought of yet. To send a message to Moscow, first a bicycle messenger pedaled to the White House and picked up the top-secret presidential response and then rode it to the nearest Western Union telegraph station. And vice versa for Soviet telegrams that weren't first read aloud on Radio Moscow. Anyway, the next day a different message comes from Khrushchev on Radio Moscow saying that America must withdraw our Jupiter missiles from Turkey before the Soviets will leave Cuba. Kennedy sends brother Bob to a secret meeting with the Russian ambassador in a goddamn Chinese restaurant in Cleveland Park to assure Boris that we will remove the Jupiter missiles if it is not made public. Right after that, a U-2 was shot down over Cuba, the pilot killed. Bob—my Bob—started a screaming fit. 'This is war! This is war!' Kennedy, bless his mittens, cooled Bob down. Meanwhile, that Navy ship was still dropping depth charges above that Soviet submarine where the Russian crew had gone crazy with the noise of the explosions and was threatening mutiny unless the commander fired the ship's single nuclear torpedo up into the belly of the U.S. warship dropping the depth charges. The Russian sub had no way to communicate with Moscow to ask permission to do this. Different stories say the captain of the submarine—I don't remember all of his name except his first name was Valentine—faced down his crew with a pistol or else Valentine was about to fire the torpedo and a sailor named Arkhipov pulled a gun and faced down Valentine. Anyway, the torpedo was not fired. The world stayed safe.

* * *

During the so-called Cuban Missile Crisis, Richard Nixon was running for governor of California and was campaigning in Los Angeles's Chinatown, the neighborhood below Dodger Stadium. Nixon was forty-nine. Fellow Californian Jack Nicholson was twenty-five years old. Faye Dunaway was twenty-one. Roman Polanski was twenty-nine years old and still lived in Poland. Nicholson and Dunaway and Polanski will one day make a classic retro-noir titled after this very neighborhood, *Chinatown*. Another actor in the movie will be director John Huston, who at the moment of Nixon's speech in 1962 was in Ireland waiting for his movie about Sigmund Freud's discovery of the Oedipus complex to open.

At Nixon's Chinatown campaign stop, a group of Chinese youngsters held up signs proclaiming 'welcome' in both English and Chinese. Nixon stepped up to a podium and noticed that the Chinese adults in the crowd were talking to each other and pointing above Nixon's head. The candidate looked up. There was a banner in Chinese strung maybe fifteen feet off the ground between two light poles. 'What's that say?' Nixon asked the Chinese politician who was going to introduce him. The Chinese man told him.

Roman Polanski's *Chinatown* ends in this very square. Private eye J. J. Gittes (Jack Nicholson), a once idealistic cop who turned existential and quit the force after failing to save an Asian girl from the Chinatown Tongs, has returned to Chinatown ten years later to rescue a white woman, Evelyn Mulwray (Faye Dunaway) and her daughter/sister from their father, the incestuous rapist Noah Cross (played by John Huston). In the resulting turmoil, J. J. Gittes sees Evelyn Mulwray shot through her eye by a trigger-happy cop. Once again, Gittes has failed to protect a woman in Chinatown.

In Richard Nixon's Chinatown 1962, he was told the banner said, 'What about the Hughes loan?,' a reference to Howard Hughes's unsecured $205,000 'hamburger' loan to Nixon's brother, Donald, in 1956.

The work of Nixon's nemesis, Dick Tuck!

Nixon climbed a ladder and tore the banner down.

In *Chinatown*, after Evelyn Mulwray is shot and Noah Cross takes his 'granddaughter,' who is actually his daughter, into his arms, one of J. J. Gittes's compatriots says, 'Forget it, Jake. This is Chinatown.'

'Forget it, Dick. This is Chinatown.'

★ ★ ★

Roswell Gilpatric remembers:

> After Khrushchev ordered the missiles to be dismantled in Cuba, I was at the White House and saw Air Force Chief of Staff Curtis LeMay with tears in his eyes telling Kennedy 'The United States has failed.' Kennedy was surprised by this S.O.B.'s words as Kennedy assumed that he was the big hero of the hour for simultaneously saving the dignity of the United States and preventing World War III. 'Why do you say that?' Kennedy asked. Curtis 'Bombs Away' LeMay answered his commander in chief with: 'We should have gotten rid of Castro and we failed to do so.'
>
> Out of all the men I have outlived, I'm happiest I outlived that repugnant half-wit.

Chapter 7

Teapot Dome, Wyoming, 1962–1963

The grandparents of Billy Burroughs had moved to Palm Beach, Florida. His grandfather would throw dimes on the back lawn and then take the boy out to search for the coins. 'The angels dropped them for you, Billy.' His grandfather constantly read Dr. Seuss's *Horton Hatches the Egg* aloud to Billy.

Florida was where Billy rubbed his young elbows with the true blue bloods of the U.S.A.—the sons and daughters of such families as the Post kids, the Kellogg kids, the Dodge kids, the Rockefeller kids. 'I once knocked Winnie Rockefeller on his fat little ass and my knuckles are still agilt,' Bill would one day write. 'Anne Woodward was a brave child. She came to school chewing gum the very day after her mother hung herself from a tree in their backyard.' The boy even knew Errol Flynn's reticent ghost of a son.

These were not the kind of children who ever appeared on *The Donna Reed Show.*

Kid violence: Billy killed an indigo snake with a bow and arrow. His best friend, Larry, shot a BB gun at Billy and missed, the BB vaporizing a rainbow garden spider. Billy took his .22-caliber rifle and returned fire, shooting Larry in his neck.

Larry survived.

During this time in his young life, Bill became petrified of the night.

* * *

It was January 1963. The British poet Philip Larkin would write:

> Sexual intercourse began in nineteen sixty-three

* * *

On January 18, the *Washington Post* reported, 'Viet Torture Reports Doubted.' The article stated that there were fifteen thousand South Vietnamese in camps or jail, 'all but a few of them rebels or suspected Communist sympathizers.' Police torture is certainly not unknown in Viet-Nam, as 'both sides play dirty here.' Concurrent with this article, the married publisher of the *Washington Post*, Phil Graham, gave a speech at a newspaper publishing convention in Phoenix, Arizona, a function he traveled to with his Australian mistress. Graham was manic-depressive. He approached the microphone and began removing his shoes. He slid off his trousers. As he continued to undress, he declared that his friend President Kennedy was sleeping with a woman named Mary Pinchot Meyer. None of those in attendance reported in print the beans Graham had spilled.

In the 'Viet Torture Reports Doubted' article: 'Members of [Ngô Dinh Diem's] official family criticize the premier with astonishing vigor in the presence of Americans.' The article mentioned that some of the incarcerated were in jail because they violated Madame Nhu's law against dancing 'The Twist.'

After the half-dressed Phil Graham was taken off the stage, Graham's assistant, James Truitt, flew by private plane with Phil's wife, Katharine, along with Phil's doctor. They found the publisher sedated in Phoenix. They bound the fellow in a straitjacket and flew back to Washington, D.C. Graham was committed for five days to Chestnut Lodge, a Maryland psychiatric hospital. At the end of the summer, Graham shot himself with a 28-gauge shotgun.

James Truitt will wait thirteen years before raising the bedsheets on Jack Kennedy and Mary Pinchot Meyer, publishing his allegations in the *National Enquirer*, doing this to get back at the *Washington Post*'s Ben Bradlee. Mary Pinchot Meyer, herself, will be long dead, having been shot in the head on the Chesapeake and Ohio Canal towpath in Georgetown in 1964. In any case, Truitt's revelations are hearsay. Five years after the *National Enquirer*, Truitt will die by bullet while in Mexico. The authorities will assume the shot was self-inflicted.

* * *

Arthur Miller had once been asked to write a screenplay based on Albert

Camus's *The Fall*. But the deal fell through. Arthur Miller's play about Marilyn Monroe was titled *After the Fall*.

* * *

Tennessee. It was freezing cold the winter of '62–'63 in Nashville. During this time, Negro college students and a few white colleagues had been holding sit-ins in a number of segregated downtown restaurants on Church Street and Fifth Avenue. One frigid afternoon in the new year, Otis Pilgrim and Baby Boo Young and Jimi Hendrix herded themselves into Grant's Discount to get some shoe polish.

'I am freezing,' Otis remarked.

'I could use some warm coffee,' Baby Boo said.

Spontaneously, the three King Kasuals were sitting at the lunch counter reserved for 'Whites Only.' The Negro counter was around a corner from the Whites' counter. Jimi Hendrix had sat down first. He was distracted. Playing music in his head. His two companions sat down as well. A white woman behind the counter—squat/hairnet/repugnant—said, 'We don't serve colored here. You boys go to the other end of the counter.'

The three all realized they had just started a sit-in.

'I just got out of the Army,' Jimi found himself saying. 'When I was in my uniform, I could get served here.'

'We don't serve Negro civilians here.'

'Hey, you have to serve us,' Otis said. 'I want a cup of coffee.'

'We don't serve Negroes here.'

'This is a public place, isn't it?' Baby Boo said. 'I don't see anyone flashing membership cards in order to sit down.'

'I'm not serving you,' the white woman said. 'This is our custom.' She walked away.

A black teenager in a waitress uniform hurried over to the three. 'You are fools,' she said with clenched teeth, glancing around to make sure she was not being observed by anyone important. 'You're why decent Negroes can't get anywhere today. You know very well that you are supposed to eat at the other end.'

She hurried away.

A pair of elderly white women sat down at the counter as far away from the three blacks as was physically possible—the black closest to the white women was Hendrix, then Otis, then Baby Boo.

The waitress in a hairnet returned. 'What can I get you ladies?'

Otis Pilgrim spoke before either white woman could answer the waitress. 'Hey, what about our order? We were here first.' Baby Boo added, 'I didn't see those two ladies show you a membership card or anything.'

The waitress ignored these statements. The two old women wanted two slices of coconut cake and two teas.

Everybody sat there.

Otis Pilgrim leaned his head forward and said, 'Excuse me, ma'am.'

The two old ladies ignored him.

'Excuse me, ma'am,' Pilgrim said again. 'Can you pass me that bottle of ketchup?'

The two old ladies peered over and then quickly looked away. They ignored the bottle of ketchup looming to their left.

'What you want ketchup for?' Baby Boo said.

'Get a cup of boiling water and make tomato soup,' Pilgrim said, standing up. He walked over to the end of the counter and reached out his arm—the two white ladies cringed—and picked up a red-colored squeeze bottle. He returned to his seat.

At that moment three policemen walked into Grant's. They walked up and down the aisle several times. The waitress talked with the fattest of the three cops at the far end of the counter. He shook his head at her. 'You can't?' she squeaked.

'This is Nashville, not Selma,' the fat cop said.

The waitress stormed away into what looked like the kitchen.

Some white teenagers came in. Each wore a thick and greasy deer-hunting red coat. Each kid had a ducktail—punks. They crowded together and muttered. Then one teenager walked up to Jimi's back and pulled his collar open and dropped cigarette butts down his back.

Jimi jumped as if he had been asleep.

'Ignore the skuldugger,' Pilgrim said and reached over and tugged the back of Jimi's shirt open so the butts fell out on the floor. Baby Boo stood up and removed the blacks' coats from the hooks on the wall and put them all on the chair he had been sitting on beside Otis. He then sat down again, this time on the next chair down.

Jimi Hendrix's radar had been aware of all this activity while he had the strongest of epiphanies concerning why he had not returned to Seattle. The Chinese and the whites and the Negroes in Seattle were a true polyglot, while the Negroes in the South were somehow more intently Negro than those blacks back home.

Everyone at Fort Campbell had said that Hendrix had the diction of a white man. This was not said as a compliment.

Jimi was fine with the way he spoke. He also liked associating with Negroes in the South. He was learning as much about who he actually was as he was learning about who he actually was not. For Jimi, the truth was that as attractive as southern blackness was, he himself was too different to fit in anywhere. He loved his guitar and he loved being onstage. He realized at that moment what he had always known—he was going to make himself famous.

That was the only way to fit in—by not fitting.

He also realized how remote he was from the Kingdom of Anger. He had never felt rage. Resentment. He had no desire to Get Even. Jimi believed in the path of least resistance. He had never fought with his father or his sergeants in the Army. He nodded his head at authority, and then went off and did exactly what he wanted while making sure he wasn't caught.

Jimi's father had told his son that according to the Bible, the punishment in hell was not flames or torture, but waves of endless anger and resentment. The waitress and the punks with ducktails and the two old women eating coconut cake—they were angry. They were already in hell. He felt above them. Literally! He was above them with his ears. He suddenly heard every sound in Grant's. The waitress stomping behind the counter. A busboy with a plastic box of silverware. The voices of the cops. The sneers of the ducktails. The sound of clatter in the kitchen. A radio was on playing Perry Como, playing music so innocuous it did not even sound like music. Then Hendrix heard the sound at the outer perimeter of his hearing. The traffic outside in the street. Jabbering of the pedestrians. Then crinkling over those sounds were guitars. He felt there must be a hundred guitars all thrashing at once, yet they were so distant a normal person at the counter at Grant's—a normal white person at the counter at Grant's—would hear this distant sound as a delicate annoyance. A buzzing fly.

No one heard those one hundred electric guitars playing at once but him. He, Jimi Hendrix. He sat at the counter silent, as was Pilgrim, as was Baby Boo. The waitress rushed by again glaring at them.

'Please, ma'am,' Jimi Hendrix said. 'We would all like some coffee now.'

Hendrix was not thinking of the words he was saying, but he unconsciously made his request in the identical diction of a white person—a white person from the Ivy League, a white person selling white toothpaste on television. Hendrix sounded so much like a white person that the waitress found herself putting three empty coffee cups before the three Negroes before she realized what she was doing.

⋆ ⋆ ⋆

Washington, D.C./Seattle, January 25.

It was Friday morning in the White House. The president walked into the breakfast room. Jacqueline and the kids were already up, Jackie and Caroline at the table, John John (as he was playfully referred to) in his high chair—each studying something in their hands. Egg cartons. Each of the three held a white egg in their hands. Both Caroline and her mother had apparently already balanced a number of eggs on their ends on the table.

'What's going on?' the president asked.

'We're balancing eggs, Daddy,' Caroline said.

'I can see that. Why?'

Both Jacqueline and her daughter said, 'For the Chinese Lunar Year.'

'This is the Year of the Hare,' Caroline added.

'Hair on your head or hare as in wabbit,' Kennedy said, deliberately attempting to speak like Elmer Fudd and failing.

'Rabbit!' Caroline shouted.

'Is this something Chairman Mao made up?' the president asked.

Jacqueline stared at her husband and rolled her eyes. 'Tell your father, Caroline.'

'It's good luck, Daddy. The quicker you can get eighteen eggs to stand, the better luck you'll have in 1963.'

'Okay,' Kennedy said. He sat down in a chair next to John John's high chair. The boy's fingers were so small next to the egg. John John couldn't get his egg to stand, but he didn't appear frustrated. 'Let me try,' the president said. He sat down. He took his son's egg. 'Let Daddy show you how it is done, John John.'

The president examined the egg. 'This is a raw egg?'

'It doesn't work if they're hard-boiled,' Caroline said.

'I think it would be easier if they were hard-boiled,' Kennedy said.

'You won't get good luck if they're hard-boiled,' Caroline said.

'Oh.' Kennedy used all his fingers to attempt to find the balancing point of the egg. The egg kept tipping in one direction or another. He picked the egg up and set it down carefully again. It wobbled. He used three fingers on each hand to steady the egg. He was sure it was steady. He held it in place for ten seconds. Then he carefully flexed his fingers off the egg. It began wobbling. He held it in place yet again. He tried to make his touch as light as possible. This reminded him somehow of playing with one of those Ouija boards to talk to the dead. Kennedy squinted across the table to see Jacqueline balance her seventh egg. Caroline was on her fifth. Kennedy put John John's egg back in the egg carton.

'No deal, dear,' Jacqueline said in her puerile voice. 'You get no breakfast until you balance an egg.'

Kennedy started to protest.

'Just one egg, Daddy,' Caroline said. 'You only have to balance one egg, Daddy. When I've got eighteen eggs balanced, I'll balance the rest of yours and John John's.'

'And how many eggs will that be?' Jacqueline asked.

Caroline thought. 'Eighteen minus one.'

'And that is?'

'Seventeen!'

Seattle. Bruce Lee was alone in a room with a basket containing eighteen eggs.

He stood in front of the table and extended his upper arms away from his chest and then crossed his lower arms in an X in front of his chest. He slowly raised his right leg behind him as he moved each arm outward like wings as he lowered his upper torso, staring straight ahead. This pose was called Looking at the Sea. Earlier, Lee had placed the large bathroom cabinet that he took down from the bathroom on the table so that its mirror could serve as a horizontal surface. There was just enough room on the mirror to balance eighteen eggs. The physics of balancing the eggs was child's play. Balancing eighteen eggs had nothing to do with gravitational pulls of the moon or the position of the sun. All eggshells are porous. One must discover three contact points on the eggshell. Glass or mirrors are not perfectly smooth under a microscope, of course. But in regard to the egg, there is no counter texture to add to the equation. One way of looking at it makes balancing an egg on a mirror much more difficult than on a kitchen table. Another way of looking at it, balancing on a mirror is easier.

The egg is all.

Lee reached out with his right hand, keeping his left arm outstretched perpendicular from his body, and picked up the first egg, barely touching it with his fingers. He did not want his body heat to transfer to the egg. He felt the yolk sinking inside the shell. He quickly rubbed his pointer finger across the bottom of the broad side of the egg. Then without thinking or breathing, he swiftly placed the first egg on the mirror and registered with his fingertips any minute adjustments that were necessary in positioning the egg. Then he removed his fingers. The egg balanced. He moved his right arm out perpendicular to his body, and then he lowered his leg and raised his body vertically and then crossed his arms in front of his chest in an X.

Then he slowly raised his left leg behind him as he moved each arm outward like wings as he lowered his upper torso, staring straight ahead. Lee then reached out with his left hand and picked up the second egg, quickly sweeping his pointer across the bottom of the broad side of the egg before placing the second egg upright on the mirror beside the first egg.

The White House. Kennedy moved his fingers from his egg. It balanced. It stood upright. No one noticed him.

'I did it,' Kennedy said.

John John cheered and bumped the tray of his high chair, bouncing Kennedy's egg to the floor.

Kennedy considered the yellow yolk spilling out of a gouge in the side of his egg. 'Well, there goes my whole year,' he said. 'Good-bye, 1963.'

'Do-overs! Do-overs!' Caroline shouted.

'There are no *do-overs* for 1963,' Kennedy said, frowning down at the egg.

★ ★ ★

John Huston had several Chinese friends who balanced eggs for the Lunar New Year. Huston would watch them and see the parallel between a balanced egg and the Gambler's Fallacy. The Gambler's Fallacy says each roll of the dice occurs independently of the previous roll of the dice. That there is no such thing as a hot streak. So too with the eggs? The third egg is like both die in a pair of dice. The egg is not aware that it is the third egg. It should be mathematically the same to balance three eggs in a row as it is to balance ten or to balance eighteen and coax the God of Luck to shine on your entire year. Yet, the egg does not stand by luck, but by the experience and skill of the fingers placing the egg on the table. This is just as the dice are dependent on the skill of the cupped hands that roll them. Various strategies were proposed of the way to hold and position the dice in your hand and then roll them toward the wall of the craps table. To make the toss a conscious act, the result not random, but deliberate. John Huston tried to educate his fingers and the palms of his cupped hands, but there seemed something unfaithful about the gestures. After all, every motion picture he ever made was influenced by luck. Good Luck. Bad Luck. Of course, there was the Hollywood unifying principle at work. A movie either made money or it did not. Huston had made movies that were plagued with bad luck; every director had. Yet he had never had one of those bad luck pictures make money, though other directors had. There were no questions to be asked about luck. You were either lucky. Or not.

Bruce Lee reached out with an egg and balanced it on the mirror. It joined sixteen other eggs all motionlessly balancing on the mirror and their reflections. Thirty-four eggs. Bruce Lee swung his body vertically and then swept up his left foot, reaching out with his right hand to place the final egg on the mirror—

* * *

Elvis Presley's nickname for Ann-Margret is Rusty Ammo.

Rusty Ammo had been born Ann-Margret Olsson in Sweden a stone's throw from the Arctic Circle. She was an only daughter. Her parents moved to the Chicago area in 1946. Ann-Margret Olsson took dance lessons. As a teenager, Ann-Margret Olsson appeared on *Don McNeill's Breakfast Club* and Ted Mack's *The Original Amateur Hour.* Ann-Margret Olsson performed at the Dunes in Las Vegas where she did a dance routine with television comedian George Burns. Ann-Margret Olsson started recording as Ann-Margret for RCA back in 1961. She had a sexy throaty voice and RCA wanted to bill her as the 'female Elvis' by having her record a version of 'Heartbreak Hotel.' She did. She made two movies. Then she met Elvis himself.

It was power at first sight. They were instantly attracted.

Rusty's parents still chaperoned her on dates.

Rusty was Elvis's alter ego. Elvis stirred up Rusty's psyche. Rusty and Elvis were both paradoxically shy extroverts. 'At heart Elvis was no saint or king, but rather a kid.' In *Viva Las Vegas*—to quote the press release—'Elvis plays a guitar-strumming race-car driver who falls in love with a swimming teacher with showbiz aspirations. They get together and discover they are competing against each other in a swimming contest.' A reporter from *McCall's* magazine wrote: 'Elvis makes a face and shakes his head. It is a flirty, cute expression that isn't in the script, but it delights Ann-Margret. She laughs and flirts right back.'

Their simpatico astonishes. The *Viva Las Vegas* choreographer wants to score one of their dances to the old Astaire and Rogers routine 'Cheek to Cheek.' The choreographer spins the song for them on a hi-fi. Rusty and Elvis consider each other. Elvis requests, 'Play it again, please, if you will.' The choreographer complies. Rusty and Elvis do an animalistic bop, bumping into furniture and shoving it aside with their hips. When the song is done, the choreographer says, 'Great. Just do that.'

* * *

March 8, 1963. Friday night. Around midnight. The TV is on. This is late for you, but tomorrow you can sleep late. You get up and adjust the rabbit ears to improve reception. You are watching *The Jack Paar Show.* This is the night Dick Nixon is scheduled to be a guest. And Nixon does show up. The two men sit facing the camera—Nixon to stage right of Jack Paar, who is leaning forward in his chair. Nixon sits a little like a priss. His ankles are crossed, his hands folded.

'Now Mr. Nixon plays the piano and he wrote a selection,' Jack Paar says. 'Would you bring the piano out here?' Nixon looks away from Paar, presumably at the piano being rolled out. Parr continues: 'Mrs. Nixon—Pat—had a tape recorder going one afternoon and she quietly said to Mr. Nixon, *Would you play that piece?* And she recorded it.'

Nixon seems bemused. He unfolds his hands, and then folds them again.

'That's okay,' Paar says. 'Mr. Nixon is aware of that. This is not one of those tricks. But the funny thing is we have hired fifteen Democratic violinists...'

The audience cracks up. So does Nixon. He raises both knees as he laughs, while Paar continues: 'We are spending more money for this orchestra than we have for [unintelligible]. And they did a concerto arrangement of this hinky dinky song you wrote.' *Hinky dinky?* Nixon smiles. 'Would you play it for us?'

Nixon reaches over with his left arm. 'Jack, let me say this.' He presses Paar's arm, while he makes expressive gestures with his right hand. 'You asked a moment ago if I had any future political plans. And if last November didn't finish me, this was because the Republicans don't want another piano player in the White House.'

Laughter. (Democrat Harry Truman played the piano.)

Nixon stands up. He is almost six feet tall, but does not look it. He is a little hunched in his sad suit. He walks to a grand piano. Sits down. Acknowledges the audience (whom we never see). Then strings and horns play an introduction. Nixon raises his hands and plays.

He plays the piano.

He sits with good posture. Nixon is certainly no Glenn Gould—stooped and humming.

Nixon sits straight and plays a... lovely melody composed of simple melodic runs. The violins repeat whatever phrase he plays. Nixon studies his hands as he moves them across the keys. The song he is playing could be movie music from the 1930s. Just a simple, kinda corny, kinda kitschy piano tune. He plays it without any dramatics or flair.

Then it is over.

* * *

On the last day of April, the Spocks were invited to a White House gala for the sixty-seven-year-old Grand Duchess Charlotte of Luxembourg. The Spocks did not pull up to the door chauffeured in a limo. They pulled up in a Volkswagen.

Throughout the evening, anxious mothers surrounded Dr. Spock asking for advice. When the Spocks reached Jacqueline Kennedy on the receiving line she softly said, 'And so. We meet again, Dr. Spock.'

* * *

In the White House, John John was raised by a nanny, just as Caroline had been. Every blue blood on Park Avenue or in Newport was nanny-raised. Every Brahmin of Boston. Not to mention every Bouvier. Every Auchincloss. Yet, Jacqueline certainly had an interest in contributing to the raising of her son. Two years before in 1961, she could not find her original copy of Spock's *The Common Sense Book of Baby and Child Care,* so a plebe on the White House staff went out and purchased the 1961 edition. Four decades down the line, the book will be auctioned at Sotheby's, tattered dust jacket and all.

The book will fetch sixty-nine hundred dollars. That is nearly fifty thousand dollars today.

* * *

It was now spring. Bruce Lee, American citizen, returned to Hong Kong to get circumcised. The day of the procedure, Bob Dylan's second record, *The Freewheelin' Bob Dylan,* was released in the U.S.A. with a cover color photo of an obviously freezing Bob walking with his girlfriend down the middle of Jones Street in the Village, dirty snow on the ground and in the background the grille of a Volkswagen Bus. Both Bob and Bruce were twenty-two years old (the Asian being the elder by six months). Viet-Nam was showing up on all young men's psychic radars. Dylan's draft number was low. Lee's was high. After Bruce Lee's successful circumcision, he returned to America and reported to the draft board for a physical. Bruce Lee was rejected because of his undescended testicle.

One of the songs on Dylan's new album was titled 'I Shall Be Free.' Two couplets went:

Well, my telephone rang it would not stop
It's President Kennedy callin' me up
He said, 'My friend, Bob, what do we need to make the country grow?'
I said, 'My friend, John, Brigitte Bardot.'

* * *

Texas, June 5. Vice President Johnson and President Kennedy traveled to El Paso to meet with John Connally in the Cortez Hotel. Connally has come a long way since the suicide of daughter K.K. Connally had always been Lyndon's protégé. Back in 1961, Johnson influenced Kennedy to appoint Connally secretary of the Navy. Connally and his wife, Nellie, moved to Washington. The high point of the appointment for Nellie was when she got to crash a bottle of champagne to christen a new Polaris submarine. Connally quit the post less than one year later to run for governor of Texas.

He won.

The 1963 tapes went something like this:

'John, I'd like to kick off my campaign for reelection in Texas.'

'I know, Mr. President.'

'You Texas folks have an increase of one in the Texas Electoral College next year.'

'Twenty-five, Mr. President. We had twenty-four in '60 and we'll have twenty-five in '64.'

'Twenty-five. That's good, John. And we want all of them. Even with Lyndon here on the ballot, we just squeaked out of Texas like three blind mice. And with Goldwater as the Republican man, we can't take any chances with the western vote.'

'I'm honored that you want to come to Texas, Mr. President. But this is a difficult time in local politics. To be frank with you, Mr. President, most Texans don't like you.'

'Now John, that's because Texans don't know the president like you and I do.'

'Don't horseshit me, Lyndon. You jaw just as bad. The more you talk about civil rights, the more the oil boys scream about lynching Communists and burning niggers in the woodpile. You got to slow down with these people. One step at a time.'

'You mean, one burning nigger at a time?'

'Now Lyndon, I know you're worried that the president is gonna dump you from the ticket. If he starts the campaign down here he can't dump you, is that your thinking?'

'Now wait just a minute . . .'

'Where did you get such a . . .'

'Now shush. Both of you. Lyndon, you know Kennedy and his Mick mouses have nothing but contempt for you and me as Texans. No use denying it, Mr. President. When I was in Washington in '61 you and your wife invited Nellie and me to functions and you always stuck us in Alaska with UN delegates from Swahili or some damn place. People who didn't speak English. Now—'

'John, you prick, hand me your telephone before I cut your balls off.'

'Mr. President!'

'Do it, you bastard. There is someone I want you to talk to. Thanks. Just a minute while I dial. [Into the phone.] Yes. Yes. This is the president. Put Bobby on. Yes. Okay Bobby, here is the governor of Texas. Kick him in the nuts. [To Connally.] Bobby wants to talk to you.'

'Hello?'

'Mr. Governor?'

'Yes.'

'I have several words to say to you: Teapot Dome. The Navy oil reserve. Teapot Dome. Haroldson Lafayette Hunt. Teapot Dome. I kid you not, do not fuck with me and my brother the president. There is enough time left in his first term to haul up a Senate committee to investigate that wondrous Connally year heading the Navy. Now, listen to my brother the president—'

President Kennedy spoke: 'Now, John, this is what we are going to do. I and Vice President Johnson are going to come to Texas and visit Dallas and Houston and whatever major cities you think in your wisdom we should visit.'

'Just a second. Lyndon, aren't you going to say anything?'

'Uh-uh.'

From the phone: 'Are you there, Mr. Governor?'

'Yeah, Bobby. Okay.'

'Also, you are going to get into bed with Yarborough and bury the hatchet.'

'Lyndon, this sonofabitch says I got to bury the hatchet with Yarborough. You got anything to say to that?'

'Just don't bury the hatchet in Yarborough's skull, John.'

* * *

Saigon. June 11, 1963. Phan Dinh Phung Street.

It's not even eight a.m. and the morning is hot. A concrete pagoda sits on the street with its entrance located down a muddy alleyway. Crowds of monks in yellow robes and nuns in gray are milling. Loudspeakers blare Vietnamese—this is a rapid language. High-pitched. Then at eight o'clock sharp, the jabbering ceases. A monk picks up a microphone and begins chanting *Na Mo A Di Da Phat*. This is a prayer. *Na Mo A Di Da Phat.* Another monk beats time on a gourd.

All the monks and nuns begin joining in the chant. The volume of their voices grows. *Na Mo A Di Da Phat.* It becomes impossible to separate the gender of the voices. Two ranks of nuns and monks begin to march back into Phan Dinh Phung Street. They begin moving up the street behind a gray sedan that is also full of monks. There are police everywhere, but all they are doing is directing traffic.

Na Mo A Di Da Phat.

The crowd reaches the intersection of Saigon's primary boulevard, Le Van Duyet. Apartment buildings line both sides of this thoroughfare. Also, a Cambodian consulate with a stone statue of a lion. Time has passed. It is now 9:20. The marchers form a circle perpendicular to the gray car. Four or five monks get out of that car. One monk opens the hood of the car (the engine is in the trunk Volkswagen style). This monk lugs out a five-gallon plastic container filled with pink gasoline. Another monk places a small brown cushion in the center of the street circled by monks and nuns.

A monk sits on the cushion and folds his legs into the lotus position.

This is the Venerable Thich Quang Duc.

He bows his big bald head. The monk holding the container of pink gasoline begins pouring it on Thich Quang Duc's skull. The container is now empty and is placed beside the cushion on the street.

Quang Duc is suddenly lighting a match...

Quang Duc becomes a pillar of flame.

The crowd of monks and nuns had been aware of Duc's intentions, but his actually burning is horrific even for Buddhists and they all begin wailing.

Burning flesh is a meat smell. The aversion to burning human flesh is psychological, not biological. Pilgrim crowds at 1692 Salem witch burnings had no aversion to the smell of cooking flesh. They would watch the witches dance in flames and still nibble snacks they had bought from vendors.

There was and is no sociological data about the smell of burning flesh in Indochina. In the center of that monk's burning head, Duc's eyes are still clenched closed, but his mouth is a pure grimace.

His burning body remains in the lotus position, his hands in his lap.

Imagine the deep control a man must have to sit in the lotus position and burn burn burn. The Venerable Thich Quang Duc's burning is real, as opposed to the holy poetry of the thirteenth-century Persian Sufi poet Rumi's cry of 'I want burning! Burning! Be friends with your burning. Burn up your thinking and your forms of expression! Burn like lovers burn!' Neither is Quang Duc doing a Blakean burn: 'Tyger, tyger, burning bright, in the forests of the night.' As for twentieth-century American burning, it won't be until next year, during the summer of 1964, when a New York City cop gets off for shooting a fifteen-year-old African-American, that all of Harlem erupts in rioting when Bill Epton, the thirty-two-year old vice chairman of the Progressive Labor Party, will shout his famous epithet, 'Burn, baby, burn!'

* * *

1963 Saigon. A journalist reported the conclusion of this public burning this way: 'Finally, Quang Duc fell backwards, his blackened legs kicking convulsively for a minute or so. Then he was still...'

Next came the fire trucks. The riot police with bayonets. Monks threw themselves in front of the wheels of the fire trucks. Monks with loudspeakers told the secular citizens what had just happened and why.

It was ten in the morning.

That night, when his compatriots burned the charred remains of Thich Quang Duc's body, the monk's heart was still intact. His heart would not burn in Saigon, just as the heart of Percy Bysshe Shelley did not burn a century before during that poet's cremation in Italy.

⋆ ⋆ ⋆

Now you've got some diamonds and you will have some others
But you'd better watch your step, girl or start living with your mother
So don't you play with me, 'cause you're playing with fire

—Nanker Phelge*

⋆ ⋆ ⋆

Saigon. Madame Ngô Dinh Nhu. Acid tongue. Acid bird. Thirty-eight years old. She wore a puffed-up Western hairdo. She mocked the burning Buddhist. She said that Thich Quang Duc had 'barbecued himself.'

BBQ monk.

Vietnamese cooking actually encompasses numerous forms of barbecues and compatible dipping sauces. The root of Vietnamese barbecue is garlic, chili pepper, sugar, lime, vinegar.

'What have the Buddhist leaders done?' Madame Ngô Dinh Nhu said at a televised press conference—her voice liquid with contempt. 'They have barbecued one of their monks whom they had intoxicated.' She smiles slightly at her own joke and adds, 'Even that barbecue was not done with self-sufficient means.' What? 'They used imported gasoline.'

'Let them burn,' she said.

'We shall clap our hands.'

One hundred years earlier, in the central highlands of Annam, a sect

---

* The collective pseudonym of all members of the Rolling Stones.

of Buddhists burned one hundred members of the Ngô Dinh family alive. Some Vietnamese Buddhists burned their aggressors instead of themselves.

★ ★ ★

So don't you play with me, 'cause you're playing with fire

—Nanker Phelge

Chapter 8

The American Embassy, Saigon, South Viet-Nam, 1963

It is summer '63.

The first lady is pregnant for the fifth time in her life. Her two sisters-in-law are concurrently pregnant as well—each for the eighth time.

* * *

Del Mar, California.

Desi Arnaz has been divorced from Lucy for three years now. He is forty-six years old. He is riding one of his favorite *baguales,* a mare. They trot in hills on his ranch that lies roughly twenty miles north of San Diego and only a few miles north of La Jolla. Desi Arnaz is now in the business of raising racehorses. *Caballos* are in his blood, as Cubans had been cowboys long before Americans in Texas or Dodge City. Arnaz is trotting toward the Pacific when he sees another rider approaching. This puts Desi on alert. It is not like anyone can just ride up to his ranch. There are fences. Barbed wire. The beach is the only approach without a barricade. The rider is close enough that Arnaz recognizes that the man is Latino. He looks too dark to be Mexican. He must be Cuban. Both men's horses scissor their ears at each other. The rider stops his horse maybe forty paces away and greets Arnaz with a raised hand. 'My name is Concepción Rubalcaba,' he calls out in Spanish. 'I come on behalf of José Simeón Negrín-Urrutia.'

Negrín-Urrutia was one of the secret moneymen in the Bay of Sows fiasco.

'Why have you come, friend?' Arnaz asks the rider in Spanish, and the rider answers, 'To ask your help in killing a prominent American.'

The Spanish for 'American'—as we all know—is *americano.*

* * *

Sunday, July 28. Jacqueline was seven months pregnant and celebrated her thirty-fourth birthday at Hyannis Port. In Washington, D.C., construction on Watergate Towne was finally permitted to begin. If Mussolini's body had been embalmed and placed in a coffin instead of having been defiled and burned, that sanctified Fascist would have placed his hands behind his head and smiled from inside his tomb.

* * *

Jacqueline's sister Lee was sailing in the Aegean Sea with her 'boyfriend,' Aristotle Onassis. The latter had just divorced his London-born wife, Tina. Lee, on the other hand, was still married to her husband, Prince Radziwill, but the woman was hoping to have that marriage annulled by the Catholic Church (just as was her first marriage).

August is a troubled month in the Aegean Sea when an atmospheric calamity known as the Meltemi blows. The Meltemi is twice as evil as the Santa Ana winds in Los Angeles. The Meltemi hurls up from Africa throwing itself upon the skin of the sea, twirling it around, making it dizzy, hurling itself around the islands howling. The Meltemi has an edge, almost a stink, suggesting that the wind is as ancient as Homer or the Medusa. Onboard the *Christina,* Lee is trying to be a perky fun girl for Aristotle Onassis even though she is neither perky nor still a girl. In fact, the woman is jittery the first thing in the morning, and every night, Lee swallows benzodiazepines to sleep. On August 7, in the middle of a particularly sour Meltemi, Lee gets a call by radio-telephone. The voice that emits is full of static. The Meltemi. Whoever is phoning tries to alert Lee that her sister has given birth. At first, Lee is overjoyed for Jacqueline. Then puzzled. This is too soon. The voice on the phone is trying to tell her that Jacqueline's baby is three weeks premature and was delivered by cesarean section. Lee drops the phone. Did this actually happen or is it a hoax perpetrated by the wind?

No. It is true. Washington, D.C. The baby is premature, but still alive. Barely still alive. Jack Kennedy, just back from a state trip to Berlin ('*Ich bin ein Berliner*'), hears this terrible news and is whisked to Cape Cod by presidential helicopter. The father and his second son are then flown to the Children's Hospital in Boston. Kennedy does not think of the baby as only a thing. This is his son, Patrick. At the hospital, President Kennedy is glued to the incubator that holds Patrick, neglecting the Affairs of State as long as a president can during the summer of 1963 when native drums beating in the distance say that the CIA is plotting something. The CIA continues to worry invasion strategies for Cuba, Castro being their favorite dog toy. Kennedy has been talking with brother Robert about disbanding the whole damn CIA and dropkicking all those assholes into the Potomac.

The president's child, Patrick, is moved to a thirty-one-foot-long hyperbaric chamber that forces oxygen into the infant's lungs. The President of the United States of America must don a surgical gown and cap before he can peer at his son through a porthole smaller than one in a motorboat.

Friday, August 9. Patrick dies of cardiac arrest. The baby has been alive for thirty-nine hours. Kennedy witnesses this terrible moment. He turns and trudges into the quarters where he's been camping out and starts sobbing.

* * *

On Cape Cod, Jacqueline Kennedy remained incapacitated on hospital pharmaceuticals and grief. Her husband would deal with Patrick's mass and funeral alone. Writer Sally Bedell Smith will report that the president of the United States gripped his son's small closed casket in both arms as if he intended to carry it himself out of the church.

Finally, Jacqueline was allowed to leave the hospital. She sequestered herself in a summer rental neighborhood in Hyannis Port inappropriately named Squaw Island. Lee Radziwill flew transatlantic from the Mediterranean to be at her sister's side, the Meltemi flying beside her airplane laughing.

* * *

'I'm going to marry Ari. Jacks, don't you get it?'

'Why would Aristotle want to do that?'

'Then Ari will be brother-in-law to the president of the United States. That's how it works.'

'No,' Jacks tells her sister. 'Aristotle will be brother-in-law to the first lady. That's how it works.'

Lee then told Jacks that Ari had extended an invitation for her to recuperate on his yacht *Christina* as his guest and sail the Mediterranean. 'Oh Jacks, tell Jack that Stas and I will chaperone you. Everything will be perfectly proper. You can't imagine how terrific Ari's yacht is. He told me we could go anywhere you want. It will do you so much good to get away from Washington for a while.'

Jacks said that she would think about it.

* * *

August 26. Nixon's failed 1960 vice president partner Henry Cabot Lodge Jr. arrived in Saigon as the new United States ambassador. Kennedy appointed Lodge for a simple reason: 'If Viet-Nam is going to be a catastrophe, let the Republicans take the heat.'

Lodge understood that the problem in Viet-Nam was Diem and the two Nhus. In Viet-Nam, those three were self proclaimed potentates. Gods. Yet everywhere else on the globe, Diem & Co. were another Flyspeck Dictator with a family of thugs.

Less apparent to Lodge and certainly McNamara back in Washington was the piss-poor administrative ability of the prime American military in Viet-Nam, General Paul Harkins (age fifty-nine). He was a pompous man who paraded forth with a swagger stick. Like Howard Hunt, General Paul Harkins also stuck a cigarette holder in his mouth. General Paul Harkins had thrown a Fourth of July party the month before and every American newsman went to partake of the free booze and the eats. Soon the press were quite obnoxicated and made up a song about Harkins to the tune of 'Jesus Loves Me, This I Know.'

We are winning, this I know,
General Harkins tells me so.
In the mountains, things are rough,
In the Delta, mighty tough,
But the V.C. will soon go,
For General Harkins tells me so.

General Harkins had a swaggering Vietnamese counterpart in Lieutenant General Ton That Dinh (thirty-six). Dinh not only carried a swagger stick, but also always wore a tailored paratrooper's uniform with a red beret tilted at a specific angle. Lieutenant General Ton That Dinh also had a giant Cambodian bodyguard.

Another South Vietnamese soldier of interest is Colonel Le Quang Tung (forty-four)—a bespectacled man who was the antithesis of swaggering Ton That Dinh. Tung was shorter than the typical Vietnamese male. He was the size of a woman. Tung was a prominent member of the Can Lao Party, Brother Nhu's undercover Roman Catholic extortion organization. Tung had eleven children. On August 21, bespectacled Colonel Le Quang Tung led raids on Buddhist temples. These actions were called the 'Pagoda Raids.' Swaggering Ton That Dinh came along as an observer 'for the experience.' Colonel Tung quietly blew up temples. Dinh actually danced, laughing in joy as the temples burned.

More than fourteen hundred monks and nuns were arrested.

Swaggering Ton That Dinh, apropos of nothing, declared to the television camera: 'I have defeated Henry Cabot Lodge. He came plotting a coup d'état, but I, Ton That Dinh, conquered him and saved the country from foreign adventures.' Ton That Dinh also said, 'Maybe in the future I'll again be governor of Saigon and fight against the Americans.'

During these days, even Viet-Nam's legendary holy carp were in peril. Far up the coast from Saigon in Da Nang, a fifty-pound carp had been found living in a pond the size of an American basketball court.

The Big Carp.

The local Buddhists believed the fish was a reincarnation of one of Buddha's prime disciples. Buddhists from the outback began pilgrimages to the pond. This would not do. Madame Nhu must not hear about this situation.

One of President Diem's cousins came down to lead an attack on the pond. His soldiers strafed the water with machine-gun fire. No giant body of a carp lolled dead to the surface. The soldiers studied the water. Just as they were leaving, the Big Carp swam joyfully near the surface and coyly made kissing gestures with its mouth.

Diem's younger brother radioed Brother Nhu for aid. Nhu sent bespectacled Colonel Tung. When Tung arrived, he stood on the shore and threw hand grenade after hand grenade into the water, producing furious blasts of water.

Dead fish surfaced. Eels too.

But no Big Carp.

Finally, Tung flung five grenades at once into the pond, throwing with such force that his glasses flew off into the water. The pond exploded in a torrent of green water one hundred feet high, the orange body of the carp at the crest of this liquid rampage. The Big Carp was ejaculated upon the land.

Colonel Tung ran to the fish and squinted at it and then kicked it to make sure it was dead. It was. He then stomped the Big Carp, both his arms raised and his mouth puffed open barking in joy.

Colonel Tung returned to Saigon very pleased with his triumph. While he went to Saigon's prime optometrist to purchase new French frame glasses, President Diem's famous paratroopers began flying helicopters up to the former carp pond at Da Nang to fill their canteens with liquid good luck.

* * *

In the U.S.A., Thursday, September 12, was the president and the first lady's tenth anniversary. They celebrated at Hammersmith Farm in Newport, Rhode Island. Jacqueline gave her husband a gold Saint Christopher's medal as Jack had left his personal Saint Christopher inside Patrick's coffin. Those who were present would observe, 'The two seemed very affectionate in a melancholy sort of way.'

That night Jacqueline told her husband of her intention to go with her sister Lee to the Mediterranean aboard the yacht of Aristotle Onassis.

Jack reacted as if she had told him that she had just posed topless for *Playboy.* 'No way. No no no. Are you crazy?' He told her that it was bad enough that the American press had been speculating about the affair between the rich Greek crook and the first lady's goddamn adulterous sister.

Jacqueline said, 'I'm going.' She did not raise her voice when she said that, but there was nothing faux-naive about how her utterance was spoken.

* * *

Those who were close to the couple reported later that something very tender and strange happened between Jack Kennedy and his wife during these last weeks of September and Jack resolved to let Jacqueline go with her sister to the Mediterranean.

All Jack's sisters-in-law despised Jacqueline and pressured him to lock her up, but this husband resigned himself to letting his wife oscillate her will. To be crude, Jacqueline had just paid for that right with her womb.

The media made note that Kennedy appeared existential during the last weeks of September. It was as if President Kennedy had become the American version of a Camus *désespoir.* The magazine *Time* wrote that the president no longer seemed driven by a sense of 'man-in-the-barricades urgency.'

At the end of September, Kennedy still had gobs politically on his plate. First, he had a foreboding about the inevitable coup d'état in South Viet-Nam. Second, Kennedy knew that by January he would likely go through what we moderns call a 'sex scandal.' As you know, Kennedy had a constant parade of carnal engagements that even if one-sixteenth were made public, would make Hugh Hefner seem like a monk. The president had spent his life knowing that common sexual morality was like a wallet, and as we know, he refused to carry that convenience. Yet, now after the death of Patrick, for the first time in his life he felt regret at betraying his wife by rutting with all those women in the frenzy of the bed.

Years from now, many historians will write in a retrospective manner that it was like during those last weeks of September Kennedy had an unconscious inkling that he was what we moderns call A Dead Man Walking. Consider that at his own father's seventy-fifth September birthday, each of Kennedy's brothers and sisters sang a song to their dad along with their gifts. Jack chose the Maxwell Anderson/Kurt Weill 1938 'September Song.' The president of the United States sang to his father:

Well, it's a long, long time
From May to December.
But the days grow short,
When you reach September.

A friend of the Kennedys told future biographer Sally Bedell Smith that it was almost as if Jack knew he was never going to see old age.

On the other hand, Jack Kennedy could have just as likely chosen that song in unconscious and dark anticipation of his old father's eventual passing.

* * *

President Kennedy addressed the United Nations near the end of September to propose a joint U.S.-Soviet trip to the moon. (Luckily for Neil Armstrong's destiny, nothing will ever come of this musing.) Afterward, Kennedy went on a working vacation in Rhode Island where the president 'directed' a home movie starring friends and their wives in bikinis. After a faux rape scene, Jack's longtime friend 'Red' Faye, wearing only boxer shorts and black socks with male garters, was filmed as if dead with ketchup poured on his chest. It has been said in reports that after November 22, 1963, this 8mm home movie will be 'locked up.'

* * *

Aristotle Onassis had wired Jacks to say that he'd stay off the *Christina* while she and her sister were aboard. Jacqueline immediately sent a telegram: 'I could not accept your generous hospitality and then not let you come along!'

Meanwhile, Jack Kennedy knew his wife's sister and brother-in-law were not going to 'cut it' as chaperones with the press. Kennedy phoned his secretary of commerce, Franklin Delano Roosevelt Jr. 'Frank, it's Jack. Open your window. You hear that? That's Dorothy Kilgallen and Drew Pearson that you hear howling at the moon.' The president then strongly suggested to FDR Jr. that he volunteer to travel with his wife, Suzanne, to act as unofficial chaperones for the Bouvier sisters as they floated upon the Mediterranean.

FDR Jr. was forty-nine. During the 1930s, FDR Jr. had been a wild boy at Harvard. He participated in car crashes and Brahmin orgies and deflowered coed after coed with the aid of bathtub gin. He was thirty when his father, FDR, died. His mother, Eleanor, had died just one year ago in 1962. Now a middle-aged man, he possessed the stodgy girth that would remind us moderns of Al Gore at age fifty-nine.

FDR Jr. told JFK, 'Yes. I will go for you.'

★ ★ ★

Jacqueline, aka Jacks, met her sister Lee at the Washington National Airport. Lee always seemed disheveled compared to her older sister. Jacks and Lee's mother, Janet Auchincloss, once said, 'Jacqueline always looked marvelously put together, while her sister Lee seemed blown out of a hurricane.' The truth was Lee was more beautiful than Jacks. Lee possessed the softer face. Lee was not as smart as Jacks in the things that Jacks was smart in, and vice versa. Together the sisters presented themselves as a comedy team with neither being a straight man or a Jerry Lewis–style fool.

The Bouvier sisters spent the grueling ten-hour flight sitting in the smoking section puffing and talking—conversing like assassins plotting; no gossip or common yack save an analysis of Jacks's switch from L&Ms to Newport menthols, the sisters speaking with enthusiasm about the aromatic qualities of that latter brand of smokes.

Meanwhile in Washington, D.C., *Washington Post* columnist Drew Pearson's 'Washington Merry-Go-Round' had continued to be a fly in President Kennedy's ointment. Pearson's newest headline read, FIRST LADY'S CRUISE CAUSES STIR.

> Much has been written in the European press about Mrs. Kennedy's cruise on the yacht of the glamorous Greek shipping magnate Aristotle Onassis, once indicted for cheating Uncle Sam and required to pay a whopping $7,000,000 fine.

As Lee and Jacks flew to Europe, Lee talked Jacks's ear off about the probability of Onassis asking her to marry him. No one expected him to marry his longtime mistress Maria Callas. Drew Pearson reached a similar conclusion:

> Onassis had only recently divorced his wife Tina Livanos, daughter of another Greek shipping tycoon, in order to marry Maria Callas, the Greek opera singer. And Madame Callas had divorced her husband in order to marry Onassis. This marriage somehow got sidetracked. Maria Callas, famous for her temper, is now reported boiling over the reported romance between Princess Radziwill and her betrothed.

* * *

October 4, Friday. The Bouvier sisters boarded the yacht *Christina* in Piraeus, the port of Athens. The vessel is the kind of opulent James Bondish yacht that Dr. No would sail. It had a seaplane on its roof. Radars. Numerous decks. Its bow was sharp. It looked like it could cut through both the sea and the air like a swordfish.

Princess Lee was telling Jacks about the movie theater inside the *Christina*. And the library. The fully operational operating room with an X-ray machine.

'What if I get an abscess in my tooth?' Jacks asked her sister.

'What?'

'Is there a dentist onboard?'

Every guest was given their own room as well as a personal maid and a personal steward. Jacks chose the room named Cyclades. Jacks's personal maid, Syllia, told 'Mrs. Kennedy' that the actress Greta Garbo had loved Cyclades too. Syllia had terrible teeth. Perhaps that was why 'Mrs. Kennedy' felt Syllia was lying about Garbo's room.

There were a handful of other guests aboard. Jet Setters. The chic set. Europeans. Jacks wanted everyone settled before she was given introductions because that was how she liked to season her traveling. And Jacks had spent most of the last two years traveling. She heard that one night when *The Huntley-Brinkley Report* was signing off, after David said, 'Good night, Chet' and the other replied, 'Good night, David.' Chet then looked into the camera and said, 'And good night to Mrs. Kennedy, wherever you are.'

Jacks was very comfortable with appearing on television as 'Mrs. Kennedy,' but had no use for watching television itself as recreation. Jacks did not even notice the device's absence in her stateroom. The woman was also ignorant of the time difference between the Mediterranean and the eastern seaboard of the U.S.A., but it was probably late afternoon in Washington. Every cabin had its own radio-telephone. It never occurred to Jacks to check in with Jack or the kids.

* * *

Gia Long Palace, Saigon. Ton That Dinh swaggered up to President Diem and asked to be appointed minister of the interior. President Diem scowled and shouted, 'Of course not!'

Ton That Dinh left Saigon to sulk in the country. Days passed. No one in the Diem administration asked him to return to Saigon.

He returned on his own, slinking not swaggering.

Ton That Dinh was called to a meeting with Brother Nhu. The morning of the meeting, Ton That Dinh was told over the telephone to leave his Cambodian bodyguard at home. Ton That Dinh was terrified as he entered Nhu's office inside Gia Long Palace. *Am I going to be shot? Tortured first?* Instead Nhu said, 'You've heard all the rumors about the coup?'

Ton That Dinh had not, but nodded anyway.

Nhu said, 'Coups are like eggs and must be smashed before they're hatched.' He gave a big Chinese opera smile. 'I'm going to stage a coup myself.' He named a date in November. 'This will be called Operation Bravo.' Brother Nhu explained that bespectacled Colonel Le Quang Tung would stage a fake revolt in Saigon. The president would take refuge at the seaside resort Cap St. Jacques.

'What will I do?' asked Ton That Dinh.

'You and your troops will remain on the outskirts of Saigon. Inside the city, Tung will see to it that mob violence will be rampant. Tung will see to it that the American embassy is stormed. The mob will kill Lodge and his wife. And then kill all the monks hiding there. Tung will then announce the formation of a "revolutionary government" composed of known opponents to my brother and my family. The radio will blare anti-American propaganda. This charade will last twenty-four hours. Then you and your troops will march into the city and crush the uprising. My brother will return to Saigon victorious. This will prove to Kennedy that the only alternatives to my brother and me are all anti-American and pro-Communist. Only I and Diem can control the population. After this "coup," all our unknown enemies will be exposed.'

Ton That Dinh gave a small laugh.

'What's funny?'

'There is a saying among the Italians that "revenge is a dish best served cold." The Corsicans even say that "revenge carried out in twenty years is revenge carried out too soon." We'll wait only until Christmas, and then hunt down and kill every last one of our enemies.'

'Ha! We'll wait only until Fish Day.'*

★ ★ ★

On October 5, the yacht *Christina* left port. Two things to know. The Meltemi almost always died by mid-September; Onassis was aboard the yacht but had not yet made an appearance. He was lying low because he was passing telegraph messages to Papa Doc, the voodoo dictator of Haiti. Now that Havana had gone Red, Onassis wanted to create a Jet Set gambling paradise in Port-au-Prince. He was in the middle of negotiating with Papa. Onassis was also actually trying to purchase the island of Ithaka in the Ionian Sea.

Jacks kept to herself that first afternoon. She wandered around the ship and poked around the *Christina*'s vast library. Onassis possessed dozens of different translations of Homer's *Iliad* and *Odyssey* in various languages. She would have to chastise Onassis when she finally met the Greek. She had been told Aristotle only read history books.

Homer was a poet.

She also found a copy of Dante's *Inferno* on the shelf. Ha! Another poet. And this one a . . . Roman.

The book seemed both indelible and incredibly rare. More a museum piece than an antique. Someone had left a playing card—the ace of spades—as a page marker in the Eighth Circle of Hell. She took the volume back to her room to read later.

There was a dinner that night. All the guests attended. Would Onassis show? Dress was casual. Stas the prince, Lee's husband, was there. He was a compact man with a thin European moustache and a receding hairline. Jacks was particularly interested to meet Princess Irene Galitzine, the Russian-born Italian dress designer. She was forty-seven. Moderns would say that she looked ten years older, although she was as healthy as aristocrats could be in 1963. She made her mark on the fashion world with her

---

* A Vietnamese holiday at the end of November.

creation, palazzo pajamas. She premiered them at a Palazzo Pitti fashion show in 1960 and received a standing ovation.

Jackie wore a pair of palazzo pajamas to dinner.

The dining room located in the hull of the *Christina* was luxurious and deceptively spacious as if the two dozen diners were sitting in the banquet hall of an ocean liner. The first course was a buffet of vegetables prepared *à la grecque* ('in the Greek style')—*aubergines* and *concombres* and *poireaux* (eggplant, cucumbers, leeks) cooked with lemon and olive oil and coriander, then marinated among bags of ice to be served cool. It was presented by a dozen waiters who served as discreetly as butterflies.

If we could glide above this dinner like angels with tape recorders, the conversations would resemble a future short story written by Lee's dear friend Truman Capote titled 'La Côte Basque,' a story containing rarefied and raw gossip spoken by the aristocrats of all aristocrats. The speakers aboard the *Christina* spoke a mixture of French and Italian and Greek and English. In particular, Jacks and the Russian-Italian princess switched between French and Italian. The princess was only one year old when her family fled Saint Petersburg from Trotsky's Bolsheviks. The princess spoke Italian like a Roman, yet French with a Russian accent, not Italian. The Radziwills and Roosevelts were listening to the Garoufalidises speak in English of the massacre of the Onassises along with other Greeks in the town of Smyrna in 1922. Prince Radziwill spoke to Princess Galitzine about their lineage. As all talkers got tipsy on the fine wine, everyone gossiped in French and Italian and English about their host, who obviously was not going to show. The Garoufalidises now only talked to each other in Greek about how they despised Aristotle associating with Americans, especially American women.

'Ari needs a good Greek for a wife.' (In Greek.)

'Mrs. Kennedy, didn't Maria Callas and Marilyn Monroe sing for your husband's birthday at Madison Square Garden last year?' (French.)

'Maria Callas sang. That other woman just panted.' (French.)

'What did Maria sing?'

'I do not know. I wasn't there.'

'What did you say?'

'I don't know. I wasn't there.'

'Why not?'

'Excuse me. Oh, waiter!'

'I only design apparel that feels good on the body.' (French.)

'Yes. I don't care for clothes that you have to think about after you've put them on.' (French.)

'An elegant woman should never look ill at ease.' (French.)

(Whispered in English.) 'I would definitely call what she is wearing *garb.*'

'The Turks made the men kneel in a line and then they came up from behind and slit their throats.' (Italian.)

'To save bullets, no doubt.' (Italian.)

'No doubt.' (French.)

'During the 1920s when liquor was illegal in your country—' (French.)

'Puritan madness!' (English.)

'Despicable *suffer jets.* Women got the vote and women made drinking against your laws . . .' (Broken English.)

'Yes. Of course. During the 1920s, Ari supplied your father-in-law, Mrs. Kennedy, with two million barrels of Scotch whiskey. Aristotle and your father-in-law became millionaires together.'

It was at this moment that in the kitchen, the cook and his assistants were placing live lobsters into pots of boiling water to scald them to death in preparation of *homard à l'américaine*. Julia Child wrote in her first book, *Mastering the Art of French Cooking* (1961), 'So many steps are involved in the preparation of a really splendid lobster [*Américaine*] no wonder it costs a fortune in any restaurant!' (Of course, no guest ever paid for a meal aboard the *Christina*. When the Garoufalidises were in a foul mood—Aristotle's sister Artemis, in particular—they muttered that all Ari's guests were freeloaders.)

The conversations below are all in either French or English.

'Some call this *l'américaine* after the lobster *province amérique* in Brittany.'

'Nonsense. Tomatoes are not at all typical of Brittany cuisine.'

'Julia says it was likely created by a Paris chef with *Provençale* aspirations who named it after the American origins of the tomato.'

'Nonsense. The tomato first came from Sardegna.'

'Nonsense. The tomato originated in Peru.'

'There's no island named Peru.'

'In South America. The Incas . . .'

'Inca dinka doo.'

'Cortez discovered that the Aztecs grew them too and brought them home to Spain. Philip the Handsome named them wolfpeaches.'

'Wolfpeaches! Strip Aristotle and I'll show you a pair of wolfpeaches!'

'Did you say sharks?'

'No, wolves.'

Everyone now spoke English, except the Greeks.

'There were so many bodies of dead Greek babies floating in the drink that sharks invaded the bay.'

'There are no sharks in the Mediterranean!'

'Are you going to doubt me? I was there.'

'No no. Every schoolboy knows there are no sharks in the Mediterranean. It's in textbooks.'

'Printed in Chicago no doubt. Famous for the sharks that swim in Lake Michigan.'

'So will your brother show himself tonight?'

'Ari is like the Wizard of Oz—*Pay no attention to that man behind the curtain.*'

'By 1965, how squalid everything will be. There'll be total depravity. My couture will be attached to crash helmets.'

'Did the pope bless your pajamas?'

'You're thinking of Helena Rubinstein. The pope blessed her lipstick.'

'Excuse me for changing the subject. Tell me, Mrs. Kennedy, it's so long since I've been to the States—do they still put little plastic prizes inside boxes of Cracker Jacks?'

Jacks answers by laughing.

'The best thing a mouse can do when he is caught in a trap is eat the cheese on the hook.'

'André Gide?

'No. Hebbel.'

'Neither of you has ever caught a mouse in your life.'

'Oh, don't be a thumping bore!'

'What do you mean, Mrs. Roosevelt?'

'When was the last time you caught a mouse? The mouse heads for the cheese on the hook, then *swack!* The hinge of the trap breaks the mouse's neck. She has no chance to actually eat the cheese.'

'I hear Ari baits his traps with *Bleu des Basques Brebis* with a smidge of *Ossau Iraty Pardou Arriou.*'

'Say that last cheese five times very fast.'

'Ossau Iraty Pardou Arriou. Ossau Iraty Pardou Arriou. Ossau Irato Pardi Arriou. Ossau Iraty Pardi Arrioh. Ossau Iraty Pardou Arriou. There.'

'You lose.'

At the end of the meal, everyone brought their plates to the deck and threw them into the sea following Onassis's decree that no one in the kitchen should have to clean a dish if the meal had been exquisite.

A fingernail moon hung in the Aegean sky. Jacks walked alone on the deck. At the poop end of the yacht, she noticed the shining blood-color star of a cigar. Someone was sitting up in the dark on a higher deck. Jacks found some steps and climbed them. She reached a dead end. She tried a door. It was locked. She climbed a ladder and shimmied across a ledge. The cigar smoker was gone.

* * *

Sunday, October 6. Madame Nhu was in Washington. Gossip columnist Dorothy Kilgallen, that fifty-year-old journalist and panelist on the TV game show *What's My Line?*, wrote La Callas Reported Heavy at Heart—

> High-flying Parisians who traveled with the Very Chic Set this past summer describe Callas as 'the most depressed dame in Europe.'

She also mentioned that Liz Taylor was living inside her yacht while *The Night of the Iguana* was being filmed on the shore of Mexico. Kilgallen also name-dropped the stripper Tempest Storm, who had left the U.S.A. to settle permanently in Europe. Kilgallen then wrote, 'Don't you adore the name of Madame Nhu's secretary, Blue Skies? She is a fast 18.'

* * *

On the morning of the second day, Jacks and Lee each took a peach the size of a cantaloupe and went deckside for a bout of breakfast sunbathing. The light still amazed. The light physically transformed Jacks's eyeballs. All colors were saturated. The bruises of purple on her peach had surely been inspired by Matisse. Then around three o'clock in the afternoon, the *Christina*'s engines were cut off and the ship dropped anchor. Lee stood and headed aft, down several levels of steps to the stern, only about ten feet above the water. Lee peeled down her one-piece green swimsuit to her ankles and stepped out and then dived off the starboard side into the sea. The water was warm. Lee did a lazy breaststroke. The sun was blinding, but you could look up with such solar clarity that surely those were individual flames thousands of miles high on the surface of that broiling star.

A launch engine started up. A small boat tailed Lee, piloted by a Greek man without a shirt, Jacks sitting at the prow. 'We're here so you don't drown,' she called out to her sister.

Lee coaxed Jacks to come into the water. The older sister stood and peeled off her suit and dived in. The pair swam for a while and then crawled aboard the launch that then headed back for the *Christina*. Jacqueline directed the Greek to head to the bow.

They hadn't bothered to peel their bathing suits back up and stood naked and called out for FDR Jr., singing, 'Come on, Franklin. Come to us. We're the sirens. Come into this sea. The sea of the sirens. Jump in, Franklin, jump in.'

* * *

The next day, Jacks and Princess Lee had gone into the kitchen to prowl. Jacks noted a jar of nutmeg. Jacks told Lee, 'If you take too much nutmeg you will hallucinate.'

'Who told you that?'

'Mary.'

'Mary Meyer?'

'Uh-huh.'

'Tell me the circumstances.'

Jacks did. The two sisters then sneaked huge tablespoons of the nutmeg into FDR Jr.'s gazpacho. The sisters watched as the man spooned up the gazpacho. He wrinkled his nose only once. He did not complain. He ate and ate and then said, 'Look at those waves! The foam is like Lustre Crème!'

Lustre Crème? Jacks said nothing aloud, but in her head she imaged FDR Jr.'s toady face on the cover of the novel *The Ugly American*.

★ ★ ★

On October 7, LBJ's aide Robby Baker resigned because the *Washington Post* exposed his 'influence peddling.' Rumors flew that Kennedy would dump LBJ from the ticket. Kennedy had supposedly already contacted Senator George Smathers of Florida. It is neither here nor there that one of Senator George Smathers's secretaries was Mary Jo Kopechne. Eventually, she would be Edward Kennedy's Mary Jo Kopechne.

★ ★ ★

On Monday the 7th of October, the third day of the voyage, Jacks was awakened around noon by the ringing telephone.

The radio-phone.

It was her sister-in-law Ethel, calling to insist that 'Jackie' return to the U.S.A. 'Your kids miss you. How can you be so selfish? Caroline has stopped eating. John John has tantrums all the time. The newspapers had just photographed little John John screaming as all hell as Jack flew away in a helicopter. And I don't have to tell you how Jack spends his time when he's unsupervised. A bus pulls up every afternoon full of blondes. Jackie? Are you there? Good. I've been reading medical articles. Well, an article. In what? A magazine in the bathroom. *Reader's Digest*. An article said the reason women have as many miscarriages as you have had is because of chlamydia. What? Spell it? K-l-u-h-m-i-d-e-e-u-h. I dunno. I can tell you that *Reader's Digest* says the name comes from a Greek word that means "cloaked." Your little Aristotle should be familiar with that! A man gets chlamydia from screwing around. He screws around but doesn't get any symptoms. He just gives the germs to his wife and when she gets pregnant, well—you know what she goes through.' Ethel paused, then added, 'Sometimes she actually gives birth'—it sounded like Ethel giggled—'. . . but she gives birth to a retard.'

The radio-telephone was a predecessor of the cell phone. 'I can't hear you anymore, Ethel,' Jacks lied. 'Hello? Hello? I can't hear you.' Then she hung up.

Jacks looked down at the table and saw that she had two cigarettes going simultaneously, both nesting in an ashtray that must be Ming Dynasty or older.

* * *

In *Moby-Dick,* Captain Ahab did not make his entrance on the *Pequod* until chapter 29. Aristotle Onassis appeared on Tuesday. Jacks was on the deck at pool's edge. She heard telephones ringing. Many telephones. The guests began running down from the deck to their cabins. Apparently, all forty telephones were ringing inside the *Christina.*

It was then that Aristotle Onassis bounced up to the deck. Jacks was the only one to see him at first. Aristotle Onassis was slight in height and stocky in body. His dress was casual—a short-sleeved shirt and baggy pants and horn-rim glasses. He smoked a Havana cigar. He held a glass full of ouzo from Mytilene.

What a powerful, powerful personality.

Soon the guests returned up to the deck one by one and Aristotle Onassis held everyone's attention. Aristotle Onassis was not just full of life. Aristotle Onassis was the source of life. You could imagine him walking through the wards of a children's hospital and all the kids jumping out of their beds and following him.

'The only rules are there are no rules! he shouted.

He announced that the first trip was to Smyrna.

Ari boomed out the horror of Smyrna, where he was born, when a great massacre of the Greeks perpetrated by the Turks took place. Horror stories. Ari's guests had heard all the horror stories from his sister and brother-in-law. But Ari made the massacre sound fresh. He narrated as Homer did, that is the horrors were not horrors, they were just statistics. Aristotle Onassis told how he only saved himself by becoming the gunsel to a young Turkish lieutenant. Ari spoke of being buggered by that Turk without shame. He gratefully became the Turk's boy because that designation allowed him to leave Smyrna intact and alive, and take a steamer to Argentina.

FDR Jr. said in English, 'Sir, you speak without shame. You are like Puccini, who described himself as a passionate seeker of beautiful women and good *libretti*.'

Onassis raised his arms over his head and clapped his hands. 'Son of a bitch, just like me!' Then he paused and smiled. 'Only I don't give a damn about *libretti*!' Then Onassis pointed at Jacks. 'The Achaeans could laugh at themselves. The Romans could not.'

It was like he was reading her mind.

'Is that why Dante had Odysseus appear in the Eighth Circle of Hell?' she asked.

'Dante is worse than Italian—my apology to Princess Galitzine—but Dante is a poet. Poets are nothing but seducers.'

'Seducers of what?' Jacks asked in a particularly breathy little-girl voice.

'Women. Men. Goats. Children. A poet would rut with an eel before eating it if he could.'

'But Homer was also a poet.'

'Homer was not a poet. He was a historian who wrote in an archaic age where there were only two ways to write, lyrical verse and grocery lists. Nothing in between.'

Jacks then said, 'Virgil was a historian like Homer and if I recall he didn't care for Odysseus either.'

'Virgil was Roman,' Onassis said. Then he said it again, 'Virgil was Roman. Dante slandered Odysseus from a, how you say, *greaseball*? Yes. I dare to say that Virgil and Dante are both *greaseballs.* As I recall, Odysseus was stuck with his comrade in arms, Diomedes, in—what Circle of Hell?'

'The Eighth Circle.'

'Odysseus and Diomedes were placed in Circle Eight of Hell to burn together forever because of their intense cleverness in deceit. The Trojan horse was deceit. Odysseus deceived Achilles into joining the war even though Odysseus knew that Achilles was destined to be killed. Diomedes stole the Palladium from Troy.'

'What's a Palladium?'—FDR Jr.'s voice.

'A statue of Athena. Shall I tell you who Athena is?'

'No. I know who Athena is.'

Jacks speaks up: 'Dante sent Odysseus to hell for those things, but Odysseus also tricked Iphigenia into returning to her father's island by lying that she was going to be married there in a big ceremony.'

'Yes. Yes. Instead, her father, Agamemnon, sacrificed her. But you know, in those days a Palladium was a hundred times more valuable than a daughter. As you know, I am a modern Greek as you are a modern American. And you and you and you—you are modern Italians. And Prince, you are a modern man of the modern world. Yet this very ship we stand upon I named after my daughter, Christina. So all this is to say, Mrs. Kennedy, that for you and me, yes! Odysseus, if he must be sent to the Eighth Circle of Hell, the inclusion of his crime against Iphigenia should make his flame burn hotter.' Then he added, 'But this is all theoretical, since as I told you before, Dante, like Virgil, was a slanderous Roman bird turd.'

* * *

Back in the U.S.A., the *Washington Post* calls Madame Nhu 'Rappaccini's daughter, Beatrice,' out of a story by Hawthorne. 'Beatrice was reared on noxious flowers and herbs that so infected her that to approach her was to be poisoned. Her touch left infection on the hand of her lover. Poison was so much a part of her nature that, in the end, an antidote killed her.'

The *Washington Post* says that Madame Nhu destroys the thing that she professes to love, Viet-Nam. Her flaw makes her visit to the U.S.A. a 'disaster for South Viet-Nam.' The paper makes the point that America is in Viet-Nam not to support the Diem dictatorship, but to defend Indochina against Communism. 'Since Madame Nhu kills only the things she loves, we seem to be for the time being, quite safe from the hazard of her embrace.'

* * *

Aboard the *Christina*. Prince Radziwill encouraged his wife's dalliances with Aristotle for complicated business reasons. He also desired to marry a woman twenty-seven years his junior, Charlotte Ford, the twenty-two-year-old daughter of auto magnate Henry Ford II (the father of the Edsel).

This marriage will never happen.

Two years hence, Charlotte Ford will become the fourth wife (thirty-two years younger) of Stavros Spyros Niarchos, yet another Greek billionaire shipping tycoon who was the archrival of Aristotle Onassis. The Ford-Niarchos marriage will end in divorce, and Stavros will return to his third wife—no need for the pair to remarry, since the Niarchoses' Mexican divorce will not have been recognized by the Greek Orthodox Church. Several years after Niarchos and Ford divorce and shortly after the third wife's death, Niarchos the Greek will marry Tina, Aristotle Onassis's first wife.

It is Tina's daughter with Aristotle Onassis, Christina, whom his yacht is named after.*

These types of complications were how things transpired for European royalty and millionaires, and Americans who got emotionally involved with European royalty and millionaires. This was a far cry from the more than ten years of situation comedies on American TV that celebrated the suburban nuclear family. Think *Leave It to Beaver* and *Father Knows Best.* Incidentally, ABC had just canceled both those long-running shows. Something was in the air, perhaps.

* * *

Dead of night aboard the *Christina.* The sky was filling with white moon-illuminated clouds. Jacks and Ari had snuggled up on the balcony on the poop deck.

'Tell me something secret and masculine about yourself,' Jacks ordered Ari.

'Tell me something secret and masculine about myself?' Onassis repeated. He thought a moment. 'I lost my virginity when I was twelve. The woman was my tutor who taught me French. Once I said to her in Greek, *Mademoiselle, you are indecently dressed. You are arousing me against my will. If you continue to dress in such fashion, nothing can stop me from violating you.* Oh, it was lovely. Sex should always be for joy. I hope that someday American women and Greek women and English women are raised to feel that carnal communication is not an unpleasant duty.'

'You have a carnal tongue, Ari.'

'I believe you have a carnal heart, Mrs. Kennedy.'

Jacks found herself saying the words 'Fish heart.'

'What?'

'Oh. My gosh. I was just thinking of a photograph I saw years ago.' She described the photograph taken by Ngô Dinh Diem.

Onassis thought a moment. 'Caviar. I worship caviar.'

'Which kind?'

'Russian sturgeon, I believe its Catholic name is *Acipenser gueldenstaedtii.*'

---

* Tina will die in 1974 in Paris of a drug overdose similar to the one that will kill rock 'n' roller Jim Morrison in Paris in 1971.

'That's Latin.'

'Exactly. There are two kinds of Siberian sturgeon, *Acipenser baerii* and *Acipenser persicus.* And of course we can't forget the *Acipenser transmontanus*, found in the Caspian Sea.' Then he pointed to the sky. 'But it can also be found in the Black Sea.'

Jacks tells how two months before, William Averell Harriman, who was now seventy-one years old and the head American negotiator in Moscow, showed up in Hyannis Port with a jar of caviar, a gift to President Kennedy from Khrushchev. Now, it had been an open secret that Kennedy had tried to poison Castro with cigars. Furthermore, Harriman had once presented Kennedy with Soviet gift wood ornaments that were installed with KGB bugs. After Jacks explained this to Onassis, she said, 'Our American appetite ruled out caution, and we all spooned up that roe. It was so exciting thinking that it may be poisoned. Or filled with LSD.'

'What is LSD?'

'A drug like the one Aldous Huxley took in *The Doors of Perception.*' Then Jacks asked, 'What time is it?'

Onassis shrugged.

'Are you sleepy, Ari? I'm not sleepy at all.'

The rich Greek told her, 'I only need maybe two hours of sleep a night. I can stay up for three days straight, but then I sleep for an entire day. I am a night bird. I am the bird of night. I fly over the moon.'

If there had been a chorus present like in ancient Greek theater, the chorus would have chanted of destiny. The chorus would tell how in 1974, Onassis will be stricken with myasthenia gravis, a neuromuscular disorder that would make it impossible for him to keep his eyelids raised. It was not that he was sleepy, the muscles in his eyelids had collapsed. Onassis will then be forced to Scotch tape them open or prop them open with blunt-ended toothpicks.

* * *

In Washington, D.C., during this time, Jack Kennedy went Christmas shopping for Jacqueline. He was also taking secret lessons to improve his French—for Jacqueline. The one thing he also did that would have enraged Jacqueline was his allowing *Look* photographer Alan Stanley

Tretick free access to take photos of the kids for the magazine, the most reproduced photo being that of almost three-year-old John Jr. peeking from a secret panel in his father's desk while his father did presidential paperwork above him.

★ ★ ★

Madame Nhu was on the cover of the October 11 issue of *Life* magazine. The article was a puff piece. The thirty-nine-year-old woman was now 'thirty' years old. And a 'Christian.' She was also 'the most determined feminist since the late Emmeline Goulden Pankhurst.' Viet-Nam was described in terms that made it seem as sexist as when the Taliban will control Afghanistan. *Life* explained that in Viet-Nam, women could not marry without their parents' consent. Then they were forced to live with their in-laws. 'Endure without protest their husbands' infidelities.' They could be 'reduced to the status of a servant to a new mistress in the house.' Madame Nhu changed all that. She 'pored' over old laws and wrote up a Declaration of Independence for Women. In the Assembly, the opposition was not large, but it was noisy. Male delegates talked interminably about the value of tradition. Just when Madame Nhu thought she had won them over in committee, they would wriggle free. 'Really,' complained Madame Nhu, 'men change their minds much more easily than women.'

★ ★ ★

Another day in the pagan Mediterranean—

The boy—the young man—was standing before Jacks and Aristotle in a perfect spot of sunlight. Behind him swirled the sea. And birds. And a pumice island with cliffs and figs and olive trees and cypresses and eucalypti.

The young man wore only sailor pants. Bare feet. No hair on his chest. He was so handsome that Jacks had an impulse to stand up and bite his shoulder.

The wife of the president of the United States did not bite the young man's shoulder.

'This young man is Roberto,' Aristotle said. 'He is only an Italian.'

Roberto shrugged.

'Hello, Roberto,' Jacqueline said in her whisper-voice. 'I am only an American.'

The young man failed to smile, yet his eyes sparkled. He glanced at Aristotle and something passed between them.

'The Gods appeared to mortals all the time,' Roberto said in English with a heavy Toscana accent. 'Men used to speak of the good odor of the Gods. With time, the appearance of Gods grew commonplace. So, the Gods only appeared to mortals disguised.'

'Thus Zeus transformed his body into that of a swan so he could experience a swan's passion while fornicating with a woman named Leda,' Aristotle added (as if this image added clarity).

Roberto continued: 'Then the Gods stopping appearing in any form unless they wanted something from mortals. The Gods grew confused about what their own needs were.'

Roberto stopped as if to see if Jacqueline had something to add or a question to ask. She had nothing to say.

'The Gods did not find the answer within themselves, so they abandoned the earth.'

'This all occurred before Homer's time,' Aristotle added.

'After a thousand years of silence, mortals called the memory of the Gods *pagan*. They now worshipped in modern fashion—they worshipped a single God who was invisible save for a moment that he appeared in the desert once as a whirlwind.'

'God's invisibility proved he was God,' Aristotle said with a smile.

Roberto: 'This God even impregnated a woman like Zeus had done with much more frequency. The woman gave the God a son who was not invisible himself. The son grew into an adult and allowed himself to be nailed to a tree. Then he too became invisible in the form of a rapacious and invisible ghost.'

'He once left the imprint of his face on a shroud,' Jacks stated.

Roberto shrugged rather helplessly and looked at Aristotle. The older man added, 'Just like a woman leaves an imprint of her lips with lipstick on a piece of tissue.'

* * *

Sunday, October 13. Washington, D.C. The Vietnamese goddess, Madame Nhu, was the guest on the television show *Meet the Press.* She said that the *New York Times* was under an evil Buddhist spell and needed shock therapy to rehabilitate itself. She also said, 'My father, who was Viet-Nam's ambassador to the United States until two months ago, has been against me since my childhood.'

Madame Nhu's father responded to his daughter at a Woman's National Democratic Club luncheon. The newspapers described him as 'soft spoken' and living 'quietly' in Washington since his resignation in protest of the Diem government. 'My son-in-law Nhu controls much more than the Secret Police. He controls everything in Viet-Nam. It is unfair to compare Nhu to Robert Kennedy who is only attorney general. Nhu is even ten times more powerful in Viet-Nam than President Kennedy is in the United States.'

★ ★ ★

The Mediterranean.

The day after Roberto's dialogue.

The sun rose again both jubilant and ethereal. Aristotle asked Jacks, 'So what did you think about Roberto's pontification?'

'It was amusing,' she said.

'You were amused?'

'I was amused.'

'Good. That is the perfect reaction for a God.' Ari lit a cigar. 'You will forgive my rudeness for calling you a God rather than a *Goddess.* The modern Greek for *goddess* is *thea,* which also means "something you can see." The whole world can see you on TV, yet there is nothing about you that is opaque. Do you understand?'

'Nope.'

'What?'

'Nope.'

'Okay. No matter. Okay. I know that I am a God. You are a God as well, but you've forgotten.' He took a hit off his cigar. 'And I say *God* in the pagan sense. The true sense. We are not invisible Gods. You and I both do what we want. Whatever we want. We want for nothing.'

'We have obligations.'

Aristotle waved his hands. 'Nonsense. Gods are not obligated to do anything, not even to be divine. Both you and I possess great wealth, no?'

Jacqueline thought for a moment. 'I suppose, yes.'

'Just as I,' Aristotle said. 'Did you toil for your wealth? Let me answer for you. *No!* Did I toil for my wealth? *No!* Wealth was an acquisition. I mean it was sport. The perfect state of equilibrium. Do you know what that is?'

'I know what equilibrium means.'

'But do you know what equilibrium is? I will tell you. Frivolity. Beauty is frivolous. Love is frivolous. The sea is frivolous. Frivolity is great delight. Emotions are for mortals. The only two emotions we Gods feel are great anger'—Aristotle raised a finger—'this is different from rage. That is for the invisible God, that gnashing of his teeth. We of pagan divinity never grow so angry that we gnash our teeth.' He lowered his finger. 'And the second emotion is mourning.'

'Mourning as in grief for the dead?' Jacqueline asked, frowning.

Aristotle chuckled. 'Not *proinos*, but *penthimos.* Not the sunshine and the early robin eating the worm, but sorrow at the death of a living thing that was not immortal.'

Jacqueline crinkled her brow. 'I don't understand.'

'You have loved a horse,' Aristotle said.

'Yes. I have loved many horses.'

'One of the things that you loved about the horse was that it did not know that it would someday die, which is another way of saying that the horse assumed that it was immortal. In this way, Death is the only thing Gods respect more than Frivolity.'

Jacqueline thought and kept scowling.

'Think about the son you just lost and let yourself weep,' Aristotle said.

She looked up in amazement. And did. Her torrent of tears was incredibly compact in a way that contrasted with, say, the melodramatic theatrical grief witnessed in an opera. And yet, as a collapsed star that is black and cold is more powerful than a star that burns hot, Jacks became the real thing, the epitome of a mother's grief.

She then stopped, turned off a faucet, and looked up at Ari. 'My husband never carries a wallet. He has so much money he doesn't need to carry money. In the same way, I have so much heart that I don't need to carry it with me.'

Aristotle smiled. 'You love yourself with all your heart. That is all that is important for a God.'

Jacqueline smiled at him. A Mediterranean smile intoxicated by the light. A smile that made the glass inside the barometer fall. 'Intellectuals feel sorry for Gods because we are so easily happy!' Aristotle said. 'It is impossible for us to be seduced. And we ourselves never bother with seduction. We are quenched and when we are not we just reach out to that which will quench us anew.'

Jacqueline reached out and touched the bone in the middle of Aristotle's bare chest. Then she drew her hand away.

He leaned his face closer to hers and said, 'We will pass the island of Ithaka tomorrow.'

'Yes?'

'I want to recite to you words that I wrote about Ithaka.'

'Poetry?'

'It is not fiction,' Aristotle said. 'It begins this way:

> "When you start for Ithaka, long for a prolonged sail of sweetness and adventure . . ."

Jacqueline closed her eyes and listened to Ari recite and as she listened, she etched his words on the inside walls of her heart. Then she murmured, 'We'll go to Ithaka and only then will I return to Washington.'

* * *

Washington, D.C. Madame Nhu lodges at the Mayflower in the heart of D.C. on Connecticut Avenue NW. She is cheap with her staff. They sleep outside of town in a cheap two-story motel in Maryland. It is nine p.m. Madame Nhu is standing with her secretary, Blue Skies, on the balcony in front of her corner room on the second floor. Her bodyguard is with her. He is solemnly holding a pair of binoculars. 'When does this vision appear?' Madame Nhu says crossly.

'Five more minutes,' Blue Skies answers.

From this vantage point, they can clearly see the screen of the Maplewood Drive-In Movie Theatre. Blue Skies has explained to Madame Nhu that in America you can watch movies from the front seat of your automobile. From Blue Skies' very first sentence explaining this, Madame Nhu stopped listening. She was bored. Madame Nhu does not like surprises. Nothing that can possibly occur on that drive-in movie screen will generate any publicity for Madame Nhu.

'Okay. It's going to happen soon.'

The bodyguard hands Madame Nhu the binoculars. They had already been prefocused, but Nhu aims them at the screen and fiddles with the focus just to be assured. Then she sees it. She sees the surprise. From this vantage point, the screen fits perfectly in the imitated vision space of the binoculars. A man is riding with a woman. Madame Nhu knows the woman is Marilyn Monroe only because she has seen photographs of Monroe in newspapers. The man is called Clark Gable, but Madame Nhu has never heard of him. What she is seeing is Gable and Monroe riding separate horses together. The horses are trotting.

Marilyn Monroe is wearing a hat.

Marilyn Monroe is wearing a Vietnamese conical hat plaited with palm leaves on her head. In Viet-Nam these hats are called *non bai tho*. The scene lasts for fifteen seconds. Madame Nhu holds her breath for fifteen seconds. Then she begins jumping up and down as Blue Skies begins jumping up and down.

'Marilyn Monroe was trying to be you!' Blue Skies hollers.

Madame Nhu raised the binoculars again.

'She is no longer wearing *non bai tho!*' Madame Nhu whines.

'I've watched this movie from start to finish. That is the only time.'

'Get them to run it again,' Madame Nhu says to Blue Skies. She looks at the bodyguard. He merely says, 'I will try.'

Madame Nhu raises the binoculars again. 'Damn!' She lowers the binoculars and then glares at them as if her will alone should make the image of Monroe on horseback wearing *non bai tho* reappear. Then she turns to Blue Skies. 'Get this Marilyn Monroe on the telephone. She'll want to speak to me. Maybe she can star in my life story.'

Blue Skies looks helpless. 'But Madame Nhu! Marilyn Monroe is dead.'

'Nonsense,' Madame Nhu says with disdain, raising the binoculars again. 'She can't be dead. She is on the movie screen.'

★ ★ ★

Saigon.

Everyone in the city knows about the coming coup. But again, no one knows whether it is a real or fake one. President Kennedy insists that the coup leaders call off the coup if they feel they cannot succeed. He worries that although the U.S.A. is not actively planning the coup, the U.S.A. is obviously copasetic with the coup. If the coup should fail, Diem will surely kick the U.S.A. out of Viet-Nam. This is why Bobby Kennedy opposes the coup. Dean Rusk is pro-coup. As is Bob McNamara.

★ ★ ★

Halloween is coming up. Adlai Stevenson talking with President Kennedy—"Texans are ridiculous, Mr. President. One hundred years after the Civil War, the Republican Party is still anathema to Texans. They don't understand that if Lincoln was alive today he'd be a Democrat. Instead of kowtowing to conservative Democrats in Texas, why don't we tell them to get the hell out of the Democratic Party and become goddamn Republica—'

Kennedy interrupts him: 'So Adlai, what happened to you in Dallas?'

'Oh that. Some John Birchers started clobbering us with placards. Extremists.'

'You were shaken up?'

'I was shaken up. I think you should skip Dallas. Or just make a speech to the rich folks, but stay off the streets. The streets are mean.'

'Lyndon ever tell you about him and Lady Bird campaigning in Dallas?'

'Yeah. Crackers in straw hats with Nixon hatbands chasing Lyndon down the street, spitting on Lady Bird.'

'Yes. And she was born in Texas! She's a yellow rose.'

'So why should you go to Dallas, Mr. President?'

'Because I am *Mr. President*. I'm going to Dallas. I'm going to motorcade down their streets.'

'Well, whatever you do, don't publicize the motorcade beforehand.'

'We don't intend to publicize the motorcade beforehand.'

* * *

Saigon. Tuesday, October 29. President Diem's brother Nhu orders the swaggering Ton That Dinh to come to Gia Long Palace. 'Why have so many army platoons moved into the swamps?' Nhu asks.

'Because it will keep the Americans quiet, sir. Otherwise, they'll start complaining that we're not fighting the Communists. I'll bring the platoons back in time to *stop* the coup.'

'I'm going to give you new orders. Infiltrate the conspirators. I know who they are—just some young restless majors. You should suggest to them that the coup be staged on November 1'—the Day of the Dead in Mexico—'Saigon will be mostly closed and the movement of troops relatively easy. This plan is called Operation Bravo Two.'

Lieutenant General Ton That Dinh begins moving troops in and out of the city. Both President Diem and Brother Nhu believe that swaggering Ton That Dinh is preparing to protect them.

* * *

When Howard Hunt's son, Saint John, will turn sixteen in 1970, his father and mother will sit him down. 'Saint John, your father doesn't work for the State Department.'

'You mean he quit?'

His father spoke. 'No, I never worked for the State Department.'

'Your father works for the CIA.'

Silence.

'The Central Intelligence Agency.'

'I know what the CIA is, Mom.'

'I am a spy. Or I was a spy. I just quit.'

Silence.

'Your father was protecting the country.'

Silence.

'I risked my life for America, Saint.'

Silence.

'I never killed anyone. Not intentionally. The only ones who got hurt were Communists. And they deserved it.'

Silence.

'Can I go?'

Silence.

'Sure, Saint.'

Saint knew that his parents expected him to be excited—like 'My dad is James Bond. Cool!' But Saint is sixteen. He thinks and feels like a teenager thinks and feels. He broods on being dragged around his whole life like a gypsy kid. Always being the freak in school. The kid with longer hair than anyone else. The kid who wore adult clothes, not blue jeans. Down the line, Saint John will say, 'It didn't mean a whole lot to me at the time that my father was a spy. It was more, *You've been lying to me my whole life about where my dad works.* All the diplomas on my dad's wall were phony.'

⋆ ⋆ ⋆

Big Fat Minh always meets with his generals as a group on Friday afternoons. On the day of the fake coup, which is also the day of the real coup, bespectacled Colonel Le Quang Tung shows up at the meeting. He has a brother in the army who comes with him. This set of brothers are not as dependent on each other as President Diem and Nhu are. Tung has said nothing about the 'fake' coup to his brother. Tung has only come to the meeting so as to not arouse suspicion. He wonders if he dare alert his brother to what is going to happen later in the afternoon.

Fat Minh arrives. Everyone is sitting at the banquet table. Fat Minh thumps that table with his fist and yells that the army is taking over—'Right now! Today! Friday!' Soldiers hoisting submachine guns rush into the room. Tung whips off his glasses and starts polishing them furiously with his shirtsleeve. *So soon? Is this the real coup? Or has Nhu prepared a series of fake coups?*

'Those who want to join the coup, stand,' Fat Minh shouts.

Everyone stands but the Le Quang brothers. Tung's brother looks at him. Tung puts on his glasses. He considers standing and going along with the charade. He looks at Fat Minh straight. Fat Minh has big eyes, eyes that almost make the jowls of his face seem quaint. His gaze is equivocal. Tung deduces that Fat Minh is serious about this coup. This is the Real

Thing. Bespectacled Tung continues to stay seated. His brother continues sitting as well. Additional soldiers rush into the room, and push and drag both brothers out the door.

Fat Minh now has a soldier lug a reel-to-reel tape recorder into the room and plug it in. Fat Minh records himself proclaiming the coup. Then each standing soldier is led to the tape recorder to state their name, rank, and support for the coup. Fat Minh's intention is for this tape to be played over the radio.

At 1:15 p.m., the siren at the Tan Son Nhat Airport signals the three-hour noonday siesta. All over the city, men and women are getting in beds surrounded with mosquito nets. In the palace, President Diem and Brother Nhu sit. They hear distant gunfire. Nhu spits out the name *Tung*. 'That asshole has started the coup three hours early.' Nhu knows he must call swaggering Ton That Dinh to let him know that his troops must return to the city earlier than intended. The voice that answers Ton That Dinh's official phone says, 'I don't know where General Ton That Dinh is.'

Nhu lowers the receiver of the phone and howls across the room at his brother. 'Where is that cow-fucking drunkard?'

★ ★ ★

In Saigon, no soldier is sure who is who.

Who is the enemy and who is our friend?

'Anyone who opposes us is the enemy' is the answer.

★ ★ ★

What about Elvis Presley? During this time, Elvis had a talk with the Colonel. He wanted the Colonel to manage Rusty Ammo (aka Ann-Margret). The Colonel said, 'I'll think about it.' The Colonel then went to the *Viva Las Vegas* director, George Sidney, to complain that Ann-Margret was getting too much face time and was trying to steal the picture from Elvis. On another burner, the Colonel was wheeling and dealing to get backing for a picture about the life of Hank Williams, with Elvis as Hank. Soon, Elvis and Rusty knew they could never marry.

Each other, that is.

Such a marriage would be like Elvis marrying Elvis, Rusty marrying Rusty. Their careers came first.

Elvis returned to Memphis.

★ ★ ★

Saigon. By four in the afternoon, insurgent artillery was gouging up the façade of Gia Long Palace. President Diem knew he had somehow been double-crossed by the army. He phoned the man he had planned to have murdered, Ambassador Lodge, to tell him the South Viet-Nam army was rebelling. Lodge told Diem that the rebels had assured him that Diem and his family would be given safe passage out of the country.

Diem hung up.

The coup generals called Diem at the palace to promise if he resigned immediately, he and his brother would receive safe passage out of Viet-Nam. 'Sir, the time has come when the army must respond to the wishes of the people.'

Until this moment, Diem knew that a coup was actually happening, yet a part of him did not believe it. Now, Diem put the phone down and casually vomited like a cat. Diem then phoned the generals to tell them that they must come to the palace to negotiate. Diem was stalling. This is how he had quashed the coup of 1960.

'Either yes or no, President Diem. There is no room for negotiating.'

Diem hung up.

Radio Saigon, 4:30 p.m. Fat Minh announces the coup is finished. He is victorious. Fat Minh demands the resignation of Diem and Nhu.

Diem telephones Ambassador Lodge yet again. 'What is the attitude of the U.S.?'

'It is four thirty a.m. in Washington, President Diem. The government doesn't have an attitude.'

At 4:45 p.m. in Saigon, Fat Minh phones Gia Long Palace yet again. Nhu answers. 'My brother is not here.'

Fat Minh impatiently signals with his hand and loyalist Colonel Le Quang Tung is shoved into the room. His glasses are broken but he is still wearing them balanced on his nose. The soldier behind him puts a pistol to the man's head and Tung begins speaking into the telephone. 'This is Tung. I am a prisoner. My special forces have laid down their arms.'

In Gia Long Palace, Nhu hangs up the phone.

Fat Minh is furious over this loss of face. He has to worry about a countercoup. He orders his bodyguard Captain Nguyen Van Nhung to take Le Quang Tung and his brother to Tan Son Nhat Airport. The brothers' hands are tied behind their backs and a jeep drives them toward the airport. The Le Quang brothers are silent. One of the brothers figures they are both going to be shot. Another brother thinks that they are both going to be flown out of the country. Then each brother changes his mind to the opposite negative or positive position. The jeep pulls off by a fence by the airport. The big engines of a large propeller passenger plane burble above them. Captain Nguyen Van Nhung says, 'Get out.'

Nguyen Van Nhung is a killer, although he sees himself as a warrior. Perhaps. He is nothing like the Greek warrior Achilles, save for one similarity: When Nguyen Van Nhung was a boy, he had a male companion he had grown up with just as Achilles had Patroklos. And just as Hector of Troy slayed Patroklos in battle, Ngô Dinh Nhu killed Nguyen Van Nhung's comrade.

Hector killed Patroklos in noble fashion with a sword.

Ngô Dinh Nhu used pliers and matches and a bucket filled with sow shit. An American commented, 'That Ngô Dinh Nhu! Doesn't give a rat's ass for the Geneva Conventions!'

Nguyen Van Nhung now takes pleasure in killing men. It satisfies the seething rage that he has felt behind his eyes ever since he was a boy.

Nguyen Van Nhung has never killed a woman and he has no curiosity about such an act.

Nguyen Van Nhung leads the two Le Quang brothers down the road several paces. They come upon two holes dug in the ground. Each brother's heart sinks. The holes are carelessly dug, but it is clear that these are sloppy graves.

Nguyen Van Nhung raises his revolver quickly and shoots Le Quang Tung's brother in the ear and pushes his body into a grave. Tung turns away and then he quickly takes off his glasses and puts them in his pocket.

A light drizzle starts to fall. It is worse than *saliver pluie.* Nhung does not shoot Tung, as the man is now muttering to himself. Tung looks up at Nhung and says, 'The names of my children.'

Nhung scowls. 'What about the names of your children?'

'I am reciting the names of each of my sons and daughters.'

'How many brats you got?'

'Fourteen.'

'Busy man,' Nhung says and puts the barrel of his gun in Tung's left ear. 'Tell me when you are done.'

* * *

By midnight, Saigon goes still.

Inside Gia Long Palace, President Diem's phone rings. He answers it. He finally hears the voice of swaggering Ton That Dinh.

Diem smiles with relief. The coup must be over. The loyalists have won!

Then Ton That Dinh begins barking, 'Ton That Dinh saved you and your brother many times, but now you mother-rapers are both finished!' (Ton That Dinh has been playing clever. If the loyalists had won, Diem would have seen Dinh as a righteous loyalist. If the coup succeeded, as it had, he was perceived as a player on Fat Minh's team.)

'It's over, mother-raper, it's over.'

Brother Nhu runs into the room holding two briefcases. President Diem takes one. The briefcases are full of cash.

At two a.m., Fat Minh telephones Gia Long Palace for the eighth or tenth time. 'I demand that you surrender.' President Diem screams at Minh and slams the phone down. He stands. He thinks a moment. He phones Fat Minh. 'All right,' Diem says. 'I will surrender and these are my terms.'

Diem tells Fat Minh that he wants a full-scale military ceremony with jets flying overhead. Diem demands that every general and major be dressed in full regalia to stand at attention before him. Diem wants a fifty-gun salute. Then he wants to be flown out of the country. Fat Minh stands listening to Diem with his mouth hanging open. Finally the fat general screams, 'While Vietnamese are killing one another I will make no guarantees.'

President Diem is about to hang up, then he says 'All right' with quiet resignation. 'I agree to a cease-fire and to offer an unconditional surrender.'

He hangs up the phone up softly.

At rebel headquarters, Minh's fellow generals all begin shouting at once. 'What should be done with Diem?' 'What should be done with Diem?' A general named Nguyen Ngoc Le howls, 'Kill the bastard.' 'No!' 'No!' 'Absolutely not.'

Fat Minh says, 'The Americans want him alive. We need the Americans. We let him leave the country alive.'

At 6:37 in the morning, a white flag waves from the south wing of the palace. The sun is rising. Already the temperature is in the nineties. Happy crowds mill everywhere howling, 'Long live the uprising!'

The innards of Gia Long Palace are Marx Brothers crazy. Rebels and civilians and even American reporters tear through Madame Nhu's underwear dressers to find pieces to give to their Saigon girlfriends.

Nhu's liquor cabinets become a paradise for the thirsty!

The *New York Times*' David Halberstam is spotted walking down a grand stairway holding a massive elephant tusk he has liberated from some bedroom. At eight in the morning, Fat Minh arrives at Gia Long Palace wearing full military dress uniform. The man has come to transport Diem and his brother Nhu back to command headquarters for the surrender ceremony—a green-covered table is waiting. The following will then be broadcast—all the generals sitting at that green-covered table where President Diem will formerly relinquish power. After the ceremony, Diem will ask for asylum. The generals will grant the request, stipulating that Diem and his brother Nhu must remain in custody until an aircraft whisks them out of the country.

Fat Minh marches through the palace, encountering that cartoon confusion of liquor and tusks. Everyone goes quiet.

'Where are they?' Fat Minh bellows.

Everyone realizes that the two Ngô Dinh brothers, Diem and Nhu, are missing.

* * *

Earlier, during the Hour of the Wolf, Diem and Nhu had entered a tunnel in the basement of Gia Long Palace and exited far from the palace in the woods near Saigon's sporting club, Cercle Sportif. Each brother hugged his briefcase of money. The two spent the final hour of the night secure in the home of Nhu's main man in the opium trade. The brothers were waiting for a car to arrive that would drive them across the river to the Cholon side of Saigon.

Chinatown.

The car never shows.

Forget it, Jake. This is Chinatown.

By dawn, the brothers knew in their hearts and sweetbreads that Saigon was now completely in the rebels' hands. Not even the Corsicans could save the brothers now. The two walked with their briefcases of money into the nearby Church of Francis Xavier. A priest gave the brothers Communion. Diem then looked at Nhu, who looked sturdy for a man who had been through what they had gone through for almost twenty-four hours. Nhu's eyes held a sense of boredom and resignation. The priest got Diem a telephone. The former president of South Viet-Nam called the Joint General Staff Headquarters. Diem spoke to Fat Minh. 'I will surrender on the condition that I be allowed to surrender honorably. My family will be allowed to leave the country. I remain as president of the country for a decent interval in order to retire gracefully.'

Minh barked, 'Yes. Yes. We will discuss the third later.'

In Washington, President Kennedy was elated by news of the coup. The casualties were minimal to everyone but the nine insurgents killed and forty-six wounded, and the four dead and forty-four wounded Palace Guard, and, finally, the twenty dead and the 146 wounded civilians. The White House claimed publicly they had known nothing about the coup. No one realized that made Kennedy seem uninformed. In Beverly Hills, Madame Nhu held a press conference wearing black sunglasses. 'The U.S.A. was responsible,' she said with seething disdain. 'I believe all the devils in hell are against us. Whoever has the Americans as allies does not need enemies.'

* * *

A month before in the Mediterranean—the night before Jacks had left the *Christina* and returned to America, the woman found herself nerved up.

She wanted to be alone. She did not want to be alone.

She wanted to wear some new green slippers she had bought on

Naxos and could not find them. She got on her hands and knees and checked under her bed, under the dresser, under the cabinet. She found a paperback. A French novel, *Le Mépris.* A French translation of an Italian novel titled *Il Disprezzo.*

Disdain.

Contempt.

She had never heard of the author. Jacks began reading. The narrator was a male Italian writer who becomes convinced that his wife has stopped loving him, that in fact she feels pure disdain. The narrator and his situation were both contemptible—Jacks identified with the wife—yet she could not put *Le Mépris* down.

Why was she reading this book? Was she meant to find it under the furniture? She left her bed and got down on her knees again with a face towel and wiped the floor under the dresser. There was no dust. Someone took the time to clean under the furniture but missed the book? She returned to the bed and read some more. The book was 250 pages. On page 141, the protagonist has been hired to write the screenplay for a movie based on Homer's *Odyssey.* Odysseus was called Ulysses in the text. This annoyed Jacks, but then the book was originally written in Italian. She read a passage where the director of the film, a man named Rheingold, tells the narrator that Ulysses never really desired to return to Ithaka, to his wife, Penelope. 'When Ulysses isn't betraying his wife with other women, he is seeking adventures that will delay him. Ulysses even dawdles.' The narrator disagrees, saying, 'If we can't trust what Homer says, who are we to believe?' Rheingold answers, 'We men of the modern world know how to see through myths.'

Jacks threw the book to the floor. Then she got on her knees and shoved it back under the cabinet. She stood and staggered out of her cabin and hurried to the deck. She searched for the light of Onassis's cigar. Nothing. She went below the deck and headed to the bar. The lights were on. There was no one there drinking. The bartender was sitting on one of the bar chairs made of the hide of whale balls, the man's head tilted back, his mouth agape in sleep. She hurried out of the bar and down the corridor where Onassis's suite was located. She stood outside his door. She could not raise her hand to knock. She turned away. She began acting as if she was being filmed. She leaned against the wall and then slid to the floor. Tears flowed from her eyes, but she did not feel as if she were crying. What she realized, what a mere novel had shown her, was that she was like Odysseus.

Jacks did not want to go home. Jacks wanted to throw her radio-telephone out of the porthole and stay aboard the *Christina* with Aristotle Onassis forever.

★ ★ ★

9:43 a.m. Saigon time. Several armored troop carriers pulled up to the Church of Francis Xavier—General Mai Huu Xuan in charge, a military man who had been demoted by Diem; a military man who detested Diem. General Mai Huu Xuan was the only military man who would accept the job of 'transporting' the Ngô Dinh brothers, as every other general of the chiefs of staff still feared Brother Nhu. After General Xuan's men pulled up to the church, they all waited inside their vehicles. General Xuan stood outside and stomped his foot. Soldiers began stepping out in tentative fashion. Then everyone stood staring at the church door waiting for the two brothers to come out. After twenty minutes, the Ngô Dinh brothers strode out of the church with purpose. They wore dark gray suits. They each held a briefcase. The soldiers stood shuffling their feet, peering down at the dust.

'Bind their hands,' General Xuan shouted. His men just stood like helpless children. Ngô Dinh Nhu gripped his briefcase of cash and smiled. At that moment, Nguyen Van Nhung the Killer got out of an armored carrier. Nhu saw him. Nhu's smile turned hollow.

Nhung the Killer walked toward the Ngô Dinh brothers.

Nhung the Killer actually sauntered toward them.

Diem stood regal, stoic.

Nhu squinted at Nhung the Killer with homicidal intimidation. The latter did not avert his gaze. Nhu peered into that other's eyes, and realized that he and his brother Diem were dead men.

Nhung the Killer grabbed the cords from a frozen soldier and tied Diem's hands, keeping Nhu in the corner of his eye. Nhu stood, tense as a cat spying a mouse.

Nhung yanked away Diem's briefcase and threw it to the ground. Nhung took hold of Diem's wrists. Nhung turned toward Brother Nhu.

At that moment, Nhu's will dissolved. He was so tired of running this country. Nhung tied Diem's hands behind his back and then threw Brother Nhu's briefcase to the ground and kicked it away. Nhung jerked Nhu's arms and spun him around and wrapped Nhu's wrists together with twine. Nhu grunted, 'Hey!' Nhung the Killer pulled tighter.

Nhung the Killer stood back to shove both the brothers toward one of the armored carriers—it resembled a roomy tank with wheels instead of tread. General Mai Huu Xuan nodded at Nhung and scooted into his jeep. Nhung the Killer pushed both brothers inside the carrier, Nhu first.

Diem's and Nhu's suitcases just lay on the ground. No one paid them any attention.

In the armored carrier, the driver was sitting in the turret. He started the engine. Nhung the Killer climbed inside and slammed shut the door. The driver took off—'Heading to Joint General Staff HQ in Saigon, right, sir?'

'Correct, soldier.'

Brother Nhu was sitting on the floor next to Brother Diem. The circulation in Nhu's hands had stopped. No new blood in, no old blood out. Nhu's hands began to prickle. It soon felt like his hands had been stung by a jellyfish.

Nguyen Van Nhung the Killer stands above the brothers and remembers his dead friend, his Patroklos. It is as if Nhu's squatting body below him were privy to the killer's thoughts. 'I mocked him, Nhung.' Nhu suddenly sneers. 'I mocked your little suck queen. I said to him, *Ha, without your gear between your legs you're as helpless as a little girl*. I turned him into a little girl, Nhung.'

The killer, Nguyen Van Nhung, implodes into a frenzy of howling guttural syllables and grabs an unattached bayonet and with a single motion squats down and plunges the blade through Nhu's suit into his belly. Nhung yanks the bayonet out and blood follows from Nhu's gut in a steady pour. Nhung hunches over Nhu, savoring the moment. Nhu's arms strain. He wants to grip his stomach and stanch the blood.

Nhung the Killer bends down and pulls Nhu's suit coat wider and again stabs Nhu through his white shirt into his wet belly. Nhung does not pull the blade out, but rips it upward following the path of the buttons of the man's shirt. Nhung stops when the blade is blocked by Nhu's sternum. Nhung the Killer pulls the knife out and tosses it over his shoulder and socks his fist into Nhu's terrible wound and begins yanking out what he finds inside, using his other hand to pull Nhu's head forward and then push it downward so Nhu must watch his own vivisection.

* * *

Ngô Dinh Diem sat in semi-lotus beside his brother, his own hands still bound uncomfortably tight behind his back. Diem stared straight ahead with an expression that was no expression. The armored carrier stopped at a train track for a train. The driver was sitting above them in the cramped space. Diem looked up and could only see the driver's sandals above him. Diem had seen few motion pictures in his life. He certainly had never seen *Psycho.* It never occurred to the man that the blare of the train had been providing a soundtrack for the stabbing of Brother Nhu much the same way Bernard Herrmann's scraping violin cry of *Shriek! Shriek! Shriek! Shriek!* had provided the soundtrack for Marion Crane's stabbing in the violated privacy of her bathroom at the Bates Motel. That shower scene is one of cinema's most essential pairing of music and image, yet Hitchcock's original intention was to have the shower scene unspool in silence, just the sound of running water. When the stabbing began, viewers would only hear a sound effect, say the sound of a knife plunging into a melon.

Hitchcock had felt disheartened about the movie he was shooting. He was actually considering giving up the ghost and turning *Psycho* into an hourlong episode of his TV show, *Alfred Hitchcock Presents.*

Hitchcock's composer Bernard Herrmann went behind the Master's back and recorded his violin squeals. Then Herrmann screened the shower scene with the new score. Hitchcock was electrified, of course. He finished shooting his movie possessing the aplomb of genius.

The Saigon-bound train passed.

Nguyen Van Nhung stood up as straight as he could. Both his arms were drenched in the blood of Ngô Dinh Nhu.

Brother Diem sat with his eyes squinted closed. He was envisioning

Soeur Angelique. He tried to picture Soeur Angelique's fingers. The girl had a scar on the top of her left knuckle. It was hardly noticeable. She had fallen into a rosebush as a child. It had been a slight ripping of the flesh. This faint scar was what made Diem love Soeur Angelique the most. The two were too shy to ever look each other in the eye. He always just watched her lips when she was talking or else studied her scar.

In the military carrier, Diem was dimly aware that his brother was now on the floor covered with so much blood it was as if a washtub had spilled. His brother's blood was soaking into Diem's trousers. The blood smelled metallic like fresh barbed wire. Nguyen Van Nhung the Killer was standing above Diem with his head tilted low because of the cramped ceiling of the vehicle. Nhung was breathing heavy like a horse. Both men's sleeves were drenched up to the armpits in black blood. Nguyen Van Nhung's hands were empty. He was still glaring at Nhu. Diem looked up at the killer's face realizing that he had never seen a man so etched in black rage. The man was moving his jaw back and forth, gnashing his teeth. Diem stopped thinking at that moment. He knew that he was next.

It won't be until the late 1970s that a collection of Diem's photographs will be exhibited at the Museum of Modern Art. Susan Sontag will attempt to write about Diem's work as she is preparing her book *On Photography.* She will be sitting at her desk in Manhattan. She will type her first sentence about Diem's photographs: 'No one ever discovered ugliness through photographs.' She types that sentence and then stares at her wall. She looks down at her typewriter and types a second sentence: 'The point is not to be upset, to be able to confront the horrible with equanimity.' Sontag looks up from the typewriter and considers the two most provocative photographs from the Vietnam War. The first, Colonel Tung standing with his arm outstretched pointing a pistol at a young man named Tse Huo Fat. The photo was taken half a second before Colonel Tung pulled the trigger, yet Tse Huo Fat is grimacing as if the bullet has already been projected into his head. Tse Huo Fat's grimace is astonishing in its awful emotional clarity.

The second photograph, of course, is the one of the naked Vietnamese girl running screaming down the road toward the camera, her skin presumably just burned by napalm.

Sontag remembers the first sentence of chapter 48 in that old semiologist

Roland Barthes's book *Camera Lucida*. 'Society is concerned to tame the Photograph, to temper the madness which keeps threatening to explode in the face of whoever looks at it.'

Sontag decides to not write about Diem's photographs because to fit them into the hematology of the Viet-Nam War would make her lose her mind. Sontag decides to write about the dead American Diane Arbus's photographs of freaks and nudists and retarded Americans instead.

Return to Saigon and see Diem, covered in his brother's blood, suddenly understanding all the pain that was in each photograph that he had sent to Soeur Angelique. Losing her was like losing a limb. Having a heart torn out. It was so obvious. Americans used a new modern term for such a condition:

Diem was a *blockhead*.

How could he be so uninvolved in his own feelings?

Diem was truly relieved when Nguyen Van Nhung reached into his jacket and pulled out a gun.

Nhung shot Diem in the face.

His brother Nhu was still twitching on his belly on the floor, the snakes of his intestines splattered on either side of him. Nguyen Van Nhung moved his gun hand to his left and shot Nhu in the skull just above his neck. Nhu's legs kicked up and down rapidly, and then he went still.

Nguyen Van Nhung reached down and wrapped his gun in Nhu's bloody shirt. The killer would retire his pistol now.

* * *

The armored vehicle stopped at the headquarters of the rebel generals. They were soon all aghast at the carnage of the Ngô Dinh brothers inside.

What was left of them.

Everyone was howling at Fat Minh. 'Why are they dead? Why are the Ngô Dinhs dead?'

'What does it matter?' Fat Minh shouted back.

General Mai Huu Xuan burst into the room and yelled with pride, *'Mission accomplie.'*

Fat Minh turned to the other trembling generals. 'Do I have to explain? I planned to spare those two and let them leave the country as planned.

But they were not in the palace when I arrived. I was made to appear as a fool. That was the final insult of the two eels of the Ngô Dinh family.'

* * *

The Mediterranean Sea.

Jacks was kneeling and weeping against Aristotle Onassis's cabin door—

She awoke in his arms. He was sitting in the hall leaning against the wall with her head in his lap.

He was wearing a black terry-cloth swimming robe.

'I heard you weeping,' Onassis said. 'What was wrong?'

'*Was* wrong?' the woman mumbled in confusion. Weren't things *still* wrong? Finally she said, 'I found that terrible book.'

Onassis didn't ask her *what* book. 'Why was it terrible?'

'It said Odysseus did not want to go home. What a terrible thought. It makes Ithaka a sham.'

'Ithaka is not a sham,' Aristotle said. 'It is true that Odysseus did not want to go home. But it is also true that Odysseus did not want to become a God either.'

'What do you mean? Odysseus was mortal.'

'He wasn't a God like you and I, but immortality is what Calypso offered him vis-à-vis Circe.'

Jacks said nothing. That statement didn't really register.

'All of Odysseus's peers wanted the transfiguration of godhood,' Onassis continued. 'Agamemnon and Hector and Achilles. Those three were semidivine. Yet, Odysseus was the one who had divinity offered to him on a silver bowl.'

Jacks frowned. 'What bowl?' Then she got it. 'You mean a silver *platter.*'

'You say tomato and I say toe-may-toe.' Onassis said that and laughed. 'Odysseus was duped into believing that an eternity of pleasure would dull his mind because truth be told he found the Gods stuffed shirts and dull. Still, he didn't want to go home either. Odysseus felt that both these intentions negated each other and he had to choose between staying a God and admitting to himself that he didn't want to go home or leaving Calypso and becoming a mortal who must sail home. It never dawned on Odysseus that he could leave Calypso and become mortal again and still not go home, but continue having adventures on the sea. Do you understand?'

'No, Aristotle.'

'I want you to go back to your cabin and think about your decisions. Washington, D.C., is your Ithaka, perhaps. You can stay here or go there. You can stay here as a God or you can return to Ithaka as a God.'

'When you say Ithaka, you mean Washington?' Jacks asked.

'Yes.'

'What are my other choices?'

'You can stay aboard the *Christina* and be a God or you can stay aboard the *Christina* and not be a God.'

'Just as I can return to Washington and be a God or be a mortal.'

Aristotle nodded.

Jacks looked around the empty hallway amazed.

'If anyone heard us talking they'd think that we were crazy as cartoons.'

* * *

Manhattan. Folk singer Phil Ochs added a new conclusion to his song 'Talking Viet-Nam Blues':

Madame Nhu meanwhile was visiting Beverly Hills
Blaming President Kennedy for her country's ills.

* * *

The Mediterranean Sea.

Jacks was in her room hunched over the radio-phone—placing a call to her husband.

Evelyn Lincoln answered at the White House, of course. Her voice got friendly when she recognized Jacqueline. Evelyn Lincoln said that Jacqueline's husband was very busy, but she was sure the president would want to speak to her.

Jacqueline was put on hold. The last time this woman was put on hold was when she telephoned the J. D. Salinger household in New Hampshire and the writer's wife answered.

Jacqueline knew what she was going to say to Jack. She was going to say, 'I'm coming home and I will go to Ithaka with you.' And he would say, 'What is Ithaka?' And she would try to explain and he wouldn't get it, but would play along.

When her husband actually came on the line—'Hello? Jackie?'—the man's wife told him, 'I've made a decision, Jack. I'm coming home. And I'll travel to Texas with you.'

Revolution 9

Dallas, Texas, November 22, 1963

Jump to the summer of 1972. A long throw past midnight in a Maryland suburb of D.C.

Saint John is now a teenager. A sleeping teenager. This eighteen-year-old is a mass of dark hair spread Rita Hayworth style across his pillow. John Lennon will shave his head in 1973, but George Harrison still has shoulder-length hair. Long hair is still cool.

Saint John's dad enters his son's room. Not a normal occurrence.

'Saint John, get up.'

Saint John surfaces from sleep into his bedroom. 'Come on. Down to the basement,' Hunt says to his son.

In the basement, his dad has two suitcases full of curlicue telephone cords, walkie-talkies, little suction cups, metal scallops with wires on one end and a prong on the other. Bugging equipment. Saint's dad says, 'I need your help and I need you to never repeat what happens tonight.'

Saint John stared at his father.

'Can I count on you?' Hunt said.

'Yes.' Pause. 'Yes. Sure. Yes, yes.' Saint felt exhilarated. *I am finally helping my father.*

Under his father's direction, Saint sprays each device with Windex before wiping it down. This obliterates fingerprints. Then father and son return the stuff into the suitcases and lug them both out to the driveway and then into the trunk of E. Howard Hunt's Pontiac Firebird. They drive for an hour into deep Maryland and stop at the C & O Canal.

Howard Hunt's official job is working for CREEP (the Committee to Reelect the President). The president is Richard Nixon, of course. Howard Hunt's Cuban men have just been arrested for breaking and entering at the Watergate Hotel. This is their bugging equipment.

Father and son each haul a suitcase to the edge of the canal and toss it into the black water.

They return to the house. Saint John says, 'God, I don't feel sleepy yet.'

'Good,' his father says. He points to his typewriter in the living room. 'Take that down to the basement.'

The typewriter is a manual Hermes made in Switzerland, built by E. Paillard & Cie, S.A., Yverdon (Suisse). His father had used it to write ten David St. John novels about ace CIA agent Peter Ward. The CIA had paid his dad to create a fictional American hero to compete against James Bond. They wanted the CIA to seem as cool as Her Majesty's Secret Service.

In the basement, Saint John watches his dad take a hammer and smash the keyboard several times. Farewell QWERTY and FGHJ and XCVBNM. Dad does not explain why. He puts the wrecked typewriter into a burlap sack.

Saint John later learns this was the typewriter his father had used to concoct a fake 'top-secret' cable postdated 1963 'proving' that JFK instigated the assassination of South Vietnamese president Ngô Dinh Diem.

Nixon's motive was to hex the Democrats' only twentieth-century saint besides FDR. Howard Hunt had sent his fake cable to *Life* magazine, but a journalist wanted proof that the cable was real. Since it wasn't, Hunt had nothing to verify it with. Nothing came of his forgery.

Howard Hunt to Saint John: 'Go across the road and throw this into Griffith Pond.'

Saint John takes up the burlap bag.

The Hunts live in a house that Dorothy Hunt named Witches Island because the gravel driveway that curls from River Road to the house lassoes a large circle of gnarled trees—a 'witches island.' The rest of the property is sumac and bamboo. There is also a stable and a rabbit hutch and a bomb shelter.

Saint John walks through the dark and hears his mother's horses whinnying loudly as if they were gathered around a microphone. The sound of smashing the typewriter must have awakened them. The horses break the immediate silence in such a way that Saint John realizes how dead quiet the night actually is. Not even crickets.

He walks down a brief slope to the pond behind their house.

As Saint has aged he has become more handsome like his father, E. Howard Hunt, in his prime. Saint John has been sent to the oldest

Episcopal boarding school founded on the Oxford system, the Saint James School in Hagerstown, Maryland. Saint John's older sister, Lisa, smashed their car. His youngest sister, Kevan, was a passenger and broke her legs and ribs. Lisa was thrown from the car onto her head. She had amnesia. Saint John will say, 'After the accident she became like Winona Ryder in *Girl, Interrupted*. Sex. Alcohol. Drugs. Depression.' Saint's parents committed Lisa to an asylum. Her father told everyone she was brain-damaged from the accident.

In the Wolf Hour, on the property called Witches Island, Saint John throws the sack with the Hermes typewriter into the water.

The splash is a swift gurgle as if the pond is not water but Jell-O.

* * *

1963, Del Mar, California. Desi Arnaz on horseback—

'You want my help to kill a prominent American? Who? Wait! No! Don't tell me! I will not get involved in any manner in any killing. Stop! Don't say another word.' Desi turns his horse around and kicks his feet against the ribs of his horse and it gallops back into the scrub.

* * *

On November 19, 1963, the newspapers in Dallas publish the route of Kennedy and Johnson's motorcade. Connally hits the roof. The route was never supposed to see ink. 'Now the damn hecklers will be out with their goddamn placards!'

* * *

November 21, 1963.

Senator Ralph Yarborough was the nemesis of Governor John Connally (and vice versa). Yarborough rode with Kennedy aboard Air Force One from Washington, D.C., to San Antonio. Yarborough sat in the back of the plane jawing with the reporters: 'I remember, boys, when Connally announced his intention to resign as secretary of the Navy and run for governor of Texas, the newspapers said, *That's good for Texas. Connally is a middle-of-the-roader. Connally fits the role of the peacemaker.* Some peacemaker, huh?'

'Senator, how do you feel about Governor Connally failing to invite you to a reception for President Kennedy in the Executive Mansion in Austin on Friday?'

'This for the record?'

'Yes. If we could.'

'For the record then, although Governor Connally failed to invite me to the reception for President Kennedy in the Executive Mansion, I hope all will join hands for the greatest welcome to President and Mrs. Kennedy in the history of Texas.' He smiled. 'Besides, Governor Connally is so terribly uneducated governmentally, how could you expect anything else?'

The *Washington Post* will report:

> When Yarborough came down the ramp at the San Antonio airport, behind the President and the First Lady (who wore a white wool two-piece suit, a black tie belt, and a black tam-o-shanter), local politicians were straining to see whether Vice President Johnson and Gov. Connally shook hands with Yarborough.

The three did shake hands. Yet Yarborough refused to ride in the same limousine as LBJ. The two Texans almost started swinging. Later, voices were raised as Kennedy read LBJ the riot act: 'These are your people, Lyndon! Control them!'

* * *

The last night of President Kennedy's life. He is sleeping alone in the Texas Hotel in Fort Worth on his special orthopedic mattress. The single mattress rests atop the larger double box spring like half a piece of Swiss cheese on a single slice of bread. The president's wife is sleeping in another room.

Sometime during the night, Jacqueline Kennedy creeps into her husband's room and leans over him to say, 'Such wonderful things are being said about me, but I'm asleep so I can't respond.' Kennedy wakes up and writes one of his 'secret' haikus—

Jackie asleep speaks,
'Beautiful things are spoken.
Yet, I can't answer.'

Next thing the president of the United States is aware of is his alarm clock buzzing. It is six in the morning. Jacqueline's visit and everything else was a dream. He rubs his eyes and chuckles. 'Me? Writing a haiku?' The president of the United States has never written any kind of poem in his entire life, not even as a schoolboy.

★ ★ ★

That morning in Fort Worth—rain. The president stood before a microphone in the hotel. 'Where's Jackie?' a Texan called out. Kennedy smiled and answered, 'Mrs. Kennedy is organizing herself. It takes longer, but, of course, she looks better than we do when she does it.' The Fort Worth crowd went Texas crazy with enthusiasm.

★ ★ ★

Later, Jack Kennedy hosts a breakfast fund-raiser. He is given a cowboy hat. He never places it on his head.

★ ★ ★

That morning in the *Dallas Morning News,* a black-bordered ad appeared that many said reminded them of a death notice. The ad cost $1,462 and was paid for by the sane sons of oilman H. L. Hunt. The black-bordered ad proclaimed that Liberals (i.e., Kennedy and Co.) were smearing Dallas. The ad promised that just as the citizens of Dallas rejected Kennedy in 1960, they would do so again in '64. The ad then asked Kennedy a number of pointed questions: 'Why was Latin America turning... Communistic?' 'Why have you approved the sale of wheat and corn to our enemies [Vietnam]?' 'Why has Kennedy allowed his brother Bobby, the Attorney General, to persecute loyal Americans who criticize you?' Finally, 'Why have you scrapped the Monroe Doctrine in favor of the *Spirit of Moscow*? The ad ended with: **'MR. KENNEDY,** as citizens of the United States of America, we **DEMAND** answers to these questions, and we want them **NOW.**'

★ ★ ★

Air Force One rolls from the sky down the runway at Love Field in Dallas while the Secret Service on the ground are fastening the clear bubbletop to the president's dark blue 1961 Lincoln Continental. Some say the bubbletop is bulletproof. Others say it only keeps out the rain. At any rate, the moment the Kennedys and Johnsons and Connallys step from the plane, the dreary sky suddenly clears like a scene in a Hollywood movie about Moses.

The door opens—

Jacqueline Kennedy is handed red roses. The woman is wearing white gloves that at times appear to be too small for her hands.

Nellie Connally is given yellow roses. She is not wearing gloves.

Jacqueline is thirty-four years old. Nellie is forty-four. Both women are wearing pink. Jacqueline knows that her 'knockoff' Chanel suit and matching pillbox hat are Tiepolo Pink. She considers Nellie's garish suit and thinks, *Four parts Pepto-Bismol with one part Campbell's Tomato Soup.* Neither woman remembers that Mamie Eisenhower was the first lady who instituted the coveting of pink.

Connally helps his wife get into her jump seat* behind the driver in the presidential limousine. Then he sits down in the right-side jump seat. He is not going to postpone sitting down to wait for the Kennedys. A few seconds later, he stands in the car so Jacqueline can scoot past him into the back seat. She thinks, *How gauche.* She can't stand Connally. In her opinion, Connally spent all morning in Fort Worth saying great things about himself while needling her husband.

Now Jack Kennedy slides in. He winces when he sits beside his wife. His back is acting up. He is wearing his brace.

He is still not wearing a cowboy hat.

LBJ is over sitting in his limo wearing *his* cowboy hat. He looks like a

---

* One of two small individual seats located between the front seat of a limousine and the back seat.

goofy rancher. When Connally finally puts on his cowboy hat, he looks as authentic as John Wayne.

Jack Kennedy knows that he can never be some Cape Cod cowboy. That was why he did not even try on his gift of a cowboy hat this morning in Fort Worth. Someone would have taken a photo. And that would appear in every newspaper tomorrow, Saturday morning—Kennedy playing cowboy.

★ ★ ★

The Secret Service are all talking into their lapels, 'Lancer is *this*...' 'Lancer is *that*...' The code name for Kennedy is Lancer. Henceforth that is how the president will be named.

At 11:55, the Dallas motorcade leaves Love Field toward downtown Dallas. It will progress through downtown Dallas and then take a quick spin down onto the Stemmons Freeway to the Trade Mart, where Lancer will give a luncheon speech to another room full of rich Texans.

This motorvation is to become the most operatic drive in U.S.A. history. It is as narratively specific as Mr. Toad's Wild Ride in Disneyland. As you learned, Mr. Toad's Wild Ride ends up in hell...

At the head of the motorcade, there are a few cars, then police motorcycles rumble. Next comes a white unmarked Ford driven by the chief of police with two Secret Service agents and a sheriff as passengers. Next is the president's dark blue 1961 Lincoln Continental, followed by the Cadillac convertible with eight Secret Service agents. Four are sitting in the car and two stand on each of the Cadillac's left and right running boards. Several wear sunglasses. The Secret Service agents who are sitting are all jiggling their feet.

Behind the Cadillac is the gray leased 1964 (!) Lincoln convertible that serves as the vice president's car. A cop will sit behind the wheel with a single Secret Service agent aboard on the shotgun side. His name is Rufus Youngblood. He is thirty-nine years old. In the back seat, LBJ sits behind the shotgun passenger, then Lady Bird on his left and next Yarborough on Lady Bird's left. The motorcade has not started and both men are already sitting with their legs spread wide like arrogant uptown Manhattan males taking up groin room on subway seats.

Lady Bird is squeezed in the middle.

Johnson sits there, briefly musing on Kennedy's dress-down the day before. 'These are *your* cowboys, Lyndon,' Kennedy had said. 'Put them in line. The Democratic Party in Texas is not going to be the laughingstock of the country.'

Well, Yarborough is riding with Johnson. Tonight Yarborough will even sit at the president's table. He even has an invite to the Governor's Mansion.

Next, LBJ thinks one of two things.

Both possible contemplations originate back in 1960, after the man accepted the candidacy for vice president. His shadow mind knew that he would never be president, but it was not until last January that this knowledge bubbled up into his consciousness. He had been too proud, too Texas proud to see the light. For three fucking years, Bobby and McNamara and even Jackie have treated him like a turd that won't go down the plumbing. The president sent him to Europe just so he would appear busy. LBJ had spoken to people this past week. They all told him the truth: 'You will never be president.' Last night was when LBJ first had his famous 'toilet' dream—dreaming he was the president sitting in the bathroom off the Oval Office, sitting on the toilet, sitting taking a Texas-size dump, and Jack and Bobby and McNamara had to cram themselves around him in the bathroom and take notes on what he was saying. When Johnson finished his crapping, he called out, 'Okay, honey!' And the men parted.

And *she* came in with a roll of Charmin...

The first possibility of what LBJ thinks next is this: The man is full of pensive melancholy. That very night he plans to tell Kennedy, 'I'm not going to run with you for reelection.'

The second possibility: LBJ is plummeting a prayer down to the devil that nothing will foul up his plan to have Kennedy shot and killed at Dealey Plaza.

In the front seat of Lancer's dark blue 1961 Lincoln Continental, the oft-mentioned Will Greer is the driver. Riding shotgun is Roy Kellerman (forty-eight), the highest-ranking Secret Service agent in the motorcade. To tell you once again, behind Kellerman, Governor Connally sits in a jump seat. Beside him and behind Greer, Nellie sits in her jump seat.

In the back seat, Jacqueline sits behind Nellie. Her husband, Lancer, sits to her right and behind Connally.

It is sixty-eight degrees in the sunshine.

Jackie is miserable. Her outfit is wool. She is swampy. Yet, remember that absolutely everyone in 1963 America uses deodorant. Americans always smell hygienic. Everyone in the dark blue 1961 Lincoln Continental smells only of cigarettes.

The motorcade starts. Cops riding motorcycles proceed in front and in back of Lancer's car. Their engines sound obnoxious.

Here come the crazies with placards right outside Love Field—

Then scattered crowds. The motorcade passes used-car lots. Junkyards. Stores to buy auto parts. This is the ugly part of town.

The motorcade passes a group of kids holding a sign:

MR. PRESIDENT, PLEASE STOP AND SHAKE OUR HANDS

'Let's stop,' Lancer commands Greer.

Greer brakes.

Lancer leans out and shakes the paws of the youngsters. A few agents of the right-side Cadillac's running board jump off and gently herd the kids away.

The motorcade continues.

Around Reagan Street, tremendous crowds. The motorcycles have to pull behind Lancer's limo. Both the men and the women in the crowd are dressed as if it's Sunday and they're going to church. The men wear suits and ties and spit-polished shoes. The women wear modest dresses or skirts. Silly feminine chapeaus on their beehive heads. Most wear high heels.

The buildings on Reagan Street are taller than the previous ones the motorcade passed—seven or eight stories. Many do not have central air-conditioning. White people dangle out of every open window cheering. Lancer is muttering, 'Thank you, thank you.' He is thanking fate for giving him cheering Dallasonians instead of crowds that spit on Johnson and Lady Bird during the 1960 presidential campaign, chasing them into some forlorn lobby at the Hotel Adolphus.

The president's dark blue 1961 Lincoln Continental turns onto Turtle Creek. This is the edge of North Dallas.

North Dallas = rich people.

Dallas is one of the most segregated cities in America, but race is incidental. The dividing line is money.

Texas is oil money.

New money.

Fantastic amounts of money.

And money likes money. The only people with money in Dallas are whites living in North Dallas, a neighborhood where, to paraphrase historian Jim Bishop, even the sewers are air-conditioned.

This North Dallas crowd is thin and quiet.

Jacqueline puts on her sunglasses.

Lancer commands his wife, 'Take those glasses off.'

She does. She holds them in her pink lap.

In another limo, Johnson, unconsciously perhaps, removes his cowboy hat.

They all continue down Turtle Creek and Jacqueline puts on her shades a second time.

'Take off the glasses, Jackie,' her husband repeats.

She complies.*

The president's dark blue 1961 Lincoln Continental now passes a nun with a herd of small children. And an angry Texan with a placard that states:

KENNEDY GO HOME!

The motorcade turns right onto Main Street. The center of downtown. Citizens turbulent with excitement, even raw joy—men, women, children, colored people. Texans will call this 'a whale of a crowd' even though Texans know as much about whales as Greeks do.

The downtown buildings here are ten and twelve stories tall. In every window—two faces, three faces. Arms waving. A continuous cry of *Jackeee* erupting block after block.

Jacqueline holds a gift—a white Lamb Chop hand puppet attached to some white flowers.

Jacqueline places both down beside the red roses.

---

* The good wife.

* * *

Up on the seventh floor of the thirty-one-story Mercantile Building at 1700 Main Street, Haroldson Lafayette Hunt stands at an open window watching the motorcade crawl along Main Street toward his viewing. H. L. Hunt is now a very old man who stands a straight six feet and carries more than two hundred pounds of pride. H. L. Hunt has lived on God's globe for seventy-four years. He had been born in nineteenth-century Illinois, finding himself the last of eight children. H. L. Hunt had been born a rambler and left Illinois as soon as he could. This meant Hunt left as a kid and has now lived in Texas for more than fifty years. This locution of time made him as much a Texan as even a man who had been titted here.

The Kennedy parade now passes below H. L. Hunt's very window—

Police motorcycles.

Now the car where the king and queen of homecoming sit.

Look! That damn cradle Catholic is not even driving his own car. H. L. Hunt believes a man should never submit to the whims of a chauffeur. H. L. Hunt drives his own damn car everywhere. He even cuts his own damn hair. If we stood with him now, no one could tell that a professional barber had not tended to his white haircut.

H. L. leans toward the open window and shouts, 'The United States serves at the pleasure of Texas, you son of a bitch.'

To Hunt's right hangs an old map of Pennsylvania made of browning parchment.

H. L. Hunt has never set foot in Pennsylvania.

Hunt hung the map to mock the memory of the oil baron John D. Rockefeller, who died at the age of ninety-seven in the 1930s, having lived thirty-seven years in the twentieth century and sixty-one in the nineteenth century. Rockefeller had become an oil tycoon, not by drilling for oil, but distilling it, procuring a monopoly on the railroads as raw oil and distilled oil were both transported by rail. In John Rockefeller's first heyday, the only American oil fields were located in the Quaker hills of Pennsylvania. Rockefeller was rumored to have proclaimed, 'I'll drink every gallon produced west of the Mississippi.'

Ha! By the late 1920s, H. L. Hunt himself owned oil fields west of the Mississippi, first in Oklahoma, then in East Texas. The Texas wells made H.L.'s fortune. Those oil beds were named Dad Joiner and Number One Daisy.

H.L. named his first oil company Placid Oil.

It was oil from Dad Joiner and Number One Daisy that made H. L. Hunt one of the richest oil vampires on the planet. H. L. Hunt can eat Aristotle Onassis for lunch or dinner. But H. L. Hunt is not a Greek wanderer. H. L. Hunt lacks Onassis's European sophistication. Caviar disgusts Hunt. He stands at his window eating a Puritan mayonnaise sandwich on Sunbeam white that Ruth, his wife, prepared for him this morning. He drove it with him to work stored in a brown paper sack.

Look down there. Look at those women dressed in pink! In pink!

Until 1958, Hunt had been a noble, but clueless, rabid foe of Communism. Then he discovered the John Birch Society. It was named after a sweet Christian missionary killed by the Red Chinese. The John Birch Society was founded by someone named Robert Welch, a man who made his fortune toiling in his brother's candy company promoting Milk Duds.

Welch's John Birch Society peeled the scales from H. L. Hunt's eyes like the skin from an onion. The John Birch Society revealed the depth of Communist conspiracy. There was conspiracy afoot in *both* Russia and the United States to create one socialist world order that would be controlled by Hasidic bankers. Those bankers now controlled everyone in Moscow and all the Eastern pansies and sodomites in New England. (The only man from Connecticut you could trust was William F. Buckley, but the word was he still peed his bed during the night and had balls the size of two Milk Duds.)

The last decent president this country had was Calvin Coolidge.

H.L. peers down again at the wives in the limousine—Nellie Connally and the Other.

Look at those two titmice. Both dressed in pink.

And the pink hearts of their husbands—

H. L. Hunt hated Kennedy aesthetically, but the fiercer hatred that H. L. Hunt erupted with toward Connally was personal.

From one Texan to another.

H. L. Hunt's man General Edwin Walker came in last in the Democratic primary against Connally for governor last year. Some punk who works at the Texas School Book Depository, which sits down in Dealey Plaza, had the red gall to try to shoot out Walker's brain one night several months ago.

H. L. Hunt raised an imaginary rifle and aimed it at the back of Connally's head. 'Bang!' Then Kennedy's head. 'Bang!' Then their pink wives. 'Bang! Bang!'

Hunt speaks out loud: 'This is what I will tell the newspapers: The myth of the indispensable man must be broken if our country is to survive.'

Then he giggles. Then H. L. Hunt bends over in a belly laugh at his own giggling.

H. L. Hunt laughs at things he says all the time.

H. L. Hunt opens the bottom drawer of his desk. He takes out something leathery and parchment-like. It is old like the map of Pennsylvania. It resembles a string of dried chili peppers. H. L. Hunt holds it in his hand like prayer beads. Then Hunt returns to his open window.

Now comes Lyndon's car.

Lyndon he likes. Lyndon is a Texan's Texan.

That Yarborough, different story. H. L. Hunt looks down at the gnarled loop he is clutching and talks to it. 'Did I ever tell you how in 1954, I hired a Neegra actor from vaudeville to drive a big green Plymouth with a big sign on the roof that said YARBOROUGH FOR CONGRESS? He would drive that green Plymouth into filling stations that had pumps for Neegras. The Neegra would pull up to those pumps and get out of the green Plymouth and then make a general nuisance of himself. Ordering five cents' worth of gas. Pressing one nostril shut with his pointer and shooting a stream of snot out of the other nostril toward the ground. He would tell everyone in a loud voice that he worked for Ralph Yarborough because *Ralph Yarborough would put coloreds such as himself on easy street.*'

H. L. Hunt laughs. He puts the gnarled loop around his own neck like a Hawaiian lei. 'Yarborough almost lost, too,' Hunt says. The billionaire sticks his head farther out the window, his chin jutting above Main Street like a Texan gargoyle.

The motorcade has almost reached Dealey Plaza.

★ ★ ★

At this moment in Dealey Plaza itself, a twenty-three-year-old man dressed in Army fatigues named Belknap is having what appears to be a dramatic epileptic fit in front of a building called the Texas School Book Depository. Most of the hundred or so people waiting for the motorcade focus their attention on Belknap. A few minutes after this, a van with HONEST JOE'S PAWN SHOP written on it comes down the street. Someone else thought they also saw Honest Joe's other vehicle, an Edsel painted psychedelically before psychedelic became a usable term. Honest Joe's Edsel has a plugged .50-caliber machine gun on the roof.

* * *

There are only several bookstores in Dallas and each only sells Bibles and other Christian books. This is why all literate Texans—10 percent of Texan adults are illiterate—join the Book of the Month Club. At least you can see Hollywood movies in Dallas. In New York City, the marquee states PETER SELLERS IN DR. STRANGELOVE. This picture is a designated classic today, but November 22, 1963, was the day of *Dr. Strangelove*'s special preview, which would be canceled.

Dr. Strangelove was a Black Comedy about Nuclear War.*

Earlier this year, when director Stanley Kubrick was finishing *Dr. Strangelove,* he heard that director Sidney Lumet was filming *Fail-Safe,* a drama about nuclear war starring Henry Fonda. Kubrick filed a lawsuit for plagiarism against *Fail-Safe.* Kubrick knew that Lumet and Fonda had not plagiarized anything, but if *Fail-Safe* opened first, Kubrick feared *Strangelove* would suffer at the box office. This is an unpleasant fact for those of us who revere Stanley Kubrick. Americans do not want to believe that revered artists can be conniving.

Dr. Strangelove is very sophisticated for Texas. Most theaters show junk. For example, five teenagers got an older brother to buy five tickets so that the kids could skip school and see two war pictures at the Texas Theatre down on Jefferson Street. The feature is *Cry of Battle* starring Van Heflin (a minor star in '63). The other flick is *War Is Hell*—a low-budget drama

---

* Today, Black Comedy implies a movie with Whoopi Goldberg. In 1963, a Black Comedy meant Gallows Humor.

starring actors nobody was familiar with in 1963 and actors everyone has forgotten today:

Baynes Barron as Sgt. Garth
Michael Bell as Seldon
Bobby Byles as Gresler
Wally Campo as Laney

Back on Main Street in Dallas, the president's dark blue 1961 Lincoln Continental reaches Dealey Plaza and makes a right on Houston Street. (For Manhattan readers, this Houston Street is pronounced *Hew-ston*, not *How-ston.*)

The president's dark blue 1961 Lincoln Continental passes the Criminal Courts Building and the County Records Building.

This is essentially the end of the motorcade. Nellie Connally says, 'Mr. President, they can't say that Dallas doesn't love you.'

She says it with a little bite. *We're not all gauche, you son of a bitch...*

Lancer answers, 'No, they sure can't.'

In the photograph above, the first curving street on the left is Elm Street. It flows by the before-mentioned Texas School Book Depository. It is a seven-story building the color of red dust containing a Hertz sign on its roof stretching in a diagonal that also proclaims the time and the temperature. It is still sixty-eight degrees.

Just below Elm is a curving ornamental structure known as the Pergola. Between Elm and the Pergola is the soon-to-be notorious 'Grassy Knoll,' which at this moment is a nameless plot of grass.

We all know the Grassy Knoll is perhaps the climax of this ride. There are supposedly Corsican gangsters/assassins hiding in the bushes with their sniper-scope rifles. The Cubans are, of course, hiding atop the buildings with level roofs on Houston Street.

Down below the Texas School Book Depository and across the street, Howard Brennan (forty-four) is standing.

There is nothing hypothetical about Howard Brennan.

He glances up at the face of the Texas School Book Depository and sees a young man at an open window on the sixth floor holding a rifle.

Howard Brennan does not respond.

Historian Jim Bishop will describe this man as a typical Texan who 'minds his own business.' The kind of Texan who is proud to say that he 'doesn't know either of his next-door neighbors.'

Behind Mr. Brennan are the teenage newlyweds, Arnold and Mrs. Rowland. Arnold studies acoustic physics in high school and works part-time making pizza pies at the Pizza Inn on West Davis Avenue.

'Want to see a Secret Service agent?' Arnold asks his wife.

He points up to the sixth floor of the Texas School Book Depository, but no one is there.

'He must have stepped back,' Arnold says. 'He was there with a Secret Service rifle.'

The man Rowland saw was a white man. Rowland looks up again and sees a dark-skinned man with a rifle in the opposite corner of the sixth floor.

Mrs. Carolyn Walther is standing somewhere between Brennan and Rowland. She notices a man at the end window of either the fourth or fifth floor of the School Book Depository. Then she thinks she sees two men standing at that window.

One holds a rifle.

She is not alarmed.

The dark blue 1961 Lincoln Continental is unmolested as it drives straight toward the corner where the Texas School Book Depository stands and makes a sharp left onto Elm Street.

It now glides perpendicular to the seven-story Texas School Book Depository building. On the sidewalk is a youth named James Worrell Jr., who has skipped classes (like the boys at the Texas Theatre) to see the presidential motorcade. A little farther down Elm, a Russian-born Jew, Abraham Zapruder, is standing on a stubby pillar at the far end of the Pergola focusing his zoom-lens camera. His secretary stands behind him so he will not fall. It is 1963 and Abraham says, 'Don't think I'm being fresh if I back up into you.'

Directly across Elm from Zapruder is a woman wearing a scarf over her head Russian 'babushka' style. She is also holding a home-movie camera. She will later be referred to as the 'Babushka Lady.'

A woman who will be referred to as the 'Lady in Red' sees the first lady playing with a little white dog in the back seat of the dark blue 1961 Lincoln Continental. As the car drives down Elm Street, a man standing at ten-minutes-to-ten in front of Zapruder needlessly opens his umbrella as Lancer's limo drives by.

The 'Umbrella Man.'

Then he quickly bounces the open umbrella up and down as if he is giving a signal.

A shot rings out.

At that first shot, James Worrell Jr. looks up and sees a rifle barrel poking out of an upper window in the Texas School Book Depository. At that first shot, pigeons in the trees take off as a flock and begin a tense circle in the sky over Dealey Plaza. Most citizens think the first bang is a firecracker or backfire.

Governor Connally recognizes gunfire.

Secret Service agents Greer and Kellerman are clueless. Only Agent Youngblood, in the front seat of LBJ's limo, hears the bang, and begins his leap into the back seat of the limo where the vice president sits.

There is a second shot.

Neither of the Connallys sees the bullet that first strikes Lancer. The first shot? The second? Both Connallys hear Jacqueline suddenly scream, 'What are they doing to you?'—Jacqueline never raises her voice, let alone screams. Both Connallys turn and see that Lancer has thrown his hand up to his neck.

'The president didn't say a word. He expressed only surprise. No pain. His eyes looked so troubled.' The governor of Texas will say this even after the Warren Commission will claim that first bullet missed the limo and hit the curb, making the second bullet 'magic,' spinning out of the president's neck into Connally's back, bouncing down and out his rib cage and shattering his wrist.

> There is no [magic] bullet. There is my absolute knowledge and my wife's too that one bullet caused the president's first wound, and that an entirely separate shot struck me.

In fact, forensics pointed to a duo of bullets hitting Connally—one bullet striking his rib cage and another bullet striking his wrist.

★ ★ ★

One of the forensic witnesses who testified to the Warren Commission was a veterinarian.

★ ★ ★

At this moment, James Worrell Jr. dashes around the corner of the Texas School Book Depository to get out of the potential line of fire.

Up in a fourteen-foot railroad tower stands Lee E. Bowers Jr. He knows that sounds coming from the Pergola or from the Texas School Book Depository sound the same because of echoes. It is just sonic confusion. He will later think that he heard four shots. Another railroad worker, Skinny Holland, is standing below the tower and sees a puff of smoke emit from the Grassy Knoll. Many others see the smoke too.

Unless that sniper was shooting with a musket, there is no modern rifle that emits that much smoke—unless the rifle has a defective silencer.

Simplest answer best answer. Most heard the first shot and thought 'Firecracker.' Perhaps it was. Some kid blew off a cherry bomb on the Grassy Knoll. Or a conspirator blew off a firecracker to confuse the acoustics in Dealey Plaza.

In Lancer's Continental—finally, Secret Service agent Kellerman recognizes the second shot as a gunshot and yells to Greer, 'Let's get out of here.' Instead, Greer starts braking, slowing the car to a crawl.

'My God, they are going to kill us all!' Connally shouts as he collapses.

In Dealey Plaza, pedestrians now start running for cover or throw themselves belly-down onto the grass.

Abe Zapruder keeps filming, not aware of what he is shooting.

Secret Service agent Clint Hill jumps off the running board of the Secret Service Caddy and runs toward the president's blue Continental.

The third or fourth shot—

Jacqueline remains stunned and aghast and helpless peering at her husband as the back of his head abruptly explodes into two separate pieces of viscera. Bishop will write, 'Dura matter, like wet rice, sprayed out of the brain in a pink fan.'

The Crack-Up.

Jacqueline screaming again, 'Jack! Jack! My God, they've killed my husband!'

A cloud of Kennedy's brain blood sprays across the windshield of the following car.

Greer, after so many years in the Secret Service, finally floors the blue Continental.

'They have shot his head off!' Jacqueline screams and turns and lunges down the trunk of the limo. Secret Service agent Clint Hill pushes her back inside.

Jacqueline holds up her arm. 'I have his brains in my hand.'

She speaks those words coldly and clearly like Lady Macbeth.

* * *

A month after the killing, the rebel comic Lenny Bruce will develop a routine about the first lady trying to 'crawl out of that car.' Adman Don DeLillo sees Lenny Bruce at Café Au Go Go. DeLillo has seen Lenny Bruce a few times. Bruce does not tell knock-knock jokes. Bruce makes sociological observations about the absurdities of modern life. Bruce is the foremost American existentialist.

Lenny Bruce walks onto the slightly raised platform stage.

Lenny Bruce is thirty-eight and has dark hair, with bags under his eyes like Roy Cohn. Lenny Bruce makes comments about Eleanor Roosevelt's 'tits' (she died in '62) and the Lone Ranger sodomizing Tonto (*The Lone Ranger* went off the air in '57). Then Lenny Bruce holds up a copy of *Life* magazine.

'I'd like to show you a few dirty pictures that relate to your daughter, or mine,' Lenny Bruce says. There is not even nervous laughter. Just voices clearing. By the way, Lenny Bruce himself has an eight-year-old daughter named Kitty.

Lenny Bruce pages through the magazine. 'Now these are some photographs of the Kennedy assassination.' Lenny Bruce holds the magazine up over his head. DeLillo is close enough to see there are two big photographs of Mrs. Kennedy trying to jump out of the limousine on Elm Street. 'I'm here to claim these are dirty pictures because the captions are bullshit.'

Don DeLillo sits at his table riveted. DeLillo does not have a companion. His wife would not come with him. DeLillo shares a table with four strangers—Negroes, three men and a woman who possesses fabulous Baby

Ruth décolleté. All smoke. The nightclub is filled with cigarette smoke like dry ice. Every guy in the place wears a tie, especially the Negroes. Everyone at DeLillo's table is very uncomfortable about Bruce ridiculing Jacqueline Kennedy.

Lenny Bruce continues: 'Here Jackie is trying to scramble out of the car seconds after her husband's head exploded.' The magazine has printed stills from the Zapruder film that Time Life had purchased for $50,000 publicly, but really $150,000 privately. Bruce continues: 'The caption says, *Never for an instant did she think of flight.*' Then Lenny Bruce shouts the word 'Bullshit!'

⋆ ⋆ ⋆

Friday. November 22.

Greer is gunning the limo down the street at eighty miles per hour. Clint is hanging on to the hood, spread-eagle. He crawls up the trunk and flip-flops into the back seat and tries to shield both Lancer and the first lady as best he can. He squints back at the follow-up car racing behind. He shakes his head at the car. He gives the thumbs-down sign.

The Secret Service driver named Kinney refuses to believe the reality of what he is seeing. Clint cannot mean that signal. After all, Kinney remembers reading that in the time of the Roman Colosseum thumbs-down meant the gladiator could live. If Nero gave thumbs-up, it meant *kill the S.O.B.*

In the right-hand jump seat in the Kennedy Continental—

One can hear the hole in Governor Connally's chest sucking air. By 1967, American soldiers in Viet-Nam will all be very familiar with that sound and call it as they hear it: *an air-sucking chest wound.*

The governor's wife, Nellie, is sitting in the driver's-side jump seat holding her husband in her lap.

In Connally's delirium, he remembers that awful phone call from Tallahassee four years earlier on April 28, 1959.

'Hello.'

'Mr. Connally?'

'Yes.'

'Your daughter Kathleen has been shot in the head.'

'My God, how bad is she?'

'Couldn't be worse,' the Floridian drawled. 'Half her head was blown away.'

* * *

This is what occurred on the day in 1951 in Mexico City when Joan Vollmer was shot in the head by her common-law husband, William Burroughs:

Burroughs's faux-gay protégé met up with his straight buddy. Those two are with Burroughs and Joan in the apartment belonging to the bartender from the Bounty.

The bartender himself is not present. He is working downstairs.

Burroughs is waiting for the arrival of the guy who wants to buy the .380-caliber Star pistol that Burroughs is selling.

Joan Vollmer is drinking Ginebra (a cheap gin) mixed with a carbonated dark green drink call limonada. (Or she may have been drinking Oso Negro gin.)

She is drinking out of a highball glass.

They all sit in that apartment. Burroughs is excited. He contemplates a new change of scenery. They will all move to South America. They will live off the land.

Joan rolls her eyes. 'If Bill is the hunter we'll all starve.'

Burroughs frowns and pulls out his .380-caliber Star pistol.

It is loaded.

'Put your glass on your head and I'll shoot it off like William Tell,' Burroughs may say. Or else, he may say the snappier, 'Time for our William Tell routine...' On either statement, Joan immediately balances the glass on her head as if she has done this one thousand nights before.

Burroughs is sitting about six feet from Joan. He raises his arm holding the gun. He aims high because the Star tends to fire low.

He pulls the trigger.

The gun bangs.

Joan's head snaps back, then lolls forward chin to chest.

She slides to the floor.

There is a little blue hole in her forehead. The blood starts flowing. The heterosexual boy hears her death rattle. It sounds like snoring. The highball glass is rolling in a circle on the floor next to a few empty Oso Negro bottles.

★ ★ ★

The Café Au Go Go in Manhattan.

Comedian Lenny Bruce looks up from the *Life* magazine photographs of Jacqueline scrambling on the trunk of the Continental convertible. 'Jackie wasn't trying to get out of the car to get help or trying to help the Secret Service man aboard.'

Next, Lenny Bruce shouts, 'No!'

Then he shouts, 'Bullshit!'

Then he yells, 'Jackie did the normal thing, man! When the president and governor got it, Jackie tried to get the hell out of there! But the magazine wants us to believe their bullshit! They want our daughters, if after their husbands get their faces shot off and they try to haul ass to save their asses—if they do the normal thing—then our daughters will feel guilty and shitty, because they're not like that good Jackie in the fantasy! It's a dirty lie to tell the people that if you're good, you stay, and if you're bad, you run, because Jackie didn't stay! Fuck it, man, Jackie didn't stay! Jackie hauled ass to save her ass! People don't stay!'

★ ★ ★

Dealey Plaza. November 22, 1963. Howard Brennan sees a gunman up on the sixth floor of the Texas Book Depository. This gunman stands in the last arched window next to the final square window.

Brennan sees that it is a white man. This man is standing six floors above Brennan and yet Brennan can distinguish that the man is smirking. This man sets down his rifle. The man then stands looking down at Elm Street. He is savoring the moment. Later Brennan will say that the gunman seemed like a poacher who had 'bagged his buck.'

All the Secret Service agents on Elm Street know that Lancer is dead. 'His head is just Jell-O, man!'

Is LBJ next?

Is this a junta?

Most of Kennedy's cabinet is at a stopover in Hawaii, planning to continue flying to attend a conference in Japan. Where was the second successor to the presidency, the Speaker of the House, John McCormack?

Where is the Bagman, the guy with the black bag that can start World War III?

One of the best-selling books of 1962 was *Seven Days in May.* It was about the American military's attempt to take control of the American civilian government.

At this moment in Dallas, America seems no better than some banana republic.

Listen! If you and I could page through some of the history textbooks boxed up in the Texas School Book Depository, they would all tell the true story of the assassination of Abraham Lincoln. The third-grade textbooks would tell the story simply and sixth-grade textbooks more thoroughly and so forth. But all the texts would make it clear that Abraham Lincoln was not shot on April 14, 1865, as part of any conspiracy theory. Abraham Lincoln died on April 15, 1865, by a conspiracy manifest.

John Wilkes Booth planned three additional deaths besides Lincoln's. Taken together these four deaths were supposed to energize the beaten Confederacy into launching a guerrilla/terrorist war again the Union. Booth intended to kill both Lincoln and Ulysses S. Grant, as the general was scheduled to be the president's guest that night. The hitch was Grant's wife detested Lincoln's wife, so Grant bowed out with respect. Thus, Booth only shot Lincoln. Then he was on the run twelve days until he was caught near Port Royal, Virginia, by the 16th New York Cavalry. Booth was trapped inside a burning barn. A soldier then shot Booth in the neck. The Yankees dragged Booth out of the barn and it took all night for him to die.

In early summer after the gunning down of Lincoln, up in Fort McNair, in Washington, D.C., two young men, as well as a man of thirty, and a middle-aged woman were hooded and hung as retribution for their heartfelt participation in Booth's plot.

The youngest to hang was twenty-one-year-old Lewis Thornton Powell, aka Lewis Paine/Lewis Payne. He did the dangle because while Booth was shooting Lincoln on April 14 at the Ford Theatre, Powell was stabbing Secretary of State Seward in that man's very bed in addition to stabbing four other members of the household as well as braining Seward's adult son with a Whitney revolver, that clubbing done at the beginning of the mayhem, rendering the revolver useless and thus perpetrating Powell's subsequent knifework. He finally fled the house on horseback into the night, screaming, 'I'm mad! I'm mad!'

Maybe.

Seward, along with the others who were injured, all survived Powell's knife.

David Edgar Herold, a twenty-three-year-old man, was hanged for assisting Lewis Powell and John Wilkes Booth in their separate errands.

A man in the prime of life, George Atzerodt (thirty), was strung up for comic relief. Instead of following Booth's orders to shoot Vice President Johnson at the Kirkwood House, Atzerodt lost his nerve and turned to liquor for solace, spending the night stumbling the alleyways of Washington skunk drunk only to be arrested when he returned to his room at dawn.

The 'mother' of the conspirators, Mary Elizabeth Jenkins Surratt, forty-two, was fitted with rope because she ran guns and provided planning-meeting locations for Booth and his cohorts. Mary had met Booth through her twenty-one-year-old son, John, a confederate of Booth when his plan consisted of 'just' kidnapping Lincoln. After the shootout at the Ford Theatre, influential Catholics helped John escape to Europe.

The four were hanged by Captain Christian Rath of the 17th Michigan Infantry, First Division, Ninth Corps. Rath supervised their roping. Rath ordered the blocks that the conspirators were standing on to be knocked out beneath their feet. The necks of Atzerodt and the woman appeared to snap the moment their bodies reached the ends of their ropes. Herold jerked for more than five minutes. Some say Powell jerked for seven minutes. Other witnesses said even longer.

After today, all those textbooks up in the Texas School Book Depository will be pulped and will mention only John Wilkes Booth as the killer of Lincoln.

★ ★ ★

November 22, 1963. Los Angeles, California. Writer Aldous Huxley, born in the nineteenth century, is sixty-nine years old and lies dying of cancer in his Los Angeles County hospital room. He knows he has only hours, maybe only moments, left before the cancer kills him. His doctor gives Huxley permission to swallow a bit of mescaline. Huxley ingests it with the hope that the resulting roil of hallucinations will assist him to achieve *moksha*—union with the Divine One.

★ ★ ★

At the Parkland Hospital in Dallas, nurses and medical personnel attempt to heave Lancer's body out of the back seat of the Continental, where he sprawls with his frozen wife. The seats are nothing but red and yellow roses and blood and brains and that damn Lamb Chop puppet, now soaked in blackening blood. Nellie Connally cradles her husband, incensed that these people do not take her husband, John, first. The governor is more accessible.

More important, *he isn't dead*. Yet.

Anyway, *that woman* will not let them touch her husband's body at first. 'You know he's dead!' Jacqueline screams. 'Leave me alone.' Finally, they take Connally out. Pull the jump seats down and hoist Lancer onto a stretcher.

Inside Parkland, Connally is wheeled into Trauma Room 2. Nellie is left outside. She is standing there as a Secret Service agent bursts into the waiting room hoisting a submachine gun. Everyone hits the floor but Nellie. In the next moment, another man in a suit runs in. The submachine-gun man spins and knocks the running man down with a lone punch—that man slides down the wall holding up his FBI badge.

In another room, Lyndon Johnson sits with Lady Bird and appears to be completely undone. He is howling and hollering nonsense.

The president is wheeled in. His is no longer Lancer. The Secret Service cannot protect him anymore. Jacqueline is sure her husband is dead and this hospital nonsense is just a formality. A nurse with a British accent reaches for Jack Kennedy's body and Jacqueline pushes the woman's hand away. Jack Kennedy is wheeled into Trauma 1. They try to keep Jacqueline out. She pushes her way in and sees a surgeon with a scalpel cutting a tracheotomy hole in her husband's throat, even though the bullet hole in his throat is the perfect size for the tracheotomy tube. One of the doctors walks in and shouts, 'My God, Charlie, what are you doing? His brains are all over the table.' Jacqueline is not offended. Of course, Jack is dead.

In another room, on a discarded stretcher, the young man named Belknap 'wakes up.' He does not suffer from epilepsy. He has a head injury sustained several years earlier after being run down by a Texas truck. Belknap calls the fits that now afflict him 'fainting spells.' The halls of Parkland are a complete chaos of panicked nurses and doctors and men with handguns. Belknap slides off his stretcher and walks out of the hospital.

He wants no part of History.

* * *

Dealey Plaza. When the shooting started everyone ran out of Dealey Plaza. Now word of the shooting is drawing citizens from downtown into Dealey Plaza.

A stream of citizens.

A reporter sees Zapruder and his movie camera.

'The Secret Service would want to see the film.'

After returning to his office in the Dal-Tex building, Zapruder was resolved to get this film into the hands of federal authorities. His business—the manufacturing of women's clothing—would be put on hold.

* * *

John Kennedy lies on a stainless-steel table in only his underpants. The doctors pull a sheet over his body and over his head at 12:46 p.m.

* * *

Café Au Go Go, New York City.

Don DeLillo could not believe what Lenny Bruce was saying when Lenny Bruce began talking about Kennedy's wife. DeLillo had left his body for a moment. Suddenly DeLillo himself is now shooting up from his table yelling, 'Wrong, Lenny! You're wrong!' Out of the corner of DeLillo's eye, he sees a burly bouncer begin zigzagging toward his table.

Bruce walks to the edge of the stage. 'Yeah? I'm wrong? I'm wrong? Tell me why?'

'You're right that Jackie was trying to get out of the car—'

'Of course she was. What's your point, schmuck? Siddown—'

'Jackie was trying to get her husband's brains back!'

'What?'

'A big piece of President Kennedy's skull blew out of the car. Jackie was trying to retrieve it!'

DeLillo says that as the bouncer reaches the table. The Negroes are staring up at DeLillo without expression. The bouncer puts his hands on DeLillo's shoulder and pushes downward. DeLillo resists. 'No, man. I'm splitting! This is rank!'

The bouncer sarcastically sweeps up his two arms to his left and says, 'This way, good sir.'

* * *

Parkland Hospital. Dallas.

November 22, 1963.

A priest arrives at 12:49 p.m. No one tells Father Huber that Kennedy is dead. Father Huber pulls the sheet from Kennedy's face and begins administering last rites in Latin—the sacrament of Extreme Unction, a useless ritual if Jack Kennedy's soul has departed his body. Most Catholic theologians believe the soul departs at the moment of death. Thus, Father Huber is giving last rites over an empty vessel. Tibetan Buddhists believe the souls of the dead linger around the body because the soul does not realize that it is dead. That is why a lama reads *The Book of the Dead* over the corpse. The words are instructions to the soul to be aware that its body is dead and to go through the bardo and reincarnate elsewhere.

* * *

In the Parkland Hospital in Dallas, yet again the persistent nurse with the British accent insists Jacqueline should wash herself.

'I'm not going to wash,' Jacqueline says. 'I want *them* to see what *they* have *done*.'

* * *

There would be no dramatic moment in the years to come, 1964 or 1968 or 1972, when it will be announced to the public that Jacqueline Kennedy's awkward crawling over the trunk of the car was indeed to retrieve a part of her husband's head, a particular piece of bone, hair, flesh, and brain that will even be anointed with a name:

The 'Harper Fragment'—so named after the person who finds the gore the next day.

* * *

Jacqueline finds herself sitting across from Nellie Connally in a hospital corridor. Nellie peers at Jacqueline with seething indifference. Nellie's husband John's right lung has collapsed. An officious receptionist struts over to Nellie Connally and tells her to fill out an admitting form for her husband. Mrs. Connally peers up at the receptionist with a look of complete disdain and dismissal, and then turns away. The receptionist walks in a complicated circle. She is confused. Her face is burning.

Then every nurse is making a fuss. One of them has found a reporter hiding under the hospital bed in Trauma 3. Two burly orderlies hurry into that room and give the guy the bum's rush.

Other nurses begin hauling sheets over all the windows to prevent potential snipers from seeing in.

Jacqueline stands up at 12:59 and returns to the room where her husband lies and kisses his naked foot. She lowers the sheet from his face. She kisses his open eyes. She then holds his hand. She removes her wedding ring and puts it over her husband's ring finger—a digit thicker than hers. Jacqueline can only work the ring down to his finger's liver point.

* * *

Dealey Plaza. Officer Craig and deputy sheriffs Boone and Moody search the sixth floor of the Texas School Book Depository. They find that this floor is in the middle of getting new tile laid. The workmen have been working from the west toward the east. There are book boxes piled in the east. The lawmen discover three rifle cartridges on the east-side floor. Craig and Boone and Moody all feel and agree that the shells are lying there to be discovered. There is nothing Sherlock Holmes about their realization. It is just a gut feeling. The scattering of the shells does not look spontaneous.

The three lawmen find an opening in the book boxes that reveals a little clubhouse in front of the window. These boxes are eighteen inches by twelve inches by fourteen inches. Many have AMERICAN HISTORY written on them. The three all walk into the nest, but three men can barely fit. They all see the rifle with a telescopic sight lying in front of the arched window.

'Don't touch it,' Craig says.

The three leave the American History box enclosure.

'Let's get Weitzman.'

'We don't need him.'

'Yes we do.'

'Yeah, we do. Weitzman has been in the sporting goods business for many years. He is familiar with all weapons.'

'Domestic and foreign.'

Moody or Boone leaves the floor to get Weitzman. Craig begins knocking on each of the American History boxes.

'They sound full.'

'Full of books,' agrees the sheriff left behind.

Weitzman now enters the sixth floor. He looks like a guy you'd call Slim with no ironic intent. He picks up the gun. 'It looks like a 7.65 German Mauser.'

Weitzman positions his body at the window where the sniper would have had to crouch. 'Tight fit,' he complains. 'Damn steam pipes up my back.'

'The sniper was probably shorter than you.'

'Height got nothing to do with it.'

It will be said that Boone now lifts up a brown paper bag from the windowsill. He looks inside and passes it to Moody, who looks inside too. 'Cleaned to the bone.'

Chicken bones. An apple core. Yet, even this mundanity will cause conflict. A reporter named Alyea will claim that the bag of bones was on the fifth floor. He knows this because he was the one who found it.

He probably did.

Surely many men who work at the Texas School Book Depository brown-bagged chicken to work. Modern CSI investigators would get the DNA off the bones and compare them to anyone who worked on the sixth floor. One year before this bloodplay in Dallas, two scientists named Watson and Crick received the Nobel Prize for their work in the discovery of DNA. This is to say, DNA is not yet a tool of America's police departments.

* * *

Parkland Hospital. Senator Ralph Yarborough was slumped in a chair weeping. Two of Connally's aides saw him and recalled to each other how Yarborough called Connally 'a wolf in lamb's clothing.'

Well, Yarborough at this moment was a lamb in lamb's clothing—Yarborough sucking in the snot in his nose, he is weeping again, and muttering, 'Horror, horror, horror,' reminiscent of the line Kurtz says in both Joseph Conrad's novel *The Heart of Darkness* and Francis Ford Coppola's film *Apocalypse Now.*

The horror. The horror.

Yarborough stands and leaves the room looking for reporters. He finds some. 'Gentlemen, this has been a deed of horror. Excalibur has sunk beneath the waves.'

Excalibur is a reference to Camelot, to King Arthur, to the Lady in the Lake—

* * *

It is ten or fifteen minutes after one o'clock. Policeman J. D. Tippit is across the river in Oak Cliff. He rushes into the Top 10 Record Store at 338 West Jefferson. The fucking Mop Tops are playing inside instead of honest Texas swing Bob Willis style. Tippit is in a big hurry. He shoves past adults and teenagers gathered around a radio listening to the news reports. The owner, J. W. 'Dub' Stark, knows Tippit and shouts, 'Have you caught him yet?'

'Caught who?' Tippit yells and hunkers at the pay phone. He puts a nickel in and dials a number from memory. He stands there. Impatient. No answer. He hangs up and forgets to get his nickel back. Then he hears it land in the coin slot. He turns and plucks back his nickel. Then he rushes out of the Top 10 Record Store and back into his police car.

Plenty of people make important phone calls during the day and the parties they are calling do not answer. In 1963, phone answering machines are as big as small suitcases and expensive. Few people own one in Dallas. Attention is spent on Tippit's futility at the telephone because Tippit will be dead in five minutes. Who was Tippit phoning? If the party Tippit was calling had been home, maybe Tippit would still have been killed ten minutes later.

Maybe not.

Tippit cruises down East 10th Street through a run-down neighborhood of clapboard houses with either dead lawns or lush lawns that no one mows.

This is Tippit's secret, or *one* of Tippit's secrets: He works weekends as a security guard at Austin's Barbecue, where he is fornicating with a married waitress. This waitress is also pregnant. Perhaps the kid is Tippit's. He is married himself. If this adultery has been discovered, it will produce at least one unhappy cuckolded husband and one betrayed and unhappy wife as well as the potential for numerous unhappy in-laws, this in Dallas where guns are as easy to procure as apples in a supermarket.

* * *

At this moment, ABC national radio is spinning the Doris Day song 'Hooray for Hollywood.' From our modern viewpoint, this song has been performed dozens and dozens of times on the Oscar telecast. It's upbeat. It's corny. It's kind of stupid. *Hooray for Hollywood. Hooray for Hollywood.* Yet, Doris Day's version starts off slow and sultry: 'Hooray for Hollywood, that screwy ballhooey Hollywood.' Doris Day pronounces each syllable of *ball-hoo-ey.* 'Where any office boy or young mechanic can be a panic with just a good-looking pan.' *Pan* is old-style slang for *face.* 'And any barmaid can be a star made if she dances with or without a fan.' This is a reference to a style of burlesque where the half-naked girl gives glimpses of her body between waves of two large feather fans she waves in her hands.

Hooray for Hollywood.

ABC radio interrupts the record and the announcer declares, 'Three shots were fired at President Kennedy's motorcade today in downtown Dallas, Texas.'

* * *

Dallas. Oak Cliff. On 10th Street, a dead cop is lying in the street.

Tippit.

He has been shot dead at age thirty-nine (like being shot at age forty-nine today). Two bullets hit his temple and two bullets hit his chest. A woman named Markham is standing barefoot beside the body. Her shoes are on the roof of Tippit's cop car. She is apparently a witness. She is at this moment a screaming hysteric sight. A cop named Jez shakes her hard and then slaps her face because he has seen this done to hysterical women in the movies.

She calms down.

She tells what happened. She heard three gunshots.

Three?

* * *

It is 1:45 p.m. at the Texas Theatre on Jefferson, about seven blocks from where Officer Tippit was shot. *War Is Hell* is what is running inside at this moment. The kids who cut school are up in the balcony.

Suddenly the theater lights go on, but the movie keeps playing. There are only about a dozen people down in the theater below.

A policeman appears up on the balcony behind the kids. He is looking for someone. The first thought in all the kids' heads is that the cop is there to arrest them for skipping school. The cop does not immediately see whoever he's looking for so he opens the fire door letting Texas sunlight pour in. Down in the theater there is a cop with a shotgun on the stage. The cop by the kids yells, 'The balcony is all clear. He ain't here.'

He was at the Texas Theatre . . .

More cops enter the theater. One chubby cop purposely struts from the front of the theater up the middle aisle. He walks past a guy sitting there and then whips around yelling, 'On your feet, you!'

A short skinny guy leaps up with his hands raised and howls out, 'This is it! It's all over now.'

There are now sixteen policemen in the movie theater.

The kids in the balcony see the skinny short guy suddenly punch the cop nearest him, and then yank a pistol out of his own pants. Then a cop punches the guy with the gun in both eyes. Another cop grabs the gunman from behind. Everyone is trying to get the skinny short guy's gun hand. His gun is a snub-nose. One cop gets his face scraped by the gun butt. None of the kids is close enough to see what happens, but the skinny short guy pulls the trigger, but a cop's hand is in the way and the hammer of the gun falls on the webbing between the cop's thumb and pointer finger.

It does not go off.

Twelve years from now in Sacramento, California, President Gerald Ford will be walking from his hotel toward the State Capitol when a young woman dressed like Little Red Riding Hood named Squeaky Fromme will pull out a semiautomatic .45 from her cloak and aim it at Ford's genitals, but an alert Secret Service agent will reach out, causing the webbing between his thumb and pointer to slip over the gun hammer, preventing it from firing.

Gerald Ford will sit on the Warren Commission, which will cover up what actually happened in Dallas on November 22, 1963.

* * *

Back at the Texas Theatre. A cop hauls the short skinny guy up and someone with handcuffs cuffs one of the guy's hands and then handcuffs that hand to the hand of another cop. Wrong. That cop uncuffs the other cop and cuffs the short skinny guy's other wrist. The skinny short guy is howling, 'Sons of bitches! Bastards!'

A cop punches the guy's head.

The chubby cop is on his knees searching under the seat for his cop cap and flashlight.

'Don't hit me anymore!' the short skinny guy screams. He sounds like a girl.

The entire audience, even the kids playing hooky, has stayed seated throughout the turmoil because the cops had told them at the beginning, 'Stay in your chairs.'

* * *

Parkland Hospital.

Lyndon Johnson gets control of himself. He is again coherent. His first thoughts appear to be a concern with legitimacy. He assumes that he is not the president until he is officially sworn in; so how can this happen as quickly as possible?

LBJ is wrong. It is not necessary to be 'sworn in.' According to the Constitution, the vice president automatically becomes the president after the standing president's death. One would think if LBJ had actually planned the shooting, he would have learned this. The Secret Service agents are now pressing LBJ to flee Dallas immediately. In Johnson's head, *I have to return to Air Force One. I have to fly from Dallas with both Kennedy's body and his widow.* He gives the Secret Service agents a look halfway between seething anger and regal authority.

'Where's the Bagman?' he asks.

All the Secret Service agents are blank.

'Get the Bagman,' LBJ commands.

They all scatter. Johnson does not know how whatever is in the Bagman's bag works; he knows he must have the secret presidential code to launch Armageddon; and he doesn't have such a code yet. LBJ just wants the damn Secret Service to be occupied and leave him the hell alone.

* * *

Officer Craig walks into the Dallas Police station. He discovers that the rifle taken from the evidence lockup in the Identification Bureau has been logged as a 6.5 Mannlicher-Carcano. This is a cheap Italian rife, so crudely manufactured that in World War II it was called a 'humanitarian' rifle because you couldn't intentionally hit anything with it. Weitzman and everyone else say, 'We must have been mistaken to think it was a Mauser.'

Not Craig. He clearly now sees the words *Made in Italy* on the butt of this rifle, not the name *Mauser* he saw on the rifle at the Texas School Book Depository.

★ ★ ★

Texans love souvenirs. In Parkland Hospital, an orderly asks Jacqueline if he can keep the president's brain-wet T-shirt as a souvenir. Imagine you are a Dallas cop in the evidence locker. What a souvenir! The Mauser that blasted the brains out of Kennedy! You take the gun and substitute another rifle that looks 'just like' the murder weapon.

★ ★ ★

Parkland. At 1:45 p.m., Secret Service agent Kellerman is waiting for the death certificate. Other Secret Service agents put Kennedy's body into a casket just brought in by a mortuary. The man is wrapped in sheets and the back of his head is missing and smearing gook on the inside of the casket.

A doctor, Earl Rose, tells Kellerman that they cannot remove the body from the hospital. 'It's the law. The crime was committed in Dallas.'

An admiral suddenly appears and starts screaming at Dr. Rose.

Kellerman and two other Secret Service agents begin pushing the casket on its roller, but a cop and a twenty-three-year-old 'Justice of the Peace' block them. Everyone is screaming.

The will of Texas will not be denied. The will of Dallas will not be denied. Testosterone coats this room like melting butter. The Secret Service agents bully the casket forward.

A Dallas cop draws his gun.

Jacqueline hurries out of a room and puts her left hand on the casket helping to propel it down the hallway.

The Dallas cop returns the gun to its holster.

They get the casket into an empty hearse. The mortician rushes up acting officious. He looks pasted together like a ventriloquist's dummy turned human. 'Where are you going?' he asks.

'To the mortuary.'

'I'll follow.'

Jacqueline crams herself in the back of the hearse with the casket. Then the hearse leaves the hospital and she sees the crowds of reporters and curiosity seekers gathered outside. She sees that the flag has been already pulled to half-mast. The hearse races down the streets to Love Field. The mortician inside the following cop car begins having a fit. 'That's not the way! What's going on?'

The hearse speeds up toward the gate in the Love Field fence. The gate opens. The hearse speeds through. The gate is closed. The cop car with the mortician inside pulls up. They are denied entrance.

LBJ is already in Air Force One. On the phone, Bobby Kennedy tells him what the oath is to become president. Another phone call. One of Johnson's old cronies, a female judge named Sarah Hughes, is now racing by car to Love Field. Lady Bird tells her husband, 'They began to lead me up one corridor and down another. Suddenly I found myself face-to-face with Jackie in a small hallway. You always think of someone like her as being insulated, protected. She was quite alone. I don't think I ever saw anyone so much alone in my life.'

'What did she say to you?'

'*Oh Lady Bird, it's good that we've always liked you two so much.*'

* * *

President Kennedy inside his casket is dragged onto Air Force One. Jacqueline's pink outfit is still drenched in blood. She refuses to change. 'I want them to see what they have done,' she keeps repeating. The female judge arrives. LBJ intends to be sworn in and then the plane will take off for D.C. Jacqueline is ordered to participate in the ceremony. 'I think I ought to. In the light of history, it would be better if I was there.'

Barely twenty people squeeze into a space the size of one of Jacqueline's walk-in closets at the White House.

LBJ takes the oath of office.

Afterward, he kisses Lady Bird on the forehead. He takes Jacqueline's hand. He gives Jacqueline a grandfatherly peck. Several men surge forward to congratulate LBJ and the tall Texan scowls them back. This is not a celebration.

The plane takes off down the runway.

* * *

It was three o'clock in the afternoon on November 22, 1963, in Dallas. People are pounding the walls in City Hall wailing, 'Not in Dallas! Not in Dallas!' Dealey Plaza is pandemonium. Cops are arresting people who looked suspicious and then letting them go. Secret Service men put Xs on their hatbands, and are allowed to go and do what they please. A woman tells a cop that she saw gun smoke coming from the Grassy Knoll. She saw everything. She even saw the first lady playing with a little white dog in the back seat of the dark blue limousine.

The cop rolls his eyes and turns away.

* * *

November 22, 1963. Air Force One. Jacqueline lingered beside her dead husband's coffin.

Presidential assistant Ken O'Donnell said, 'I'm going to have a hell of a stiff drink. I think you should too.'

Jacqueline asked, 'What will I have?'

'Scotch.'

'I've never had a Scotch in my life.'

'Now is as good a time as any to start.'

* * *

Cornish, New Hampshire. The Salingers' TV is blaring assassination news in the living room. In the kitchen, Claire Salinger is playing Mouse Trap with her seven-year-old daughter, Peggy, and three-year-old son, Matt. Mouse Trap is a three-dimensional Ideal Co. 'board game.'

Claire and Peggy and Matt take turns rolling a single die and move their red/green/blue mouse markers the appropriate number of spaces on the twisting path of the red-and-blue playing board. Depending on the square where each mouse lands, a miniature plastic Rube Goldberg–style 'cause & effect' machine is constructed. Matt has a predictable three-year-old's attention span for this portion of the game. To placate the kid, when the mousetrap is constructed, Matt always gets to activate it regardless of whether it is his or his sister's or mother's mouse sitting on the Trap Spot.

The kid activates the contraption by turning a small handle connected to a vertical red-colored plastic dial containing prongs. This turning sets off a chain reaction. There is nothing further the child has to do but watch. Matt does not sit back and watch, but continues turning the crank as if this turning keeps the whole contraption in motion. Of course, the kid is only three years old. The prongs on that red dial mesh with the corresponding prongs on a horizontal yellow dial.* This dial in turn spins and bumps a pole that hits a green plastic boot that is propelled outward to kick over an upright yellow bucket. Inside the bucket is a small steel ball the width of a single piece of M&M's candy. The bucket tips over and the steel ball zigzags down a seven-tiered trough. The trough is blue. The steel ball continues its roll down a horizontal curving plastic gutter. The gutter is red. The color makes the gutter seem vaguely anatomical. Finally, the steel ball hits a yellow pole that propels upward a green plastic hand, palm-up. The upward motion of the hand tips a gumball-sized marble on a plank. The marble then free-falls into a miniature red bathtub, rolling into a large hole located where the drain should be. The marble lands on the upward side of a blue plank. This causes the downward side of the plank to shoot upward, striking the toes of a green plastic figurine of a man in a full-bodied bathing suit circa the 1900s.

The plank hits his toes hard enough to flip the figurine into the air backward. He lands in a large yellow tank empty of water. The tank is connected to a yellow-ratcheted pole where a red dome-shaped 'trap' balances precariously at the top. The vibration of the diver landing in the tank upsets the balance of this red trap and it clatters down the pole entrapping a red or blue or yellow mouse sitting in the Trap Spot.

Springing this contraption delights Matt to no end, even if it is one of his own mice that gets trapped. All in all, the three Salingers spring the trap thirty times before sister and mother let Matt win the game.

The television is still blaring bad news from Dallas. At one point, J. D. Salinger walked into the kitchen and opened the refrigerator and peered inside. He shut the refrigerator without removing anything. He looked at the Mouse Trap playing board with the mousetrap fully constructed and said, 'Dealey Plaza.'

---

* That second dial is reminiscent of the Aurora plastic model of the Hunchback of Notre Dame chained to a circular dais.

* * *

Jack Kennedy's secretary was on the airplane that was carrying President Kennedy's corpse back to Washington. Evelyn Lincoln had been with Jack Kennedy for more than ten years. These were still the Della Street years (Della Street being fictional lawyer Perry Mason's combination secretary and Girl Friday). She sat. There were no tears in her eyes. She sat and wrote a list of who could have done this to her boss.

The first name she wrote was 'Lyndon—'

The second was a group, 'KKK—' followed by 'Dixiecrats—'

Then the name 'Hoffa—' followed by the 'John Birch Society.' She wrote 'John Birch Society' without the dash.

Next she wrote 'Nixon.' Then 'Diem'—obviously she meant Kennedy was killed in retaliation for the coup death of Diem in Saigon.

She wrote, 'Rightists.' 'CIA in Cuban fiasco.' 'Dictators.' And 'Communists.'

During the time Evelyn Lincoln took to compile her list, Jacqueline had the brainstorm that the funeral should follow the pattern of Abraham Lincoln's. In fact, seven hours from now, special assistant to the president Arthur Schlesinger Jr. will be combing through the stacks in the Library of Congress with a flashlight (the lights are set to an automated timer) searching for specific details about Lincoln's funeral.

* * *

By dinnertime time in Dallas that Friday night, a cop finally figures out about the little dog that crazy woman said the first lady was playing with. It was that damn Lamb Chop hand puppet. From a distance, the lamb looked canine.

* * *

That night in Washington, D.C., Haroldson Lafayette Hunt checks into his room at the Mayflower Hotel, a fifteen-minute cab ride from President Johnson's mansion, the Elms, on 52nd Street NW. Hunt flew in from Dallas that afternoon. The FBI in Dallas had even rushed him to

Love Field in an unmarked car. Haroldson Lafayette Hunt is the richest man in the world, but he has never considered buying his own jet. He flew Delta. He sat in first class, of course. In those days, first class was really first class.

Why is H. L. Hunt here in Washington on such short notice? There will never be an official answer. He even has his people establishing his presence 'incommunicado' down in Mexico.

Lyndon is a Texan. Hunt is a Texan. Texans stick together.

H. L. Hunt finishes unpacking and then awkwardly, with grunts and heavy breathing, lowers himself to the burnished carpet of his hotel room. He balances on his hands and knees and begins to creep. He slowly and methodically creeps on his knees among the legs of the furniture in his room in the Mayflower Hotel.

* * *

It is now after midnight in Washington, D.C.

Jacqueline is no longer first lady.

Johnson has assured her that she and the kids can stay in the White House for at least a week or two. She is now up in her bedroom finally taking off her pink suit. Rolling down her nylons. They reek. Not of sweat, but of bad meat. Her pink outfit has many sticky black patches of dried blood mixed with dried flecks of Jack's brain.

Jack was the one who had discussed her wardrobe for the November 22 luncheon. 'Be simple—show these Texans what good taste really is,' he had said.

* * *

Arthur Miller's *After the Fall* was in rehearsal at the ANTA Washington Square Theatre. After the president was pronounced dead on TV, word got out quickly that Broadway would go dark. All performances were canceled. Producers and theater owners were now furiously meeting and burning up phone lines planning when the theaters could open again.

Arthur Miller sits in the empty American National Theatre and

Academy off Washington Square, slouching in the first row sharing a bottle of Glenfiddich with the play's director, Elia Kazan.

Miller speaks. 'Everyone says Maggie is Marilyn.' The cadence of his voice is slurry.

'How could Maggie be anyone else?' Kazan answers.

'You fucked Marilyn 'fore I did, Cap'n. Your mistress-wife Barbara is playin' Maggie. How could you allow that if Maggie was Marilyn?'

'Arty, I just shtupped Marilyn. You married her, for Christ's sake.'

'Lemmy tell you again, that Maggie is not Marilyn.'

'And Louise is not Mary?'

'Mary who?'

'For Christ's sake, Arty. Mary your first wife.'

'Lemmy tell you—I once took a trip to Hollywood and told Mary that while I was out of town I met an attractive woman and I wanted to go to bed with her, but I didn'. Mary wouldn' lemmy forget that for a year.'

'That's rough.'

'A whole year. Pass me the bottle, Cap'n.'

'Slow down. Slow down.'

'Why? There's plenty more where this came from.'

'So Arty, I suppose that Holga is not based on Morath?'

'No, sir. Their European background is the same. That's it.'

'Christ, Arty. Holga says, *I had a child and it was an idiot and I ran away.* That's not about Morath giving birth to Dan?'

'Oh fuck. Holga is not the only woman in the world who gave birth to a retard.'

'Did you hear what you just said?' Pause. 'I've gotta go take a piss.'

Kazan leaves. Kazan returns.

'Okay, Cap'n,' Arthur Miller says. 'Okay. Okay. Let's change Maggie's costume.'

'Change Maggie's costume?'

'Yeah.'

'To what?'

'Let her wear the cheapest, most gaudy blond wig that money can buy.'

'Are you out of your mind? Why not just hang a sign around Maggie's neck saying, *I am Marilyn Monroe?*'

'I believe in giving the people what they want.'

★ ★ ★

Arlington National Cemetery, Virginia. All night Robert McNamara had been outside, wearing only a trench coat as he stumbled among the graves with the chief gravedigger searching for the perfect spot to plant Kennedy. The gravedigger's name was Portimos. The man was McNamara's age and was not literally a gravedigger; he was just the highest-ranking staff member at Arlington who could be located on such short notice.

McNamara had no idea what he was looking for. An elevated piece of land—clear land so mourners could pay respects for hundreds of years to come. There should be trees nearby, but not close enough that their roots could break into the president's casket.

Bucolic was the word that described what McNamara wanted. *Bucolic* was not a word suitable for nighttime use.

Portimos had no aesthetic sense of grave location. In frustration, McNamara told the man, who was at least as old as McNamara himself, the gravedigger joke from *Hamlet*.

Portimos didn't get it.

This pair must have scouted forty acres by now. All night it had been cold enough to see one's breath. There was no moon; it was as if the escaping respiration was illuminated on its own accord.

It was also quiet in the cemetery. McNamara understood the term *dead quiet* as the two strode between rows of quiet white arched gravestones, each reaching just above their kneecaps.

Portimos had a flashlight, but whenever he turned it on the light irritated McNamara, who told the gravedigger to turn it off as the flashlight was not bright enough to illuminate anything anyway.

McNamara glanced at his watch for the tenth time and almost slapped his own forehead as he realized that he had set it to Texas time ever since the president had flown away on Air Force One on Thursday. Dawn would come one hour sooner than McNamara had been figuring.

Soon.

McNamara even sensed that the birds had started singing. McNamara turned east toward the city. He was positive that the dawn was almost discernible. McNamara told Portimos to shine his flashlight on the map McNamara was holding.

'There's one last ridge to search,' McNamara said.

Portimos glanced at the map exhaling a fist of breath and then insisted that the only way to reach that area was to walk down a hill and circumvent a treed area.

'According to this map, this tree line is just a shallow row of oaks.'

Portimos ignored McNamara and just trudged down the hill, turning on the flashlight to guide his way. McNamara faced the trees and walked toward them. Then he walked between them. Most of their leaves had fallen. McNamara felt and heard crackling under the soles of his shoes. The sun was not up, but there was enough peripheral light to make out where he was going.

It was much colder among these trees.

McNamara stopped and ran his finger along a tree trunk. The map said these were oaks, but McNamara was sure they were dogwood. McNamara had a sudden memory of being in a southern tavern and someone put a nickel in the jukebox and a mournful hillbilly began braying, 'I feel just like a dogwood tree / someone came and carved a cross out of me . . .'

McNamara realized that he was a dozen, maybe two dozen trunks in to what should have only been a short row of trees. He turned around. He could not see anything but the dim outline of timber. McNamara considered retreating back to the open land, and then rejected this consideration. He continued in the direction that he had been heading. There was no bush. Just trees. Just the crunching of leaves. He counted how many trees he was in—thirty. Now forty. He stopped and decided to wait until the sun rose.

He leaned against a trunk.

Did he want to go to sleep? He closed his eyes. He thought of the beginning of Dante's *Divine Comedy.* So many published translations have Dante 'waking up' in that dark wood, that dark forest, that forest dark, that gloomy wood, that shadowed forest. McNamara suddenly remembered a Sunday afternoon more than a few years ago—his Ann Arbor book group when he had made everyone retranslate the beginning of *The Divine Comedy.* McNamara recalled Carl Djerassi's translation. Djerassi had read his version of Dante's beginning and McNamara nitpicked it to death.

McNamara felt sudden regret. Not big regret. Just slight regret. McNamara was sorry that he had not appreciated the hard-boiled brevity of Djerassi's translation. For the first time since McNamara came to Washington, he wondered if he should have told Djerassi good-bye.

McNamara only wondered that for a moment and put it out of his mind. He recited Djerassi's translation of Dante out loud to the dogwood trees:

'In the middle of my life I found myself lost in a dark wood, the right road lost.'

Epilogue

Reciting Poetry with Aristotle Onassis

Washington, D.C., Sunday night, November 24, 1963.

The dignitaries begin arriving for President Kennedy's funeral on Monday. Charles de Gaulle will be there. Emperor Haile Selassie. Prince Philip. Jacqueline's immediate family will attend. There is only one guest that Jacqueline Kennedy invited who does not fit into either category of family or dignitary. Aristotle Onassis flies to Washington, D.C., at Jacqueline's request.

No one says anything to Jacqueline about Onassis's presence. Not even Bobby. In all the chaos and the turbulence, she spends a half hour alone with Onassis.

* * *

'I don't think that I could have orchestrated Jack's funeral without understanding what you told me on the *Christina*.'

Onassis did not say anything. He was a God. So was she. They understood much without talking, of course.

'I asked you here in private, Ari, to have a moment where we can say your poem again. Together. Both of us.'

He eyed her a long time. Without moving his eyes, he first saw her face and hair. Then her eyes and nose and mouth. And then just her eyes.

'Ari, you are the only one who can understand.' She said those words in her Monroe little-girl voice.

Ari boomed out, 'I will say it.' Then commanded, 'You start.'

She cleared her throat awkwardly, as if she had never given a speech before or spoken on television. 'When you start for Ithaka,' she said in a gentle voice, 'long for a prolonged sail of sweetness and adventure.'

The next lines Onassis recited. 'Don't be afraid of the Lestrygonians and the Cyclops and Poseidon steeped in rage—' (In particular Ari pronounces *Lestrygonians* as if it was the most sublime word a Greek could ever speak.)

Jacqueline continued in a firmer voice than she had used before: 'They never appear if your spirit stays empyreal.'

Onassis then said, 'Lestrygonians and the Cyclops and Poseidon only appear to foul minds, never upon a pure sail.'

Jacqueline: 'Hope that your sail is long. Every morning is bathed in the joy of summer. Hope you sail into ports for the first time.'

Onassis: 'Browse at Phoenician markets, and acquire mother-of-pearl and coral and amber and ebony . . .'

'And sybaritic perfumes of all kinds,' Jacqueline added, stretching out the word *sybaritic* until it almost sounded five syllables long.

'As many sybaritic perfumes as you can,' Onassis repeated quickly, making *sybaritic* sound like the word *cigarette.* Then he commanded: 'Visit as many Egyptian cities as you can. Learn as much as you can from scholars—never crowding Ithaka from your mind.'

'Ithaka is your destiny.' Jacqueline said in a tiny voice paradoxically containing alarming authority based on its slightitude.

Onassis continued: 'You must not hurry the voyage at all, best for it to last for years. Anchor at the island only when you are old—old and rich with all that you have experienced along the way.'

'Have no expectation that Ithaka will make you rich,' Jacqueline said. 'Ithaka gave you that beautiful voyage. Without Ithaka you would have never even set out your door.'

'Ithaka has nothing more to give you,' Onassis added.

'Ithaka has not deceived you if you find her poor,' Jacqueline recited.

'You will now be wise with experience,' Onassis said gently. And then recited the last line with no inflection at all.

'You will finally understand what all Ithaka means.'

* * *

The next day, that Monday, the day of Kennedy's funeral—November 25, 1963—a telegram arrives for Jacqueline Kennedy. It was sent by Madame Nhu. Her telegram read in its entirety:

NOW YOU KNOW HOW IT FEELS.

About the Author

David Bowman was born in Racine, Wisconsin, on December 8, 1957, and his interest in writing first emerged while he was studying music at Interlochen Arts Academy High School, where he graduated with honors. He briefly attended Putney College in Vermont before moving to New York to write while working as a bartender and a clerk at a bookstore. His works include *Let the Dog Drive*, *Bunny Modern*, and *This Must Be the Place*. He was shortlisted as one of *Granta*'s best novelists under forty, and as a journalist, he interviewed musicians as diverse as Lou Reed for the *New York Times Magazine* and Kris Kristofferson for *Salon*. He died, too young, from a cerebral hemorrhage in 2012 at the age of fifty-four.